SPY CHASER

Three Gripping Espionage Thrillers

DEREK THOMPSON

JOFFE BOOKS

Published 2016 by Joffe Books, London.

www.joffebooks.com

With thanks to Anne Coralie for the book title.

ISBN-13: 978-1-911021-26-1

BOOK 1:

STANDPOINT

Chapter 1

Thomas Bladen focused his binoculars on a block of shipping containers far below the lookout. As a prolonged ferry blast carried across the port like a cry of mourning, he surveyed the slate sky, tracking a gull as it veered across and crapped on a Bentley. He smiled for the first time that day: welcome to Harwich. If he hadn't been so far away — and on surveillance — he'd have thrown the bird some bread for a second run.

The laptop bleeped — another image stored. He bent towards it amid the stench of damp and decay of the near-derelict room. His colleague, Karl McNeill, lightly tapped a window and made a customary grunt of approval. Thomas ignored him.

"Hey Tommo, check out the red-head; eleven o'clock — by the blue sports. I'd do some deep cover work there, right enough. I'd even forego the overtime!"

Thomas glanced over and grimaced. *Prat.* After putting the binoculars down carefully, he attended to his camera, readjusting it six inches to the right. Then he squeezed the button and watched as another square of panoramic mosaic gradually uploaded to the screen.

"I don't know why you bother with that old bollocks, Tommo. Overkill if you ask me, and the job's not even on yet."

"I like to be thorough," he held a finger up to keep Karl at bay. *And I don't like to be disturbed.*

"Hardly worth it though, for a Customs' promo, unless you're after impressing the boss?"

Thomas paused and moved the camera again. *Here it comes.*

"But then, weren't you and Christine co-workers *and* playmates before she became boss?"

"That was a long time ago." He stared at the sequence of images before homing in on the sports car. "She's married," he announced with satisfaction.

"Who? Christine Gerrard?"

"No, your dream date in the blue sports. I see a wedding ring."

"I wasn't looking at her fingers."

The room fell silent again; Thomas preferred it that way. *Magnify the row, scroll right and* . . . Something snagged his attention; he stopped on square 34, captivated by a lone figure leaning out of a four-by-four, with high-powered lenses.

"Karl, how many spotter teams are on today?"

"Jeez, pay attention. Customs are on the ground, Crossley's lot are on the far side and then there's us two, in the penthouse."

"'Course, yeah." He tried to ignore square 34 and fell back into the rhythm of the job, while Karl rustled a newspaper and muttered something about tits.

"Tommo, didya ever think, when you signed up with the SSU, that you'd one day rise to the third storey of a genuine shit-hole?"

He smiled without turning round. "Well, I had my hopes . . ." Adjusting the magnification, he took a clear shot of the four-by-four's number plate. As he worked, his fingers tingled, or else he imagined they did. Whoever the stranger was, he didn't appear on the duty roster, and Thomas was a man who didn't like surprises. He photographed what he could, collecting details — an expensive shirt, an ornate wedding band and a designer watch. One thing was clear — this gate crasher wasn't short of a few quid.

The walkie-talkie crackled into life; mystery man would have to wait. "This is Control; we have a green light. Repeat; we have a green light."

Suddenly professional, Karl called in their readiness. Thomas had seen that metamorphosis many times now and it still fascinated him.

"Thing is," Karl mumbled, leaning towards his eyepiece, "if they gave us rifles instead of cameras, we could sort out the bloody smugglers ourselves."

"Thank you Rambo; maybe that's the reason they don't arm us?"

At the next ferry horn, Thomas checked the time and turned to catch Karl's big performance, watching as he scrunched his face up, cartoon style.

"Thar she blows!"

The ferry slowly manoeuvred into port and they watched from their vantage point, primed like racing dogs in their traps. Thomas tried to concentrate, but that tingling feeling kept pulling him back to the lone spotter — still there and focused in the same direction.

The slow tally of vehicles and pedestrians snaked out into a warm Essex afternoon; a dark blue Customs van inched forward to greet the traffic. After three cars passed, the van doors slid back and four uniformed officers fanned out. The lone spotter tensed up; Thomas could see his binoculars twitch to attention.

A white Transit was diverted to one side. The driver brandished paperwork, but it made no difference. A Customs Officer took his keys and unlocked the back doors.

"Got ya, you bastard!" Karl hissed triumphantly.

The Customs team removed several boxes and the Transit's suspension lifted. Thomas focused in on the driver. He'd be making his excuses now, trying to bullshit his way through by talking about a party or a restaurant or stocking up for Christmas — in June. But he looked more nervous than he ought to be.

"Nicked!" Karl growled with relish, and popped open a celebratory can.

Thomas laughed. Typical Karl: enthusiasm of a Labrador and the loyalty of a Premier League footballer on the make. Last assignment, he'd been Benefits Fraud team, through and through. Now it was HM Customs, providing fly-on-the-wall footage for in-house use. Karl seemed to love it all, but as far as Thomas was concerned, the Surveillance Support Unit was just a cheap labour source for any government department in need.

Other vehicles slowed, as if to enjoy the spectacle. One, a red Astra estate, held back the queue for a few seconds, prompting a chorus of car horns. Thomas rattled off a couple of shots then switched over to binoculars, picking up his walkie-talkie.

"Control, from Team 3; the red Astra exiting — worth investigating? Over."

"Control, from Team 2 — suggest we ignore that," Ann Crossley over-ruled him. "It's just a family. The driver must have porn stashed under his seat!"

Thomas wasn't convinced, but he knew when to hold his tongue and kept the Astra in sight. As it jolted forward, a rear window lowered a few centimetres. It drew level with the Transit, and a short piece of pipe poked out. On instinct, Thomas panned left, framing the Transit driver's face; the man looked like he'd seen a ghost. It was over in seconds. Even after the driver slumped to the ground and the red car had dissolved into the traffic, no one else seemed to react. But it had burned into Thomas's brain, in slow-mo. He tasted the fear and helplessness, and swallowed it down.

The walkie-talkie blared into life. "A passenger's collapsed. Ambulance required *immediately*."

Something clicked at the back of Thomas's mind. Square 34! He shifted the camera along; there was only one empty car space —

the four-by-four was gone, but the ferry was still unloading. He darted from square to square, tracking along the car lanes until he found it. He clicked frantically, no time to focus, hoping he'd get something useful.

Karl jammed an earpiece to his face and embarked on a running commentary. "Jesus, they think the poor bastard's been shot. He's still breathing; not much blood loss — can't have been much of a weapon."

Thomas shuddered. Karl made it all sound matter of fact but then, he reasoned, for someone with Karl's military background, it probably was. "So," Thomas felt the sweat trickle down the sides of his face, "when do you start your new job as a Samaritan?"

Soon, the view was choked with blue lights and sirens, as an ambulance and the police put in an appearance. Thomas watched through the window, without magnification; he no longer felt like taking a ringside seat.

"What about that, Tommo?" Karl spluttered gleefully. "I can't work out where there's a clear line of sight — unless it was at close quarters — like maybe a zip-gun? Hey, it could have been your family from the red estate! Crossley's going to look pretty stupid at debrief. What a shot though, if it was, I mean — moving vehicle and all; even *I* couldn't have done that, in my day."

"Your compassion's overwhelming."

"Still," Karl pondered aloud, "it's not much of a hit if he's still alive."

Unless that was the intention? Thomas recalled the haunted look on the driver's face. "Well, anyway, it's not our problem," Karl picked up the walkie-talkie and called for authority to stand down. "Right Tommo, are you coming for a late lunch before we head back? This will be the worst promotional content ever made. What's the betting it all gets mysteriously lost in the editing process?"

And even as Karl said it, Thomas decided that some of his own footage, especially the four-by-four, wouldn't make it into the report. Rule number one: Don't get involved. Rule number two: If you have to get involved, get involved alone.

"You *coming*?" Karl insisted.

"Nah, you go ahead. I'll be here a little longer."

"Suit yourself. I'll see you back at base."

Or, as they both knew better, The Railway Tavern in Liverpool Street.

* * *

Thomas sat perfectly still for a couple of minutes and breathed in the silence. Out the window, he could see things returning to normal down there.

He took new shots of the area around square 34 and lined up the rows above and below. Half an hour later, Photoshop had smoothed out any inconsistencies. It was like Spot the Difference for idiots, with the four-by-four missing. And only the new version would be available for public viewing. As soon as he'd finished, he pulled out his mobile and hit the redial button.

"Miranda Wright," she sang.

"Hi, it's Thomas."

"What can I do for you, my darling?"

He savoured her voice like a warm cognac. "I'm after something," he said, opening a file on his laptop.

She gave a filthy laugh and he drew the phone in closer.

"I need a number plate checked . . ."

"Well, it'll cost you — dinner tonight."

"Done; and listen, make sure this is kept anonymous." He read the letters out phonetically, emphasising each number, the remnants of his Yorkshire tones lost in cool precision.

"Eight o'clock it is then — you can pick me up at work."

"Thanks, Miranda."

"Don't thank me till you see where we're eating. And dress up for a change!"

Chapter 2

Karl performed a slow handclap as Thomas shouldered the door to the office, a bag in each hand.

"You took your time — I waited a good hour for you."

"I'm sure you managed to prop up the bar without me," Thomas said, "I had to do something with my laptop."

Karl grinned. "Maybe it's all those weekend wedding shoots, clogging your hard-drive."

Thomas nodded wearily and eased past him to his desk — Karl, on another fishing expedition. "What time does the boss want us in?"

"Five o'clock, amigo."

He sighed; it was still weird sometimes, thinking of Christine as *the boss*. Cutting it fine though — Miranda would go spare if he was late again.

"Fancy a pint later, Tommo? The rest of the gang are going, but they never stay long . . ."

"Sorry," he cut him off. "I have plans."

Karl baulked. "Normal people don't have plans. They eat, date, drink themselves stupid; but you have *plans*. Do you know, it's been a year since we started working together and I still don't know you."

Thomas nodded, half-listening. Something was bugging him, besides Karl's attempts at camaraderie. Real tip of the tongue stuff. He'd seen something familiar today — only he didn't know quite what it was. "We'll do it sometime soon, Karl; Scout's honour."

"That's more like it!" Karl sounded almost convinced.

Thomas unpacked his laptop, loaded the report template and made a start.

* * *

At 5 pm prompt the office door at the far end of the open-plan room swung open. Karl waited at a respectful distance, while Thomas set his screensaver password then led the way. Karl followed closely behind, muttering *paranoid* in a pretend cough.

The rest of the team were already in Christine's office — they had been there for nearly half an hour. Thomas shared a *who-knew* glance with Karl. Then he nodded to Christine with the briefest of smiles, taking in the sight of her. She looked every inch the professional. And two years on, he could still recall every one of the inches beneath that tailored suit.

Christine broke eye contact and cleared her throat. "I'll make this brief. As you know, we've lacked a permanent Senior Officer for months now. I'm delighted to tell you that Bob Peterson will be our new SIO from next week."

Thomas felt her words like a fist to the guts. This would be the same Bob Peterson who had taken Christine under his wing — coincidentally, a short while before the big break-up. And Bob had most likely helped himself to a whole lot more besides.

It took a moment or two to realise that Christine was still talking. "—Bob's a good man; I served under him about eighteen months ago."

He narrowed his eyes. *That was a new way of putting it*. He cleared his throat; Karl's eyebrows nearly scraped the ceiling.

Christine blushed, but stuck to the script. "Bob wants to do individual reviews as soon as poss, to get to know you all. Right; I gather we had some drama at Harwich today — Karl?"

Karl gave a concise account, leaving out the redhead and the lager.

Christine made notes as she listened, avoiding Thomas's glances. "Okay everyone, thanks for your time. Karl, Thomas — reports by ten, tomorrow. And thanks to everyone else for completing them today. That's all."

Thomas blew a breath from one side of his mouth. *Creeps.* Trust the brown-noses to get their reports in early. Strange though that no one had mentioned the red Astra. He dismissed the thought and focused on the way the strip-light glistened off Christine's lipstick, sensing the moisture gather on his own lips. Funny, it wasn't like him to play happy memories in the workplace. Christine opened her mouth to speak again, but he was through the door before she'd got a word out; nothing like paperwork to take the sting out of bad news.

Karl sidled over to his desk. "Sure you won't join us now?" There was an edge to the voice as if he was really saying: 'I see your pain and I want us to understand each other better.'

Thomas considered. Maybe. More likely, it was a case of: 'Please don't leave me with these tossers.' Either way, Thomas sat and watched them go. He had nothing against Karl personally; he actually liked the bloke. They were different to the others in their Surveillance Support Unit team; everyone else around them had a degree and a career-path, using the SSU as a way of picking up contacts and experience. Karl had transferred in from the Army — glory days that he never tired of talking about. Which was still a step up from Thomas's own route — via a humble Civil Service desk job and a love of photography.

Christine Gerrard's door yawned open. He swivelled round and the neon glare stretched across the carpet. "I had a feeling you'd still be here."

He leaned forward, lacing his fingers together tightly. "Just making the most of the quiet." He hated lies, his own most of all. But if he'd said, 'Still taking in the good news,' it would have meant a round of questions and answers. And he didn't have the stomach today.

She leant against the doorframe, stroking the carpet with her shoe. Every second swing, her leg escaped from the pleats of her skirt, which only served to remind him of everything Bob Peterson had cost him. Christine tilted her head to one side, as if to read his thoughts. "Listen. We're okay, aren't we, about Bob Peterson? I had no say in it."

"Sure, why not?" He yielded the words with some difficulty. She nodded and retreated into her office, closing the door. He slammed the laptop lid shut; maybe he'd ring Karl some time about that drink.

Chapter 3

Thomas glanced at his watch as he got out of the car; just made it. *Caliban's* — in garish green lettering — reflected in his windscreen. Inside, Miranda was draped against the bar; she looked edible. "I like a man who comes on time." Her laughter, even at his expense, thawed his edginess in an instant. She took pity on him. "Care to guess where we're going, then?" Sheryl, the manager, stopped fiddling with glasses and waited for his response.

He never fared well in front of an audience. "Not fussed."

"My, how you sweep a girl off her feet. Last of the great romantics." The women cackled like a hen party at a strip-show, and Miranda peeled herself away from the bar. "Come along then; you drive and I'll navigate."

Twenty minutes later, they were at a restaurant in Shoreditch, surrounded by marketing execs and multimedia entrepreneurs. "What do you think, then?" Miranda whispered. "The chef here wants out and I'm looking to bring proper food to Caliban's."

He nodded, took another slice of the tuna and followed it down with a mouthful of wine. "It's good."

She pivoted forward and passed a folded piece of paper across, like a love note. "So, here's my side of the bargain."

He cupped a hand over hers, palming note and hand.

"And there was me thinking you were only after my body." She leaned back, her cleavage tilting away, out of range. "Hey Thomas, remember that first meal we had together, in Leeds?" She squeezed his hand then retreated to her glass. "You were really trying to impress, that night; you 'ad the strongest curry on the menu and all that Yorkshire bitter. It was a classic — they told us to leave when

9

you got too pissed, and then you stood up and said every true Yorkshireman could hold his drink. But you still chucked up on the way home!"

It was a familiar script. He knew his lines as well as his cues. "You wore your purple skirt and those bangles we bought at that wholesale place. And tons of pink eyeshadow. Everyone stared when you spoke because you sounded like a Londoner off the telly."

"Oh yeah? Well, what about when you started making up Cockney rhyming slang then puked over your denim jacket?"

He grinned, recalling their *apples and blurrgh*. "Wonder what happened to that jacket? They're back in fashion now."

"You gave it to me, after I made you dry-clean it. I've still got it somewhere . . ." she sighed, and he downed some wine to avoid looking at her. "Anyway, open your present."

He unfolded the paper and read it slowly. *Bollocks.* His knife clattered to the plate and the missing synapse fired up in his brain. It was that distinctive wedding band; and now he knew exactly where he'd seen it before. Even so, he read the paper again, in the vain hope that he was mistaken. Fat chance.

"Problem?"

"Yeah, you could say that," he bit at a nail. The mystery four-by-four was registered to a Robert Peterson in Southampton. "Miranda, you remember me talking about Christine Gerrard . . ."

Her face soured. "Wonder Woman, you mean."

He yielded a weary smile; Miranda remembered everything. Wonder Woman, because, when it came to Christine and Bob Peterson, he'd always wondered.

"What's the trouble?"

That was unexpected — a touch of genuine concern. "Dunno. May be nothing. But the vehicle you got checked for me belongs to that bloke Christine used to work for." Now was his chance to say more or say nothing; he settled for nothing.

She studied him for a good half minute. "Look Thomas, I can't pretend I'm her biggest fan, after all you told me, but you know you can always speak to Mum and Dad if she's in serious bother."

He loved the way she liked him to know that he was *still* considered family, even though the two of them were no longer together. "Well, let's leave it for now." He took another sip of wine, imagining that snidey bastard Peterson tangling with Miranda's family. What a clash of cultures that would be: Oxbridge player versus the East End's finest.

"Hey," she lifted her glass and the colour of the wine reflected in her eyes, "let's go dancing!"

"Can't; I have to work later."

"Civil servants don't work nights."

"This one does."

"Oh, go on, Thomas; it's been ages since we went anywhere."

He didn't mention that it was hardly surprising, since she'd been seeing some second-rate footballer for the last couple of months.

She made puppy eyes at him and wriggled in her seat.

"Alright," he relented. "As long as I'm in bed by one-thirty."

"If I didn't know you better, Mr Bladen, I'd swear that was a come-on."

One of these days, Miranda, these games of ours are going to hurt someone.

Chapter 4

Beep beep beep. He forced his eyes open, took a second to focus then flailed in the direction of the alarm. He rolled over slowly and surveyed the empty side of the bed. *Ah, Miranda.* He stretched under the duvet and adjusted the bulge in his boxers. How was it, he wondered, that two people could have such a complicated . . . he searched for the word. Relationship?

In the kitchen, he picked up her coffee cup from the night before and studied the lipstick print. She might have stayed, if he'd asked, he told himself as he placed it carefully in the sink. Only he hadn't asked.

By eight-thirty he was in the office, looking and feeling as if he'd pulled an all-nighter. He slumped at his desk and typed up the notes, closing his eyes now and again to recall the details. It still didn't make sense. He opened another document, copied out a few separate sentences and saved the file for Karl — the lazy bastard. He was in the middle of a tricky combo, yawning and trying to rub some life back into his face, when the main door opened.

Ann Crossley nodded curtly and took up her seat on the other side of the room, without a word. How cheery. But then, what more could he expect from another Foreign Office wannabe?

An email pinged in from Karl, entitled: 'Help!' It read: *Hung over, please cover for me. Should be in by 9.30, but if not, ring me. Thanks.* It was sent at 2 am. Even Karl's emails were late.

* * *

12

'Doctors,' Christine Gerrard had once told Thomas, back when they'd shared a bed as well as office space, 'doctors assert that coffee on an empty stomach is bad for both the digestion and the liver.'

They don't know shit, thought Thomas, as he waited impatiently while the vending machine spat out a chemical cappuccino, the perfect concoction to kick-start his working day. A chocolate bar helped, too; it saved on sugar in the coffee for a start.

Right. Time to do some thinking. He took the spoils back to his desk and unlocked his drawer to get a writing pad. He drew three overlapping circles — like a maths problem — and labelled them Docks, Christine and Bob. Then he stared at the page for a few minutes before adding in squiggles and notes.

So what did he know? First off, it would be a cruel twist of fate if Bob Peterson had just happened to put in an appearance at the docks that day. Unless . . . unless he was sussing everyone out, ahead of his appointment? Now there was a thought. Maybe Christine knew, and they both wanted to crosscheck the reports with Bob's own observations? He bit into the Twix.

It was a reasonable assumption, but full of holes. It had been a routine assignment — they weren't even front of house — so why would Peterson bother? He boxed in Bob's name and started shading, inking him out of existence.

Maybe Bob Peterson's snooping around Harwich was some kind of payback for the fateful day Thomas had made his surprise visit to Christine's executive development weekend. *Who mentors someone in a country hotel, for Christ's sake?* His breath caught in his throat at the memory and he laid the pen down, spreading his fingers wide. It had all been a misunderstanding, surely? So why had he wanted to lay Peterson out — and still wanted to now?

Crossley was mumbling on the phone. She met his eyes and bent her head. "We're back today, sir; same positions. My team are on their way there now." She paused and covered the phone. "Where's Karl?" she hissed.

"He had some personal business to sort out." That was weak. He fired an email off to Karl: *Get your report done and get your arse in here; we're going back over to the docks.*

And where was the lovely Ms Gerrard? No sign of her. Nine-fifteen and all's definitely not well. *Ping.* Karl had responded:

Ha ha. Report's already done and attached. Please print without changes then meet me onsite; and pick up some painkillers on the way. You're a pal!

Thomas opened the attachment, reviewed, edited and corrected Karl's speed typing then added the extra sentences. After printing both reports, he sealed them in an envelope and slid it under Christine's door.

Karl's sallow face lit up as Thomas rattled the plastic container. "Thanks Tommo, you're a life saver. I got you the usual — sausage and egg on white, no ketchup. " They exchanged gifts solemnly, like a battlefield Christmas. "Listen Tommy, sorry for taking the piss about Christine. Honest to god, if I'd known that Bob Peterson was coming in to run the show . . ."

Thomas accepted the half-apology with a shrug; it was his own fault really, for confiding in best buddy Karl that one time. He devoured the sandwich and tried to put all thoughts of yesterday behind him.

"Anyway," Karl's voice lifted a little, "I met this wee lass in the pub last night and for a while I thought I was in love . . ."

Thomas set up his camera slowly, making Karl wait for the cue to conclude his shaggy pub story. "Go on then, how long for?"

"About three pints."

Introducing . . . Karl the stand-up. Thomas could almost hear the *boom cha* in his head.

After the previous day's drama, it felt good to get back into routine. Vehicles came and went without incident; order was restored. Customs were more visible today, making it easier to get decent shots. By lunchtime, the Customs team they were following had unearthed four rampant alcoholics, three pornographers and a couple of illegal immigrants — a good morning's work by anyone's standards.

Karl nipped out for a comfort break, leaving Thomas alone with the soothing sound of the gulls. He made the most of the time, reviewing the day's mosaic, happily without Bob Peterson.

The mobile rang, the same default ringtone as the day he'd bought it.

"Hey you; it's me, Miranda. Well, say something then."

"Hello?"

"Very droll. Look, you *will* be at Mum and Dad's on Sunday? You did promise and they haven't seen you in weeks . . ."

"If I promised then I'll be there."

"Great. You can collect me from Caliban's at one-thirty."

"Your wish is my command."

"Careful or I'll hold you to that, and then where would we be?" Thomas grinned to himself. "In trouble."

"See you, babe." Miranda hung up.

He was still staring into the past when Karl returned with fresh rations.

* * *

By late afternoon, Karl had recovered sufficiently to regale Thomas with another instalment of Army Adventures. This time it was peacekeeping in Kosovo. Early on, Thomas had learned two things about Karl. Firstly, that he enjoyed talking about his time in the Forces — a lot — and secondly, that he didn't like his monologues interrupted.

Karl spoke with gruff fondness about his regimental comrades, but his anecdotes tended to lack specifics such as places and names. Thomas had pieced together that Karl left the Army suddenly, and his transfer into the SSU had been down to some string-pulling. Strangely, Karl's trips down memory lane never ventured anywhere near the point, two years ago, when he'd actually joined the Surveillance Support Unit.

There wasn't much for their Customs team to do between ferries, so that left plenty of downtime for conversation. Thomas knew just which buttons to push, and soon Karl was waxing lyrical about Black Mountain and an Irish adolescence spent avoiding The Troubles and chasing anything in a skirt.

Thomas met him halfway, offering up childhood summers in the Dales and on the Yorkshire Moors. "So why did you come down to London then, if Yorkshire was so idyllic?"

This, Thomas knew, was Karl's way of saying, 'So what were *you* running away from?' He didn't miss a beat. "Nothing to keep me there. And I'd met this London lass."

Karl cheered. "Hooray! Thomas Bladen isn't a virgin after all."

He flipped Karl the finger and continued. "My uncle ran a local newspaper in Leeds, and they needed a cub photographer and general dogsbody. I wasn't getting on at home and I'd been taking pictures since I was a boy . . ."

"Sounds like a match made in low-wage heaven. So, what about the girl?" Karl edged forward a little in his chair.

"This girl, right, she wanted to be a model. And my uncle, well, he always had an eye on the next chance; so he sets himself up as an agent. Nothing suspect, mind."

He paused; did he really want to go into all this now? But Karl was waiting, like a toddler gazing at an open packet of biscuits. "Okay, she was about my age and didn't know her way around, so my uncle suggested I look after her. Then we got together, left for London, and moved in with her folks . . . the end!"

"That's not much of a story!"

No. It wasn't. Not when you missed out that it had been Thomas's idea to look out for Miranda, and with good reason. Or the part where his uncle's friend wanted her to do topless poses and wasn't keen on taking no for an answer. Or the finale where Thomas lamped him, broke the guy's nose and got the sack.

Karl pushed for more. "So you got to London, delivered the princess to the grateful king and queen, and all lived happily ever after?"

"Yeah, for a few years anyway."

"Come on, Tommy; and then what?"

"And then all good things came to an abrupt and frosty end."

"Sure, that's a sad story. Methinks you left all the best bits out." Karl laughed deeply, and Thomas found himself joining in, even though he didn't get the joke. "Still, at least you've got your old pal Karl to tell your troubles to."

"We must be grateful for small Murphys."

Karl took a bow. "Listen Tommy, if you're at a loose end over the weekend, you're welcome to come by and share a few cans."

"Not this weekend — I've got a wedding shoot booked."

"Really?" Karl's brows almost knitted together.

"Uh-huh." Better to lie than admit he was having Sunday dinner with his ex-girlfriend's family.

Ann Crossley's voice broke through on the radio. "Team two to team three. We've been asked for a Friday round-off with our Customs colleagues, as soon as this next ferry is unloaded. Refreshments will be provided!"

Karl sat to attention, nodding furiously. "You up for it, Tommy Boy?"

He shrugged.

"Okey dokey, Ms Crossley," Karl responded, giving Thomas a thumbs-up. "We'll join you as soon as we've packed our toys away." Another ferry horn blared out. "So, it's drinks at the captain's table, eh? And maybe we can find out about yesterday's gun-crime statistic."

"Karl, can you do me a favour and not ask? I think it's best if we leave it."

"That's all very well, but my report sang our praises and scored us a few points against the rest of Ms Crossley's groovy gang."

"No it didn't — I changed it."

Karl raised his chin. "Now why would you do a thing like that?"

Thomas sighed and scratched at his neck. "You know how Crossley is. After all, *we* were the ones to pick out that suspect car — not that it's proven," he backtracked. "So it's less complicated if we leave it out and stay 'on message.'" He made finger speech marks, the way Crossley did when she was running a brief.

"Well, well, you've got it all figured out. Right oh, mum's the word."

Yeah, thought Thomas, but for how long? "Look, tell you what, why don't I give you a ring on Saturday and sort out a get together?"

Karl nodded and glanced out the window. "Here they come, last of the high-rollers!" He yawned and tracked the first vehicles off the ramp. "Now, that's an expensive-looking van. What do you think Tommo — see that great big silver thing with the logo and details on the side? It's a classic double bluff; it's so in your face it couldn't be bent — what do you reckon?"

Thomas stopped taking photos of the Customs team and panned right. He almost dropped the camera when 'WRIGHTS — the Wright Way to Do Business' glared into view. *Oh Jesus: Miranda's brothers' van.*

"How about we buzz the team on the ground to give them a tug? A tenner says the van has been back through here in the last three weeks.

Thomas rested his camera in his lap and squeezed his hands together to stop them trembling. "I wouldn't bother." True, in a dishonest sort of way.

"But come on — the Amsterdam ferry!"

"Nah, we could be wasting everyone's time. No one wants to be stuck here, filling out unnecessary paperwork on a Friday. Let's leave it to Customs — it's *their* call."

Karl tilted his head, tick-tock fashion, weighing it up. "Fair enough."

Thomas felt the sweat clinging to the small of his back. He picked up binoculars and flicked around the Customs officers to see if anyone seemed interested in the silver van. Then he swept along the lane of traffic for a suitable decoy. "Control, from team three," he kept his voice calm and controlled, "there's a blue sports car, six vehicles down the line. It may be nothing, but it looks like one in the car park that went out yesterday." He could feel Karl scrutinising him and turned slowly, matching him in a staring contest.

Karl reached for his walkie-talkie. "Driver was a red-head; large wedding band and a humming bird pendant." He watched Thomas's face the way a cat looks at a baby bird.

Thomas went back to his binoculars, hardly breathing until the silver van was clear. The static burst from the walkie-talkies made him flinch. "*Control to teams two and three; we're doing a check on the blue sports car, over.*"

Karl clicked off. "I'm not sure what just happened there, Tommo," he set his own walkie-talkie down carefully. "But I'll tell you this for nothing, as a professional courtesy: it's a fool who underestimates me."

"Never have, never will," Thomas replied, smiling until his face hurt.

Chapter 5

Thomas burst awake like a swimmer breaking the surface, gasping for air. He lay there panting. *Jesus. Never again.* That was the worst thing about drinking too much: it always brought on the nightmares.

First, he'd had one of his classics — finding Christine and Bob Peterson together at the country hotel. Only, in the dream, he confronted them instead of letting Christine shoo him on his way. Now, he pushed past her and landed one on Peterson from the off and didn't stop until Peterson was a bloody pulp. Usually he'd wake up then with his fists clenched, but this time it tipped over.

Back in the house in Yorkshire; he and Patricia, kids again, huddled under the blanket as he read his Beano annuals aloud by torchlight to drown out their father's rage downstairs. The jagged tension, building in degrees to an explosion of crockery or a door slam, followed by the muffled silence of their mother's submission. Then the slow, heavy footfalls up the stairs until their father reached the very top step, the one nearest his bedroom. They always held their breath together beneath the blanket, listening. And just when he felt he couldn't hold it any longer, the scene exploded into thousands of tiny mosaic pieces.

He snatched at the clock: eight thirty. It was Saturday, a day of leisure, and he was a little disappointed. The previous night gradually revealed itself in a blurred montage of images. Karl had been drunk too — he had an almost medical susceptibility to alcohol. In a parallel universe he'd have been a good, cheap date.

Memory stirred. What time had they arranged to meet today? And wasn't there something about bringing his passport? He shook his head to loosen the memories, and pain signals rebounded from all corners of his brain.

He was drifting through the supermarket with the rest of the drones at ten o'clock when a text came in from Karl: *Good craic last night. Don't forget driving licence & passport. 3 pm Holloway Rd tube.*

He filled his trolley with whatever came to hand and added in chocolates, flowers and a quality bottle of wine for Sunday. Couldn't very well turn up at the Wrights' place empty-handed. As he pulled away, he checked the rear mirror and did the thing he always did, driving a full circuit around the car park, just to make sure no one was waiting for him. So far, no one had been.

On the way home, he pondered Bob Peterson again. Say Bob *had* been checking on the teams. Why that Thursday, particularly? The high-street gridlock soured Thomas's thoughts as he waited at temporary lights. Maybe Peterson wasn't there for them at all; maybe he was watching the ferry? But he was there well before the ferry arrived. Two things out of the ordinary had happened that week — the shooting on the Thursday and then Miranda's brothers coming through on the Friday. The lights changed to green and he put his foot down. And what the bloody hell did Karl need to see his personal ID for today?

Karl was already waiting outside the underground station when Thomas arrived, at five to three. He looked in fine shape, untarnished by the previous night's excesses. Lucky bastard.

"Great to see you Tommo; you won't regret this — got your documents?" Karl seemed really chuffed that he'd turned up, as if that were ever in doubt — pub promises being the social equivalent of signing in triplicate.

Thomas tapped his coat emphatically and followed Karl to his car. He watched as Karl checked casually around the vehicle. Old habits died hard.

Inside, the Ford Fiesta smelled overpoweringly of oranges.

"Hop in," Karl said cheerily, flinging an old newspaper on to the backseat.

"Did you murder Mr Del Monte and stash the body in here?"

Karl nodded and smirked.

"Oh, right. Yeah, 'scuse the aroma — I spilt a two-litre carton last week. It's dried out fine but . . . anyway, I quite like it."

Before Thomas could comment, Karl thrust in a CD of the Undertones, cued up a track and then did a murderous accompaniment to 'Perfect Cousin.' Karl would have made a perfect cousin himself — if only he'd taken a vow of silence. He waited until Karl had slaughtered the song to the very end.

"Okay I give up. Why the ID?"

"You'll see," Karl winked.

Top of the list of things that Thomas hated was surprises; second was more surprises. And the smell of oranges was now a possible contender for third place. He stared out the window as the streets of Camden flickered past, his mind rushing through the possibilities: white slave trade, booze cruise to Calais . . .

Karl tapped the wheel in time to the music, more or less, attempting to harmonise with the singers in places a lesser man would fear to tread. After a twisting series of back-roads, the car came out into a nondescript industrial estate. Karl parked and switched off the engine. "I thought it was high time we got to know each other properly, now that we're acquainted professionally. And where better than at a club where we can unwind and be ourselves?"

Thomas nodded dumbly. *Drinking club? Strip club? Poker club?*

Karl got out and stood in front of the car, swinging his keys.

"Come on, then. Are you gonna sit there all day?"

Seeing the look of glee on Karl's face, he took his time. Karl showed his driving licence to the security camera then had him do the same. He pressed his hand against the reinforced steel door as Karl held it open. This underworld was clearly members only.

They went inside and Karl smiled at him briefly, as if he had passed some test of brotherhood. They crossed the lobby and walked up to a desk surrounded by reinforced glass. Karl took out his two forms of ID and pushed them through the drop chute. A woman retrieved them and kept them below eye level. When they were returned, with nary a smile, Thomas followed suit. This time she requested £40 for a visitor's pass, which she informed him did not include the cost of equipment.

Thomas glanced at Karl and handed over two twenties. *Thanks a lot.* And he was still none the wiser. It could be an S & M club for all he knew.

"Right, Tommo," Karl slapped him on the back, "Welcome to the club!"

An electronic buzzer hummed and clicked, releasing a door at the end of a short corridor. On the other side, to the left and right, there were rows of doors. Thomas breathed deep; the air tasted subtly of smoke and machine oil. He keyed up his other senses and became aware of a muffled *thud thud* in rhythmic succession all around him.

Karl twisted the handle on a side door and pushed. A woman stood with her back to them, legs slightly braced. If their presence distracted her in any way she didn't show it, as she emptied her weapon into the target with calm precision. Thomas nodded to himself. *So that was it — a Gun Club.*

She placed the pistol on the counter, removed her ear-defenders and turned around. Thomas could see that all her actions were exact and measured. She smiled their way and Karl shifted his weight side to side, like a dog waiting for treats.

"Glock, I presume?" he asked.

Thomas figured that was for his benefit.

"You know me so well!" she leaned forward and tapped Karl's shoulder. He reddened.

"Teresa, this is Thomas — my pal from work."

Thomas flinched; he never mentioned the '*w*' word.

Teresa eased past Karl and checked a small screen on the wall behind him.

"I'm done here. The bay's free for another hour. I'm off to the bigger equipment," she made it sound like a gym. "Maybe catch you gentlemen later, in the bar?"

Thomas got the door. Teresa picked up her Glock 9 mm, removed the magazine and checked the weapon. She seemed to take her time about it, and Karl didn't seem to mind.

Thomas waited until Teresa had gone.

"Glock?"

"The choice of champions! Standard law enforcement issue, 9 mm; seventeen in a clip," Karl sounded like a survivalist train-spotter. "Now, wait here while I go get *us* some equipment and practice material."

Left alone, Thomas looked at the end of the bay. Terrorist targets glared back at him. An options menu on a small wall screen told him there were fourteen pistol bays — one was closed and one designated private — clearly, a busy day today. The bigger equipment, as Teresa had politely put it, was another eight bays' worth of fire-powering fun. He was about to venture into sub-menus when Karl returned with two cases.

"Right then. Before we start, a few ground rules."

"Who uses this place?" Thomas cut in.

"Mostly armed forces and police, that sort of thing — current and former."

"And all this is legal?"

Karl raised an eyebrow.

"I'd hardly bring you otherwise, now would I?"

"And Teresa; is she . . ."

"Now, now," Karl waved a finger. "The first rule of gunfight club is that nobody asks what anyone does. Members expect confidentiality. You of all people can appreciate that."

Karl ran through the essentials: only one person at the yellow line; no talking while using the equipment; loading, operating and emptying; the stance; breathing and squeezing; ear-defenders on unless everyone's hands were empty. It was a regular Handguns for Dummies.

Karl had a Buddhist-like calm, if you could forget about the firearm. Stripped of banter and bravado, he was a man in his element, comfortably loosing off rounds in tight formations until the magazine was spent. He put his weapon down and shifted the headgear.

"Now, you; and remember to allow for the kickback."

Thomas stood at the line and felt the cool weight of a Browning in his hands. The ear-defenders cocooned him, sealing him in with his thoughts. He gripped the handle tightly and watched the tiny, almost undetectable tremor of the barrel. The paper circles awaited him, and he leaned forward slightly, breathing into his stomach as he crushed his finger against the trigger in a single, fluid movement. Then he waited, statue-like, as the dulled whine of the bullet echoed in his head. After three more shots, he stopped and put the gun down. He was, even by his own estimation, shit.

Karl clearly thought that laughter didn't count as speech.

"It's fine — for a beginner and all. Let's try something a little more provocative."

At the flick of a button, terrorists swivelled towards them in a ragged line. Karl took the stand and quickly got into his stride. Head and heart, just like in the movies.

"Now you."

Thomas stepped up and something clicked in his psyche. When he looked into the anonymous, printed faces, his mind went slipstream. He saw teachers, the Neanderthals at school, Bob Peterson and his own father. And now, when he pulled the trigger, he was rewriting history, redressing the balance of power in his head.

He finished the salvo and placed the gun down, touching it gently like a talisman. The targets bore the conviction of his thoughts; every one a body shot.

"That was much better, Tommo. I think we've found your brand!" Karl applauded. "Better than many I've seen, picking up a gun for the first time."

"Thanks," he acknowledged, justly pleased, except it wasn't the first time.

* * *

The bar was actually a café, which was a relief. Guns and alcohol hadn't sounded like a good mix. Karl pointed him to a couple of comfy chairs and went off for coffees. Teresa waved from across the room, keeping her distance. Thomas glanced from table to table at the crowd — singles, couples and groups, and presumably every one of them proficient with a gun. He didn't feel reassured.

Karl seemed different somehow, since the shooting practice. But then, Thomas reasoned, thirty-six rounds from an automatic pistol would do that. "Right then Tommo, what's on your mind?" Karl blundered up and slapped a tray on the table.

"What . . . what do you mean?"

It was a well-practised stalling technique; if in doubt, act distracted. He reached for a cup carefully, but Karl didn't look impressed.

"Come on, Thomas, cards on the table. I've brought you into my confidence, shown you part of my secret world . . ." Karl grinned and eased back in his chair, ". . . How about returning the favour?"

Thomas peeled his back away from the vinyl upholstery. Every breath seemed to spread the dampness.

"I'm not sure what you're on about. You've obviously invited me here for a reason — if it's to join your private army, on today's performance, you'd best put me down as a driver," he searched Karl's face for a punchline. "Beyond that, I'm clueless."

Karl smacked his lips. "You can play that innocent abroad line as long as you like, but I don't buy it. Something *happened* yesterday — I'm not sure what."

Thomas felt himself blushing. *Stupid bastard.* He tilted his head towards the coffee. *Yeah, that'd work, hiding in the coffee steam.*

"Anyway," Karl continued, sipping at his cup, "I'm pretty sure you're clean, so I guess that puts us on a level footing, *whoever* you represent."

It sounded like a cue.

"Sorry, you've lost me — who I represent?"

"Come on now, Tommo, enough with the games. Why else would you be in the Surveillance Support Unit?"

"How d'you mean?" Thomas leaned forward, leading with his jaw. "It's just a job, that's all; forget the mission statement and the badge — we're the hired help. All right, I grant you most of 'em are more ambitious, but not me or you, right?"

He stopped short; Karl was staring at him intently, still as marble.

". . . And I s'pose it's also a proving ground for the likes of Ann Crossley and Christine Gerrard, on their way up the greasy pole?"

He'd run out of things to say and opened his palms flat. If there were any aces in this conversation, he didn't have them. No one spoke for a good minute, before Thomas braved the silence.

"You were expecting more?"

Karl toyed with the sugar sachets.

"Shit. You really *don't* know, do you?"

"Not yet . . ." Thomas narrowed his eyes.

Karl slumped back in his chair and gazed at his hands.

"God, Tommo; what a pickle of bollocks. Let's take a step back. You've been in the SSU for . . ."

"Two years," he filled in the blank even though Karl already knew it.

"Okay, well it's a little bit longer than that for me, and I started in West London. Some time ago, I was asked to participate in a *covert review* of the SSU, from the ground. There were concerns about information going astray . . . And before you ask, I don't know what — and even if I did know, I wouldn't tell you."

"So how are you involved in all this?"

"Not at all, officially. I'm just a pair of eyes and ears, as you've probably figured out. But I thought, after that van yesterday, that you were definitely . . . you know . . . representing some other party as well."

"I just felt they were innocent."

"*They*? You have a good memory," Karl blinked slowly.

Thomas swallowed hard; he could feel the heat at his armpits. They finished their coffee in uncomfortable silence.

"Look," Karl said eventually, "I messed up, okay; I read the signs wrong. You don't socialise, you doctored my report; you convinced me to let someone go through at the docks — Christ, you may even have picked out a gunman. It all added up to you being in the SSU for more than a mortgage and a pension."

"Like you, you mean?" Thomas was still adjusting to the idea that Karl had another life going on.

Karl soon tired of being stared at.

"Let's not let this screw up a perfectly good working relationship, eh Tommo? What do you say?"

"Deal," Thomas stretched out his hand. "As long as you introduce me to Teresa when I bring the drinks back."

As Thomas stood in line, watching as Teresa ambled over to their table, he had a revelation. Right up there with gravity, the faked moon-landing pictures and real men not liking opera. He rushed the coffees back then excused himself to the gents. He locked the cubicle door behind him, sat on the toilet lid and took deep, slow breaths. His pulse pounded in his ears. This was something he hadn't felt in a long time: fear. He speed-dialled Miranda's mobile and stared at the graffiti on the inside of the door. Even at a gun club, there was apparently someone willing to do the nasty with strangers for ten pounds. Some helpful soul had even added pencil drawings.

She picked up first ring.

"Miranda Wright — at your service!"

"Hi, it's me. Listen, I'm going to ask you a question; it may seem a bit odd."

"Are you okay, Thomas?"

She must have sensed the concern in his voice; she'd cut straight through the usual double-entendres.

"I need to know if an Irish guy has been at Caliban's recently, asking questions. About five-foot eight; short, reddish-brown hair. Check with Sheryl and *be* discreet."

"I'll ring you back."

"No," he insisted, "just text me."

"Okay. I'll come over later tonight. You don't sound good."

"Fine."

Back at the table, Karl was in full flow.

"All Ulster men are romantics — it's the Celtic blood; poetry is in our veins."

Thomas took his seat; the hammering in his chest had slowed a little.

"I thought that was Guinness?"

Karl's eyes lit up at the prospect of a joust.

"Whereas, your Yorkshireman . . . he has no finesse. It's all whippets and coal."

Teresa turned towards Thomas. He pulled it together and went for broke:

> "Because of the light of the moon,
> Silver is found on the moor;
> And because of the light of the sun,
> There is gold on the walls of the poor.
>
> Because of the light of the stars,
> Planets are found in the stream;
> And because of the light of your eyes
> There is love in the depths of my dream."

"Well, well," Karl mimed applause. "Is this a hidden side to you, Tommo?"

Thomas smiled; more like a poetry book from a Leeds charity shop. One he'd bought, back in the day, to impress Miranda. Even now he could recall one or two, word perfect. The poet Francis Carlin would have been pleased, had he not been dead for a hundred years.

The three of them found an easy rhythm of conversation, where nothing much was said, but everyone seemed to gel. Teresa continued to play one off against the other. Thomas saw early on that he was on to a loser; where Teresa was concerned, Karl was smoother than a vaselined billiard ball.

As he watched Karl in action, it was hard to believe that his buddy was anything more. As if the previous conversation had never taken place. Then the text came in from Miranda. One word: *yes*.

Chapter 6

Miranda's car was already at the end of his street. At first he felt relieved and then reality started to dawn. The charade he'd kept up for the last couple of years was about to come apart at the seams. He slowed, weighed down by the conclusion that he was as big a liar as Karl.

She waved from the car as he approached. *God knows how long she's been waiting. Probably turned up, got no answer at the door, saw the car and decided to stay put, bless her.*

The car window slid down.

"About time; shift your arse — this takeaway will be stone cold!"

It was all he could do to stop himself from kissing her.

She followed him inside and he heard the clank of the wine bottle in her coat pocket. With the oven on and the meal reheating, Miranda sprawled out on the sofa, leaving a deliberate space. He opted for the armchair and perched forward, cupping a loose fist.

"Are you gonna tell me what's up, then?"

He rubbed a knuckle on his chin. This was it: the end of life as he knew it. "You know how I never talk about work? Well, it's time to break that rule."

Miranda reached for her wine. Maybe she was trying to inoculate herself against bad news. He copied her, on the off chance that it might work.

"What . . . what do you think I do for a living, Miranda?"

She frowned.

"We agreed that I'd never ask, just like you never ask about Mum and Dad's business. You told me that you take photos and that's good enough for me. I dunno, stuff like accident investigations, crime scenes, maybe? One time you also mentioned delivering packages . . ." she looked up, studying his face. ". . . And you said that it was all government work."

Which he translated as: 'Is it *really* government work?' He took a gulp of wine and felt the heat rise to his face. *Let's try a different approach.*

"Remember a couple of years back, when your dad was being fitted up by that dodgy copper."

"Course I do. Your pictures saved his bacon. What's that got to do with your work?"

Sod it, shit or bust.

"That's sort of what I do for a living, some of the time. You know, photographs, where people don't know about it."

Miranda sat upright.

"What? Like some sort of spy?"

Nervous laughter followed, as if she wanted to be wrong about this.

"Not exactly," he looked away. "I do *surveillance* — pictures, film, audio."

The buzzer went off in the kitchen. Miranda got up. For a moment or two, he wondered if she'd be coming back.

"Look Miranda," he called out to the kitchen, "I owe you an explanation."

The only reply was the clattering of the oven door. Miranda returned with a tray full of tins. She spooned out the food and put his plate down beside hers.

"Is it dangerous, then?"

He'd seen her like this before, calm and controlled — on the outside. He shook his head and tried his best light-hearted smile — the sort people use at funerals when they've got nothing useful to say.

* * *

He started at the beginning — a straightforward Civil Service job, at State House in High Holborn. That much she already knew, but he sketched in some of the detail. The Patent Office was on floors three to fifteen, with the Royal Navy occupying ground to two. He mentioned the Russian gift shop across the street that everyone thought was a front for a spy-ring. Ironic now, all things considered.

He glided over the backdrop to that time, when he and Miranda had separated, and the trench warfare that led up to it — no sense in raking up the past again. After the split, his lowly desk job had kept him going, somewhere to while away the day until he could photograph the underbelly of the city. Even lunchtimes had been spent taking pictures — in nearby Bloomsbury, or the odd panoramic shot from the thirteenth floor of State House. Hiding from life, like every other pen pusher who thinks — or hopes — that they're destined for something better. And his personal pipe dream, back then, had been that the right portfolio could get him on to a national newspaper.

There had been one particular man in the building who shared his fondness for unorthodox hours — an inhabitant of the fifteenth floor, where mere mortals weren't allowed.

Comments in the lift about his choice of camera — the one he brought to work religiously, as if to say 'fuck you' to lifer colleagues — led to an invitation to photograph the skyline from the top deck, and the chance to show his wares to someone who shared his passion. That was how he'd met Sir Peter Carroll, founder and patriarch of the Surveillance Support Unit, although Thomas didn't know that at the time.

A few weeks later, an opportunity arose for some weekend overtime as a stand-in cameraman. And, he freely admitted, a little bit of intrigue and interest in a Miranda-less existence. Wind forward two or three months and he was called up to the fifteenth floor for a formal interview with Sir Peter and two lackeys, under the watchful eye of a painting of Churchill.

He ended his monologue, swerving past any mention of the assignments themselves. Miranda's eyes looked capable of swallowing him, as if she were physically seeing him in a new light. She drained her glass and set it down carefully on the table.

"Mum and Dad aren't gonna like this."

He nodded rhythmically; she was right. John and Diane Wright took a dim view of the establishment, and here he was, coming out of the secrecy closet. And when all was said and done, they were still family to him.

An uneasy silence hung over them. Miranda finished her meal with the same fixed expression, as if she wanted to slap him, hard. He couldn't really blame her.

"So why tell me now?" she paused and folded her arms. "And how long has this been going on?"

He put his cutlery down; his appetite had died.

"A year or so."

"Bollocks!" she glared at him, "I don't believe you."

"Well, maybe eighteen months, give or take."

She was still glowering.

"Look, it's no big deal — I just work in the background."

"Right, so what's the story with the Irish geezer you were asking about?"

He blew out a long breath; crunch time again.

"I think someone might be checking up on me."

She started laughing; he hadn't expected that.

"Serves you bloody right — one of your lot is he? Or MI-27!"

She turned away and a part of him died inside. Instinctively, he reached out and touched her arm. Her face changed. Scorn gave way to concern; that made him feel worse.

"Why don't you tell me about it — I'll go stick the kettle on."

"I was at Harwich yesterday and I saw your brothers' van coming off the ferry from Amsterdam. It was definitely Sam and Terry. I kept Customs off their back."

"No point me asking what *you* were doing there?"

"My job. Look Miranda, I'm trying to help. The place is crawling with Customs and Excise at the moment. Whatever the boys are doing, they can't do it there."

She opened her mouth to speak, but Thomas headed her off at the pass. "I don't care what they're up to. I just wouldn't want any trouble for them."

She nodded, as if he'd just flashed the family loyalty card at her. "And the Irish geezer?"

"Like I said, he could be investigating me."

"Could be?" she sounded exasperated. "For what — is he interested in the family?"

"Honestly? I don't know."

"Well, you better bloody well find out."

"Okay," he conceded. "But will you help me warn the boys off, tomorrow?"

She picked up the remote control and flicked through television channels. If she'd been a cat, her tail would have been twitching. She settled on a made-for-TV film of no interest to either of them. He stole glances at her as she sat there, avoiding eye contact. Surely he could trust *her* of all people?

Out of desperation, he snorted like a horse and she stifled a smile; she always liked that. He nestled into her side of the sofa and felt her leg against his. Her handbag started buzzing.

"Mobile," she said, deadpan.

Still not out of the woods yet then.

"Hi Sheryl, how's business — many punters in?" There was a long pause. Miranda's eyes narrowed. "Oh, really. Alone?" she looked daggers at Thomas. "Keep him there . . . no, if he looks like he's gonna leave, chat him up and spike his drink. I'm on my way." She snapped the phone shut. "Your Irishman is at the club right now. Get your coat."

The car grumbled menacingly; Miranda held the wheel like it was a lifebelt.

"Either you sort this today, or I will."

It wasn't a request; it wasn't even a threat. But he could feel the walls going up around her.

"When we get there I'll take the side door — you go in and speak to him."

He knew what else was coming.

"Miranda, don't call your brothers."

They stopped at the lights, opposite a billboard for a building society. An old advertising slogan popped into his head: *because life's complicated enough.*

* * *

Miranda parked. He touched her shoulder lightly, but she shrugged it off.

"You better deal with this, Thomas."

He pushed the swing door: high noon, in uptown London. There were maybe a dozen punters in the room and Karl was sitting in full view of the bar, reading a copy of *Private Eye*. He seemed engrossed in his magazine, chuckling away, giving every indication that he was enjoying himself enormously.

Miranda appeared behind the bar and Sheryl sidled over to her, flattening her New Yorker tones to a whisper.

"He's been drinking a pint of shandy for ages."

"Shandy?"

"Yeah, when he ordered it, he said that's what real men drink these days!"

Karl laughed aloud suddenly as if he were listening to every word.

Miranda opened her mobile, selected a number carefully and held the phone up as if she was trying to get a signal. Thomas read her, loud and clear. Resolve this now or the Brothers Grimm would turn up, like working class cavalry. He couldn't blame her. Nothing was more precious to the family than Miranda. He held on to that thought and tried to walk tall to the bar, clocking the cover of *Private Eye* — Tony Blair grinning like The Joker.

He ordered a drink — Southern Comfort and lemonade — which Miranda made sure he paid for. Glass in hand, he drew up a chair and faced Tony Blair. Karl didn't stir.

"What are you doing here, Karl?"

"Can't a man enjoy a nice quiet drink and a read of his comic?"

"Cut the bullshit, I'm not in the mood."

The magazine lowered like a drawbridge.

"I've been asked to tell you, as a friend: the conversation we had earlier today — it never happened. It's off limits — comprendez?"

Thomas knew now how an ant felt under the magnifying glass. His *friend* was threatening him. For a second or two, he thought about smacking him one. But Karl was becoming a more unknown quantity every minute.

"Then this place is off limits too. Understand?"

Karl smiled a conciliatory smile.

"Agreed. I take it that the staff are out of bounds as well?"

No laughs today. They sipped their drinks in unison. Thomas felt the tension reach out across his shoulders. He held his position; hard, unyielding and still close enough to lamp Karl if the need arose.

"One more thing Karl — there better not be any bugs here."

Karl reached into his pocket and Thomas flinched; they both saw it. Karl pulled out a small plastic case, and slid it across the table.

"As a show of good faith. On Monday, we reset the clocks and it's business as usual. Deal?"

"Deal," Thomas lifted the lid for an instant, clocked the electronic device then closed it carefully.

Karl drained his drink and rolled up his magazine.

"Well Tommo, I must be off. It's been grand. See you at the office," Karl picked up his glass and took it over to the bar.

Sheryl started towards him but he carried on walking.

"Nice meeting you . . . Miranda, isn't it?"

Thomas remained at the table, with his back to the bar, until Karl had gone. The door was still moving when Miranda sat down to join him.

"He won't come here again."

"Thanks," she said quietly, staring at the table.

His face softened and he rolled back his shoulders, like a boxer winding down after a successful bout.

"And Thomas," she was close enough to kiss him, close enough that he could smell her body's scent below the perfume; "Don't bring your work into my life again."

The blood drained from his groin in an instant. He palmed the plastic box into his pocket, locking eyes with her all the while.

"I think I'd like to sweep this place for bugs, as a precaution. It'll be Monday before I can get the equipment."

She nodded; maybe she was adapting more quickly than he'd expected. *Leaps and bounds.* Yesterday she only knew he was a photographer; today he was Spiderman.

She snatched his glass away as she got up from the table.

"You know your way home."

He swore under his breath and thrust his hands into his jacket, crushing his hand against the box until his fingers were numb.

* * *

31

Ten-thirty at night, the doorbell rang. He paused the film — a black and white comedy more than sixty years old. He was still smiling as he checked the silhouette through the glass.

Miranda didn't move; she kept that model profile thing going on, knowing its effect on him. He managed to open the door without ripping the handle off. "We never got to dessert," she said, slinking past him, with an overnight bag over one shoulder and a carton of vanilla Haagen-Dazs in her hand.

Chapter 7

Thomas blinked, in the Sunday morning half-light. All around him was the faint, unmistakable scent of ice cream. He pulled a spoon from under his shoulder and stretched his arm out, contacting Miranda's leg. *Oh yeah.*

She stirred, looked up at him like the cat that had got the ice cream and rewarded him with a delicious smile.

"Well, we haven't done that in a while."

She crossed her thigh over his and shifted closer — but not too close — honouring their unspoken rule: whatever happens today is only for today. And now it was tomorrow. He shaped a hand around her breast, but she held it to one side: down boy.

"Let's just sleep a while."

He closed his eyes and tried to think of something other than sex. Karl came to mind first, and he wondered what a therapist would make of that? Where did he stand with Karl now — could they really *reset the clocks*? He twitched and Miranda playfully slapped him to lie still. And what was Bob Peterson really doing on the scene?

Miranda groaned in protest.

"Look, if you really can't sleep," she flicked his erection and paused, opening her eyes wide to see his reaction, "Milk and one sugar, thanks."

He disentangled himself and reluctantly left the bed, glancing down at his misplaced enthusiasm. Not today, by the sound of things. The kettle took its time so he waited in the kitchen, taking the pistol stance and handling a lethal fork while doing replays in his head. Something else he hadn't told her about.

Miranda was feigning sleep when he returned to the bedroom, breathing a little too heavily — always a giveaway. He plonked the tea down and started gathering up clothes from around the floor. Along the way he lifted the ice-cream lid and flung it into a bin.

"Aren't you coming back in again?" she pouted, drawing back the sheet like the world's best show and tell.

He didn't need a map and directions.

* * *

Miranda's mobile alarm sounded at ten-thirty.

"Get up you lazy bastard — I've got things to do. I need to stop by the club."

It was funny, the way that Miranda sometimes avoided calling it Caliban's, even though she'd named the club herself. All part of her dumbed down, East-End girl made good façade. She had done well for herself though, opening Caliban's a little more than a year ago; purchased largely with her own money from a lucrative modelling contract in Bermuda, plus a contribution from Mum and Dad — which Thomas always read as: other people's money.

She always smiled when she saw her photograph on the living room wall; it was a spontaneous walking shot, from the streets of Leeds, taken with an old 110. True, it had dated, but somehow that just added to its eighties charm. Sometimes he'd move the photo around, just to try and throw her off guard, but it was always on one wall or another. Christine Gerrard, in her time, had hated that picture; another reason to treasure it.

Miranda stood before the picture gallery, head cocked to one side and a thin smile upon her lips.

"If you follow me down to the club, I can drop you back there after dinner." The subtext: you're going home alone tonight.

On the drive over, whenever they paused at traffic lights, he could see Miranda glancing back at him. Once or twice she gave a sly wave in the rear mirror, but her face was distant. Another clock reset, it seemed.

He parked at Caliban's and followed Miranda to the back office. Sheryl was her usual indispensable self — coffee ready and waiting as they entered. He sometimes liked to think that she was the daughter of an American crime family, with the Wrights as part of an underworld exchange programme. But he never asked; everyone needed secrets.

Miranda settled at her desk and pored over the accounts. He left her to it and went into the pool room across the way. Sheryl followed him.

"Fancy a quick game?" she racked up the balls and bent forward enticingly.

He mustered an eggshell smile.

"Sure, why not."

And it was a quick game. Sheryl played to win; she meant business. Small wonder that Miranda had appointed her as manager of Caliban's. Best of three became best of seven and still the balls were sinking faster than his self-esteem. Part way through game six, 4-1 in Sheryl's favour, Miranda appeared at the door. Sheryl looked over and they shared a glance. With that, she killed the remaining stripes with clinical precision and then iced the black.

"He's all yours," she called across to Miranda.

"Thanks for keeping him entertained," she winked, heading for the door.

As Thomas passed by Sheryl, she touched him lightly on the shoulder; "She tells me everything, you know."

He hoped she was joking.

Outside, he transferred the chocs, wine and flowers to Miranda's Mini Cooper. She took one look at the bouquet and shook her head.

"They're past their best — we'll pick up something better on the way."

Fair enough. He liked to make a good impression with Mum and Dad, especially today when he'd be delivering an avalanche of bad news.

* * *

The Wrights' house screamed *working class with money*, from the expensively paved drive to the retro coach lamp at the door. They'd dispensed with the wrought iron gates a couple of years back, after a police raid took them off the hinges. Miranda's brothers — Terry and Sam — had already arrived, their BMW and Peugeot parked side by side; they shared a large house out towards Canning Town.

Miranda pulled out her key — all three children still had keys — for a while, Thomas had one too, but he'd turned his in when Miranda had left for sunnier climes. Dire Straits' 'Brothers in Arms' was playing through the hallway like mood music. Thomas almost waited at the door until 'Money for Nothing' kicked in — a family anthem if ever there was one.

Diane, mother to the clan, waved and disappeared into the kitchen. Miranda peeled off to the living room to meet with the rest of them, but Thomas carried the spoils to Diane. Even in profile, she was a fine-looking woman and her genes had generously found their way to Miranda. Diane turned and smiled. "Sit your arse down and pour us both a glass of wine."

Bliss. No pretensions, just honest to goodness real people.

"How's things, Thomas?" she glanced up as she basted the chicken, and winked. She'd left off the rest of the sentence, which would have run: 'How's things, Thomas, with you and my daughter?'

"Not bad," he blushed and Diane smiled again. He knew both she and John still held out a fragile hope that Miranda and he would one day get their act together. As John had succinctly put it, "Stop fucking about and settle down." One Christmas, John had got so royally pissed that he'd declared: "I sometimes wish I had another daughter, so you could start again from scratch."

Thomas survived his gentle interrogation and sauntered on through to the others. John and the boys gave a cheer at his arrival. Miranda kept her distance. "How's business, Thomas?" John asked casually, just as always.

Miranda looked daggers at Thomas. Yeah, John would get an answer and a half today. She retreated into the kitchen, morphing from successful businesswoman to mummy's helper in the blink of an eye. They weren't a throwback family, just traditional. Presents under the tree and Queen's speech at Christmas; cemetery visits on Boxing Day and sovereign rings for the boys' twenty-firsts.

John picked up a remote control and the wall slid back, revealing a TV screen that almost qualified as a cinema. Highlights from the last West Ham game flooded the room. Thomas watched with mild interest. He'd been to a few games with the boys over the years, but it didn't really light his candle. For a while he'd even tried following the York City club, out of loyalty to his home region. But deep down he still believed football was for people who didn't have the balls for rugby.

Sam had once had a trial for West Ham youth team, straight out of school. Somehow this still entitled him to offer comment on every pass and volley. Terry, not to be outdone, punctuated every unsuccessful manoeuvre with 'bollocks' or 'that was shit,' the two brothers relishing their double act. John looked on proudly at his sons and Thomas, if he could have, he'd have taken a hundred photographs from all angles to capture the feeling forever. The boys looked up to him, the parents thought the world of him and Miranda — well, he didn't even have words for what they had between them.

At the table, with John carving, Thomas made an extra effort to join in with the banter. For a while he could forget his painful duty and just enjoy the company; that and Miranda rubbing her foot up against him under the table. But by the time the dessert bowls were passed around — no vanilla ice cream, thankfully — he had a sinking feeling.

"So," he broke the easy chatter. "I've, er, got a bit of a problem." The clan all shifted in a little and he cleared his throat. "I was at Harwich last week — I saw the van come back from Amsterdam."

John Wright shot a surprised look to his sons. Thomas carried on. "The thing is, well, it's not a good place to do business right now."

The boys hadn't said a word. John was first to speak. "How d'ya mean, Thomas?" John's voice had a quiet authority. Or maybe it just seemed that way because Thomas had never seen him in a rage.

Miranda shifted her foot away and sat up a little straighter. "Thomas was working there, Dad, taking pictures."

John nodded, eyes narrowing. Terry piped up. "No sweat, we didn't get stopped or anything."

Miranda cut in. "No, and that was thanks to Thomas."

He gaped at her, open-mouthed — so much for trusting and sharing.

She clocked his face and turned beetroot, whispering to herself: "Bollocks!"

"That'll do, thank you," Diane stopped eating.

John sat back in his chair, scratching his chin as he looked over at Thomas. "Do you want to talk about it?"

Thomas nodded; at least he'd been given a choice. "I was on a film assignment for Customs & Excise — a training film." So far so good, successfully tiptoeing the line between truth and bullshit. "Someone with me wanted the van checked, but I persuaded him not to bother."

He felt Miranda squeeze his hand under the table; he couldn't tell if the clamminess was his or hers. John took a sip of his beer — somehow he'd never made the conversion to wine. "And when was this exactly?"

Thomas looked along the table to Sam and Terry. "On Friday."

John leaned forward. "I told you two to leave it well alone — how many trips has it been now?"

"Five, Dad," Sam said.

A stranger might have itched to know what they were carrying. Thomas, he was just happy that they'd got through without incident.

"Well, thanks, Thomas. Do we owe this Customs geezer anything?"

He shook his head quickly.

John looked straight at him, like a dog deciding whether or not to attack. "So what's the problem, then?"

Thomas twisted his paper napkin. "There's this bloke at work — another photographer — only . . . only he might have taken an interest in my private life."

"Do you want me to sort it out for you?" Sort *him* out, more likely.

"No, it's taken care of now," he looked to Miranda for encouragement. "But I'd be a lot more comfortable if you'd let me check your house over for . . . electronic devices."

"You mean like the Old Bill might use?" John's face twitched.

Thomas swallowed. "Well, it's probably nothing; I'd just like to be sure."

"It's alright, Dad," Miranda pitched in, "he's doing the club for me as well."

Diane stepped into the fray. "Hold on, let me get this right, Thomas. Someone's been checking up on you and you think they might have planted stuff here, in our home? What kind of business are you involved in?"

"Mum, give him a chance. It's just a precaution."

But Diane was having none of it; it wasn't hard to see who Miranda took after. "No, let's have it all out in the open. You involved in drugs or something?"

The Wright family creed: no drugs or prostitution or porn. Some might say that wouldn't leave a lot to profit from, but they'd be very wrong.

"Alright," Thomas tapped the table, "here it is. About a year ago I changed jobs — still Civil Service but I became a *specialist* photographer." He stressed the word so that hopefully it would say things that he wouldn't have to. Diane recoiled like he'd just punched her.

"Well, you never bloody said! Did you know about this, Miranda?"

"No Mum," Miranda admitted in a quiet voice, "I only found out yesterday."

Thank you, Judas.

"Hold up," John raised a fork. "If we're gonna talk about this, let's get comfortable." Like a sofa would make it all easier.

John mainly listened and didn't ask too many questions. Everyone else picked at Thomas like he was the day's special.

"So let me get this straight," Terry laughed. "You've been leading this secret life for over a year and you never told us!"

He shrugged, like a desperate plea for clemency.

"Hey, give the boy a chance," John calmed the mob. "Never mind what he kept from us, for a minute; he still did the boys a favour and we're in his debt."

"Just let me sweep the house for . . ."

"Intrusions," Miranda chipped in helpfully.

"Well," John concluded, "that's about it. Miranda, why don't you and your mother make us all some tea."

Oh bollocks, Thomas thought; here comes the real discussion. John waited less than five seconds after the kitchen door closed. "I don't like deceivers, Thomas, but I respect loyalty. The main thing is that you still looked out for Sam and Terry. I appreciate that. All I want to say is this . . ."

Thomas braced himself. John and the boys leaned in as one.

"How much do you think we could charge to check out other people's places for these intrusions? I know plenty of people who would be interested in that sort of service."

"Hey Dad, I could get some cards printed."

Thomas looked over at Sam. God help him, he was serious.

* * *

Miranda seemed unseasonably chirpy on the drive back to Caliban's; a marked difference from Thomas who felt like he'd lost a tenner and found a black eye. "Cheer up, babe, it'll be fine."

He rubbed a thumb against his forehead in disbelief. "Your dad wants to offer a counter-intelligence service to the criminal fraternity, your brother wants to get me business cards and your mum probably hates me now."

"Nah, I talked with her while you four were playing *The Godfather*. She knows it wasn't personal, what with you not telling *any* of us."

Seconds out, round two. "Look Miranda, it's the Official Secrets Act not a bloody Cluedo game."

"So, do you *like* your job, then?"

Now there was a question he'd never been asked. Not even Christine Gerrard had drawn that one out of the hat, come appraisal time. "Most of it, yeah. But I don't like the idea of being at the other end of the lens."

Miranda squeezed his thigh. "You used to pose for me though!"

In the club's car park, she turned off the engine. He wanted to say something meaningful; he been thinking about it all through the drive over. The best he could offer was: "Look, I'm sorry."

She kissed him matter-of-factly on the cheek and that hurt more than anything else. And she'd know it. Nothing pained him as much as Miranda drawing away again.

He trudged towards his car and consoled himself. Not a bad weekend, all things considered. He'd played with guns, had some great sex, shared a family meal and admitted to the people he cared about most in the world that he'd been lying to them for months. Oh yeah, and found out that his best mate at work had been spying on him. Roll on Monday.

Chapter 8

He got into the office early and flicked the main lights on. At the far end of the room, Christine's sanctuary was ablaze like an electric fly-killer. Ann Crossley's chair had a bag hung over the back of it so someone had already started playing brown-noses with the boss. But then, today was the big day when Bob Peterson joined the gang. In all the weekend's excitement he'd almost forgotten that piece of joy.

At 8.15, the impossible happened; Karl had somehow twisted the space-time continuum and arrived before most of the rabble. As soon as he was in the door, he marched over to the vending machines. Good to see that military training hadn't gone to waste. Then he appeared at Thomas's desk with coffees and two Twixes. "I, er, think I may have been a bit over-dramatic. All quits now?" Karl put the goods down and extended his hand. Thomas reciprocated, grabbing the payoff before Karl changed his mind.

Karl had clearly been at a different 'prioritise your work' seminar. First on his agenda was clearing out the spam emails from the web filter, with occasional commentary. "Jaysus, you'd think they could at least *spell* sperm? Fancy writing it with a 'u'!"

"Why do you bother reading them?"

"I don't read *all* of them — I just find some of titles intriguing. Lookie here Tommo; what do you reckon? Genuine herbal Viagra from Naples!"

Christine's door opened and the sound of chatter and laughter floated out. Thomas and Karl exchanged a customary glance of contempt. Ann Crossley strode out, with all the confidence that a Cambridge education could buy, even if it had diluted her native Cardiff accent along the way.

"Good morning, gentlemen!" she crooned and returned to her desk.

"Ann, have you lost a few pounds by any chance?" Karl asked.

She glanced over herself admiringly. "Well, yes, as it happens."

Karl daggered in with lightning speed. "Because I found a fiver on the carpet."

"Karl," she scowled, "you can be a real prick sometimes."

"That's because sometimes only a real prick will do!"

She huffed and fired up her laptop.

"Why do you do it, Karl?" Thomas shook his head. Karl just flashed a grin. Out of the corner of his eye, Thomas saw a figure filling up Christine's doorway. The elusive Mr Peterson was surveying all that he owned. Thomas snapped a Twix finger in his teeth and stared at the screen, waiting for the inevitable call to visit the grown-ups. He managed a good five minutes of stoic activity under Bob Peterson's gaze, including Karl's emails declaring that Bob Peterson must be a busy man if he had time to engage in a one-way staring contest.

At eight thirty a mobile alarm went off; Bob Peterson cleared his throat. "Thomas, could you pop in please?" The poor sod was obviously a slave to the clock.

He drained the last of his coffee and picked up a notepad and pen. He imagined, for an instant, that Bob Peterson had been one of the targets he had fired bullets into. It helped put a smile on his face.

He sat down and tried not to react as Christine closed the door and sat closer to Bob than he would have liked.

"Thomas, glad to have you on the team."

He noted the lack of a pronoun — a good way to spot liars and sociopaths. Even so, he made the supreme sacrifice and shook Bob's hand.

"I've arranged to see everyone over the next couple of days, but I really wanted an opportunity for the three of us to, er, clear up any lasting misunderstandings."

"Do you mean the one about me *not* knowing you two were carrying on together before Christine and I split up?"

Bob and Christine exchanged an 'I told you so' glance; Christine folded her hands earnestly. "Thomas, we've been through this. Bob's interest in me was purely professional — when will you get that into your thick . . ." she paused and Thomas touched his tongue to his lip. The next words used to be: working class. But patronising the lower ranks would never do in front of her boss.

"—Head?" Thomas offered, generously. He had to be smart, smarter than Peterson, anyway. He glanced at Bob's hand — same ring as he wore at Harwich. As clear as the blow-up he'd printed at home. He swallowed his pride and did what needed to be done.

"Look, can we start again? My stuff with Christine is all in the past, but your arrival stirred things up a bit for me."

"Sure, sure!" Peterson beamed as if he'd just successfully hidden a pair of Christine's knickers in his back pocket. "I've checked through your record, Thomas, and it's exemplary. I'm sure we can work together — I'd hate to have to lose you from the team."

Thomas made no attempt to hide his shock. He looked straight at Christine, who seemed similarly surprised. "I'll wait to hear from you, then."

"Absolutely," Peterson opened the door, as if he was making a point. "Don't go too far; I want the whole team in at 9.30."

Thomas returned to his desk with a face like thunder. Christ, he'd really made a mess of that; nearly played his hand too soon. He went over to Karl. "Fancy a walk? I need some air."

"Be right with you Tommo, just closing down. Don't forget to lock your laptop."

Something else he hadn't done properly.

* * *

Karl ushered him to a café five minutes away. They both ordered a full breakfast. "I take it that your tête à tête wasn't all you hoped for?"

"I made a complete dick of myself," he shook his head slowly. "I accused him of sleeping with Christine before we'd officially split."

"Don't be expecting a good appraisal then!"

Two preposterously large mugs of tea arrived. Karl waited until the waitress had turned her back then made pretend swimming strokes over his tea.

Thomas just sighed; he'd lost his sense of humour.

"You know, Tommo, I loved and lost this girl, once. We were both stationed in Germany and we got together quickly. It was all brilliant and then I had to go back to Blighty on some urgent family business."

Thomas stopped drinking tea and paid closer attention.

"Anyway, she bumps into this officer on base, while I'm gone — turned out that she'd had a bit of a thing with him, over in Cyprus." Karl rotated his finger to show the passing of time. "So I get back to barracks and there's another fish in my kettle, so to speak."

Thomas had already decided that Karl made these phrases up. "How long were you away, Karl?"

"Long enough, evidently. I wasn't very mature about it all. And unfortunately for me he was a nastier fighter," Karl lifted his sweatshirt to reveal a series of white scars.

Thomas gasped.

"Listen now, I was no angel either. We wrecked the bar, apparently. I was certainly pretty wrecked at the time!" He winked then calmly took a sip of tea before he continued. "Anyway, not to be outdone, I tried a different tack and sent some photos of them together to his wife. Did I mention he had a wife?"

Thomas remembered that Bob Peterson was married, too. "And?"

"His wife divorced him. And later on, so I heard, the 'Officer and Bastard' married my lovely Jennifer." Once he'd stopped talking, the waitress returned; Karl's face lit up like a beacon. "Beatrice, you're a sight for sore eyes. Your husband is a very lucky man!" He was rewarded with a demure smile and the all-day breakfast — so named because it could take a slow eater all day to finish it.

Further conversation was parked as they made their way through a meal fit for a king — a king who enjoyed mushrooms, eggs, tomatoes, sausages, bacon, toast and beans.

Thomas clapped his hands appreciatively. "That hit the spot."

"You can always rely on your uncle Karl to make things better! Come on now or we'll miss the party."

* * *

The team filed into Christine's office, all clutching pen and paper. Karl had brought along his Homer Simpson pad and novelty snake pen.

Bob Peterson introduced himself and shook everyone's hand warmly. It was the usual 'we're in this together' speech, with a potted history of where he'd been working before and the assurance that he wasn't going to bring in change for change's sake — which always meant the exact opposite.

Christine chipped in here and there, as if they were a double-act already, and managed to not look in Thomas's direction. At one point Peterson made a joke about Sir Peter Carroll and asked Thomas not to repeat it the next time he saw the 'old man upstairs,' a blunt reference to Thomas having been interviewed by Sir Peter himself. Thomas swallowed his pride and smiled on cue.

Later, Ann Crossley asked about an accelerated development programme and Peterson agreed to look into it. Thomas managed not to mention that Christine herself had done something similar. So far, so good.

Karl wondered aloud what had made Peterson come to their branch of the SSU. Peterson laughed it off without committing himself. Thomas had been listening through a haze of indifference, but now he saw an opening. "So Bob," he adopted a matey tone, "how was the move up from Southampton?"

"A nightmare — still a work in progress!" Peterson grinned. "Most of our things are still in storage — I was working in Southampton right up to Saturday night. We're still waiting to exchange on the house so I guess I'll be commuting, unless one of you has a spare floor?"

Laughter all round. Thomas laughed too, at Peterson's audacity — the lying bastard. Gotcha! Christine's face was a study in marble. Then an alarm bell went off in his head. What if she and Peterson were engaged in their own little re-enactment society?

Later, Thomas sat at his desk, deep in thought. He had what he wanted — Peterson's denial, even though the photo proved he'd been at Harwich — but he didn't know what to do with it. 'Bang to rights' as Sam or Terry would put it. He smiled at himself. How ingrained the London-isms had become after years of living there. Even his accent was more East End than Yorkshire, these days. On those rare occasions when he contacted his own family, the first thing they usually said was that he gone 'all southern.'

Karl had stayed on for a few minutes — probably a prelude to his assessment. Thomas watched as he walked out of Christine's office, holding up the Simpson's pad as a face. Karl, his only ally — someone he still didn't know if he could trust.

"How did it go, then?"

Karl took a deep breath. "Fantastic, Tommo. They're thinking of putting me up for the George Cross."

"You're a funny man, Karl McNeill."

"That's just what Bob Peterson said — now are you sure you weren't listening at the door?"

Thomas held up a hand, Honest Injun style. His mobile bleeped; a text from Miranda: *Thanks for a lovely weekend. M. x.* He blushed and switched off the phone, remembering to pick up a sweeping kit from Stores, for Caliban's and the family home.

Chapter 9

Karl drove out to the docks with Thomas riding shotgun. He didn't say much to Karl; he was too busy thinking.

Peterson didn't need to lie; he could have mentioned being at Harwich, now that he'd met the team. He could have explained it as an informal assessment before taking charge. But no; something smelt fishy and Peterson was a week-old prawn.

By the time they arrived at their hidey-hole, overlooking the action, Monday weather had really kicked in — a drab, half-hearted downpour that set the mood. They sat, munching on sandwiches and peering through binoculars like schoolboy birdwatchers. Matter of fact, Thomas could identify the different gulls — Herring, Common and both types of Black Headed Gulls; not that he thought Karl would be interested.

Karl soon declared he was bored of scoping for women and went back to *Private Eye*. Thomas took to staring out at the sky, or what was left of it, as rain sprayed the windows in rhythmic bursts. It was, to quote Karl: "Shiter than a field of slurry." Clearly, the man had the soul of a great poet.

After a further hour of struggling together with the cryptic crossword and generally wasting taxpayers' money, the walkie-talkie spluttered into life. "Control to all units; we're calling it a day. Come down and get some close-ups."

* * *

The Customs teams went about their work, with little regard for the *Floaters* — a moniker the SSU had never managed to shake. The filming was supposed to be impromptu sequences, but as every good

45

photographer knew, off-the-cuff material needed a lot of preparation. A dry lens, no reflections or glare, no inadvertent staring into the camera; it took time to stage that level of spontaneity.

Karl did the bare minimum and homed in on the youngest and prettiest Customs Officer. He swaggered about, displaying the subtlety of a Great Dane with a hard-on. Thomas drifted along behind him to witness the charm offensive at close quarters.

"Ah me, I do so love a girl in uniform!"

The woman turned, saw Karl's beaming face and lifted her shoulders. "You must be the Floater everyone's been warning me about." Before Karl could answer, she flashed a smile. "So how do you want me?"

Karl did his thing, manufacturing life-like shots under cover from the rain. Thomas was regulated to bag man, moving equipment while the maestro was in full flow.

"By the way, whatever happened to the shooting victim?"

Thomas jerked to attention behind Karl; very slick, right in the middle of a sequence — classic misdirection.

"Funny you should ask." Little Miss Flirtatious turned and made a Marilyn Monroe pout for the camera. "The way I heard it, he was whisked off to a private hospital somewhere."

Karl moved from behind the camera and looked directly at Thomas, just for an instant — a regular Holmes and Watson moment. "Hey," Karl knelt down near her to change his data card, "I wonder where all the booze in his van went?"

Karl's supermodel looked over to Ann Crossley. "She supervised it."

"Well then," Karl chortled, "We'll be alright for the Christmas Party! Okay sweetheart, I'm all done here — I just need to get the steam off my lens."

She gave him a little wave and went off to join the others, glancing back a couple of times on her way.

"You know, the camera really loves her."

"Looked like it wasn't the only one." Thomas folded his arms.

"Come on now, Tommy. I was working my subject, like any good photographer."

Thomas squatted beside him while Karl put his trusty Nikon to bed. Thomas eyed it suspiciously. He preferred a Canon; but they'd had that debate many times over.

"You look pensive, Tommo — what's eating you?"

"I don't do *let's pretend* very well, Karl. And you heard what she said . . ."

"Just keep to your boundaries and let me do my job."

Thomas stalled him, arm outstretched. "But what exactly *is* your job?"

Karl walked around him. "Don't go there, Tommo; don't go there."

* * *

17.45 on the dot, as requested. Christine's door was already open. Thomas knocked politely on the frame; *start as you mean to go on.*

"Thomas!" Peterson cried delightedly, as if they were at a class reunion. "Come in, have a seat."

On the desk was a fan-spread of reports, all bearing Thomas's name.

"I understand you and Karl McNeill were on duty when the firearms incident took place at Harwich?" Before Thomas could reply, Peterson added, "But there's nothing in your report."

It was a pawn-to-king-four gambit — obvious, but effective. Thomas responded in kind. "I keep my reports factual and we were concentrating on the Customs Officers." *Facts.* A light went on in his head. If he had any snaps of the red car heading up the exit lane, he'd probably have the registration number too.

"And these?" Peterson pawed at one of the mosaic shots. "What are these about?"

Thomas shrugged it off. "Just background detail. I like to set up early and get a feel for the location."

Peterson stalled for a second and Thomas caught it. "Christine tells me that you have real potential."

She shifted forward in her chair. "Bob and I have discussed this, and we think you're ready for development. It means additional training in Staffordshire and it could open doors for you in the future."

Thomas wore his best fake smile. Christine continued, "We'll need a decision by the end of the week — there's an opening next Monday."

Peterson was staring intently at the mosaic photograph from the day of the shooting. Thomas kept his eyes firmly on Christine, which was no great hardship, and leaned back a little to keep Peterson in his peripheral vision. No doubt about it though, she was looking really good today.

"One thing I would like to ask you," Peterson slapped the photograph down. Thomas jolted awake. "What's your opinion of Karl McNeill?"

"He's very good at what he does; seems to read people well," Thomas played it safe and stayed vague.

"But what about personally? I gather you two socialise from time to time."

Thomas concocted a cross between a laugh and a cough, each as fake as the other. "Well, we have the odd drink, now and again — I met him last weekend, as it happens. I get the impression there's more to Karl than meets the eye. But I s'pose we all have our little secrets."

Christine became a study in scarlet and Peterson dropped his pen, which rolled off the desk; they both froze. Bingo, right on the money.

Thomas decided to push his luck. "If you don't mind, I need to be away soon; I have a date I cannot break." *Yeah, looking for bugging devices in Dagenham, followed by a takeaway curry for six.*

"Oh." Christine looked surprised. Not disappointed, he noted; just surprised.

"That's fine." Peterson extended a wet-fish handshake. "Thanks for your time and your candour. Let Christine know about the training."

* * *

Miranda always said that men couldn't multitask, but Thomas found that London traffic always afforded him time to think. So a burst water main at Burdett Road was practically a gift. By the time he'd ploughed through to take a left at Bow Common Lane, he'd found one thought that he just couldn't shake. And it wasn't a good one.

Peterson would have scheduled an arrival time at Harwich that day and known precisely where he'd parked; probably the vehicles around him too. He was a pro after all. Then Thomas had given him — bloody *given* him, mind — a mosaic showing the whole panorama without Peterson's four-by-four in it. As good as saying: 'I know you were there and I'm keeping it to myself at the moment.' Stupid, really stupid.

And now, suddenly, he was trainee executive material when earlier in the day he'd been facing the heave-ho from the team. Peterson had him snookered; not accepting the training meant showing his hand and accepting would put him at arm's length.

Desperate times and all that; he swung the car into the first available space and fetched out his mobile. "Hey, Karl. Listen, any chance of a chat at the club, some time soon? Wednesday? Nice one; see you tomorrow."

The Wrights left him to go about his work. All except Sam, who followed him around like a lost sheep: nothing new there. When Thomas had first brought Miranda back to London, Sam had only been about thirteen. Talk about hero worship. Thomas had rescued Miranda from the clutches of doom. Or more precisely, from the paws of Butch Steddings — modelling agent and all-round scumbag. Even now, Thomas and Miranda still used the word *Butch* as code for something dodgy.

By 21.30 Thomas had his feet up and John Wright was handing him a beer. All clear, no trace of Karl's handiwork on the premises. And sadly, no sign of Miranda either. If she were playing hard to get she'd put in a cup-winning performance tonight. No reason to expect her at Caliban's on Tuesday night either, for his next debugging booking. The only bit of good news that night was that no one had mentioned the business potential of Thomas's new career.

By the time he got back to the flat in Walthamstow, it was close to midnight. The answering machine light was flashing insistently. He put the electronics case down in the hall, set the two door locks and hit the magic button.

"Hello Thomas, it's your mother. Just ringing to see how you are and when we can expect a visit. Your sister and the kids send their love and so do me and your dad." No names just titles — nice.

The next message was Miranda. "Hi, sorry I won't be there tonight or at the club. Sheryl knows the score."

He dithered for a second then stabbed the delete button. "Of course she does," he seethed in the dark, "you tell her everything."

Chapter 10

Karl held the heavy metal door open as Thomas stepped through. It felt as if that door was shielding him from the outside world. Once the formalities were dispensed with, Karl led him to a bay and went off to procure the equipment.

He leaned against the wall and gazed out at the targets, seduced by the stillness. A perfect backdrop to the maelstrom of his own thoughts.

Karl soon returned with two Browning 9mm pistols. "You won't find any answers staring down there!"

So there were answers to be had? He opened the case and, under Karl's supervision, primed the weapon and took the stand. He closed his eyes for a moment and let the roar in his ears carry him. The barrel wavered. Sweat massed at his brow and his armpits felt sticky, as if the growing web of deceit and half-truths was oozing out of him.

He sighed, took aim and squeezed the trigger. Somehow he'd expected the first shot to settle him, but it had the opposite effect. The barrel shuddered — no chance. He flipped the safety catch and put the gun down.

Karl stepped up beside him and put a hand on his shoulder. "It's all about being able to close in, to focus on one thing. No distractions or prevarications. Because if it came to it, that's what the other guy would do." Karl nudged him aside and drained the magazine without breaking a sweat. "Now, try again."

Thomas lined the target up. His stomach contorted and he fought against it, making himself breathe steadily to counter the nausea. It all came back to him then, the first time he'd held a gun.

* * *

1984. Maybe not the dystopia Orwell had predicted, but in Yorkshire, a police state nonetheless. Night after night, woken up by the sirens; the procession of policemen, like the invading Roman army they were learning about at school. At first it was exciting; they played at *Blake's 7*, from off the telly, space rebels against an evil, galactic federation. Or else they tried to get close to the horses.

But the screw quickly tightened and then it wasn't fun at all. When coalmining collapsed, so did the world they all knew. There were arguments at friends' houses and rows at home; relentless shouting and door slamming. School became a refuge from home.

Every day his dad swore vengeance on 'that heartless tyrant bitch, Margaret Thatcher.' It was the first time he'd seen his father so full of hatred. In some ways, childhood fell away. The older kids talked about a revolution. They hadn't covered that in class, so it didn't all make sense.

And then there was that day, playing around in the greenhouse. That's when he found it, wrapped up in newspaper and hidden in an old rucksack: a real gun. Next day his dad came home unexpectedly, caught him red-handed. He really went off on one; raged at him, threatened him — his own son — to keep his mouth shut about the pistol and to never go in the greenhouse again. Thomas had been so frightened that he'd pissed himself, right in front of his dad. Even now, just thinking about it, his face burned.

* * *

He swallowed hard and heard the echoes of his own laboured breathing. How long had he been standing there? *Just pull the fucking trigger*. One, two, three, four in rapid succession, gunning down his shame and the past. As if that was ever really possible. "Done," he called aloud. As he stepped back, he saw Karl leaning casually against the wall, watching him. "Peterson and Christine asked what I thought of you, yesterday. I told them you were dependable."

Karl nodded and packed away the pistols, game over. Thomas waited for him in the corridor. Maybe it had been a mistake coming here this time. The strangled whistling of a familiar tune made Thomas turn — 'I Shot the Sheriff' — Karl of course, the stupid bastard. "Come on amigo, something closer to home," Karl passed him a larger case.

Thomas balanced the rifle comfortably, nestling it against his shoulder. The weapon smelt different, and the realisation amused him. He wriggled his face closer in to the sight and inhaled then released. The crosshairs barely moved as he levelled up and fired. He felt the recoil in his shoulder and shrugged a little, preparing for the next one. Now he saw the hole, placed close to the inner ring. Five shots followed, each within an inch of the original.

"Very good. Amazing what a little time and preparation can accomplish. Now, step aside and let me show you what a professional can do!" Karl was still a much better shot. He made short work of the remainder of his ammunition and lowered the rifle with a sigh. "The bar, I think."

* * *

"Drink up Tommo — nothing worse than cold coffee."

He swayed the cup mid-air. "Peterson wants to send me on some special training next week. I reckon he wants me out of the way."

"I'm not surprised. Remember that wee Customs lass I was doing so well with?"

Thomas arched an obligatory eyebrow.

"She's been reassigned — she told me when I rang her last night; did I mention I picked up her number before we left? Anyway, it looks like someone's having a bit of a clear out."

"Well, I'm staying put."

Karl gave him the kind of look that *he* used to give his sister Pat when she still believed in the Tooth Fairy. "Think so? A quid says they split up our dream team within a fortnight."

They both did mock spits and shook hands on the bet. Thomas toyed with the rim of his cup. "When I was a kid, I used to pray at night for Jesus to end the Miners' Strike and save their jobs," he sucked in one cheek. "Yeah, stupid, I know. But I was ten. It was the last time I ever thought about relying on anyone else."

"Hey though," Karl brightened, "just imagine if he'd ever achieved it. We'd have got him over to the six counties on the next ferry out!"

"Look, I owe you an apology, Karl, for thinking you were prepared to . . . you know . . ."

"Fix up your drinking hole? Understandable, under the circumstances."

Karl wiped his face with a napkin. "Listen, I know you feel you're in the middle of everything, but — and don't take this the wrong way — stick to what you're good at and leave well alone."

Thomas pondered that for a second. The problem was, he was already involved.

* * *

He didn't sit down to eat until after 10 pm; a cheese omelette with bacon bits in it and bread that was only good for toasting. He cleared away methodically and switched on the immersion heater. Now or never time. He drummed on the desk while the laptop fired up and didn't linger on the default image: Rievaulx Abbey, beset by lightning. Sifting through the unused images folders, he found what he was looking for — two pictures of the red car at the port. Not his best work by any means — slightly blurred, though enough detail across the two frames to put together a complete registration number.

He dialled Miranda, without thinking of the time, and asked another favour.

"That depends. If it's for your job, the answer's *no*." She sounded distracted, probably by all that background music.

"Are you in a club?"

"What?"

He was pretty sure she'd heard him and wasn't that a man's voice close by? "Are you with someone?"

For a few seconds there was silence then he heard a familiar tone. "I've got to go, Thomas. Just text me whatever you need. Bye."

The room went cold. He sat for a while, staring into space, taking it all in. Sleep was off the menu now — a familiar part of the pattern. He washed up and sent Miranda the text. Then he grabbed his car keys and an SLR camera, promising himself that he wouldn't end up outside Christine's flat again.

To begin with, he just drove around, looking for a prospect. The radio was tuned to some late-show, where the emotionally stunted could unburden their souls. And in between the confessionals, a talk-jock served up a hearty stream of platitudes.

'That must have been awful for you. Do you have a message for any listeners in a similar position?'

"Yeah," Thomas spoke directly at the radio, "get a life." *Like he had a life?* He flipped the station to something more melodic and cruised the City of London to the tunes of the eighties; happily cocooned until The Human League struck up with *Don't You Want Me?* Ouch; too close to home.

Thoughts crept into his brain, or out of it. Was Christine still single — had he imagined some sort of buzz between her and Peterson? He smiled, taking his own bait: only one way to find out. No harm in taking a drive by her flat later. Driving past without stopping didn't really count. He glanced down at the camera, mute beside him on the passenger seat, like his conscience.

At Archway he pulled over and took the tripod from the boot. He found a suitable position, set the camera up and started timing the traffic. After twenty vehicles, he opted for a timing of seven seconds. He waited, enjoying that delicious sense of anticipation. Despite all the technological progress, at heart it was *magic* — that's what it was. A moment in time, in all its shame and glory, captured forever.

He was reverently packing everything into the boot when he heard talking. He cocked a fist and moved to the blind side of the car, crouching to get a better look. It was a woman, stumbling along the street towards him, having a conversation with herself. From the look of her, she was maybe seventeen; seventeen going on twenty-five. And she'd had a skinful.

"Alright mate?" she grinned as he stood up. "'Ave you got the time please?" She was too drunk to be scared of approaching a stranger at night. But that was okay because he was scared enough for both of them.

"It's late — you should be at home."

She started laughing and teetered about like a Jenga conclusion. "I missed my lift and I'm too skint for a taxi. I got college tomorrow . . ."

Hook, line and sinker. "Alright," he conceded, feeling he'd been played like a cheap violin. "Do you need a lift somewhere?"

"Nice one," she gave him a wavering thumbs-up. "Ever heard of Battersea?"

He nodded wearily. *No good deed goes unpunished.* In the end, he crossed the river, found the nearest cab office and left her there with a tenner. Better that than explaining to an irate family that he was just a Good Samaritan, and nearly twice her age.

By the time he was safely over the Thames, he'd given up on Christine's and opted for home. As he parked up, he noticed the small handbag in the passenger door. Brilliant — something else to be sorted out. He opened it carefully, as if it was a steel-sprung trap. There was a passport-sized picture of two schoolgirls; all grinning smiles and too much lipstick. Also inside were a college card and timetable, a door key, a nightclub matchbook, two tampons and a packet of condoms — one missing. Clearly, a woman for all seasons. He noted the college address; another good deed for tomorrow then, before work.

Chapter 11

Thomas got waylaid by traffic on the way to Battersea Technology College. He left the bag in a padded envelope at reception, with a note suggesting she be more careful in future.

In the office, Karl was already sifting his junk mail for gold. "Tommo, come and see this. Why would any man want to increase his sperm by 500%? Hey, unless he was a donor and paid by volume!" Ann Crossley looked over without saying anything. Karl called Thomas to one side. "When are you telling Christine that you won't require the key to the executive wash room?"

"No time like the present," he glanced at her door. "May as well get it over with."

"Don't be too long — I'll get the coffees in," Karl stood up and wandered towards Ann Crossley. "Can you imagine a man with five times the sperm? Where would he keep it all?"

Christine was on the phone. She saw Thomas approach and waved him in. "Okay Bob, leave it with me and thanks again for your time." She put the phone down and did her best to bury a smile. She used to do that with him, when they were exchanging glances at work, back in the day.

"I thought I'd tell you right away that I won't be taking up the training offer."

Christine frowned. "I think you're being very short-sighted. Bob went through your files very carefully — and despite your macho display — he was impressed by what he saw."

I'll bet he was. Thomas pushed his tongue against his lower front teeth to make a poker face.

"You're making a mistake, you know."

And there was something about the way she said it that made him pause and sit down. The best defence might not be attack, but it was better than no defence at all. "I was in your part of the world last night — I nearly popped round."

Christine did a good impression of a rabbit caught in headlights. "I was busy," she snapped, "and you shouldn't assume I have no life of my own."

It all sounded a bit Jane Austen from where he was sitting, but he got the message loud and clear: stay away. Which only made him more determined.

* * *

At Harwich, in the afternoon, Crossley radioed in; she sounded smug. "Thomas, Christine wants you to ring immediately. You're to report to Sir Peter Carroll, first thing tomorrow morning. Top priority."

Thomas relayed the news. Karl sucked a tooth. If he'd played his cards any closer to his chest, he'd have worn them as a tattoo. "Well now, Tommy Boy; looks like I just won a pound. Another two says Crossley knows more than she's saying. Has Sir Peter ever asked for you by name before?"

"Now and again. I've done the odd pick-up, up north. Maybe he thinks southerners get a nosebleed if they venture further than Watford."

"Yeah," Karl stared ahead, "or maybe you've pissed somebody off?"

It was the first time Thomas had visited Main Building in Whitehall. He'd seen Sir Peter in a few buildings since State House in High Holborn. It was as if the old man couldn't settle. And every time, including at Whitehall, Sir Peter kept his distance from the various offices of the SSU.

The security guard eyed Thomas up and down. In most governmental buildings, Thomas knew, security had been contracted out to agency staff — the engines of bureaucracy made safe on minimum wages. Main Building was not one of those places. Glancing left to right, he counted five people in the reception area who stood or sat ramrod straight and took their duties very seriously; no skiving with the television on here. Most, if not all, would be armed.

"Thomas Bladen?"

He nodded and held up his ID. Despite the twenty or so years since the SSU had existed, there was still a hard core of resentment and mistrust from the *real* security and armed services. Chummy here, sneering back through the reinforced glass, was clearly not a member of the SSU fan club.

"Hand please." Fingerprint checks had already been introduced, last time he'd attended Sir Peter. And even though he had nothing to hide — nothing that would show on a hand scan, anyway — he still twitched a little as the scanner went about its business.

An escort appeared, to take him up to the top floor. No conversation in the lift, not even a gripe at the weather. And above them the cameras silently filmed every nuance; despite working in surveillance, Thomas could never get used to that.

The lift rose to the top floor, which made him smile; some things never changed. A grey carpet extended before him, complemented by grey walls and a series of identical navy blue doors. The only way to tell them apart was by the acronyms — ATFA, SA2A and NORAD Liaison. This was *need-to-know* taken to extremes. They rounded a corridor, he and the silent wonder, along the dog-leg, past FRD, CIA — *surely not* — and then finally a door labelled SSU. The escort knocked curtly then opened the door for him. "I'll be back to collect you."

100% pure charm.

Sir Peter Carroll was sat behind his desk in a navy blazer and tie; he had a look of the Cheshire Cat about him. "Thomas, good to see you!" he stood and extended his hand, but that was as much as he moved. Behind him, the familiar portrait of Sir Winston Churchill adorned the wall, with a great cigar in his mouth and a paperweight of a spitfire by his hand. *There's no place like home.*

Thomas had seen that painting maybe a dozen times, most of them at State House when he'd been showing off his photographic prowess. "How can I help you, sir?" He knew the old man would like that.

"Thomas!" Sir Peter elongated the name in mock disapproval. "Will you join me in a whisky?"

He nodded, happy to accommodate his benefactor. They sat for a minute or two, savouring their drinks. Thomas had never been sure how far the informality thing stretched; it had all been pretty loose before he'd joined the SSU but he'd never pushed it since he joined the payroll.

"I'd like you to collect a package for me; from Leeds."

A Yorkshire pick-up. Coincidence? Thomas didn't subscribe to them. "Where do you want it delivered?"

"To me, here in Whitehall — Highly Classified."

He nodded; if Sir Peter were studying his face for a response he'd find none.

"You'll leave for York from St Pancras station, Friday morning. I thought you'd appreciate the chance to spend time with your family up there."

Terrific. Must remember to book the street parade.

"Retrieve the item from an office in Leeds on Monday morning. Then straight back here — understand?" Sir Peter lifted an A5 brown envelope from an in-tray and picked up a telephone to summon the escort. "So . . . what do you make of Bob Peterson?"

"Don't know much about him," he played dumb. "I gather he's been working out of Southampton." *Give or take the odd bit of moonlighting.*

Sir Peter laced his fingers together, like a judge about to pass sentence. "Not really your sort, eh, Thomas?"

Thomas shrugged and stuck with his glass.

"I'm sorry you turned down the training — Bob was very keen."

Blimey; good news certainly travels fast.

"It's sensible to get Bob on side," Sir Peter leaned across his desk. "Winning a war is easy — that just takes superior forces. But winning the peace . . . ah, that takes superior intelligence. Do you follow?"

"I think so, sir." It all added up to a cryptic pitch for *be nice to Bob*. Three raps on the door brought the conversation to an end.

"Monday," Sir Peter said as the guard closed the door behind him.

Outside, Thomas felt for the envelope; he knew better than to open it on the street. Even though, on past experience, it would only contain travel times, an address and a named contact. It was still before eleven. He rang Christine to check what she wanted him to do next; back to base it was then. On the way over he called Karl.

"Ah, the happy wanderer! How did it go?"

"Fine thanks. Listen, turns out I'll be away this weekend — when do you fancy meeting at the club?"

"Well now, let me check my packed social calendar . . ." Karl paused for about three seconds. "Yep, this week's good — pick a day."

"How about tonight? — I know it's short notice . . ."

Karl backtracked like a Lamborghini slammed into reverse. "The thing is, Tommo, there's this senorita."

"It wouldn't be Teresa by any chance, would it?"

"A gentleman never tells. Why don't we make it Thursday night?"

"Done."

* * *

The office seemed deserted when Thomas arrived. The team would still be at Harwich. And Peterson, with any luck he'd be under a bus.

"Hi there," Christine poked her head out of her door, "fancy a bite to eat?"

He blinked a couple of times; did a comedic search behind him.

"Come on, you must be hungry?"

"Sure, why not — I've just got to make a call."

"Great! I'll power down and get my bag."

It had been a long time since they'd strolled along the Thames together. The water shimmered in the sunlight; slow lazy bow waves brushing the banks as the tourists motored up and down. Given the choice he would have lingered awhile to watch how the shadow lines sliced across the concrete. But it was Christine's gig so he kept quiet and played follow my leader.

He remembered the bistro, a spit away from the Tate Modern. It had been the site of that first try-out lunch with Mummy and Daddy. No surprise then that Christine made small talk about her parents; people who wouldn't make space in a lifeboat for him if the ship went down in flames — in shark-infested waters.

"Anyway, enough about me; how are your family, Thomas?"

The *coincidence* bell rang so loud in his head he could hardly hear himself think. He muddled through with a mixture of old news and half-truths, grateful when Christine claimed them a table.

"Here, this is good. A great view of the North Bank."

They agreed to share a bottle of wine — her treat. He quickly got into the rhythm of their non-date. There was nothing at risk here since not only had she no interest in him romantically, he still had Bob Peterson marked down as her bedtime companion. On those terms, he could afford to relax and enjoy himself.

"I really do wish you'd think about the training, Thomas," she had a certain way of saying his name that could still set his teeth on edge. The tone dragged him back in time, just before the ice age had set in. He avoided a skirmish by drawing on the healing power of wine. "I know Bob's appointment was a shock . . . but that shouldn't stand in the way of your future. Hmm?"

He smiled. As the early afternoon sunshine picked out her auburn highlights, it was easy to recall what he'd first seen in her, two years before. By dessert he'd noticed her legs again. *Best stop now, Thomas, before your tongue runs away with you.* Christine, oblivious to his gaze — or used to it — was enthusing about her parents' stables, where she still kept a horse.

He replayed the first time he'd met her mother, when she'd inquired pointedly: "Do you ride at all?" And the killer line he'd never delivered: Only your daughter. Cue canned laughter. Not for nothing had Mrs Gerrard later described him as coarse, behind his back of course. Guilty as charged.

His mobile went off. He made that stock face that all people do, suggesting they're irritated by a call even when they're secretly delighted.

"Hi babe. I've hit a problem with that number. Sorry about last night . . ."

He cut across her. "Sorry, you've caught me at a bad time. Can I ring you later? Great — speak to you then." Touché Miranda. He switched the phone off, pre-empting an abusive text.

Christine ran a fingertip around her wine glass. "Girlfriend trouble?" she lifted her head square to his.

He leaned out of the sun. "There is no girlfriend. How about you?" He said it casually and glanced to one side to give her space to respond.

"Me? No, no girlfriend either. My lesbian phase ended at boarding school." She kicked him playfully under the table, tapping her handmade Italian shoes against his brogues. "This is fun, isn't it? We should do this more often; we are friends after all."

He adjusted his crotch under the tablecloth and then raised a glass. They clinked a toast, friends forever. Or for the time being, anyway.

* * *

He didn't ring Miranda back until the evening. Either she couldn't or wouldn't pick up, so it was at least an hour before she returned the call. Another hour, in which he cooked or worked or went to the toilet, with the mobile at his side.

"Hey babe, how's it going?"

He kept it low key. "Yeah, fine; sorry about this afternoon, I was involved in a work thing."

"No problem," she managed to make it sound just the opposite. "That number you gave me doesn't exist. Hello? Are you still there?"

"Yeah, I'm here, Miranda."

"I'll read it back to you in case I got it wrong."

He checked on his computer as she spoke. "No, that's the one. Not to worry." Except that now, he was really starting to worry.

"Listen, fancy coming over for Sunday lunch? Just me this time!"

"I can't. I'm off to see the folks."

"Blimey, hell's finally frozen over! How long you away for?"

"A long weekend." There was a pause. He squeezed the phone closer, to hear her breathing.

"Well, if you fancy some company up there . . ."

If you only knew. "The thing is, it's also a work trip."

"Oh."

That was a conversation killer. She said to get in touch if he needed anything and left him to it. On the lounge wall, a seventeen-year-old Miranda gazed back from a hazy St Paul's Street, Leeds, in the summer of 1994. The warmth of her smile lit up the frame. He closed his eyes and tried to pour himself into that photograph. No such luck.

He didn't ring his family until Thursday morning; no point building the visit up if he could play it down. His mother started planning an itinerary while they were still talking. And she said that his father would be pleased to see him; she made it sound like a solicitor's appointment.

Of course, he'd stay with them — they wouldn't dream of him booking somewhere. He made a note to cancel the hotel in York. She closed the call with 'give our love to Miranda,' even though the break-up was years ago.

* * *

Karl was uncharacteristically quiet, had been all day. It was as if someone had super-glued his personality shut. Thomas had tried several approaches without success. Still, today was Thursday, so at least they would be able to talk on neutral ground.

Funny, the way Karl never questioned why he kept going back to the gun club; he'd never really asked himself that either. It felt safe, in a way. Not like being around Miranda and her family, but a different kind of sanctuary. Or maybe it was just Karl. He understood the pressures of the job and the demands it made. You became guarded, even to those closest to you.

"Are we still on for tonight, Karl?"

His oppo looked up from his eyepiece and gave a thumbs-up. "Roger that!" It still sounded like a watered-down version of Karl. "Got your jim-jams packed for tomorrow, Tommo?" It was the first time he'd mentioned the pick-up job.

"Uh-huh."

"Well, be careful, okay?"

"Karl, I'm touched, I didn't know you cared."

"Listen, laughing boy, just keep your wits about you."

Strange times indeed.

By the evening, Karl's introspection pills had worn off. They practiced with a Browning and a Glock, and then Karl nipped out for a .44 Magnum. Thomas felt completely intimidated by the sight of the thing — like that time he and Miranda rented a porn film. Still, he rose to the bait and made a complete arse of himself, to Karl's evident joy.

"Are you sure now you're not related to Clint Eastwood?"

More like Clyde the monkey. Later, Karl was his usual chatty self; firearms seemed to give him a new lease of life. By the second pastry, conversation had turned to the marital status — or otherwise — of their colleagues.

Karl was in the chair. "Crossley — not a chance; either plays for the other side or she's saving herself."

"What is it with you and her, Karl?"

"Let's just say we had professional differences in the past. And despite her best efforts, I'm still here. We've buried the hatchet and all, but I doubt we'll ever be pen-pals."

Okay, crunch time. Thomas took a slip of paper out of his pocket. "I know I was supposed to mind my own business, but I did some checking on our mystery red car and the number plate's a fake."

Karl lowered his plate. "I can't say I'm not impressed. Even so . . ."

"Come on Karl, this is all wrong," Thomas raised his fingers to count off the points. "First someone gets shot and they take him to a private hospital. Ann Crossley removes the vehicle and the woman who told us about it gets transferred. Then the car I thought was suspect turns out to have false plates."

Karl gazed at the ceiling as if seeking inspiration. "I'll tell you what, Tommo, seeing as how we're trusting each other. I'll make you a deal. I'm gonna write something down and put it in an envelope. Don't open it until we get together again on Tuesday. If I'm right, I'll let you in — I mean it. But if what's written down is totally wide of the mark, will you agree to let all this go?"

Like that was ever gonna happen. "You're on; I do love a magic show."

"Me? I'm Ulster's answer to David Copperfield, so I am. Now, sit yourself here while I find some stationery."

Thomas relaxed a little; he was starting to feel like he belonged. Teresa came over; it was easy to imagine her in a uniform. He was still lost in the 'regulation skirt' when she coughed, bringing him back to reality.

"Where's Action Man?"

"Action Man — brilliant!"

"Because he tries all the equipment here."

Nought out of ten for deduction.

"So, are you thinking about becoming a member?"

Now there was a thought. Might also be his best chance of finding out about Karl. He shrugged.

"I'm sure someone could vouch for you."

"Is that how it works, then?"

She smiled enigmatically; too keen. He noticed a cluster ring on her right hand; could have been an old engagement ring. She flexed her hand then massaged her neck self-consciously. "Coffee?"

He shook his head. If he had any more coffee today he'd be able to walk to Leeds.

"Well, well, this all looks very cosy!" Karl had tiptoed across, doubtless using his Action Man skills.

"I'm trying to find out your little secrets."

"That shouldn't take long — simple man that I am."

Yeah, right.

"Here you go, Tommo. Remember, not to be opened until Tuesday."

The envelope had a daub of wax on the back; blue wax, like a birthday candle. He held out the envelope, wax side up. "Just making sure."

* * *

Back at the flat, he packed a bag and threw in an AGFA Isomatic 110. Because sometimes he just liked to take snaps. Round about midnight, he put down *The Adventures of Sherlock Holmes* and cut the light.

He always thought that if his father was called upon at the Day of Judgement, it was the one thing he could say in his defence: that he had introduced his son to the great works of Conan Doyle. Tonight he'd made a point of re-reading *The Red-Headed League*, a classic study in misdirection. And come to think of it, Karl had reddish hair too.

He lay on the bed, pondering the incongruities. 'Oh, give over, Thomas; it's just a story,' he could hear his mother chuckling. Even as a child, he had always had 'a head full of questions.' He got undressed and eased into the cool sheets, wondering if Miranda were sleeping alone tonight. Or Christine, come to that.

In the early hours of the morning, a car alarm went off. He dragged himself to the window to check. Unlikely it would be his own car, since: a) the only reason anyone would break into it would be to fit a better stereo out of sympathy and b) he never put the alarm on.

A few doors along, a yellow Ford Escort was revving up for all it was worth, the throaty rumble making the window tremble against his hand. A young woman was stood at the kerbside, arms folded. He caught the gist of it straight away; Sharon didn't love Kevin anymore, but Kevin wanted to prove his love by pissing off her parents and all their neighbours.

He flicked the curtain behind him to get a better view. An RS2000, with four round headlights — four of them! How did a toe-rag like Kevin afford a car like that? Probably wasn't even insured, never mind the bloody tax.

Tax — of course! He shrugged away the curtain and let it fall back into place. *Thank you, Kevin.* The wall-clock showed it was nearly two. He didn't bother putting the light on; hopefully this wouldn't take long.

He fired up his personal laptop — where he kept copies of *all* his photographs. Stuff for work, recent shots that had never made it into his official reports, even a set of wedding photos for Miranda's cousin. All filed, in an orderly system. It only took a minute or so to navigate the folders and subfolders — red car, four pictures. Two of those were partials of the front, at an angle. He magnified the appropriate sections, and positioned them side by side onscreen. Together, they formed a Rosetta stone, a complete registration that differed from the number plate.

He basked in the blue-green glow of the laptop, staring at the pictures; he was getting good at this. Unlocking a drawer, he lifted out a surfboard key-ring — a Bermuda present from Miranda. He pulled the thing apart, inserted the memory stick device and uploaded the crucial files. Now he'd sleep like a charm — mystery solved.

As he crawled back to bed, checking that the alarm was still set for seven, he wondered if Kevin was back in Sharon's good books now. He hoped so; as far as Thomas was concerned, he'd earned it.

* * *

By seven forty-five, he was out of the flat and walking up Hoe Street — that still made Karl laugh — for Walthamstow Central Underground. The walkway was littered with rubbish bags, discarded cardboard and old newspapers. He fell in step with the rest of the ants, swerved around the offer of a free newspaper and disappeared into the maze of platforms and walkways, unaware that someone else had fallen into step with him.

He surfaced at Kings Cross and headed straight to the ticket office at St Pancras. In the queue, he picked up a text from Miranda: *Have a good trip. Mx.*

And although he'd memorised Monday's reporting instructions, he still pressed his hand lightly against his jacket. He could feel Karl's magic envelope there too. The train was called early so he made the most of it, grabbing a copy of *Private Eye* on the way — just to see what Karl found so amusing.

Once Thomas had passed safely through the barrier, the person trailing him made a call. Sir Peter Carroll liked to be kept informed.

Chapter 12

Thomas left the train at Leeds, for a one-man nostalgia tour. It was a routine that he'd never deviated from over the years. Starting off with the Indian restaurant on Merrion Street where he'd taken Miranda for their first meal together. The place was closed; he pressed his face against the tinted glass. The décor had changed again. It was classier now; looked like there was a bigger fish tank too. He preferred it before.

Next stop Hyde Terrace, the bed-sit — sneaking in with Miranda after hours because the landlady on the premises ran a *respectable* property. Except when her gentleman friend came over on Wednesdays and Saturdays. Good old Christian hypocrisy — a little piece of home. He wondered if she still owned the place and if she'd recognise him as one of the teenage lovers she'd threatened to call the police on; probably not. He settled for a slow walk past.

He had a love-hate relationship with Leeds. It marked the transition between Pickering and London. Leeds was where life had begun to take shape. Being away from home, that first job with photography, meeting Miranda; the good things. But Leeds had also felt soulless; and all that grief with Miranda and Butch Steddings was like a bitter echo of school life. Yep, nothing like revisiting teenage angst for working up an appetite. He'd never tell him, but cafés without Karl just weren't the same, so a pub lunch was the order of the day. Caliban's aside, he wasn't a huge fan of pubs. But the Angel Inn scraped through on atmosphere alone. Thanks to *Private Eye* and a problem with the sandwiches, he lasted a full forty-five minutes.

And finally, on to the main event: the Art Gallery, along The Headrow. Portraits fascinated him; the way they captured something of the inner person and revealed it forever. He'd tried to paint Miranda once — it was rubbish, of course. But the actual process, the way he'd been able to study her for hours and to see how the light changed her features — well, it was almost a religious experience. She hadn't taken the piss either, not even when he'd said he wanted to be a professional photographer one day.

He checked his watch — time to go — and skirted around a gaggle of college girls outside, slowly smoking themselves to death. He made the station in plenty of time, unlike the delayed Scarborough train.

* * *

At York, he saw his mother standing by the car, as he exited, looking out for him. She waved enthusiastically and he reciprocated with a slow hand. If he'd been any more non-committal he could have doubled as a stunt pope. His father remained in the driving seat, hands on the wheel.

After the obligatory greetings they joined the Friday traffic, slipping across the Lendal Bridge and along the A64 before it clogged up for the evening.

"How's sis?"

"Now, Pat'll be coming over later," his mother changed the subject without drawing breath. "She said to say that Gordon sends his apologies. He's been working long hours and doesn't think he'd be at his best."

Thomas studied the veins on the back of his hand. "How are they getting along these days?"

His father let out a deep sigh, but his mother kept to the script. "He moved out for a few days last month — said he needed a bit of room to himself. He's under a lot of pressure, you know." She said it earnestly, as if to convince all three of them.

Yeah, right. The only pressure Gordon was likely to feel was in his elbows, when he was on top of some tart in Whitby. "Why didn't anyone tell me Pat was having difficulties?"

Thomas's father half-turned. "Because you're never around — not for *this* family, anyway."

And there it was: gloves off, round one.

"Come on James, let's not start."

Father and son stared at each other through the mirror. No one spoke again.

* * *

It was hard to get too worked up about seeing the house, which had been his second childhood home, and he'd left in his teens. But it

67

still held ghosts. He rolled his eyes at the memory of that final-straw row with his dad, over 'drinking and backchat.' Maybe one drinker was all the house could bear.

As soon as they got inside, his mother rushed straight into the kitchen to put the kettle on. It was like he'd never been away. Tea, the great panacea for fractured families, now with added digestives.

Thomas and his father sat in the parlour glancing in the general vicinity of each other. Stalemate. Thomas knew his father would crack first; a childish power play, but one he excelled at. All it took was time, and he could wait.

"So, 'ow's life in London?" his father relented.

"It's okay." Hardly the response of the year, but anything too enthusiastic or dismissive would invite further discussion. *And we wouldn't want to use up all that sparkling banter on the first day, now would we?*

After tea, his father tried again. Rugby — Malton & Norton's season compared with York then football — Leeds United getting robbed again in the final minutes. Thomas didn't bother to remind him that he'd lost interest in sport years ago, not counting the odd West Ham game.

Everything had settled by the time Pat's key rattled in the door. "It's only me." It sounded like she'd brought the little ones as well.

Thomas tried to recall when he'd last seen them and reached into his pocket for some guilt money.

"There he is!" Pat pushed the door to, beaming as if she'd just won the lottery. He eased out of the chair and opened his arms. She squeezed against him, the way a limpet fights against the tide. "It's really good to see you," she whispered, sniffing back tears.

Gordon. That little shit. One of these days he'd get through to him, using Gordon's head for Morse code.

The kids kept their distance at first, hardly surprising as he rarely saw them. All it took was a few words of encouragement from Pat and a few silly noises from him. Pound coins helped as well.

"I thought we could all have tea together," Pat suggested. "Me and Thomas could walk down to the chippie."

He nodded, seduced by the thought of getting out of the house. Fish & chips — a feast for the prodigal son.

"Here," his father held out some notes, "If you eat at my table, you're my guests."

And that about summed it up for Thomas; he was a guest. As soon as they shut the door behind them, leaving the kids hammering on the old piano, Thomas blew out a breath like an over-inflated balloon.

Pat laughed and grabbed his arm, winching him in close. "I have missed you though. You should come up more often."

"So I hear."

She looked away and pulled him towards the gate, still arm in arm. There had always been an easy peace between them, despite their differences. Pat had moved four streets away, settled down and continued the family line. Whereas Thomas, he'd abandoned them all, changed his accent and become a stranger. Pat never questioned that — she understood his reasons.

She waited until they were stuck in the queue outside the fish & chip shop. "How's Miranda?"

"Still single," he paused, reading between the lines. "As am I."

She shook her head faintly, as if she didn't believe any of it; sisters — too clever by half.

He waited until she'd paid for everything and stopped her at the door. "I'll pay for this lot. Give Dad his change, no need for him to know. I'm sure Mam can use a little extra."

She gave him a playful punch and he doubled up in mock agony. "You always were a silly beggar! Come on, I'm famished."

* * *

It was a typical family scene, three generations eating together; adults with plates on knees, but children up at the table; a bottle of ketchup passed around and hot, sweet tea to wash it all down. Except, for Thomas, it was as alien now as that terrible weekend he'd shared with Christine Gerrard and her parents. It wasn't that Pickering was smaller — no, it grew bigger with each infrequent visit. But the house, rooms and inhabitants alike — they all seemed narrower.

He walked Pat and the children home afterwards, doing a stint as Uncle Piggy-back. He didn't go inside though, not if Gordon might be around. It was Pat's life after all, and lamping someone rarely solved anything. As he wandered back the long way home, a police car blared in the distance. He smiled broadly for the first time that day; he'd make time to see Ajit before Monday.

Ajit was the only school friend he'd bothered to stay in touch with. They had two things in common: a love of photography and a secret they'd never discussed.

No one cared much when Ajit joined the class in 1988, except the throwbacks — and every school had them. It was racism all right, but with a twist. It wasn't the fact that Ajit was Asian, just that he'd come from Lancashire. Or so they said. School life was a proving ground for every would-be alpha-male fuckwit. Thomas had experienced a little of that himself when they moved to Pickering, after Maggie Thatcher broke the miners in two. But any son of a miner was hailed as a hero, even though all he'd done was stand in the street in York, collecting money for them.

Day after day, Thomas had watched Ajit run the gauntlet; watched as the gang formed into a leader and four lieutenants. Thomas knew it wasn't his fight. He and Ajit were both members of Photography Club and shared a few laughs, but that was about it. Still, wrong is wrong, when all's said and done.

Originally, he'd only meant to scare off the main bully, give him a bit of a thump to show him what it felt like. That was how it started, anyway. But it developed a life of its own. He followed the ringleader, and trailed the group to where they smoked and drank cider after school. He bided his time, did nothing while the shoving and the tripping up and the sly punches on the arm continued; just stood and watched. He and Ajit even fell out over it. 'Some friend you are!' Ajit had snapped. Some friend indeed.

On that final, momentous night, he'd gone out fully prepared: black jacket, gloves and balaclava. That Friday, he'd waited in the shadows; even pissed in a bottle to avoid leaving evidence, and chucked it over the wall into the fields. Over an hour, sitting there in the dark, watching. And the more he waited, the stronger he felt. Like he was invincible.

The lad had ambled right past, half-cut on cider. He'd crept up behind with the speed of a cat, swiped him across the head and kneed him in the back, almost climbing on top of him with the momentum. Then, as the boy went down screaming, Thomas scrambled over him and legged it.

The screaming followed him as he'd crossed the road; not that it troubled him any. He scuttled into the first alleyway, pulled off the balaclava and folded it carefully into his pocket. He heard a front door slam and somebody call out in panic, but he kept on walking; he walked tall. A few streets on and he heard sirens; ambulance or police, could have been both. It didn't matter; for the first time in his life, he'd seen justice.

When he came home, his mother was watching television. His dad was still down the pub — nothing new there. "Cup of tea?" he said it in a quiet voice and his mother obediently scuttled to the kitchen, leaving whatever she'd been watching.

He opened the stove door and carefully placed the balaclava inside, as if it were a funeral pyre. Then he knelt and watched as they burned, feeling the heat against his face. When his mother returned, the smouldering embers were still visible on top of the coal. She didn't ask; mothers never do.

He'd stayed up later than usual even though he was tired. Pat was over at a friend's; she tended to do that on Fridays. She was a smarter girl back then. His father came back after closing time, reeking of beer and resentment.

Things escalated quickly, and this time Thomas stood between his parents, blocking his dad's approach as he swayed around the room — big mistake. The slap caught him unawares and knocked him to the floor. He sat there in a daze, unable to hear what was being said for the roar in his ears. His mother was a statue, no help there.

He remembered getting up and readying his fist. Even though he'd likely get a good belting afterwards, this time he was going down fighting. But his mother intervened, grabbing him roughly by the shoulders to move him to one side. Children hitting their parents back, that was crossing the line.

"Go to bed, James," she'd seethed and his dad had meekly complied.

Thomas had watched with a mixture of amazement and contempt.

"You shouldn't interfere," she'd scolded, as she checked his face for injury.

"Someone should."

"You watch your tongue. He's still your father when all's said and done." Then she sat down to watch the television, as if nothing had happened. "He doesn't mean it, you know," she'd said later without looking at him. "It's just, sometimes . . . the drink brings it out o'him. His dad were the same."

Thomas didn't reply. He rubbed his cheek until the side of his face was sore. Hopefully he'd have a bruise there next day; either way, he'd never forget.

Saturday's local paper ran a front page about a violent attack that had left a boy in hospital. Suspected skull fracture, facial abrasions; cracked ribs. Not quite what Thomas had bargained for, but he wouldn't lose any sleep. On the Monday, a policeman came to school assembly to talk about personal safety.

No one messed Ajit about any more. Nothing proven of course, and the rest of the bullies were hardly likely to speak to the police. On the Wednesday, Ajit didn't come to Photography Club after school. And on the Thursday he caught up with Thomas, alone.

"Look Thomas, don't take this the wrong way, right, but I can't hang around you for a while. My parents want me home straight after school, what with the attack." Then Ajit lowered his voice. "Listen, right, I don't know if it were you or it weren't you. I don't want to know. I'm grateful — he got what was coming to him. But that's an end to it. That's all I'm saying."

Three weeks later, Ajit returned to Photography Club; the pack leader never came back to school. Rumour was that the family had moved away, fearing a vendetta.

The breeze stirred and he touched the side of his face. It was turning cooler. Odd really that he'd ended up working for the government and Ajit had become a police officer — something for a psychologist to chew over.

* * *

Saturday was market day and his mother was in her element, showing off her *visiting* son to every shopkeeper she knew. Then tea and a bap at the new Victorian tearooms — a contradiction that only he found amusing. He sacrificed Saturday afternoon on the altar of television, sat there with his father watching every sport known to man.

It all unravelled after dinner — he should have seen it coming. Leeds had dropped points for no good reason and he'd made the *mistake* of bringing in a bottle of whisky as a peace offering. By the time he'd got back from seeing Pat and the kids — with Gordon still playing the invisible husband — the bottle was half-empty; or half-full, if you happened to be an optimist. Either way, it didn't take long for old resentments to surface, on both sides.

"What right do you have to judge me, eh? You swan about up here when you feel like it, like some great conquering hero. And you look at us like we're the shit off your shoe. You know your trouble, eh? You're a bloody snob. Ever since the day you met that London tart and you abandoned us."

Twelve years had added weight to the grudge. It was all calculated, of course, in the expectation that Thomas would stand no criticism of Miranda or her family. So he withdrew into himself, waiting for his father to implode. Silence had always been his weapon of choice and he'd honed it like a sabre.

His father crossed no-man's land to deliver another volley. "When we stood shoulder to shoulder . . ."

Thomas winced. *Here we go again . . .*

". . . Shoulder to shoulder as they closed pit after pit — the working man were at war. Months we stood together, while that daughter of the antichrist laid this country to waste. Neighbours — begging for 'andouts, looking in supermarket skips for food."

Tears of bitterness rained down; he wiped them away with a fist. The other hand stayed tightly on the glass. "And when I heard you'd got a job wi' 'The Government,' the very people all working-class folk had been at war with, I were bloody ashamed."

There it was: the cold truth.

"You've betrayed your own class, Thomas; turned your back on your roots. I mean, who are you? Who the bloody hell *are* you?"

Thomas looked to his mother, sat quietly, staring at the carpet. He wondered if she felt the same way. He headed for bed. It wasn't even nine o'clock, but he was exhausted. The whisky had been manipulative; he knew that. But you have to know where the bleeding comes from before you can cauterise it.

He read for a while, too agitated to sleep. Once Sherlock Holmes had resolved *The Eligible Bachelor*, he sent two texts. One to Miranda, which read: *Can I come home now?* And tried to tell himself he was joking. And one to Ajit, to try and arrange a meet-up. Then he turned out the light and sank into a dreamless sleep.

* * *

He woke early on Sunday to the sound of sparrows scrapping on the roof outside. His eyes felt tight against his skin; he'd been crying in his sleep — hadn't done that for some time. He rubbed his face as if he could disguise the evidence.

Tiptoeing around the house reminded him of stolen weekends on the moors. A note left on the table — back on Sunday — and two days of absolute freedom. Ajit's dad would drive them over; sometimes there'd be three or four of them, the car jammed to the gills.

Time check: seven thirty. He crept out quietly. It was a fair distance but he didn't mind the walk; the exercise was good for him, it made him feel grounded.

Ajit was late finishing his shift. Thomas waited in the foyer, sipping machine coffee. The notice board was a library of misery: rabies, terrorism, drug abuse, domestic violence — he read that one twice — and HIV. He figured if you read all that for too long, you'd never want to leave the police station.

The desk sergeant picked up a telephone, nodded to whatever he was hearing and cleared his throat. "Ajit will be out in a bit. You the one from London?"

Thomas smiled grimly, primed for the put-down.

"It's a bit different up 'ere — more sense of community, like. I dare say you've noticed that."

He didn't bother mentioning he was a Yorkshireman by birth; his accent would have made it sound like a mockery. *Sense of community? Easy words.*

The secure door buzzed and clicked — just like the gun club. Then Ajit sprang the door wide with one large hand. He had a smile to match. "Thomas, my man!"

They did a round of macho handshakes and shoulder slaps, until the sergeant asked them if they wanted to be alone together.

"How long you up here for?"

"Heading back tomorrow."

Ajit led him out to the car. "You could have stayed with me and Geena."

"What? And miss playing Happy Families?" He turned abruptly and saw a brown car waiting at the junction. There was no traffic at all. "Could you call it in for me?" He felt the blood draining from his face.

"What's got into you, Thomas? Are you in some sort of trouble?"

"Can you just call in a PNC check — as a favour to me?"

Ajit reached for the radio. Thomas had already pulled out a small pair of binoculars and started reciting the number plate. Ajit stared, open-mouthed. "Bird watching," he explained.

The check back came quickly. "'s all right, Thomas, it's one of ours! Out of town CID. I wonder what they're doing, coming over the borders!" Ajit peered at Thomas closely, as if he could see past his defences. "Right then, 'ave you got time for a walk in the wilds? 'Cause by the look of it, the town don't agree with you."

Thomas brightened. "Aye, that'd be great. Mind if I drive — it makes a change from London."

"You never did take to being a passenger."

Too true.

* * *

Ajit filled the passenger seat; he looked as if he'd been poured into the car. It was a different story at school, but a growth spurt at the end of his teens had provided a Sunday rugby side with a formidable prop forward. Now, when he laughed, the whole car seemed to shake. Although, Thomas thought, that could just be the suspension.

Thomas began to relax in his friend's company. When he'd decided to leave Leeds and go with Miranda to the brighter lights of London, Ajit had been the first person he'd told. It was the kind of easy friendship moulded by years, that doesn't require regular phone calls; where a missed birthday or a late Christmas or Diwali card is no big deal. Now, driving out across the North York Moors, they were like teenagers again.

"Did tha hear about the Hasselblad on sale at auction, down in London?" Ajit was as excited about the camera as a virgin on a first date.

"Hear about it, I went to view it at Sotheby's!"

"Yer jammy bastard!" The car rocked again.

They parked up on Ferndale moor and raced up the ridge like children. Thomas was light on his feet, but Ajit powered past him like a steam engine. From the ridge, the land swept out towards Rudland Rigg. Thomas half wished he'd brought a kite.

"So, come on then, London boy, what sort o' bother are you in?" Ajit made a playful jab at Thomas, which he fended off with a slap.

"You know I work in the Civil Service . . ."

"Aye. Patents or summat?"

"Well, I transferred; I'm a photographer now."

"You lucky beggar. Is it leaflets and that, or something more exciting?"

Thomas took a long breath. "Outdoor work, mainly."

"Nice — buildings or forestry?"

So much for the 'trail of breadcrumbs' approach. "Mainly people; the sort who don't know they're being watched."

"By heck, Thomas Bladen, you're a dark horse."

Thomas caught the way that Ajit's face froze for an instant; maybe he was remembering a time that he'd rather have forgotten.

"Are you allowed to tell me who you work for, then?"

He blew a dandelion head and watched as the spores drifted at the mercy of the breeze. "SSU — Surveillance Support Unit."

"Blimey, who'd a' thought it; one of them coverts. I won't say owt, obviously." Ajit gave a wink the size of Catterick. "Still durn't explain your bit of bother though."

Thomas pushed the binoculars to his face and said nothing.

Ajit seemed to take the hint. "Give us a go, then," he swung wide towards Rosedale Abbey. "Buzzards are out — Geena and I come up here regularly."

"I thought the suspension was a bit worn out."

"Give over!" Ajit gave him a shove and continued tracking the buzzards. "You know I'd help you, Thomas, as much as I can of course," his voice warbled with concern.

Thomas smiled for about a second. Even now Ajit believed in the letter of the law; he admired that in a way. "Thanks Aj; I'll let you know if I need you."

They stood side by side for a long time, gazing out across the rich moorland; neither one spoke. Then Thomas sighed and the spell was broken. He wanted to tell Ajit that it was good to be back, despite everything, but there was no need.

"Right then, me little Cockney Sparra, let's get you back to the bosom of your family."

"And you back to Geena's."

"I'll bet that sort of wit goes down a storm in London."

"I have to ration the tickets to keep the crowds down."

Ajit contorted himself into the driver's seat. "Don't give up your day job."

No chance of that now, not when it's getting so interesting.

Ajit declined the offer to come in and say hello to the folks, but he asked after Pat and wished her well. Back in the mists of time, he had gone out with her for a short while. After Thomas had left for Leeds, of course.

"Is that you, Thomas?" his mother cooed. She knew perfectly well it was; she'd been standing at the curtains when the car pulled up. "Door's on the latch. Come in, kettle's already on."

He grinned; one day, scientists would research the psychic ability of mothers to know when to make tea. "Is he up yet?"

"Well . . . your father's not feeling too great. He's asked if you'd like to go over Fylingdale this afternoon . . ." she waited, hands apart in nervous tension, clapping them together triumphantly at the answer she'd hoped for.

Afternoon. Wow; must be a hell of a hangover this time.

"He doesn't mean it, Thomas, you know that. You're his only son when all's said and done and he just wishes you were back here; we all do. Oh, I know too much has happened for you to want that — you've got your own life now — I'm not stupid. But it doesn't stop us wishing."

Thomas slid an arm around her waist. "You're a very wise woman."

She looked him up and down. "Wise enough to know not to bring a bottle of whisky into the house. He can't 'andle his drink — never could, lets all the demons out. I think you did it on purpose," she gave him a mock slap on the arm. "Come on, sit yourself down — I'll make your favourite breakfast. I've got in smoked bacon and eggs."

His father didn't surface until after one, announced by a groan; he couldn't tell if it was the door or his dad. James nodded carefully, acknowledging them both in one sorry movement. On the table was a steaming mug of tea and a paracetamol. He lowered himself to the chair as if it was a hot bath and took his medication. "I'll be right as rain in a bit." He looked as if he'd slept in the rain.

Thomas put the newspaper down and enjoyed the spectacle of his dad trying to tackle some toast. It might have been his imagination, but his mother seemed to have made it extra crunchy.

* * *

Eventually, they made it out to Fylingdale; Thomas ended up doing the driving, as his father didn't feel up to it. He pulled in by the side of the road so that the wind buffeted the windows and gently rocked the car. When he was a kid, Thomas had been told that this was the Weatherman helping him to sleep.

Despite the wind, Thomas left his jacket open, enjoying it against his skin. He closed his eyes, lost to the elements and swallowed by the moors. And his first thought — the only one that came to mind — was wishing Miranda could feel this now, beside him.

His father tapped his arm. "Remember that old bunker we found on't moor? They've opened it up to the public — I'll show you."

'We found.' Close enough; Thomas and Ajit had uncovered the hatch in a thicket, running around like crazed puppies. His father had shouted, 'give it a rest or go play somewhere else.' And so they had. Ah, hangover weekends, such a staple of childhood memories.

At first they thought they'd discovered a secret tunnel into Fylingdales airbase — Fylingdales, USA, as some locals called it. He remembered Ajit and him writing a letter to the base commander about doing a school project on it. Then a nice man from the USAF came to Photography Club with a wings patch for each of them and a donation to the school. It turned out that the bunker didn't go anywhere; it was an isolated installation built as a test.

Seventeen years or so later, the sealed door had been exchanged for a lockable one and the Cold War relic was now a freebie tourist attraction. They managed a five-minute tour, grabbed a leaflet and set off across the moorland. Thomas didn't say much afterwards, but he noticed his dad wincing with the exertion of the walk. He stopped and waited, made like he had cramp.

"Yer taken any good photographs lately, Thomas?"

He smiled, knowing that *good* automatically excluded talk of London skylines. "Aye. I went to Wales for shots of the red kite. I'll send you prints if you like."

"Yeah, do that. Wales in't so far from London, is it?"

A subtle way of reminding him that Pickering was about the same distance. He conceded defeat by changing the subject. "We'll need to make tracks soon or dinner'll be burnt to a crisp."

They both laughed. As if Thomas's mother would ever let that happen. Growing up, Thomas often wondered what she'd seen in his father, although he'd been a muscular man in his younger days, when he worked the pit. At times like this though, when his dad laughed, then he understood.

He slowly shook his head. Fathers and sons; they made the hundred years war look like a skirmish. On the way to the car they passed a family making their way up the slope, the boy screaming with laughter as his dad raced on with the boy squarely on his shoulders. Thomas had to look away.

Chapter 13

The family had given him a good send-off, Sunday night. A light tea and then a round of happy — i.e. highly edited — memories; photo albums all present and correct. Pat brought the kids; Gordon even put in an appearance later on, to take the children home. Dad was off the drink for the night; he only usually drank on Fridays and Saturdays. Maybe that was why Thomas had always hated Fridays.

Ajit came over first thing Monday morning, like the cavalry. Destination: Leeds. Geena waited in the car and Ajit stood at the gate, as if he were guarding Thomas's only means of escape.

His dad raised a hand in greeting from the front door. "By heck, Ajit, you'll be needing a bigger police car soon."

Thomas eased past his folks and called his goodbyes. His father had a love-hate relationship with Ajit. Loved the man, but hated what he'd become — another rant for another Friday night.

"Have a safe journey, son, and don't forget about sending those photographs."

Son — blimey, one for the diary.

Geena moved to the back seat, but not before she had swarmed over Thomas. "Come 'ere, you big lump."

He glanced at Ajit. Compared to *him*, he wasn't even a lumpette.

"So," Geena piped up as soon as the car pulled away. "'Ave you told him, then?" Ajit said nothing. "Three months gone!" she cried, "You're gonna be an uncle, Thomas!" She ran a hand where the bulge would appear.

Thomas didn't ask why he was only finding out now; secrecy seemed to be catching. "Crikey, what did your dad say, Ajit? Has he fixed a date for you, then?"

Ajit flexed his lips and launched into a parody of Mr Singh senior. "Ajit, now see here, I'm an 'onourable man with an 'onourable son . . ."

Thomas stared hard at his friend. "You 'aven't told *him* yet either, have you, you great pudding?"

"Men — you're bloody useless," Geena laughed even as she said it. "Leave it to the women — I've already told your mam."

"What?" Ajit instinctively turned round to her.

"Eyes on the road, you big lump," Geena pushed out her hand.

Thomas had a flash of inspiration. "A month or two from now, you'll both be great lumps!"

Geena leaned in, between the front seats. "Yeah and it wouldn't hurt you to do a bit o' settling down."

Ajit looked daggers at her. She made a 'What have I said?' face and fell silent. Thomas reached for the radio to drown out his thoughts.

* * *

At Leeds station, he separated out a rucksack and stowed the rest of his stuff in a locker. He'd completed a walk past on the Friday so he knew where the office was — a typically drab MoD building. The security process was less sophisticated than Whitehall, but no less formal. After an ID check and sign-in, he was shown to a side room. Away from family and friends, old ideas returned to haunt him. Like how he'd got the gig for a Yorkshire pick-up at all. Perhaps this was Peterson's revenge? If so then Sir Peter Carroll was in on the gag. Anyway, he was here now.

Just about the time he'd started counting ceiling tiles, a woman entered the room — mid-thirties, not big on words. Her epaulettes identified her rank as a captain — good to know he'd learned something from Karl. He found himself unconsciously closing his legs and straightening his posture. She might have been in Leeds, but her accent was pure South East England, as if the two of them were on an exchange programme. "This way if you please, Mr Bladen."

He followed her down three flights of concrete steps. His breath hung in the air; the basement was big on atmosphere, but small on heating. And the blast-proof doorframe only served to remind him of the Fylingdale bunker. The Captain produced a swipe card and approached the keypad. He instinctively turned away until he heard the last of the bleeps.

She levered the door mechanism and swung it, beckoning him in without speaking. Inside the room were two safes, a table bench like something out of a school science lab and a couple of chairs. It all looked like a full-sized logic problem. While he took a seat, the good captain produced two keys, which she held up one at a time, as if she was performing a trick. He almost clapped. She inserted a key into the safe on the left, in precise movements. The mechanism gave way with a *clunk* then she pulled back the reinforced door and started unloading the contents.

It was money, a lot of money. *Holy shit.* The packets of currency piled up on the table.

"That's fifty-three thousand pounds."

No it wasn't. He pressed his palms together, as if to stem the sweat. *Jesus.* He focused on the mound of sealed packets. That indefinable itch was kicking in. "Can you count them, please?"

She did as he asked, counting the *fifty-seven* packages out, just as he had the first time. Next thing he did was glance around the room for CCTV. What the hell was going on? She seemed genuinely perplexed, but that cut no ice with him.

"Check again."

"The requisition order states that fifty-three thousand pounds are to be couriered and that all contents are to be cleared from the safe." She waved the paperwork in the air — it could have been in Greek for all he cared. On the shelf behind her was a single DSB — document security bag. He stood back and watched while she bagged the goods like an upper-class bank-robber. Then he noticed the split in the bag. He took a deep breath and tried to ignore the adrenaline racing in his veins.

"I can't take it like that. Don't bother sealing it — I'll need a new DSB."

Her head flicked up. "It's the only one we've got here. I'd have to go all the way upstairs. You have your rucksack in any case."

She pronounced it *rook-sack*, as if it were an exotic object. And she clearly wasn't used to being given orders by civilians. Tough. He didn't waste words. "I'm not taking that package in that DSB. So either you get a new bag or you can stick it back in the safe."

"But you'll miss your train."

He did a double take. *Miss my train?* Two years he'd been fetching and carrying for the SSU. No one at the collection point was supposed to know the courier's travel arrangements. It shouldn't have been possible.

She broke eye contact. "Very well," she blushed scarlet, "Wait here."

"I'll wait outside, thanks. And best lock the door with what's in here."

She wavered then thought better of it, ushering him out quickly. Once the door was reset, she rushed upstairs two steps at a time. He pressed himself against the wall, felt the cold surface hard against his skin. He touched Karl's envelope through his jacket and wondered if this was all some kind of sick joke. Maybe that was it; someone would be out soon to admit to the wind-up.

A minute or so on and he started to wonder if they'd abandoned him down there. *Think Thomas, think.* He could always leave — just walk away and call it in as a no-show. But that frisson of fear was also exciting; it was like the feeling he'd had that first time at the gun club. As if there was a bigger picture. And knowing that, he had questions that needed answers. Like since when did the SSU act as bagmen for currency? And if they'd always been, since when did they start sealing confidential packages in front of the courier?

The Captain clattered back down the stairs — she looked as pale as he felt. She handed him the DSB then remembered that she had to unlock the door again. His going off message like that must have thrown her completely — not part of the plan, whatever the plan was. His paperwork was duly signed and countersigned then she bundled him out of the building. What had really burned the stew was his insistence on keeping the ripped DSB as evidence. If looks could kill, she would have been a soldier. Then again . . .

Outside, in the street, he pulled the rucksack in tight over his shoulder and sprinted for the first taxi he saw. He directed the cab to the Art Gallery and stood at the roadside until he was sure it had gone. A large coffee helped to stave off the shock. He threaded through the crowds and took his place in the taxi queue.

* * *

At the station, he retrieved his bag and had another coffee. All in all, he'd done well. Neither DSB was sealed — a simple sleight of hand distraction before both bags went into his rucksack — or was that rook-sack? He laughed into his coffee. A profitable retirement as a stage magician; Karl could be his assistant. Karl, in a non-speaking role — now that *would* be magic.

The London train was late, leaving him too much time for introspection; the coffee wearing off didn't help his mood either. Ajit and Geena — shit, they were starting to behave like adults. Okay, Ajit had always been responsible. But, a baby! And Pat looked all set to become a one-parent family in the not too distant future. Mum and Dad were the same of course, like that was supposed to be a comfort. And to top it all, *he* had just played Secret Squirrel and walked off with fifty-seven grand — with four of that unaccounted for. Watson, we have a problem.

The tannoy finally delivered an indifferent apology and announced that the train was in. He quickstepped up to first class and tried not to look smug as the poor bastards in standard walked further down the platform. He found his reserved seat and quickly abandoned it for another, which had no seat behind him. A few rows away a student — by the looks of him — settled in and upped the volume on his earpieces. Thomas counted to twelve and stared out the window, eager to be free of Leeds; he didn't relax until they were on the move.

A few minutes out of the station, as if answering a scratchy mating call, the train manager appeared and made a beeline for Grunge Boy, checked his ticket and pointed him towards cattle class. Thomas couldn't help but smile; nice try kid.

As Grunge Boy approached, he mouthed something that looked like *wanker*. Thomas gently angled out the tip of his boot. Grunge Boy was too busy flipping Thomas the finger and went down like a sack of shit.

He grinned; the bloke looked a lot grungier, face down. Then he noticed how straight the back of his hair was and a wave of panic swept over him. For a moment, he considered checking him for ID, but he calmed himself and laughed it off. "Are you alright, mate?" He figured Grunge Boy must be okay if he was well enough to keep swearing.

Thomas smelled her perfume before he saw the woman — something a little more upmarket than he was used to. She asked without words if the seat opposite was taken. He did the polite thing, shook his head and scanned the rest of the carriage for options. Sod it, he was settled now and the journey was less than three hours — he could grin and bear it. It was an attractive perfume after all, on an attractive woman.

"Ooh look — matching rucksacks!" she lifted hers up from the floor to show him. He patted his own rucksack on the seat beside him and tried to quell the warning bells in his head. Any fishier and he'd be in Whitby harbour.

He had to admit it; first class really *was* first class. True, it was more of a finger bowl than a mug's worth, but the coffee was good and strong — and free. He glanced up at the woman opposite, now deep into her copy of Feng Shui Gardening. Hardly reading matter for spies. He sighed, remembering the game that he and Miranda used to play in Leeds — the name game. Pick any stranger and give them a name based on an arbitrary feature or characteristic, usually the first thing you notice. The advanced version involved picking occupations and back-stories.

Chelsea Girl — as in the flower show — looked over from her magazine and made a half-smile. Maybe this was how spies went on the pull. Maybe he was thinking about everything a tad too much. He hid himself in *The Return of Sherlock Holmes* and left her to it. He loved the way that everything in the stories had a purpose — no excess fat. If only real life were that reasonable.

When the remainder of Moriarty's gang were safely under lock and key, Thomas put the book down to rest his eyes. He couldn't shake the high strangeness of the morning. Had he done the right thing in taking charge, back in Leeds? Perhaps it really was some sort of test? More likely Sir Peter Carroll got his kicks from moving pieces around a board, playing Churchill in his war room.

Thomas had always felt, deep down, that the old man had a soft spot for him, what with being a civilian and everything. Once, back in State House, Sir Peter had waited patiently while Thomas had spent fifteen minutes setting up a skyline shot at sunset. Not a word spoken until the magic moment was captured. Come to think of it, he'd given Sir Peter a print of that.

Right; time to get busy. He launched from his seat, stepping carefully over Chelsea Girl's stylish feet as he headed for the toilets, rucksack in hand. He did wonder if he'd be mistaken for a pornographer in need of a quick fix, but needs must.

Even in first class, there was someone incapable of flushing the toilet, or keeping their first class piss off the seat. He slammed the lid down and pulled a pair of gloves from his jacket. Best not to put fingerprints on the money while he was transferring it back to the old, torn DSB. Yep, all fifty-seven thousand, still there. It weighed less than he'd expected, not that he was in the habit of ferrying huge amounts of cash around.

Someone tried the lock from outside. He didn't bother responding; he had other things to think about. He'd keep the unsealed DSB and add it to the bugging device that Karl had given him in Caliban's; he was fast building a trophy spy kit. He checked the rucksack was secure, flushed the toilet and opened the door, only remembering to take off his gloves halfway down the carriage.

By London, he and Chelsea Girl had totted up less than five minutes of conversation — a personal best in stonewalling. He let her exit the train first and gave her a couple of minutes' head start.

* * *

Sir Peter was very specific about the delivery time — which left a conundrum. How do you kill a few hours with fifty-seven grand to look after? Simple really — you take it to the movies. Leicester Square was a 'phantasmagoria of cinematic entertainment' — he'd read that once on a tourism leaflet. He picked a foreign film with subtitles. Miranda had made him sit through a dozen foreign films when she'd returned from Bermuda. But once he'd seen *Rififi*, he was hooked.

Sadly, this wasn't even *Rififi's* second cousin. After two and a half hours, the tortured Breton artist had left her diplomat husband and set sail for Tangiers with her daughter and a cat called Filou — like the pastry. At least, that's what he thought had happened; he'd tuned out for a while, absorbed by the soundtrack of his thoughts, trying to make sense of a *very* difficult day.

He arrived at Main Building with twenty minutes to spare. He'd decided to check in early, then kick his heels in the foyer, maybe count some tiles. He approached the reception desk, relieved to have finally made it.

"I have a personal delivery for Sir Peter Carroll." He passed his ID through the slot.

The woman on the other side of the glass looked him up and down. Nothing like a hearty welcome, and neither was this. A colleague beside her picked up a telephone and a round of military whispers ensued. It was a quick game. "Sir Peter Carroll is no longer in the building."

He took out his orders and studied them again; there was no mistake. "Can you check to make sure?"

Again, the look that told him he was about as welcome as Karl on Ann Crossley's honeymoon. He put the bag down and massaged the sweat into the back of his neck. "Is there any way of reaching Sir Peter?"

"Sir Peter," she stressed, as if to reclaim the name from the lips of an infidel, ". . . is unavailable." There was a long pause. "Is there someone else I can call for you?"

"Forget it," he narrowed his eyes, "I'll come back tomorrow."

Outside, the screech of London traffic brought him to his senses. He checked his watch; still time to make it back up to Leeds, but the building would likely be closed. Why hadn't he rung ahead when he'd first got to London? Easy answer: because he'd never had to before.

His mobile held five numbers now: Miranda, her parents, her brothers' place, Karl and the Pickering homestead. And by his own reckoning that was probably two numbers too many. His thumb hovered over the choice of speed-dials. No contest, under the circumstances.

John Wright picked up immediately. "Yorkshire Tourist Board." Funny man — he must have clocked the caller. "Alright, Thomas, how was your time away?"

"Good, thanks; not long back. Listen, all right to pop over tonight?"

"You're always welcome! Bring some money — we'll play some cards."

Bring some money; that had to be the understatement of the decade. "Nice one, John," he fought to control the shake in his voice. "I'll train it up and grab a cab at the station."

"Don't be daft. Ring from the train and one of the boys'll meet you."

"Thanks mate." He began to breathe easy again. The boys would be there too. The Wrights' home was the safest place he knew. And there was always the chance that Miranda would put in an appearance, especially if he texted her.

Back at his flat, he decanted dirty clothes, picking up clean ones and his personal laptop. He was in the middle of deciding whether to take along a camera when the phone rang. Fantastic, Miranda must have got his message.

"Hello?" Silence. The kind of metallic silence where you think you can hear whirls and echoes, but really there's a cavernous emptiness. He waited, a minute or more, his heart pounding as he strained to pick up clues — breathing, background noise, anything. He put the phone down and straightaway drew the curtains. *Easy, Thomas.* Probably just a wrong number, some old dear, as deaf as a post, who'd misdialled.

The phone started up again, its tinny, synthetic sound reverberating through the flat. He crept to the window — nothing in sight either direction. The phone was still ringing relentlessly: number withheld. Now he was really freaked. Whoever it was, he'd answered before so they knew someone was in. Stupid — he might as well have hung a banner outside: 'cash available to good home.'

The racket from the phone died; the silence afterwards was deafening. He tiptoed to the front door and double-bolted it. There was only one choice — he could either stay there with a bagful of money or make a break for it.

He grabbed his rucksack and bag — no time to change now — and went to the back door. He pressed his face tightly against the frosted glass and waited. There was no sense of any movement out there. The door opened with a creaking click; he never oiled it on purpose. He locked up and took the metal steps two at a time, down to the excuse of a garden. His eyes scanned the debris — bingo, just what the doctor ordered. He grabbed a piece of wood that had been dumped there and weighed it — good enough to do some damage.

The gate swung back and bounced a little against the back post. Another pause, listening out into the open space, breath held, straining for clues. At the point where he needed to breathe again he stepped into the back alley, club in hand. Fear was turning to a simmering rage. He slammed the gate shut and took practice swings with the stick. But all that lay before him was a few old dustbins, half a motorcycle and the usual mixture of newspapers, discarded milk bottles and dog shit.

He trod warily, the stick primed by his side. Nothing stirred except his own overwrought imagination. At the end of the alleyway he dropped the stick and broke into a gallop. Call it instinct, call it paranoia; call it what the fuck you like, he had to get away from there. As he closed on Walthamstow Central a bus drew by and he was so hyped up that he got on — and stayed on — just to give himself some time to uncoil. He sat downstairs near the exit and rode the bus all the way to Leyton Underground instead.

He didn't phone the Wrights until he was climbing the stairs at Barking. Terry, the elder son, was there in minutes. How Terry could afford a BMW remained a mystery to him; the Wrights' business dealings were as unfathomable as the Atlantic, and probably as treacherous. Two poor sods waiting for taxis looked on with envy as Thomas opened the car door; he couldn't blame them. Silver and chrome bodywork, sixteen valves, two hundred Nm of torque, and all the other specs that had meant nothing whatsoever to Thomas when Terry described them in loving detail. But it looked the business.

He climbed inside, squeezed his bag behind him and kept the rucksack on his knees — he felt like a first day pupil holding his satchel.

Terry talked as fast as he drove. "So this American geezer rings up and offers me a '67 Corvette — imagine that!

At that moment, all Thomas could imagine was his last coffee churning in his stomach. Terry interrupted the anecdote for some toe-curling cornering. "And I said to him: I'll give you fifteen grand, subject to sight, and he says . . ."

Look at the road; look at the road.

"American geezer, he says to me: 'Son, you got yourself a deal.' Stupid yank got the year wrong. Turns out it's a '78, but I reckon there's enough parts in the wreck to turn a profit."

"Wreck?"

"Yeah — totalled. Dad's gonna come with me to check it out, then we'll strip it down at the yard. I know this, erm — whatcha call it — installation artist. Poncey modern stuff — great body though."

"What, the Corvette?"

"No, some mate of Sheryl's; comes into Caliban's now and again."

Thomas nodded carefully; his head was spinning.

"Yeah, she uses the car parts in her sculptures. I wish she'd use my parts."

Hand off crotch; both hands on the wheel!

The BMW arrived at Chez Hideaway with a final flourish of brakes that set Thomas's teeth on edge. Diane, matriarch of the Wright clan, was waiting at the door. Terry fetched Thomas's bag from the car.

"Thomas, come inside love — you're as white as a sheet."

And no bloody wonder after Steve McQueen's performance. He went in to the living room and looked for Miranda; it was too much to hope for, but that hadn't stopped him hoping. John met him with a beer in his hand. "John, could I 'ave a private word?"

"No problem. Come through — pizzas are on their way."

He followed John to a side wing of the house, rucksack in hand.

"We can talk here in my office — I work from home some of the time now." The room was as silent as a Mafioso on trial.

Thomas glanced around the room in surprise. It was spotless, orderly, not what he'd expected. No dodgy shipment receipts, no unpaid bills from the Revenue and no rolls of twenties — like *he* could talk, today.

"Take a pew. Now, what can I do for you?"

No easy way to do this. Thomas pulled open the rucksack and the ripped DSB to afford John a generous view.

"Fuckin' 'ell, Tom — this is s'posed to be a friendly game."

They laughed together. And as Thomas leaned back he saw three frames up on the wall. In the centre was a classic photograph of the whole family. He remembered the occasion well; Miranda had made him go shopping with her. Not that watching Miranda try on a succession of figure-hugging dresses could ever be described as a burden. He'd been the photographer, plumping for a 90mm lens on a 35mm camera.

To the left of that was a framed newspaper clipping: LOCAL BUSINESSMAN EXONERATED IN POLICE INVESTIGATION. Thomas turned away quickly before the blush took hold. That had been the closest he'd come to owning up about his day job, around a year ago. His back twinged just thinking about it. Two hours in situ, waiting for a copper so bent he could have doubled as a corkscrew. Waiting in shitty weather and poor lighting so he could capture the moment when Bent Cop tried to collect a pay-off, to avert a watertight but spurious case.

Yeah, lots of risk on that one, especially from the work side. Still, he'd achieved a natty set of black and whites — he preferred them for detail in crap lighting — and a half-decent sound recording, good enough for the police anyway. John, his brief and some senior officers all received an anonymous set of photos. Only the police received the sound recording.

He sensed John watching him, but his curiosity was in overdrive. The third frame really surprised him. Circa 1990: *Meet the*

Parents, East London style. It must have been one of their first nights out after he and Miranda had come down from Leeds. The composition was too wide and contrived although it had a sort of naïve charm; it looked like a snapshot in time, a moment of stillness that couldn't last. Thomas and Miranda, front and centre, sharing a shy clasp at the very bottom of the picture. Diane and John resting hands on their shoulders. A tight-group foursome that still evoked a sense of belonging. Jesus. He'd be reaching for a hankie soon.

"I keep 'em up there to remind me what's important." John smiled and clapped him on the shoulder. "So if you're in some sort of bother, you only have to ask."

Thomas kneaded his forehead. How do you follow that? With the truth — most of it anyway — starting with the pick-up in Leeds, down to the silent phone calls in the flat. John listened, perfectly still, as if several grand in a rucksack was nothing new.

"Well, you know you can stay here, as long as you want. Terry or Sam can drop round the flat tomorrow and pick up some of your gear."

A nice idea, but not a solution. "Nah, I'll be fine once I get rid of the money." On cue, they both looked back into the bag.

"I s'pose it *is* real?"

Thanks, John; something else to obsess about.

John leaned back against his chair. "Okay, here's what I think. Stash the money in my safe for tonight and we'll consider the subject closed. You sleep on it and make sure you take some photos, as evidence."

Sound advice. When the deed was done, John let out a belch that would rival anything the Harwich ferry claxons could produce. "Better out than in. Right then," he clapped his hands together. "Let's go play some *cards*. I feel lucky!"

Everyone in the family knew that Diane was the cards maestro. Popular rumour — and the couple encouraged speculation — was that John and Diane had first met at a casino. One version ran that Diane was a croupier and John the hapless punter. Another, that John had played dumb to win her over — unlucky in cards and all that. The romantic in Thomas was happy to believe either.

He followed John into the living room. Lounges were something other people had — in smaller houses.

"Where's the bloody pizza — I'm starving. Thomas, do the honours will you; drinks and glasses in the usual place," John waved him past. The doorbell rang. "About time!" John roared over the chaos of chairs, crockery and glasses all moving simultaneously.

Diane looked over for an instant. "Thomas, be a dear and see to the door."

88

He passed four beer bottles over to Sam, mid-waltz, and headed for the door, wallet at the ready.

Miranda was stood before him, laden with pizzas. "Special delivery."

He stood at the door, doing the algebra in his head: sight + sore eyes = Miranda.

She deposited the pizza boxes on the hall table. "Mum said to come over; she was worried about you."

Must remember to up the size of Diane's Christmas present this year. He slipped his arms around her waist and pulled her close, breathing her in like oxygen. He was about to speak when she closed her mouth over his. She tasted of ripe cherries and vanilla again. He closed his eyes and lost himself in her scent, her touch, her sanctuary.

"Put him down, sis; some of us need *food.*"

He felt her hand leave his back, probably to flip the finger at Sam. And then the heat of her smile against his face. He was safe, cocooned from the world in the bosom of the family: Miranda's family.

Chapter 14

The two strangers hunched down into their car seats a little more tightly to drive out the cold. The younger man rubbed his hands together, like a character straight out of Dickens.

"Can't you put the heater on, just for a little while?"

"Nikolai," the older man said in a disparaging tone, betraying the slightest trace of Mother Russia, "To be too comfortable would dull your senses. Have some more coffee if you wish."

"It's *Nicholas* — you know that," he scowled at the thermos flask by his feet, but didn't dare voice his displeasure openly.

The older man tutted and pressed the button for the dashboard clock. Within the next two hours, four identical snatch burglaries would take place across North London — starting now. "It is time," he opened his mouth wide to pronounce the name, "Ni—cho—las," ending with a malevolent hiss. "Take this and remember, he will be alone and unarmed."

The younger man made an audible gulp. He reached for the gun and held it flat in the palm of his hand, as if weighing the outcome of the enterprise.

"Only shoot if you have to, but try not to kill him. Such things attract the wrong kind of attention."

Nicholas put on a balaclava and slid out of the car, pistol thrust into his pocket. He padded across the street, a door-ram enforcer hanging at his side, scanning left and right like a night-time road safety ad. He mounted the steps in two stretches and paused at the door, listening for a television or a radio. It was unlikely that the owner would be awake at this hour; that gave him the element of surprise.

A prior visit to a similar property, a few streets away, had given him the dimensions of the flat and the distance to be covered inside. He let go of the gun and it sagged in his coat, spoiling the well-tailored lines. He swallowed hard, took a couple of steadying breaths then swung back the enforcer with both hands, penduluming into the door with an almighty crash.

The older man heard the sound and smiled in the semi-darkness. Two minutes at most. He hummed a little tune and flexed his gloved fingers like a concert pianist, calmly screwing in the silencer on the barrel. He released the car door and stepped outside in the chill of the early morning, resolved and unconcerned — no loose ends. A sound at the rear of the car caught his attention and as he turned, the handle of an automatic pistol smashed against his skull.

A finger pointed at the figure slumped on the pavement and then to the back of the car. The man on the ground yielded a low moan, which drew no one's sympathy. A canvas bag was placed on his head, hangman-style, and the body searched. The weapon was extracted and the body placed in the car boot. The leader directed his two colleagues with more hand gestures, and then crept across the street. He checked the safety on his pistol was off and nudged the door gently; the splinters of wood whined in protest. He stepped inside, keying his senses to the slightest sound or movement.

Nicholas was still in the living room, getting his bearings. He moved towards what should have been Thomas's bedroom and cocked his head, listening for breathing. The door was only pulled to, which gave him an extra second and a greater advantage. He grinned in the dark; his first field assignment was going like clockwork. *Surprise, domination and victory* — he heard the words in his head like a school motto. He flexed his shoulders to psych himself up even more, lifted the gun and rushed the door.

"Right!" he felt by the wall for the light switch. "Give me all your money — *now*!" The bed was empty; sheets neatly tucked in at the corners. "Shit!" he gasped aloud.

Before he could get out another word, a 9mm Browning pistol pressed tightly against his temple. "Don't even fucking think about it," Karl McNeill snarled into his ear.

Nicholas dropped his pistol as if it were molten lead. Karl slammed a knuckle ring into his face, smashing him to the floor. Then he knelt on his arms, ripping off the balaclava. Nicholas was barely conscious, which left little reason for the punches that followed. But Karl delivered them anyway.

"Karl, that's enough," a woman's hand pressed into his shoulder.

He eased himself up and turned to the man beside her. "Get him out of here and I want this damage cleared up pronto — call a team in." And even though he knew now that Thomas wasn't at the flat, he padded the rooms searching for him until Teresa ordered the stand-down. His hand smarted where the ring had cut into his own knuckle and the pulses of pain danced with the adrenaline tremor that ran through his body like a fever. "Where are you, Tommy Boy?"

Chapter 15

John Wright was already sorting out breakfast at six thirty in the morning, whistling a Beatles tune like John Lennon could never have imagined. Thomas walked into the kitchen and raised a nanosecond grin at the idea of John and Karl forming their own covers group — touring prisons to punish the inmates.

"Morning Thomas, what can I get you?"

It was a longstanding morning ritual. Diane liked a lie-in until seven-ish so John took her in the customary tea and toast. Thomas used to have a similar arrangement with Miranda, only his service was a little more personal. No Miranda today though — she'd left around eleven the previous night. Thomas conjured up the memory of her at the front door, like a child recalling their favourite Christmas.

"Tea and some toast would be great, thanks John."

"Are you sure about going into work today?"

He shrugged. What else *could* he do? The best thing would be to ring Christine, explain that he'd be late on-site and head over to Whitehall again to get it over with. He nodded at the thought — must ring Karl as well. That magic envelope had been burning a hole in his brain since he woke up; at least one mystery would be settled today.

Sam bounded into the kitchen while Thomas was still crunching toast. "No Miranda?" The youngest of the Wrights was as matter-of-fact about the whole Thomas-Miranda thing as the rest of the family. Ten years of will-they-won't-they had worn their expectations down to a smooth, frictionless finish.

"Nah, she went home last night." Thomas crunched his toast.

"Oh," Sam sounded disappointed for him. That made two of them.

93

* * *

When Sam dropped Thomas off at Barking station before eight, Thomas had the semblance of a plan. He'd make his calls and squat at Whitehall. Sir Peter would turn up eventually and, if he didn't, Thomas would wait it out. Maybe it wasn't very professional, but then nor was leaving someone holding a stack of money.

On the way down to the platform, he checked the mobile. Pat had sent a text thanking him for coming up — a technological first for her. And there was one voicemail alert. The call had come through in the small hours. Maybe Sir Peter was apologising? Unlikely, as he didn't have his personal number; at least, Thomas hadn't given it to him.

Standing on the stairway he jammed the phone against his ear, oblivious to the lava flow of people around him.

"Thomas, this is Karl — where the hell *are* you? Is everything all right? Ring me — it doesn't matter what time. Ring me *immediately*."

Thomas didn't waste any time.

"Tommo, thank God! Are you okay? Can you talk? Are you alone?" It was like a podcast of Question Time.

"I'm fine. I can talk for a sec — I'm about to get on a train. "

"Great, how long will it take you to get to St James's Park?"

"Fifty minutes, tops."

"Okay, I'll see you there. We've had a bit of a situation. And I'm afraid I've had to change your locks."

Karl rang off; Thomas stumbled down the steps in a daze. Change the locks? Why would someone need to get into his desk? The penny had dropped by the time he got down to the platform.

* * *

Karl was waiting by the ticket barriers, moving rhythmically from foot to foot. Thomas raised a hand and Karl dashed forward. "Am I glad to see you!"

"What's been going on, Karl?" Thomas stood, ignoring buffeting and abuse as people tried to move past or through him.

"Not here; let's walk," Karl escorted him out to the park. "We'll take a stroll to Marlborough Gate. They do great coffee and I'm buying."

He watched as Karl checked around them while they walked. It made a change for someone else to be twitchy. "All clues gratefully received."

"Oh right, I was forgetting. Tell you what, why don't you open that envelope I gave you."

Thomas passed the envelope over for Karl to examine. No reason, other than to see if Karl would check it, which he did. Karl handed it back and looked suitably pleased. Inside was a single page with four sentences, in Karl's own fair scrawl, which read:

1. FIRST THEY'LL TRY TO BRIBE YOU.

2. THEN THEY'LL LEAVE YOU WITH THE MONEY.

3. THEN THEY'LL ROB YOU.

4. NOW YOU'VE LOST THEIR MONEY, THEY OWN YOU.

Thomas read the note three times; he could see Karl scrutinising him out of the corner of his eye.

"So, Tommo," Karl sounded nervous; "Marks out of ten as a clairvoyant?"

He swallowed hard and folded the paper back into the envelope. "Spot on — for the first two."

Karl nodded and went off for the coffees. Thomas slumped on a bench and gazed out at the park, the sports bag containing the rucksack crushed between his legs. How the bloody hell could Karl have known what would happen? Two explanations came to mind. Either he was involved in this whole mind-game *or* he'd experienced something similar.

Karl returned, passing him a steaming cup. "It's Javanese, apparently. And lookie here," he rattled a paper bag, "muffins."

Thomas reached into the bag and squinted at Karl. "Can we cut to the chase? Am I in or not?"

Karl picked at a muffin and sent a piece arcing over to a waiting pigeon. "Rules first, Tommo. I will tell you as much as I can, but there has to be . . ."

Thomas didn't feel like accepting anyone else's rules today. "It happened to you as well, didn't it?" Okay, it was a bluff, but a reasonably deduced one.

"Uh-huh." Karl swigged back his coffee. "I was offered two grand, by way of an unaccountable surplus. You?"

"Four."

"Well, I suppose that's inflation for you!"

"And what did *you* do, Karl?"

"I took it — too right I did!"

Thomas choked on his coffee.

"Calm yourself, Tommo. I took it as evidence. All safely under lock and key somewhere. I wasn't smart enough to stay away for the night like *you* evidently were." Karl peered at him like he was a science exhibit. "No, but I rang ahead and had some old army pals let themselves in with a spare key. So when two thugs turned up to rob me of the readies, I had my own welcoming committee. Next day I turned up to the rendezvous with the cash, minus my £2k cut of course."

"And what happened to the two guys who came a-calling?"

Karl sipped at his coffee more slowly and stared into the distance. "You're better off not knowing."

Thomas felt dizzy, as if the park was closing in on him. He took a mouthful of sweet, doughy muffin and squeezed it down. "What happens now?"

"Well," Karl reached into his pocket then held a closed hand over Thomas's, "firstly, these are yours." He dropped three keys into Thomas's waiting palm. "Remember items two and three on my list? You had your own visitors last night and they weren't bringing you chocolates and flowers. Don't worry, the new door's top quality and nothing's been taken so there's no real harm done."

Are you taking the piss? "Except someone knows where I live."

Karl sighed. "Time to grow up, Tommy Boy. You wanted in — it goes with the territory. You can't expect to wander around in the dark without stepping in some shit."

"Thanks for that," he whistled into his coffee. "I'd better complete my delivery — I'll see you over at Harwich. We'll talk about this again."

"Indeed we will."

He binned the coffee carton and got up to go. The bag seemed heavier now, and so did life.

Karl called after him. "Cheer up, Tommo, you're in good company." His voice dropped a tone. "And listen, we don't discuss this on the job; we can't be sure it's safe there."

Thomas nodded and trudged off towards Whitehall, jingling his new door keys on their leprechaun key ring. His brain was in meltdown so he started small, one step at a time. First, he'd see what Sir Peter had to say about the money. Then he'd consider telling Karl about the tax disc on the red car. And then he'd reveal Bob Peterson's appearance at Harwich on the day of the shooting. It had all the makings of another fun-packed day.

He crossed back over the lake and followed the path to the gate. A police officer crossing the park stopped in her tracks and watched him as he moved about with his large sports bag. Mindful of the small matter of fifty-seven thousand pounds on his shoulder, he approached her, flashed his ID card and spun a line about looking for Main Building and being lost.

Outside the park, he noticed a sign for the Cabinet War Rooms and Churchill Museum. Ironic to think of Sir Peter Carroll's office, close by, with that painting behind his desk. Maybe he'd moved there for the souvenirs.

* * *

The same security staff faced Thomas as he entered the building; on a whim he saluted and they returned the compliment. They were more attentive now. All branches of the armed forces, potentially, supplied personnel for the SSU. But, like one of Karl's secret squirrel rules, people rarely volunteered where they'd come from. It used to drive him mad, but today, facing Whitehall's answer to the Spanish Inquisition, it suited him fine.

Soon he was in a lift with a different silent wonder as escort. His eyes drifted towards the escort's holstered weapon. The guard followed his gaze and tapped the holster confidently. Thomas decided to chance his luck.

"Browning — thirteen rounds," he paused for half a second; "Plus one in the chamber."

The guard smiled and relaxed. The soldier stood at ease. And all thanks to a quick round of Name That Gun.

"You were here yesterday, Mr Bladen?"

"Call me Thomas. Yeah, Sir Peter got called to a meeting; he asked me to come back today. I got some right stick about it at the office — I don't suppose anyone could tell me what his meeting was about so I can cover my arse?"

Soldier Boy smiled and shook his head. Thomas had thought it unlikely the guard would hand over a guest list, but it was worth a try. "If it helps any, Thomas, I know that Sir Peter left Main Building around eight pm. I escorted his chauffeur upstairs to collect some papers."

Thomas faked a smile to avoid sneering.

The escort knocked at the door and ushered Thomas inside. Sir Peter was up and out of his chair before Thomas had reached halfway across the plush carpet. "Thomas, my dear boy," Sir Peter grabbed his hand and shook it keenly. "I must apologise for yesterday. Simply unavoidable. Come take a seat."

Thomas sat down and waited. If in doubt, play it straight.

"So, how was your trip?"

"Fine, sir. Everything went to plan."

Sir Peter seemed to rise up from his chair a little. Thomas pressed his tongue against his lower teeth, rendering his face expressionless. He reached down to his bag and opened the zip, squeezing the handle to stop himself from shaking.

Sir Peter was very still, like a bloated cobra.

"Actually, there was one problem . . ." he kept his head bent forward. *Nice and steady, Thomas, don't blow this.* He lifted out the torn DSB from his rucksack in one fluid movement and thudded it down on the desk.

97

Sir Peter's mouth lowered about a foot. Thomas fancied that even Churchill behind him looked perturbed. "The DSB they provided me with was torn. I made them count the money out in front of me." That part at least was true.

Sir Peter stared at the sealed, torn DSB — the solid blocks of currency poking out like expensive building blocks in a substandard toy bag.

Thomas lifted his face level. "I'd prefer you check the contents, sir, if you don't mind." *Chew on that, Winston.*

Sir Peter broke the seal on the DSB and methodically stacked the currency on his desk. He counted the pile out loud, ending on 'fifty-seven.' "Yes, most impressive — I'd like you to accept a token of my appreciation."

The top two slabs were separated and slid halfway across the mahogany. Thomas had already considered the possibility of a second buy-off and decided what to do about it. "I really couldn't, sir — I was just doing my job."

Sir Peter sighed through his nose, as if he were deflating. Still a cobra, but not quite so bloated "Surely there must be a camera that you've had your eye on?" The old man wore an encouraging smile, like a disguise; his hand rested on the £2000, poised to push it forward.

Thomas didn't need a rethink; two grand could buy a whole lot of camera, it was true. But the two grand would also be buying him. And anyway, it would be suspicious to accept £2000 now when he'd turned down £4000 back in Leeds.

"I wouldn't feel right, sir. Besides," pause for big smile and grand finish, "there's no need."

Sir Peter returned the £2k to the pile and patted it affectionately. "Well done, Thomas, you've passed. It's a little test I have for when people show particular promise. I always knew my confidence in you wasn't misplaced."

He glanced over to the window, but there was no sign of a curly tail.

Chapter 16

He left Whitehall with a mixture of feelings. For all his bravado, he was really no further forward. There was too much going on. It was like playing several games of chess simultaneously — and losing them all.

Christine Gerrard had surprised him when he'd telephoned in, offering to drive him over to Harwich as soon as he was free. She'd gone on site for jobs in the past, but the timing was suspect to say the least.

Her Mercedes looked conspicuous by the underground station. He reached for the car door and breathed in a heady mixture of French perfume and the sound of Grieg. She smiled at him, but kept her sunglasses on.

He caught his perplexed look reflected in her face: Grieg. He wasn't big on classical music; it just wasn't something that floated his boat. But he'd always had a soft spot for Grieg; well, maybe not *soft* exactly. Grieg had been the musical accompaniment to a backwoods romp with Christine in this very car. He brushed the leather seat for an instant, lost in the memory of flesh against hide.

She drove off before his seatbelt was on and he waited for his underwear to settle before he spoke. "Thanks for the lift." Hardly repartee of the decade. Funny thing about Christine; it took him time to thaw around her. Partly the whole 'my boss is my ex' thing and partly because they both knew he'd been an absolute dickhead when they'd split up. It was as if she held a silent moral victory over him.

Eventually Christine removed her glasses; she looked tired.

"Everything alright, Chrissie?"

She shrugged. "Let's talk about something else."

He steered the conversation to safer waters, encouraging talk about her parents, their fancy horses and their fancy house. Then he listened as she recited the genealogy of their prize nags, with bloodlines going back a hundred years. It was the only topic where Christine ever really seemed to come alive, and by Harwich he felt he knew every horse personally.

A text from Miranda came through as they neared the port; she'd got him the new details for the red car's owner, based on the tax disc. He shut the mobile off afterwards.

"Secret admirer?" Christine looked piqued.

He mustered a hangdog expression. "No, more's the pity. Unless Karl counts?" He pressed his hand into the upholstery.

"I had it professionally cleaned," she shot him down in flames.

Yeah, but for whose benefit?

She parked the Merc at Harwich and they sat for a while, windows down, saying nothing. Christine seemed on the brink of speaking a couple of times, but somehow never crossed the line. He watched the gulls at play and wondered what would have happened if he hadn't been so attentive that first day. He knew the answer already — everything would still have happened, just without him knowing.

"Did you turn down the training because of me, Thomas?"

What? "No," he yawned and stretched in the seat. "It's just not my style."

She crinkled her nose. "Surely you don't want to do this your whole life?"

He felt the smile rise across his face. "It'll do for now. Time I was getting back to work." He led and she followed, which almost made him nostalgic. The stairwell harboured old packing material and a fire extinguisher that had seen better days. Good for Christine to see where they'd ended up. They climbed the stairs and he found himself whistling Grieg. As they rounded the last corner she gave him a quick jab in the back and he stopped.

"Ah, so you've brought my boy home!" Karl set down the remains of a baguette.

Thomas braced himself for her reaction to the mess, but she wrong-footed him and went over to Karl. "Thomas has been given additional clearance . . ."

Since when?

". . . He'll be accompanying you on the next out-of-hours pick-up. See that he's briefed when the time comes."

"Will do," Karl's tone bordered on reverential.

She touched Thomas on the shoulder as she left. "And Karl, clean this place up; it looks like a pigsty."

"Ma'am," Karl replied.

They both played statues until Christine's footsteps faded from earshot.

"What the hell was that about?" Thomas almost tripped on the words.

"It's called playing the game, Tommo."

* * *

"Is it a pint for you, Tommy Boy?" Karl hadn't come to life until the evening.

"Uh-huh." His brain ached with the effort of thinking; competing thoughts echoed back and forth.

Karl returned with beer and crisps. Karl loved crisps; maybe it was his Irish genes — Thomas had been afraid to suggest. "Right then," Karl ripped open two crisp bags and spread them on the table, "now we can talk!"

Best start off with an easy one. "So, is Christine in the know?"

Karl crammed a handful of cheese and onion into his mouth and filled the gaps with beer. He sat for a moment, a look of contentment on his face. Then he chewed thoughtfully and swallowed. "Is she bollocks! But she thinks she is, which has its uses. Of course, you'll know about her family — rather well connected. Confidentially," he snatched another clutch of crisps, "I think she finds the idea of all the cloak-and-dagger stuff a bit of a turn-on."

Thomas hurriedly dived into his drink.

"But never forget, Tommo, there *is* a dagger. My advice? Tell Christine nothing; she'll follow orders. Whereas we, amigo, we're the cloak within a cloak."

Now seemed like a good time to share the red car's true registration, seeing as how they were amigos and all.

"I'll look into it," Karl promised.

"No need; I've got the details here," he passed over a beer mat with small, neat handwriting on it.

"My, my, private sleuthing — how very enterprising. How about we check it out this weekend — if you're free?"

Thomas smiled; Karl was very good at this. In only a few words, Karl had acknowledged that he had his own sources, decided the next step and sniffed around his weekend plans. "Fine by me, Karl." He put down his pint. "Now, tell me more about who ruined my door and how you managed to stay one step ahead of all this."

Karl bowed at the table. "You see, you're a bit of an odd fish, Mr Bladen. You're not ex-forces, but you're secretive and *wonderfully* unambitious. As you'll recall, I originally had you down as a mole for another outfit. Like as not, other people think the same. So when Ms Crossley said you were wanted by the big cheese, and you said you'd got a free ticket up north, I put two and two together. I'm guessing there was a ripped DSB waiting for you?"

Thomas raised a glass to him, recalling the comedy of errors in Leeds.

"It's standard MO from what I can tell. Not sure how Sir Peter slots into all this. Anyhow, the difference in my case was that Crossley found out I'd taken the £2000 — I still don't know how."

"And my visitors?"

"Well, they weren't selling *The Watchtower*. The newbie was sent in and the seasoned pro was waiting outside, across the street." Karl's voice dropped away as if he were considering how to continue the sentence.

"How did you . . .?"

"Let's just say I try to prepare for all eventualities. I won't kid you, Tommo, they meant business; they had *guns*."

Thomas touched his hand to his mouth then felt stupid about it.

Karl raised an index finger. "Of course, they don't have them anymore — I have them safely in my box, with the others!" He winked and took another gulp from his glass. "If you'd feel more comfortable I can let you have a piece of equipment for home."

Thomas blinked twice very slowly, as if that would somehow refocus the picture. But it was already becoming horribly clear.

Chapter 17

Thomas flicked another page of the novel and glanced out the windscreen; there was still nothing to see. Just an ordinary street — typical Saturday morning tedium. Every breath drew in the stench of orange combined with petrol. But at least he was past the gagging stage. Karl had his feet on the dashboard and a tabloid open across his legs with a bag of crisps in his lap — quite the multitasker.

Thomas shut his paperback. "So why are we staking this house out?"

Karl interrupted the pen moustache he was lovingly adding to a topless model. "It goes like this," he held up a loose fist in preparation.

Thomas mentally rehearsed a suitably impressed face.

"Thinking this through logically, all we know about the car is two things. One," Karl's index finger shot up like a nose-picker, "the red car probably held the shooter at Harwich. And two," his middle finger rose up to join it, "Ann Crossley had the victim's van taken away — now why would she do a thing like that?"

Thomas shrugged; it sounded like Karl had it all figured out anyway.

"Before we go in with our size nines, we need to know a little bit about the car and its owner. So we require a plausible reason to go knocking on their door."

Thomas nodded. "Seems reasonable."

Karl shifted his crisps and folded the newspaper. "But you know what seems *unreasonable*, Tommo? Why wouldn't you report the number plate to your superiors? And check this — surely the false number plate will eventually flag up somewhere on CCTV and be checked?"

Thomas felt his mouth drying out, like a lazy dog in the heat. "Then why exactly are we here now, Karl?"

"We," Karl stared at him intently, "are a team within a team. Which means what we're doing today doesn't get back to Christine — strictly off the record. And you, my mystery man, need to tell me what I'm missing. Because I know there's something."

Thomas pushed back into the passenger seat, increasing the scent of oranges. "Right . . ." he drew out the word to epic proportions, making it sound like three separate words, "time to come clean. Remember on the day of the shooting, when I asked you how many spotter teams were on?"

"Aye, so I do."

"Well, I saw someone with field binoculars, down in the car park. He was watching the ferry; and as soon as the shooting went off, he scarpered, pronto."

"Interesting," Karl tried to refold his newspaper, gave up and then scrunched it behind him to the back seat. He went back into stare mode.

"I managed to take pictures of the car number-plate and the driver. But there's a complication."

Karl opened one hand flat as if demanding the pay-off.

"The watcher was Bob Peterson, no question." The inside of the car reverberated with sighs.

"Well, you're obviously in the right job; you're a one-man secret service, so you are."

"Wait; you haven't heard the complication. I doctored the watcher out of my mosaic photo for my report — before I was certain who it was. I wanted to check it out on the quiet. Christine wouldn't have known any different but . . ."

Karl grinned and waved a hand up like a zealous schoolboy. "But Bob Peterson must have shat a brick when he heard that you took mosaic shots. Especially when he saw the mosaic from that morning and found he wasn't in it!"

"Yeah, you could say that."

When Karl set it all out before him, he didn't feel quite so impressive.

"So, what then? Uncle Bob tries some damage limitation? Offers you executive training, but you don't bite. Then you get sent to Leeds for the Cashback Challenge."

He considered that. "I wasn't sent by Bob though; Sir Peter Carroll. . . so it must follow that Bob Peterson spoke to the old man."

"Hang on, Tommy; if Ann Crossley was on the ground with a spotter team, then why does Uncle Bob need to be there at all?"

Thomas opened his mouth to speak, but Karl silenced him with two more raised fingers. "Because, Dr Watson, either something different was due to go down that day *or* the shooting was planned and Peterson was supposed to report back afterwards."

Thomas ran a thumbnail between his teeth. "Dr Watson?"

"Come on, Tommo, give me some credit. I've seen a battered copy of Sherlock Holmes poking out of your coat on at least two occasions — I'm no stranger to the great man myself, I might add. It should be recommended reading for the spy about town."

Thomas felt a chill. "And is that what you are, Karl — a spy?"

"Now, you know as well as I do that the Surveillance Support Unit merely assists the work of government agencies, including the security services." Karl raised an eyebrow. It's been documented in Prime Minister's Question Time."

Round and round in circles. Thomas was fast acquiring the mother of all headaches. "So now what?"

"Now, we give the good people at number 129 a wake-up and shake-up call. If you'll excuse me . . ." Karl rescued his mobile from a collection of old car park tickets and chocolate wrappers. Then he pulled out a photocopy of a car magazine classifieds page, with one ad circled and several others crossed out. Thomas gave it the once over; he'd never heard of the title. Karl looked extra pleased with himself. "All my own handiwork — see, I can use computers too! This was my back-up plan; and as sod all has happened in the last hour and a half, we might as well go with that."

"I don't get it."

"Watch and learn, Tommy Boy. Read me the phone number off the ad, will you? If no one answers, we'll have to pay the house a visit." Karl dialled and his voice morphed into leafy Sussex. "Ah yes, hello, I'm ringing about the hatchback — is it still available?" He nodded to Thomas at the reply. "Really? Are you sure — I have the ad here in front of me. Well, that *is* very strange. What a pity; I was planning to pay cash."

Thomas watched the lines furrow on Karl's face like a well-ploughed field. It seemed all might not be going to plan.

"Yes, I was in South London anyway. Erm, well, that . . . er . . . might be interesting. I certainly appreciate the offer. Well, naturally, what the tax man doesn't know!" Karl faked a laugh that would have been at home in Uckfield. Let's say, what, ten thirty? I'll just get a pen. One moment . . ."

Karl held a hand loosely above the mouthpiece and looked away, out the window. ". . . Jessica, Daddy's on the telephone. Go and join Mummy by the till." He lifted his hand free. "Sorry about that. Right, fire away."

Thomas winced — poor choice of words. He watched Karl cradle the mobile under his neck and jot down the address he already knew, on a space near the fake ad.

"That's lovely. Ten thirty it is then. Oh, yes of course: it's . . . Bob Jefferson." Karl went to drop the mobile back into its nest then thought better of it and dialled a number from memory. "It's Karl. I need some money — a couple of grand should suffice. Okay, make it three; and a smart jumper, and a pair of driving gloves. Looks like I'm buying the car. No, I understand. Yes, he's here with me now."

Thomas blanched.

"I'll be at the café on Jerome Street — call me when you're ready. Quick as you can, please." Karl cut the call. "Well, Mr Bladen, seems like you're my lucky charm — that's a turn up for the books. You'll have to drive this back yourself." He beamed like a cherub who'd just won a card game. "Café time — and the apprentice spy always pays."

Thomas watched as Karl tucked into his all-in-one breakfast with gusto. It looked like three breakfasts, all in one. Not that the portion size seemed to slow Karl any. Thomas, on the other hand, was finding that a conscience wreaked havoc on his appetite so he played safe with a large mug of tea and a meagre two eggs on toast. He jabbed at the eggs so that they bled yellow and swept the plate with toast, sluicing the yellow into ketchup. "What about the family with the car?"

Karl managed to cram sausage, bacon and beans into his mouth, and still talk. "The car may give us something useful, but the family is our best lead, so we'll keep a watchful eye."

Thomas set his mug down. "That's not what I meant."

Karl's mobile rang, breaking the deadlock. He checked the number, didn't pick up. "That's me away — I'll not be long. Don't let them take my plate."

Thomas was speed-dialling Miranda before the glass door had finished rattling. He gazed past a window sticker featuring a dancing sandwich, out to a grey Saturday morning. "It's Thomas. Listen, what are you up to this weekend?"

Miranda ran through her schedule at Caliban's, running on into a visit to the gym and a DVD at home. He didn't interrupt; he was happy just to hear some normality. "I might have a date Sunday evening, but we can meet during the day if you like?"

Ouch. He rubbed a thumb across his chest, as if testing a wound. Served him right for making assumptions. "Right, yeah," he smarted. "Tomorrow daytime it is, then." He felt his face tightening. No one spoke for a good ten seconds.

"You're such a dick. Of course I'm free — unless I get a decent offer *today* at Caliban's?"

He blew a breath down the phone: stand-down from DEFCON 3. His jaw unwound into a smile. "So I'll maybe see you later — or tomorrow." They both laughed at how crap he still was at all this. He felt like a fish that's hooked and reeled, thrown back after a few panicky gasps, but unable to resist the lure again.

"Goodbye, Thomas!"

He parked his breakfast and acted as Lord Protector when the waitress made a play for Karl's leftovers. Could you even call yourself a waitress turned out in headphones and ripped jeans that showed your underwear?

The café door pinged; in walked Karl nouveau — V-neck sweater and driving gloves. "Ta da!"

Thomas gawped, couldn't help it. "What are you supposed to be?"

Tonight," Karl slid back on to his vinyl chair, "I'm going to be . . ."

Thomas didn't give him the satisfaction. "So," he reached for his second mug of tea, "did you get the other thing?"

"All safely on board," Karl reassured him, squeezing his jacket pocket as he folded it by his feet. "Anyways, let's saddle up. I want to put them on the back foot when I'm there, so you ring me on the mobile — family emergency — in say, six minutes." Karl winked and Thomas narrowed his eyes as he sipped his tea. Karl looked affronted; his fork stalled above his plate. "What?"

The tea didn't help Thomas's mood. "You're very good at this."

Karl swooped down a fork, scraping the plate. "This," Karl whispered like a gas leak, "from the man who takes secret photos and does his own background checks on Bob Peterson. You're pretty good yourself," he took a bite, ". . . for an amateur."

Thomas raised his mug: touché. He left Karl to his washing-machine impression and went to find the gents. The waitress lip-read his request and flicked her finger towards a door with a hazard sign on it. *Number one for customer service.* He nodded his thanks and tried not to stare at her t-shirt, emblazoned with: 'Don't even think about it.'

Karl walked up to the house, glancing at the red estate in the drive, which he noted had been cleaned. A pity, but the forensics team were on standby so there was always hope. He rang the doorbell and straightened his jacket, making sure his sweater was proudly on display. If you could be proud of a golfer's reject.

He heard a brief exchange on the other side of the glass, aware he was a good fifteen minutes ahead of schedule. Then silence, and the door opened about a foot wide. "Bob Jefferson, we spoke on the phone — I managed to get away sooner. Jessica's being difficult so my wife dropped me off a little early. I hope that's okay?"

107

The woman smiled faintly. She looked tired. "Here's the ad I mentioned," he showed her the photocopy and waited while she studied it, right down to the shopping list he'd added at the bottom in blue felt tip.

She passed it back and nodded. "Won't you come in?" He clocked the accent — not a native South Londoner. Probably an incomer, the sort who called Streatham *St Reatham* or described Balham as 'just off the Kings Road.'

* * *

A man came down the stairs. It had to be a man, judging by the heavy footfalls. "Hello."

Karl's trained ear registered the slight twang on the second syllable.

The woman tensed, turning to her husband. He led from there. "We are keen for a quick sale. You mentioned cash on the phone? Let me show you the car and we can discuss the price."

Brief and to the point. The wife — she had the ring on — picked up her child and opened the door again. Karl played for time and went into a long spiel about his niece looking for a car to drive across France with friends from Uni. And how the friend with the car had dropped out and they were looking for a hatchback, but a car like this was really far more practical. He loved this part, getting into character, spinning a yarn and seeing where it took him, always with one eye on the bigger picture.

He let the seller see that he knew nothing about cars, asked a nonsense question about transverse engines and checked whether it took diesel or lead-free. The seller warmed to him, or his ignorance — same thing really. It was a classic con: let the victim think they're conning you; it rarely failed.

Karl's mobile chimed in, with a TV ring-tone so awful that he almost cringed himself. He made the obligatory embarrassed face. "Yes, hello darling; I'm looking at it now — you know I think Beatrice would love it. No, we're still discussing the details. I won't be long. Can't you just keep Jessica settled? Well, I can just join you at home, can't I — if she's really that bad."

He faked a huge sigh. "Right. Yes, I understand. Just give her sips of water. I'll be as quick as I can. No, no, you stay there — I'll drive over." He paused, as if suddenly aware of his mistake. "I'll, er, make my own way back." He switched off his mobile and did his best impression of the word 'agitated.'

The husband laid a hand on his shoulder. "Children are a constant worry because they are our precious jewels." He then started the car up and let Karl try out the driving seat.

Karl managed to shave £50 off the asking price and insisted they shook hands on the deal. All very proper — minus the receipt — and in record time.

They stood at the window and watched him back down the drive. He paused to wave and wondered, just out of devilment, how long they would wait there. By the look on their faces as he glanced up for the final wave they'd have waited forever, just to see him gone. He drove to the corner and flashed his lights for Thomas to follow him in his own car; mission accomplished.

* * *

Thomas had nurtured a faint hope that Karl would guide him to some secret bat-cave lair, but it was short-lived. After a twenty-minute drive through Saturday traffic, Karl led him instead to a supermarket car park. Tucked away in a far corner, a woman was waiting by a silver Ford. Karl parked a few spaces away and Thomas followed suit.

"Tommo, you remember Teresa."

She smiled, as if she knew something about him that he hadn't disclosed. He resolved to quiz Karl, some other time, about what that might be.

"Good work Karl. Nice to see you again, Thomas."

And that was that. Karl handed over a package — Thomas figured it was the remainder of the money, plus the gloves and the jumper. Then they got into Karl's car and left the scene. In the wing mirror he saw someone else get out of the Ford and walk around the red estate. Karl glanced towards him, not the slightest bit interested.

"Not our problem, Tommo; our part is done."

"No point my asking who Teresa works for, I suppose?"

"None at all!" Karl chuckled, and Thomas wondered if Karl even knew himself.

Chapter 18

Thomas pressed the intercom button and stared up at the CCTV camera. He hated being this side of the lens, always had. Too many childhood memories of his dad telling him to 'stand up straight' and 'at least try to look like you're enjoying yourself.' It was probably why he'd got into photography in the first place — to regain a degree of control.

"Why, Mr Bladen, what a pleasant surprise!" Sheryl's nasal tones smacked of a cheesy New York cop series.

He turned his face from the camera and listened hard for the steps down the back staircase. The fire door released and Sheryl stood before him, leaning against the doorframe, pop video style. She looked him up and down. "Great to see you, Thomas."

He rolled his shoulders self-consciously. Was she attractive? Absolutely. To use a Karl-ism: she could probably wake the dead in their trousers. And boy did she know it. She probably had an exclusion order from the mortuary. And the clincher, for ten points — was he interested? Not for a second.

Maybe that's why she played so easy to get. It didn't help that his defence was to close down. That seemed to make her try even harder to get a reaction. He liked to think that Miranda put her up to it — for sport — but he worried, deep down, that it was just Sheryl. Male customers loved it of course. A little piece of authentic Brooklyn right before their eyes; and Sheryl was the little piece.

He thought about the morning's activities as he followed her upstairs, mainly to distract himself from her backside; the sucking and popping of Sheryl's trademark chewing gum punctuated their journey up to the office. She had once told him that she chewed gum

110

to keep her mouth moist and supple. He'd never felt the same way about spearmint again.

* * *

Miranda was busy looking at colour swatches. "Hey, you're a man. What do you think of this?" She held up a colour card with a thumb across it.

"It looks like lilac."

"What an insightful eye for detail. I can see why you're drawn to the camera. Fancy a coffee?"

Sheryl took her cue and slinked past him, timing a bubble pop by his face.

"I don't know why you get so uptight around Sheryl; she likes you."

"Maybe that's what I'm uptight about."

"Lighten up, Thomas, and don't flatter yourself; it's just her way. I can see you find her attractive so what's the big deal? Blimey, if I was a man, *I'd* fancy her."

"I never said I fancied her."

Out the corner of his eye he could see Sheryl's jeans straining as she walked away.

"Anyway, what have you been up to today?" She was still staring down at the mass of colour charts and strips of material. But Thomas had played this game before.

"Oh, nothing much. I, er, went to help someone buy a car."

"Really? Terry and Sam could have got you a good deal. Anyone I know?"

He paused for maybe a couple of seconds; a couple of seconds too long. "Just someone from work."

Miranda didn't turn, but her back arched forward just that little bit more. Then she slapped a hand on the desk and Thomas felt the three-minute warning go off.

"Why don't you just *ask*, Miranda?"

"Because I'm not sure I'd like the answer."

Sheryl returned and placed the coffee mugs beside Miranda. "Um, I hope this isn't a bad time." Sarcasm dripped off every syllable.

Thomas could almost feel the heat from Miranda's glare. Maybe that was why he was sweating. Miranda looked up at Sheryl, completely unfazed. "Just a few issues with trust."

"Miranda!" Sheryl raised her eyebrows and tut-tutted dramatically. "You can't trust men, honey — you know that."

111

Thomas looked daggers at her as she left the arena. But she just winked at him again and mouthed: 'she loves you really.' At least, that's what it looked like. It could have been 'she loves you rarely.'

"Jesus, Thomas, why did you have to take that bloody job?"

He moved behind her, gazing at the back of her neck; that smooth, lightly tanned neck that he loved to run his lips over. He laid a finger on her skin and traced a river, enjoying the familiar tingle that ran up and down his spine and settled in his groin. Miranda shrugged free.

"Knock it off; I'm not in the mood. I'm serious. Why would you want to go and do a job like that — and hide it from me?"

Tread carefully, he told himself; don't answer too quickly. This is an exam level question — and it's pass or fail, with no retakes.

"Do I need to remind you? I took the Civil Service job so we could work near each other. And not long after that you decided to call it quits."

They reached for their coffees and he noticed that her mug read 'The Boss' while his was 'The Hired Hand.' Nice one, Sheryl.

"Be honest, Thomas; neither of us was happy with the way things were."

He drew back, cradling his mug. "I was happy."

She gave it a second's consideration. "Bullshit. You just couldn't stand the thought of me being with anyone else." When she said it like that, it sounded like a bad thing. "And let's not forget we'd split up at *least* once before then."

Ah yes, the infamous drought of '97 to '98. "So that's why you went to Bermuda — for a whole year?"

She didn't flinch, didn't even break her stride. "I needed breathing space — we both did. The only difference is, you used yours to get off with Christine *at work*."

'Get off with' wasn't the term she normally used. But hey, Sheryl was only next door, like as not listening to every word. Not that he cared too much what Sheryl thought.

He resisted comment. Resisted mentioning that Miranda had hardly taken a vow of chastity over in Bermuda — or when she returned. Time to tone things down a bit. "Why are we having this conversation?"

"Because you're shutting me out, Thomas. Mum was in a real flap about you, that night at the house — I know you talked to Dad about something. You used to confide in *me*. Well, I thought you did — before I discovered your secret life." She put her face right in front of his.

Jesus; Sheryl must be lapping this up.

"And remember how we first got together? I trusted you. I told you about that scumbag, Butch Steddings; about the way he was coming on to me to do his dodgy photos."

"I know," he felt his knuckles itching, partly from outrage and the lingering memory of lamping Butch. The haunted look in her eyes brought him back with a bump. He put a hand to her cheek. "But this is different, Miranda."

"No it's not. You're frightened, Thomas. I *know* you. Is it that Irish bloke?"

"No," he took a breath, tried it again more confidently. No, it's not Karl."

"Well what then?"

It could have been the reflection of the strip light, making her eyes glisten like that. He pressed his hand against her face, felt the warm flesh against his fingertips and wished she could understand by osmosis.

"I'm not gonna leave this alone, Thomas. And don't think I give a shit what Sheryl hears. So either you tell me now or we are going to have a major falling out." She sighed, and leaned a little against his hand. "If you can't be honest with me, then I've got no room for you in my life — it's your call."

There was steel behind those blue eyes. He picked up the reference straight away. When she'd returned from Bermuda, he'd told her about Christine. Then Miranda had got involved with some city trader, probably just to piss him off — which it had. Worse, the stockbroker believed in spreading his options. As soon as Miranda found out, she'd dropped him like a lead weight. Once Thomas had showed her evidence of a wife.

He felt ashamed that it had come to this. Miranda was probably bluffing — she'd come around in a few days or a week or so. But . . . but he'd have to tell her sometime. He took another deep breath. "Two blokes turned my flat over while I was at your parents' place. They were hardcore — after some money they thought I had. They smashed my door and they came tooled up."

Miranda paled. "Is this to do with Karl?"

"Not like that! Karl took care of it; he was looking out for me."

Miranda brushed his hand away. "Maybe I should speak to Karl, then."

"No, don't do that." Too quick, too edgy; he knew she'd pick up on it.

"So what do I do, then, Tom?" She never called him Tom, not since Leeds and Butch Steddings.

"Just be yourself. The same loveable pain in the arse you always are."

"Flattery'll get you nowhere."

113

He didn't believe that.

She put her arms around him. He leaned in and squeezed her back towards him, as if he could dissolve her flesh into his.

"Well you better not make any more enemies, Thomas Bladen. Because if anyone messes with you, they'll answer to me."

He didn't doubt that for a second.

He finished his coffee and pretended to be interested in her colour schemes. Then he made his excuses and headed for home, alone — probably for the best. He picked up a Chinese on the way, and a carton of milk — company for the old one seeking asylum in his fridge. He wondered if Karl had similar relationship problems? Was there even anyone special in his life? Special — Karl would piss himself at that.

The TV had little to offer so he dived back into the pile of DVDs towering on the floor. Something edifying and life-affirming — *Shaun of the Dead*, the perfect accompaniment to prawn chow mein and special fried rice. Miranda had long since educated him on the perils of factory-farmed chicken, but he figured it would be pretty hard to do much to a prawn other than catch and eat it.

It was a great film; he'd seen it before at the cinema with Miranda. But the joy of DVDs — for him, anyway — was the extra features. How it was done, deleted scenes, notes on cinematography and special effects. Sometimes all that was better than the actual film.

Some time after ten, he gave up the ghost and turned off the DVD. The TV channel kicked back into life at way past a reasonable volume. He dropped it down a few notches on the level and did a double take. Sir Peter Carroll was on screen — large as twenty-two-inch life — pontificating about some political debacle.

It was too good a chance to pass up on. He reached over and dialled Karl.

"Hello?"

"Karl, it's Thomas. Quick, turn on the TV — our beloved leader's doing a turn."

"I know; I'm watching it already. How sad is that!" There was a pause. "Is everything okay, Tommo? Only you've rung me on your landline — you've never done that before. Are you going all touchy-feely on me?"

He took a breath, remembering he was *number withheld* on all his calls. They watched Sir Peter run rings around the other guests on the late night current affairs programme. Even the presenter was no match for the double-talk, counter-pointing and justifications. It was like seeing Freddie the Fox perform a gig at the henhouse.

Karl, who followed politics more closely — i.e. more than almost no interest whatsoever — offered his own comments and managed to predict a couple of Sir Peter's responses.

Thomas had only caught the tail end of the programme and after fifteen minutes, Karl was humming the national anthem tunelessly as the studio lights dimmed.

"So, Tommo, what's on your mind?"

"I dunno, Karl. These last weeks; I'm starting to lose the plot."

"Now *that* I don't believe for a second! What's really bothering you?"

"How do you cope with it, Karl?" he eased his shoes off and flexed his feet. "All the secrecy and the pretence and the—"

"Lies," Karl chipped in. "That's would be the word you're looking for. It's the price you pay for knowing. And once you know, things are never the same again."

"For a second there, you almost went into *The Matrix*."

"Aye, it's not a bad analogy. Only it's debatable whether we're the dudes in black vinyl, or Agent Smith. Listen, do you fancy getting together tomorrow — I'll meet you at midday, same tube station."

"Yeah, that's sounds good. Thanks mate."

"No problem. By the way, I'm glad you rang actually. Don't make plans for next weekend — we're working. I'll tell you all about it when I see you."

"What?" he sat bolt upright on the settee. "No, tell me now."

"I don't think so; phones have ears. Good night, Thomas."

* * *

Sir Peter Carroll's Daimler glided away from Television Centre. The roar of the traffic seemed to echo the applause of the studio audience. Even his opponents had congratulated him on his mastery of the subtleties of the situation.

He swirled his whisky glass and let the aroma pervade his senses. Outside, the streetlights and car lights prismed against the tinted windows. He checked his watch and smiled.

As soon as he reached for the phone, his chauffeur raised the glass screen. Sir Peter waited until the screen sealed him off before he dialled the first number, even though Trevor had been with him for years.

"Ah, good evening. I wish to get a message to Yorgi. Ask him to ring me tomorrow on the office number. He'll know who it is."

The woman sounded fearful at the mention of Yorgi's name. In the background he heard a man's voice — it could have been Yorgi, but he doubted it. No matter, he had no interest in Yorgi's personal life. He closed the call and settled his glass. Then, phone still in hand, he lifted an address book from his blazer pocket: 'P' for Peterson.

"Robert? Oh, yes, if you would, thank you. Ah, Robert, it's Sir Peter. You did? Why, thank you! Now, Robert, I'm ringing for an update on the Harwich consignment. Yes, I saw that you'd put Crossley on to it. Good, definitely a step in the right direction. I think we'll be ready to move soon, now that we've got the full team on board. Long time coming — indeed! Have Crossley get an update, first thing Monday. Capital! Now, what's the latest on the poor driver?" He scrawled down some notes and put an asterisk against Ann Crossley's name.

"Right. Send Crossley to my office Monday morning — she can update me there." He ended the call and tucked the address book back in his blazer. He signalled to Trevor that the screen could be lowered. Then, he dialled home.

"Yes, hello darling. Really? It was good of you to watch. No, don't wait up; you know how these things work. The PM likes us seniors to take every opportunity to make friends with the media. I'll be back late — I'll use the spare room. Night, night." He stared out at the blurred lights of London and his smile reflected back in the glass like a malign crescent. "Trevor, I think I'll drop in to The Victory Club."

The chauffeur nodded; Sir Peter enjoyed the deferential bob of his head. It was the little touches that made Trevor such a treasure. Their eyes met in the mirror. "Very good, Sir Peter."

He reached for his whisky and smiled again. If tonight's girl at The Victory was anything like the last one Yorgi had provided, it would be.

Chapter 19

"You've got to be able to trust your instincts, Tommo," Karl swivelled left and right at the first click of the target turning face on. "Do you want a go — it's not so different from taking high-speed photos. Okay, maybe with nine mills instead of a data-card. But the principle's the same."

There's a comfort. All those years that Thomas thought he'd been honing his camera skills he'd actually been secretly training to be Super Shooter. The idea played in his head like a disturbing version of *The Karate Kid*: wax on, wax off, and reload.

Karl laid his pistol down. "So, I'll save you the trouble of avoiding the topic of next weekend. We're away to Suffolk for a pick-up."

"And is this for our side or their side, or doesn't it matter?"

"See, Tommo, I told you that you'd get the hang of it eventually!" Karl grinned like an idiot. "But seeing as you've asked, this is a special request from our beloved leader."

"Dress code: casual?" Thomas straightened an imaginary tie.

"Dress code: damp-proof — we'll get kitted out from Stores on the Friday, before we leave work. You're going to be the water baby."

They spent less than an hour on the range. As Karl reminded him, time flies when you're firing guns. Afterwards in the café, Thomas scanned the horizon for Teresa. Someone as organised as Karl would be sure to have arranged a meeting.

"Relax, Tommo. She'll be here presently."

He picked at the pastry crumbs on his plate. So they were doing Sir Peter's private dirty work — and look where that got him last time.

Teresa made a play of waving as she came over, but she looked agitated. "Things have moved forward unexpectedly."

Even Karl seemed a little put out.

"There was a disturbance at the target house last night. A neighbour called the police and an ambulance out, to a domestic. It seems Yorgi went ballistic — if you'll forgive the phrase — when he came back and found the car was missing."

Thomas felt like raising a hand, to remind them he was still there. "Who's Yorgi?"

Karl and Teresa gave him the kind of look that made him wish he wasn't. "Our likely Harwich shooter," Teresa explained, glancing at Karl.

"He has a name," Thomas said slowly, reciting his thought aloud.

"And a reputation to go with it," Teresa replied.

Thomas kept quiet now while the grown-ups talked, picking up the odd snippet, here and there. Yorgi was evidently a big shot — again with the puns — and Teresa's report suggested he had left the country after the incident.

He felt his mind start to drift — funny how things bobbed to the surface when you weren't concentrating. Now that he thought about it, he'd never seen any photographs from the year Miranda spent in Bermuda. Well, okay, a few 'here I am at the beach' pics, but no proper work photos of any kind. His mood soured; he tried to tune back into the conversation, just to escape himself.

"So what do you think, Thomas? Could you speak to them?" Teresa had lowered her voice.

"I'm sorry?"

Teresa and Karl both eased forward towards him. Teresa was still in the big chair. "With Yorgi away, this is our best chance to make contact with the brother again and offer him a lifeline — think you're up to it?"

Thomas could feel their eyes on him like sunlamps and sensed his face smouldering. "I can try." Jesus, he wasn't even convincing himself.

"Top man!" Karl patted him on the shoulder. "Right, come on then, Tommo; no time like the present."

Teresa sat in the back of Karl's car. The scent of oranges was starting to fade; now it was more Earl Grey tea than breathable vitamin C.

"So what do I say, exactly? I mean, what am I allowed to tell them?" It was the third time of asking — different ways, but the same question. Karl looked ready to pop a vein.

"For fuck's sake, Tommo! We've been through this. They let a gunman use their car as a sniper's post. And we've got the car now. There's not a lot *to* say."

Maybe Karl was right to be pissed off. When Thomas heard himself, he sounded like an amateur — well, he *was* an amateur.

Teresa played peacemaker. "All we're trying to do is offer them protection — if they want it. Let them know that there's help available. But don't spook them."

Karl hardly looked at Thomas for the rest of the journey. It reminded him of Ajit, back at school, when he'd been accusing Thomas of something, but wouldn't come right out and say it.

As they parked up, Teresa handed Thomas a scrap of paper. "Tell them they can ring here at any time, if they need us."

He nodded and gripped the note tightly, casting a last, quizzical look at Karl as he opened the car door.

* * *

Teresa waited until Thomas was at least five cars away. "What's the problem, Karl?"

"I can't put my finger on it. I mean, I trust him right enough. I'd stake my life on him not working for anyone else, but . . . well, there's something about him. I don't think we ever get to see the real Thomas Bladen, and that worries me. When it comes down to it, we don't know his capabilities."

"You'd not recommend recruiting him, then?"

"No, not yet. He's more useful to us as an outsider."

"How much have you told him?"

"The usual — only as much as we need him to know."

107, 108, 109 . . . Thomas counted on, just like he used to do when he was a child. Useless figures that kept his mind occupied; stopped him from too much thinking. His sister Pat used to tease him about it.

"You'd spend your whole life counting, given half a chance!"

But that process of measuring and timing; that's what had kept him sane when Dad went into his rages or when Mam had disappeared into the kitchen to dry her tears or to get the swelling on her face to go down. Numbers.

115, 116. He could see the house looming ahead. Surely Teresa could have told him exactly what to say, how to couch it all? He felt his stomach turning over. If he didn't get himself together his first words would be: 'Can I use your toilet?' A fine spy he'd make! He

119

laughed at himself and squeezed the little piece of paper ever more tightly.

His legs dragged as he walked up the short drive, the sweat congealing against his skin. He remembered the time he'd first brought Miranda back to his digs in Leeds. How they'd both been too nervous to discuss how far they wanted to go. And how he'd ached for her. It wasn't just the rush of hormones and Thunderbird wine, but a need to connect with her, to anchor her to him so that she'd never leave Leeds, or him. *Yeah, nice one, Thomas.* Now he was at the front door with a gut ache *and* a hard-on. *Brilliant.*

He pressed the bell, realising that he'd missed a chance to copy Teresa's magic phone number for himself. He heard voices approaching — a man and a woman — and hoped to God that was sweat running down the back of his legs.

The door slowly opened. "Can I help you?" she said, even though her voice suggested the opposite. It was the same ice blonde that Karl had described. Refined, with a hint of yummy mummy — to use Karl's apt description.

"Can I come in? It's about Yorgi, sort of."

She stared at him for a moment and tilted her head back, directing a stream of something Eastern European behind her. Best guess, she'd figured that he wasn't Masterspy, but maybe that gave him a slight edge. The husband squeezed in beside his wife; the door didn't open any further.

"There's no one called Yorgi here — you have the wrong house."

Yeah, so the Eurospeak was a happy coincidence? He pressed his hands together and touched his lips then immediately felt foolish. He looked like his mother, back when she used to pray at home. An idea came to him. Not divine inspiration — more like desperation. He was never going to see these people again, right, so what harm was the truth?

He reached into his wallet and prised away his driving licence. Behind the ID card was a cut-down photograph, of him and Miranda. Typical adolescent photo-booth stuff; she had her arms around his neck, practically clinging to him. And he had a smile like he'd just found a fifty-pound note. The fact that she'd just grabbed his groin before the flash probably helped.

"This is Miranda. I know it's hard to protect the people we care about."

The couple studied the photograph for a long time; in the end he got so nervous they might snatch it indoors and lock him out that he asked for it back. His pulse was still racing as he tucked it carefully back into his wallet.

The door arced open. "What do you want, Mr . . . ?"

"Bladen. Thomas Bladen." Yeah, he'd thought about bullshitting them like Karl had insisted, but they just seemed like two scared people who had been dealt a crappy hand.

They sat on the sofa opposite him, their son at their feet. The man did the talking "You and Miranda have children, *Tomas*?"

"What? No," he shook his head to emphasise the point, hoping it would also cool his face off. "Look, I'm just here to offer assistance."

"Are you with the police?" the yummy mummy reached down, hoisting her son to her lap.

He shook his head again. "Look, any chance of a drink and can I . . ." he stood up and the sudden relief on his bladder made him exhale loudly.

She pointed him upstairs.

He heard the rattling of glasses as he closed the door behind him. Karl would probably have searched the bedroom; Karl wasn't there though. He checked the bathroom mirror. What a state! 'Are you the police?' That was a joke. Not unless CID stood for something completely different.

It seemed to be the longest piss of his life, as if his body was ridding itself of his fear. He flushed, did all the usual stuff and filched around in the wastepaper bin. Bingo — loo roll holder. He split the cardboard tube and copied out Teresa's helpline number. Then he peered at himself again in the mirror and splashed more water on his face.

Downstairs, a glass was waiting for him. He turned it around and the little boy cooed as he watched the light dancing, fascinated. Smiles all round.

"Supposing my husband and I needed help — what would you want in return?"

"Me? Nothing. I'm here as a messenger," he unfolded the piece of paper and passed it over.

The drink reminded him of the chocolate liqueurs they used to have at Christmas, in Pickering. Just the right side of sickly sweet. The couple studied Teresa's piece of paper for a long time. Or maybe they just didn't want to make eye contact, with him or each other. Yeah, they were rats in a trap all right: poor bastards.

"Look," he took pity on them, "Yorgi might be mixed up in some trouble, but you seem like good people." Okay, nought out of ten for subtlety, but it conveyed the gist.

The man cleared his throat. "Tomas, do you have brothers and sisters?"

"Yeah, a sister — Pat; she's a couple of years younger than me." What was he doing — why not draw them a bloody picture? He took another sip of alcoholic goo. The more he thought about it, they were *all* being used.

"Yorgi is my brother — my . . . half-brother; my name is Petrov and I am the younger in the family. When we were growing up, Yorgi was always the leader. He made the rules and I followed him. I learned very young not to challenge him."

Thomas said nothing. He noted the wall clock above the crucifix and decided to give himself five more minutes, tops. The wife stared at him as if she could pierce the façade and see into his soul. He fidgeted in the chair.

"How much trouble are we in, Mr Bladen?"

Now he felt like they were playing him. All he had to fall back on was the truth. "The authorities know about the incident." He watched their faces fall. "The victim survived though and you may have been unwilling accomplices." *Unwilling?* Jesus. He'd as good as accused them of complicity. *What a prat.* He rubbed at his forehead and closed his eyes. "I'm sorry; that came out wrong. What I meant was that so far there is no direct evidence against you."

Petrov raised a defiant hand. "He told us to face forward and to drive, said if anything happened we'd lose our son. We didn't know *what* he was planning."

Thomas looked from face to face. Chances were, they *knew*.

"Tomas, what would you have done?"

He said nothing, tried to hold their gaze.

Petrov patted his son. "I have always done what I could for Yorgi, but for many years we were apart. Then a year or so ago, he tracked me down . . ."

Thomas sat up: interesting choice of words.

". . . He leads a different life. Mixes in circles I would be afraid to. You understand?" Petrov reached for his wife's hand. Only now, as she turned towards him, did Thomas notice the reddening down one side of the face and the way Petrov shifted his weight away from one side of his ribs. "Alexandra and Lukas are my family. I must put them first. Will the people at this number understand that the way you do?"

He couldn't answer, didn't feel anything but shame. He couldn't pretend that he didn't care. And caring meant doing something. "Here," he wrote out a mobile number on the newspaper by his feet and ripped it off. "This is *my* number. Just in case."

His hand wavered and his stomach churned with raw emotion. "I have to go now," he stood up carefully as if his balance might be off; in a sense it was.

Alexandra lifted little Lukas aside and saw him to the door. Thomas followed her gaze to the crucifix. He blushed, caught in the act. "Bless you, Thomas Bladen," she kissed him on the cheek and then closed the door behind him.

It didn't feel cold outside, but a couple of tears gathered in his eye. He flicked them away casually, as if they were nothing. And as each step took him further from the house, he felt a growing sense of exhilaration.

He got back into the car and Karl started up the engine without a word. He ventured nothing and withstood their scrutiny; decided he'd sit this one out. Karl lasted until they'd cleared the Thames.

"How did it go?"

He took a breath and kept things simple. "They seemed pleased to have a contact number; I think they'll be in touch."

Teresa tapped Karl on the shoulder. "Anywhere around here is fine." Karl nodded and checked his mirror, pulling in along Queen Victoria Street.

Thomas watched them, saw the way Karl looked at her and how she avoided him. No goodbyes, not even a thank you. If he had to guess, there'd been *words* in the car while he'd been delivering a lifeline. But did that mean . . . nah, couldn't be. Surely Karl was smarter than that?

He watched with Karl as Teresa disappeared up the cut through to St Paul's. They sat for a while, the grumbling engine and indicator clicks marking off the seconds. Finally, Karl tore his gaze away from the side street. "Fancy a drink?"

"Sounds like a plan," Thomas parodied him.

Karl didn't react. He gazed out the windscreen, dull eyes watching the crowd in vain. Thomas could almost feel his longing.

"Yeah, a pub would be great," he emphasised, spurring Karl into activity. Jeez, what a pair of fuck-ups they were. Karl had fallen for Teresa, and Thomas, in his day, had all but set up house with Christine Gerrard. Women and power — it was like mixing your drinks: no good would ever come of it.

In a pub in Stratford they found a quiet table; Karl sat facing the door as usual. Thomas did the honours and got half a pint for himself and a pint of shandy for Karl, along with crisps; last of the big spenders.

Karl took a sip and smacked his lips theatrically. "Tell you what, Tommo. I'll do another little magic trick. Are you ready?"

He felt dread creeping through him.

"You gave them your own number, didn't you?"

Thomas coughed into his drink and kept his head down.

"It's okay, Tommo, I understand. It's an obvious rookie mistake — you felt sorry for them, right? I'd have done the same, at the beginning. I won't mention it to Teresa, but I need you to let me know if they ever do contact you. Deal?"

He wondered what else Karl had deduced about him.

Karl leaned back and stretched; he seemed to have cheered up no end. "You see, Tommo, we're not so different, you and I."

Chapter 20

Miranda had arrived early. Every night on the phone since Sunday, she'd been trying to talk Thomas out of this mysterious weekend job, the one he still hadn't explained. Maybe face-to-face she stood a chance of getting through to him.

She sat in the car, two streets away, flicking through a professional catering magazine that she'd already littered with notes and doodles. Thomas figured in a good few of those scribbles, not that he'd have known. She was the princess — naturally — and Thomas the face in the corner, sometimes just a pair of eyes, watching from a distance. Blimey, how accurate had that turned out to be!

More flicking, to a feature: a stylish eatery in Berkshire. She nearly drooled over the décor and the fancy name: *panache*. Thomas had suggested she call *her* club Miranda's — a talent for the obvious. But Caliban's was her private joke. At school, she'd loved *The Tempest*, ever since she'd caught her name in it, and had weathered the piss-taking of the other girls. The boys of course were more malleable — not for nothing did Miranda translate as 'the admired one.' Rough times, though.

She doodled some more. Whatever Thomas was mixed up in, it would be a stroll in the park compared to a gaggle of spiteful, hormone-addled bitches. *Addled* — she smiled at that; one of Thomas's words that had crept into her vocabulary. She fingered her neck-chain, following it round to her name, shaped in gold, and tapped it distractedly. Yeah, the only time that name had lost a little of its sheen was when her mum had told her about a chain-smoking casino croupier — the one she'd been named after.

This was bloody silly. She had emergency keys to the flat — *new* keys at that — just as he had to hers. But ever since the heavies had busted in while he was away, Thomas had cranked up his paranoia a notch or four and passed it on. "Sod it," she stuffed the magazine in the glove compartment; she'd take a walk past — what harm could it do?

* * *

Thomas found a parking space at the end of the street. He waited a minute, checking front and back; nothing much was happening. He reached for the sports bag on the passenger seat, containing a waterproof bodysuit, a torch so bright it could almost illuminate Karl's cryptic messages, a length of rope and a pair of walkie-talkies. He checked again — all quiet on the Western Front. Time to move.

He clocked the figure in the distance almost as soon as he closed the car door, watching as the loner crossed the street towards his flat then stopped still. He hugged the bag close and picked up the pace, moving from car to car, crouching low. Closer, and he could make out a woman in a long coat; she had her back to him and her hair was either short or tucked under a beret. She looked like she was auditioning for a French Resistance tribute act.

He used the trees for cover; good solid forest trees that some planner had approved decades before and which now bulged up tarmac and pavement in the struggle for existence. *That's it, keep looking away from me; stay like that.* He cantered across the road and snaked behind a delivery van; the woman still hadn't moved.

Ducking back down, he loosened his grip on the bag and tried to settle his breathing. Who? *Shit.* What if this was Teresa, and Miranda turned up? He went for broke and sprinted the remaining distance, dropping the sports bag and grabbing her shoulders in one fluid movement. "Right!"

Miranda gave a short yelp and turned her head. "Jesus, Thomas! You frightened the life out of me."

His heart was beating so fast that he struggled to find the words. "Don't ever stand in the street like that again."

Miranda paused, as if weighing up whether to slap him. "You arse!"

Somewhere, a bugler sounded the retreat. His head began to clear. "Sorry," he held up a hand, "I just got a bit freaked. Let's go inside."

"Well," Miranda headed on up the steps. "As long as you're not worried that people will see us."

She used her keys before he could object. He let it pass and carried on into the kitchen. Listening hard, he heard Miranda close the front door and then bolt it. So far, so salvageable.

She slumped into a chair and dumped her bag on the table. "I did bring you a present, but I'm not sure if you deserve it now."

When he returned, he was carrying two glasses of wine — his own only half-full — and the bottle tucked under one armpit; one hundred per cent style.

"What's this — are you cutting back?"

He smiled sheepishly and handed her the grown-up glass. "Can't overdo it —I'm working tomorrow, remember."

She took a sip and pursed her lips, although he knew it was a good wine.

"Look, about earlier; I know I was a dick but I'm only thinking of you, okay?"

She didn't skip a beat. "Then tell me . . ."

He shook his head. "The less I tell you, the less you have to worry about."

"Is this the way we're going to live now?" She pulled a DVD case from her bag, tapping it rhythmically against her arm. "Still not sure if you deserve this . . ." The tone was playful and when he looked at her all 'puppy-dog,' she seemed to melt.

"It's not porn, is it?" Hardly likely. That one time they'd watched a porn flick together he'd sat in mute embarrassment, feeling a mix of betrayal and arousal. Getting turned on by other nubile women on the go, while your girlfriend was in the room with you, was hardly a declaration of love and devotion. And besides, those guys on screen were a lot to live up to.

"It's *The Thirty-Nine Steps*. And before you say anything, yes — it's the *original*. Seemed appropriate, what with your new life as a spy."

That lit the whole box of fireworks. "Let's get one thing straight, shall we?" he clunked his glass down hard. "I'm not a bloody spy."

She leaned back in silence, and he felt really stupid. Like the time in Leeds when he'd got drunk, taken a leak in the park and soaked his own shoes. It was time for a tactical withdrawal. "I'll go sort out the grub and then we can watch Robert Donat kick arse. Help yourself to the telly." A polite way of saying: end of round one and back to your corners.

* * *

The bolognaise was already prepared — real stuff, no crap. Made to a recipe of Pat's and freshly dug out of the freezer the night

127

before. He kept the kitchen door open and listened as the TV erupted into life; a comedy, by the sounds of it and so sharp that a laughter track had been added. "Shouldn't be long," he called out.

There was silence from Miranda. Either the comedy was more riveting than it sounded or she still had the hump, big time. Or both. Not much else he could do, other than watch the pasta simmering, and think. Why were he and Karl going to Suffolk? He jabbed at the frothing pan with a fork, submerging the strands. How far did he want this work with Karl to go? So what if Peterson was bent? He grabbed the fork from the saucepan and held on to it until the heat reddened his fingers. No, Bob Peterson had lied to him; and Sir Peter Carroll had tried to set him up. He deserved some answers.

The TV volume rose — advert time. He smacked his lips appreciatively as the garlic and beef flirted with his nostrils. The way to a man's heart and all that — and hopefully a woman's too. "Pasta's almost done," he relayed the news. "I'll come in for a bit."

"*You've Been Framed*, I think," Miranda stared at the TV, deadpan.

He perched on the edge of the sofa and sipped his wine. He saw right away that she'd topped it up, but he let it pass. On TV, a child ran into a transparent patio door and bounced back two feet. The studio audience laughed and winced; Western Civilisation — coming soon.

Nothing more to be said, he nipped off, returning with a bowl of salad; quite the little Jamie Oliver. *Try something new today.* Yeah, like not having another argument.

The bolognaise was good when they got there; even Miranda said so. They ate and relaxed — or at least, relaxed hostilities. Onscreen, Robert Donat grappled with conspiracy, paranoia and false accusations. Thomas knew just how he felt.

Miranda nudged him, mid-film. "Bet you didn't know that in the book, there's no female lead at all."

"Maybe it needed improving."

She patted his leg: good answer.

By the end of the first bottle of wine, they'd moved past the talking stage. She sat close and ran a finger up and down his arm; he could feel the tremors in faraway places. As they watched the dying minutes of the mystery, Robert Donat finally figured out his enemies' plan and how to stop them. As the credits rolled, Thomas grabbed the remote and peered at the screen, checking through names mostly forgotten. He wasn't a film buff particularly, but sometimes, when he spotted a cameraman in a really enjoyable old film, he'd search them out on the net and see what else they'd done.

"That was champion," he sat back.

Miranda squeezed the arm she'd been teasing. "What shall we do for a second feature?" It sounded like a come-on. Then again, everything Miranda said sounded like a come-on.

"Well . . ." he stretched the word out like bait. She didn't respond; she wasn't biting. Jeez, he'd have to ask. "Are you stopping tonight? He cringed at the words — about as romantic as a six-pack of lager.

"Maybe," she smiled, and chuckled.

He turned to her and her eyes sparkled in the reflected glare of the TV. There was a heavy pause — the tipping point of desire — then his lips found hers. He was greedy for her and she seemed eager to follow his lead. He moved a hand under her buttock and tilted her towards him. He felt the shape of her mouth change and slid his left hand behind her, to the small of her back.

Her fingers burrowed beneath his shirt, ranging over his torso. An idea came to him, but he killed it dead. Since Leeds, there had been one unwritten rule. No talking — during sex or foreplay or canoodling. No declarations of love, no verbal requests.

He levered her on to one buttock and she took the hint, rolling with him in one uneven lollop. He shifted down the cushions by about a foot and she swung one leg over his, pinning him to the sofa. Now, as they kissed, they moved in rhythm, their pubic bones rising and falling against each other. He lifted her t-shirt and circle kissed her navel and stomach, enjoying the no-man's land between two leisure parks.

He could feel waves of pleasure rippling between them. She moved faster, taking control, as he'd wanted her to. He started to unbutton her jeans as she rocked, and he tried to shut out the calls of despair from his bladder: bad timing 'R' us. She bore down on him, her out-breaths reduced to faltering gasps. He gave up on her jeans, thrusting with his hips, willing her to climax before his bladder burst. He drew her closer as she came, drawing her head towards his and moving his tongue around hers as the last shudders freed themselves from her glorious body. "Now you," she said breathlessly, shifting back on to the sofa.

The relief from his bladder was like a gift from God. As he turned to her, she was undoing the last of her jeans buttons. "Hold that thought — I really need to pee." He heaved himself up with difficulty and staggered to the bathroom.

He heard her grumbling in the other room, but the call of nature would not be ignored. His body took a while to respond, as if it resented the unused hard-on. At last, everything flowed, and flowed; and flowed.

He finished up and washed his hands. His reflection looked flushed. He grinned at himself; he felt like a teenager again, copping off with Miranda on the bedsit put-you-up in Leeds. As he opened the unlocked door he repeated her words to himself — now it was his turn. By the time he'd taken half a dozen steps, he was back at full mast.

Miranda was standing in the living room. Her jeans were fully fastened and she was putting on her coat. He did a double take — twilight zone style — staring at her crotch as if he could hypnotise it back into action.

"What's going on?" His question slammed against her granite expression.

"Your boyfriend called. He'll be over in an hour. Thanks for everything."

"You don't have to go . . ." he paused, wondering if he could possibly steer the sentence towards: 'we could still have a quickie before Karl turns up.'

"What, hide in the bedroom? I don't think so, Thomas. I'm not the hiding type."

He caught sight of his mobile phone on the table. "You didn't . . ."

"Relax Thomas. I didn't speak to him and break your little code. He sent a text."

Yeah, a text that you read. "Look, I'll call you over the weekend."

"We'll see," she didn't look convinced.

He followed her to the door. "Look, Karl wasn't supposed to be coming over until tomorrow evening."

"Careful Thomas," she faced him down. "You're giving away your secrets."

As he went to kiss her, she turned her face away. "Sam'll pick me up. I'll come back for my car tomorrow sometime."

There was nothing left to be said. He settled for "I'll make it up to you," but she was already down the steps and away. She didn't look back.

Back inside, he rechecked the sports bag, tidied up and waited for the call.

"Tommo, it's Karl. Are you free to talk?"

I am now, thanks to you, you bastard. "Yeah, all packed and ready to go."

"Great — everything's gone haywire. Bring a decent sweater; they say it's gonna be a cold night."

Chapter 21

Karl had given precise instructions for the pick-up: on a corner, three streets away, in twenty minutes. His timing was exact, stopping just long enough for Thomas to get in the car and jam the bag behind him.

Karl seemed to be in a chipper mood. "We're driving to Minsmere Bird Reserve, like proper wildlife photographers. And no shag jokes," he grinned. "Now sit back, pick an album and enjoy the ride. Status Quo or Queen?"

Thomas slept for most of the journey. Karl wasn't saying a lot and there were only so many times he could hear Karl singing about 'Having a good time.' He dreamt that he and Miranda were back in the flat, arguing. Then she'd slapped him and walked out. He followed her to the street, to find Karl, Christine, Bob Peterson and Sir Peter Carroll, all slow clapping as if they'd caught him out at something.

He shuddered awake and tried to clear his head. "Are we there yet?" he tried his best child-in-car voice.

Karl glanced sideways, didn't reply.

Fair enough, he'd stick to questions. "Have you been here before, Karl?"

"Aye — once; it's a good drop off point."

Karl was true to his word; it had taken two and a half hours non-stop. The car slowed to a halt, facing a metal gate. Thomas waited; maybe this was the pick-up point and all the gear in the bag was just precautionary.

Karl got out and unlocked the gate, waving Thomas through so he could close it behind them. A more inquisitive person might have asked where Karl had got the key from, but Thomas was just about up to his limit with curiosity.

Karl reclaimed the driving seat; he sounded edgy. "Okay, here's how it works. I lead and you follow. We wait for the drop, retrieve what we came for then hightail it out of here, lickety-split."

"So if this is so easy-peasy why am I here as well?"

"Hold on there, Tommy Boy," Karl manoeuvred the car up the dirt track. "Nobody mentioned the 'e' word. And it's standard procedure to have two bodies for night-time retrievals."

Thomas checked his watch and chewed his lip. "How long are we waiting for?"

A cloud drifted across the moon, edging silver as it crowded out their only natural light source. No music now and no conversation, as Thomas watched Karl staring through the windscreen, checking the wetland for who knew what.

"You'll never get a submarine through that."

Karl smiled, but didn't respond. As he'd managed two cold pies, a large bag of crisps *and* taken a dump somewhere in the swamps, perhaps he was considering his next activity.

Thomas sat beside him, wearing the wetsuit. He felt like a mascot for safe sex. "I still don't see . . ."

Karl raised a finger then tapped his watch. "Sshhh. Any time soon."

Thomas released the car door on command and swung himself out. The water lapped gently, close by — water he would have to get into. Karl seemed very calm now, with a night-scope strapped to his head, like a malevolent cyborg.

The droning engine cut into the night with increasing fervour as it approached. Thomas moved to the water's edge and waited for Karl's signal. The red and green wing lights flickered through the clouds as the plane circled over and released its cargo. Soon a small, white parachute glistened silver as it spiralled down towards the water. Karl twitched like a cat, tracking the parachute's descent in jerky movements. Out on the water there was a muted *splosh* as the package landed.

"Now," Karl hissed.

Thomas slipped into the water, forcing through the mud and weeds that conspired to strangle every step. Soon he was in up to his thighs, half-wading half-floating in the cold gloom, gliding towards the quarry. He couldn't hear Karl anymore; it was just him, the water and each laboured gasp as he closed on the box — the parachute and cords lifeless as a dead jellyfish.

As he laid a hand on one corner, he heard a popping sound and water kicked up about a foot in front of him. By the third shot, he was rooted to the spot in panic. He did the only thing he could think of, pulling himself underwater, letting the roar of pressure in his ears drown out the screams in his head. In the murky half-light of his torch, he saw the strands of cord and dragged the box towards him.

Bad idea; the impacts in the water increased. And they were getting closer. Ice chilled his veins. Christ, he was going to die. He thought about Miranda, thought about what a shit he'd been to her. Saw his father and mother sitting in the living room in Pickering, curtains drawn; imagined his father gazing into a glass: 'I knew he'd come to no good when he went to London.'

He held on to a breath past the point of reason, heart pounding, eyes bulging, raging against the injustice of it all. Finally, as his senses started to fade, he thrust through the surface, fighting for breath.

"Get your fucking head down!" Karl bellowed.

As he plunged below again, he heard returning gunfire. At least Karl was looking out for him — a reassuring thought that only lasted while the pressure intensified in his chest. Until the heavy heat stretched out across his collarbone, numbing his arms, choking him. Despair quickly filled his lungs as the oxygen ran out; the abject no-win terror of being shot above the water or drowning beneath it. "Argh!" he surfaced again, flailing his arms to get balance. Only now did he realise that he'd become disorientated and was a good ten feet from the package. It bobbed further away with every second, taunting him to choose between safety and failure. With a great gulp of air, he made his choice, propelling himself towards it, closing his mind to the chaos around him as he hit the water like an ironing board. He clawed blindly at the box, swearing at the strain of keeping hold.

Then he felt it, the smouldering poker against his arm; a fire even the water could not cool. White-hot light blinded him, skewering his brain awake. This was pain he'd never known before. But, then, he'd never been shot before.

His legs buckled and the mud slammed into him. He grabbed the package with his good arm as he went down, kicking wildly to make for the reed bank. Birds scattered in the commotion, but he stayed put, keeping low, clasping the package between his knees. He forced himself to breathe through his nose, gritting his teeth to try and block out the pain. He felt like his arm was hanging off — he didn't want to look, didn't want to know.

He could hear Karl, blazing away with one, no two weapons. Round after round; he lost count of the relentless rhythm — the sound seemed to fade in and out of his head. Then he heard the sound of glass shattering and the shooting stopped.

The water seemed to swirl around him. He felt his pulse go into overdrive; his hands were shaking. He wished that he were armed, so he could track those fuckers down and stick a bullet in them. But he was trapped. He couldn't let Karl know he was okay without giving away his own position; couldn't leave the cold, cloying water for fear of being shot again. As Karl might have said: he was properly fucked.

A hollow *thom* broke the silence then the sky high above the water lit up like magnesium. Karl's flare arced down and faded on the far side of the water.

"It's clear!" Karl called out plaintively. "Are you there?"

He turned in Karl's direction, but all he saw were blotches of light. Lesson four in how to be a spy: never look directly at the flare. He waited a few seconds, still terrified of the enemy in the dark.

"Come on, Tommo; we don't have time for this — do you have it?"

He dragged his limbs from the mud's grasp, suppressing a scream as his injured arm brushed against the reeds. Just before he clambered out, he dipped his hand into the water and washed the tears from his face.

Karl stashed the package behind the driver's seat then handed him a bath towel. "Right then, let's get a look at you."

He needed help to ease his arm out of the wet suit. Even the night air hurt. He stood flinching, eyes closed as Karl carefully touched around the wound. Karl murmured to himself and reached back into his car.

"This will hurt."

Thomas coughed back laughter. "No need to treat me with kid gloves."

Karl shrugged and poured out something that smelt like meths. Thomas braced himself, fist drawn tight to stifle any reaction. When the cloth touched his arm he thought it had caught fire. "Fuck!" he shrieked, both at the pain and the way the tears ran from his eyes.

"Hey Tommo, no points for bravery here — you did the courageous bit earlier." Karl finished dressing the wound and handed him a small bottle. "Take one of these every couple of hours while the pain is bad. Only one, mind; these are not your usual headache tablets!"

They stood grinning together, like boys who'd just completed a dare. "Are you sure you still want to play this game? Come on then, let's go finish the job." Karl opened the passenger door and helped him in, still dripping water and slime.

Thomas nodded, unable to speak, blowing huffing breaths as he edged into the car seat. His arm felt like someone had crushed it in a vice; Karl assured him it would feel worse the next day. Some comfort.

"Shouldn't we have checked their car?"

"No point, Tommo. Odds on, it's stolen. Three cheers for Robert and Lizzie, eh?"

Thomas squeezed his eyelids. Maybe delirium was setting in; Karl was making no sense whatsoever.

"In the glove compartment."

Thomas reached forward with difficulty. Inside were two handguns.

"Robert and Lizzie — the Brownings!" Karl milked his 'ta-da' moment.

Thomas laughed breathlessly and slumped back. Even with the heat on full, his legs were getting numb from the damp. He tried pushing the waders down his legs, but his left arm shrieked in protest.

"Take it easy. I'll keep the heat full blast and get us there quick as I can. But I'll not break any speed limits. Imagine trying to explain two guns in the glove box and a wet man beside me trying to get his trousers off."

Thomas smiled and rolled his head away. He felt like he was sinking into the chair. Delayed shock, come down; call it what you will, he needed to sleep.

"You get some shut-eye; we've a way to go yet."

He closed his eyes. It seemed as if Karl was talking and then the radio struck up with 'You've got a friend.' Then blackness.

* * *

Thomas felt the car rocking from side to side. Scratch that; it was Karl, applying the gentle art of persuasion.

"Time to wake up."

He opened his eyes; it looked like they were in a concrete wonderland and Karl was the tour guide.

"We're in an underground car park — I won't be long. I'll stick your bag on the backseat. You did bring a change of clothes like I told you?" Good ol' Karl — he thought of everything.

Thomas blinked in the muted neon glow; his eyes ached. First things first, he reached for Uncle Karl's all-purpose painkillers. Then he wriggled his way out of the car and squelched a few steps. His nervous cough echoed into the distance; he seemed to be alone. He did a quick scan around for CCTV then dried himself off with the bath towel one-handed and got changed with as few sudden movements as possible. There was no mobile signal and the time on the clock meant they were probably in London.

He gathered his wits and headed into the shadows for a piss. Nothing seemed real, the world rendered pleasantly numb. As he stumbled back to the car, he saw holes in the driver's door; they looked like bullet holes. He yawned, managed to clamber into the back seat and lay there in the shadows.

Memory and pain collided in his brain. At the lake, in the worst of his panic, he'd feared that Karl was actually firing at *him*. He giggled in the dark, overwhelmed by everything but unable to stop thinking. He mustn't forget that Karl had probably saved his life tonight. He sniffed back the emotion. Of course, Karl had put him in danger in the first place, but no one was perfect.

Next thing he knew, something squeaked — maybe a door — and somewhere in the gloom, someone started whistling 'I Shot the Sheriff.' As Thomas sat up, Karl waved, like he was just back from the shops. He held up a couple of packets and passed them through the open passenger door.

"Jesus, this car smells like a marsh! Our leader's very pleased with our performance tonight — he sent us these with his compliments."

"Hush money?" Thomas took the oblong envelopes and weighed them with his good arm.

"Danger money, more like! So how's the walking wounded?"

Thomas grimaced and waved a hand tentatively. He had so many unanswered questions he could scarcely count them. "So what did we risk life and limb for, exactly?"

Karl put a lot of irritation into one sigh. "I didn't ask; I don't need to know. Now be a good boy and open my envelope."

Thomas clamped the envelope between his knees and tore at the paper. He ran a thumb through a run of £50s and £20s. "I make it at least a couple of grand, maybe three."

"Which means, Tommo, that whatever we fished out of the wet was worth more than five grand to Sir Peter Carroll."

"And the sniper?" Thomas lifted his arm a couple of inches.

"He was probably just a hired hand, warning us off till somebody else turned up."

"*He?*" Thomas tilted as far as the seatbelt would allow.

"In my limited experience, Tommo, women don't miss. Come on now, enough with the philosophising. Let's go find ourselves a drink.

* * *

If the pub's name wasn't enough of a clue, then the military crests and insignia on every spare inch of wall were a dead giveaway. The landlord had greying ginger hair and a ruddy complexion. Thomas took him for a former sergeant major, still crimson from years of shouting; somehow he couldn't see a former officer working this hard after demob to earn a living.

"Mr McNeill!" the landlord all but saluted. "Always a pleasure!"

136

Thomas hung back; no one paid him any attention. Karl crossed to the bar, leaving him in the centre of the saloon, like a deodorant commercial.

"A shandy for me and a whisky for my associate."

Thomas felt unreasonably disappointed; not comrade or oppo, just associate. He listened with envy as Karl fell into easy conversation with Mein Host. No point standing around — might as well be comfortable. He grabbed an empty table with a view of the bar. The tabletop reeked of polish, but he couldn't see any evidence of it; even the beer-mats had formed an unhealthy attachment to the veneer.

Karl took his time coming over. Maybe it was tough leaving his army pals behind. Once or twice he looked in Thomas's direction and then carried on with his conversation. No matter — the extra time gave Thomas time to clear his head.

"Your very good and continued health, Tommo."

He managed a smile, lifting the whisky up to the light, and breathed in deeply through his nostrils. Even good whisky couldn't stop his stomach churning at the thought of cold, gushing water closing over his head.

"I know how you're feeling, Thomas," Karl lowered his voice. "There's not a man or woman here who hasn't been where you were, hasn't asked themselves at some point: Is this the end?" Karl leaned forward and produced a packet of crisps from his pocket. "The thing is, this is what we do."

There was no answer to that, but still the need to say something. "How scared were you then, when it was all kicking off?"

"Are you kidding me? I was like a brick factory on overtime. I get a sweat just thinking about it — if I hadn't brought Robert and Lizzie out for the night . . ." Karl broke off and did his customary plague-of-locusts routine on the crisps. "Look Tommo, I know it's a lot to deal with, first op and all."

"I don't know if I'm really cut out for this." It sounded so much clearer, out loud.

Karl put the crisps down and straightened his back against the chair. "Well, only you can make that choice. But meantime, the packages will *still* come and go, Bob Peterson will *still* have lied to you about being at Harwich and Sir Peter Carroll will *still* be playing tin soldiers with the rest of us. Come on, aren't you still the teensiest bit curious to know what the fuck is really going on?"

Thomas managed a grin and sank the remainder of his whisky. Karl had a point. But so had the bullet that had almost gone through his arm.

* * *

137

Thomas closed the front door and bolted it. He felt like never opening it again. He sat in the dark, hugged tight against the cushion, reliving the paddle from hell. It wasn't long before he reached for the phone.

"Ajit, you awake? It's Thomas."

"Hiya mate, 'ow's it going? Let me just take this downstairs — Geena's asleep."

Thomas pulled the phone close and lifted his feet on to the sofa. Only Ajit and Miranda could keep a meaningful conversation going for longer than twenty minutes. He knew because he'd timed it. And right now he needed to talk.

He chatted with Ajit for over an hour, about nothing in particular; the latest on Geena, the joys of Yorkshire policing and the glory days of Pickering; anything and nothing to keep his thoughts at bay. "By the way," he added as things wound to a close, "I still have your *Blake's 7* annual somewhere. I saw it when I was last having a clear out." This, Ajit would know, was boys' code for 'I'm still thinking about you,' and it sufficed.

Last thing before bed, Thomas counted out his money from Sir Peter. Three grand, tax-free — nice work if you could get it. Or not.

Despite the previous day's excesses, Thomas woke early on Sunday morning; a fireworks-in-the-brain, no prisoners, wide-awake start to the day. His arm stung like a bastard and try as he might he couldn't get his body to settle. The alarm clock glowed 6.45 defiantly. He popped one of Karl's magic pills with a swig of cold tea and then got himself ready, using his left arm as little as possible. There was no pretence of putting a camera in his car; he knew exactly where he was going — across London to the well-appointed streets of Highgate. Time to start separating truth from fiction.

The traffic was non-existent so early on a Sunday. He remembered driving out to Enfield once to photograph a pair of foxes; this wasn't so different. When he got to Christine's street, he parked up, engine running. Did he really want to do this? Was it any of his business who shared Christine's bed these days? True, he reasoned with himself, but if he backed off now that would mean he had a problem with it. The words 'painted' and 'corner' formed a trio with the painkiller to cloud what little judgement remained.

He pulled out and moved into second gear, rolling down the road at a steady ten mph, scanning both sides. There were several four-by-fours on the rugged streets of Highgate, though not the one he was looking for. Instead of relief, he felt a gnawing disappointment; it was there somewhere — he was sure of it. He dug out a street atlas and rested it on his knees, tracing a grid pattern, two streets away in every direction.

And suddenly there it was, the bonnet stone cold. The same vehicle from Harwich, the one Peterson probably used for taking the wife and kids shopping. So now what? He got back in his car and stared into the distance. Too early to ring Christine and anyway, what would he say? 'Hi, I happened to be in the area and I see you're shagging your boss who's married.' Yeah, that'd be a vote winner come his next assessment.

He thumped the steering wheel, sending shockwaves up his bad arm; it concentrated the mind wonderfully. He needn't say or do anything for now — he'd leave it to Karl. Speed-dial number 4.

"Morning mate, I couldn't sleep."

Karl sounded like an advert for *Grumpy Bastard* magazine. "Well why don't you get a bloody paper round? Do you know what time it is — what do you want?"

"I've got some information on Bob Peterson — he spent the night at Christine's flat; just thought you should know." He rang off: mission accomplished.

An hour later he was crashed out on the sofa, lullabied by the TV. He slept deep and heavy, waking by degrees as the mobile shrieked for attention. *Not now, Karl, bugger off and leave me in peace.* The mobile gave up then bleeped. He yawned and looked across at the clock. Blimey, it was evening — so much for Sunday. He rolled his neck from side to side and carefully hauled himself up to sitting. Still bleary eyed, he thumbed through to voicemail.

"Tomas, it is Petrov. You must help us; come quickly. Yorgi has contacted us — I am very afraid."

Fuck. He scrambled off the sofa and grabbed the cash envelope, his mobile and his keys. On the way over, he pulled Petrov's number from the mobile and stored it for speed dialling.

He made good time into South London and called in his progress. Alexandra answered, calmer than her husband, but definitely freaked. He told her to get packed and be ready to move as soon as he got there. From the little sense she made, he gathered that Yorgi had phoned them out of the blue — pissed, high, or paranoid; possibly all three; ranting about a hospital and unfinished business with a traitor. And then he was coming for them.

South of the river and every traffic light, every fuckwit incapable of doing thirty mph on a thirty road, all piled on the minutes and the pressure. No point calling Karl now, he was practically there.

He beeped the horn three times as he pulled up. A curtain snatched back, then the family made a run for the car, dragging as many cases as was humanly possible. They didn't look as though they planned on coming back. He popped the boot and revved up to encourage them, flicking his gaze between the windscreen and his mirrors. As he pushed into the car seat, primed for the off, the clamminess of his shirt squished against his back. He shivered and smiled; he was almost enjoying this.

Petrov ushered his family in the back and climbed in beside them. He seemed to take a last remorseful look at the house then Thomas met his eyes in the mirror. Time to go. For all the fire in his blood, Thomas drove sensibly, keeping to the speed limit and watching all directions. Petrov and Alexandra said nothing; he preferred that.

As they crossed London Bridge, the enormity of his actions began to sink in. He didn't have a plan, beyond getting them away from there. He flicked on the radio for inspiration, but it was in short supply tonight. *Jesus, another tailback.* In a city that never sleeps, why did all the insomniacs have to drive? His passengers sat, trance-like, as he battled through the traffic. They hadn't said a word, not even to ask where he was talking them; a question he was quietly asking himself.

His first, impossible thought had been to head to Miranda's parents. Without question they'd help him, but it would mean dragging them deeper into his murky world. That was the word for it: *murky.* His second choice was less inventive. Pick a hotel at random; any hotel would do, but the more upmarket the better — and room service was a necessity. It had to be somewhere Yorgi couldn't trace them to. He settled on Paddington, only because he and Miranda had once spent a weekend there playing tourists. And besides, the station afforded a range of escape options if he really couldn't protect them.

The engine rumbled to a standstill. He glanced down at his mobile and thought about Karl. There was every reason to ring, and few not to. Petrov had called *him* though. He reckoned he could sort things out for the time being with less fuss. Behind him, Petrov's family hardly made a sound, but their expectations massed around him like the roar of a West Ham crowd. He didn't bother turning round. "I want you to stay in a hotel until I figure out the next step. You'll need to remain in your room. Order whatever you need, but *stay put.*" He took out an even thousand and handed it to Petrov's bewildered wife.

"Why would you do this for us?"

He swallowed; he didn't really have an answer. Not without going into all the history with Ajit and . . . He stopped short. Maybe Ajit could provide police protection if he got them up to Yorkshire? The idea shattered before his eyes. *Wake up; this is more than you can handle. You need help; you need Karl.*

Alexandra paused from her whispered conversation and stared through the mirror. "How long must we hide there?"

"I don't know, probably just for a couple of days." He shouldered the door and breathed in the rush of air. "Remember, don't contact anyone except me."

They looked settled in the car. Tough. He emptied the boot and picked up a couple of bags, ready to start walking. "Let's get on with it."

Chapter 22

'Opportunities multiply as they are seized.'
Sun Tzu, The Art of War

Yorgi folded the book flat and closed his eyes. It was not enough merely to read wisdom; one had to imbibe and absorb it. He blinked against the harsh neon strip light and moved uneasily from the chair, holding the kitchen table to steady himself. His breath still tasted of vodka and his head bore the pitiless, unrelenting pressure of a hangover.

In the corner of the room, a black bin-liner sat and waited, serenaded by two flies. He wrinkled his nose in disgust, but did not consider moving it. He took a pub glass out of the cupboard, wiped it with his hand and ran the tap, squeezing his eyes closed to bear the whine of the pipes. Then he reached to the broken tiled ledge behind the sink and took the last of the painkillers. The box said *fast acting* so he sat still for three minutes. Only now was he ready to face the front room.

The table was upended — that much he did remember — but the extent of the devastation was a shock. He recalled speaking to Petrov; even the thought of his half-brother's name was like taking a candle to a fuse. His head throbbed to the rhythm: Pet-rov, Pet-rov. He picked up an armchair and turned the cushion over to sit. There was little point; it was filthy, either side. Peasants might live like this; he would not. He nodded to himself and grunted approval. It was settled; he would increase his fees, work the girls harder. He sniffed hard by his shoulder — taking in the stench of sweat and vomit. It

142

was a disgrace, he told himself, unconsciously resurrecting his father's voice in his head — not Petrov's lineage, but his *real* father.

"Yes Papa," he promised aloud, "I will complete my chores and better myself." He unbuttoned his shirt, pushed the sleeve back over the grime and rubbed his watch glass; the smooth, domed surface always made him smile; transporting him back to Amsterdam. He had only been pimping back then, when opportunity had presented itself. How the American tourist had begged and pleaded. But showing mercy to your enemy disrespects him. Sun Tzu understood that. So, once he had taken the man's watch and sneered at his flabby white body, he'd brought the knife easily to flesh.

In the shower he mentally relived the scene, enjoying the steady throbbing between his legs. The way the fat American had collapsed on the floor, squealing, oozing blood across the pale carpet. It was all so vivid, so *alive*. The frozen horror on the girl's face, making her gleam like an angel; like a religious statue. He sucked in the shower steam, felt it hot in his lungs as his memory wound on. That sense of absolute power as he'd fucked the girl on the bed, oblivious as to whether the man lived or died beside them on the floor. At that moment he had become a god, made in his own image.

He tilted his face to let the suds run down the length of his body and squirted shampoo around his pubic hair. Water spattered off his erection as he closed his eyes, moving his hand, slowly, teasingly downwards. Images of girls — so many girls, willing and unwilling — danced around him in a kaleidoscope of pleasure. Yes, Yorgi; yes. Now, as his hand found rhythm, the images were interspersed with the flashbacks of violence — the heavy certainty of the trigger or the knife handle. Pleasure and pain; pain and pleasure. At the point of orgasm he dug his nails hard into his penis, sending a delicious chord of agony and ecstasy through his body. When the pulses of semen had stopped, he relaxed his grip and gazed down at the savage marks on his flesh, like the bite of an animal.

He finished his shower and shaved, adding cologne to sting his face awake. A pair of trousers and shirt that had been hanging up for days gave him a respectable and inconspicuous air. He put the watch back on and checked the time: seven o'clock. Time to gather his things — the old clothes he would dump; another skin shed. A charity shop would meet his needs for the time being. He'd paid cash in advance for this hovel so no one should be visiting for at least another two weeks. By then, Mr Svenson — the name he'd given to the greedy bastard who'd made £500 out of him — would be long gone.

At Victoria station he stashed his bag and walked away with only a small carrier, stuffed in one side of his coat. He kept the silencer in the other pocket. He knew that the van driver, Dechevez, was in a private room on the third floor. But beyond that he knew nothing more than when he'd first encountered him at Harwich. Then, it had been a warning. Now, a permanent resolution was required. That it concerned politics was of no interest to him. Politics, he considered as he passed the hospital signs, was just another business — profit, loss and opportunity. Dechevez — whoever he was — was simply no longer profitable to someone.

* * *

Yorgi slipped through the open door at the side of the hospital and went straight to the basement. The stifling heat and the noise of the boiler took him back to his time at sea, stoking the engines and avoiding the attentions of the drunken louts who liked to use young boys as playthings. He remembered hiding behind the hottest pipes, risking a scalding rather than something far worse.

He went deeper into the hospital basement catacombs and pressed a hand to the boiler pipe, resting it there until it felt like the paint was searing his skin. A sharp reminder of what he had endured. His ears picked out the shuffling gait ahead of him and the squeak of the trolley. He hid in the shadows and fitted the silencer.

The cleaner shuffled past then stopped, just beyond the alcove. He let go of his trolley, paused and turned. Yorgi stepped out of the shadows like a panther, closing on his victim like the predator he was. Yorgi thought, for an instant, that the look of dread hinted at some kind of recognition. The idea amused him — that this was one of the people he'd trafficked to freedom, only to come back and claim him when the situation required. He levelled the weapon, surprised to hear a native tongue.

Sun Tzu wrote of turning every situation to one's advantage by reading the signs and acting accordingly. Yorgi believed knowledge was nothing unless it was tested in practice. He made the cleaner take off his overalls; promised him mercy as long as he didn't piss them in fear; a promise Yorgi had no intention of keeping, especially since they may have met before. The man stood before him in his underpants and vest, weight sagged forward a little, hands clasped together as if in prayer. Yorgi smiled and the man relaxed a little, smiling back. The first shot to the head — hygienic and efficient; the second, to the heart — just because he could.

He dumped the body in a laundry trolley and wheeled it out of sight. Only then did he change into the uniform; the overalls were baggy enough to fit over his clothes — a bonus, as was the ID card. When Yorgi smelt a foreign sweat against his clothes and skin, he felt a sense of transformation, as if he now inhabited the dead man's shell, claiming him. His mimicked accent might have sufficed to get to Dechevez, but this new persona offered a better disguise. Small matter that the photo bore little resemblance to him. A cleaning trolley and a hangdog expression would grant him anonymity, and people would see whatever they expected to see.

He exited the lift at the third floor. The air reeked of sickness and disinfectant; the heat smothered him like a blanket. He pushed his watch up his sleeve and wiped the tiny beads of sweat from his face. He started mopping along the corridor, head down, humming softly. The latex gloves were a little loose and he knew that later they would make his skin itch. But it was a minor inconvenience.

As the dry linoleum retreated and the room numbers counted down, he felt the thrill of anticipation and his erection pressing tightly beneath the overalls. He looked into the distance at the Asian nurse who was bent over, reading, and thought about what he'd like to do to her. He watched her for at least a minute until she looked up and gave a nonchalant wave in his direction. He responded in kind then furtively felt for the bulge through his pocket.

When she moved out of sight, he pushed the trolley closer and peered through the door-glass for the first time. Dechevez was there, sleeping like an innocent. Yorgi leered at him, his teeth reflecting in the glass like fangs. He turned towards the trolley and drew out the gun, keeping it at his blindside.

He waited, head down, watching as the pretty nurse picked up a folder and left his field of vision again. Barely breathing, he reached for the cylindrical door handle in small, precise movements. He felt the handle give way and the door ease in. Heat wafted around his face. He remembered then, as a young boy, his father coming into his room; stealthy, loving and unannounced. He always looked forward to those goodnights, but could never stay awake to catch him no matter how hard he tried. He would just open his eyes and Papa would be there, like Santa Claus, at the edge of his bed.

Dechevez sighed softly. Yorgi heard his father's voice again: 'Sleep well, Yorgi; you are my good boy.' His eyes glistened as he squeezed the trigger, his lips forming the words: 'I love you, Papa.' Dechevez's body twitched against the pillow and the blood seeped down the side of the bed, pooling on the lino.

Yorgi fired again, just to see the head jerk a second time, like one of Papa's wooden puppets. He hummed as he closed the door, carefully spraying polish over the aluminium handle and door plate and wiping it tenderly. Then he collected up his cleaning implements, pushed the trolley round to the lift and left it there. As he headed for the stairwell he heard the lift door ping behind him and a murmur of voices carried along the corridor. He removed the ID card from his jacket, looked at the name and whispered his thanks to the original owner.

Outside, he acknowledged the other cleaning staff gathered by a side door to smoke. He declined their offer to join them and muttered 'newspaper,' waving casually behind him as he reached the corner. He removed his overalls in the nearby public toilets and packed them into a carrier bag, ready for the nearest recycling bin. The ID he would keep — a souvenir of his own inventiveness. He felt for the watch underneath his overall sleeve; it was time to settle things with Petrov. And for that he'd need a vehicle.

Chapter 23

"Tommo, we got us a situation."

Thomas watched himself in the café mirror as he answered the phone, staring back in dismay; he looked rough. "I'm listening, Karl."

"I've located the hospital, but it's bad news; two dead — professional hits. One's our shooting victim from the docks — Dechevez — and the other's a cleaner. The police haven't found a connection between them yet and we're trying to keep a lid on things until they do." Karl's voice was unemotional; he could have been reading from a script. "The cleaner was Yugoslavian or . . . something Eastern European. I guess he'd be a former Yugoslavian now." Karl had probably rehearsed that line.

"What's the plan, then?"

Karl didn't respond immediately. "There's something else. I'm sorry, Tommo. There was a fire in South London, where you did the home visit."

Thomas caught his reflection, nodding needlessly.

"The house is completely gutted, apparently. I don't see how anyone could have got out of there alive," the line went quiet.

Thomas let out a gasp. "It's okay, Karl. I've got them! Petrov rang me — I put the family somewhere safe. This is down to Yorgi, isn't it?"

Karl ignored the question and let out a whoop of joy. And then it hit Thomas like a smack in the face; he'd done something amazing. He touched his neck where the crucifix chain used to rub, back when he'd worn it to please his mother.

"Are you still there, Tommo? Wherever they are, they're not safe; we need to bring them in."

Now came the familiar dilemma: to trust or not to trust.

Karl wouldn't wait. "Are you there? Listen to me. Yorgi is a Grade A psychopath. I've seen the file. If he's killed twice today, he's probably tying up *all* loose ends."

Thomas felt a creeping sense of doom. "But I told Petrov not to call anyone."

"Come on now — where did you take them?"

"Near Paddington — I cut through the City to save time."

"No!" Karl wailed, "Central London — the congestion charge; there are vehicle recognition cameras everywhere."

"I don't understand. If Yorgi's working alone . . ."

"That's just it, Tommo. These people are pros — they'll have connections. You better give me the details and pray Yorgi hasn't got to them first."

Thomas threw some money down on the counter — the way they do in films — and ran back to the hotel. Thank Christ he hadn't driven off anywhere. He pushed the glass door, ignored the night porter and made straight for the stairs. He took them two at a time, rounding the final flight at the Fifth Floor, and slammed through the fire door. Left hand corridor, down towards the end. He knocked politely then thought better of it, banging with his fist. "It's Thomas, open the bloody door." He stepped back and sized it up; it looked tougher than he did.

"Alright, alright; you'll wake Lukas," Petrov scolded him. The door unbolted and then the latch turned — at least they'd done something right.

Thomas pushed his way in; Alexandra lifted her head from the sofa. "We couldn't sleep so we watched television. Too much has happened; tell him, Petrov," she looked daggers at her husband.

Petrov carefully closed the door then slicked back his hair with his fingers. "I over-reacted, made a mistake. Yorgi telephoned on my mobile and apologised. He wants to make amends, to drive over and collect us, but this Alexandra does not want."

"Your house was burned down," Thomas blurted it out in one breath. No warning, no preamble; no point.

Petrov pressed a hand to his forehead and staggered to a chair. "How?"

Alexandra didn't say a word. She ran to a side room, where Thomas figured Lukas was sleeping.

He was glad she'd left the room; it made things easier. He stood over Petrov. "The fire was deliberate and Yorgi's killed two people today." And there was something about Petrov's face; a knowing look in the eyes that told Thomas this wasn't the first time. "Does

148

Yorgi know where you are?" He felt his legs start to tremble. "We have to go, *now*."

Petrov leapt to his feet. "Is impossible. My wife needs to sleep. Besides, I have told him nothing. He does not know where to find us." He held up his mobile phone as if it was the evidence that would clear him.

The green light shone out to Thomas like a taunt. Oh Jesus: the mobile. As traceable as a number plate, with the right equipment. "When did he ring you?"

"About ten minutes after you left."

Thomas's mind raced through the maths. Ten minutes, plus fifteen minutes or so, equals thirty minutes max; plenty of time to be on the move. And if Yorgi could access information on the hoof . . . shit. "Get up," he snarled. "We're leaving."

Petrov's mobile rang; they both just stared at it. Thomas's senses went into overdrive; his first instinct was to grab the knife on the room service tray. Futile in itself, but a sign of how scared he was. His breath came in shallow bursts. *Think Thomas, think.* He grabbed Petrov's mobile and switched it off with a strangle hold. Reality kicked in: get out, go to ground and rely on Karl. He clicked his fingers at Petrov and pointed to the side room. Next, he turned the TV off and rang Karl.

"I'm organising a team, Tommo. In the meantime you'll have to improvise."

Improvise? Thomas felt the sweat trickle down his back. He gave Petrov another few seconds, mainly to avoid arguing with him. The bedroom door opened, and the family was ready to leave. They looked at him the same way they'd done at the house — as if he had all the answers. He tried to draw strength from that.

"Right," he held up a hand, as if he might grasp a passing plan, "got it. Here's how we do it. Petrov, you go alone. Alexandra, you take the boy. Yorgi is expecting three people together. Petrov — swap jackets with me; quickly."

It was bollocks, but it was a start. It gave them something to cling to; the delusion that he knew what he was doing. He and Petrov emptied out personal belongings and made the switch. Now came the tricky part.

He unlocked the door. An inch open and all he could hear was his own breathing and the television from next door. He emerged slowly, signalling for them to follow. But at the turn in the corridor, he had a flash of inspiration. "Stay in the room until the bells start."

Alexandra narrowed her eyes. "What bells?"

He blinked twice and ushered them away. "Just be ready."

He ran to the fire alarm and punched it hard, harder than needed. The sting in his knuckles felt good though; it seemed to sharpen his senses. He heard the alarm echo along the corridor; guest doors opened at random and a few simply closed again straight away. Stupid bastards.

Petrov and Alexandra wasted no time in joining the throng on the stairway. Thomas timed it and fell in close behind. He tapped Petrov's shoulder at the last landing so that he could pass him. Alexandra had already slowed up by the fire door, with the child in her arms. She looked lost.

He gently grabbed her elbow and steered her out into the street. The police were already in attendance — maybe Karl's doing, he couldn't be certain. He told Alexandra to stand by the police car. Petrov, if he'd kept to the plan, should be making himself invisible. Only Thomas — wearing Petrov's jacket — walked around slowly as if dazed by the chaos around him. He took his mobile out casually and hit the speed-dial. *Now, Karl.*

"I'll be on-site in ten minutes, max. I got some of the boys in blue to help out. Stay in the crowd, Tommo. Believe me, Yorgi is out there somewhere. Be safe."

Thomas didn't feel brave now, or clever; he just felt sick to his stomach. Like he was in one of those nature programmes where the gazelle stands around waiting for the lion to strike. This was insane. *Easy, Thomas, just drift away from Alexandra; find a different policeman and ask some stupid questions.* Anything to let Yorgi see that *Petrov* was smart enough to stay out of harm's way.

The police officer brushed him off and took a call on his radio, so much for Plan A. He listened without being obvious — something about sending everyone back in again. A firefighter approached, with a face like thunder.

"Some twat set off the alarm. We've scoured the ground floor upwards, just waiting on the basement. I'll give you a shout when the Incident Controller gives the okay to return."

This was where the plan unravelled. Still no Karl, and Petrov out there in the crowd — no doubt keeping an eye on Alexandra even though Thomas had told him to stay clear. They were bound to go in together, which pretty much defeated the object. He couldn't keep them out on their own, in the open; couldn't get them away, as his car was around the block. In short, screwed from all angles. He could slug the copper to create a bit of a commotion? Think again; the guy didn't look as if he took any prisoners — maybe trigger a car alarm on one of the Mercs, then? Yeah, and what good would that do?

The mobile rang; he grabbed at it as if it were a lifebelt.

Karl was breathless. "I'm at the back of the crowd; get them ready."

"*Ready?*" Thomas hissed. "I split them up for safety — there are over two hundred people in the street."

150

"Well, you better get a bloody move on. I couldn't get a pick-up in time so I'm their ride out of here."

The firefighter reappeared, had a few words with the police officer and raised a hand to sound the retreat. The residents morphed into grumbling cattle and moseyed on in.

Thomas picked out Alexandra easily. She had followed instructions and stuck by the police car. As he approached, she was in conversation with one of the cops. "Ah, here is my husband!"

He swallowed hard and hoped that the boy didn't start screaming. "This way," he all but scooped her up.

"Where is Petrov?" she whimpered.

"I'll find him in a minute. Come on," he pulled her arm roughly. They swam against the tide of returning hotel guests until Thomas caught sight of Karl's old banger in the middle of the street. His heart skipped a beat; he had to steady himself against Alexandra as he led her to the car. She stared at Karl; he stared right back.

"It's okay, really," Thomas insisted, craning the door wide and nudging her towards it. "I'll go and get Petrov."

He spotted his own jacket heading back into the hotel and elbowed his way through. Other guests had made for the complimentary drinks; Petrov was rooted to the spot, standing in the bar like the ugly one at a Valentine's disco.

Thomas zeroed in. "Alexandra and Lukas are already in the car — we'll take you somewhere safe." The way he said it, he was barely selling it to himself.

Petrov's face was as blank as the décor. Thomas eased him outside. Karl pulled up and Thomas shouldered him to the car like he was an invalid. "I'll sort your cases out later."

Petrov opened his mouth, but he didn't speak. Thomas reached for the front passenger door.

"That's okay Tommo — I'll see you back in the hotel bar for a wee chat."

As Thomas sat down in the bar, he felt the damp patch cold on his back, clinging like a dirty secret. He shifted forward and glanced around the room. For all he knew Yorgi could be any one of them — no saying he had to look like Petrov. Yeah, he argued with himself, but Yorgi was a professional. Ergo, he'd have seen Karl driving off — he'd hardly be hanging around now. *Ergo?* For an instant he thought of Christine, all lips and Latin. He squished against the chair again and felt a droplet trickle down his spine to rest in the crack of his arse. He grimaced and pulled his top away. Sod this for a game of soldiers, he'd nip out to his car and get the sweatshirt from the boot. On the way out, he grabbed an empty beer bottle for comfort.

After all the commotion, the streets outside seemed unnaturally quiet. There was still traffic — this was London after all — but it was reduced to glaring lights and shrouded shapes. The side street was jam-packed with parked cars. He stuck to the shadows, avoiding the sickly orange glow of street lamps where he could. He moved quickly, keeping his wits about him.

He paused three vehicles from his car, and gripped the beer bottle more tightly. It might have once held extra strong lager but it wasn't strong enough to take on a bullet. He smiled in the gloom; knowing exactly what he was doing: gallows humour. He took a breath, sucking it down like a smoker getting a fix.

Despite the bollocking awaiting him, he wished Karl were there. As if on cue, his arm throbbed through its dressing. Enough stalling. He took a final glance around then stepped smartly to the rear of his car. The boot catch gave way with a sigh; he reached in without bending his head, feeling his way around for the sweatshirt. For a split second he was going to change in the street, but he suddenly felt more vulnerable than ever. He didn't want to let go of the bottle so he did a bit of a juggling act and slammed the boot down hard. *Good one Thomas; Mr Psycho might be out there but that ought to scare him off.* He jogged back to the hotel, kidding himself that his panting was due to being out of condition, not blind terror.

* * *

Yorgi watched closely as the stranger fumbled about in his car then ran back towards the hotel. This was a new factor, an unknown quantity. Killing him now would achieve nothing. No, this man had chaperoned Alexandra and Lukas out of the hotel; and he would be the best way of reaching them again. He might need a little encouragement, but he would cooperate. As for Petrov, well, he could be persuaded to do anything. Yorgi leered in the darkness, remembering how he'd forced Petrov to shoot a rat on the farm. Petrov had shaken and bawled; how he had pleaded! He had done it in the end though. They always did what he wanted in the end.

He pressed his watch close. Sometimes, when he felt the glass against his ear in the night, he fancied he could still hear the American screaming. He lowered his hand and moved the battered copy of Sun Tzu's *Art of War* from his lap. A phrase was underlined: *'A man who knows when he can fight and when he cannot, will be victorious.'*

The traffic was a distant hum through the glass. He reached for the device and left the car, walking along the street with the transmitter nestling in his palm. The gun remained in his pocket, in case anyone was foolish enough to disturb him. He found the place, underneath the chassis near the driver's door. He pushed the apparatus up against the metal, making sure it was secure. Then he disappeared into the night to await victory.

Chapter 24

Thomas returned from the gents with his old clothes knotted together. The bar was still busy as he threaded through, holding the bundle down like a secret shame. He stuffed it under the chair, bought drinks and crisps and left them untouched on the table, feeling like a kid waiting outside the headmaster's office.

Karl arrived ten minutes later; Thomas figured he'd passed Petrov on to someone more senior — Teresa perhaps? Karl spotted him at the door, but didn't acknowledge him. This did not look good. He sat down and took his time about it, sipping at his pint of shandy before he spoke. "We're in the shit. Yorgi wasn't picked up; he's gone to ground."

Thomas opened a packet of crisps methodically. "Isn't that a good thing?"

Karl glared; wrong answer. "Grow up, Tommo; he's a fucking killer. We've no way of knowing when he's going to pop up again. Meantime his brother and that lovely wee family of his are looking at relocation and a new identity; and all because you fucked up."

Thomas jerked back as if he'd been sucker punched. "Hey, if it wasn't for me, Petrov might still have been at the house when . . ."

Karl was having none of it. "First, do you really think he'd have stayed there waiting if you hadn't agreed to pick him up? And second, what the fuck were you thinking of, not informing me? We're supposed to be a team!"

Thomas clenched his fists, under the table. "We're a team, Karl? Then who are we working for, huh? Who did you hand Petrov over to? We're a team when it suits you."

Karl closed in on him. "For two pins, I'd knock you down where you stand."

"I'm sitting down though." Not a flicker from Karl. All Thomas felt from him was a heat-haze of anger.

Karl kneaded his forehead, as if he was trying to massage the words into place. "Look, you're plainly out of your depth in all this. You're a *liability*."

Ouch. Thomas gulped back the shock along with the lager. There was nothing else to be said. He put his glass down — definitely half empty tonight — and started to stand.

Karl pulled at his arm. "Hey," he snarled, "we're not done yet! Petrov thinks you're some kind of saint so you'll be in on the interrogation — we're giving him a day or so to soften up. In the meantime we need to get a few things straight, once and for all." He pointed a finger dagger at Thomas's chest. "You need my help; Yorgi getting away like that looks worryingly suspicious from a certain angle."

Thomas launched himself to standing. The glasses rocked on the table, their contents swirling like miniature tempests.

"Calm yourself, Tommy Boy," Karl lifted his drink and took another sip. "This fiasco has put us both in a difficult position. I suggest you take a day off tomorrow — ring in sick — and have a serious think about your position." Karl sat back and looked away: class dismissed.

Thomas grabbed his clothes from the floor and made for the door. His arm was stinging again, but there was a kind of comfort in that. He was on the phone to Miranda before he'd reached the car.

"Thomas — it's late; what's up?" Straight to the point. He played vague. Wrong move; more questions were the last thing he wanted, and Miranda knew him too well. "Bad day at work?"

Four little words which translated neatly as 'serves you fucking right.' Before he had time to think, they were bickering down memory lane; trudging through the past in the search for survivors — his possessiveness, his secretiveness, that footballer she'd been *banging* — a word he knew would exocet through her defences. She told him to grow up and sort his life out. Sort it out? He didn't even know what his life was anymore.

He cut the mobile off mid-sentence. His arm was screaming now; he popped a pill and wondered how he'd ended up like this — Miranda, Christine and Karl, all blocking him like chess pieces. Shit, there was only Ajit left, and he was on the other side of the thin blue line.

The worst part of it was that he blamed himself. Oh sure, he'd make his peace with Miranda somehow and get back on side with Karl. Petrov and his family though, that was something he couldn't fix — didn't even know where to start. It was Big Boys' stuff. And there was something else too.

Yorgi was the first person he'd been afraid of since leaving Leeds. Okay, maybe Miranda's dad to a point, but Yorgi was a *killer*. The word made the blood slow at the back of his neck. What if . . . no, he didn't dare think that way. He'd move carefully on this now; phone in sick tomorrow, like Karl had suggested, and get his head together. He breathed a little easier and put the car radio on to drown out his thoughts.

* * *

Ask most Londoners and they'll tell you that driving is a necessary evil; a means to an end, but not a pleasure. Thomas loved it though; for him a car brought freedom. Even if he wasn't out working or taking his own photographs, sometimes it felt good to just get in the car and lose himself in the maze of London streets. A full tank of petrol and a bag of crisps, and he was a happy man. And after the day's shenanigans, what better way of winding down?

He left Paddington and turned up through Maida Vale, breezing through Kilburn. Irish Town, as Karl had christened it — and he ought to know. Kilburn High Road ran into Shoot-up Hill, worth the journey for the irony value alone. He sang to the radio, laughing at the realisation that his rendition of 'Eye of the Tiger' was as murderous as anything Karl could produce.

And okay, maybe he hadn't planned it consciously, but when the first sign for Highgate appeared, it all seemed to make sense. If he could just straighten out the whole Christine and Bob Peterson thing, it would be a start. Then maybe he could recover some credibility with Karl. At the very least he'd unsettle the happy couple and that could only be a good thing.

The closer he got to Christine's flat, the more malicious he felt. After all, hadn't Bob Peterson's appearance at Harwich been the detonator? The defining event that had bollocksed everything up? So this could be payback time.

He parked, switched off the ignition and made himself comfortable. He wouldn't bother to check for Peterson's vehicle — no point: guilty as charged. He punched in Christine's number and paused for a second on the send button. Game on. He held the phone lightly to his ear and crossed his feet. At the fourth ring he suddenly remembered the time. Oops.

"Hello?"

"Hi, it's Thomas; hope I'm not disturbing you," he winced — about as subtle as a hammer at an osteopath's.

"Thomas? Er, what can I do for you?" the curtain flicked back, silhouetting Christine against an orange glow. She looked good, even at a distance in a five second show.

"I just fancied a chat. Listen, I know it's late, but how about I come over?"

The line went silent for a moment; the kind of silence that a hand over the receiver makes. "I don't think that's a very good idea, do you?"

It was too much to ask that Bob Peterson would put in an appearance at the window. He'd settle for something less tangible, like an admission.

"Are you out there somewhere, Thomas?"

Shit. Peterson was probably right next to her, might even be listening for his reply. *A large plate of 'backfire' to table four.* He swallowed and stared up at the window, which showed a silhouette of Christine and Bob.

"I'm waiting, Thomas."

"I just needed to talk with you tonight. There have been developments." Jesus, what was he saying? But the idea had already formed. "I think something is going on with the department."

For an instant he thought he heard Christine gasp. Or maybe it was static.

"Look, I'm not far from your place; I could drop over — I won't stay long."

"No!" she yelped, "we've been through this before, Thomas. If you've got anything to say to me you can say it now or it'll have to keep until tomorrow."

Fuck it: in for a penny, in for a pound. "It's about Bob Peterson."

No reaction; she was good. If he knew her like he thought he did, the next words would be brief and measured.

"What about him?"

"I'd rather tell you face to face."

"Thomas, don't piss me about. I could have your mobile trigged before you got half a mile away. If you've something to say . . ."

"You do know he's married with two kids?" He winced.

"Grow up Thomas, and keep your nose out of my personal affairs."

He bit his tongue. "I'm just looking out for you, Chrissie."

"I can look after myself. And don't ring me here again, Thomas — I mean it. The next time you call me at home it goes on your report — do you understand? It's been a long day; I'm going back to bed."

"Is that alone?"

"Last warning, Thomas. Whatever you think you know, you'd best forget it. This ends here, but you are all out of favours now." The line went dead.

He hung up and exhaled deeply into his hands. Stupid bastard; what was he doing? He grabbed up the mobile again and speed-dialled number 1. "Hi Miranda, it's me again. Can I come over? It's been a lousy night."

"Do you know what time it is?"

"Late?"

She laughed. "Get some sleep, Thomas; it'll all be better in the morning."

"But your bed is so much more comfortable than mine . . ."

"Suit yourself."

He sat there for a minute, trying to think straight. Was she toying with him? She'd done that once before, and he'd arrived to find the lights out and the door locked. "Well," he told himself in the dark, "there's only one way to find out."

Chapter 25

Thomas rang the bell in shrill, insistent bursts.

"Alright!"

He squinted as light erupted, framing her blurred outline through the glass.

Miranda peered back at him, her face pressed against the frosted pane.

"Do you know what time it is?" she opened the door a degree, and instinctively he strained to see where the frayed silk dressing gown ended and her thigh began. "I wasn't sure if you were serious about coming over, when you rang."

"Well, here I am," he waited awkwardly, leaning against the door, matching her resistance. Then, as if he'd finally decided what he really wanted to happen, he pushed a little more until he felt her hand relent and the door swung in.

"Lock up, will you?" she walked off to the bedroom without looking back.

He brushed against the coat hooks; there was a man's jacket there. He slammed the door and flicked the switch. The only light now was the pink glow at the end of the hall.

"I see you've had a visitor," he called out from the shadow, tasting the venom of his thoughts.

"It's my brother's — Terry left it here. Jesus, still as paranoid as ever! Now get your arse in here; I've got stuff to do tomorrow morning."

He slipped off his shoes. "What's Terry up to these days?" His voice wavered, caught between relief and shame. She was right, still the same demons; if anything, he was worse since Christine. Something else to blame her for.

Miranda was still undressing in the bedroom. He pressed up close behind her, watched her smile and tried to fathom that look as he spread his fingers across her breasts. He touched his lips to her neck, traced a circle of kisses behind her ear. She smelt of expensive soap and perfume.

What sort of a person wears perfume on the strength of a phone call? The same kind who turns up at one-thirty in the morning, with nothing but a hard-on.

"You could've shaved."

He sighed, no arguments tonight. Besides, actions spoke louder than words. His hand travelled down between her thighs. Miranda gasped and pushed her buttocks against his groin. She leaned back, draping over him and her hair fell across his face. He studied their reflection: it looked like a still from a low-budget porn flick.

She laughed as she turned to face him and he was startled by a momentary wave of contempt. This was so easy for her. 'Sex is sex,' she'd said in the past. 'Don't confuse it with something more complicated.'

He discarded his clothes methodically, and joined her on the bed. He wondered how much activity the bed had seen since he'd last been there. Then he reached for the lamp and snapped it off, shutting out his thoughts.

He was greedy for her, eager to wrap himself in desire. But he wanted her to want him, really yearn for him; he needed that tonight. He tasted her skin, ingested the perfume's acrid undercurrent and let his tongue travel the length of her body, slowly and tentatively, as if it was a forbidden journey. Soon they moved together rhythmically as only familiar lovers can. Yet the closer they became the more he felt like an outsider.

"You're hurting my arms."

He relaxed his grip, jarred back into the moment. He was rough with her, knew that he wanted a reaction. A sudden image of Christine and Peterson, together, rose up to taunt him and he pushed hard into Miranda as if he could drive away his demons. He heard her breathing change and synchronised his body to hers, matching the frenzied thrusts to the rhythmic rocking of her hips.

"Not yet," he heard her whisper breathlessly, as she arched her back.

His mind detached itself from the scene; he became a voyeur while instinct took the lead. And then, when he felt her whole body meld around his and her low moans built to fever pitch, he tilted upwards and burst inside her.

They remained still, a tide of release and tenderness washing between them, until he slumped on top of her with a heavy sigh. She held him close and he lay there, still panting, his dry lips savouring the sweat on her breast. He felt a tear forming in his eye and lay motionless, as if he could deny its existence.

"That was epic!" she congratulated him, stroking his hair affectionately.

He knew she'd expect some salacious compliment in return, but he wasn't in the mood tonight.

"Would you rather have been somewhere else?" she read him like a book.

"Sorry," he conceded and untangled himself from her.

"Is it still about Christine — do you wanna talk about it?"

He rolled carefully on to one side and traced Miranda's face in the dark — that knowing, beautiful face. Then he kissed her; a long, tender kiss, as if to pour himself into her lips and escape his own identity. A lesser man would have called it love. But it was more than that. "I'll tell you in the morning," he promised, pulling her towards him as he closed his eyes.

Chapter 26

Thomas yawned in the gloom. He stared, bleary eyed, trying to make sense of his watch without disturbing the thick curtains. It was either five to eight or twenty to eleven. He leaned across and stroked behind her ear, certain that Miranda was awake and ignoring him.

She wriggled free from his fingers. "Listen, any chance you could drop me off at the club on your way into work? I left my car there last night and I'm picking Terry up from the airport today. I can give him his coat back too, if you like?"

"Very droll. Just take my car — I'm calling in a sickie."

"Wow. Hold the front page. Do you wanna come with me, then?"

"Nah, I'll just hang around here for a bit and meet you later at the club."

She paused, as if in mid-thought. "Well, lock up after you and no going through my underwear drawer when I'm gone."

"You know me so well."

"Indeed I do, Mr Bladen. Speaking of which, what brought you to my door last night — welcome as it was." She slipped out from the duvet and into a dressing gown. "Something about Christine wasn't it?"

She knew bloody well it was. He sighed and tapped at the bedside table with his index finger.

"If that's Morse code, I never went to Spy School." She was still smiling.

"Christine's involved with this married bloke; and he's bad news."

"Brave Sir Knight to the rescue?" she raised an eyebrow.

162

"Not quite."

"Can't Karl help you out?"

He felt her studying his face. He shook his head.

"Lovers' tiff?"

"Something like that," he braced himself for some righteous piss-taking, but it never came. That was Miranda, full of surprises.

"Well, I'm here if you need an ear. And don't forget," she gazed in the general direction of his groin, "I keep all your secrets."

He waited until Miranda was in the shower before ringing in. Christine's office phone was diverted to her mobile. She sounded relieved; it was a short call. Karl had been spot-on — a little breathing space would do everyone a favour. After he'd rung off, he tried the bathroom door — locked. He felt peeved; no reason to be but there it was.

* * *

Sir Peter Carroll took the call in his limo. "I've seen the picture — it's definitely our man. Yes, indeed, very delicate. I'm certainly not aware of any affiliations. No, Yorgi, best you remain where you are — I'll handle things from here."

The call ended. Trevor, the driver, glanced up in the mirror and read his employer's mood well enough to say nothing. Another number was dialled.

"Nicholas, I have an opportunity for you to redeem yourself. I want you to supervise a collection — Thomas Bladen." Sir Peter could almost hear Nicholas salivating over the phone.

"Thank you, Sir Peter, we'll pick him up before he gets to Harwich."

"Excellent. I'm relying on you Nicholas — don't let me down again."

* * *

Miranda waited patiently at the lights, studying the pedestrians as they herded past the front of the car. Ever since Thomas had come out of the spy closet, she'd practised extra vigilance. Still, with a family background like hers, she was pretty vigilant anyway, especially where men were concerned. As a teenager, having boyfriends had been a dangerous pastime — for them. Back then, secret assignations and sneaking about were second nature. If anything, Thomas's cloak-and-dagger act had brought on a touch of nostalgia.

A young mother pushed a stroller out just as the lights started to change. Miranda sat, primed, ready to flip the finger behind her if anyone dared beep. Mother and child; it made you think. Her biological clock wasn't even building up to a tick, but that hadn't always been the way. Once . . . well, one day when she'd come to terms with what might have been, she'd give it all some thought.

The second the mother reached the kerb, Miranda put her foot down, narrowly beating the change back to amber. She stole a final glance in the mirror then powered through the traffic. Eager for distraction, she flicked on the radio and re-tuned it to something closer to the last twenty years.

The green Peugeot she'd kept tabs on had been two cars back for a good five minutes now. Probably nothing in it, but she pulled in and watched as it passed without slowing down. Better safe than sorry. Back when Dad was first under suspicion, when he was being fitted up, the Wright family had sat down together and drawn up a set of rules.

Simple stuff: mistrust everyone; say nothing; if at all concerned, go to a public place — preferably with lots of CCTV and people. Thomas had said similar things that morning, like an echo of her dad. Although he did play poker better.

* * *

Nicholas arrived promptly at Great Portland Street. He'd prepared a briefing, but it was very clear, from the moment he opened the conference room door and laid eyes on them, that he was more passenger than leader. No round of introductions here. Everyone knew their place — and their distance.

"Shall we?" he headed for the stairs, crossing his fingers that they followed him. He took the front passenger seat in the people carrier and said nothing until they were on the move. The GPS tracker showed that the car was southbound, corresponding to the map onscreen. His job, he now realised, was to relay the data and coordinate the team. So why was the blue dot travelling further and further away from Harwich?

He considered ringing Sir Peter to check. No, he could manage things. Besides, how hard could it be to pick up one SSU man? He touched lightly at his cheek and felt the last vestige of bruising from where he'd taken a beating in Thomas Bladen's flat. He blushed at the memory of waking up in the undergrowth of a roundabout, stripped to his underwear. Shameful, but he'd weathered that storm. Whereas his accomplice had never been seen again. "Get a move on; I think he's giving us the run around."

The driver obeyed him and he felt his silent companions behind him twitch to attention. "I'm Nicholas, if you didn't already know." Now he was in his stride, captain of the team.

"Alice."

He looked round at her and stared, as if to say 'really'? She didn't flinch. Alice, it was then. Jack declared himself, but the driver — a much older man — said nothing. No matter, Nicholas was used to dealing with servants. No one ventured any further information, which didn't surprise him. Scratch the surface of most departments and the protocol was the same.

They were making progress against the target vehicle and it didn't take a science degree to pinpoint the destination: Gatwick. They still had the element of surprise and the advantage of numbers, if it came to that. So what was Bladen up to? Sir Peter evidently didn't know; this could be the coup he'd been looking for.

He swapped hands with the tracker unit and felt the clamminess between his palms. "Good luck everyone; we're nearly there." He saw Jack and Alice share a glance of disdain — so much the better. He wasn't there to be liked; he had a job to do. The numbers on screen whittled down as they approached the short stay car park. He already had the number plate and gestured as he saw the vehicle parking up; gestured because he was too wired to speak.

* * *

A people carrier with blacked-out windows drew in front of Miranda's car. She heard the doors as she delved into her handbag for her mobile to ring Thomas and let him know she'd arrived. As she rifled through her things, she ran through a shortlist of opening lines and settled on: 'Are you still inside?'

Before she could dial, her driver's door opened. She turned to see a youngish man in an expensive suit. "Yeah, what do you want?"

He looked lost for an answer. She reached over to pull the handle in, but the light began to fade. Behind her, someone was blocking the passenger door. Panic time.

Posh Bloke had stepped back, allowing a woman to crank the door wider and start pulling on her arm. "Where is he?"

As Miranda felt herself being dragged out of the car, she went limp to conserve her strength. Then she grabbed the edge of her seat and pulled herself down towards the gear-stick. As soon as she was close enough, she kicked hard against the passenger window, right at the chink in the pane that Thomas had never got round to fixing, driving her boot heel into the glass with a roar. The window splintered on the third kick; a pity that light block had the sense to move in time. Now she rolled on to her stomach and let the woman pull her out, waiting until she was past the steering wheel to swing, left-handed. Not her finest work, but three years of kickboxing — and running a bar — did the job.

"Wait!" Posh Bloke held up his hand, like a teacher intervening in a playground brawl. "We're here to help you. Thomas sent us. He's in trouble."

Miranda ceased struggling and the woman let go. They ushered her into the people carrier. If this was the cavalry, they had a funny way of showing it. As everyone climbed aboard, she copped the driver sending a text. No one else seemed to have noticed.

"What about my car?"

Posh Bloke seemed subdued again. "It'll be taken care of."

Next question. "Is someone going to tell me what's going on?"

Either they were stonewalling her or something was amiss here. Eyes darted back and forth, but nobody answered. Posh Bloke seemed to be the one in charge; she'd have to work on him. She played the game of pluses and minuses in her head, as much to organise her thoughts as to try and stay calm. Pluses: they hadn't hurt her, they'd mentioned Thomas and they didn't seem like hardened criminals — and she knew what *they* looked like. Minuses: Thomas must have sent them to her and she didn't know what the deal was.

Nobody spoke to her as the people carrier sped clockwise around the M25. She wasn't bothered; she had plenty to think about. How did they know how to find her, especially as she'd been driving Thomas's car? A shame about the window though — she'd better let Thomas know she was safe. "I need to make a phone call."

"Later."

Well, that was brief and to the point. She toyed with the idea of just opening her mobile, but something told her to stay submissive and bide her time. The woman beside her winced as she practiced opening and closing her eye. Yeah, as Sheryl at the club would say, in her native Brooklyneese: 'suck it up.'

Eyeball — no one had introduced themselves, bar the merest sniff of an ID card, so she had given them her name — Eyeball's face changed. She seemed more focused and detached. Miranda almost felt bad for punching her — sisterhood and all that.

"How well do you know Thomas Bladen?"

Miranda smiled inwardly. Outwardly she stayed as blank as a new canvas. All Thomas's paranoia was finally bearing fruit. "We go way back."

"And what do you know about his work?"

This was like painting by numbers. "He's a government photographer — and he delivers packages." *Too much information maybe?* She glanced ahead and read the A road as they turned off. Eyeball leaned over and touched her leg.

"I know this must all seem strange to you."

That was a first; good cop and bad cop all rolled together, making: average cop. Miranda nodded and bit at her fingernail. Dad had said he used to do that in police interrogations, to accompany whatever crap he was feeding them.

Eyeball continued. "It's just a precaution, you understand. Thomas's cover is at risk and he wanted you kept safe until we have things under control."

Miranda dug her nail hard into her hand, to stifle a response. They were lying, and badly. Firstly, Thomas didn't have any cover. Secondly, he was *intensely* private, so how would they know about her? And thirdly, if Thomas had been in any kind of trouble, he'd have contacted the family first.

But here she was, in the company of strangers, and he did have that bandage on his arm the previous night, so something didn't sit right. "Does Thomas know I'm with you?"

Eyeball swallowed and took a breath then swapped glances with Posh Bloke. "We'll contact him once you're at a secure location."

Miranda narrowed her gaze and dug her nail into her palm again: jackpot. She sat back and took stock; she was sandwiched between two of them — no chance of getting out. Best play the dumb blonde for now and try and hold it together. "Yeah, that makes sense. Do you think I could just leave him a message? Only I was supposed to feed the dog later and he might worry if he gets back and Butch . . ."

Eyeball leaned forward and Posh Bloke mumbled approval. "Alright, but keep it short — you can use my mobile." Eyeball opened her phone, punched in the digits from a piece of paper and passed the phone over.

It went straight to his office voicemail. "Hi Tom, it's Miranda. Erm, something's come up so you'll have to sort Butch out yourself today. Sorry." She returned the phone with a smile; it was up to him now.

Eyeball gave her a funny look. "I need your handbag, as a precaution."

The silent wonder on her left wriggled in his seat; no, he squirmed. Even he didn't fall for that line.

"Okay," Miranda handed her bag over.

Posh Bloke signalled to the driver and they pulled in at the next lay-by. He seemed quietly agitated. When they stopped he got out, walked a few yards ahead and got on his mobile. Whatever he was saying, he didn't look happy.

Eyeball leaned in close again. "We need to find Thomas urgently — do you know where he is, Miranda?"

"He wasn't working today so he lent me his car." Then she thought of something else. Oh bollocks, Terry would be waiting at the airport.

Eyeball seemed satisfied with the explanation, unlike the Silent Wonder. From the look on his face, he had less of a clue than she did.

After five minutes or so, Posh Bloke stormed back to the vehicle. His face was a picture — a portrait depicting 'pissed off.'

"We're to go here," he announced to the driver, passing him a note. The driver seemed unperturbed, switching on classical music as he rejoined the traffic. Posh Bloke said nothing more, but his face spoke volumes.

Chapter 27

"Anything I can get you, Thomas?"

If Sheryl leaned any further over the bar, her breasts would tumble out to greet him. "That's okay," he flustered.

Caliban's was practically empty. He felt like a teenager on a blind date, trying not to look conspicuous as he watched the minute hand inch its way round for the umpteenth time. He thought about ringing Miranda, but she'd probably be driving. He turned the mobile over and pretended he was fiddling with the casing instead.

"Wanna shoot some pool?"

"Sure," he'd never sounded less sure of anything in his life.

"Relax, Thomas. I don't bite."

No, he thought as he followed her, but you do look capable of nibbling.

"You and Miranda go *way* back, don't you?"

He smiled; that was the phrase they always used.

"So how come you two never quite got it together?"

He made a dumb face in the absence of a convincing explanation, and racked up the balls. The first two games went to Sheryl with ease — he barely got a look in. He turned the third game around and somehow snuck in the black, more by luck than judgement.

Sometimes when she looked at him, he wanted to ask her things — about Miranda, about herself; about why a girl from Brooklyn should wind up managing a bar in East London. But he let it go, same as always. For a while, he kidded himself that he was capable of winning, but Sheryl's soon shattered any lasting illusions.

"Did you grow up in a Pool Hall?"

169

"Pretty much! You're not too bad though."

He chose to take it as a compliment. As he bent down to take a shot, his mobile trilled into life — it was Karl.

"Thomas, are you free to talk? It's *urgent*."

"Sure," He felt the blood run cold up his neck. He shouldered the phone and moved to the main bar for better reception.

"Where have you been today?"

"Nowhere. I was out last night and I'm at Caliban's now."

"Tommo, your car's been picked up at Gatwick airport. There's damage to one of the windows, keys still in the ignition. Were you there?" It sounded like an accusation.

"No, I lent the car to . . . to a friend."

The line went silent. "Stay right where you are and I'll come get you."

The room seemed to spin; he grabbed at a chair and it shrieked. Sheryl rushed over and the shock on his face reflected on hers. He sat down before his legs buckled under him.

Sheryl quickly rejoined him with two whiskies. "Talk to me."

He shook his head.

"Is it Miranda?"

"They found my car . . . abandoned . . ."

Sheryl put a hand to her mouth. "I'll ring Diane."

"No!" he barked. "Let me take care of this. Karl's on his way." He downed most of the whisky in one go and felt the bile swirling inside him. Sheryl looked at him, as if she could see the turmoil inside. He realised that he didn't even know what to tell her.

They sat, huddled together like victims in a lifeboat, neither one speaking. When he wavered and felt he was on the verge of tears, he pressed into his wound, choosing pain over emotion. Sheryl's eyes were brimming; she just stared at him, silently, searching for something to cling on to.

* * *

Karl burst through the door. He pulled the chair back and hoisted Thomas to his feet. "Come on, we have to deal with this."

Sheryl looked up at him and Karl laid a consoling hand on her shoulder. She stared back at Thomas, wide-eyed, in disbelief.

"I'll be back later — I promise."

He shuffled to the car in a daze, Karl's hand at his back. Karl didn't speak until they were on the main road. "I'm sorry, Thomas; it doesn't look good. Your nearside window was broken — from the inside."

"Miranda had the car."

Karl didn't press him on it. "How much does she know?"

"Just the basics — and she knows about Christine." It felt easier to talk when Karl was asking the questions.

"What about her?"

"I went over to Christine's last night, to confront her about Bob Peterson. She warned me off, said it was my last chance."

"Oh Jesus, Thomas. You couldn't leave it alone, could you?"

In the silence that followed, Thomas's psyche began to regroup. "How did you find my car?"

Karl upped the speed. "That's not important now. I checked your office voicemail today — I always check it."

Thomas shot him a glance.

"Miranda left you a message about dealing with Butch."

He felt his mind shift a gear. Butch: Miranda was in some kind of trouble.

"The thing is, when I checked a little later, someone had deleted the message. I reckon someone doesn't want you to hear from her."

Thomas pushed his hands together, prayer fashion, and touched the index fingers to his lower lip. "You've got to tell me how to fix this."

"I'll do everything I can, Tommo, you know that. First, we're gonna pick your car up and get the window fixed. Tomorrow, when you go in to work, nothing has happened. Got it? If these bastards want anything, they'll be in touch."

Thomas nodded slowly as if punch drunk. "Did someone follow her?"

"They didn't need to. Somebody put a tracker on the car. I suggest we leave it there. So if you need to go anywhere private, you take a cab from now on."

Thomas covered his face with his hands, blotting away the tears.

"I don't know if I can do this, Karl. I don't think I'm strong enough."

"You have to be, Thomas; you've no choice."

He closed his eyes and tried to sleep, but Karl's supernatural silence only amplified his thoughts. Why would someone take Miranda? And what the hell was he going to do about it? He lashed out and punched the glove compartment, jolting himself into some sort of clarity. "Unless they'd been planning this . . ."

Karl still said nothing.

He looked around, aware he'd just said the unthinkable. Who the fuck were *they*? No, wait, he was on to something; or maybe he just wanted to believe that. He put his hands together again and rocked back and forth. "I've only done two things that would make . . ." his voice cracked. "Two things. I contacted Christine and I helped Petrov get away from Yorgi." As he said Yorgi's name, he felt sick to

171

his stomach, as if his intuition had suddenly whispered *yes*. "For Christ's sake, say something, Karl."

Silence again, apart from the pounding in his head. He looked around and saw the signs for Reading. Well, bollocks to it, he'd had enough. "Stop the car, I want to get out," he already had his fingers on the handle.

"Tommo, just relax, we'll be there soon . . ."

"I said, stop the fucking car. Now!"

Karl pulled hard left and crushed the brake, screeching the car to a lopsided halt. "Listen to me; we have to do this by the numbers. I know you're scared right now, but so far there's no indication . . ."

Thomas raised a chopping hand to interrupt.

"That's enough!" Karl roared at him.

He fell back to his seat, defeated.

"Look, Tommo, I've dealt with this shit before; I grew up with this kind of coercion. When they want something, they'll be in touch. Until then, we sit tight."

He let go of the door and the car resumed its journey, snaking its way to an industrial estate on the outskirts of Reading. As they approached a set of nondescript units, Thomas recognised his car coming off a flatbed trailer to a waiting team of overalls.

"We'll give them half an hour — come on, let's take a wee walk."

Thomas looked through the glass; it felt safe in Karl's car. Somehow, if he went outside, he'd be accepting all this. Karl walked around to the passenger door and waited.

* * *

The pungent stench of rubbish and diesel couldn't disguise the chill in the air. Thomas rubbed his arm self-consciously as they walked. Karl still wasn't saying much and as for Thomas, he didn't dare open his mouth for fear of screaming.

Karl's destination soon became clear, as the white, mud-spattered caravan gradually got closer. "You need to eat something," he insisted, pointing to the bargain garden furniture.

Thomas flopped into the chair and pressed his fingers hard against the plastic's rough edges. He looked over at the counter; exactly how did his *best buddy* fit into all this?

Karl brought over a couple of teas and enough sugar to fell a racehorse. "Get it down yer. Burgers are on the way."

Thomas didn't protest. He hugged the polystyrene cup and tried to reason out his options. He didn't know where Miranda was or who had taken her. Okay, he had suspicions about this Yorgi, but that's all they were. The sound of nearby traffic lulled him into some kind of

172

mental pause. She hadn't screamed, 'Come and get me,' on her phone message — according to Karl anyway. No, she'd mentioned 'Butch' instead: private code for dodgy dealing. And the car window was a smart move, but what did it mean? Had she'd been taken against her will, yet still somehow able to make the call?

Two plates clattered down on to the table. Thomas opened his eyes; bloody stupid — polystyrene cups, but proper plates. At first sight, the burgers churned his stomach, and then hunger took over as his instincts kicked in.

"Okay," Karl bit into his burger savagely; "you take the car to work tomorrow. And if anyone treats you differently, it's a fair bet they're involved."

"And then what?"

Karl chewed on a piece of burger that was putting up a fight. "Then we get a better idea of who we're up against."

Thomas tilted the bap away so that the fatty juices didn't run into his mouth.

"Come on, Thomas, think about it. Miranda left a message for you on your office phone. Nigh on two years, we've worked in the same office, and have you ever taken a personal call there? No, because neither she nor anyone else has your number; am I right?"

He nodded; he was already putting together a shortlist in his head of anyone he'd encountered since he'd joined the SSU. And while it didn't exactly give him hope, it gave him a focus.

The burger was sliding down nicely. He felt more grounded, more settled, confident enough to take a chance. "Karl, I need to ask you something," he kept his voice low and his gaze down. *Here goes* — "And if I don't get the truth, I'll go to the police."

It was a terrible bluff, so shit that Miranda's dad would have spotted it at a poker table. But he was desperate and it might, just might, rattle Karl a bit.

Karl took a long sip of tea. Thomas took the silence as consent to continue. "Is Miranda's disappearance connected to the missing information you're after?"

Karl inclined his head.

"Jesus, Karl!" he erupted, overbalancing the chair behind him as he stood. He was a dozen steps away when he heard Karl scrabbling behind him.

"Wait up, Tommo, please." Karl drew level and laid a hand on him, shifting his eyes about like a guilty schoolboy. "Look, I honestly don't believe Miranda is in any immediate danger. And what I'm about to tell you, well, you wouldn't have believed me before now."

"I'm listening," Thomas conceded, and carried on walking back to his car, with Karl trailing alongside.

"I don't know how well you know your European history, but the ending of World War Two was a messy one."

Thomas laughed spontaneously, surprising himself.

"Anyways, after the boys finally put their toys away and buried their copious dead, the key players decided that steps had to be taken to avoid making it a hat-trick of stupidity."

Thomas stopped in his tracks.

"Now, whatever you think of the European Union's track record, the wars have at least been kept regional. It doesn't take a rocket scientist to see that a few years down the line, a United States of Europe is a real possibility."

"And the point of this bollocks?" Thomas felt his fist tightening again.

"Some people aren't willing to wait a few years; important and influential people with something to gain, throughout Europe and beyond. That's the kind of information I've been looking for."

Chapter 28

The technician greeted Thomas and showed off her handiwork on the side window. "Good as new," she joked, as if she'd just done him a favour. He let it slide and collected his keys.

Karl tailed him back to a service station off the M25. When Thomas came out from the gents, Karl was kneeling by his car at the driver's side. He didn't seem at all embarrassed to be caught in the act.

"I was just checking the tracker on your car — it's still active. Remember, anywhere you don't want people to know about, use alternative transport."

Thomas joined him by the wheel, determined not to comment on the gizmo Karl had in his hand.

"I need you to trust me, Tommo," Karl whispered, close enough that Thomas could see the fret lines in his face. "Don't go off doing anything stupid. And don't forget, we're talking to Petrov after work tomorrow, so get a good night's sleep."

Yeah, that was Karl: the wellspring of compassion. Thomas opened the driver's door, nudging Karl out of the way. "And what do I tell Miranda's family? Her brother's already messaged me asking why she wasn't at the airport."

Karl shoved his hands in his pockets. "I'd, er, appreciate it if you stalled them for a while. A missing person report will only complicate things."

"Yeah, but for who?"

"For all of us, Tommo. We all want the same thing," he faced him. "Miranda safely home and the people who did this held accountable."

He paled at the thought of lying to Miranda's family. That was a complete no-no. But the alternative was equally unthinkable. So he made a pact with the devil. "Three days, Karl — tops. And understand this: I may not have your connections, but if word hasn't reached me that Miranda's safe . . ." he couldn't finish the sentence because that sickening feeling rushed up to gnaw at his guts again.

Thomas sat in the lay-by and stared at his mobile. The car rocked as another juggernaut thundered past. As he switched the phone on with one hand, he was wiping away tears with the other. The most precious thing he had with the Wrights was trust and now he was destroying that. For a greater good perhaps, but it was still a betrayal. As the phone dialled out, he wondered, if he could do this, then what else was he capable of?

Judas time. "Terry? Hi, yeah, sorry mate, I've been really busy at work. Ah, mate, total balls-up. Miranda had to go out of town, short notice . . ." the monologue went on, each line more forced and implausible than the last. Maybe Terry would just assume they'd had a huge fight, and Miranda had swanned off to the coast, like she'd done before. All he could do was act vague and leave Terry to join the dots for himself.

Terry seemed to accept everything he said; it was like taking a sick dog to the vet's on that long, final walk. When the deed was done, he needed a drink. And where better than Caliban's, where he could pimp the remainder of his soul by persuading Sheryl to back up his story.

He'd barely stepped through the door before Sheryl called him over. "Let's go through," she raided the scotch optic with two glasses on her way up to the office. The barmaid smiled at him; nothing seemed out of place as he passed. But he still felt like a condemned man.

Sheryl closed the door. "Have you found her?" she thrust a drink into his hand as if it was some kind of truth serum.

He shook his head.

"So what the *fuck* have you been doing since you left here?"

He let her anger run its course. She had a right; and yes, Miranda deserved better — far better than him. And something told him that when it came down to it, when Karl and all the monsters had finished playing their games, it would be left to him to pick up the pieces. So he cut the crap and told her straight; about Terry, about how he'd lied to buy Karl and him a little more time. And he pleaded with her to just let things lie for three more days.

Sheryl took a last gulp of scotch and set her glass down. Her hand trembled a little, but she raised her head to look him in the eyes, slowly and deliberately. "If anything happens to Miranda, you're a dead man."

176

He chose to take that as agreement to his request and started to reach out to her hand, then thought better of it.

"Is this to do with that Irish guy — the one you had a showdown with?"

There it was again, that uncharted territory: to trust or not to trust. "Sheryl, don't take this the wrong way, but I can't talk about it with you."

She swooped for his glass. "Hey, the only reason I'm even listening to you now is because I know that's what Miranda would want. If it was down to me I'd make a couple of phone calls and . . ." she blinked twice slowly, ". . . well, I'm sure you can figure it out."

On the drive home, he added Sheryl to his mental list of people to keep at a distance; hard to do when he'd promised to ring her mobile, twice a day — without fail.

* * *

Back at the flat, there were no messages — too much to hope for. He took the Leeds photograph of Miranda off the wall and propped it on the table. Just sitting there, he could hear her laughter merging with the sound of traffic, the scene ablaze with sunlight and the promise of happy ever after.

The oven pinged and he returned to the present with a thud. Only now did he remember that he'd put a cottage pie on. He took another shot of Southern Comfort to dry his tears.

He fired up his laptop and ate beside it, going through his usual anonymity server for untraceable web surfing. It wasn't hard to get lucky on the conspiracy sites; everything and everyone had an opinion, and by Christ they were going to share it with you. After twenty minutes of being distracted by 9/11 theories he set about his search in earnest, following trails that led to the Bilderberg Group and the New Holy Roman Empire.

After that jaunt to La-La Land he narrowed his quest to historical documents relating to Europe from 1945 onwards. What he wanted were facts, and they seemed thin on the ground. Finally, he located a 1946 speech given by Winston Churchill, in Zurich. There, in black and white, was the phrase 'United States of Europe,' along with the proposal to first set up a Council of Europe. Maybe Karl was on to something after all.

Chapter 29

The mobile went off at 6.30 am. Thomas spasmed awake from a nightmare and made a wild grab for the phone.

It was Karl, with nothing to report. He repeated the need for a veil of normality and reminded him about seeing Petrov after work: he was business-like, and, in a way, Thomas drew strength from that. If Karl was used to dealing with situations like this, then maybe everything would turn out okay.

Now wide awake, he showered and dressed, stared at Miranda's photo for longer than was healthy, and then was out the door. The seven-fifteen traffic offered little resistance — so much the better for the two-hour slog to Harwich. Perhaps someday they'd get a surveillance gig in Chingford. He noticed that the radio had been retuned — it was obvious who'd done it — and he couldn't bring himself to change it back.

Desperation was a strange thing; he'd learned that from his mum when his gran was dying. When you're trying to negotiate with the Man in the Sky, you'll offer up just about anything. So, by the time the first sign to Harwich had appeared, he'd resolved to cherish Miranda on her safe return, the way he'd always meant to. In the last chance saloon of life, he was still asking for one for the road.

* * *

Miranda liked to sleep in; that whole 'up before the dawn' insanity was Thomas's thing. Unless it was for bedroom athletics, she'd always opt for easing herself into the morning. Today was different though. It wasn't every day you found yourself the honoured guest at a bona fide cloak-and-dagger convention.

She'd turned in early the night before and now it was some God-awful time, and here she was, sat up in bed wide awake and thinking about Thomas. Okay, so they'd bullshitted her about being sent by him, but that didn't mean he wasn't in trouble. She went back over the previous day's events again, to fix them clearly in her mind. The same things stood out — the driver stashing his mobile as they got in the car and Posh Bloke losing his rag in the lay-by. And repetitive questions about not much in particular. Conclusion: either something was wrong or they were really shit at this. Or both.

The night before, she'd asked how long her stay was likely to be and all she'd got back was a few nervous glances. She smirked now as she pressed her back against the pillows — maybe the answer was classified. She'd get some sense out of them today. The woman, Eyeball, seemed like the best candidate for new friend.

She slithered out of bed and threw on an oversized dressing gown — blue towelling, not very chic. No harm in having an early morning wander, maybe watch a little satellite TV. She turned the door handle with infinite care — no sense in disturbing anyone else. As soon as the door clicked she heard scuffling in the corridor and caught the last moment of Eyeball launching from a chair.

"Good morning," Miranda opted for friendliness first. Eyeball — and that eye certainly shone today — nodded blearily; she looked as if she had spent the entire night on the chair. That was a worry. Miranda ambled over, smiling like she was back on a Bermuda fashion shoot, and made a mental note to check if the windows were locked.

"Would you like some breakfast?" Eyeball said it like she meant it.

"That'd be great," Miranda retraced her way to the kitchen.

Eyeball tagged along like the less attractive one on a double date. Miranda filled the kettle and tried the thing that usually worked on men — Thomas being a rare exception: keep them focused on one topic then switch channel suddenly to get a straight answer.

"If I'm staying tonight I'll need more clothes . . ." she stopped there, hoping Eyeball would suggest that she pop home to fill up a suitcase or an overnight bag. No dice.

Instead, Eyeball asked for her sizes and promised fresh clothes, later that morning. They sat together at the breakfast bar, drinking tea and eating toast, like the new girls at boarding school. Eyeball must have been bottom of the pile, she reasoned. Because, let's face it, you don't get the top brass strapping their arse to a chair for the night.

A till receipt was still on the work surface — Miranda clocked yesterday's date before Eyeball tidied it away. *Okay then, back to Project Best Friend.* "Look, I feel really bad about your eye, er . . ."

Eyeball glanced at the open door and replied, "It's Alice."

Alice Eyeball, it was then. "Alice, I don't suppose there's a gym around here? I could do with working off last night's curry."

A bloody takeaway — hardly James Bond. Useful though, Miranda recalled, as Alice rinsed the cups. The round-trip for the pick-up was about forty-five minutes so they couldn't be that far from civilisation. The trouble with country lanes was that they all looked the same. With all the excitement the previous day, after leaving the M25 the rest was a bit of a blur. Unless they'd dropped something in her curry.

She told Alice that she ran a pub, which seemed to rattle her a bit. Probably because it meant another closely supervised phone call. She smiled again, remembering the one from last night. Ringing home was a tricky one. A calculated risk as Mum could have blown it, but she was brilliant.

'Okay Miranda, thanks for phoning. Did you want Butch taken care of while you're away, or is Thomas looking after him?' Even the way she had told Miranda: 'Take care and I'll see you soon.' It still sent a shiver of delight up and down her spine. Mum was on the case.

* * *

Thomas looked out across Harwich and tried to concentrate. Just him and the gulls, not so different from the day Bob Peterson appeared. What if he'd been less attentive that day? What if the shooting and Peterson had been all someone else's problem — Karl's, for instance? What if . . . and then a flashbulb went off in his brain, illuminating what was already there.

The door opened downstairs, shortly followed by the strains of 'When Irish Eyes Are Smiling.' Karl huffed and puffed up the stairs, depositing his cases on a table with his usual lack of care. "Grab hold of these sandwiches while I do a sweep of the premises."

Thomas watched as Karl went to work, checking for other people's devices: surveillance on the surveillers. Karl worked quickly and methodically around Thomas, as he stood in the centre of the room, sandwiches in hand. Finally, Karl pronounced, "Clear!" with a dramatic flourish.

The morning soon filled up, with tracking shots of Her Majesty's Customs and Excise at work in a busy British port. Thomas even fitted in a couple of brooding skylines. But whenever he stole a glance at his companion, Karl was looking right at him.

"It's alright, I'm not about to crumble into pieces." *Not in front of you, anyway.*

"I know that, Tommo. No news, I take it?"

"Shouldn't that be my line?"

Karl shrugged with just his face. "Investigations are continuing. And just so you know, as soon as we get what we want from Petrov, we're shipping the family far away."

Like that was supposed to make him feel any better? Before Thomas could respond, the walkie-talkie crackled.

Karl made a face approximating 'intrigued' and nodded to whatever was being said. "Thanks Ann, out."

Thomas furrowed his brow and Karl was immediately on the defensive. "What? Can't I extend a little professional courtesy to my esteemed colleague?"

Thomas shook his head in mock disgust. Clearly, somewhere along the line, they'd had words and put their childish spat to rest.

"Anyways, she was letting us know that Christine will be on-site shortly." Karl sat bolt upright, like he'd been stung in the arse. "Hey, shift; get your lens on the staff compound. Let's see if she so much as twitches at your car."

Brilliant. He and Karl took up position, two cats after the same canary. Christine Gerrard's Mercedes glided up to the compound gate. She flashed her ID at the attendant — who looked like he couldn't give a shit — and veered left where there were still spaces. Thomas's heart was racing; unless she was planning to vault the fence she'd have to walk back past his car. If she even coughed beside his replacement window he'd have his first genuine lead.

Come on, come on; out you get. Any second now . . . nearing the front of the car . . . He held his breath and pushed hard against the viewfinder, swallowing Christine's face. She had a faraway look about her, as if she'd rather be somewhere else. Closer . . . and . . . *nothing.* The moment passed. She crossed the bonnet and walked beyond Karl's shit-heap of a car without blinking an eyelid.

"What do you think?" Karl was still tracking her.

"I don't think she faked that."

"Well," Karl looked up with a wry grin on his face; "You'd know more about that than me. Okay, she's eliminated herself from our inquiries — for now."

Thomas smiled back, a small crumb for Karl's ingenuity. He liked the sound of 'our inquiries'; it made him feel less alone.

Christine headed straight for their block. Karl made a half-hearted attempt to tidy away the remnants of breakfast and his newspaper, but as soon as he heard the door downstairs he busied himself with his camera.

She clip-clopped up the steps, clearing her throat by the doorway. Thomas turned, catching Karl out the corner of his eye following suit.

"Gentlemen, we're downscaling our presence here — by two."

Thomas looked over at Karl. Was downscaling even a real word?

Christine crossed the threshold. "Karl, why don't you take a break — I'd like a private word with Thomas."

Karl nodded gladly, as if he'd had the same idea himself. "I'll go over to see Ann Crossley — call me there when you're done," he rattled a walkie-talkie.

* * *

Christine waited until they were alone. "After our last conversation, I thought we'd better have the next one face-to-face."

Uh-oh. Suddenly she reminded him of her mother doing the 'And what are your intentions towards our daughter?' routine.

"I don't know why you're so fixated with Bob, and not that it's any of your business, but yes, we are seeing each other on a casual basis."

Seeing *to* each other, more like. But he wasn't going to rise to the bait this time. Instead, he separated his Bermuda key ring methodically, detached the cover and applied it to his laptop's USB port. Christine stood beside him while the software whirled and opened the folder.

"Bob Peterson was here on the day of the shooting," he clicked on a series of folders and opened the one named Uncle Bob. As if to emphasise the obvious, he'd superimposed a black frame over Peterson's four-by-four.

Christine stared at the screen for maybe a minute. Thomas handed her the gift of silence. She looked shaken. And if he were honest, he was savouring every second.

"Has Bob seen this?"

Thomas opened up the file marked *Uncle Bob V2.0*. "No, I filed this version with my report. But he probably realises I saw him there," he paused, hoping that if he gave her enough space, she'd say something about Miranda or his car; a forlorn hope.

"Where is this going, Thomas? I mean, what's brought this on?"

He stood up; they were almost toe-to-toe. "I have a friend who's in trouble." He stopped and looked into her eyes. "I think it's connected with Bob."

Her demeanour changed; she came over all Florence Nightingale and pressed his hand tenderly. "Bob's okay, really."

"Come on, Christine, he lied about being at the docks — in front of all of us."

"Well . . ." she seemed to struggle for logic, "he stayed with me that week."

"Yeah, but you're not in the pictures. And the only day Bob turns up on site — unannounced — happens to be the same day someone is shot."

"You're surely not suggesting Bob was behind that?"

He pushed his hand up a little and felt hers firm against it. "No, Bob wasn't behind it. I think I know who's involved. But I don't believe in coincidences."

Christine stalled; it was as if a cloud of doubt had settled on her face. He imagined her asking herself the same question he had: was Bob the witness or the lookout?

"What kind of trouble — it's not Karl is it?"

"No, it's not Karl. But I can't say any more — I don't know who I can trust."

"Hey," Christine squeezed his fingers, "you know you can trust me!" She seemed to gaze at him in a way that she hadn't done for a long time. "It's a woman, isn't it?"

Bollocks. "Chrissie, can you just leave it please?" He felt tears welling up and withdrew to the window, coughing to stop his voice from cracking.

She took the hint. "Alright, I'd better be going, Thomas. If you want to talk, you know where to find me. I promise I won't say anything to Bob."

He kept his back towards her, staying that way until he heard the door close. As soon as he composed himself, he rang Sheryl. "Hi," he kept the tone sombre; "no, nothing yet, but I'm a little closer to figuring out what's going on. I'll call you this evening. And Sheryl, thanks — you know."

Karl sauntered back within minutes of the call. Anyone would think he'd been watching Thomas through binoculars. "So, we're leaving Harwich soon," Karl was trying his best to be subtle. "What did Christine drop by for?"

Thomas parked himself on a stool. "I called her at home."

Karl's face was blanker than usual.

"I was pissed off with you and myself, after our discussion in the hotel bar. So I took it out on Christine. I rang up and slated Bob Peterson, reminded her that he was married. Less than bright; I think he was in the flat at the time."

"You don't think Peterson is anything to do with . . ."

"Miranda? No, and I'm pretty sure Christine's clean. She came here to smooth the waters. And if I really thought Bob was responsible, I wouldn't be standing here now."

Karl stated the obvious. "Not Christine or Uncle Bob — the list grows shorter."

"Maybe Petrov will have some suggestions when we speak to him."

Karl feigned disinterest, but his body language screamed 'fuck off.'

* * *

At four o'clock on the dot, Karl was packing his equipment away, having got Ann Crossley to cover for them. "Here's how we play this," Karl sounded masterful. "First we drive back to your gaff because that's where you're supposed to be. Then you transfer to my car and we go talk to Petrov."

Thomas brightened a little. He was in the game, though God knows what they expected him to get from Petrov. Still, anything was better than sitting in that flat alone.

He parked down by Lloyd Park, on the opposite side of the road, to avoid scraping bird shit off the roof later on. He moved his stuff into Karl's car — quicker than taking it into the flat.

Karl welcomed him into the dry passenger seat, inviting him to check out the glove compartment. No guns this time but there was a choice of albums. Thomas opted for something reflective — ACDC's 'Let There Be Rock,' which Karl seemed to appreciate.

Karl swung out to the North Circular, picking up the A10 north.

"What do you want me to say to Petrov?" Cut to the chase; always the best way of dealing with Karl. Even if it meant shouting over 'Whole Lotta Rosie' as it fried the speakers.

"There's no subterfuge here," Karl notched the volume down. "We need to know everything about Yorgi; where the red car was before Harwich, past haunts, anything."

Thomas nodded and twisted the volume back up. What *he* really wanted to know was whether Yorgi was capable of kidnapping Miranda. That question made him shudder.

Chapter 30

Thomas zoned out for the rest of the journey; Karl left him to it. Somewhere, between drifting off and Karl nudging him awake, he remembered Sir Peter Carroll's very first pep talk about loyalty and confidentiality.

"We're here," Karl sounded apologetic.

Thomas soon saw why. It was one of the ugliest buildings he'd ever laid eyes on. The sign at the front — next to 'cars parked illegally will be clamped' — read 'Conference Facilities.' It all looked like a very bad joke.

"It's a converted telephone exchange."

"Shame they never converted the outside — it looks like a prison."

Karl nodded. "Or a fortress."

"And Petrov's family have been living here?"

Karl waved a scolding finger. "Uh-uh. More than you need to know."

Thomas tried not to stare at the CCTV cameras. They reminded him too much of being at Caliban's.

Teresa met them at the front steps. Thomas took it as read that she already knew all about Miranda; he wasn't about to confide in her in any case. They threaded past a series of doors to one with a sign that read 'occupied.' She gestured to Thomas to go in first.

Petrov leapt up from his chair, with a look of rapture. Alexandra was there at his side and Lukas was in the corner, playing with some toys on a rug. It looked like a Social Services training film. "Tomas! It is so good to see you!"

They shook hands enthusiastically; Alexandra kissed him on the cheek. All hail the conquering hero. Teresa and the quiet one on her side of the desk seemed to relax.

"You are well, yes?"

There was a question. He swallowed and let out a breath. Then replied, "Yes, I am well," with all the enthusiasm he could conjure.

They all sat down and the silent wonder — Thomas labelled him the Handler — took orders for drinks and left the room. Teresa started recording, assuring Petrov and Alexandra that they were assisting of their own free will and were not obliged to answer. Nonetheless, it was clear where this was going; they may as well have had a tick list.

How did Yorgi contact them? Why did he contact them? What were they doing in Europe? Where did they meet him? Where was he likely to be now? Teresa's formidable line of questioning didn't take long to put Petrov on edge. Several times he shot glances at Thomas, a searching look as if to say, 'Why are you allowing this?'

By the time they reached a comfort break — Teresa did a neat line in irony — Thomas had just about reached the end of his tether. Petrov was in danger of clamming up and that didn't suit his needs at all.

The tape was switched off; he had nothing to lose. He put his mug down and leaned across the table. "How dangerous is Yorgi?"

Teresa made a mad scramble for the 'on' button and glared at him. Tough shit.

"Very dangerous. Tomas, I tell you the truth; Yorgi fears *nothing*." Petrov sat back a little, as if to consider his own words. "Well, except snakes. One time I saw him scream at the sight of a snake on the farm and when I laughed, he nearly broke my arm."

Thomas wasn't sure how you could nearly break an arm, but then he recalled that he'd nearly been shot. Karl nudged him to carry on.

"Have you ever met anyone with Yorgi? Or maybe you spoke to them on the phone?" He almost said 'at the house' then he remembered that they didn't have a house any more

Petrov nodded. "On the phone; maybe twice. An older man — British, not foreign."

"What kind of British?" Karl pitched in. "Like me?" He sounded like he was trying to prove his own innocence.

Alexandra searched the ceiling for recall. "He was English, well-spoken; and he called from a mobile."

Thomas smiled at her. Less use than nothing, but it was a step in the right direction. "Why would Yorgi still want you — want to see you, I mean? You told me before, that you sometimes didn't hear from him for months."

Petrov and Alexandra shared a none-too-subtle glance and neither responded.

Thomas took a sip of tea, felt the warm liquid swirl around his mouth yet still leave it parched. He knew he would have to be quick and concise before they bundled him out of the room. He felt a cold numbness at the base of his skull, spreading down his body. There was only one question he was interested in now.

He turned his head away slightly, certain that if Karl saw his face clearly he'd spot something was amiss. He cleared his throat and took in a great gulp of air. "I think Yorgi may be holding a hostage, someone important to me . . ."

Alexandra covered her face. Petrov gaped at him, and Thomas remembered showing them Miranda's photo at the house.

"No!" Alexandra called aloud and little Lukas stopped to look up at her.

Karl leaned his arm across Thomas's chest, as if that would somehow stop him speaking. Petrov and Alexandra launched into an argument, in a language Thomas didn't understand. Now Alexandra was crying, shrieking at Petrov who kept waving his arms to shush her. Thomas flitted from Petrov to Alexandra, waiting for them to revert to English. When they did, he wished they hadn't.

Petrov made a last comment in his native tongue and wiped a tear from his face with a handkerchief. His face was red and sweaty. "Yorgi would not take hostages. I am sorry — if Yorgi took your friend, she is dead."

Thomas felt his whole body convulsing; there were voices around him, but they all blended into one chaotic chorus. His breathing went into overdrive. He pushed against the table and propelled himself up, lunging for the door. His stomach congealed as he ran along the corridor, snaking back to the main door. He only just made it outside when the wave of nausea and abject terror hit him, like a force ten gale; he retched and retched, until his stomach seared, until the tears were dripping off his face.

When he was done, he staggered away from the pool of vomit and sank to his knees, closing his eyes against the world. He'd never felt so alone, his life so utterly devoid of meaning. He'd fucked up the one beautiful thing in his life, and he'd lost her.

It was futile, but the next thing he decided to do, as he choked back the despair, was to send a text to Miranda's mobile. Maybe her killer would read it, maybe no one ever would; but his last act to her would be one of contrition.

He fumbled the security code on his mobile first time and had to try again. As the screen lit up the text icon appeared. He gulped again and wiped the blur from his eyes. Was this the final text they'd let her send, *made* her send? Oh God, anything but that. His hand trembled as he thumbed the button — he had a voicemail.

His first instinct was to switch the phone off, shield himself from any more pain. But that was just cowardice. He owed her more than that, so much more. He input the code with a cold resolve and braced himself for the worst.

"Thomas, it's Diane. Miranda called me earlier about Butch."

He dropped the mobile. Miranda had phoned today — she was still alive! It couldn't have been Yorgi. He started laughing — at himself, at the absurdity of a second chance, at all the stuff his mother used to tell him as a child about God's mercy. He fingered his neck where the crucifix used to be and felt the sweat, sodden against his armpit. She was alive; Lord have mercy, Christ have mercy.

He texted Diane straight back, in no fit state to speak to her: *I can't talk now — I'll come straight over.* It was weak, but it was honest. He glanced at the mud and puke and snot all down himself — Diane would understand.

His mind was racing as he walked back. Whoever had taken Miranda was the enemy — and enemies had to be dealt with. It may not have been Yorgi who did this, but it had to be connected with him.

Karl opened the door; Thomas pushed past him. He felt like a man redeemed — a man on a mission. He returned to the interview room and shoved the door. Everyone turned; Petrov stared up at him as if he'd never expected to see him again.

Thomas stood over the table and faced them down, slamming his palms against the wood. "I'm only going to ask you this once — what does Yorgi still want with you?"

Petrov shrank back. "He gave me a package to look after; I should have left it for him at the house."

Chairs scraped behind him, but Thomas didn't react. He glared at Petrov as if he could incinerate him by force of will. And Petrov evaporated. "It is in my case. I never meant to keep it. I thought it would be something to bargain with, if we needed such a thing."

Thomas gazed around the room with a look of contempt. It seemed like everyone was holding out on him. As he made for the door, Karl stood aside.

"Tommo, I'm so sorry; I didn't know . . ."

"I need your car — now."

As he pulled into the Wrights' drive, the first thing Thomas noticed was the lack of cars. The doorbell only managed three chords before Diane was standing there.

"Jesus, Thomas, you look like shit."

"Where is everyone?" he was starting to feel mildly freaked.

"I sent them out for a while; said I wanted time to myself. By my reckoning, you've got a couple of hours to get your story straight, right after you tell me what's *really* going on."

She walked off, letting the door swing in; he followed her inside. "Let's cut the bullshit, Thomas," Diane was already pouring herself something strong. "I know all about Butch and your little code — Miranda told me what happened a long time ago."

He turned a shade of scarlet.

"Something's up — I get that. So where's my daughter and what's going on?" Diane pushed a drink across the table to him.

The sudden heat in his stomach brought him to his senses. He told her what he knew, which wasn't much. It was work related — his work — 100% personal. And he was going to sort it. He'd made another decision on the way over. Fuck Karl and his cloak-and-dagger antics; he would go and see Sir Peter Carroll, do things properly through official channels.

She took it surprisingly well, listened attentively until he'd finished then got up to go to the kitchen. He heard a kettle switch and followed her in.

"Look Diane, I never meant for this to happen . . ."

She span round and slapped him hard across the face, sending him flying. "Don't you *dare* make excuses to me; you should have come to us at the beginning. We're your family, Thomas — don't you ever forget that. Now, you better take care of this and deliver Miranda back to me, or we will deal with them and you."

He got up from the floor and tried to regain some dignity; he didn't know whether to stay or go. Diane had frozen him out; the way she looked at him, he was nothing to her. That was even worse than the shame. "You know where the door is."

He wanted to apologise again, to extract an ounce of forgiveness from her. But who was he kidding, he couldn't forgive himself so why should she? He got to the front door and went to open it, but she blocked him with her arm.

"If anyone has threatened her or hurt her, they're never going to hurt anyone again. I want your word — swear it."

He felt his jaw harden. "You have my word." As the door slammed behind him he thought, just for a second, that he heard her sobbing.

189

Chapter 31

Thomas drove back to the flat and tried to pacify himself in front of the TV. Any relief about Miranda was tempered with an aching sense of loss, of still not knowing where she was. Added to that, Petrov had lied to him — a man he'd put himself on the line for. And for all Karl's efforts, if Yorgi was holding Miranda, well, Karl was just as powerless and clueless as he was. It all added up to a very poor starting point. He couldn't settle, roaming the channels, wondering whether Karl would bring any more super-duper painkillers when he collected his car. And speaking of killers, was that *his* destiny now?

Karl turned up an hour or so later. They sat in Thomas's flat, the TV turned low in the background, not achieving a great deal. He put Karl straight about Diane's phone message, early on — no point torturing the poor guy. But Karl had little to share in return.

"Honest to God, Tommo, we're doing our utmost." Which was like saying: 'A' for effort, 'F' for achievement.

Thomas sat back in the armchair. Karl was sitting pretty much where Miranda had been, last time at the flat. "Did you get the package from Petrov?"

Karl shifted on the cushion. "Yeah, it's a sealed DSB — can you believe that? Teresa's speaking to her people tomorrow about what we do with it."

That hurt. *Yeah, no rush or anything.* He decided to leap the ravine. "Only you and Christine knew I wasn't working when Miranda was taken — from my car."

Karl banged his cup on the table. "Now wait a minute . . ."

Thomas held up a hand. "So they *can't* have been after Miranda. I mean, why *then*, the day after we spirit Petrov and his family away? And if they'd had the tracker on my car beforehand, they could have picked me up *with* Petrov at his home."

Karl calmed down. "I see your logic. Then the tracker must have been put on your car at the hotel or later on. But who else, other than Yorgi, would be interested enough in Petrov to want to get hold of you?"

"Dunno. Someone who's interested in Yorgi? Or working with him? It's the same thing from our perspective. Maybe *our* was stretching things a bit, but he was softening Karl up for the biggie. "Miranda's missing and she's still at risk. It seems to me that Petrov and the DSB are our best leads. I want the DSB."

Karl's eyes widened. "And just what are you intending to do with it?"

"I'll take it to Sir Peter Carroll. He has connections — MI5, Army Intelligence; I don't care who. I just want Miranda back. There could be something in that DSB that leads to Yorgi." The thoughts came thick and fast now; "Perhaps it's Yorgi they want and they think I can give him to them."

Karl scratched his teeth on a knuckle. "What you're asking — the DSB . . . it's not something . . . it's not my decision. I can speak to Teresa later, but even then . . ."

Thomas looked at Karl, really looked at him. Did he already know what was in the DSB? Had Karl been playing him for a fool?"

"Well, I'm going to see Sir Peter tomorrow, with or without the DSB."

"Look, I understand where you're coming from, Tommo. You do what you need to," Karl held up his hands. "I just wouldn't want you to be disappointed if your 'special relationship' with our glorious leader isn't as special as you think it is." He checked his watch. "Look, you've had a hell of a day so I'm going to piss off and give you some breathing space."

Thomas tossed Karl his car keys.

"All I'm saying is: don't be too hasty. I'll talk to Teresa and get back to you."

* * *

"Hi Sheryl," Thomas kept his tone measured, leaving little space for her to interject. He focused on the things that he wanted her to know, starting with the biggest and the best. "Miranda called home today; no, Diane told me. Yeah, it's great news. I'm seeing someone official tomorrow . . . yeah, straight after, I promise." It was gone one when he finally mustered the energy to go to bed.

He put the call in to Sir Peter's office at seven thirty next morning; he'd been thinking about it since six. In the intervening time, he'd come up with nothing by way of a story, so he'd stuck with the need to see him urgently. He'd still head over to Harwich and play the waiting game.

When he got on site, Karl wasn't there. Ann Crossley was none the wiser on his movements. At ten thirty, Thomas rang him on his mobile, but it was out of use. Christine was the next logical choice; she had mixed news.

"Karl has been assigned elsewhere and is subject to a lockdown. Sir Peter Carroll has asked me to pass on an open invitation to Whitehall." She sounded bemused.

Thomas had once been subject to a lockdown. Standard procedure on some assignments — all contact with the rest of the team or anyone else expressly forbidden. It was the closest they ever came to secret squirreling.

He weighed up the situation. An open invitation was a definite plus; unusual too, given Sir Peter's fondness for protocol. What about Karl? True, Christine had warned them that the job was coming to an end — bloody suspicious timing though. His own lockdown had been a three-day stint with the Serious Fraud Office, but lockdowns of just a day had been known; all the more reason to follow things up with Sir Peter in the meantime.

* * *

The sun glanced off Main Building, illuminating it against a photogenic blue sky. In other circumstances, he might have stopped to admire it. Not today though.

After reporting at reception, he gave his details and took a seat. He tried playing it out in his head, sifting the facts to choose what he wanted to share. Someone was missing and somehow he'd got mixed up in helping the brother of . . . He backtracked; how could he explain knowing that Yorgi was a gunman? He was still juggling the facts when he noticed someone standing over him.

"I'll take you up now."

No hello, no introductions; this was evidently the kind of person who smiled on the inside, if at all. There was no eye contact in the lift; just the definite sense that this guy thought Thomas was the shit on his shiny boots. Another warm welcome extended to Floater colleagues in the Surveillance Support Unit.

As the lift door opened, he felt a rush of excitement. This was the big step that would bring Miranda home. He should have done this when it first all kicked off. And besides, he'd already passed Sir Peter's loyalty test; this was like repaying his trust.

The escort left him at the door. He knocked confidently. Sir Peter opened the door and welcomed him in. "Thomas, your message sounded important. I've cleared my appointments for the next hour or so."

Brilliant. Just what the doctor ordered.

"It's a little early for a drink — I thought perhaps a coffee?"

Thomas smiled as he sat down. Now for the tricky part, keeping Karl and Teresa out of it. Bob Peterson was the logical fall guy, by process of elimination. That and the fact that Thomas thought he was a snake.

Anyhow, big breath and straight in at the deep end. "I'm in trouble, sir. A friend of mine has disappeared and I think it's connected with something I saw." He'd barely got two sentences out when there was a rap on the door. He almost jumped out of his chair.

"It's just the coffees. Come in!" Sir Peter boomed.

Once he had a cup in his hand, Thomas resumed his story — the edited version. Harwich — Bob Peterson — the red car — Petrov — Yorgi — his missing friend. There were gaps wide enough to park a bus in. He didn't explain how he'd tracked Petrov down or why he'd kept it all to himself. But the old man was still listening, which was a good sign.

Sir Peter had stopped making notes, right at the point where Miranda went missing. He put a spoon in his cup and stirred it slowly, rhythmically tapping the cup three times. Then he put the spoon down in a precise fashion and laced his fingers together, like some mafia don. He seemed to grow in stature. "Now then, Thomas, why don't you tell me *all* about it?" A self-satisfied leer lit up his face like a Halloween pumpkin.

Oh fuck. Thomas tried to quell the trembling in his hand as he put his cup down. He understood now, and felt sick at his own stupidity. Behind the desk, even Winston Churchill seemed to be smirking at him: *checkmate*. Then the penny really dropped — the Churchill speech, off the net, the 'United States of Europe' speech from 1946. Jesus, short of taking an ad out in the papers, the clue had been in the painting all the time.

Sir Peter puffed up his chest and cleared his throat. "Let me be frank, Thomas. I'm extremely impressed by your resourcefulness and I regret the recent turn of events. But I believe I can bring about a mutually satisfactory conclusion. Will you let me help you?"

Thomas's first instinct was to hurl the bastard through the window and watch him crash to the concrete below. But this was the real world and he was all out of options. "What do you want?"

"Supposing Petrov had something that didn't belong to him; something we could exchange for Miranda."

Thomas froze. He hadn't mentioned Miranda by name.

"Can you get it, Thomas?" the voice was insistent.

He closed his eyes and drew breath. "I'll talk with Petrov."

193

"I'm sure you'll be very persuasive. Shall we say twenty-four hours? And Thomas, it would be better for *everyone* if the package remained unopened," Sir Peter slid out a desk drawer and retrieved an A4 Civil Service envelope. He passed it across, but before Thomas could break the seal, Sir Peter brought the meeting to a close. "I think that's all we have to say to each other at this juncture. Goodbye Thomas — twenty-four hours. It's best if we resolve this without Yorgi's involvement."

He had to use the chair to stand. He felt Sir Peter watching him as he staggered for the door. A guard was waiting in the corridor. Thomas shuffled along behind him in a daze, brown envelope in hand like hospital bad news. At the lifts, he felt his insides shatter. "I need the gents."

The guard stood outside the main door, like a bouncer. What did the guy think he was going to do, swim down the u-bend to freedom? He leaned against the sink and ran the tap to try and drown out the hissing in his head. A spasm brought up a clump of brown-stained sick. It reeked of coffee and fear. He let it slide down the plughole then splashed some cold water over this face. He left the tap running and dried his hands.

And now for the envelope. It was sealed tight; not last minute, and still wet with spit, but something planned in advance. Inside were photographs. The top one was a herd of people, slightly blurred, moving away from the camera. A sign on the wall settled the mystery: Walthamstow Central. He looked more carefully at the centre of the picture; and there he was, merging into the crowd.

He flicked through the other photographs frantically, half expecting the worst. He wasn't disappointed; there was Pickering — his parents' house, Pat and the kids. Those bastards had everything on film. The last shot was the final dagger through the heart. A telephoto lens of him and Ajit, sat in a car by the police station. It had been a rat trap from start to finish.

He sneered at his reflection and shook his head. His eyes were red from lack of sleep and the tears he was holding back. He slipped the photos back into the envelope, turned off the tap and opened the door.

* * *

Back on the street, everything seemed larger than life; everything except him. As he looked over his shoulder, Main Building soared above him, all-powerful, impregnable. On impulse, he opened his mobile to try Karl again. Did he dare? It would be a disciplinary offence if he got through — both for him and Karl. He was completely screwed.

He walked over to the park and sat down on a bench, the open phone still in his hand like a weapon. They might be watching him, even now. He hunched forward, pretended to play with the buttons and glanced around. The only people nearby were a woman with a baby in a stroller and two college kids playing with a Frisbee. The stroller could be a disguise for a directional microphone and a camera, with the students waiting for him to move. *Yeah, right. And maybe the Frisbee was a hover camera.*

He cradled his head and leaned forward, tasting bile. Through the chink of light between his fingers, he watched people ignoring him. He needed coffee; he had a lot of thinking to do.

The espresso he bought from the coffee stand in the park didn't taste so great, but its effects were undiminished; such were the restorative powers of premium caffeine. He needed a plan, fast. He sipped rhythmically and went through a list in his head.

Point 1: Sir Peter Carroll had said they'd prefer that the package wasn't opened. So who had the package now? Answer: Teresa. But he could hardly ring up every Intelligence office and ask if a Teresa worked there. But . . . he did know where she'd been — he could go back to the building where they'd interrogated Petrov. Someone there must be able to get hold of her. He took a bite of the muffin as a reward and held the sugary stodge in his mouth until it melted.

Point 2: Get some time off work. He couldn't be in two places at once. Christine would sign it off, and if she took issue with it he could always refer her to Sir Peter. He texted her to say he was coming in for a chat when he picked up his car. She responded immediately that she'd wait in for him.

By the time he got to the park gate he breathed a little easier. At least he knew what his next steps were. One glance back told him that Buggy Woman and the Frisbee Kids were either holding position fantastically well or they were just innocent civilians. If there was such a thing anymore.

Chapter 32

Thomas felt safe among the crowds — buoyant amid a sea of tourists, shift-workers and pickpockets. True, the mass of CCTV cameras threw him a little if he thought about it too much, but he'd already reached his paranoia limit for the day.

The next train was three minutes away so he grabbed a bench and tried to lose himself in the giant poster opposite. A suspiciously attractive couple beamed down on him, extolling the virtues of some European bank he'd never heard of. 'Small savings and big decisions,' they smiled. He mused on that; it was the big decisions that everyone was afraid of.

The open plan office at Liverpool Street was deserted; no surprise, as it was the middle of the day. He'd harboured the tiniest of hopes that Karl would be around, but a lockdown meant restrictions on contact, movement and behaviour.

Christine's light was on and the door open, so he didn't think twice about approaching. Inside, she and Bob were reading through files. They seemed to be looking for something.

Thomas quickly stuffed the envelope of photographs inside his jacket and zipped it tight. He rapped on the door. Bob looked up, gave him a half nod of recognition and returned to his reading. Christine did the talking. "Hello Thomas, please come in. Bob and I are just finishing up."

Of course you are, he thought. He said nothing, watching from the door as they continued their synchronised folder stacking. Then he grabbed a seat in one corner, a good vantage point to see who was the most unsettled.

Eventually, they took the hint and gave up on their search. Bob Peterson didn't look happy about it though, which pleased Thomas no end.

"Back in a mo," Christine explained with a grin, "call of nature."

It was a little informal for Thomas's liking. And judging by the look on Peterson's face, he felt the same way. Thomas looked him over, trying not to appear like the aggrieved ex.

"So," Bob glanced at the top folder on the pile, "how's Harwich?"

That was all it took. The red mist that Karl used to joke about became a sunburst. Thomas leapt the distance between them, grabbed Peterson by the lapels and slammed him up against the door. A mountain of folders seemed to scurry for cover.

"Fuck Harwich!" Thomas snarled, through a haze of rage. "When all this is over, I'm coming back for you."

"What the hell is wrong with you?" it took Peterson a moment to take it in. He started thrashing about, but Thomas had him pinned.

It had been pure instinct, nothing more, and already he was wondering what was wrong with him. Peterson struggled a second time then, before Thomas even realised it was coming, his fist blasted through his arms with an upper cut. Thomas took it on the jaw and reeled backwards, dragging Peterson with him to the floor, only twisting at the last moment to try and cushion his fall.

Peterson wasn't going down without a fight. And there was a score to be settled. Juvenile? Definitely, but Thomas felt that Uncle Bob had it coming on two counts: one, playing away with Christine — no doubt in his mind at all now — and two, Peterson was somehow the starting point of all his troubles.

* * *

Christine opened the door to find the two of them locked in combat. The main punches had already been traded and now it was about who could rough who up the most. At first, she didn't speak. Thomas was glad of that. It might have distracted him from his main intention of hammering the shit out of Peterson.

"That's enough!" she slammed the door. Then she pointed to two chairs in either corner of the room and they both complied.

Thomas looked first at Peterson and then at the mess. And he couldn't help smiling. He'd finally fulfilled a personal ambition and landed some punches on Peterson, even if he had taken a few knocks himself. His only regret was that he hadn't drawn blood; maybe next time he'd staple Bob's ear.

For a while there was silence. Christine bent down to retrieve some of the paperwork. She looked pained, which pained Thomas. Just because Peterson was an arsehole, it was no reason for her to suffer.

He stood up; in all the excitement he'd almost forgotten what he came there for. "I need some compassionate leave — I'll be on the mobile." He spoke directly to Christine, ignoring Peterson altogether.

Christine looked down at the floor and waved him away like he was too much to bear. He straightened his jacket as he walked out, patting the envelope as he closed the door behind him. He called Diane on his way out of the building.

"It's Thomas. I'm off work now . . . indefinitely, until this is sorted out. Nah, I'll tell you face to face when I have more info."

"That's good news, Thomas, because you're going to be busy."

* * *

He drove out beyond the North Circular, ditching the car at Hatch End. Best to assume the tracker was still working, like Karl said. He jumped a cab at the station — finding the old Telephone Exchange wasn't difficult; there couldn't be too many buildings that ugly.

"Wait here," he waved a £20 note under the cabbie's nose.

The car park was empty; gates locked. Nothing fancy, no barbed wire or anything to excite the interest of your average industrial burglar. He looked back at the cab, figured the driver was engrossed in his horses — or the £20 — and launched himself over.

The place seemed deserted; even the conference centre sign was gone. A quick scout around the perimeter confirmed that the good guys — if that's who they'd been — had left without a trace. Bollocks.

The cabbie didn't seem surprised to see him back so quickly. He folded his paper away and unlocked the passenger doors. Thomas was still catching his breath as he tumbled back on to the seat. "Any idea who owns this place?"

"No, guvnor, it's been shut for ages. We used to get quite a bit of trade there; you know, corporate knobs with their laptops and that. You, er, interested in buying it or something?"

A chink of light in an otherwise shit day. "Well, not me," Thomas went into bullshit mode. "A mate of mine is looking for office space round here. He's small time with big ideas." He raised his eyes in mock disdain.

"As you'll likely be a big tipper, I'll tell you who the estate agent is when we get to the station."

Cheeky bastard. He checked his watch; still time to ring them. As soon as the driver had sodded off at the station to spend his big tip, Thomas dialled from a super-duper phone box. Funny how things changed; he almost missed the smell of piss and sweat. He leaned against the metal back-plate and sighed. He and Miranda had once shared a knee trembler in a phone box, after missing the night bus, one stormy night in Balham. No chance of anyone repeating that here unless they enjoyed the open air.

"Yes, hello, I wonder if you *can* help me. An associate of mine recently rented a property in Larchall Road — the converted exchange building. I was supposed to meet them, but my flight was delayed and I was wondering . . ."

Wow, stonewalled straight away. Karl had made this stuff look so easy. "You haven't? Well no, what about . . . no, right . . . I see." If only West Ham had as good a defence.

The senior partner had handled all the arrangements and she was now on holiday in Canada. Hence: no names, no contacts and no yellow brick road.

He got in the car and headed south, with only the radio for company. It was all going pear-shaped again. He had Diane and Sheryl pulling his strings from one side and Sir Peter the Bastard on the other side. *Ping*: small savings and big decisions. He'd seen that ad before, at Holloway Road tube. He'd even had a discussion about finances, in which Karl had revealed his own astute investment strategy: *saving is for pussies*.

Thomas allowed himself the luxury of a smile. Now he had a way forward again, sort of. He could find his way to the Gun Club but would they let him in? He pulled over and stared at the *A to Z* intently, like an ugly man checking out the foreign bride catalogue. Nope, it wasn't coming together at all. The only thing for it was to drive down to the tube station and retrace his steps.

* * *

The industrial estate was half full with cars. He remembered that Teresa had been driving a silver coupé the day Karl had bought Petrov's red estate, but it could have been a hire car. And of course, he hadn't made a habit of carrying his driving licence and passport around, so getting in might be a tad tricky. Three men got out of a BMW; for a second he thought he'd seen one of them before. But he could hardly wave and explain. They glanced in his direction and didn't glance again. This was getting him nowhere.

He walked up to the thick metal door with as much confidence as he could fake. The camera stared at him implacably. He pushed the intercom and said that he'd been there before and was looking for a member named Teresa. He let go of the button and waited. Nothing happened.

He tried again, a different pitch — same basic facts and that he needed to speak to her urgently. He held up his SSU ID card, for good measure. Finally, he got a response: "You must have the wrong place." Now he was getting seriously pissed off, and desperate. He hit the button again. "Look, I don't have a lot of time. If she's there, I need to see her; she'll know what it's about. Be a good girl and stop fucking me around."

He did elicit an immediate response, but 'if you don't go away I'll call the police' wasn't the one he hoped for. He took a breath. "Look, I'm sorry for behaving like a twat. But it's really important and I *have* been here before, more than once — you can check your records against my ID and name. And I've got nowhere else to go so I'm just going to sit out here in my car and wait until she turns up - today, tomorrow, whenever. I'm not going to cause any trouble, and if you want to call the police, then you go right ahead."

He took a step back, raised a hand as if he was being sworn in on a jury, and backed away slowly to his car. Then he drove around the car park, clocking the security cameras on poles, and managed to find a space facing the door.

Sunset came and went; evening crept upon him, a staring contest with a steel door that was only interrupted by the occasional visitor and an emergency piss in an old lemonade bottle. He tried the radio for a while, but it took the edge off his concentration. Even his survival ration granola bar — the only food he'd had all day — couldn't lift his spirits.

He figured he'd fucked his job now; he couldn't see how Christine and Peterson would keep him on the team. In the unlikely event that Christine took his side, he'd given Peterson the ideal excuse to prise him out. *Stupid, Thomas; really stupid.* He closed his eyes for a few seconds, and fantasised that he and Miranda were running over the North Yorkshire Moors.

Tap, tap, tap; tap, tap, tap. Jesus! They must have called the police after all. He turned to the window, ready to surrender. Teresa was standing outside. He pushed the sealed piss bottle under the passenger seat before he lowered the window.

"You shouldn't have come here."

Okay, not the welcome he'd hoped for but he still felt like hugging her. "I was desperate. It's become . . ." he searched for the right word. ". . . complicated." Yeah, if complicated was another word for meltdown.

"What's the problem?" Teresa stopped short. "Have you been in a fight?"

"Yeah, with Bob Peterson." He figured she knew who Peterson was. Heck, maybe she'd always known. He passed over the photos in the envelope and waited for comment. Then he got tired of waiting and told her about Sir Peter Carroll. After all, what did he have to lose now? He was all out of friends on this.

"You drive," Teresa insisted. "We'll go back to yours."

"What about the bug in my car?"

She held up two fingers, like a victory salute. "Bugs, plural. That's how I'm here. Karl's been keeping an eye on you."

He couldn't help, but smile. Karl: the wily little Celt.

* * *

It wasn't difficult to understand what Karl might see in Teresa, apart from an air of mystery. She was very capable and clearly didn't take any shit. Once inside the flat, she assumed control, drawing the curtains before she did a sweep of the living room using a hand-held detector. He left her to it, put the kettle on and dug something resurrectable out of the freezer — two portions.

"Karl thinks very highly of you," she carried on talking with her back to him. "But he's worried you'll do something rash about Miranda."

No mistake there. He'd already decided he would sort out whoever was involved — every last one of them. "So how did Karl send you to find me, exactly?"

She snapped the portable shut and turned round. "Simple," she tilted her head to one side. "He knows the OS ref of the indoor firing range and he tracked your car."

"What about the lockdown?"

Her face was calm, as if she could say much but was choosing not to. "It only takes one text to me, on a throwaway mobile — *T at CLUB*." She paused and folded her hands together. "Then smash the mobile and it's like it never happened. You just have to make sure you don't get caught."

He felt his mouth form into a wow. Karl had been covering his back after all. The kettle clicked, breaking the spell.

"I'll just sweep the other rooms, starting with the bathroom."

"Sure," he nodded, waving a hand behind him. "It's just off . . ."

"I know where it is, Thomas; I remember from the last time I was here."

The wow expanded into a cavern. Of course, Karl had saved his bacon before, at the flat, when he'd had the good sense not to be there. Teresa must have been involved.

He made the tea. "So what's the deal with you and Karl?" his voice seemed to echo through the flat. There was no answer, but he felt sure that she'd heard him.

* * *

It was strange, eating dinner with another woman. Having another woman in the flat at all, come to that. Christine Gerrard, in her time, had never been a fan. She always seemed to treat the east of London like some sort of infection.

The food settled him, helped his thoughts to fall into place. "Has the DSB been opened?" he hovered, mid-fork, waiting for her answer.

"No, not yet. It's sealed and there's no tag inside — we X-rayed it."

He swallowed. "Have you made a decision — do I get it?"

She made a smacking sound with her lips; he doubted it was the quality of the food. "It may contain vital information about the cartel . . ."

He nearly countered that but he could see, by the way her eyes flickered, that she was still thinking it over.

". . . And can you afford to trust Sir Peter Carroll?"

The room went very cold. Any optimism he'd been nurturing, including the comforting notion that a simple trade-off could be made, was dangling by a thread. Teresa was right of course. How could he trust these bastards, when he knew what they were capable of — two corpses at the hospital, Petrov's house torched, and counting.

"I'm sorry, Thomas; it could be too valuable to lose," she sounded like a bank manager, turning him down for a loan.

Desperation wrote its own scripts. "What if we copied it first? You'd keep a copy and I return the original." Okay, it was feeble, but at least it *was* a plan. It wasn't as if they'd come up with a better option.

"We know it's a document box," she backtracked, softening her voice. "The paper may be heat and light sensitive. Photocopying or scanning is just too risky."

"What about photography?"

"I don't know Thomas," she flicked the hair from her face. "I don't know. And besides, once we open the DSB, the seal is broken."

He tapped his chin. "I might be able to solve your problem." *Your problem, good one: reverse psychology for beginners.*

Teresa listened as he told her about the DSB he'd kept from Leeds. Maybe it wouldn't be an identical match, but if it meant having something to exchange for Miranda and not, he'd take that gamble.

"Now," he gathered up the plates; "I've also got a couple of ideas about special paper." No sense losing momentum while she was still malleable. "How about doing the photography in a darkroom?" He gestured out towards the hallway. "Or I can try one of my Internet buddies, see if they know anyone with a *Starlight* camera."

Buddies — that was stretching it a bit — a bunch of ultra-competitive snappers and geeks, who would tell you where to find equipment, as long as you knew what you wanted in the first place.

He dumped the plates in the sink and fired up his laptop, waiting until he'd cleared the minefield of password and security protection before he brought Teresa screen-side.

"Great for night shots," he pulled up a couple of images from a folder. She didn't respond, but that was fine — he was impressed enough for both of them. "Someone hired one for me once; back when I thought I'd be the next Andy Rouse."

She stared at him blankly and he sighed, appalled.

"I'm supposed to contact Sir Peter tomorrow so I need an answer."

She was quiet for so long that he thought he'd finally met his match in the silence game. He studied her as she stared off into space. The way her hair fell, just above the collar-line; the slightly muscular legs and that cluster ring on her right hand. If she noticed him watching her, she didn't seem at all perturbed. He wasn't perving or anything, he told himself. He just wanted to weigh up what sort of person he was investing with his last few ounces of faith.

Teresa turned suddenly, catching him off guard. He felt a pang in his heart — Miranda used to do the same thing. Whoa, *used to*? He swallowed hard, deciding at the last minute not to punch himself.

"I'll tell you what," Teresa narrowed her eyes, "Why don't you give me a few minutes and I'll make a couple of calls?"

He headed for the kitchen, pausing along the way to lock his laptop. He turned the radio on and did his domestic thing to the soothing sounds of Seventies Soul, courtesy of Dobie Gray and others. Except, tonight, they weren't so soothing. Suddenly, for no reason at all, he recalled the first time he saw Miranda naked. How she'd made him close his eyes. And then, for the only time in his life, all the clichés had been true. So beautiful; the sort of enchantment that made him want to cry, then and now. He looked skyward and closed his eyes.

* * *

Teresa returned after a handful of songs; long enough for him to pull it together again. "My people have agreed to let you take the DSB to Sir Peter Carroll, once the document is copied to our satisfaction. After that we'll monitor the situation closely."

Very generous of them. With Sir Peter firmly in the frame and copies of the papers safely tucked away, they had very little to lose. Whereas . . .

He thanked her and tried to warm it up. Things were improving. He had allies now, although the odds were still stacked against them. He stopped mid-thought. "I need a car tonight."

"I'll arrange something, and I'll be back tomorrow with the package."

Chapter 33

Teresa had given her assurance that the car wouldn't be tracked. He wasn't sure if he believed her, but he was in no position to be fussy. The Wrights knew to expect him. On the drive over, he ran through different versions of what he wanted to say, but in the end he decided to let them take the lead.

When he arrived, the driveway was full of cars — a packed house tonight. He stood outside for a moment, trying to get a grip on his fear and his bowels. He took another breath as he held his hand over the bell. This was going to be rough. He pressed the button lightly, reminding himself that they were the ones really suffering here.

"It's open," Diane's voice wavered from behind the door.

He gave it a tiny shove and it released inwards, drawing the light from the kitchen through the open inner door.

"We're in here."

It took all his courage to step across the threshold, knowing as he did that he was turning his back on everything he had selfishly tried to preserve.

Well, best not keep the family waiting. He pushed the living room door and went in. Sam and Terry looked up from their armchairs; neither spoke or acknowledged him. Diane was sat on the settee with Sheryl next to her, holding hands as if it was the only thing keeping each of them together. Miranda's dad, John, was nowhere to be seen.

"Come sit down," there was kindness in Diane's voice and he felt wretched at that; it was something he hadn't earned and didn't deserve. Sheryl wouldn't look at him, but if he was honest with himself it was one less face to deal with.

There was no point beating around the bush so he told them what he planned to do. To get a package which *someone else* — he stressed that — had kept secret from him and deliver it in exchange for Miranda.

It was less an interrogation than a series of silences, speckled with short exchanges. Mostly, they wanted answers he couldn't give. What was it all about? Why Miranda, or him? Why couldn't he let the family deal with it? Someone — Sam or Terry, it all got lost in the stillness and the unspoken fears — passed him a drink. As if he'd won it on merit by his responses. He gripped the glass so tight he thought it might break, wanted it to break and pierce his skin so he could feel something as acute as the pain on their faces.

"I'm so sorry," he hung his head and waited for the room to swallow him. The tension wrapped around him like a physical pressure. It was harder to breathe now. He felt tears forming. Not now, Jesus; they'd think it was staged. He took a gulp from the glass and pinched the tears back, rubbing his eyes clear. He kept his head down, not wanting to read their expectations.

"Thomas," Diane spoke his name and she sounded like a stranger. "John wants to see you in his office." She didn't say *now* but that's what she meant.

He finished his glass and set it on the floor; last drink for a condemned man. His limbs dragged like dead weight as he walked through to the other side of the house. It was quieter there, and devoid of comfort. There was a line of light under the closed door. He knocked twice and went in.

* * *

John Wright was hunched over his desk, hands crushed together. Thomas felt his shoulders sink, almost smelt those Saturday dinners again when his dad had come home, spoiling for a fight.

The main light was off and the desk lamp shone away from John, casting him in shards of shadow. The hands on the desk didn't move at all. Thomas stood in no man's land, waiting for sentence to be passed.

"Close the door," John managed to convey resolve without menace. The room shrank around him.

Thomas waited for John to speak again — he had little to say, himself, other than repeat what he'd said to the others. In the semi-darkness, he could still make out the photographs on the wall — small comfort.

John's hands moved to his face and he blew his next breath through his fingers; the breath was long and laboured. "You found Miranda in Leeds, kept her safe and brought her back to us." He nodded for Thomas to sit opposite him. "Diane tells me that Miranda is in trouble because of you." It wasn't a question because they both already knew the answer. "When you came to London and we set you up in a home together, you made us a promise. Do you remember?"

Of course he remembered. One simple sentence: he'd never let her down. No matter what happened between them in the future — and God, how prophetic that clause had turned out to be — he'd never let her down. "I know."

John took a sharp intake of breath. "You've always been a man of your word, Thomas, and I look upon you as one of us." John was struggling with the words, raw emotion choking every syllable.

Any moment now, Thomas thought, that fist would come flying across the small space between them.

"Diane says this has to be handled a certain way — and it has to be done by you." He took another long breath. "Miranda is our little girl, Thomas; she's precious. So I expect you to do what's necessary."

Thomas tensed up, half closing his eyes against the light and whatever was to come. He heard a drawer being opened and then a thud on the desk. He looked down to see a pistol, light gleaming along its edge. John nudged the gun over to him with the heel of his hand.

Holy shit. John was stone-cold serious. Thomas reached forward and touched the barrel, felt the metallic chill seeping into his skin.

"Do you know how to use it?"

Thomas took the gun, slipped out the magazine and checked the chamber was clear. He also noticed that the mag was empty. As he looked up, there was a thin smile on John's lips. He swallowed and let the gun rest in his hand; he had just crossed the line, on a one-way ticket.

John leaned down and lifted a carrier bag onto the desk. Inside was a shoulder holster and ammunition. Thomas weighed the gun in his hand and, as if demonstrating his side of the pact, loaded the weapon. This was a moment that would live with him forever, like scar tissue that appears healed. But it's always there, beneath the surface.

Chapter 34

Not long after Thomas returned home, Teresa was at his door. He checked through the curtain first — she was alone, though logically she must have come with someone to take back the Audi.

She watched him as he gazed forlornly out of the window at her, as he looked past her in the vain hope that Karl was around. Nothing doing. He opened the front door, car keys in hand. She edged forward and he stood aside.

"I won't stay long," she seemed almost cheery. "I've got good news."

Yeah, Thomas thought; maybe she'd found some affordable body armour to go with his new gun. He put the kettle on and joined her in the lounge. She perched on the edge of the sofa arm, hands together.

"I'll bring the DSB over to you tomorrow evening." There was a 'but' coming. ". . . But we'll need some extra time before you give it back to them."

He felt his jaw dragging down. The kettle clicked; he ignored it. "You want me to put Miranda at further risk?" He felt his shoulders hardening.

"If the information is useful, we'll have to act before the cartel gets it back."

He made a break to the kitchen. Teresa followed him.

"Look Thomas, I know this is all—"

Thomas rounded on her. "You don't know shit. This is business as usual to you people, but for me, it's personal."

Her next move was textbook — the reassuring hand on the arm. "If you tell Sir Peter you can get the DSB in a couple of days, and that it's still unopened, he'll accept that. Why wouldn't he? He'll still get exactly what he wants."

She negotiated the cups and spoons through trial and error as he sat and watched her. Maybe she could tell he wasn't convinced, still not a card-carrying member of their gang. "Let me put this another way," her voice moulded into concrete. "We need two more days, with or without your cooperation."

He blinked a couple of times, waited for the heat across his face to subside before he spoke. She beat him to it.

"This isn't a game, Thomas; this is life and death to our operatives. The contents of that DSB could save lives."

He nodded without saying a word.

"I'll be back here tomorrow, around six."

All he could do was sit there like a statue and listen to the door closing behind her.

* * *

The dream returned that night — the arguing downstairs, him and Pat cowering under the covers together and that terrible silence when their mother capitulated. As if the world had ended. Pat, crying and shaking under the sheets, as the heavy *thud thud* grew closer on the stairs. He was holding her tightly again, so that she couldn't feel his own trembling.

The hollow *catch* as Dad gripped the door handle. And even though it hadn't moved, you knew he was there because his legs stole the light from underneath the door. The handle turning, the light switch driving out the comfort of shadows, and then the footfalls to the side of the bed. Pat's nails, digging into his skin so hard that he wanted to cry out, only Dad would just call him soft and take a swipe at him. He could smell the hand on the sheets, stinking of shame and self-loathing

But when the covers were snatched away, it was Miranda at his side, warm and sensuous. And Dad wasn't there in the room this time: it was Sir Peter Carroll. He was speaking, whispering as his hand stretched towards Miranda.

And Thomas couldn't move; he was paralysed until somehow he remembered the gun. The sweet, silver pistol with the magic star on the handle; the one that meant he was the sheriff. He reached under the pillow and as soon as he felt it, he drew out the gun and thrust it into Sir Peter's face.

Sir Peter took a step back in the dream, standing there, daring Thomas to 'be a man.' His eyes blurred, but he wiped them one-handed, the gun still at arm's length to ward off evil. Then his fingers slowly closed together and *pow,* the gun went off.

Thomas shocked awake, rigid against the bed with tears spread across his face. Slowly, he regained movement in his limbs, felt the muscles in his shoulders and back release. It was a little after five in the morning; he flipped the mobile on, in case there'd been word from either Miranda or Karl. Then he ran for a shower to avoid the disappointment.

After toasting the last of the bread, he took John Wright's pistol from where he'd hidden it in the kitchen and re-examined it — no serial numbers or distinguishing marks. It might never have been used before, but he doubted that. He tried on the shoulder holster, adjusted it a couple of times and nested the gun. He must have stood in the middle of the kitchen for a minute or more, no quick draw bullshit or confronting the mirror. No, the only thought going through his brain was whether John had started like this himself; whether one unfortunate situation had turned an honest man into . . . into someone like *him*.

He ditched the holster in a drawer and stowed the gun away carefully. The mobile phone had nothing for him. Only six o'clock now; way too early for Whitehall.

So many times in the past he'd worked his way through London, cursing the traffic as he inched ahead, bumper to bumper. But today, when he wanted the drive to take forever, nothing doing. He parked at the work compound, just to keep his car handy, and went walkabout. He'd brought along a Pentax Optio to kill some time.

London, before the rush, was a different place altogether. The city breathed softly before the hordes invaded; the haze lifted off the Thames in the first light of morning. Walking beside the Embankment, lulled by the lapping water, it was easy to forget just how much shit he was in and how deep.

The police launch prowled along the Thames as he watched, lens poised; the sun burst through the mesh of steel and brick and glass behind it to light up the skyline. He drank it all in — better than espresso. When did he last do this? When did he last feel such a connection to London? He couldn't remember. It was Miranda's city, but it was also his.

By the time he'd had his fill and grabbed a coffee at St James's Park, it was just after eight. He felt limbered up after all the walking and, thanks to the coffee, as sharp as a blade. Grateful too, that he hadn't followed his gut and brought the gun along.

A few miles on foot had given him time to reflect a little. No one had suggested that Thomas was anything more than an innocent in all this; and basically that's what he was. As long as he played it that way and didn't come across too cocky or clever, why wouldn't they give him a couple of extra days?

At first glance, Main Building looked closed for business, but the door gave way and the security staff squared up to him from across the polished marble flooring. He moved to the glass screen, stated his name and flipped them his ID.

A receptionist directed him to the hand-scanner and checked a list of names. Yep, there he was, all present and correct. Sir Peter wasn't in his office yet, so he waited in the foyer, with an early morning broadsheet for company.

Coming from Yorkshire, Thomas was no stranger to the class struggle, but never was the divide more clearly defined than in the newspapers — insightful information for the movers and shakers, and tits and celebrities for the plebs. Oh, he liked a tabloid as much as the next man, but it didn't equip you for understanding the bigger picture. Take today — a Benelux corporation was holding strategic talks with a French business partner, ahead of a meeting with representatives from the EU Commission. *Jesus.* The more he read, the more it seemed like Karl's mythical Superstate was already in place.

After fifteen minutes of isolation therapy, a guard came over: Sir Peter would be ready for him shortly. Okay, final run through of what he was going to say. The DSB was unopened; no, he hadn't seen it and yes, he would bring it to them in a day or so. As to anything else, he knew nothing: if in doubt, say nowt.

He stood and stretched. Sir Peter might have him on CCTV that very minute, just watching him sweat. Not a very comforting thought. He heard boots on marble and turned to face them; it was show time.

The journey to the lift took place in customary silence. He thought maybe he'd seen this guard before. As they exited the lift, he realised where — at the gun club. He nodded and smiled as they entered the last leg of the corridor. The guard paused and looked him up and down, as if trying to place him. "Are you ex-mob?"

Fortunately, Thomas had had the benefit of Karl's education: mob, for military. He tilted his hand noncommittally: *could be.*

Three raps and away, leaving Thomas standing there like the last virgin in a nightclub. Sir Peter took his time about answering; he probably thought he was piling on the pressure. This was Pickering all over again, but now the bullies were grown up and infinitely more savage. It would be harder to get away with it this time; a shove into the pavement wouldn't quite cover it.

Thomas knew the score. For the terrorised, it went one of three ways. You resigned yourself to it, withdrew as much as you could and survived, day to day. Or else you crumbled, lost hope; gave up on yourself. But if there was still some part of you that they hadn't got to, hadn't chewed up and spat out, you bided your time and then you struck back, hard.

He heard Sir Peter's voice and meekly entered the office. Meek: that was the watchword. And no need to fake the unease; he already had that in spades.

Sir Peter offered him a chair, all very civilised. It was bloody obvious that he didn't have the DSB with him, but they went through the master and servant formalities. He delivered the agreed message and then asked if there was news about Miranda.

It seemed to throw the old man. Even though he'd been listening attentively before, that one small question upset the apple cart. "I'll see what I can find out for you, Thomas." He looked at him differently after that, like Thomas was a simpleton.

Thomas thanked him, said how grateful he was and shook his hand. It sealed the deal. Two days' grace and the promise of a telephone call later that day — quite a result. At this rate, he decided, he might even let him live, when it was all over.

* * *

Two days to put together a plan; afterwards, there would be no going back. That was fine — it meant he had nothing to lose. He made straight for the Victoria line and waited on the platform, fantasising about earning a crust as a freelance photographer — *every snapper's fantasy*. Maybe he and Miranda . . . The soundtrack in his head stopped abruptly. She'd probably never want to lay eyes on him again. Like he said . . . nothing to lose.

He made it to the office just after nine. Hopefully, Christine would be in and he could set the record straight, come clean about Miranda and everything. There was even an outside chance that Christine could help him, somehow. Because, now that he thought about it, there *was* something he needed. First though, he had to fetch something from the car, something he'd bottled out of at Whitehall.

Christine's office light was a lone beacon. He glanced around at the empty desks, shrouded in shadow; he'd miss this place, even the crap coffee from the machine. He thrust his hand into his jacket pocket and opened the box one-handed, positioning the bug ready for attachment. Christine's door was closed; he knocked, tentatively. But the voice that answered was Bob Peterson's.

Always have a Plan B, and preferably a Plan C as well. Karl called it The Dorman Rule, after a bloke he'd met in a pub once. Plan B was to proceed as planned. There was no Plan C, short of walking away.

He opened the door with his left hand and tried to play nicely.

"You're the last person I expected to see, Thomas. What do you want?"

Count to ten. This was too important to screw up for the sake of scoring a few points. "Bob, can I sit down, please? I need to discuss something."

Bob Peterson gestured to a chair opposite, ever the genial host. Thomas drew close and slipped out the bug under the table, leaning forward earnestly as he applied it to the underside of the desk.

"Christine isn't here!" Peterson sounded triumphant.

"When's she back?"

"I don't know."

"Look, it's really important that I speak with her."

Peterson laced his fingers back behind his head and breathed in deeply. "Anything you've got to say, you can say it to me. I run this team, remember? Christine's been temporarily transferred."

Thomas gave the bug one last touch for safety's sake and brought his hands to his face, like a poor impression of *The Scream*. "Bob, I need your help . . ." Now he was totally winging it, leaping from word to word at twenty thousand feet. "They've got Miranda and they want the documents from Harwich."

Pure bloody guesswork, but Peterson twitched at the 'H' word. *Shit or bust.* "On the day you were there, Bob, the day I photographed you." *Now, just rest a minute and see what happens.*

Peterson's face turned a sickly shade; he folded like a bad poker player. "If you've got something they want, just give it to them — for all our sakes."

"I need to know Miranda's okay — can you get a message to her?" Subtext: are you involved, you bastard?

Peterson wiped the sweat from his lips and stared at the desk; he looked like he wanted out, in a bad way. "Why did you have to get involved? I mean, you're not with SIS or anything. You're a bloody civilian!"

"Hey, I was doing my job. And then you turn up at this office . . ." *And pause again to let Peterson fill in the blanks.*

"I was sent here, Thomas," Bob Peterson raised his hands like a beggar. "You think I wanted to be at Harwich, or here? I've a wife and family, for God's sake — you're not the only one with something to lose."

Thomas's immediate reaction was 'tell that to Christine.' But he kept his mouth shut. Peterson was just a pawn in someone else's game. "Do you know where Christine is?"

He shook his head; he looked like he wanted to cry. "She took a call early this morning, at the flat. They came and collected her — she looked pleased . . ."

Well at least they were past the pretence; he almost warmed to Peterson for that.

". . . In a people carrier. I was told not to contact her — executive orders, you know where from."

And he did know, now. All roads seemed to lead back to Whitehall.

"Thomas, you can't fight these people. Do what they want and maybe they'll leave us all alone."

He considered that for maybe half a second. "Yeah, and maybe they won't." It was time. "There's something else; I want you to sign out a vest for me."

Peterson's eyes widened. "Body armour?" He gulped. "I can't issue you with a weapon — there's no way . . ."

Thomas shook his head slowly, crediting him with enough intelligence to figure it out. "I only need the vest."

Peterson made the call and signed the chit for Stores. It was a shame that Bob's voice was so off-key, for the recording. Still, Thomas could always edit it afterwards; he was good at that.

"What . . . what are you going to do?" Peterson handed over the chit, like a signed confession.

"I don't know. It depends on Yorgi . . ."

The face before him drained; it was like someone had slit Peterson's throat. So, Bob was in deeper than he'd imagined. He knew that if he stayed any longer, he'd end up asking questions about Yorgi; things that would only weaken his resolve, the way that Petrov had crumbled every time his maniac brother had got in touch.

"One more thing," he stopped at the door. "If you *can* get a message to Miranda," he paused, trying to think of something more meaningful than 'I love her.' "Her dog's very ill; tell her that Butch will have to be put down."

214

Chapter 35

"So," Thomas said to himself in the car, "that went well, all things considered." On the seat beside him was the latest, lightweight, standard-issue body armour. It had pinched a bit under the arm when he'd tried it on, but he could live with that. If things went badly — and he had a nasty feeling that things could get very bad indeed — it might make the difference between living and not living.

All reason told him to go back to the flat and stay put, but he was past the point of reason. As the car escaped from the gridlock of Liverpool Street, instead of heading east for Walthamstow he turned north, ploughing through trendy Islington, dodging scooters and Smart cars, through to the Angel where he picked up the A1.

One thing was nagging him, something Peterson had said about Christine. She'd looked *pleased*. Not coerced, not under duress: pleased. A pound to a penny then that she had to be involved. Stupid of him to have trusted her; she'd always been a career woman. Bob was probably just her stepping-shag to something better.

He drove on to the *Welcome Break* and re-stocked the car with snacks and petrol. On the way out he powered up the mobile, ever the optimist. And on to Plan C. If Christine was involved, there was one person sure to know. A person so close to Christine that she even discussed her sex life with her. As he'd found out before, to his cost.

* * *

There are some journeys in life that a person never looks forward to — the dentist, funeral directors, and the STD clinic. Thomas had added Gerrard Hall a couple of years back, when he and Christine had been involved. In what her mother apparently still referred to as 'the social experiment.' Okay, so the imposing house wasn't actually called Gerrard Hall — except by him — but it might as well have been. The class divide again, large as life.

On the drive over, he worked through his pitch. Christine was missing and no one was talking. But if she'd gone willingly, surely she must have been expecting it? Another of Sir Peter Bastard's little exercises, perhaps?

The sign for the village of Ampthill triggered all kinds of memories. Meeting her parents for the first time; the great sweeping drive, Christine beside him — poised but nervous; the house staff looking at him with disdain, like she'd found Heathcliff in a ditch. He laughed at himself as he drove along, remembering his dire attempts at fitting in — the diamond-patterned sweater and the new jacket: priceless. All he'd needed was a pair of plus-fours and a silk cravat.

The sight of the gates sobered him. He pulled over and stared through the bars. The CCTV cameras were an innovation; they must really be serious about keeping the oiks out. This would not be easy; any inquiries would not be well received coming from him, oik that he was. He checked for voicemail and came back empty-handed.

A Land Rover towing a horsebox passed him and the passenger swivelled round to get a good look. The sticker on the back said: 'I slow down for horses.' Big deal. 'I give blood for horses,' now that would be a sacrifice.

He started up the car and fell in behind at a respectful distance. He breathed in the great expanse of greenery and tried to prepare himself for the inevitable welcoming committee. The horse saviours peeled right, towards the stables; he waved them off.

The car made that wonderful sound on gravel, the one that reminded him of horse drawn carriages, and *Pride and Prejudice*. In the Gerrards' case, class and prejudice. He couldn't even cut Christine some slack on that score.

One of the staff was on him before he'd opened the door. "Excuse me, sir, but this is a private residence — can I help you?"

"I'm here to see Mrs Gerrard — Francesca."

The underling scuttled away. A curtain flickered ever so slightly behind one of the drawing-room windows. He waited outside and listened for whinnying from the stables. There was the faint whiff of horseshit, which he'd always found appropriate on those few occasions in the past when he'd been allowed to cross the threshold.

The butler, or whatever he was, returned, his back bent forward slightly as if in permanent deference. Most likely his family had come over with the Gerrards when the Normans arrived on their expansion tour of Britain. "If you'd like to come this way, sir." The last word sounded a little like cur.

Francesca Gerrard was waiting for him in the doorway. Everything about her was tailored; tailored skirt, tailored cardigan, tailored smile. A string of pearls circled her neck, knotted and extended to her waist like a pendulum. "It's been a long time, Thomas."

It was a cool reception, bordering on frosty. Not like when she'd come on to him, that one time, when the champers had flowed on Christine's birthday. A polite, but firm hand extended in his general vicinity. "Why don't you come through?" she walked off, leaving him little choice other than to stand there, gathering dust. The manservant nodded to her and retreated to the shadows.

The room that Thomas found his way to was like an American vision of liddle-biddy ol' England. Mahogany furniture fought for floor space with oak and ash. Displayed in one corner of the room was a suit of armour. He wanted to go over and lift up the visor, do the classic joke: anything to calm his nerves. She seemed in no rush to hear what he had to say; which made him even more nervous.

A servant arrived, with an extra cup, placed it on the tray and glided out.

"Please make yourself comfortable."

As if that would ever be possible here. He caught the look on his face in a mirror, and blushed. He was behaving like a lout and with no good reason. He was, in truth, a snob. Christine had seen that from the off. Maybe that had been part of the attraction.

"I take it you're here on business?"

"Ah, yes. Mrs Gerrard — Francesca, I really need to see Christine."

"I'm afraid that's not possible."

He squinted: interesting choice of words. "Is she here?" he glanced in the direction of the stables.

She looked worried for a moment then recovered her stone façade. "Christine is very discreet about her career, but one gets a sense of these things."

He sipped his Earl Grey and tried to keep a lid on his temper. "Do you know where Christine is? I have to talk to her." The words came out like a threat.

"After the damage you've done, I hardly think she'll want to speak with you." Francesca snorted, like one of her precious horses.

He tried her words on for size. What damage had he done? "Look, Francesca, I don't have time for this."

He launched out of the chair, and through the open French doors, round to the courtyard at the side of the house. All the while, yelling for Christine. One of the stablehands rushed up to see what the commotion was.

"It's alright, Stewart," Mrs Gerrard appeared by the arch.

The stablehand took a long hard look at Thomas, who shook his head slowly and flexed a fist. Today, he was not in the mood.

Horse-boy retreated and Francesca sauntered towards him. "Christine isn't here; satisfied? She's working on something clandestine," she paused, "but you of all people should know that." Her hand lifted to catch her jaw.

He couldn't help yielding a tiny smile at her discomfort.

"What's going on, Thomas?"

His mobile rang and they both jumped. "Thomas, it's Ann Crossley. Karl asked me to look out for you. You need to get out of there *now*."

He left Francesca standing and sprinted around the side of the house, back to the car. The manservant was bending down close to one of the tyres. "Touch it and I'll break your face!" he hollered, rising a fist to show he wasn't pissing about.

It bought him the precious seconds he needed, better for everyone. Given the choice he would have run him over, no question about it. The car roared into life and wheel-span, showering the hapless butler with gravel.

He saw the blue sedan approaching at speed; it wasn't budging for anyone. At the last moment he swerved wide, churning up the carefully tended lawn like a protest vote. He heard the car screech to a stop behind him, but he'd already veered around it, gunning towards the open gates to rejoin the road, his heart thumping in his chest like war-drums.

* * *

Thomas opened the driver's window; he needed some air. What the hell was going on? Nothing made any sense. If this was Sir Peter's people, they'd already know he'd agreed to get the DSB so why the intercept? If it was Yorgi — he took a deep breath — how would he know where Thomas was? Maybe Francesca Gerrard had arranged some secret signal to bring in the heavy mob? He tried to stick to facts. How many had he seen in the car? Two, he thought. But you don't stop to do a headcount when someone's trying to run you off the road.

Back on the A1, with no sign of the blue sedan following him, he turned his deductive powers to the phone call. Karl had said he was on better terms with Ann Crossley so that made sense, sort of. And Karl might have told her about the legit tracker on the car, same as Teresa. So why were all his allies keeping their distance?

When he got back to the flat, there was a message waiting on the machine, blinking insistently. The voice was measured, under control. "It's John; ring me with an update." He cleared it off, poured himself a Southern Comfort and stood for a while, gazing at Miranda's photograph. "I won't let you down," he whispered.

It was early in the day for a drink, but he figured he'd earned it. The need to ring John back pressed hard upon his temples, but the sweet, sharp taste on his lips won on points. He moved the chair round to face the door; too much thinking — that was the problem.

And what about Teresa? If Karl was an enigma, then Teresa was a sphinx under witness protection. Maybe that was the draw for Karl — a mystery deeper than himself.

He dug out a notepad and pen and wrote down all the names, hoping it would help: Karl, Teresa, Ann Crossley, Sir Peter Carroll, Bob 'scumbag' Peterson and Christine Gerrard. Then he scrawled lines between them, linking some and excluding others. He stared at the page until his eyes ached, as if he could solve it like a logic puzzle. But all he noticed was that he'd extended the double 'r' in Gerrard, making them look like a pair of legs. His arm throbbed and his head hurt, and he was all out of ideas.

Chapter 36

Eighteen . . . nineteen . . . twenty . . . done. Miranda eased back on the exercise bike and glanced over at the wall-length mirror; a good workout. The sweat dripped from her headband and had stained her top like heavy raindrops. She was alone, save for 'Pumping Classics 3 — music to shape and tone to.' They left her alone in the exercise room because there were no windows, hence no way out. At this rate she'd be super-fit again; she visited three or four times a day, for short bursts, just for something to do.

She'd surprised herself by how quickly she'd adjusted to the regime; and maybe disappointed herself too. Three days? Four days? It all blended into one. Everywhere she went was supervised, except the bathroom, the bedroom and the gym. Though no doubt someone was always close by. This was like the worst health club in the world; talk about killing with kindness. No one had threatened or mistreated her; they just kept her under watch and interspersed the boredom with twenty questions; the same twenty questions.

Mainly they asked about Thomas; otherwise it was the Irish bloke, national security and random stuff that made no sense whatsoever. And always there was the suggestion that Thomas was in real danger and that her information could be vital. No one seemed to know how long she would be there, or the specifics of why Thomas was in trouble. Or else they weren't saying.

And what did *she* know? Well, there was one tarmac lane to the front of the house and high fencing around the estate. A walled garden extended to the back of the house with a single arch at the far end and some trees beyond it. Not that she'd ever got close. Whenever she was outdoors, someone always stood back there, supposedly to check it was safe for her. At first, the mixture of bullshit and bureaucracy had been amusing — for a day or so. The thick glass on the sealed bedroom windows was the first wake-up call.

The exercise bike bleeped as the last of the dials powered down, so she relaxed her grip. Alice Eyeball had promised to try and find out more about Thomas today, but that was hours ago. Face it, Miranda, she told herself, until they find whatever they're looking for, you're stuck here.

She checked her no-run make-up and pressed her palms against the glass. Maybe this was one of those two-way mirrors like the police were supposed to use. Like Elvis. She put a finger on her sweatband, traced it down the side of her face and diagonally across her top. If there was a perv watching, he was very quiet about it. Then she sniffed at her shoulder and wrinkled her nose. Funny really, the way her own sweat reminded her of Thomas, the scent of their bodies after their favourite exercise routine.

Time to hit the showers. She wiped the bicycle seat then grabbed the door handle. Alice was standing in front of her like an apparition.

"Jesus!" Miranda flinched.

Alice jumped back about a foot. "Sorry, didn't mean to startle you," she blushed. "Somebody's on their way here to see you."

"How long have I got?"

"She'll be here in about twenty minutes."

It would have to be a quick shower then.

* * *

After making herself presentable, she sat down on the bed and picked up her notepad. The one they gave her to write down anything important she remembered. The one she was certain they checked whenever she left the room.

How many former couples still bother to recall where they met and what they know about their ex's job? Play twenty questions at least twice a day and it soon comes back to you. This was the sanitised version, of course. No Bladen family back-story — nothing about the blazing row with Thomas's parents when they first met her or their jaw-dropping opening line: 'Are you pregnant?' No, this was the family-friendly set. Met in Leeds, moved back to London, Civil Service, break-up, SSU: neat and tidy as a stashed roll of £50s.

Alice was at the bedroom door again, so she picked up the notepad and brought it out with her. Alice led the way to the interview room. "In here please," she said, standing back a couple of feet. She didn't stick around either.

Sod it, Miranda thought; I'm not knocking. The catch turned quietly and the first thing she saw was a dark-haired woman looking out the window, talking on a mobile. Her lips formed the words 'fucking 'ell.' Her mouth ran dry. The world of strange had just acquired a new territory. She reached back and pushed the door until it clicked.

The woman at the window looked round and abruptly finished her call. Miranda couldn't be certain, but the last words sounded like, 'Thanks Bob.'

"Hello, you must be Miranda!" All smiles. Miranda played Simple Simon and mirrored her. "I'm . . ."

Yes, Miranda beamed; I know who *you* are.

". . . Christine. I work with Thomas. I've come for a little chat."

Miranda sat on the sofa and wondered how long she could keep a straight face. She'd only seen Christine twice before — and one of those was at a distance. But you never forget your ex's *new* girlfriend — you don't need a notepad for that. The first time was when Thomas had arranged back-to-back pub meets. And even though she'd teased him about staying in the bar, in the end she'd scarpered out the side door, just in time to peer in through the window.

Seeing Christine brought it all back — how jealous she'd been at the way Thomas had got on with his life while she was in Bermuda; had got on Christine, that was. Horses, that had been it; she smiled at the recollection. Christine was into horses. She'd pranced into that pub like an Arabian, all high-headed and flighty, trotting round the bar as if she owned it. Not a way to win friends in Whitechapel. And Miranda herself? Well, a thoroughbred of course. Yeah, ancient history now, but all the same she had to catch her breath when Christine leaned forward to speak.

"I can only imagine how difficult this must be for you, Miranda."

Miranda opened her notebook, as if she was rehearsing a play. Christine flattened her hand over the page. "Thomas hasn't been himself at work lately — you've probably noticed that, too?"

Miranda tilted her head back and nearly laughed. "We're not a couple."

"I'm sorry, I thought . . ." Christine seemed to give the sentence up as a bad idea.

Miranda turned the spotlight round. "Have you talked to Thomas?"

Christine did the 'eyes to one corner' thing. Sheryl at Caliban's reckoned it meant whatever came out next was either a memory or a lie.

Miranda got in there first. "I know you and Thomas were involved."

222

Christine nodded. "I thought as much; the way you reacted just now . . ."

"Then let's cut the crap," Miranda chucked the notepad in her direction. "That's as much as I know. Now, have you spoken to him; is he okay?"

Christine surveyed the pages and without looking up, whispered, "He saw one of my colleagues today." She put a finger to her lips and glanced at the door.

Miranda watched as she carefully tiptoed over. A second's pause then she wrenched the door open; no one was behind it. "Good," Christine turned and smiled; "now we can talk a little more freely."

It was stupid and clever at the same time, but Miranda knew this was the first person she'd seen who definitely knew Thomas. And maybe cared about him too, in her high-handed, flighty way. "Would that be Karl or Bob Peterson?"

Christine blanched; Miranda fought hard not to gloat. That ought to burst the balloon. "So now we understand each other, why don't you stop fucking me around and tell me why they're keeping me here?"

"He said you were confrontational," Christine managed a sliver of a smile.

"Look, let's get on with this — we both want the same thing, for Thomas to be safe."

"*Thomas*?" Christine went a funny shade again.

* * *

Christine ordered coffee and Posh Bloke acted as a waiter. When he'd gone, she scanned through Miranda's notepad again and went down a different line of inquiry. How did Thomas get on with his family? That one drew a wry smile, from both of them. Next it was: how often did Miranda see Thomas? That was a weird one. And then the topper: why was Miranda driving his car that day?

Miranda gulped at her coffee wearily. "What're you actually after?"

"Alright," Christine closed the pad and passed it back to her gently. "What if I were to say to you that Thomas is suspected of corruption or espionage?"

"Bollocks," Miranda erupted, "I don't believe it."

"Good — neither do I." That sounded like a confession.

"So why am I stuck here, then?"

Christine rolled her shoulders back, as if she was trying to shrug off a great weight. "It appears that Thomas helped someone steal a package."

"The ones he delivers for work?"

"Hmm." Christine stopped short of confirmation. "Only this one was being carried by someone else."

"Can't help you there," Miranda pulled down the shutters. "But I do know he was worried about *you* — because of this Peterson bloke. He's the bent one, by the sound of things."

"Listen to me very carefully," Christine brought a hand under her mug. "It would not be in your interests to repeat that to anyone."

Miranda tilted her head to one side and stuck out her jaw. "You don't scare me; you're just a posh bitch in a suit. What are you supposed to be — the heavy?"

"No," Christine looked down at the floor, "not me," her voice wavered.

For a moment, Miranda felt something for her other than contempt — only for a moment though. "I think we've both said enough, don't you?"

Christine conceded the point. "Yes, why don't we draw a line there; we can always speak again later. I brought some DVDs over."

"Great," Miranda bubbled with mock enthusiasm. "Let's go watch a film together," she searched her brain for something apt; Thomas would have been brilliant at this. *Got it.* "How about On Her Majesty's Secret Service?"

Judging by her face, Christine was not impressed. "Look, Miranda, we're on the same side — let me prove it to you. I was given a message today, relayed from Thomas." She paused and lowered her voice. "It's bad news I'm afraid; your dog's very ill."

"My what?" Miranda flinched back against the cushion.

"Thomas said that Butch would have to be put down." The room went deathly still. Christine moved back to the window.

Putting Butch down? How? Was Thomas mounting some sort of rescue — did he know where she was being held? Shit. They were all armed here; they made no secret about that. Even Alice Eyeball was packing a piece.

"I'm very sorry about your dog; was he old?"

Miranda closed her eyes and tried to focus. "Er . . . yeah. I . . . I need to lie down for a while."

Chapter 37

The shrill ringtone on Thomas's mobile sliced into his brain like a steak knife. He woke, all arms and legs, sending his notes across the floor. He stabbed at the green button, working his lips to try and dispel the gummy, stale taste in his mouth. "Hello?"

"It's Teresa; open your door."

He checked the curtain; she was alone. In her hand was a small holdall.

"What kept you?"

"Sorry," his head felt muzzy, "I was asleep."

"Have you been drinking?" she pushed straight past him like she owned the place.

"Only a couple. Listen, Christine Gerrard has done a disappearing act." He'd expected some kind of reaction. But no, Teresa was too good for that.

She opened the holdall and carefully removed the Document Security Bag. "Over to you, then," she put it down and folded her gloved hands together.

"I won't be long. Try not to search the place." Not even a glimmer; not a flicker of warmth. Karl must really suffer on cold nights.

His initial trepidation faded the moment he closed the darkroom door and latched it. No surprises there. Whatever crap the world was throwing at him, all he needed was a camera or a darkroom and he was transformed. Christ, even his dad became a better person when cameras were introduced into the equation.

He snapped on a pair of latex gloves and broke the seal on the yellow DSB. Under the red light it looked a murky orange brown.

The box inside was untagged, just as Teresa had promised. He slid the lid off and immediately turned the pages upside down. Stupid as it sounded — even to himself — he wanted to be able to say he hadn't read any of it. Not deliberately, anyway.

That was easy for the first four pages — two in French and two in German. After that he focused on the top left and top right letters, now inverted, to get the focus. He checked after every photograph that the camera's infrared dot was still off in case it marked the paper. He kept his movements controlled and precise; his teacher from school Camera Club would have been proud.

Once he'd reset the box and sealed it in the new DSB — the one from Leeds — he felt the sweat nestling between his shoulder blades. The photos were fine, but he was a wreck. He unlatched the door and went out, still wearing the surgical gloves. "It's done."

"You've been in there for thirty minutes — what took you so long?"

Jesus; talk about ungrateful. "You wanted this done right, didn't you? I'll set up the printer for you."

She followed him to the laptop. "I'll need your camera data-card as well."

Of course you will. God forbid you should start trusting me now. He connected everything up, set it to print and walked off to the kitchen. "Call me when you're done. Do you want any tea?"

"No thanks; I had some while I was waiting."

He took his tea and loitered near the doorway until she called him back. All done and dusted, pages printed and enveloped; data-card removed. As if it had never happened.

"Thank you, Thomas." She looked relieved, already putting her coat on. "Remember what we agreed. At least two days."

Well, *agreed* was putting it a bit strongly. He walked her to the door. "So what do I do, then? Ring up Whitehall in a couple of days' time and tell them Special Delivery?"

"You'll need to figure that out for yourself. Whatever it takes, we *need* those two days. Ideally we'd have preferred more time, but under the circumstances, we're willing to compromise."

He felt like punching her face in — that, or crying. She opened the front door and pulled her holdall close. He pondered its cargo, and tried to forget that the pages included names, addresses, account-like number strings and some sort of contract.

"And this is where I return to the shadows; goodnight, Mr Bladen, and good luck." She'd only taken a few steps outside when a car started up, flicked on the headlights and pulled up parallel to her. In the blink of an eye, she was gone.

* * *

He bolted the door and stood in the centre of the living room. After all the tension, the silence in the flat seemed forced and unnatural. He waited for a moment, until his breathing had subsided. Then he reached into his back pocket and pulled out a second data-card, twin to the one he'd handed over to Teresa. *Clever boy.*

At that point he didn't really care what was on it; it was collateral. He had recognised one upside word though, in French: *état* — state, in English. United States of Europe, maybe? He checked the clock — time to make that call.

"John, hiya mate. I got your message. Tonight? Sure. I've got a couple of things to do before . . . right . . . I understand. I'll be in a cab in ten minutes." A minicab to Dagenham then; no expense spared.

Camera, secret data-card, gun and ammo, clothes, DSB, toothbrush and shaver, laptop and Sherlock Holmes book — everything for the modern spy about town. Thanks to traffic, it took almost an hour to get to Dagenham so he opted for the station. £45 all told, but the cabbie did throw in a series of free lectures on the way.

About the class divide, the racial divide, about what a pain in the arse lazy good-for-nothing sons were and how all the bloody immigrants coming over here were ruining everything. And all to a musical backdrop of what he now knew to be Bengali Asian Fusion. And every second or third sentence from the driver rounded off with 'Do you get me?' which he quickly learned didn't require an answer, as it made no bloody difference.

* * *

It was a surprise that Diane was the pick-up. The only time Thomas saw her at the wheel was when they were going out for the evening and John had decided to make a serious assault on his own liver.

She didn't have much to say, which was fair enough. He was probably the last person she wanted to see so he didn't push it. She seemed to thaw a little by the time they reached the house, but it was hard to tell; at least she was prepared to look him in the face now.

Sam and Terry's car spaces were empty; it looked like dinner for three, unless Sheryl — the other member of his fan club — was putting in an appearance. As they went inside, Diane told him, "Dinner will be ready in fifteen minutes." Which played in his head as: you have fifteen minutes to give us some good news.

He cut straight to the chase and dug out the sealed DSB, reminded them how he'd acquired it and why it would secure Miranda's safe release. It all sounded foolproof until he noticed the gun, amongst his things in the bag. If Diane had seen it, she didn't

227

react; it might have been business as usual for her, given the nature of *their* business.

After the DSB, he handed over the data-card. "It's an unauthorised copy of whatever's in the pouch."

John held the little case carefully at its edges. "We'll keep it safe for you."

Over dinner, Diane pressed him on how the transfer would be made; an answer he still didn't have. John Wright had ideas of his own. "Take the boys with you, as back-up."

Diane slammed her cutlery down.

Thomas read her face and winced. "It's fine, John, honestly."

"No." John looked first at him then at Diane. "You misunderstand. I insist."

In all the years Thomas had known him, John had never done *menacing*, until now. Not even when Thomas had turned up on their doorstep as a stranger, with Miranda on his arm. Forthright and unequivocal, maybe, but never this.

"The boys will be waiting at the scrapyard, first thing tomorrow."

Thomas had to force down the rest of his meal; hungry as he was, he couldn't dislodge a bitter aftertaste. He skipped the post-dinner drink and followed them to the comfy chairs, for more questions.

He offered up Bob Peterson's promise of getting a message to Miranda. Then Diane had to spend ten minutes talking John out of making a personal visit to Uncle Bob. Which reminded him . . . "Can I use your internet?"

John and Diane pulled up chairs behind him; he didn't comment. First, he picked up an anonymous server, then he took a slip of paper out of his wallet and set it on the keyboard; no point being coy now. He touch-typed a URL and went through the appropriate security, clicking on 'telephony,' and upped the volume. "This is a recording of all Bob Peterson's calls from Christine's office, today."

There were seven calls in all. The kick-off, provoking a chorus of obscenity from everyone, was Bob Peterson ringing Sir Peter Carroll's office to warn him that Thomas had requested a protective vest. The reply was dismissive; Thomas was being cautious, nothing more. He was just an amateur.

For some reason Thomas couldn't fathom, that still cut deep. Two calls later and it was Christine ringing in on Peterson's mobile. The sound wasn't brilliant, but Miranda was mentioned, with Peterson relaying the message about Miranda's dog Butch.

"Huh?" John said. Diane reached forward without a word, pressing Thomas's shoulder: the boy done good.

Thomas went through the calls sequentially. Peterson kept trying to extricate himself. "I've got a wife and child!" he pleaded, the signal swooping and dipping as the mobile moved about.

"Well then," the line on the recording suddenly cleared; "You'd better think about them very carefully."

Poor sod. The caller was male, well-spoken, mid-twenties. The sound quality dipped again, as if a moment's grace had passed. Then the voices went metallic and Thomas started to lose the thread. But one word pierced the cacophony: *Yorgi*.

He felt sick to his stomach; it as good as proved that he'd been on the right track since Petrov. He blinked back a tear and stayed schtum because he couldn't deal with their fear as well as his own. Because if it was Yorgi, then Miranda was in more danger than they could imagine.

Now what? He opted for distraction. "I'll leave the log-in details here, for tomorrow," and listened to the sound of his heart pounding against his chest. What would Karl do? He stared at the screen, catching sight of John's inbox, scrunched up onscreen and half-filled with porn and spam. Karl would improvise, that's what he'd do.

"Could you give me a few minutes please?"

John and Diane took the hint, left him to it and moved over to the sofa.

* * *

He worked quickly, without an audience.

Step 1: Set up a webmail account with a slew of random numbers and letters.

Step 2: Get the six-digit Ordinance Survey reference for the Wapping scrapyard.

Step 3: And here was the bit so clever that Thomas grinned as he was doing it — translate key words into something that would pique Karl's curiosity.

Irish Gaelic was a bit too obvious so what about . . . Kosovan Albanian. A quick internet search and he plumped for two words, cutting straight to the point: betejë and shpëtim — battle and rescue. He figured Karl would have picked up at least one of those words out there during his army days; he was counting on it.

In the body of the email from his seemingly random email address, he put in a message: *'Are you looking for gud time, big love? Order now.'* Then he added *'0800'* followed by the OS reference. He kept the title as informative as he dared: *'Sexi Kosovo Girls betejë and shpëtim . . . spurm.'* An easy to find reference to tomorrow, a few more keystrokes and away the email went, hopefully winging its way to Karl's spam email folder, where only Karl would see it. *Job done.*

John or Diane had put the telly on; though neither of them seemed to be watching.

"I'll get her back." Now seemed a good time to make outlandish promises. It was one he'd made himself. He had a Plan B. If the worst happened — and he'd confronted that nightmare frequently since Miranda had been abducted — he would track down and kill everyone responsible. No question; no messing; no macho bollocks — no exceptions. He gasped for air and swam to the surface of his thoughts. "I'll need more ammunition."

Diane actually smiled at him.

Jesus. He felt like he'd just shared dinner with the Grissom Gang. "I just want to say that I really appreciate you letting me deal with this."

John crossed his legs. "For now," he looked away at the clock. "Right," he decided aloud, "you better turn in for the night; early start tomorrow. You're in Miranda's room."

Thomas dragged himself out of the chair, said his goodnights and took his bag off with him. The door still had Miranda's nameplate on it. He almost knocked; he felt like an intruder.

Closing her door behind him, he stared at the bed, bag still in hand as if he wasn't sure whether he would be staying. Now and again, they'd shared that bed — in their crazy on-again, off-again merry-go-round. He approached the duvet and ran a hand along one edge reverently.

Either Miranda had stayed there recently or Diane had left a trace of her favourite perfume to really twist the knife. He closed his eyes and inhaled deeply, imagining her in front of him.

He checked the en suite — for no reason other than to be away from the bed. The figure in the mirror looked haggard and drawn; he barely recognised himself. He closed his eyes again and tried to feel Miranda close behind him, the soft pressure and heat of her breasts against his back; her laughter at his 'oh so serious' face and the sparkle in her eyes under the starry ceiling spotlights.

He wanted to pray, the whole shebang. To kneel down right now on the bath mat, asking for intercession and atonement for his sins. But the thing that stopped him cold wasn't a lack of faith — patchy as that could be. No, he still didn't know what he'd done wrong in the first place, not where Miranda was concerned.

He brushed his teeth, did the necessary and confronted the bed. He chose Miranda's side of the duvet. And okay, he wasn't proud of it or anything, but the bedside cabinet was just too tempting. And it wasn't like he was going to search through the whole room or anything. But he was restless and it was still early . . .

The top drawer was a mass of little yellow post-its, built up over time. He flicked through, tracing Miranda's neat, round handwriting with his fingertips. Underneath that little memory sculpture, he found some old lunch menus from Caliban's and even one from its former incarnation. Was chicken and chips ever really that cheap? This was stupid, he told himself, and carried on anyway. Just the top drawer, he promised himself, digging deeper past the tampons and some paperback called *Perfumed Garden*. Below all that was a 'confidential counselling' leaflet with a date and time scribbled on it. He blushed and lifted it out, along with a couple of postcards — both from Bermuda, from Miranda. One, to Mum and Dad, read: *Everything will be alright. Miranda x.* The other, to the whole family, said: *Looking forward to coming home again. I love you. Miranda x.* He put everything back in order and shut the drawer.

Chapter 38

Miranda, Christine and Alice sat on the sofa together. In any other setting, this could have been a mid-week girls' night in — complete with chick flick, pizza and red wine. Posh Bloke, now identified as Nicholas, had been a right misery about the choice of film; he'd claimed his share of the deep-pan and left them to it. Jack had stopped for a while then announced he was going to patrol the perimeter. Silently, Miranda presumed, like he did everything else.

It was an okay film — they'd let Miranda choose it. When Jack had fetched it back with the food, it was missing a label, a receipt and a bag. Maybe they'd shoplifted it to order. Still, she'd resolved to make the best of it.

Everyone laughed or held their breath at the right places; they just didn't speak to each other, except to move the goodies around. Just at the point in the film where the sassy-yet-caring girl-next-door realised that her best friend was a better match than the scuzzball of a boyfriend, a small green light in the wall flickered into life.

Christine jumped up, barked a code word to Alice and shouted for Nicholas and Jack. It didn't take Brain of Britain to work out that all was not well. "Jack — comms room, now!"

Miranda sat and watched the mayhem play out. She wondered if Christine had spoken like that to Thomas; maybe she still did during office hours. Then the penny dropped: they had a comms room — probably hidden cameras outside. What if Thomas was out there?

She stood up — on the pretence of stretching — and hugged herself like an orphan, in the centre of the room. Alice had her gun drawn and looked very, very scared. "You'd better go to your room."

The door sprang wide open, almost as wide as the look on Alice's face.

"Oh, for heaven's sake, stand down," In a single sentence, Christine turned Alice into a child.

Miranda looked at Christine through narrowed eyes; what was really going on here? Christine twitched and broke eye contact. Nicholas strode into the room like a lion. He did everything but spray the place, and by the look on his face, he was thinking about it.

"May I have your attention everyone; my colleague will be staying with us for a couple of days."

The stranger waited at the doorway until he had everyone's attention. "Ah, my dear," he crossed the floor to Miranda and extended a well-manicured hand. "Such a pleasure. You may call me Yorgi."

She accepted graciously — no sense getting off on the wrong foot. Nice watch, if you were into retro.

"And you," Yorgi clicked his fingers at Nicholas, "you will join us in the interview. The rest of you are not required." Then he laughed; the kind of laugh that makes you check where your children are.

Miranda found herself complying, meekly following them to the interview room. No one else had moved. Earlier, she'd thought that she and Christine had made some kind of connection. Well, maybe that was just a mind game to soften her up for the big one.

* * *

Yorgi didn't take prisoners. Initially he was all charm and sophistication but, Jeez, the cruelty in that man's eyes. He looked at her with the cold gaze of a predator; a woman gets to know the type, if she's unlucky.

At first Miranda figured she'd ride out the storm and basically wear them out. But this guy was good; he asked the same question ten different ways. No drinks, no comfort breaks and no one to help her. Nicholas seemed to relish every minute, watching the master at work. And even though she knew she had nothing more to tell them, after an hour in their company, she wished she had.

"You must think!" Yorgi banged the desk again. Nicholas jumped too. Yeah, for all that alpha male act, he was as frightened of this bloke as the rest of them.

"Did Thomas mention a package — a delicate matter of security?"

She shook her head again then remembered his insistence on verbal responses. He made Nicholas write everything down, questions and answers. "I need the loo," she was shocked by how small her voice was. She waited while Yorgi considered her request, didn't leave the chair until he pointed to the door.

"Four minutes. No more."

Nicholas marched her to the toilet; he looked smug, repeating the time span as if he'd thought it up himself.

She remained on the toilet seat afterwards, watching as her legs twitched. The tears came without warning; she pulled at the loo roll and dabbed her eyes furiously. Not now, not when that fucking savage was trying to break her down. She pinched at her arm — an old trick to displace her weakness in front of her brothers. God, she wished they were here now. She checked her watch — it was going to be a long night.

Chapter 39

Thomas jolted to attention as John rapped on the door and called out 'six o'clock.' He yawned and rubbed his eyes; he'd been awake for ages. He recalled being a boy, woken up on Saturdays for his paper round. Looking back, it always seemed to be raining — or snowing — everyone else still warm in bed. His dad would make him a mug of hot, sweet tea to see him on his way. 'Mustn't let 'em down, Thomas, mustn't let 'em down.' Those words seemed to have followed him around his whole life.

He showered, using Miranda's gel, even though he'd brought his own along. Then he dressed and sorted through the bag for the fifth time. Shit — no protective vest; he'd left it at the flat. Well, he weighed the pistol in his hand; if push came to shove he'd just have to get the shots in first.

Diane was milling about in the kitchen; she looked like she hadn't slept a great deal either. She kissed him on the cheek, same as she did all her children, and he felt his stomach twitch. Breakfast was a welcome escape from the possibility of conversation, and Diane had done him and John proud. She sat down with them, nibbling at the world's smallest piece of toast.

John ran through the itinerary. "This early, I reckon an hour will be plenty."

Thomas kept his thoughts to himself. An hour? Just to go ten miles up the A13. What was John planning to do, make him walk there?

Diane saw them to the door. The way that she and John held each other took Thomas's breath away; he thought that kind of certainty only existed on television. It brought him up short — didn't he and Miranda used to have that kind of relationship? He turned away, but not before he heard John promise Diane that it would all be okay.

"Bring them all back safe, Thomas," she sounded like she was sending him off to war — and maybe she was.

* * *

John didn't say much until they were on the A13, joining the other poor bastards travelling into work.

"I put extra clips in your bag while you were in the bog."

Thomas smiled. He would have made a joke about firepower if his guts weren't churning. He wondered about the gun again — about where it had come from, and its history. His stomach flipped another somersault; better off not knowing.

"Can I ask you something, Thomas?" John didn't wait for permission. "Where'd you learn to use a gun? At the house, you seemed to know what you were doing."

"Indoor firing range."

John looked disappointed. Thomas thought about showing off his flesh wound, as credentials; bloodied in battle, as Karl would say. Yes . . . Karl. Would he have read the email by now? Would he even be able to act on it if he had? Great — something else to stress about.

"Listen . . ." John kept his eyes on the road. "What are you going to do when all this is over? I can't see you keeping your job if you pull a gun on 'em!"

Yeah, that's right, John; lap it up.

The lights hit red; John turned to face him. "Only, me and Diane were talking last night. And, if you needed a job, we could take you on, part-time, like — with the family. 'Cos sometimes people come to me with the sort of problems that someone like you can handle."

Wow. Thomas locked eyes with John for a second or two. He felt the heat rise up his face and choke him. After all the shit he'd brought on Miranda and the family, they were still willing to chuck him a lifeline.

"No, er, need to commit yourself right now, Thomas."

The lights turned green and his guts did more gymnastics. Back in Pickering, Ajit's dad used to take them out on the moors. Often, on the way back, he'd wish that the car would break down, just to delay getting home. Or he'd count down every ten trees or street lights, surrendering territory in batches of ten. He was doing it *now*; he didn't realise it at first, but he was still wishing for something he couldn't have.

* * *

"We're here," John kept the car running. "I'll check that website for any more phone conversations from that Peterson bloke and ring you if anything turns up."

The breezeblock walls of the scrapyard were covered in graffiti, making it look like a techno-fortress. Thomas figured Sam and Terry weren't fussed; he remembered Sam's fondness for the spray can in his teens. What goes around, and all that.

Above the wall was a layer of corrugated steel. Some of that had been colonised by Street Artists Anonymous too. The E1 posse might be feerlezz, but he didn't rate their chances if they ever went over the fence into the yard.

The door set within the main gate was open and waiting. He banged on the panelling and announced himself.

"Hey Thomas, how's it going?" Sam could always be relied upon for a warm welcome. Terry though, looked like he was sizing him up. Sam elbowed him sharply.

"Alright, Terry?"

Terry sniffed aloud, like a Rottweiler gauging the scent of a rival. "Are you sure you're up to this?"

Up to this? He took a few steps forward, into their domain. No question, because when it all came down to it, he'd *have* to be. He dropped his bag by the door. "I am, if you two back me all the way."

Good answer. And true, as it goes. John Wright was a shrewd man. Now there were three chances of getting Miranda out, and if it all went pear-shaped he had people he could trust implicitly.

He closed the door behind him and drew the bolt across the gate. Terry led the way, through the scrapyard, deep among the junk-filled skips and piled up cars. In one derelict cul-de-sac, a series of crude targets had already been set up, ready for practice.

It took less than half a clip to realise that drawing from a shoulder holster was too slow. It was Terry who nailed it — too clumsy, too telegraphed; the way Thomas moved one arm across and the other instinctively backwards to give better access to the weapon. Plus, he'd hopefully be wearing a vest and that might slow him further.

He reverted to the basics and once he'd cleared a row of targets, both brothers seemed to lose their scepticism. Okay, they weren't slapping him on the back or anything, but they listened now when he gave instructions for repositioning new targets. He shot from standing, kneeling, lying down; a crash course in 'aim and fire' — not 'think then aim then think and fire.' Think too much, on this occasion, and it could be the last thing he did. He yawned; fatigue and the constant spectre of fear were taking their toll.

Sam came to the rescue. "Don't worry, Thomas, I'll make us all a brew."

Yeah, nothing like a nice cuppa after a hard day's shooting.
They sat on planks raised up by milk crates, staring down at the makeshift targets — two shop dummies and beer bottles on poles.

"When are you ringing the geezer to make the switch?" Sam sounded so much like a cinema gangster that it was painful.

Thomas turned it over in his brain. Teresa wanted two days' grace so was that the day after today? And how was he supposed to stall everyone? He scuffed at the ground with his boot. "I'll contact him later today." Sam and Terry nodded in unison and the three of them sought refuge in their mugs of tea.

* * *

All Thomas heard was a *click*, far behind him. It was the only warning before a shot rang out, shattering one of the beer bottles. The boys dived for cover; Thomas threw himself on the ground and scrabbled for the handgun, which he'd zipped up in the bag. He was still fiddling with the handle — jammed, naturally — when he heard the boots crunch against the ground towards him.

"See here, Tommo, is this a private party or can anyone join?"

Thomas saw Sam and Terry standing on the periphery, gripping metal bars: futile but admirable.

"Karl McNeill, at your service," he took a bow and holstered his weapon, which looked like one of his beloved Brownings.

Sam and Terry gave each other a strange look, dropped their weapons and approached him.

"Terry and Sam, I presume? Is there anything left in the pot; I'm gasping!" Karl released a rucksack from his back and cricked his neck in several directions. He was dressed head to foot in black.

"What are you supposed to be?" Thomas thought it best to get in early.

"That's a fine welcome for a man who's driven half the night to be here. Seriously, how are you, Tommy?"

After tea, Sam and Terry did the decent thing and buggered off to the nearest café for supplies. Thomas set up new targets — under Karl's instruction — and Karl unveiled the contents of his rucksack — a veritable armoury.

"So you obviously got my clever message. How did you get away?"

Karl laughed, rat-a-tat-tat style. "Well, my mammy wasn't willing to write me a note so I did what any decent pal would do — I walked off the job."

"Really? Shit." Thomas floundered for words. "So what's going to happen?"

"Hey, don't sweat it, Tommo. We have other things to sweat about. Bottom line is, Miranda's caught up in someone else's fight — that's unacceptable. You let me worry about my blistering career. Some things are more important."

Thomas gulped some tea down to soften the lump in his throat. "So where have you come from then, if you've driven half the night?"

"Hey, hey, Mr Bladen," Karl weighed the two Brownings in his hands, squinting one eye. "That's confidential information. I'll have you know that I've signed the Official Secrets Act."

"Twat."

Karl answered with a volley of two-handed gunfire, blasting bottles in all directions. "So how are you gonna tell Frank and Jesse James about the two-day hiatus?"

Thomas curled a lip. So, Karl had been speaking to Teresa as well. "Dunno — any ideas?"

"As a matter of fact, I have," Karl exchanged weapons with Thomas for a try-out, "but I'm not sure you're gonna like it."

Thomas followed Karl's drill to the letter, first kneeling then crouching, coming belly down to the ground, walking straight ahead, and all the while shooting. Karl was a natural; no, scratch that, he was an *un-natural*. His hit rate was mesmerising, against an assortment of bottles, headlights and shop dummies.

"You're really serious about taking down these bastards?" There wasn't a trace of mockery in Karl's voice.

Thomas laid the weapon on the ground — safety on — and brushed dust off his jeans. "Yorgi's definitely involved and he's not the negotiating type." He relayed the fruits of his intelligence gathering.

Karl poked his tongue out and licked his upper lip. "Hear me out now," he made the pistol safe and passed it over. Thomas put it on the ground. "If we're getting Miranda in exchange for the papers, *and* taking care of Yorgi — assuming he's there . . ."

"Oh, he'll be there," Thomas felt a shiver run down his spine.

"You need to be somewhere safe; a place you know well. Your life could depend on it. And hers."

Yeah, thanks for that. Thomas opened his hands to catch some more pearls of wisdom from Guru Karl.

Karl got the message after a few seconds. "Oh, right. If it was me, I'd make the exchange somewhere secure — only one road in and out."

Thomas wiped the sweat from his neck. "Yeah, but it's not that simple, is it? They've got Miranda — I can't take any chances; if anything . . ."

Karl brought his hand down hard on Thomas's shoulder, as if anchoring him. "Do you trust me, Tommo? I mean, *really* trust me? I see a way through this, but you'll need to do things my way."

Thomas looked around him; everything was still. There was that feeling again; a sense that Karl knew this was coming and had always known. Still, weigh that up against any other options — precisely none — and what else did he have? Nowt. "I'm listening."

"You have to dictate the terms. Name the place — and state your price. If you give them a price, they'll have you down as a rank amateur — which you are not. This gives us a certain, minimal advantage."

Thomas picked up the empty mug and stared inside. He felt like crying, and he could have filled it to overflowing. "I don't know. I can't afford to fuck this up," he heard the panic in his own voice.

Karl play-punched him on his good arm and shook his head dismissively. "It's like automatic doors. You keep right on walking at a steady pace and they just open — because it's what they're supposed to do." He did an exaggerated slow march on the spot.

"No guarantees though," Thomas wasn't smiling.

And neither was Karl. "No, Tommo, no guarantees."

He dropped the tin mug, the hollow clatter echoing in his brain. And shielded his eyes with his palms. He asked for guidance in the darkness, a solitary waiting, throbbing in his chest. But all he felt was the breeze stirring against the backs of his hands and all he heard was the hiss of his own breath. He lowered his hands and sighed. "Okay, how's this going to work, then?"

By the time Terry and Sam returned, the guns were stowed away and Karl was making stick drawings in the dirt.

"Who wanted the runny egg?" Rely on Sam to break the tension.

* * *

Thomas sat down with Sam and Terry, as Karl repeated the plan for their benefit. As it was the second time he'd heard it, his mind began to wander. With hindsight, it was easy to see the choices he had made as inevitable. The mind played tricks, picking out key pieces of information and stringing them together like second-hand pearls. Wrap the parts in meanings they never had before and hey presto, it's destiny. But mostly it was just making the best of a difficult situation at the time, and wanting to feel good about it.

Karl did some keypadding on his new state-of-the-art mobile and the Internet flashed up the bunker, not too far from Fylingdale; the one that Thomas and Ajit had rediscovered as kids. It was closed, Saturdays and Sundays. One road in and the same road out;

surrounded by open moorland. Even Thomas had to admit that the location was damn near perfect.

Terry raised a few objections while Sam wanted to be convinced. Thomas watched as Karl sold it to them; how the setting, time and place would work in their favour. Except he referred to it as 'securing the objectives.' It was a new side to Karl, decisive and with a certain, clinical eye. If the army was missing him, Thomas figured, it wasn't missing a mere squaddie.

Once the boys were on board, Thomas made the call to Dagenham. Diane and John didn't take the change so well — not at first, anyway. And bringing Karl's background into the picture seemed like the desperate act of a desperate man. Thomas was past caring; he just wanted it all sorted.

It still sounded a bit sketchy in his head. Karl and the boys would dig in on the moors. Then Thomas would make his call to Whitehall, giving details of the exchange and adding a £40k fee to the mix. He could follow Karl's logic that Sir Peter would deduce he was a greedy bastard, and that Thomas had probably sent the document up country, ahead of time. But what if they just sent the police — or worse — round to his mum and dad's, or Pat's? Karl's logic to the rescue again; so what, they wouldn't find anything. No, but they might take a few doors off in the process. Anyway, the plan was set and there was no going back now.

* * *

Thomas was alone again, but not abandoned. He loitered for an hour in Wapping Gardens, near the scrapyard, and then at the Turk's Head Café, cradling a coffee he didn't need. He figured it was a better option than waiting around Wapping Underground, trying not to look suspicious. The last thing he wanted was an over-zealous copper doing a bag search.

When it was time, he took the tube to Victoria and wandered the station complex, psyching himself up for action. If he didn't commit soon, the spare-any-change brigade would bankrupt him. He chose a phone stand to use and waited for it to be free. Which phone made no difference at all, but every little firm decision was a toehold on reality. He slid in his card and dialled the number from memory, in slow, steady movements.

As the number connected he checked the time — Karl's team should be well on their way now. The phone picked up on the third ring — no switchboard interrupt or invitation to leave a message. He stalled for a second, led with his name — always a strong opening — and took the plunge.

"So, Thomas, what do you have for me?"

He closed his eyes. "I can get the DSB to you in a couple of days' time."

"I see," the voice was non-committal. "How do you propose to do that?"

Half-truth time. "I'm to await a phone call at home and then I'll be texted a time and place." In his mind's eye, he saw Sir Peter scribbling notes down in red ink. "I go there alone and collect the package then we do the exchange and I leave with Miranda." He tried not to sound too authoritative, but hey, he wasn't asking permission either.

Sir Peter Carroll rasped down the phone. "That's settled then — I'll await your next call." The line went silent.

Thomas fought the panic and followed the plan. "There's one more thing." *Steady now, not too eager.*

"What's that?" It sounded like the old man had tapped a spoon against a cup, like he was waiting for a punchline to a joke he'd already heard before.

"I'll need £40,000, for services rendered."

"I see."

Can two words be made to sound smug? Those did. He hoped Karl was right — better they had him down as a chancer, than as honest and predictable. The line cut off while he was waiting for a reply.

Chapter 40

Miranda woke up with a migraine. Not a drink hangover, but a stress, dehydration, unable-to-sleep headache from hell. She hadn't had one of those in years. Last time? Probably the break-up with Thomas; the final break — a funny memory to dredge up. Doors: that was it. Those bloody doors slamming in the night and someone messing with a portable TV or radio in the corridor outside her room. And all that shouting — some bloke yelling at the top of his voice. Who was she kidding: it had been Yorgi.

She stumbled to the en suite and ran the tap, scooping the cool, stinging water to her face. It was the crying that did it; always gave her a bloody headache. The bathroom cabinet had been thoughtfully stocked with the female guest in mind — tampons, painkillers and cotton-buds. She snatched a couple of tablets and sank her head below the tap, pushing past the nausea by focusing on the craving for water.

A quick shower, then she changed into her gym wear — well done, Alice. It was a masochistic never-fail cure: exercise. True, you felt like shit for three quarters of the time, but afterwards, if your head hadn't exploded, you were in a better shape to face the world. She stuck a body spray in her waistband, ditched the lid — funny how they all looked so phallic — and opened the bedroom door.

The corridor was empty — hardly surprising after last night's aggravation. Even so, she tiptoed past every door to make it to the exercise room on the far side of the house.

The strip lights flickered with an angry buzz, gleaming off the shiny surfaces in a riot of light. She gave her eyes a moment to adjust, then began with a few warm-up stretches, progressing to practice falls and rolls on the mat. Back when she'd spent time in Bermuda, she had started kobudo defence classes. Her commitment had more to do with a guy she'd been dating, but now and again she still went through the kata at home.

Soon she was getting into her stride and the painkillers were kicking in. She flicked the CD player on, turned the sound down slightly and cycled like a maniac. The blood started pumping, and she turned her thoughts to the previous night. That Yorgi bloke was really unhinged. If Christine hadn't finally intervened, he'd have probably kept her there all night. But . . . Christine had left her there in the first place. So much for her promise of friendship. Jesus, this bloody CD — she must know every beat of every track by now. Maybe it was time to send Alice shopping again.

The shift of air, as the door opened inwards, broke her train of thought. She turned behind her — stupid really as she was facing the mirror — and there was Yorgi, looking like he'd had an argument with his suit, and lost.

He didn't speak, just stood with his back against the door. Miranda lifted her feet off the bike, swung over it and jumped down; the bike whirred on. "What do you want?"

Yorgi seemed to look beyond her, as if it wasn't really her he was seeing. In two words: coked up. She edged back and felt the sweat running between her shoulder blades. He was whispering to himself now; maybe it was deliberate, to freak her out. If so, he was succeeding. "I asked what you're doing here."

He snapped out of his torpor and glared at her, opening his mouth to a sneer. Miranda narrowed her gaze; flicking her eyes over him, fixing the vulnerable points in her brain the way that her sensei had showed her, long ago. She moved out into the middle of the room, facing him. Then it happened.

In a second, he had leapt the distance between them and had his hands on her shoulders, pressing down with such force that her arms felt weighted. He leaned in close to her face. "I have had a hundred dogs like you," he hissed, the words spattering against her skin. "Now, I ask you for the last time — where is my package? Does Tomas have it?"

She felt her face flush at Thomas's name and looked away, trying not to react. But Yorgi swung his face round to fill her gaze. He reeked of sweat and rage. Yeah, that was it: rage. And he was barely keeping a lid on it.

His hand drove into her collarbone and at first she resisted, pushing back as if to pretend it wasn't crushing into her. Then she relaxed and the weight of him toppled her off balance. Now he looked at her differently, as if she'd awoken something in him that was even more dangerous. Every woman knows that look, and what it means. Dread and anger mixed inside her like the elements of a Molotov cocktail. And the flame was coming.

He moved his hand down to her breast and flattened against it. She smacked it away, full force, and a malevolent leer rose up on his face. "I will enjoy teaching you . . ." he squeezed with his fingertips, digging into her flesh.

She kept her gaze on him, implacably hidden behind mental defences she hadn't had to use in a long time. A slight shift to one side and her leg was primed. At the first movement, his hand came down hard to block in front of his groin, but she crosskicked and slammed into his knee with the top of her foot.

Yorgi let out a roar of pain and fell to the floor, dragging her down with him. He was bigger and heavier. Despite his pain, he used his descent to his advantage, pinning her down and straddling her. Red fury burned in her eyes as she rocked him from side to side with little effect. "Now I give Tomas a message you will both remember for a *long* time."

Miranda pushed her arm forward, across and below her abdomen. He cackled with laughter, as if he relished the struggle. With a grunt of determination, she stretched her fingers, slipped into the waistband and palmed the bodyspray. The adrenalin was in full flow now; she wanted this fucker dead.

He bore down on her and she felt the obscenity of his bulge against her clothes. He pushed again, burrowing his nails under the elastic of her leggings.

She bent her neck back, drew down a snort of phlegm and spat in his face with all her might. He withdrew his hand to wipe it, and she took full advantage, emptying as much spray as she could into his eyes. He screamed and clawed at his face.

She swung a punch at his throat, but hit wide of the mark, catching a glancing blow against his chin. At the same time, she wrenched one side of her body up, screaming at the effort. He fell to the right and she dragged her legs out from under him.

"You bitch!" he choked through his hands, launching at her blindly from the floor — half grabbing, half flailing, crashing the two of them into the full-length mirror. They rolled together, mid-trajectory, and he hit the glass first, bearing the brunt as shards blasted from the wall.

She felt for her balance, sensing him crumple. But Yorgi had only folded momentarily to arm himself. She saw the blade glint against the ceiling lights as his hand swung towards her face. She dug her elbow in hard, twice in succession, against whatever flesh she could contact and swerved to one side as his hand arced in.

As she rolled on the glass-strewn floor she heard the crackle of fragments and curled in tight to protect her face. As soon as she came out of the roll, she leapt for the door and wrenched it open. Outside, she pulled the door to and stood behind the frame, frantically bracing herself for the tug-of-war.

"I kill you, you whore!"

She leaned back to counter jam the handle and bellowed for help. What the fuck was wrong with everyone — were they all deaf?

"Tomas and Petrov — they are dead men!"

She shuddered at every syllable. Then a shot rang out, dead centre of the door, blasting a hole through like a tiny explosion. She screamed and pulled her arm rigid until the bicep burned. The only way this bastard was coming out was if he shot a hole big enough to climb through. The stench of scorched wood and hot metal stained the air. A second shot burst out the door, splintering against the opposite wall.

At last, she heard people galloping towards her. Christine got there first. "Quick, come with me," she pulled Miranda away and threw an arm around her.

Only now did Miranda feel the flecks of glass in her hand and the sting as she brushed them aside.

"Nicholas, keep him here. You'd better sort this out — *now!*" Christine demanded, half-carrying Miranda away. Yorgi was still yelling as Nicholas attempted to placate him from the other side of the door.

Miranda made it as far as the kitchen and retched in the sink. Christine stood back, but she could feel her staring. "You've got to get away from here."

"You *think?*" That was all Miranda could manage before another bout of vomit erupted against the stainless steel. Not so stainless now. She felt her legs buckling and gripped the side of the sink unit.

"Come on," Christine insisted, "we don't have much time."

Miranda turned, and for a moment she thought of striking out. But by the time she had chambered her knuckles, Christine had moved out of range.

"Miranda, hurry, please!"

She followed the voice through to the lounge. Christine was unlocking the patio doors.

"Right," Christine's voice sounded shaky. "Take my phone . . ." she fumbled about in a small shoulder bag. "Give me your hand — quickly," she scrawled four numbers on Miranda's arm. "My cashcard — and there's twenty pounds." She thrust plastic and paper into Miranda bloodied hand. "And you better take this."

Miranda looked on in amazement as she passed her the gun. "Why are you doing this?"

Christine hyperventilated a little as she searched for the words. "Just go and don't stop — I'll say you overpowered me . . . get out while you still can."

And that was all Miranda needed. Adrenalin flooded her muscles and the survival instinct drove her past the pain, past the terror and through Christine. Afterwards she'd try to rationalise it as giving Christine an alibi, but right that second Christine had simply become another obstacle to be dealt with. She struck with a well-aimed heel of her hand, contacting under Christine's chin with a satisfying *thwack*. Christine went down like the proverbial sack of shit, but Miranda didn't wait around to watch the finale. She launched through the doors, straight across the grass, barrelling towards the arch at the far end of the garden. She flew like a Valkyrie, gun primed. Like Mum used to say, when they'd really misbehaved as kids: all bets were off now.

Chapter 41

06.30.

"Yes, this is Sir Peter — do you know what time this is? *What?* No, you did the right thing calling me, Nicholas. I can be in Whitehall . . . let's say eight o'clock. Take command up there under my authority and keep Yorgi under control — whatever it takes. Medicate him if you have to. Who was the senior officer? Christine Gerrard. Right, here's what I want you to do. Widen the search and put a surveillance team on the girl's parents' home."

Sir Peter glanced over at his wife trying to get back to sleep. He turned his back to her, and whispered. "Monitor Bladen's phone — I'm sure you don't need me to tell you of the difficulties the organisation faces if she makes it home before we get the package back. Do we understand one another, Nicholas?" He placed the receiver down and sat up in bed.

"What is it, Peter?" his wife fumbled for her bedside lamp.

"It's nothing, dear, just work. I need to go to Whitehall urgently." He didn't wait for an objection; too many years had passed for one to be raised. He picked up the telephone again. "Phillip, how soon can you have the car here? Forty-five minutes will be fine."

Chapter 42

Thomas span the plastic token in the air, pleased that he'd stored the DSB in a locker at Victoria. Just in case someone came knocking on his door before he left for Yorkshire. Everything was in play now and all he could do was wait at the flat. Teresa had dropped off the radar altogether; Karl, Terry and Sam were en route to somewhere Karl had promised 'would be close enough to the bunker to see Miranda's smile.'

He wandered, room to room, staring at the pictures as if they were an exhibition of someone else's life. And hadn't it been that, really? Leeds was a world away; the Miranda he knew — carefree laughter, sardonic wit and a lithe body with visiting rights — that was all gone now, surely? Somehow he'd overstayed at the theatre of life and seen the magician packing the tricks away; he'd never be so enthralled again, nor fooled so easily.

In the kitchen there were more photographs: a couple of panoramic views of the moors, at dawn and dusk. He remembered spending a whole day on that. For reasons he still couldn't fathom, it had to be dawn and dusk on the same day. The entire photography club had been there, all sandwiches and flasks, and a sneaky lager for him and Ajit that he'd found at the back of the Christmas cupboard. The photos were amateurish, but there had been potential in them; the composition of the shot, two trees together silhouetted against the orange glow; the way he'd waited and only taken two frames of each. Just two frames a piece in a crazy shit-or-bust challenge to his own abilities.

Looking at the pictures now opened a narrow window to the past. He could just about glimpse what it was to be a teenager again, to be outdoors and not be afraid or isolated or . . .

He coughed, as if to attract his own attention. Another photograph, lower down, cradled his reflection and he stared at the tears without reproach. Well, almost without reproach. "Finished?" he asked himself aloud.

* * *

Later that morning a text came in from a mobile he didn't recognise. *'Get new mobile, text us here with our names. Kosovo Girls.'* At last, something to do. He grabbed the bag and took the car; might as well give them some activity to track.

The salesman looked all of seventeen, but that didn't stop him trying to sell mobile-phone insurance and a host of accessories that only served two purposes — to delay Thomas and to really piss him off. Once he'd escaped his clutches, he found a camping shop and bought a compass. Not quite a Silva, but a decent enough copy.

Back at the flat he dug out the old maps — the ones that only saw daylight once a year at most, ready for the joyful family reunion. It was a deal he'd hatched with himself, many years ago — every time you spend a little time with the Bladen clan, I'll let you out on the moors.

The new mobile fired up with a little fanfare, which was the first thing he changed. He followed Karl's instructions and programmed in the Kosovo Girls number; he was in Karl's hands now.

The landline call came soon after. "Thomas? John." This was minimalism played to Olympic standards. "How's it going? The boys are in Scotland for a few days, on a fishing trip . . ."

He winced: way too clever.

". . . And did I tell you that Uncle Robert's been unwell — last I heard. I might pop round there, just to see if he needs anything."

He gulped. Did John Wright have enough information to track Bob Peterson down? Well, Bob would have to fend for himself.

"Anyway, have a good weekend and remember, Monday night is poker night. Everyone's expected."

The call ended. Thomas put the phone down and unclenched his teeth — a stupid, unnecessary risk. That settled it; he'd ring Sir Peter Carroll now and then get his arse up to Yorkshire.

"Hello Sir Peter, it's Thomas. I've just received a call — I've been told to head up to Yorkshire tonight. I'll pick up the DSB, then hand it over to you tomorrow. Hmm yes, I'll drive up. And Sir Peter, I really appreciate what you're doing for Miranda and me." The line nearly choked him. "Now, let me give you a handover site for tomorrow morning — I'll be there nine-thirty." He rattled off the OS reference, matching the red circle on his old map.

* * *

By the time he got to Victoria to retrieve the DSB, everything he needed had been transferred to a large rucksack, including the vest. Uniforms were funny things; hill-walker or vigilante — it all depended on what you kept beside your Kendal's mint cake.

Back in the car he hung an old St Christopher over the rear-view mirror. He didn't have the balls to string JC up there yet, but he was willing to take any help he could get.

Three hours into the drive to Yorkshire, the mobile flashed so he pulled over. It was Karl, in his own inimitable style: *'Dug in. drive safe, no speeding!'*

Mum and Dad had been thrilled to hear he was going to be in the area for a couple of days. Well, not thrilled; pleasantly suspicious was closer to the mark. Understandable though, considering he'd generally rather walk through nuclear waste than spend time with the Bladens. And he wasn't very subtle about it.

As much as he'd wanted to, he knew it would be wrong to drag Ajit into everything. Ajit would want to help through 'official channels.' But that was the kind of thinking that had dropped Thomas in the shit in the first place. Although, now that he came to think about it, a copper like Ajit could be useful under certain circumstances. Thomas weighed it all up as he exited the last services, before leaving the M1.

Chapter 43

Be it ever so claustrophobic, there's no place like home. And, if Thomas were honest, Pickering was no place like home either. If it weren't for the fact that he was bloody tired he'd have driven out, anywhere, rather than do the reunion bit now. But, as things stood, he was all done in. Not just the driving, tortuous as that had been, but the endless mental coin flipping; the absolute conviction that this would all be okay, followed by an all-consuming dread that it was all beyond his grasp, no matter what he did. It put a whole new sheen on: 'Are we there yet?'

The homestead curtains twitched as he was parking up; Mum had probably been waiting there for the last half hour, watching cars. He took a long breath and swung the rucksack over to the driver's side, checking that the box of chocolates had survived the journey intact.

His mother was at the door while he was still three feet away. He switched the rucksack to one hand, opened his other arm and engulfed her.

"It's good to see you, lad."

He used to scoff at the way she could produce tears — once he accused her, harshly, of manufacturing them to order. Today, he had to stay focused to stave off his own. His father smiled from the armchair and they did their usual strong father-and-son handshake act. Bladen senior waited until Thomas's mother had skipped off to the kitchen to re-boil the kettle.

"It's grand to see you, Thomas. Is everything all right?"

"Not exactly," he replied, then suggested they talk later, in private.

"Are you, er, stopping long?" His father stared at the rucksack, which Thomas had pressed tightly to his leg.

He pulled out the chocolates and placed them on the floor.

"Helen, come look at what Thomas has brought us."

Blimey, who is this impostor and what's happened to my real dad?

Pat put in an appearance later, with the kids. Gordon even managed to travel four streets to pop his head round the door when he came to take them home. It was like Thomas had slipped into a parallel world, where no one was using the next person in line for emotional target practice.

Karl was there at the back of his mind, but all he could do was wait for an update. So basically, he was Johnny No-mates for the night. He'd fed the family a vague story about being in the area for work — another half-truth that Karl would have been proud of.

His mother said she was going round to keep Pat company, while Gordon nipped out for a few jars. It sounded staged, but Thomas didn't care. He sat, statue-like until the door closed behind her.

"So," James carefully shut the hall door behind him, "what's to do, Thomas?"

He'd played it out so many different ways in his head, but however he began there was no easy opening. He unclipped the top of the rucksack and looked inside. "Why don't you sit down, Dad; this is complicated."

"Look, if there's summat troublin' you lad, just spit it out."

Easy words. He made two false starts, opening his mouth without speaking.

"Come on, Thomas, why are you really here? I don't buy all that rot about being here for work."

He nodded and pulled the drawstring closed. "It's Miranda, Dad. She's being held by someone — because of me."

"Is it drugs?"

Thomas erupted. "Of course it's not bloody drugs — what do you take me for?" Right, bollocks, he'd let him have it all, chapter and verse. First, the photograph at the Harwich, then Petrov's car, and then Yorgi. It was all loosening up inside his brain and oozing out like molten wax. He didn't know if his father was really listening — it almost didn't matter because now he was talking he didn't want to stop. Karl, Bob Peterson, Sir Peter Carroll, Christine — he knew they'd just be names to his dad, and quickly forgotten. But he wanted to get it all out now and lay it bare before him.

It took nearly half an hour to get to the present day, how Karl and the boys were already out on the moors, risking life and limb to help him bring Miranda home. And how he was really in Yorkshire to make the exchange.

His father had said very little. He seemed to wait until Thomas had run out of commentary. "And you've not thought of going t' police?"

Thomas raised his hands, clawing at the air in sheer frustration. "What did the police ever do for you, Dad?"

"Aye, I know; I'm only saying, like. But . . ."

Thomas reached into his rucksack — it was time.

"But won't it be dangerous?"

Thomas smiled; his dad was a master of understatement. He pulled out the bulletproof vest and passed it across.

"Blimey, there's nowt to it; doesn't look as if it'd stop a cough!"

They both laughed; it cut through the tension like a cleaver.

"And that's why," Thomas lowered his voice even though there was no one else in the house, "I wanted to talk to you in private, because I need your help."

His father leaned in and the flickering fire reflected in his eyes. "I'll do anything I can."

Hold that thought. "I need the gun," the words plummeted to the floor.

"Now, look . . . Thomas; I can see how you're fixed . . ."

He stood up and his father looked ever so small. "Don't fuck me around — is the gun here or not?" He could hear the desperation in his own voice and he felt ashamed. He hated feeling like that, hated being there, asking for help from the one person who'd never been any help to him, ever.

His father hadn't spoken for maybe a minute.

"Look," he reached into the rucksack again and drew out the .38 automatic. "These people don't mess around. I need the gun you kept in the shed."

His dad looked up at him one last time, and sighed. "Wait here."

Thomas called after him, making sure they understood each other, once and for all. "Make sure it's loaded."

He put the vest and pistol away, and stared into the flames, close enough for the heat to sting his eyes. At least, that's what he told himself.

His father took a good five minutes. Thomas was in no rush though, as long as he got what he came for. A second weapon could make all the difference.

"Here," his father put a rolled up cloth on the table with a soft thud.

Thomas picked it up, trying the weight for size. When he looked up, his father's face was frozen. "Did I do summat to make you like this?"

"No, Dad," he spoke through his hands, just like he used to as a boy when he'd been caught out at something. "You've always told me about the Miners' Strike, about the struggle against Thatcher and the government. It's my turn now, Dad; *I'm* the one fighting and these bastards," he felt the tears falling but he didn't care anymore; "these bastards have got Miranda and she . . ." Fuck, he couldn't even say the words. He choked on a breath and looked up. His father was wiping his face with a hankie.

"Now, I need you to do summat else for me, tomorrow — have you got some notepaper and an envelope?"

His father watched as he wrote out a letter to Ajit, detailing where he was going and when and what was going on. If it all went to shit — and he pretty much expected that, one way or another — at least the police could clear up the aftermath.

"I'll tell thee something, Thomas, and I've never told a living soul. That little gun there has only been fired twice. I took it down to the allotments one time and fair scared myself to death with a single bullet. And of course the other time . . ."

Thomas sniffed and stared at him blankly.

"Bloody 'ell son, don't you remember?"

He shook his head, as if he could deny the truth.

"It was you, yer daft bugger. I caught you in the house messing around with it and, well, we'd had words the day before. You only went and pointed the bloody thing at me and it was loaded. You couldn't have known that of course."

Thomas felt the heat roasting his cheeks. He *had* known; he was sure of it.

"Aye, bloody thing went off and shot a plate from the wall. It were like something out of Spanish City Amusements at Whitley Bay! Anyhow, you were so scared, you peed yourself and to tell the truth I think *I* might'a done as well!" His father folded the hankie and dabbed his forehead. "Look, I hope you know what you're doing."

A cog rotated in his brain; there was something else to take care of tonight. "I'm going out for a couple of hours." He picked up the Makarov pistol in case his father changed his mind and added it to the rucksack. It felt good to have it, as if he were reclaiming it from the nightmare.

"Are you out seeing Ajit, to drop off your letter, then?"

"No," Thomas raised a stop hand, "he doesn't know I'm here — he mustn't get the note until tomorrow morning. Tell Mam I'll not be back late."

He drove to York, for no other reason than that it was a good distance from Pickering. Far enough away for a DSB pick up, if there'd actually been one.

He wandered among the crowds — there were always crowds in York, no matter what time of year. Always a group of twats in Viking helmets and club sweatshirts, who thought they were able to hold their drink.

Despite his own prejudices, he opted for a busy pub — something with sport splashed across a widescreen TV. He squeezed through the throng and made straight for the gents, emerging a few minutes later with the vest on, under his sweatshirt, for practice. He settled for a pint of shandy and found an abandoned table at the far end of the pub. Nearby was an old man with a Border Collie at his feet. They were like two refugees from the twentieth century — the old man clinging to his pint of bitter and Thomas pawing over a hiking map of Fylingdales Moor.

A woman arrived with a buggy and commenced her double experiment, trying to poison her kid with cigarette smoke and mobile phone radiation. "Come on, Crystal, say hello to Daddy."

Thomas watched and swapped raised eyebrows with the old feller. The poor little mite in the buggy didn't stand a chance. Daddy was probably on the other side of the pub somewhere, stuck in the crowd. Or in a young offenders' centre.

He sighed into his shandy and puzzled over the map, a map so old that the bunker tourist attraction wasn't even printed and had been added in by felt-tip pen. One road, in and out. He looked at the surrounding terrain and access roads; it would entail at least a two-mile walk, maybe more; something else to factor into his non-existent plan. He put his glass down on RAF Fylingdales.

How was this supposed to work, exactly? Just walk up and say, 'I'd like my girlfriend back please?' And what about Yorgi — Yorgi was *bound* to be there and he was, by any reckoning, a nasty piece of work. No wonder Petrov had wanted to keep hold of the DSB. And where were Petrov and his family now? All safe for the night, no doubt, and with no idea what was going on all because of them

He took another gulp of shandy. How do you solve a problem like Yorgi? The more he thought about it, the more he felt his stomach shake. A man who feared nothing — Petrov had said so. Well, almost nothing. Maybe the Yorkshire Police Air Support could drop a crate of snakes on him . . .

The pub crowd cheered at a goal or a try or a foul; they were leaping up and down like a troupe of morons so Thomas couldn't tell what the payoff was. He raised a glass to them anyway, for living for the moment — lucky bastards.

Time for home; he'd been there long enough for an imaginary pick-up. He folded the map carefully and re-tied the rucksack. The barman received his glass, and exchanged it for a sneery look. Yeah, do come again.

* * *

Out in the car, he had another attack of the dreads and slipped the .38 between his legs. Unlikely anyone would try to lift the DSB from him, but better to be prepared. He checked his reflection. Is that what he'd become — a walking worst-case scenario?

Nothing happened on the drive back to Pickering. If the Eurostate Cartel had planned to storm the car, they'd obviously thought better of it. Karl probably had it right. All they wanted was the package back; Peterson had fallen meekly into line so why wouldn't he naturally do the same, especially as he'd asked for a forty grand disturbance allowance? And if they did stop him tonight, what was he gonna do — start a shootout on the A64? Good point. He stuffed the .38 back in the rucksack and pushed it out of reach.

Ma and Pa Bladen were watching TV when he got back. James glanced up and tried to wink reassuringly. But try that when you're terrified, and a tenner says it will look like a facial tic. "I was telling your mam, I'm thinking o' getting a dog."

"Thomas," his mum made his name sound like an alarm call, "your dad says you're off early morning — are you coming home tomorrow, then?"

He had to walk to the kitchen so they couldn't see his face.

"Kettle's not long boiled, if you're making," his mother called out.

He brought back a tray and noticed his dad had forsaken the armchair to squeeze in beside her on the settee. Wonders would never cease.

Thomas set the tray down. "Yeah," he started, smiling as his mother mock-frowned at the word, "I'll be back tomorrow."

Dad reached for his cup. "I were thinking, Thomas, 'appen I might drive out with you, tomorrow morning, and get a bit of fresh air. I've already rung work and taken tomorrow off, especially."

"Ooh, that's nice, Thomas; you turn up out of the blue and your father's already taking holidays. You should come up more often."

Thomas blew on his tea.

"That's settled then, lad," his dad sat back.

* * *

He lay in bed, letting pixel thoughts scatter and reform of their own accord. It wasn't long after ten — he'd turned in early, on

257

account of the long drive. He tried to picture Karl and the boys —
sleeping underground. But all he could see when he closed his eyes
was Miranda.

Some time after eleven he picked up a text: *Bunker road now
closed for repairs. Don't take chances tomorrow. Kosovo Girls
Brigade.*

Chapter 44

The wall clock read six thirty.

"Do you want some breakfast, Thomas — a bit o' toast maybe?" Thomas's dad stood by the kitchen doorway. It could have been a father and son day trip but for the ominous rucksack on the table. "All set then?"

They moved to the front door. "Don't forget the letter, Dad . . ."

"It's in safe hands, Thomas."

There was no small talk in the car until they reached the great outdoors. His dad was the one to break the silence. "You don't have to answer, but is this what you do for a living, like?"

He felt for his dad, trying to fathom all this out and come up with a new picture of the way things were. He shook his head, offered up as much explanation as he thought would help and directed them along the map. There were no police roadblocks to contend with, no suspicious vehicles with blacked out windows. In fact, the roads were so clear it was as if no one else existed.

For a few minutes he lulled himself into memories of the two of them out on the moors, photographing the sun as it struck the heather at dawn. He still had a print of that one somewhere, back at the flat.

"Here's good — don't stop until I tell you. And don't hang about afterwards; straight to Ajit at the police station."

"I could come with yer, Thomas; the two of us, together, like." There was an edge to the voice, like ice cracking on a pond.

"No, this is something I have to sort out. You taking my car away will really help though, honest." Hopefully it would buy him a little extra time when they tracked it to the police station.

"If they . . . if they harm a hair of your head, I'll not rest . . ." his father was crying now.

"I know," Thomas shook his hand; he didn't know what else to do.

The car rounded a hill and disappeared. He cleared the road and swung his binoculars wide. If he was really lucky, he could still pull this off. He had Karl and the Dagenham Duo on his side — so why were his guts still churning up like Robin Hood Bay in a spring tide?

It took an hour or so of scouring the moorland before Thomas found the habitat he was looking for: a pond. What was it the teacher used to say in Photography Club, at school? *Take every advantage.*

'It's possible, sometimes, to be so still that you almost merge into the landscape. Photographers and birdwatchers, the good ones anyway, they know how to do it. It takes patience and planning, but if you're really lucky all that hard work pays off.'

Thomas remembered his teacher's speech and tried to take comfort. His muscles were past numbness, beyond cramp; he'd been crouching in the same position for a good ten minutes now, glancing sideways on, as the grass snake wove through the grass. He fixed it with his gaze, as if he could magnetise it to the spot while he inched the canvas bag forward by degrees. He felt a bead of sweat slide down the side of his nose, trickling over skin cells, gathering pace. But he didn't dare flinch in case it broke the charm. The grass snake licked ahead of it, unaware of the converging bag. A little closer . . . and . . . bingo!

He flicked the forked stick, lifting the wriggling snake high into the air, twisting and contorting it to keep control. With his other hand he moved the bag underneath — the one with the DSB in it — and brought the two together, pulling the drawstring of the bag with the snake safely inside. Then he allowed himself the luxury of a smile and touched the crucifix at his neck.

As he stood up and stretched, he felt the .38 pulling a little in its shoulder holster. Not to worry; it wouldn't be for much longer. He took a celebratory sip of water, apologised to the snake and checked his compass bearing. Time to get walking again.

* * *

The entrance to the bunker beckoned, like a doorway to the Underworld. He surveyed the site through binoculars and tried to imagine Miranda down there, counting the minutes to freedom.

He squeezed the fear down into the pit of his stomach, telling himself silently, over and over, that they were *all* on the same side. That Sir Peter had entrusted him with the recovery of the sealed DSB.

Entrusted, coerced — what was a word between friends? Their only interest was in recovering the DSB; *his* sole concern was Miranda.

Only one thing for it now: to set things in motion. "Hello, it's Thomas Bladen." There wasn't an echo on the moorland, but the words seemed to magnify. He announced himself again just to make sure he wasn't startling anyone. And hopefully Karl would now know he was on site.

As he walked forward into view, someone surfaced from the bunker — a suit. Thomas raised a hand in greeting and forced a smile upon his face. The suit half-turned and Sir Peter Carroll emerged, shadowed by another man.

Thomas advanced a few more paces until Sir Peter raised a hand. "That's quite far enough, Thomas. I must say, you've picked a fine spot — reassuringly secure." There was bravado in the voice yet somehow Sir Peter didn't have his usual unassailable confidence.

He watched the old man and kept his smile high, forcing it until his mouth ached. "I've got the package here. When can I see Miranda? " He lifted the canvas bag high and held it out to one side.

The other man beside Sir Peter shifted his feet, the bodily equivalent of licking his lips. This must be Yorgi; he wasn't massive, although he looked formidable. And even at that distance, Thomas could read him: a face unencumbered by conscience.

Thomas took another pace forward. Sir Peter stalled him again. "First things first. I think we'll have your weapon on the ground; we don't want any accidents."

Hook, line and sinker. Thomas reached under his arm slowly and tossed the .38 to the ground with his thumb and forefinger. A pity, nonetheless.

Yorgi seemed much amused, but he already had his gun drawn so he could afford to be jolly. "And now the bag, if you please," he affected a bow.

Thomas felt the tension in his throat, squeezing the words out in single file. "I need to see Miranda." But the next face he saw was Christine's, rising from the depths of the bunker. His legs turned to lead.

Yorgi was laughing now, waggling the gun towards him like a taunt. "Now, smart boy, give me the fucking package or I kill you."

And they say manners are a thing of the past. Not now, he told himself: no distractions. This was it then. He backed his arm up for a half-decent throw.

"Quickly," Yorgi sneered, or you'll never see your whore again."

He felt his breath turn to fire. Chances of making the distance without being shot — very low indeed. Willingness to try anyway — almost absolute. Almost. He fed on the rage and helplessness that

261

swarmed inside him and drew them down, until he felt a strange sense of stillness, as if the world was narrowing in. Yorgi, prick that he was, had done him a favour; he had brought Thomas into what Karl called 'the kill zone.'

The bag sailed through the air and landed near Yorgi's feet. He grinned like a ravine, lowered his gun and retrieved the bag.

Thomas inched his hand up the side of his jacket to the pocket: shit or bust.

"What? You think you are smarter than Yorgi; you and that piece of shit, Petrov? No, Tomas, you are a fucking moron. Your precious Mi-ran-dah isn't even here! But I made sure I fixed her for you."

Yorgi opened the bag and shoved his hand in. Any . . . second . . . now . . . "Argh!" he screamed and snatched back his hand.

Thomas took his cue, drew the Makarov from his pocket and fired. No hesitation, no deliberation; aim, shoot to kill.

Yorgi jerked backwards, dragged into a spin by a shoulder wound. But that didn't stop him returning fire.

Thomas was momentarily stunned by his own incompetence. Then he heard the blast as the bullet slammed into his chest, smashing him down. He felt the ground punch him in the head and a clamour of voices swirl around him as the blood oozed down his face.

He must have been dreaming; Miranda was calling his name. He dragged himself to sitting, gasping for air, just in time to see Miranda materialise from the sidelines like some glorious angel. Then it all got very frightening indeed.

"You bastard!" Miranda roared at Yorgi and shot him, square in the chest.

Yorgi went down, but Thomas knew a pro like him would have a vest on as well.

Thomas heaved himself to standing, screaming with the pain; waving Miranda frantically aside, out of the line of fire. She didn't get it and started running towards him.

Yorgi jerked back up mechanically, wide-eyed and bloodied, like a homicidal marionette. Suddenly there was gunfire overhead, seemingly from all directions.

In the confusion, Karl barrelled through the scrub, slamming into Miranda side-on as he carried her to the ground. Yorgi's second shot went wide of the mark and whizzed past Thomas's head.

Karl rolled away from Miranda and recovered to face Yorgi with one of his Brownings drawn. Thomas dropped to one knee and kept his gun hand level.

Yorgi remained absolutely still, blocked by two weapons. His face twitched, like a trapped animal; Thomas figured Yorgi wasn't ready to call it quits yet. Yorgi turned to Sir Peter, pushing the barrel into the old man's face. "I take my package and I walk away."

Thomas was still wondering if Karl could make the shot when Karl abruptly lowered his Browning. Yorgi emptied out the bag and then he looked directly at Thomas. His gun wavered for an instant. "This isn't over, Tomas."

"Yes it is," Sir Peter's voice was as clinical as his marksmanship.

The bullet slammed into Yorgi's skull in a flash of red, propelling him to the ground as blood and brain matter pumped free. Sir Peter Carroll stood rigid, flecks of Yorgi's blood glistening against his face and clothes.

Karl holstered his gun and helped Miranda to her feet. She took his hand reluctantly and looked across at Thomas. He ran to her, clutching his chest on the way — it hurt like a bastard. Then, as Karl stood aside, Thomas gritted his teeth and squeezed Miranda hard against his jacket. She felt cold, in every sense. He breathed her in, pressing her face against his neck, and watched Karl surveying the scene.

Karl turned to face him. "Well, turned out nice again." He threw his one-liner away and advanced on Nicholas, who was already by the package. "Hey, hey," Karl called out, "don't make me shoot you. Leave it be." Then he looked over at Christine, who nodded to him.

The air crackled; Christine lifted a walkie-talkie from her back pocket. "It seems a local man drove through the road barricade; Jack and Alice have been detained by a policeman on the scene. Police Air Support is on its way."

Sir Peter Carroll lowered his head. Thomas pointed at him, the Makarov still in his hand. "He goes down for this, Karl."

"Hold on there, Tommo . . . that's not the way these things work. If this goes public, we all crash and burn — that'll be the end of the SSU and all those Euro bastards vanish into the night."

Thomas had already started walking. Miranda was at his side, her hand in his. He'd seen enough, heard enough and had enough. Karl shouted after him. "I'll sort it, Tommo; I promise. No loose ends. Leave it to me — I know how these things are done."

Miranda nudged Thomas as they crossed Christine's line of sight. He watched as the two women eyed each other silently. Miranda dropped a cash card, a gun and a mobile phone at Christine's feet, and then pulled Thomas away.

Chapter 45

It had been seven days. A whirlwind of events that, as Thomas lay listening to the birds outside, almost seemed like they'd happened to someone else. As he rolled over on one side, the bruise in his chest reassured him that it definitely had happened to him. He caught the alarm clock on the first bleep — he'd been awake for ages anyway. It was his second morning back at the flat.

Sam and Terry had taken Miranda back to London after a hotel overnight. He'd wanted to drive her home, but she made it very clear she didn't want him around. So he'd stayed on in Yorkshire for a few days, just until the official story unfolded: Eastern European drug trafficker apprehended, following combined operation between police and security services. He left after that — he couldn't stomach any more lies.

He'd been ringing John and Diane's twice a day, to check on Miranda. There had been a suggestion she might go abroad again but, thankfully, Diane had talked her out of it. Said that what she needed was the family around her.

Give her time, they told him — and that was about all they told him. Did they blame him? Not as much as he blamed himself; that wasn't possible. John reassured him that he'd be welcome at the house, in time.

And Karl? Well, Karl was another huge disappointment; he'd showed his true colours in the end, and tidied everything up. John Wright even got his gun back, apparently. Last Thomas had heard, Karl was back at work, resetting the clocks once more.

As he lurched out of bed, the previous night's phone call with Karl stung his ears. 'Trust me, Tommo, I've got your back covered.' Yeah, right.

He showered and then stared at himself in the mirror. The bruise on his chest had come up a fine shade of purple. Right about where the heart was; Yorgi was a true professional to the end.

Today was the big day — off to Whitehall to face Sir Peter Carroll. As he grabbed his coat off the peg, he noticed two brown envelopes on the mat — minus addresses or stamps. The A4 photographs were a mixture — some colour, some monochrome. There was a woman going about her daily life — at the shops, with her children, and a family photo in a park. As to the black-and-whites — well, not quite porn, but the couple weren't holding a raffle. Not unless they'd found a novel way to pick the winners. Sir Peter Carroll was evidently more athletic than his physique suggested. It looked like some sort of downbeat hotel or a motel, and it definitely wasn't the woman from the colour shots. The very last photo was different to all the others — an outdoor scene, long lens — Sir Peter's gun up against Yorgi's head.

A small card fell out of the envelope. He bent down to read it and a lump came to his throat. 'I never break a promise — K. See you back at work soon.'

He ditched the card, checked the other envelope — a copy of everything — grabbed Exhibit A and headed out the door. At Walthamstow Central he filed through the gate with the masses and enjoyed the rich travelling experience that was the Victoria line.

He walked past the lockers at Victoria and shuddered. He needed coffee, a double espresso. As he savoured its umber goodness, a text message came in: *Dinner tonight? Caliban's — 8 pm. Don't be late! Give Karl my regards. Mx.* Wow. He texted back a glib comment and marched right into Whitehall, holding up his ID like a badge of honour: Floaters Anonymous.

"Are you delivering that?"

He glanced at the resealed flap. "Yes, it's for Sir Peter Carroll's eyes only."

A guard escorted him towards the lift, same as ever. The door pinged open and a half-familiar face greeted him. It took a second to place him — Sir Peter's chauffeur. They exchanged the briefest of smiles and Trevor — that was the name that had eluded him — subtly tapped his own chest as he passed, mirroring where Thomas held the envelope over his bruise. By the time he'd turned around, Trevor had gone.

* * *

265

Three raps and there he was, back in the spider's lair.

"Please take a seat, Thomas."

He leaned forward and passed the envelope. If Sir Peter had looked pale before, by the time he'd viewed the contents he was positively anaemic. "What . . . is it that you want?"

Thomas smiled, a little smile to let the old man know that things were about to change. "These are *my* terms. You'll sign an executive order today, prohibiting Karl and me from being moved to separate teams without your express consent — which, of course, will be up to Karl and me. Bob Peterson's to be transferred immediately — I don't care where — and Christine Gerrard promoted in his place."

Sir Peter shrank back in his chair, like a slug at a salt-fest. As Thomas looked up, even Churchill's portrait seemed shocked at such audacity. Well, bollocks to them both.

"Are we finished, then?"

The cheeky bastard. "No, there's the small matter of forty thousand pounds outstanding — for Miranda." He put his hands on the hallowed desk. "And let's be clear: if you or your representatives ever take an interest in the private lives of anyone associated with me again, *you'll* wish they hadn't. You can keep the photos — they're copies." He stared at Sir Peter, waiting until the old man broke eye contact; it took about thirty seconds. A voice in his head muttered 'overdramatic,' but he shushed it silently.

"So now what, Thomas? I presume you know about my new working relationship — with Mr McNeill's associates?"

It wasn't a surprise, but it still left a bitter aftertaste. Karl had explained the rationale: run Sir Peter Carroll as a double agent; preserve the SSU, blah blah blah. It stank, however you pitched it, even if Karl was right and it suited the greater good.

"What happens is that I collect the money and then I'm out of here."

The bundles of notes were lifted from a safe behind the desk, all ready and waiting; he didn't bother to count them. Sir Peter handed them over solemnly, like a school prize; Thomas stashed them in a carrier bag.

"I hope you're not thinking of leaving the Surveillance Support Unit. You're a resourceful man, Thomas. I can always use a good man like you."

Thomas picked up the bag. He was halfway out the door when he turned and looked back. "Not any more."

THE END

My thanks to the following people:
Christine Butterworth, David Brown, Elizabeth Sparrow, Helen Rathore, Jane Pollard, Jeremy Faulkner-Court, Kath Morgan, Martin Wood, Michael Wise, Richard Coralie, Sarah Campbell, Sue Louineau, Susie Nott-Bower, Villayat Sunkmanitu and Warren Stevenson.

BOOK 2:

LINE OF SIGHT

Summary Report - In Confidence

Subject: Thomas Bladen.
Thomas transferred to the Surveillance Support Unit from a civil service desk. Despite initial suspicions, he does not appear to have any intelligence agency affiliations and his civilian status is confirmed.

While on a recent shared assignment with HM Customs, he witnessed a punishment shooting by Yorgi — a hitman who worked for the Cartel on a freelance basis. Thomas showed considerable initiative and assisted me in investigating the incident and collecting evidence of the Director General's duplicity. This was instrumental in helping to expose Sir Peter Carroll, and constituted a major intelligence coup for us. Sir Peter, while remaining head of the SSU, is now also being run as a double agent against the Cartel.

Inevitably, there were risks in using a civilian in such a high-profile operation. However, it was too good an opportunity to ignore, as Thomas had met Sir Peter prior to joining the SSU, and had actually been interviewed by him.

In an effort to mitigate some of the risks, I gave Thomas rudimentary firearms training and enough information to gain his trust. Unfortunately, we underestimated the extent of the Cartel's influence within our own department, which led to the abduction of another civilian, Miranda Wright — someone with close connections to Thomas Bladen.

The situation reached a crisis point in Yorkshire, as detailed in my separate report. Although neither Thomas nor Miranda was injured in the concluding firearms exchange, both have been affected by it.

Thomas and I will continue to work as a unit, and this arrangement has executive approval from Sir Peter Carroll. Following a review with our Senior Intelligence Officer, Christine Gerrard, Thomas and I have been removed from 'front line' assignments for the time being.

My recommendation is that Thomas (and Miranda, for that matter) should not be put under any surveillance by our organisation, and that I should remain the sole liaison point.

Thomas has proved to be a valuable asset with excellent surveillance skills and good deductive reasoning. He has an affinity for counter-intelligence work and I believe that his civilian status may give us a tactical advantage in further assignments.

Karl McNeill, Surveillance Support Unit.

Chapter 1

Thomas Bladen rested his camera on the dugout shelf and gazed across the terrain. He took a breath and held it, pressing his fingers against the rough grain of the wood, as a delicious tension gathered in his chest. This was the moment when his world came alive.

The *plom plom* of mortar fire broke the stillness of a perfect autumn day. Birds scattered, as if they knew what was coming; they didn't have long to wait. Smoke bombs detonated on cue, followed by thunder-flashes and industrial firecrackers: the works. Karl McNeill, Thomas's fellow surveillance operative, kicked off his own 'dud-da-da-*dah*-da' version of *Ride of the Valkyries,* while they waited for the photogenic armour to appear.

"See here, Tommo, they're late!" Karl tapped his watch. "Trust the bloody Mechs to screw up the schedule."

"Hush." Thomas squeezed closer into the camera eyepiece. He'd chosen a gorgeous opening frame and didn't want to miss a second.

The ground shuddered underfoot as the prototype C12 Battle Buster — to quote the corporate bullshit Karl had already accidentally trampled on — erupted into view. Then, as the air around them seemed to throb, the C12 revved over the crest of the hill like a foundry worker's fantasy.

All conversation in the dugout ceased. Thomas and Karl did what they did best. True, it wasn't quite surveillance if the tank commander knew you were there — more like PR — but the job still had to be done.

As the vehicle rumbled past, its pennant and aerial swinging wildly, Thomas got what he'd come for, rattling off a series of camera shots that he'd later compare with Karl's for their customary competition. Then he reached for his coffee, sipping steadily at the rich, bitter liquid.

"It's show time." Karl waggled a finger like a baton. Somewhere, beyond their vision, a turret should have been turning.

Thomas closed his eyes and tried to visualise the barrel — raising steadily, rotating and firing. He squeezed his eyes shut at the thought of the powerful recoil, and imagined the shell spinning relentlessly towards its target. There was nothing to see from their position, but they could hear the armour piercing payload; slicing through the air until . . . *pow* . . . the target was obliterated.

A tannoy shrieked into life. "Ladies and gentlemen — the C12." Somewhere, out of earshot, a gaggle of arms dealers — all legitimate, if such a thing were possible — would be offering polite applause and reaching for their chequebooks.

"Well, Tommo, that was the last vehicle before lunch so . . ."

An expectant pause. . .

". . . So I'd say it's *tanks* for the memory!"

Thomas cringed. Karl had probably been crafting that gem all morning.

Jesus. So much for that celebrated Irish wit. Northern, or southern? Thomas had never broached the whole Irish thing with Karl, not once in the eighteen months they'd worked together. Come to that, he didn't actually know where Karl's religious loyalties lay. A Proddy most probably, given Karl's time in the British Army. Still, somehow he couldn't picture the teenage Karl with either the Queen or the Pope for his bedroom pin-up.

* * *

The clouds parted, as if bestowing a benediction. Thomas breathed easier as they walked over to the mess hall. After an entire morning trapped in cramped conditions, contending with plastic furniture, extended delays, Karl's inescapable gas attacks and his delightful sing-songs, a stroll in the open air was a feast for the senses.

Alongside their security colour-coding the badges read 'Official Photographer,' and they kept their camera cases close at hand. According to Karl, the only opportunist greater than a squaddie was two squaddies.

While the posh folks might be enjoying canapés and sipping Pinot Grigio, for the commoners it was mess-hall fare with those self-same squaddies. Not that Karl seemed to mind; no, he was in his element — back amid a sea of khaki and camouflage, as if his two and a half years in the Surveillance Support Unit had never happened.

"You bloody love all this, don't you?" Thomas raked through his stew half-heartedly.

"Hey, this is just another job. Glorified PR lackeys — that's what we are." But his eyes shone as he gazed around the room.

"Really?" Thomas put his fork down with a clatter, causing the boys at a nearby table to stop and look over. "What if you could turn back the clock, jack all this in and go back to the army?"

Karl chewed his stew slowly. "Well, leaving aside the challenge of time travel, I'd have to say . . . no."

Thomas raised an eyebrow of dissent. "Bollocks."

"What, Tommo, and miss all the fun we've had together? Not a chance." Karl beamed his hundred-watt smile, but Thomas wasn't buying today.

He looked past Karl's pudding and the thrum of the mess hall slipped away from him. He was back on the Moors, and that psychotic bastard, Yorgi, was taunting him again. He was standing there, helplessly, flinching at the flash of sunlight and the blinding realisation that Sir Peter Carroll was raising a gun and . . .

"Hey." Karl clicked his fingers in front of Thomas's face. "You were zoning out on me there." The missing word was *again*.

Thomas nodded, pushing his plate away; nothing quelled your appetite like the memory of an execution. There was probably a diet plan in that somewhere: Monday to Friday, eat two good meals a day, then every weekend witness a shooting. The pounds will drop off, mainly through the night-sweats.

Karl drew in a breath. "I know how you feel, Tommo, sure I do. I was sixteen when I first saw a man die, right in front of me. . ." Karl fell silent, long enough for Thomas to know that a punchline wasn't on its way.

"Come on, Karl," he gestured towards the exit. "Let's call this meeting of Depressives Anonymous to a close."

Karl pushed his chair back. "Go on then, Mr Bladen, what goodies can we look forward to after lunch?"

Thomas pawed through his notes. "Helicopter demo — rooftop rescue. Then a couple of armoured cars and after that some small arms."

On cue, Karl retracted his hands into his sleeves. "Like these?"

Thomas quashed a smile. *Dick.*

* * *

Back outside, Thomas stretched in the sunlight. It wasn't all bad there; even army bases had trees. If you could ignore all the military hardware and square bashing, you were left with a lot of land. Probably some decent wildlife too, if they'd had the time to explore.

"You know, Tommo, you can always talk to someone — me, for instance."

Talk to someone? Yeah, that was how they'd got this gig. A post operational review with Christine Gerrard, after the business on the moors, and since then it'd been weeks on the surveillance equivalent of light duties.

No, the only person Thomas wanted to talk to was Miranda; it had been her life, not his, that had been threatened and turned inside out — and all because of his shitty job. Even now, just thinking about her, he felt the shame smouldering inside. Oh, they still met up and spent time together, but he couldn't quite forgive himself. And he reckoned she felt the same way.

"Right, Tommo," Karl held his camera case out at a jaunty angle. "What say we posh ourselves up and crash the arms dealers' bistro? How much do you think one of them earns?"

He smiled briefly. Almost two months on, and Karl was still putting in the effort, still trying to convince him it was business as usual. Never mind all the lies and double-dealing — the people they'd saved and the ones they couldn't. In Karl's eyes, it was all gift wrapped and put away — for the greater good. Well, fuck that for a game of soldiers.

Karl's mobile chirruped for attention. "Dearie me, I've told them never to ring me at the office." He hit the button on his work mobile. "McNeill here. Uh huh. We're out by the flagpole. Yes, ma'am, will do; McNeill out," he put his case down. "We've been reassigned, Tommo; we're to wait here — Christine Gerrard's express orders. Someone else will carry on our good work this afternoon. Transport's on its way — *special request*." He straightened an imaginary tie.

Thomas screwed up his face, as though he'd just caught wind of a bad smell. Minutes later, they heard the unmistakable growl of a Land Rover. Thomas turned towards the sound and paled, the combination of camouflage and blue lights registering a unique kind of menace, even to civilians. And judging by Karl's face, the military police weren't to his taste either.

The Land Rover screeched to a halt beside them; both MPs had that standard-issue wasp-chewing face. Thomas had grown immune to the contempt that the forces and the police reserved for the Surveillance Support Unit — they were often referred to as *floaters,* and a lot worse besides.

After checking ID cards, the MPs muttered between themselves then radioed in. The sergeant eyed them from the Land Rover. "Yes sir, we've got them."

Thomas nudged Karl, who didn't respond. The sergeant was calling the shots now. "Get in."

276

The vehicle swung away from the main buildings in a wide arc. Thomas hadn't ventured out this far before; they'd been limited to authorised areas only. A tarmac road wound through oaks and beeches, only he didn't feel so keen on nature now. The Land Rover rumbled on without a word, until a guardhouse loomed, with a heavy-duty gate that could only mean they were entering a more secure area.

He glared at Karl, willing him to say something. But that didn't happen until they'd passed the checkpoint.

"Would someone like to tell me what's going on?" Karl sounded rattled.

The MPs didn't even turn around. Thomas wanted to speak, but the words jammed in his throat. If Karl was holding back then they really were in trouble.

"Should I be phoning my boss — or a lawyer?" Karl's face was now an angry shade of red, a tribute to the soldiers' scarlet caps.

Thomas recalled that Karl had never explained how he'd come to leave the army and join the Surveillance Support Unit. Maybe this was unfinished business.

One of the MPs twisted round and barked, "No calls."

A minute or so later, the vehicle reached its destination, close to a nondescript door where the flaking grey paint screamed *underfunding*. Thomas followed Karl's lead and went into the anteroom without a sound. The door closed behind them.

Chapter 2

"Don't take this the wrong way, Karl, but is this anything to do with you?"

He was silent for a moment as if weighing the evidence. "Tommo, I've never even been here before. What the hell could I have done?" The voice was uncharacteristically shrill — odd to see him in a flap. But then, as Karl had once told him in a waltz down military memory lane: you don't fuck with the Red Caps.

Thomas let the matter drop and fell back on instinct, circling the small room. *Stick to the details.* There were two small windows — in need of a clean — and nothing to see outside. A stack of chairs occupied one corner of the room — with another three along one side of a large table, and a single chair facing them, court-martial style. He glanced Karl's way then thought better of it. There was no phone there, not even a socket. And right now he really needed to hear Miranda's voice.

He took out his mobile and punched in the security code. Karl's eyes bulged. "What are you doing? Don't be stupid!"

Jeez. He cut the phone and scanned the room again. This whole set up didn't feel good at all.

The sound of footsteps echoed outside, coming closer. Karl's face screamed, 'I told you so,' as he stood to attention, ramrod straight.

Thomas slouched against the table; no point pretending that he was army stock, and right now he was glad not to be, if this was how they treated their own.

The door swung in and a green jacket filled the frame. "At ease," the officer declared, glancing at Thomas as if he were shit on his shiny boots.

He looked the uniform in the face. "And you are?"

Karl took the hit. "Don't be a prat, Tommo; this is Major Eldridge."

He made a mental note: Karl and the major already knew each other.

"My apologies for your unorthodox mode of transport, gentlemen, but I had to get you here quickly. We're in a fix, Karl, and your presence on the base is fortuitous to say the least.

Yeah, but who for?

The major closed the door carefully. "There's been an accident in one of the test labs and I need an *objective* record, before the investigation team gets onsite. The corporate junket across the way has made things a little difficult for us — can we talk freely?"

Both the major and Karl looked directly at Thomas. He swallowed and sat up properly, bringing his hands together as if in contrition.

"I want both of you to get as much photographic evidence as you can without disturbing anything. You'll have half an hour at most, and then they'll be here to take the body away."

"Body?" Karl glanced at Thomas, an unspoken question hanging in the air: *Are you sure you can handle this?*

Thomas felt his face burning and cleared his throat. "We'll need forensic suits, and I suppose we're subject to a lockdown?"

"That's correct, Mr Bladen. Your things are being brought across now. Lockdown will be in effect for twelve hours. As a courtesy, you have a couple of minutes to attend to any personal business; then I'll need your phones and keys, etc." Major Eldridge finished his speech and left the room.

Thomas didn't waste any time; he speed-dialled Miranda before the footsteps outside had receded. "Hi, it's me. Listen, I'm really sorry, but something's come up," he sighed in time with Miranda. "I can't get away tonight." His eyes rested on Karl. "Yeah, he's here as well . . . you know I can't talk about it." He was still preparing a comeback line when Miranda hung up. He switched the phone off and placed it on the table carefully, as if it were toxic. Karl shrugged, by way of consolation, and copied him.

The good Major returned so promptly that Thomas wondered if he'd been standing right outside. "If you'd like to follow me."

Thomas smarted. *As if they had a choice.*

* * *

279

Thomas carefully secured the fastening at his neck. In other circumstances this would have been comical — he and Karl kitted out in white romper suits. But behind that door — a very heavy door, he noted — was some unfortunate's final resting place.

"I'll come and collect you in thirty minutes. Be ready."

Thomas let Karl lead the way in; he could feel the pit of his stomach extending away as he stepped over the threshold. Flung across the floor on the far side of the room, a starburst of blood and shrapnel. Beyond the bench, fragments of flesh and metal were embedded in the wall, and below it, the remains of a woman lay slumped back. He stared at her — at what was left of her — transfixed by the gaping hole in her skull. She looked like a grotesque sculpture; only partly human, something a twisted adolescent might have sketched on his bedroom wall.

"Must have been a faulty breach mechanism," Karl kept the chat to a minimum.

Which was just as well. Thomas didn't feel like talking. He stepped carefully around the debris and tried to tell himself that this was just another job. He'd done crash scene photography before, mangled wrecks with limbs poking out. But this was of another order; this was *carnage*. He fell into the rhythm of the job; get the footage and then get out. There was so much blood though, and an eerie mix of body fluids, smoke, and a trace of perfume hanging in the air like a lament.

Suddenly he was twelve again, off to see his grandma's body, in the Chapel of Rest at Scarborough. His mam had said he didn't have to, but he knew she'd be proud of him for going through with it — his younger sister, Pat, had waited in the car. As soon as they'd gone inside, it was there. Not a smell exactly, more an instinct; a sense of being in the presence of death. The natural urge was to run, far and fast, but he hadn't run then and he wouldn't now.

"Poor wee thing," Karl's voice cracked. "She must have been a bright girl to be working here."

Thomas's mouth was parchment dry; he nodded and looked away. The glass in the wall clock was smashed, zigzag lines raging across its surface. The slow ticking seemed to Thomas a travesty — a machine persisting when something more precious had not survived. He heard Karl behind him, clearing his throat, as if to say: *let's get on with it.*

He ignored him and closed his eyes, reciting the Our Father silently for the deceased. Then, remembering where he was — and who he was — he swung the camera round and began framing shots that would likely haunt him forever.

"Tommo, see that metal casing over there; well, what's left of it. Unusual magazine."

He took the hint and photographed it from different angles, then eased the casing over with a pencil. It slipped and clattered around the floor; for a few seconds it was the only sound in the room. Then he put a foot on it and turned to Karl. "Is all this . . . normal?"

"Nah," Karl grimaced. "Totally wrong, like a fucking *bomb* has gone off." He clicked his fingers then drew a finger to his lips. Thomas watched, wide-eyed, as Karl produced a mobile phone with a camera, and passed it over. "Get everything you can."

Emotion soared in Thomas's chest; for a moment he couldn't breathe. He felt the heat radiate across his face. Karl wasn't prepared to let this go. And neither was he.

At the far end of the testing range, a single target waited. He pressed the retrieval button; the whirring mechanism took its time, drawing the paper towards them like a spectre. There were holes — lots of holes — and several different sizes. He was no mastermind where ammunition was concerned — he relied on Karl for that. But even he could see that someone had re-used the target.

He summoned Karl over and continued taking both official and unofficial pictures. Then he pointed to a scattering of different-sized shell casings, but Karl didn't say anything. Finally, when Thomas thought he couldn't stand another minute in that claustrophobic hellhole, Karl banged on the door. "I think we're done here."

Major Eldridge was waiting on the other side. "We've put you in a secure area for the night — I'll get some food sent over, not that you'll feel like it. I realise you've got exhibition footage that needs to get to your liaison team so perhaps you could burn that to discs and then let me have your data-card."

Thomas blinked hard at the apparent slip of the tongue: data-card, singular.

* * *

"So, this is us," Karl shouldered the door of the shared quarters; two beds, micro wardrobes, a table and chairs, a TV and the usual facilities.

"May as well sort out the laptops now." Thomas dropped his stuff on the bed and opened his laptop bag methodically. He set both machines up and cabled them together, quickly shuffling the Army Demo footage between screens before burning it to a DVD. Once he was satisfied that the disc worked, he wiped the original material from both their data cards. Karl seemed happy to let him get on with it, opting for a shower and a shave.

Checking that the room door was locked, he went through the test lab photos, for quality and clarity. But each photo took longer than the one before, and he began to feel more like a voyeur than a technician. Those images marked the end of a woman's life, the moment the lights went out for good. He stared at the collection filling his screen; it was only the sound of the shower cutting off that brought him out of it. He rubbed his face and finished the job, burning all the footage to a single DVD, for the major. God only knew what Karl wanted done with the pictures on the mobile.

Karl emerged, half dressed — thankfully his lower half — with a towel around his shoulders. As Thomas looked over, he saw the silvery scars of a bar brawl etched on Karl's torso. Karl brushed his hand over them for comedic effect, as if they were crumbs. "All done, Tommo?"

He nodded, and offered up the mobile that he wasn't supposed to have.

"Nah, you keep it for now, just in case." Karl slumped on one of the beds.

Thomas left the laptops powered up for the major's scrutiny and flicked on the TV to drown out his own thoughts. It wasn't helping. "Tell me, Karl, what are we really doing here?"

Chapter 3

Thomas stood at the window, staring blankly at lights in the distance and tracking the occasional plane as it blinked across the sky. Normally, he'd have checked out the view through a lens, but he wasn't in the mood tonight. Neither he nor Karl had spoken for at least twenty minutes. Karl had raided the drawers to unearth a soft porn flick, a duff comedy and a slasher horror — none of them had stayed on long. Even Karl's quip about the porn film containing extras had failed to warm things up.

It was a relief when someone knocked on the door, bearing room service, even if Major Eldridge was right behind the squaddie. Once the Catering Corps had departed, the major loitered over the open laptops. The two discs lay side by side; one labelled up as *exhibition footage and stills*, the other left untitled. He picked them both up as if weighing them, and then put them down again.

"Just the one copy of each?"

Karl nodded curtly. "Sir."

The major opened his mouth to speak, and then sighed, delivering his next words with precision. "I'll check your laptop logs *now*."

Thomas watched him closely as he performed all the cursory checks before lifting just the test lab DVD, so that the strip light rippled against the casing. "Now your laptops are clear, I won't need to see them again. I . . . er . . . I think I'll go and rustle us up a bottle of scotch." He turned to face Thomas and Karl; his face gave nothing away. "I'll be no more than ten minutes." He gave the accident footage DVD back to Thomas. "When I return, I expect to see the laptops stored away. Do we all understand one another?" The door closed.

"What the bloody hell's going on?" Thomas leapt over to lock the door.

But Karl didn't answer; he was too busy breaking another blank DVD from the packet to make a copy.

By the time Major Eldridge returned, with a serious bottle of single malt whisky, Thomas had the additional copy of the DVD safely stored in his jacket. Karl and Major Eldridge conducted a decent assault on the whisky, while Thomas watched from the sidelines. Around 11 pm, when, despite all the army reminiscing, Thomas had learned nothing new about Karl at all, Major Eldridge stirred from his chair. He shook hands with them and pocketed his two single DVDs, but lingered by the door.

"I wanted you to see this."

Karl took the photograph and passed it to Thomas. It was a passport-sized, first day at work picture with short, dark hair framing her face and brown eyes staring out on the world. A hint of a smile played on her lips. He burned the picture into memory and returned it.

"I appreciate your efforts today, gentlemen. And I suggest you leave the base at first light." His voice had the quiet authority of a man who was used to giving orders. Karl saluted and even Thomas felt a stiffening of his shoulders. Whatever terribleness had gone down in the lab, this was a man of honour. Either that, Thomas mused, or he was a man with something to hide.

After giving the comedy film a second try, they turned in for the night. Karl rolled over on his mattress, creaking the springs. "Tommo, you awake? Can I ask you something?"

"If you must," he huffed. Maybe Karl could talk him to sleep.

"What do you think the major wants us to *do* with the copied DVD?"

Thomas wriggled about to try and get comfortable. "Could be he's just thinking on his feet — a little insurance policy for the future."

"Nah, you don't get to be a major without being able to think strategically. He wants us to have it, but why?"

Outside, unfamiliar sounds speckled the vacant landscape. It could have been a distant owl, but more likely a car horn — some lucky bastard with a less complicated life, off to see his girlfriend. Thomas's thoughts flew to Miranda, and then back again to the base. "I can't help wondering what we're not being told."

Karl shifted again on the mattress of a thousand squeaks. "Aye, some wee girl is on the slab tonight and I reckon her family will get everything but the truth. I think she — and they — deserve better than that. Maybe that's where we come in. Nighty night, amigo."

* * *

Thomas was already awake when some joker banged on the door at stupid o'clock. By the time he got it open, the only thing greeting him was their mobiles and keys in a cardboard box on the floor — very hospitable. He gave Karl a nudge and got himself together.

It was still dark outside; their Land Rover was ready by the door. "You better drive, Tommo, I'm not feeling too clever today."

He passed up the chance for a comeback line and took the helm, taking pity on Karl's head and opting for something light and classical on the radio.

Karl didn't stir until the motorway services, apart from sporadic bouts of snoring and sleep chewing. He finally opened his eyes as they pulled up, yawning and stretching, like Belfast's answer to Bagpuss.

"Coffee?" Thomas was already half out the door.

"I'll sit here if it's all the same to you; a large coffee, a copy of *Private Eye* and a packet of biscuits. Thank you very much." Then he switched radio stations, as if to declare that he'd officially regained consciousness.

Past the plastic double-doors, Thomas called Miranda. She was her usual razor-sharp self.

"They've let you out then!"

He waited a few seconds in case another gem was coming; turned out there wasn't. "Yeah, all done and dusted. On my way back to civilisation now."

"And should I ask?"

He grimaced — a fingernails-on-blackboard face. She knew better than to ask. "Industrial accident — with a fatality."

"Oh," she gulped. "I'm sorry."

"Look, let me make last night up to you — what're you doing later?"

"Is that an offer, Mr Bladen? Saturday night at Mum and Dad's."

He grinned, anticipating her next line.

"You're welcome to join me . . ." Somehow she managed to turn the word *join* — even at Mum and Dad's — into something salacious. ". . . If you're not too busy saving the world, that is."

He shifted away from the wall as a woman struggled past, baby in her arms. It struck him then that this was something the girl from the test lab would never get to do, and he felt a chill go down his spine.

"You still there?" Miranda's tone was insistent.

"Yeah, sorry. I'll be home in about three hours, once I've dropped off laughing boy. I'll sort out some clean clothes and head over."

"I can pick some stuff up for you to save time. Then you can drive straight over to Mum and Dad's . . . if you like."

She sounded like a carer. It still hurt, however unintended. Miranda had been the one held hostage, just months ago, but people were still treating *him* like an invalid, tiptoeing around him in conversation. As if everyone else but he was adult enough to deal with it. Jesus, he was drifting again.

"Er, yeah, thanks Miranda — that'd be great. See you when I see you." He picked up the supplies and trudged back, taking pains to keep out of everyone's way.

"You took your time — were you grinding the beans?"

He managed a half-smile and got back in. Karl looked him up and down. Thomas hated that. Karl was a master of deduction.

"Tommo, do you call out in your sleep?" Karl asked.

He closed his eyes momentarily. "Let's not do this."

Karl was still gaping at him.

Jesus. "Alright. On those rare occasions when someone else is around, I've been told I do sometimes call out in my sleep."

Karl nodded at him, aha style, and slurped at his coffee.

"I was like that after my first tour. . ."

Thomas watched him ease back into his seat and waited. Karl seemed to breathe by osmosis, to avoid interrupting his own delivery.

". . . So you see, Tommo, in the end there's nothing to be ashamed of in seeking help. Talking it through is the best way of getting to grips with your feelings and dealing with them."

Thomas put his coffee cup down. He'd had ten minutes of this and they were still in the bloody car park. He tried breathing slowly to stay calm; fat chance.

"You really wanna know how I feel, Karl? I feel like I should have killed that bastard Yorgi, the second he uttered Miranda's name. And I wish to God I had. I dream about that time on the moors, over and over. Sometimes I get him first and sometimes he gets me. And sometimes he shoots Miranda, and that's when I wake up screaming. I ought to have protected her from the consequences of my job, but I didn't — I fucked up. And now, half the time I can barely look her in the face."

Karl seized the first opening. "You have to be able to move on, Tommo."

"Bollocks." He nearly said, 'you weren't there,' but Karl *had* been there. Matter of fact, Karl had been the one who'd protected Miranda after Thomas took a bullet. By his reckoning, that made Karl twice the man he was.

Karl munched on a biscuit theatrically. "Right. Hear me out," he pleaded, spraying digestive crumbs across the dashboard, "and I'll not interfere again — I promise." Karl's face bore all the sincerity of an insurance salesman, but Thomas was eager to be convinced. "Look, I know a person who can help you; someone like her helped me when I needed it."

Thomas felt his back muscles relaxing. "You?"

"I haven't always been the calm and composed man-about-town you see before you today. When you see your oppos slotted, or you find yourself doing things you despise, well, it takes its toll. But a good medic can ease you through that — help you get it all into perspective."

Thomas started the ignition. Karl put down what was left of his biscuit.

"Christine Gerrard asked me to keep an eye on you, to let her know whether you're fit for duty. She'd arrange a referral, no questions asked."

Thomas gripped the wheel. When did everyone become so interested in his wellbeing? A better question might have been when did *he* stop caring? He huffed in time with the revved engine. Karl was right, no change there.

"*Fine.* Book me an appointment with the nut doctor; anything for a quiet life."

Karl smiled beatifically, and retrieved his biscuit remnant from the dashboard.

* * *

The radio formed the only soundtrack for the rest of the journey. He dropped Karl off at Holloway Road tube, the pick-up point where Thomas used to join him on their visits to the gun club. But guns were a completely different prospect once you'd seen what they could do to flesh and bone. Once you'd seen a dead body, all that intellectual reasoning and hand-eye coordination practice was just so much play. He waved Karl away and didn't stop until he reached that part of the urban sprawl he knew and loved as Dagenham.

Chapter 4

Although it was a work vehicle, Thomas still felt slightly sheepish rolling up to John and Diane Wright's place in a 4 x 4. The house was a working class des res, large and imposing. It screamed two things: a) we made it here the hard way and b) if you don't like it, you can fuck off. John Wright reckoned there were more *business people* — as he liked to refer to the better-heeled criminals about town — around Dagenham and Hornchurch than there were in Parkhurst and Wormwood Scrubs prisons combined. Which reminded Thomas to take all his bags out before he locked the car.

Time was when he had his own front door key. Back when he and Miranda were more of a firm fixture than a series of friendlies. Simpler days, before he'd left his Civil Service desk job and joined the Surveillance Support Unit; before he'd got mixed up in all that secret squirrel stuff. Anyway, no use standing on the threshold like an apprentice Jehovah's Witness, best get indoors.

The doorbell twanged a chord in his heart. This was his second home, more so than his native Pickering, despite his Yorkshire roots. The Wrights were more a clan than a family, with the boys, Sam and Terry, making up the remaining forty per cent of the mix. But the jewel in the crown for all of them was their Miranda.

It took Thomas a moment to realise that the door had opened. Sam was standing there impatiently. "You coming in or what?" Sam swung a playful punch and helped him with his bags. "Mum, where do I put Thomas's stuff?"

There was no answer from the kitchen. Small wonder. The sleeping arrangements all depended on whether Miranda was stopping over. It was more than ten years since Thomas had turned

288

up on their doorstep — in the heart of London's East End in those days — with Miranda in tow, having pulled her away from the clutches of a dodgy photographer in Leeds. A mate of Thomas's uncle — and the one Thomas had lamped good and hard.

And since he'd escorted the fair Miranda home, they'd treated him like a prince. They'd even helped them set up home together, but young love and bad habits didn't make for reliable foundations.

Sam dumped Thomas's bags in the hallway and led him into the living room. John Wright looked up from a table covered with a mess of wires and components.

"'Ere, Thomas, have a go at this — you're the electronics wizard."

It sounded more like a dare than a request. It was only months ago that Thomas had told them what he *really* did for a living, so it was still fertile ground for piss-taking.

"Come on," John vacated his seat. "You work out what this is s'posed to be and I'll get you a beer."

There was a glint in his eye as he sauntered off to the kitchen. Thomas looked down at John's pet project, recognised a capacitor and a circuit board but not much else. Jesus, some components were glued to the motherboard. He fiddled with a couple of wires and they came away in his hands.

"So what do you reckon then?" John could scarcely contain himself.

"I *reckon* you're having a laugh!"

John set the beers down and erupted into laughter. "As soon as Miranda told us you were coming over, I put something together."

Thomas weathered the chorus of good-natured abuse and drifted away to the kitchen. He always felt like a lost sheep when Miranda was absent, and her mother was the nearest substitute. Diane gave him a motherly hug, which in no way detracted from the fine figure she cut in her skinny jeans and fading blonde locks, as she turned back to the oven. "She'll be here soon," Diane said, matter-of-factly. He felt his face simmering. "So . . ." Diane faltered.

No one said 'how are you?' or 'how's things?' anymore. Miranda must have drilled them. Neither did Karl, come to that. He knew they'd all spoken about him, about how he was coping. Maybe he'd get them each a Support Worker badge for Christmas, and make it official.

Diane found her thread. "So . . . it's cards tonight. Texas Hold 'Em followed by Blackjack, and then we'll see who's got any money left!" She touched him lightly on the shoulder and kept her hand there. "And no cheating!"

He laughed. Given Diane's croupier past, that seemed unlikely. Unless you counted those Christmas sessions, where Diane dealt and John inexplicably held the only hand with picture cards.

A key crunched in the lock and he started, caught between trying to act cool and the desire to rush to the front door.

"He's in 'ere." Diane bellowed as the door creaked open. Then she went off to sit with John and the boys.

Miranda entered, doing her slinky walk, swinging a box of chocolates provocatively. She could look sexy filling a shopping trolley. "I see Mum's keeping up the subtlety night classes. Alright, babe?" She moved closer and he felt his body responding to a wave of heat between them. He basked in the warmth of it, their feet almost touching. "Did you miss . . ." she began, but he finished the sentence for her, with his lips.

Time with Miranda always felt different; tensions longer, emotions more intense. He gave himself up to the moment. When they separated she pressed her hand to his chest, to the place where Yorgi's bullet had struck the body armour during the shootout. The heat from her palm penetrated right through him, making his back sweat.

"Hard day at the office?"

He moulded his hand over hers, filling the gaps between her fingers, and squeezed.

"Knock, knock." Diane rapped against the doorframe, beaming. "No spectators allowed — caterers only I'm afraid!"

* * *

Dinner was a simple affair: shepherd's pie and veg, followed by apple crumble and custard. The chocolates and spirits didn't come out until the boys had cleared the table and laid a green baize cloth over it reverently. As John always said: if you're gonna play cards, do it properly. Ironic, given that John was one of the worst card players known to man. Well, to Dagenham. His occasional lucky flourishes only seemed to coincide with Diane's stints as dealer. No, he was definitely not one of life's high rollers. How he'd ever lasted long enough in a casino to hook up with Diane in the first place remained one of life's enduring mysteries.

In deference to Thomas's lack of preparation and ready cash, John declared it a chips and IOUs night. The stakes were the usual, enough to keep your interest but not silly money; it was a family game after all.

The cards flew thick and fast, with the chips moving round the table several times. He sat to one side of Miranda, so she couldn't read his face. And, if he was lucky, he might get the odd furtive leg squeeze.

"'Ow's your Irish mate, Thomas?" John didn't look up from his cards.

Miranda's hand rested reassuringly on his thigh; he cleared his throat. "He's fine." Nah, they deserved better than that. "Actually, Karl bumped into an old army mate; I think it shook him up a bit." *Yeah, that and the dead body.* "I think the bloke is after a favour, as it goes." He tabled a couple of cards to be exchanged. "Well, you know Karl!" He looked right at John.

Miranda intervened, reaching for the box of chocolates, which she waved under his nose. "Something to nibble on?"

He selected a toffee and wondered if the question counted as a promise.

* * *

The clock read eleven fifteen. "Right then," Diane drew the cards together and formed them into two fans, merging them flawlessly. "Let's see the final scores."

Thomas was down twenty quid and he'd got off lucky. Fortune — or Diane — had favoured Sam. He collected the IOUs and sat back in his chair, hands interlaced like a Mafioso. "Why don't we all just call it quits?"

John smiled sadly and shook his head. "No, son, cards is cards. You win and you collect, simple as that." He said his goodnights and headed off to bed. Diane followed a minute later, reminding the boys to leave the room tidy.

Miranda turned to Thomas amid the hubbub of cards, chips and glasses being moved away. "I believe you owe me a hard centre," she raised an eyebrow. "I'm off to bed." She could still make him blush on command. He followed her out, picking up his bag on the way.

"Try and keep the noise down, sis," Terry pleaded.

Miranda was completely unfazed. "I'll do my best," she called behind her. "But so will he, probably, so I'm not promising anything."

Chapter 5

Miranda paused at her old bedroom door, smiling coyly. It was only when she relented and moved to put her arms around him that he noticed the ring. *So much for observation skills.*

"Blimey."

The old engagement ring, from the days when love's young dream had leapt the crevasse to formal commitment. Even if it did end up jumping back again a few months later.

"Hey," she scolded him, "I do still wear it now and again."

Yeah, like now — on the right hand with the stone palm-side. He swallowed that thought and delved beneath the curtain of her hair, landing lightly on her neck. Forget the G spot; Miranda had an N spot. He let his fingertips do the talking, gently kneading her flesh.

"You know," he paused, just to gaze at her. "I've never quite worked you out."

"That's the plan," she laughed and kissed him, flicking her tongue into his mouth.

She tasted of brandy and chocolate, rich and exotic, like a good liqueur. They didn't speak of love or commitment as they fell onto the bed; no one spoke at all. In the wordless pact of familiar lovers, nothing needed to be said.

* * *

He twitched awake in the early hours, startling her. She cradled him, and he lay there, listening to their breathing in the dark, trying to push back the creeping dread. He felt as if something had been lost; wondered if she felt it too. He agonised over whether things could ever be the way they had been.

Later, when he surfaced once more, he heard the birds outside and struggled at first to work out where he was — curled up in a ball, submerged beneath the covers. Miranda's legs were warm against him, and he raised his mouth to her stomach, uncertain whether she was awake. He let his hands travel freely over her body.

Sometimes he wished she'd play hard to get. But they weren't kids any more.

"When you're done playing Gulliver's Travels down there, remember that Dad gets up early. So if you're thinking of a rematch, we'd better get a move on." That was Miranda, just like her mum: all subtlety.

* * *

By the time Thomas made it to the kitchen, Sunday breakfast was in full swing. Miranda would follow at a discreet interval; he never understood the logic, but that was true of so much about her.

Diane was usually the hostess with the mostess. However, John Wright liked to do Sunday starters. Diane was at the table, mug of tea in hand with a magazine in front of her. "Morning, love. You stopping for dinner today?"

"I'll see what Miranda wants to do." Or, more accurately, what Miranda wanted him to do.

"Why don't you nip out for a paper and get a bottle of something — make it red, we're having beef. Oh, and a couple of cans for John."

Good plan. A seal of approval from Diane would overrule Miranda's contrariness. "Okay — I won't be long. Anyone else want anything?" Sam shot into the kitchen like a puppy at the jingling of a lead. "I'll come too."

Thomas grabbed the keys for the Land Rover and got ready to face the day. Dagenham had lost none of its charm. The cul-de-sac was as silent as a politician wired to a lie detector. The lawnmower brigade wouldn't be on duty for at least another hour.

He stood for a moment eyeing up the vehicle. These days he didn't take chances, not since a tracer on his car had led to Miranda's abduction. Who gave a shit if people thought he was paranoid? Let's face it — he *was* paranoid — it was an occupational hazard.

He did a circuit of the Land Rover. Nothing untoward; cancel the red alert in his head. But . . . but then he did a double take, as his brain caught up with him. There was a cylinder attached underneath, and he'd never noticed it before. His mind raced, rationalising the irrational. He wasn't scared exactly but it didn't make any sense.

He whipped out his mobile and phoned Karl.

"Hi-de-Hi there, Tommo. What's shaking?"

Idiot. "I've got a problem — the Land Rover's been tampered with."

"I'm listening . . ."

He sent Sam back indoors, told him not to come out again. If it was a bomb, it was the least covert bomb in the history of incendiaries. He described the container to Karl and tried not to sound freaked out.

"I'll come straight out, if that's okay. It doesn't sound like an explosive device and I can't see why someone would have put it there overnight."

Before, then?" Thomas flashbacked. "Maybe when we stopped at the Services yesterday?"

"Nah, I stayed with the vehicle. Granted, I was a wee bit hung-over, but I think even I'd have noticed someone playing Meccano."

Thomas stared at the canister and felt the world retreating.

"So I'll pop over, then, Tommo?"

"Quick as you can — I'm sure you know the way."

The notion of a visit from Karl caused quite a stir in the Wright household. Less, Thomas reasoned, because Karl was a newcomer to their lives and more that they'd probably spent time him when Thomas had convalesced in Yorkshire.

The family loitered in the living room, making small talk. Then John disappeared abruptly into his office, returning with a mobile and a pissed-off look on his face. "'How long is Karl gonna be? I could do without all this."

Thomas didn't have any answer; he was too busy reminiscing. Medical books and the Internet might tell you that a flesh wound from a bullet doesn't take long to heal — a month or so, tops. And less, for the chest bruise, where Yorgi's precision had hit the padded vest, dead centre. But the mind . . . Jesus, that was a different story altogether. Google that one and settle into a comfortable chair.

When the doorbell rang, everyone jumped — the way they do in cheap dramas. John cast a glance at Thomas; he took the hint and went off to deal with it.

Karl flashed a smile as the door opened. "Clean your car, mister?"

Thomas felt his jaw relax a little as he fell into the game. "Yeah, you could as it happens; there's a terrible stain on the underside." He held back by the door as Karl circled the vehicle slowly.

Karl finished his lap of honour and scratched at his chin thoughtfully. "Might be better to do this somewhere private. The boys have a breaker's yard down Wapping way . . ."

Thomas teetered on the doorstep, weighing it up. Karl had been down there once before; another incursion into his territory. But what other option was there? "Wait here — I'll speak to Sam and Terry."

Five minutes later, the whole Wright clan emerged, with Thomas leading the way. Karl nodded to them each in turn, saving a small smile for Miranda. Thomas tried not to look too bothered, and failed.

* * *

A two-vehicle convoy left for Wapping. John Wright rode with Thomas and Karl in the Land Rover, following Sam and the rest of the family. Thomas felt squeezed again; he was getting used to his work and personal lives overlapping, but this was so far outside his comfort zone it could send back postcards.

John was clearly enjoying himself immensely, swapping jokes with Karl like they were old pals. Thomas figured they probably had more in common; Karl had been in the army, and John was definitely 'a man's man.' Meantime, here he was again, on the outside.

John slapped his hands together as he delivered the next punchline. "And the feller says: 'Don't look at me, I brought the music!'"

Karl's laughter could have shaken the chassis apart. "Come on, Tommy Boy, let's have some of that native Yorkshire wit."

John threw him a wry glance. This was a new one — Karl and John teaming up against him. He told them the one about the blind man giving his dog a biscuit. And then made a stab at a joke about the whistling prostitute with the glass eye. They left him alone after that, which suited him fine. All the better to check the mirrors, just to make sure there was no third car anywhere.

* * *

Terry got out to unlock the gates, and then both vehicles drove right into the yard before he bolted the gates behind them. Everyone decamped; Thomas watched as Sam went off to make a brew. Jesus, this was turning into a real family outing.

Karl and John carefully detached the canister and laid it down on a piece of tarpaulin. Everyone else unconsciously backed up a step. "I just want to say," Karl started unscrewing the cap at one end, "here on in, we keep this amongst ourselves."

Thomas felt a dull sense of familiarity thudding against the inside of his forehead. He muscled to the front. "You know what this is, don't you?"

"Well," Karl removed some packaging then retrieved the first part of a contraption. "Let's just say I could hazard a pretty good guess. He delved back in and extracted the other pieces. "Ladies and gentlemen," he stepped back from the spread of pieces and carefully put down the handle, "I give you . . . the smart gun."

Thomas clocked that Karl was wearing gloves. Then he gazed down at the tarpaulin, and saw the shadow of clouds as they passed overhead.

Miranda sidled up to him and pressed her hand against his back. "You okay?"

He sighed. "I think I could do with that tea now."

Sam did the honours. Thomas grabbed a mug and sniffed the milk — passable, even if it was that sterilised crap. He beckoned Karl away from the family. "I think you were bang out of order getting them involved — couldn't you have taken the canister off to your *own* people?"

Karl took a long, slow sip of tea and wandered off towards an avenue of cars piled five high. Thomas trailed him like a sullen spouse. He could see Karl was searching for something; hopefully, a decent explanation.

"Tommo, you do trust me? Surely to God you've learned by now who your friends are?"

He conceded that one with a nod.

"Okay, here's the deal. I can't get involved — not with a weapon. The footage from the lab, well that's different — I know my superiors won't like it, but they'll wear it."

Thomas knew straightaway that he wasn't talking about the head of their unit, Christine Gerrard. He meant Karl's *other* job in counter-intelligence.

"The weapon is your business now, Tommo. And you'll need back-up — people you can rely on."

When Karl put it like that, the Wrights were the natural choice. "Then what *are* we doing out here?"

"Me, I'm looking for a replacement bumper for my car — mine's cracked. And you happened to know someone who could get me one at short notice."

Typical Karl — always one step ahead.

"What's my next move then?"

"Well, don't try and assemble it or fire it. And don't leave any prints." Karl waved his hands, Al Jolson style. "You know, a scrapyard would be a great place to hide something, don't you think?" He pointed casually to a suitable wreck, then started heading back. "From now on, Tommo, unless I tell you otherwise, I don't want to know."

Thomas was still counting hubcaps when Miranda sought him out.

"All sorted?"

"Champion," he used the exaggerated Yorkshire accent that always made her laugh. It worked like a charm and he threw a loose arm around her.

"Well, this is a Sunday with a difference — is Karl coming back to Mum and Dad's for dinner."

"Don't ask me, Miranda — I just work here."

* * *

In the end, Karl collected his bumper, caught a ride back to his car and sodded off home to Kilburn. Thomas wasn't sorry to see him go. Another line had been crossed, and there was no way back. But that didn't mean he had to like it.

Chapter 6

"More pudding?" Diane waved a dish under Thomas's nose.

He glanced up and concocted a smile about as substantial as a meringue. He could feel the weight of their attention fixing him to the chair. He blew out a sullen breath and leaned back.

Miranda stared hard at him, appalled. He blinked a couple of times in the hope that she could read him better than he always claimed.

"Why are you being such an arse?" That drew a few chuckles around the table.

He glanced around and folded. "Look, I'm a bit weirded out by the idea of Karl on friendly terms with you all. I'll get used to it." *Only because I reckon I'll have to.*

"How long do you think we're gonna have to keep the pod, Thomas?" Sam was almost quivering with excitement.

"Dunno. But don't go touching it, or it'll need to be wiped again," Thomas scolded playfully. He paused and thought for a second. What was he really worrying about? Someone had wanted him and Karl — let's face it, *Karl* — to have a copy of footage from the lab accident *and* what looked like part of a test weapon. Okay, so it wasn't a normal couple of days for most people, but this was the game he was in now. He found a smile. "Anyone fancy another round of cards?"

The Wrights all cheered, as if Thomas had just returned from a dragon quest, wearing a new scaly waistcoat.

* * *

Thomas surveyed the IOUs ranged before him, like a happy bank teller. And now that he'd resolved to speak with Christine Gerrard the following day, about Karl's counsellor referral, the mosaic of his life was starting to make sense again.

He was down to a two-hander with Diane; he figured she was holding two pairs — one of them royal. All he had to do was hold his nerve . . .

Then a mobile went off. The Wright household shot glances at one another. They took their cards very seriously. It wasn't about the money or even the winning; it was about the playing. With them, card games were like catechism to a Sunday School teacher; you didn't mess with it.

"For fuck's sake," John huffed. Everyone settled on Thomas.

"Don't blame me; it's not mine — that's not my ring-tone."

Miranda didn't stand on ceremony; she reached into Thomas's jacket, slung over a chair, and lifted out the offending phone — Karl's camera phone from the army base.

It took him a moment to remember how the phone had got there. He held his hand out and she passed it over with a sneer. "Hello?" he blushed, hot under everyone's gaze.

"You've got to help me . . ." a woman's voice trailed off, punctuated by the sound of heavy traffic. "I've no one else to turn to."

Thomas gulped. The phone bleeped. *Bollocks. Almost out of battery.*

"Hold on," he looked round frantically. "I need a charger, *quickly*."

Sam dashed over to a sideboard, scrabbling in the top drawer until he fished one out. Diane slapped her cards down and ran to the kitchen. She and Sam converged on Thomas, so the charger could be plugged into the mains.

"You still there?" his breath caught in his throat, snared on the fear in her voice.

"I can't stay here — I'll ring you." The line went dead.

Blood drained from his face. He checked the caller number and phoned back. The ringing echoed in his head. "Quick, check out a number for me on the Net," he pointed to Miranda, like she was a servant.

She did as asked, scowling all the while. The prefix was in Middlesex, west of London. Thomas put the mobile down and chewed on his lip, lost in thought. First, the photos on Karl's mobile — superfluous, as it turned out, because Major Whatshisface had allowed them to copy the footage; then the container hidden under the Land Rover. And now some woman ringing on the mobile that Karl had suggested he hang on to. It all sounded like a set-up.

"I've got to go out. Terry, you wanna play this hand — it's a good 'un!"

"Where are you going?" Miranda's antenna was on full alert.

"Not sure." That was half true, softening her up for the rest. "I'm going to head over Middlesex way and wait for another call."

"On the phone you didn't know you had?" her voice was brittle.

"It's Karl's phone, okay? I forgot he'd left it with me."

Miranda snatched it up from the table. "So I shouldn't expect to see any pictures of you on this?"

Wow, that was a novelty — Miranda, the possessive one. In an instant he remembered what photos *were* on there. He stood back and let her get on with it.

She scrolled through the menu options like an aggrieved wife on the prowl. He knew what was coming. She wanted him open and honest? Fine. When she got to the pictures, she gasped and stared at the phone, open-mouthed.

"What is it?" Diane responded instinctively to Miranda's distress.

"It's a dead girl," Thomas beat her to it. "That's what I dealt with on Friday."

Miranda looked up, pale as chalk. "Then who the bloody hell just rang you?"

"I've no idea. That's what I intend to find out." He grabbed his stuff and headed for the door. Miranda was a step behind him. "You drive and I'll navigate."

Chapter 7

Thomas watched the road carefully as they sailed down the A13 towards the A406 North Circular Road. Better that than risk a row with Miranda.

"So, she could be anywhere in Middlesex?"

He let it pass, wishing the mystery woman would get her finger out and ring back. Karl's mobile had been left at the house to charge up, with the calls forwarded to his; which meant Miranda was also phone monitor.

"And why couldn't Karl locate the Middlesex number for you?"

She had a point. But no, Karl wanted to be kept out of this and he reckoned there was a reason for it beyond some old army loyalty.

Rain spattered against the windscreen, drowned out by the heavy rhythm of the wipers. There was a comfort to it; steady, regular, purposeful — all the things he wished he were. Instead, he felt trapped. Miranda's being there at all was bollocks, and they both knew it. He gripped the steering wheel. *Even a moron can travel the A406 unaided; it's a fucking circle — how hard can that be?* And when he got there, what use was a navigator if he was just driving around?

"I wish you'd talk to me."

He glanced over, then back to the road. "What do you want me to say?"

"Say anything — tell me why you're doing this."

He opted for a soft sell. "You know me; I'm a sucker for a damsel in distress."

She was quiet for a while and he fooled himself into thinking he'd got away with it.

"I have nightmares too, y'know, Thomas . . ."

He didn't; and it pained him that not only had she never said, but he'd never considered it.

". . . I thought Yorgi had killed you when I saw you go down. I thought it was all my fault."

He felt a lump in his throat, forced it down. There were tears in her eyes. He sniffed and his own eyes prickled in response. "I failed to protect you, Miranda — I don't know how to get past that . . ."

He changed lane and checked the road signs, letting the wave of emotion subside. Miranda put her hand against his, on the steering wheel. "Just don't shut me out, and we'll call it quits, okay?" She laughed through the tears.

When she took her hand away, he craved it like an addict. There was no eye contact after that until his mobile rang. Miranda seized it without hesitation. She didn't waste time with niceties.

"Where are you? We're on our way . . . right, got it . . . good idea — a public place. Try and stay calm . . . oh, it's Miranda. Dunno; blonde hair, brown boots, jeans — I'm wearing an engagement ring . . . yeah, and the bloke? Typical scruff-bag! We'll be there as soon as we can. Promise."

Before Thomas could add his own two penn'orth, she'd closed the call and pulled out her own mobile. "Dad? No, everything's fine. Can you get Terry for me a minute? Terry? Go look up a pub on the Net — Abrook Arms, in Uxbridge. Yeah, ring me straight back."

Thomas blushed. It was a funny time to be proud of her.

She looked up at him. "What?"

"Dunno, just a different side of you, I s'pose."

"Different, good?" she pouted.

He conceded a smile. When Terry rang back she was ready, pen in hand, and scribbled furiously into her address book. Now she could really navigate.

* * *

They pulled up outside the Abrook Arms, still in mid debate, with him losing on points.

"All I'm saying is, you could have checked with Karl and found out *why* you're doing his dirty work. Or maybe you already know something?"

There wasn't a lot he could say. The mystery call to the mobile could have been a set-up by someone who wanted the smart gun — or who wanted it *back* — and here he was, walking into the lion's den. But for all that, he was glad to be doing something about it, especially with Miranda riding shotgun.

The pub door squeaked open. The place wasn't exactly heaving. In the far corner, a live band was knocking out a decent rendition of 'Try A Little Tenderness.' One sweep of the bar told Thomas who the Mystery Caller was. She'd be the only one sat alone, clutching her chair, mousy hair drawn back into a bun.

Miranda clocked the woman as well. She waved her left hand in front of her, with the engagement ring transferred to its former position. Any hammier and it would have come with salad in a roll. Thomas nudged her and she pointed him towards the bar for three drinks, doing a sexy walk for his benefit. One of the band almost got his tongue caught in his guitar strings.

The drinks came quickly, thanks to lack of competition at the bar; and by the time he arrived at the table, Miranda was finishing the introductions.

"Wasn't sure what to get you, but I figured you looked like a rum and coke."

Point of fact, she looked like a frightened child.

They moved away from the band to another table; they stuck out as strangers anyway, so there was little point pretending they were there for the music. Plus, they had a lot to discuss.

Mystery Caller was first to speak. "Can we just go?"

"Finish your drink first," Thomas took control. "You look like you could do with it. And it creates less attention."

"He's right, Jess," Miranda piped up, lifting her driving licence off the table. "Have you eaten?"

Jess didn't answer. The pub crowd, such as they were, cheered after a few intro chords. Thomas watched as a few fans joined in with 'Everybody Needs Somebody To Love.' Unfortunately, some of them were vocally on a par with Karl.

"Blimey — must be Wilson Pickett night!"

Jess looked at him blankly and he smiled to himself at her inadequate musical education. Their rapport was non-existent so he left her with Miranda and went in search of crisps. You could never have too many crisps; he knew that because Karl had done the clinical research.

He was still congratulating himself on how well he was handling everything as he ferried them back. Then he saw Jess crying. Not just crying, she was bawling her eyes out. Miranda was doing her best, but whatever Jess had been holding on to had reached the point of overspill.

"It's time to make a move," he got up, keeping hold of the crisps and leaving Miranda to shoulder the woman out of the pub. He hung back, checking to see if anyone had taken an interest. Only the barman was looking around, most probably hoping for customers. Thomas nodded in thanks and took the glasses over.

303

"Is she alright, mate?" The two women were out the door by now.

"Yeah, just a bit of boyfriend trouble."

The barman murmured something and went back to staring into space.

Although Jess had been upset in the pub, the sight of the Land Rover really made her lose it. It took all their coaxing — and most of that was down to Miranda — to convince Jess they really were there to help her.

Miranda accepted a back seat, with all the grace of a pub brawl. Once everyone was aboard, Thomas passed out the crisps, banking on a comedy moment to lighten the load. He made straight for the North Circular.

The crisps gave Jess something to do, which made the conversation a little easier. He wanted to start with something simple, and to avoid, 'Why did you call me and who the hell are you?' for as long as possible. Unfortunately, Miranda hadn't attended that little briefing in his head.

"So come on, Jess," Miranda soothed her as they snacked on Salt & Vinegar together, "what made you ring *us*?"

Jess paused, mid crisp. "He said, if I made it out safely, I was to ring that number and someone would take care of everything." She stopped, gauged their faces and did a fair mime of the word *terror*.

Thomas's brain was spinning like a bicycle freewheeling downhill — lots of whirling and no control. "You did the right thing, calling us," he insisted. "We'll find somewhere safe for you and then we can get to the bottom of this."

No one seemed to feel like talking anymore, so he put the radio on and found something easy-listening; not classical — he wasn't trying to put them to sleep — but nothing too boisterous. It also freed him up to concentrate on the driving and ponder what his next move was.

Miranda drew in a breath, a big one; the sort of breath that could only end in a sixty-four-thousand-dollar question. As ever, she didn't disappoint. "Jess, can you tell us what kind of trouble you're in?"

Jesus. Why don't you use a loudhailer and be done with it? Part of him was appalled, but another part was fascinated, seeing Miranda in action. It was a new side to her, and though he'd never tell her, he preferred it; they were a team again.

"I was there on the base, when it happened."

Oh shit; that opened a trapdoor. He caught Miranda's eye in the mirror, aware that he could stop this right now, but Jess might not give him a second chance. "Did you see the accident?" he kept his voice low.

"No, I was on my way back in. But as soon as I heard the explosion, I knew. I panicked and hid away; tried to pretend it wasn't happening."

He could hear the way her voice fluttered as she spoke. He dug his nails into the wheel to drown out his own memories. "I need to know everything, Jess."

She didn't reply and he waited it out for a while, letting the radio soundtrack fill the void. Maybe now was the time to mention he was her only option.

"Do you have clearance for this?" Her voice grated.

God knows. "Absolutely — we both do." He smiled reassuringly in Miranda's direction. That winning Bladen smile; it could open locks on a good day, and today was definitely an improvement on yesterday.

Jess took a few long breaths, as if she were rhythmically bringing details to the surface. Then she tilted her head back and began. "The prototype weapon was designed to utilise a range of ammunition without the need for modification." It sounded like she was reading from a cue card.

Bingo. That explained the unusually colandered target. He nodded appreciatively for her to continue.

"The UB40 will support urban ground troops."

"The what?"

"The weapon is designated the UB40 — Urban Ballistics. It was some sort of in-joke apparently."

She didn't look like she'd be laughing for a long while. He snorted contemptuously; they must have pissed themselves, down at research central. UB40, like the old unemployment benefits form, because all other firearms would be out of a job.

"Its working title is the Scavenger, but the branding hasn't been decided yet." She paused then added as an afterthought, "and my contract is ending soon."

Alarm bells rang in his head at the words *brand* and *contract.* Clearly, not your everyday MoD personnel.

"Who do you work for, exactly?" This was starting to feel like an interrogation.

"Engamel Solutions, of course."

Never heard of them. He played to his strengths and said nothing. Glancing in the rear mirror, he noticed Miranda was sat very still. Hopefully she wouldn't feel inclined to ring her family and update them. She looked moody, probably pissed off because he and Jess were talking shop now. And it might not help that Jess wasn't exactly hard on the eye.

"So," Miranda leaned towards the gap between the front seats; "How did you get off the base?"

He smiled. Clever girl; cleverer than him, evidently.

Jess went a funny shade of pale. "I can't say."

Miranda was having none of it. "Can't say or won't say?" There was an edge to the voice. Even Thomas shifted a little in his seat.

"Pull over — I want to get out." Miss Tiny Tears became Miss Belligerent.

Miranda, he knew, did not like to be challenged, and especially not by a woman. He glanced in the mirror and Miranda was staring right at him, nodding.

He slowed down.

"You're free to leave us at any time," Miranda huffed. "But whoever got you out clearly didn't give a shit about you . . ."

Nice. Always try the softly-softly approach first.

She qualified her statement, "You've no belongings and they dropped you off in Uxbridge, alone. You don't have any close family nearby . . ."

How the bloody hell did she come up with that?

"Because if you had, you wouldn't have rung us . . ."

He grinned, tilting his head away so that no one else could see. The woman was a genius.

". . . So let's stop pissing around, shall we? We're here to help you, but you've got to trust us."

Jess released her grip on the door handle. "Okay," she whispered. "I was told to ring your number and not to speak to anyone else. Am I in a lot of trouble?"

That's what he'd been wondering. Had she been freed for her own good or for someone else's? Either way, it was time to intervene.

"At this point we're only interested in uncovering the truth." He tried to convey a sense of authority and understanding.

No one spoke again until the signs for Edmonton.

"Where is she stopping tonight, Thomas — Walthamstow or Bow?"

Good question. "My place — Walthamstow." The next sentence leapt past his brain and out his mouth. "Jess, you can have my bed; I'll kip on the sofa."

Miranda smacked her lips. "Sounds like three's a crowd."

"That's not what I meant," he retreated, catching a glimmer of a smile to his left.

But Miranda rang ahead and secured a pick-up from her brother, Terry, telling him to bring the rogue mobile with him. Her tone was measured, in control, and Thomas could feel the shutters coming down.

Chapter 8

"So have a good evening, then." Miranda swept out of the flat, slamming the door behind her.

Thomas tried desperately to change the subject. "You must be hungry, Jess — do you want a takeaway or shall I see what's in the freezer?"

Jess sat hunched on the sofa, hands on knees. She lifted her head a little and managed to shrug her shoulders.

Time to work that old Bladen magic. "Here," he tossed the remote control over to her and then turned on the TV. "You have a play and I'll see what's available on the food front." A thought popped into his head. "If you want to ring anyone . . ."

Her eyes flashed awake from their stupor.

". . . I'll get you a throwaway mobile — I've got one put by. Don't use the landline while you're here." Which begged the question: just how long was he planning to keep her here?

In the end, he settled for a takeaway curry, phoned in the order and took a walk. Doubtless, she'd use the throwaway mobile the second he was out the door and he was fine with that. Maybe she'd arrange her own safe house somewhere else. Given Miranda's parting glance, that might be safer for everyone.

The Indian takeaway was empty, if you didn't count the fish tank and the badly tuned television on a bracket, leaning precariously out of the wall. An adolescent pushed through the beaded curtain and nodded with a flick of his head.

"Alright, boss?"

Inwardly, Thomas cringed. The day that he became anyone's boss, his dad would disown him and then he'd disown himself. He reminded the lad of his order and sat down on the torn vinyl chair, flinching as his hand touched the chewing gum that some thoughtless bastard had left there.

He rifled through a small pile of newspapers and picked up a daily, raising it in front of him, so he didn't have to watch the youth gazing up at the TV and tutting. There was nothing about the accident in the paper.

* * *

Fifteen minutes later he was on his way, wondering what the benefit was of ringing ahead. As he got to his front door and fished for his keys, he made contact with Karl's rogue mobile phone in his pocket. Questions floated up before him. *Assuming Karl didn't know Jess — she hadn't actually asked for him by name — who would he have given the number to? And when?* He stood on the doorstep, keys in hand, mulling it over. The only person they'd really spoken with was Major Eldridge. A light glimmered at the back of his brain. *The only time he'd been away from Karl was at the motorway services, on the way home.* Something definitely smelt funny and it wasn't the Peshwari naan. Time to go indoors.

"It's me, Thomas," he called out from the hallway.

The only noise was the TV. What if . . . he grabbed the door handle and burst in, the takeaway bag swinging wildly in one hand. Jess jumped about five feet in the air — just as well she had the sofa to land on. He held up a hand by way of apology and she took the hint, dropping the TV volume.

Dinner was a muted affair; they were strangers after all. He steered clear of alcohol in case she got the wrong idea. She said that she'd rung her family on the mobile and told them she'd be unavailable for a few days because of work. Assuming that were true, it sounded like she'd been coached, which suggested she'd made another call beforehand.

"Does anyone know you're here?"

Her face was a cross between startled and indignant. He took that as a no. As he was clearing the plates, she stood and stretched, arching towards him.

"Mind if I take a shower?"

He blushed, told her it was fine and then remembered that he ought to change the bed linen for her. Might be better to do that later though or she could misread that as well. Jeez, no wonder he never had any female visitors apart from Miranda. He clicked his fingers. Shit, no change of clothes for her either. Well, he could spare a sweatshirt or something; maybe stretch to a pair of boxers.

He waited until the pipes were running, dug out some spare clothes and left them in a neat pile outside the bathroom. Then he went and hid himself in the front room, closing the door.

Left to his own devices, he slipped back into what Karl called *job mode*. First thing he did was check the call register on the new mobile. No one had rung her back and she had indeed made two calls, not one — ten points to the blue team. He grabbed a pen and noted down the numbers. Duplicitous, certainly, but no more so than ringing up to ask for help and then only giving him half the story.

He heard the pipes shuddering to a halt. She must have been in there for a good fifteen minutes. The door clicked and eased in slowly. Jess had done the thing he secretly loved; she'd pulled his baggy T-shirt down to make it into a dress; well, almost. He didn't dare wonder whether the boxers he'd left out for her were on active service.

The DVD he'd picked out was one of Miranda's — *Sex & the City*, Series Two. Before, according to her, they all became full of themselves. He repositioned his armchair so that Jess sat to one side of him — less chance of gawping at her legs, which she'd thoughtfully folded under her on the sofa.

"Have you got anything to drink?"

Clearly, not a request for tea or coffee. He nodded, crossed the room diagonally, like an inebriated crab, and fetched out two cans of beer and half a bottle of Southern Comfort. As he passed a can to her she leaned towards him and the top of her T-shirt hung forward suggestively.

"Thank you for everything, Thomas."

Her eyes followed him back to the sanctity of the armchair, and she looked a little disappointed. He pressed play on the DVD and let the opening credits roll. It didn't help his conscience that one of the characters in the show was called Miranda; it was like God was sending him a warning.

"Are you and Miranda an item, then?"

He looked up from the screen and blushed. Did anyone really talk like that? *An item*, like a pair of trousers? Good analogy actually, he congratulated himself with a sip of Southern Comfort. Like trousers — joined at one end and apart at the other.

"It's complicated," he confessed. And back to the screen.

"Only I noticed one of your photographs," she gestured outside, towards the bathroom. "She's wearing the same ring, so I presume you gave it to her?"

This was getting less fun by the minute. "Ancient history." He coated his tongue in Southern Comfort to smother any more words at birth.

Jess laughed out loud and nodded in agreement, in places where he merely smiled. Chick flick material, as Sheryl, Miranda's bar manager, would say. More laughter now and even a glass raised to the TV. It was like the battle of the sexes, waged with volume control.

He was gradually losing interest in the antics of the sassy-yet-vulnerable-yet-sexy-yet-needy women on screen. And simultaneously, he was in danger of gaining interest in his houseguest. So he excused himself to go and find pillows and a duvet for the sofa. Jess didn't seem to mind; she was lost in the show, or maybe in an alcoholic haze. Either was fine if it kept her calm and at arm's length.

He stashed the bedclothes outside the bathroom, and went in to brush his teeth and have a final pee. When he emerged, Jess had set the bed up for him on the sofa and commandeered his armchair; legs folded under again, preventing a private view. The latest episode was just winding up.

"I'm going to bed soon; busy day tomorrow," he yawned dramatically and skirted the edges of the room to pull a Sherlock Holmes book from the bookshelf.

"Well, if you're sure." She stood up in one fluid movement and leapt the gap like a gazelle. Without another word, she put her arms around him and drew him close, in a hug to write home about. As he put a supportive arm at her back he felt the absence of a bra, and quickly snatched his hand away. Her breath smelt sweet, like nectar.

She planted an emphatic kiss on his cheek, just beside his lips — willing him to taste it, tender and ambiguous. "See you," she said, swaying gently on her way to the bathroom.

It took a moment to collect his wits from his underwear.

"Er, the yellow toothbrush on the stand is a spare," he flustered. He waited until she came out before getting under the duvet. It felt strange. A bit like waiting for Miranda to come to bed, only, he reminded himself over and over again, Jess was going to one bed and he was on the sofa for the night. Finally, the toilet flushed and the sink hissed, then the door unlocked.

"Can I ask you one more thing?"

He didn't reply.

"Have you ever been in love with someone who's married?" Her face was a mermaid's, far from home. He shook his head. "Take my advice then, it isn't worth it. They never leave."

Unable to follow that, or to fathom it, he mumbled a goodnight and turned to 'The Adventure of the Illustrious Client.' It seemed about right, somehow.

At first there was just a dull sense of recognition, of something being out of place. It took maybe a moment or two to register — the door at the far end was open. He rubbed the bleariness out of his eyes and met her silhouette.

"I couldn't sleep. Mind if we talk? Kettle's already on, if you want one?"

Make yourself at home, why don't you. He used her time in the kitchen to put on his jeans and get his act together. When she returned, he was sat up.

"Should I ask what the time is?"

"About three — I'm really sorry," she said earnestly. "If it's any consolation you weren't exactly restful yourself — I heard you calling out in your sleep."

He couldn't argue with that and didn't want to get into it, so he shunted up to the far end of the sofa and she played bookends at the other, cradling her tea like it was holy water.

"I couldn't stop thinking about Amy."

He was all primed for a 'Who's she?' when Jess added, "and how she died." She was overwrought and tired, so it seemed only natural to move across and put a comforting arm around her. In contrast to before, her lips were tentative, innocent almost, as they found their way to his. She smelt clean and, for want of a better word, virginal. He gently guided her face away.

That was when he saw the light glowing from his mobile. He reached over and flipped the cover. Miranda's text was brief and to the point: *Soz about earlier. Maybe I'm in need of something — chocolate! Mx.* He shut the mobile and smiled at Jess, a reassuring smile that suggested they probably both felt foolish but no real harm had been done. And now that he had steered away from a whole lot of further complications, he pulled the duvet back over himself, turned away from her and tried to get back to sleep. "I'll see you in the morning."

Chapter 9

Thomas's mobile alarm kicked in at six thirty. He made a slow lunge to kill it and the events of the previous day came barrelling towards him, a close escape from his own stupidity. Sure, she had looked cute, but so what? He grabbed the cups and started out for the kitchen, almost colliding with her outside the door.

"What did they say would happen after we picked you up?" He played dumb, but deliberately said *they*, to see how she responded.

Jess furrowed her brow. "He told me . . ."

Well, that narrowed it to half the population.

". . . That I had to stay hidden for a while because of the inquiry. And that the base records would show I wasn't there that day."

He carried on walking and, to his surprise, she followed him.

"Let me guess," he was freewheeling now, but he had experience to draw upon; "an untraceable payment appears in your bank account in a few days' time and you take a long holiday somewhere warm until this all blows over?"

Her mouth opened but nothing came out. He took it as a subliminal hunger message and put together a breakfast of toast and scrambled eggs.

"You wouldn't have been taking advantage of me, you know, last night."

He piled the toast high and avoided eye contact. She hadn't finished.

"No one would have known."

He took a huge bite and rolled it around his mouth. It needed more brown sauce. "*I'd* have known."

Over breakfast, he ran through a comprehensive set of dos and don'ts — mostly common sense. Jess, in turn, gave him a shopping list. For a second or two he considered enlisting Miranda's help, and then thought better of it.

It was all getting a bit domestic for him, so he got ready for work, reminding her not to open the door or go near the curtains.

"I'll ring you on your mobile. Stay safe." Not very gracious perhaps, but he'd taken the precaution of locking his bedroom and the dark room. Just in case she got through the rest of *Sex & the City* and needed further entertainment.

His watch read seven thirty as he opened the front door. A chill autumn breeze sharpened his senses. Across the street, an elderly woman was pooper-scooping the strenuous efforts of a West Highland Terrier; and the poor beast was still in mid strain.

"It's alright, dear — I'm cleaning it up."

Unclaimed dog shit was the least of his problems — where the fuck was the Land Rover? Karl was his first port of call; he sounded chipper, right up until Thomas dropped his bombshell.

"I'll come straight over."

"No," Thomas's breath caught in his throat. "I'll handle it — I just wanted to let you know first."

"Well," Karl stretched the word out, "you'd better call it in to Services and let the boss know."

"Will do — I'll see you in the office later."

He vaulted the steps to his door and fumbled for his keys. His heart was thumping. Why take the Land Rover? Was someone expecting to collect the canister? And what would they do when they found it wasn't there?"

"It's alright, it's Thomas — I'm alone," he yelled along the hallway.

Jess opened the living room door. "What's going on?"

Now was not the time to play twenty questions.

"The Land Rover's been taken. Don't make a sound." He pulled out his mobile again. "Christine, it's Thomas. I have a problem — the Land Rover's gone."

She checked some details, but didn't pass any other comment.

"Yeah, just about to call in Services — I'll fill out a statement when I come in. No, once I got home."

He ended the call on the edge of politeness; the sweat was already gathering at his neck. Jess smiled from the sofa, as if to suggest she wasn't really a whole heap of trouble.

"Jess, if you even *feel* under threat today, call the police."

She looked frightened. Tough — welcome to the world of consequences.

He double-locked the door from the outside and hotfooted it to Walthamstow Central tube station. If anyone planned on following him they'd have to be bloody quick today. Even so, he changed trains twice and surfaced one stop early to walk the rest of the way to the office.

* * *

Karl greeted him just inside the door, vending-machine coffee in hand.

"I listened out for your footsteps on the stairs, great heffalump that you are. We, er, need to have a little chat."

Thomas tried to avoid a pained expression and pushed past him. The main office was empty, not a soul around and even Karl's laptop was off. Christine Gerrard's office light was aglow and the door was closed. From where he was standing, it looked like she had guests.

"We're in here . . ." Karl led the way.

We?

". . . And by the way, Tommo, you look like shit."

Christine got up as Karl opened the door. Ann Crossley, another member of the team, edged her chair round so they could all squeeze in. Karl grabbed a spot at the opposite side of the table — all very cosy.

"What's going on?" Thomas looked at them each in turn: Karl, who'd become his closest ally in the Surveillance Support Unit, protecting him to the point of risking his own life; Ann Crossley, who had once warned him when he hadn't even known he was in danger; and Christine Gerrard, who had put aside their own tangled past and helped preserve the integrity of the SSU when things had turned ugly, out on the moors. None of which explained this little summit.

"Thing is, Tommo . . ." *So Karl was the messenger.* He sounded almost apologetic. ". . . We all thought it was time, after everything that happened earlier this year, to settle a few things."

Thomas waited it out, feeling no obligation to make it easy for them. He was done asking questions anyway. That faculty was already stretched to the limit, trying to figure out what had happened to the Land Rover. And what the hell he was supposed to do about a fugitive, a weapon he wasn't supposed to have, and footage of an industrial accident that didn't seem to have any purpose?

In the end, Christine played her seniority card. She started by reminding Thomas of things he already knew — a classic way of placating people and asserting some kind of normality. He nearly laughed at the thought: *normality.*

She covered old ground quickly — how there was still a faction within multiple government departments — including the SSU — that supported a fast track to a United States of Europe.

Even now it sounded like bollocks. Or it did, until he remembered Sir Peter Carroll and the set up with the money and the ache in his chest, where Yorgi the hit man tried to plant a bullet, seconds before Sir Peter put him down for good.

"You know of course that we each report to different agencies."

He nodded dumbly. In his experience, dumb usually worked. Christine took the bait.

"And now that you know we're on the same side . . ." which sounded a lot like 'now that you have proved yourself.' ". . . we only need to have this conversation once. You know Karl served in the army, Ann?"

Ann Crossley sat back and lifted her head proudly. "Naval Intelligence."

Christine's whole posture seemed to relax, as if the effort of pretence was over. "And before I met you Thomas, I spent two years in the Foreign Office."

Blimey. He looked daggers across the room. He already knew about Karl's background, but Christine's bombshell . . . Somehow that little nugget had failed to come out during the year he and Christine had shared a duvet.

Every statement threw up more questions. He let the opportunity pass — he had enough to think about. Christine was still talking, so he tried to refocus.

"Whereas you, Thomas, have a purely civilian background." The way she said it made it sound like some sort of infectious disease.

"But that gives you a certain objectivity and independence, which could be advantageous."

For two months, ever since Yorgi had been surgically removed from the equation and the whole bad business put to bed, he'd been kept away from their in-house counter-intelligence. He knew it was still going on; that became obvious when Karl was late or didn't show up for an entire day and Christine never said a word. Although God only knew who Karl actually represented. MI5 maybe?

Anyhow, it didn't take Brain of Britain to realise that the three of them were assessing him to see if he was still capable of playing a role.

"The explosion at the test facility has unfortunate implications."

That'll be a great comfort to the victim's family. He made the supreme effort and bit his tongue.

"Karl cannot get too involved in this matter, so Ann will provide any support you need."

Now his feelers were twitching; he let his tongue go. "Support for what?"

Christine steamrollered his comment like it was soft tarmac.

"Tomorrow morning, you will report to Sir Peter Carroll in Whitehall."

"Now wait a f . . ."

Christine gave him her *know your place* look, the one that always stopped him in his tracks. The one her mother had tried at that disastrous 'Happy Families' Christmas with him and Christine at the big house. The only time he'd ever missed Christmas with the Wrights — when Miranda had been abroad.

"It's out of my hands, Thomas. Karl would be seen as too partisan."

Karl hadn't looked at him since he'd first sat down. He shot the big feller a glance, but Karl wasn't receiving loud or clear.

"Okay, that's all. Dismissed." Karl and Ann rose to their feet immediately, and were at the door before Thomas had shifted his chair. Christine raised a hand.

"Thomas, can you hold on for a minute?"

Ann closed the door carefully behind her. Thomas watched as she and Karl went over to her desk, talking all the while. Best friends forever, or was that supposed to be Ann and him now?

"A couple of things . . ." Christine attempted one of those efficiency smiles — pragmatic and energy saving. "Firstly, yours I believe?" She opened a drawer and picked out an audio surveillance transmitter. "I found it under my table after Yorgi . . . when Bob Peterson was still in charge."

She flushed scarlet and he sunned himself in the afterglow. Bob Peterson, her former boss and her former shag.

"I won't ask what it was doing there or how you came by it."

He accepted the bug and pocketed it, along with the battery, which she'd thoughtfully separated. He hadn't thought to check the secure web server for sound files. Or maybe Karl had fixed that too.

"Look," Christine softened her voice, touching his arm with her fingertips. "Karl told me you'd agreed to speak to a professional about what happened with Yorgi. I've cleared your schedule for this afternoon — no sense delaying, now that you've made up your mind."

She held up a business card that he snatched away, like a petulant child. Her perfume wafted across; Clive Christian, if he wasn't mistaken. Some things never changed. Which made him wonder whether she'd stopped seeing the very married Bob Peterson, especially since he'd pressured Sir Peter Carroll to transfer Uncle Bob out of London. Like Jess had said, they *never* leave.

316

* * *

Karl had stumped up for lunch; condemned man's last meal and all that. A pub lunch, naturally, with Karl sticking to shandy. It was an olde worlde pub with thoroughly modern prices. They sat, cheek by jowl with dozens of anonymous suits, arranged in orderly fashion like a factory farm for diners.

"I've noticed a certain scrutiny from you today, Tommo."

Thomas put down his panini and licked the mozzarella from his hand. "It's nothing. I'm just surprised about working with Ann, that's all."

His unspoken question burned in his eyes — when did Karl get to know about it?

Karl raised a glass to his heart. "I'm touched by your loyalty. Rest assured it'll be a temporary state of affairs. Word is that you're going into uncharted waters."

"Come again?" The hackles on his neck rose up.

"I believe Major Eldridge has requested your attendance."

Thomas took another bite of panini, hit raw onion and crunched it up. The sharp, sour taste suited his mood perfectly. "But I thought you two were buddies?"

"Well, we served together, right enough. And I'd go so far as to say that he's a decent man. It's the former that's the problem, if you get my drift?"

He didn't. The onion was lingering, so he rinsed it down with the last of his orange juice — couldn't very well see the shrink, reeking of onion. "So what will you be up to while I'm playing *fetch* with Sir Peter Carroll tomorrow?"

"I'm out for the day — compassionate leave. My mammy's unwell."

He caught his breath. To all intents and purposes, Karl never even had a family, until now.

"Is it serious?"

Karl managed the smallest of chuckles and rubbed his forehead, spiking his brown hair. "You could say that; she's dying."

"Shit." Not the most eloquent message of support, but it spoke volumes.

Karl checked his watch. "You'd better get your skates on or you're not gonna make it to Harley Street on time. Nothing but the best for our boys and girls. And listen, give me a bell later — let me know how you got on, okay?"

"Roger that."

Karl smiled on cue. "And get some chewing gum; this close up, you smell like Onion Boy."

"Listen, if you, er, want to talk any time — or meet up — just give me a call."

Karl waved his shandy towards him. "Come on now, will you ever fuck off? Please — before we start doing hugs and high fives."

* * *

He left Baker Street tube and took his chances crossing Marylebone Road, before checking in with Jess. She was quieter, and he'd expected that. You might be able to cope with incredible challenges and stresses, but it all caught up with you eventually. Shit, that's why *he* was there. She had nothing to report — if he could believe her. Which he didn't.

He counted the street numbers until he found a column of buzzers with the name he was looking for: R. Kyriacou. He tapped his feet self-consciously and glanced up the street. *Right then, here goes nothing.*

The buzzer was answered immediately, confirming his name and appointment time. The voice sounded just short of warm, non-judgemental. The door clicked and he slipped inside, climbing the lacquered stairs in rhythmic strides.

On the third floor, he branched out to the left, where a woman was waiting. Her glasses hung on a chain around her neck, and her expression was neutral.

"I'm the two thirty." A pointless repetition of his intercom intro, which might have been why it drew no response. "I'm here to see Mr Kyriacou." Sudden thought: was it shrinks who didn't use the term *doctor* or was that surgeons?

"That would be me, and it's Ms Kyriacou."

A brilliant start. He followed her in. No padding on the walls — always a good sign. At one end of the room was a wall-length bookcase, which puzzled him. If this was a place of work you couldn't possibly find time to read all these; it felt like a pose. Maybe it impressed the rich clients.

"Can I get you a tea or coffee?"

He sat down with a mug of tea and a biscuit. Thankfully it wasn't a 'you don't have to be mad to work here, but it helps' mug. He took a good look around; this could almost be someone's living room. There was a faint roar of traffic; he tuned in and let it carry him inside. It reminded him of lying on a ridge as a boy and cupping his ears so that the wind blew past in a continuous sigh.

"Shall we start, Thomas?"

If he took what she said at face value, then she knew nothing about him, other than his name and that he worked for a government department. This was, she explained, a confidential referral service for people such as himself.

"Now, how can I help you?"

Chapter 10

"You see, Tommo, I told you there was nothing to fear!"

He pulled the mobile back a little and smiled at the mouthpiece. "We'll see. I've been booked in for eight sessions and apparently I'm dealing with a trauma."

"Just the one? Jeez, what a lightweight!"

He checked his watch. "I can get to Liverpool Street for four thirty, if you're allowed out for a quick drink?"

"Aye, sure enough. I'll see you in The George then."

Next stop, Regent's Park. The pocket camera was like a toy, compared with the day job, but he couldn't let the opportunity pass by. As he crossed the busy road again and risked the wrath of cab drivers and cycle couriers, he was already getting a sense of what he wanted to photograph. This was the way he had worked when he was still chasing a role on the dailies; the jolt of inspiration and the anticipation of pulling it off; joy or disappointment — no middle ground.

Conscious of time, he'd chosen an easy win — a black and white of a lone tree beside water. It was a curious thing, photography; you could learn a lot about the snapper from their compositions. He preferred landscapes, except for shots of Miranda. She wasn't exactly his muse, but after twelve years or so of skirting around each other, it wouldn't do to break the set. He'd told himself that the bleak moorland photos he loved so much were a reaction to the day job, until he remembered that he'd always taken those kinds of pictures. He found a suitable cherry tree and rattled off five snaps from different positions. If any of them worked out, he'd add the best to his wall and give a print to Miranda.

Jess didn't pick up when he rang her mobile again. No sweat, he'd be home before seven pm. She was probably in the loo; as far as Thomas knew, he was the only person who carried the mobile *everywhere* in case of a call.

* * *

"I tell you, Mr Bladen, the office has been damn quiet without you this afternoon." Karl shook a couple of crisp bags to simulate excitement.

Thomas sat down and passed the pocket camera over.

"Hmm . . ." Karl scrutinised the Regents Park pictures. "Number four is probably your winner. I suppose by then you knew what you were doing, and by number five you were getting sloppy." High praise indeed from Karl.

It felt like a Friday, on a Monday. Karl talked him through the Case of the Disappearing Land Rover, of the efforts (minimal) and the progress (non-existent) to locate and recover the vehicle. At least the paperwork had been completed. And it was satisfying to know that they'd deprived some schmuck of the *special feature*.

Karl dismissed any theorising on who and why and how. That could wait till another day, he insisted; this was just a wind-down meet-up. A couple of times the conversation stalled and Thomas primed himself to mention Jess. But when it came down to it, he couldn't do it. Karl had enough on his plate with his mother. Still, there were things that needed to be said, and there was only one place where he knew Karl would talk freely.

"How about we get together, one evening this week at the gun club?"

Karl's face seemed to glow momentarily. That or it could have been the light reflecting off his shandy. "Really?"

"Sure. Why not?" Thomas put his hands together in mock prayer. "My therapist did say I should confront my fears."

"Fantastic. You don't have to participate if you don't feel ready."

"We'll see."

Just the thought of the club and the cold weight of a gun made his hands sweat. But seeing the unexpected joy on Karl's haggard face almost made it worth it.

Two drinks on and Thomas realised that he hadn't bought Jess anything to wear. He blushed, because the idea of it conjured up all kinds of complications. He turned the conversation to the following morning's meeting in Whitehall.

Karl listened for a while and cut in at the first opportunity. "I understand how you feel about Sir Peter Carroll. The words *snake* and *poisonous* come to mind. But the art of politics," he nodded in Thomas's direction, "which I accept is not your bag, lies in shaking hands with the person who just tried to stab you in the back."

Thomas consoled himself. Besides, Karl's shadowy friends were now running Sir Peter Carroll as a . . . was it a double agent or a triple agent now? Whatever it was, it made his head hurt.

As he was leaving, Thomas had another thought. "Is Major Eldridge married?" Apparently he was, although Karl never said if it was happily.

* * *

He caught the overground train to Walthamstow Central and negotiated his way through the drifters and delinquents who treated the space outside McDonald's as their personal territory.

No one paid him much attention and that was how he liked it; he could have been any other pen pusher trudging home, rather than a recent collector of unclaimed weapons and people. He cut down a side street to cross Forest Road and gave a nod to Lloyd Park. How many years was it since he'd proposed to Miranda by the Yew tree there? Still not long enough to forget that she'd deflated his big moment by telling him that Yew trees were connected with death and graveyards. So much of life, he pondered, as he popped into the convenience store for milk and bread, was fixed by tiny events — like pixels in a digital frame. Even now, as he wondered whether it was insulting or considerate to buy tampons and deodorant for his houseguest — it was all down to having Karl's mobile when the call came in. If only he'd given Karl his phone back.

What was it the therapist had said? 'Trauma can make us examine our values and our choices. Often, traumatic events are entirely out of our control. But what we do subsequently can be influenced by them.' He wasn't quite sure how that applied to toiletries, but it was something to think about.

* * *

Instinct wasn't something he often laid claim to; he preferred to think of it as being observant, reading what was there for anyone to see. It was all in the details. As he approached his flat, he knew straight away that something wasn't right.

He stood outside, checking life's pixels. And there it was, the join on the curtains — seamless. Beyond neatness and beyond how he'd left them that morning. He checked the front door — locks intact, not a scratch on them; hinges the same. A familiar sinking feeling settled in his stomach as he unlocked the door; if he was right, there wasn't much point in announcing himself.

He dropped the shopping by the door and flicked the lights on. It was very quiet. The front curtains had been bulldog clipped together. He tried the back door then spotted that the nearby window was unlocked. Not a sign of Jess about the place, or her original clothing. Part of him was worried, but he couldn't see how anyone could have broken in and taken her without leaving any traces behind.

One sideboard drawer was slightly out of line from the others — and £40 adrift. The missing cash he could live with, but leaving his flat vulnerable was a cardinal sin. He noticed the post on the coffee table, so she must have been there when it came, at around eleven. His brain shifted up a gear. Of course, she could have been anywhere when he spoke to her earlier on the mobile. *Well, done is done; now what?* He flipped his mobile and dialled the most-called number.

"Miranda Wright, who wants to know?"

"It's Thomas. There's a problem. Jess has disappeared; she got out of the flat while I was at work."

"So your sexual magnetism repels as well as attracts?"

"Yeah, very droll," he snapped. "Meantime, one woman is dead and another one who was at the scene is out there alone."

There was no response for a few seconds. "How do you know she's alone?"

Good question. "I double-locked the doors, front and back; no forced entry." He could hear keys jiggling in the background.

"Doesn't mean someone didn't collect her; or she could have gone out to meet someone."

Maybe she was on to something.

"So why ring me? Are you planning to form a search party?" That was Miranda, all heart.

"I didn't know what else to do . . ."

"Yeah, you did," there was a snarl in her voice. "Ring Karl — it's his mobile, he can deal with it."

He thought about Karl's mother and shuddered a little. "No can do, Miranda. It's *my* problem."

"I'll come over, if you want."

"Thanks."

* * *

There was a definite swagger as Miranda waltzed in, an hour later. He'd put on dinner for two — a freezer special — and brought out a bottle of wine, Miranda's favourite, from the back of the cupboard. She was in a triumphant mood from the off.

323

"I knew she was bad news; the way she turned on the waterworks to order."

He choked a little and scuttled off to the kitchen.

"Fess up then," she called after him. "Did something happen?"

Crockery clattered.

"Look, it's no skin off my nose. We're not exclusive to each other . . ."

He nearly dropped a plate. *We're not?*

". . . But we ought to be mature enough to be honest with each other."

He was never any good under pressure with her. "Alright. We kissed. Well, that is, she kissed me."

"You poor defenceless man. And I suppose you fought her off to protect your honour."

"Hey, don't take the piss. I stopped things going any further if that's what you're looking for."

She was only a few feet behind him. Close enough to hear her sighing. "You're so easily manipulated . . ."

He didn't know if she meant him or men in general.

". . . Pathetic . . . make a man feel like Sir Galahad and he'll whore himself out and be grateful to do it."

It took all his self-control not to retaliate with: *Is that how we got together?* Somehow he managed to dish up without smashing anything, and carried the food through with a face like thunder. It was hard to know what was pissing him off more — the fact that Miranda was talking like this, or that she was probably right about him.

They ate and watched TV without talking; not exactly a dazzling evening. He wondered why she'd bothered coming over at all, and then remembered that she'd given him a choice — some treat that had turned out to be.

By mutual consent, they gave up the ghost at half past ten. He performed his ablutions and waited for her, but as he followed her into his bedroom she paused at the threshold. "I'll get you the duvet for the sofa."

He felt his mouth open about a foot. She feigned surprise. "Surely you didn't think . . ." Game, set and match to Miranda.

He collected the folded bedclothes by the door and hunkered down on the sofa again. For a while, as he lay there, he thought about how he'd feel if Miranda had shared his bed one night, then snogged some stranger the next. He fired off a jovial text to Karl, and tried to sleep without thinking about what he was missing.

The click of the bathroom light disturbed him around midnight. He woke to a face full of cushion. The door at the end of the room was open; the bedroom glare bled across the carpet.

He heard the familiar hiss of the tap running in the bathroom. He shifted position on the sofa and saw a naked Miranda heading into his bedroom. She stopped and turned in the doorframe, cutting the kind of silhouette that would chase a man to his dreams and leave him there weeping.

"G'night then, Thomas."

He was still gazing forlornly at the illuminated carpet when the door closed firmly, consigning him to darkness. He lay there, breathing in her perfume as it wafted through the flat. Even if he didn't have visitation rights, his bed had been well and truly scent-marked.

Chapter 11

He took Miranda in a cup of tea at seven am and didn't stick around to chance another rejection. Later, in the shower, he thought he heard her trying the locked door. He emerged, towel tightly around his waist, determined not to have a row.

"You coming over to Caliban's after work?" Miranda was waiting for him.

Caliban's — her bar in the East End; it sounded like an invitation. If he'd been any more confused, he'd have had to ask for directions.

"Sure, unless I get another call to deal with."

"Up to you. Your loss."

Ouch. Wrong answer. He skipped breakfast and the offer of a lift to the station, leaving Miranda to lock up with her own keys when she was done. He thought about Karl, and then about how he'd feel if it was *his* mother. A big question. He wasn't close to her anymore, or his dad, unlike his sister Pat — who lived a few streets away. No, family had never been his strong suit, unless it was Miranda's family — as his own were quick to point out.

* * *

St James Park tube was his exit from the underworld. Despite the heady concoction of heat, machinery and teeming crowds, he loved it below the surface. A million micro dramas and all you had to do was take notice. Miranda reckoned it was his father's miner genes, desperate for expression.

And of course, where there were crowds, there was coffee. Life always felt better when it had an espresso tinge to it. He waved the little cardboard cup under his nostrils like a connoisseur, his nose tingling with delight. He alternated between choc-chip cookie and coffee, promising himself a salad at lunchtime by way of penance.

Main Building in Whitehall felt smaller than when he'd last been there, as if Sir Peter Carroll's exposure and deflation had taken it down with him. He entered the lobby and paused, enjoying a moment of confidence. Well, almost. Karl's cryptic comment about *uncharted waters* didn't sit too comfortably.

He walked across to a wall-mounted screen, tuned to News 24. Same old shit; war, dodgy politicians, public scandals and celebrity toss. *Oh, to be in England.* Still, it was a good five minutes before he could tear himself away, and only then to check the time. Mustn't be late. Ten minutes to go. May as well check in.

After the usual round of Guess Who, he put his ID away and placed his hand on the scanner. All present and correct. A kindly guard told him to go wait by the seats and someone would come to fetch him.

He sat down and toyed with his mobile, hopeful that Karl or Miranda might have something to say. Then he remembered the piece of paper with the two numbers Jess had called. His hand gravitated towards the beige phone on the glass table. What harm could it do? Answer: none because he was calling from Whitehall. He figured the first number would be the most interesting, given how Jess had described her message to the folks. This would be the *prep* number, hopefully. The second ring had barely kicked in before it was answered.

"Cecil Eldridge. Hello?"

Blimey. He gulped under his breath and slowly leant forward to cut the call without attracting attention from the front desk. Then he lifted his finger clear and nodded as if he were still in conversation, playing out the last of it as his security escort arrived.

"Mr Bladen? If you'd like to come this way?"

The escort was stony quiet as they made their way up in the lift. Usually that bothered him, but he was glad of it today — more time to think. Why would Jess ring Major, or rather, *Cecil* Eldridge? And if he answered his mobile without his rank, that suggested a very personal number. But Jess, from what she'd said, wasn't even on the official payroll. No, she was contracted to that outfit . . . Engamel Solutions. Something else he ought to do some checking up on.

Top floor, lift doors open, turn right and compensate for the bounce from the carpet. No CCTV up here, just in case the MI5 bloke along the corridor fancied a quick chat with the CIA liaison office. The idea made him smile momentarily.

Now he was at the door. Tappety-tap; it was *The Three Little Pigs* in reverse.

"Come in."

The sound of Sir Peter Carroll's voice sliced through Thomas's composure. Tension slid across his shoulders like an ice floe. The escort abandoned him outside and went on his way.

He turned the handle, taking a deep breath to resist the urge to smash the man's face in.

"Hello, Thomas." Sir Peter's tone was cautious, and he was keeping to his side of the desk.

He took comfort in that; they were both finding their feet in this brave new world. Sir Peter may have founded the Surveillance Support Unit and Thomas may have been a mere underling, but since Sir Peter's collusion with the United States of Europe movers and shakers, *Mr* Carroll also did the bidding of Karl's people.

"I've ordered coffee — it should be here presently."

He took a seat and nodded, without offering a handshake. He winced at himself. *Skating very close to looking like a dick.* Whatever had happened, Sir Peter was still the boss.

The boss rested his fingertips on the edge of his desk. Maybe it was meant to be some show of honesty. Fat chance. "I'll come straight to the point. You and Karl McNeill were asked to capture supplementary evidence at the test facility, following an equipment malfunction."

Thomas felt his mouth open and his right hand — the punching one — start twitching. "I think you mean the scene of the fatality."

Sir Peter's face was blank, and pale. Either he hadn't known or he was doing a bloody good impression. He cleared his throat and lifted his fingers away quickly, as if the desk had a built-in polygraph. "Something has gone missing from the facility and a light touch investigation is required. Suffice it to say, this is not something the military police need to concern themselves with at the moment."

Two knocks on the door. Sir Peter shifted a gear to benevolent host and coffees were served. When the orderly had closed the door behind him, Sir Peter put his spoon down with infinite care and patience. Thomas took it as a sign that bad news was coming.

"Major Charles Eldridge has requested your assistance. He requires a surveillance officer — specifically, someone without an armed forces background."

"But Karl and I always work together — you signed the executive order."

"And I'll continue to honour it."

Honour? Do me a favour.

"However, in this case, Karl has already agreed it would be in everyone's best interests if you dealt with Major Eldridge alone, wherever possible."

The penny was dropping. Everyone's best interests implied that Karl wanted things this way as well. He could live with that, even if it did mean cosying up to Ann Crossley for a while. "There's something else, isn't there?"

Sir Peter smiled, a thin-lipped rat-in-a-corner smile. "There is a certain commercial interest in this investigation, but that can wait. Now, Major Eldridge will be here in a few minutes. When you are dismissed, I want you to leave the building and return in one hour — is that clear?"

He shook his head infinitesimally; wheels within wheels. It shouldn't have come as a big surprise, but somehow it did. Sir Peter was still a wheeler-dealer, still playing political poker and managing to cash in early.

When Major Eldridge put in an appearance, Sir Peter and Thomas were looking at photographs together. A love of photography had sparked their first conversation, back when Thomas was a pen-pushing civil servant. And, to a degree, photography still sufficed as a neutral zone.

"Sir Peter, Thomas." Major Eldridge nodded curtly in lieu of handshakes.

That was okay, courtesy seemed to be off the menu today. The good major explained that he had asked for an independent support officer — he didn't mention surveillance at all. Thomas waited until the *any questions* part of the programme.

"Who's the commercial interest? And what are my responsibilities there?"

Major Eldridge straightened his jacket. "The prototype weapon is being developed by a consortium: Engamel Solutions. It's likely that they'll want to speak with you."

Sir Peter glanced at his watch. "I think that'll be all for now, Thomas."

"Very good, Sir Peter." He rose and glided to the door, like a butler on casters. It amused him to think that Sir Peter would know this was sarcasm, while the major would see it as deferential. Perhaps they'd compare notes afterwards.

* * *

Out in the park and safe from prying eyes, Thomas checked his mobile and picked up a *call me when free* text from Karl. He wasted no time.

"Hey, Tommo, how's the new job?"

"Plenty of perks — free coffee, ginger nuts, duplicity. So where are you now?"

"I'm watching the front of Main Building — I thought you might want to accidentally bump into Major Eldridge on his way out."

"How did you know he—?"

"Come on now, Mr Bladen, credit me with some intelligence — forgive the pun."

"I've been instructed to go back there in an hour so I shouldn't imagine the major's going to emerge any time soon. I'll come over to you."

Karl wasn't looking his best. It didn't take Sherlock Holmes to realise that his mother's impending demise was hitting him hard.

"I, er, don't know what to say."

"That's okay, Tommo, I know you're the sensitive type." Karl took a breath and touched a finger to his bottom lip. For anyone else you'd say he'd just had a thought. But Thomas knew that Karl was *always* thinking. "Let me make it easy for you. She has cancer — last time I spoke with the doctor, she said Ma had maybe two months . . . and I won't be going to the funeral."

He nodded. Karl hadn't taken his eye off the entrance to Main Building, but now he was sitting up. "Tell you what, Tommo. Better get your skates on. Your new army friend is strolling for the border. Time to make like a Yorkshire Terrier!"

* * *

"Major Eldridge!" Thomas gasped as he made it across the road.

The major turned slowly and his face softened in recognition. "Thomas, just the man. I wanted to speak with you privately, later."

He smiled and read him like yesterday's news. *Yeah, maybe I could ring you on your personal mobile.*

"I look forward to working closely with you."

"Me too — may I call you Cecil?" It was either clever or stupid, but he was determined to squeeze something useful from their micro meeting.

And while Major Eldridge barely flinched, his pupils did a Latin tango. He recovered sufficiently to pass on his phone number — not, Thomas noted, the number Jess had called him on. He considered asking the major how Jess was and *where* she was. Maybe not though, just in case the major had nothing to do with it after all and it spooked him.

He bounded back to the park like a kid who'd just been given a new football. Karl was waiting on a bench, hunched forward, sharp as a cat. "Good meeting?"

"You could say that," he felt his smile engulfing him. "By the way, I meant to return your mobile — from the base."

Karl pocketed the phone without looking at it. "Did Major Eldridge ring you? I gave him the number when we stopped at motorway services. I figured it best he have a private number."

Confirmation then of how Jess knew where to call. "No, nothing from the major . . ."

"And yet?" Karl frowned, sitting back and narrowing his eyes.

He tapped out a rhythm on the bench. "Someone else called; turns out there were two technicians at the test site. The other one left the base and wanted assistance."

"Very interesting," Karl congratulated him. "So the major must have slipped her the number."

Thomas blew out a breath. "Well, that might not be all he's been slipping her. After me and Miranda picked her up, she rang the major on his personal mobile — I checked."

Karl ran his tongue along his teeth as if scraping away the taste. "Hmm, messy. If Major E snuck her off the base then he's probably also responsible for the Land Rover cargo. That's a lot of risk for a man in his position. I won't ask where you've stashed this woman."

"Jess," Thomas dropped in his little pebble and then Karl made a show of lightly cupping his ears. He sprawled out on the bench beside Karl. A jackdaw scrambled to the ground a few feet away and eyed the two of them curiously.

"See now, he's a *real* scavenger. Know something, Tommo? I can't help thinking the major was using me as a mule. First the weapon components and now this *Jess* — it was my mobile she rang after all.

Yeah, Thomas thought to himself, the one you conveniently left with me. He scuffed the ground with his heel and the jackdaw jolted to attention. "I thought you weren't getting involved?"

"I'm not." Karl's voice was flat, non-negotiable. He filched about in his pocket, dug out what looked like half a peanut and flicked it over to the waiting bird. "But let me know how you get on."

Thomas was still mulling over what the hell he was supposed to do about it all when Karl stood up and brushed his trousers. "I've always trusted Major Eldridge — that doesn't mean you should." The jackdaw erupted into comment like a trained stooge.

Thomas's mobile trilled; a simple ringtone; the most nondescript on the list. He nodded to Karl and dove in. "Hi, Miranda, what's shaking?" Sometimes he was so smooth he could barely keep the phone in his hands.

"She's turned up again, at the flat. She wasn't expecting to find me here though." Miranda's tone all but screamed 'I told you so.'

"Did she say where she'd vanished to?" Thomas upped the volume a little; making sure Karl caught every word. "See if you can get her mobile on the quiet and check the call record. I need to know who she's called. Okay, speak to you later. Thanks." He cut the call, turned to Karl and waited.

"Quite the little team, you and Miranda. A fella could get jealous."

Thomas pointed to a tree. "Quercus coccinea."

"Is that your privileged Yorkshire Secondary Education coming through?"

"Nah, it's my 1987 encyclopaedia and a school project on oaks in Britain."

"Ah yes, the scarlet oak. And don't look so surprised; haven't I always told you we have lots in common? Right, I'm out of here — see you around, unless you're clubbing tonight?" The sort of club that welcomed Glocks, Smith & Wessons, Brownings and Colts.

"Sorry, got a date I can't break."

Karl smiled sadly and walked off towards the trees.

* * *

As soon as the call came through from Sir Peter's office, he rushed back. The same escort shadowed him in the lift, did the customary three knocks at the door, waited for a muffled reply and then scarpered. Before Thomas could get to the handle, the door opened and the face behind it was that of a stranger.

"Hey there, you must be Thomas. Come on in."

He extended a hand mechanically, like a dog giving paw, while Sir Peter Carroll watched from behind his desk.

"Thomas, this is . . ."

"Michael Schaefer," the man announced himself, heavy on the volume. "Please, call me Michael — Engamel Solutions."

As John Wright might have put it: fuck a duck. And a Texan duck at that, by the sounds of things. Thomas took up the empty chair — no coffee, he noted — and waited for someone to speak.

"This is very delicate, Thomas." Sir Peter ran his finger along the edge of the desk. "I need you to establish an audio presence on Major Eldridge."

He took out a notebook and listed the requirements. It helped to quell any lingering inclination to ask the wrong questions — and there were so many to choose from. Okay, so it wasn't the first time he'd provided internal surveillance for a government department. But — and this was a biggie — the major was MoD, unlike the SSU. And laughing boy wasn't even on Her Majesty's payroll.

"Now, Thomas, Christine will need to be briefed, to some extent; strictly on a need to know basis." Which meant Christine would get the wafer thin version.

"Michael will be my personal representative in this matter." Sir Peter waved a conciliatory hand towards Schaefer as Thomas looked on. In this poker game, a Corporate seemed to beat a Title.

"Ya see, Thomas . . ."

Ah, it speaks again. Well, drawls.

"Engamel Solutions knows Major Eldridge is of the highest calibre. We just want to be . . ." he looked to Sir Peter for the right word.

"Doubly sure?" Thomas pitched in.

"Absolutely! I can see you're the right man for the job."

Thomas shot a glance across the desk and then went back to note taking. Two devices, preferably. One in the major's office and anywhere else would be a bonus — car or home. *No pressure then.* "How will I get access to the base?" *Best to identify the mountains from the off.*

Sir Peter took in a breath, as if he were competing for oxygen, and released it sparingly though a sickly smile. "Major Eldridge has requested your support while the investigation is being conducted."

He couldn't hold back a murmur of discontent. *Since when did the Surveillance Support Unit offer that kind of support?*

Schaefer's smile was pure Osmonds; Thomas nearly shielded his eyes. "If you have any out-of-scope expenses, this ought to cover it." An Engamel envelope wafted across.

He looked to Sir Peter, as though appealing for a free kick from a referee. Sir Peter didn't stir.

"What happens if the major doesn't need me on the base?"

Sir Peter shifted a little in his expensive chair. "Major Eldridge's home and private apartment addresses are also in the envelope."

* * *

Outside, Thomas rang Miranda for an update. "Sorry, I couldn't talk earlier — long story. What's the latest?"

"I'm on my way to Caliban's; Jess is with me."

"*What?* Are you insane? She should stay at the flat."

"And we all know how successful that was. Look, Thomas, I have a business to run. At least this way I can keep her company."

He stopped walking and stared out at the skyline. "Is Butch involved?" It was their personal code for anything dodgy, coming from Butch, a hands-on photographer Miranda had encountered in her youth — and whom Thomas had given a beating.

"No," she chuckled. "Butch ain't around — stop worrying. I'm varying my route and staying glued to my mirrors. Catch you later, hon."

He smiled and closed the phone. *Hon*, the way her bar manager, Sheryl, addressed all the male customers, flinging it about like free sachets of salted peanuts.

Chapter 12

It was weird, being in the office without Karl. Ann Crossley — his designated backup — sat on the other side of the room with nary a second glance. Or a first one. He returned the favour and typed out some notes, anonymising the major to *Target* and detailing the reporting instructions that Sir Peter had laid out. Times New Roman didn't make it any clearer, so he mentally filled in the elements that would not be documented.

Someone — the major was still the frontrunner — had wanted him and Karl to receive parts of the UB40 Scavenger. Someone — again, the major was favourite — had spirited Jess away and given her Karl's number to ring. Since then, Karl had washed his hands of it all *and* the Land Rover had gone walkies. On the plus side, he still had the Scavenger bits, and Jess, and footage from the accident. But what the bloody hell was he supposed to do with any of it?

He looked across to Ann for inspiration and coughed, like a teacher trying to catch out a daydreamer. She surfaced from whatever thoughts she'd been immersed in and pointed to the vending machine.

She was so different from Karl. If he had to put a finger on it, she tried too hard — the model of efficiency and bugger-all instinct. Karl might be a little rough around the edges, especially where paperwork was concerned, but he got things done. Ann? He wasn't sure if he would trust her to pick up some shopping.

"Is this an official coffee break?" he cracked a thin smile and it shattered on very stony ground.

"How did your meeting go at Whitehall?"

So many meetings, so little sense. "I've been assigned to the MoD."

She selected two coffees. "Come on," she pushed the doors and stood at the stairwell.

He caught the door in time and followed her, tapping his security pass to make sure it was there. The lock clicked hard behind him. Ann held a plastic cup out, perhaps as a peace offering. There was no enmity between them; they just weren't close, like Australia and Africa. He glanced up and down the stairwell. It always struck him as strange that the Surveillance Support Unit occupied only a couple of floors in buildings that belonged to other government departments.

That was one of Sir Peter Carroll's masterstrokes when the SSU was formed in the 80s, intended to integrate with other departments. Didn't work of course, other than to localise the disdain. Nobody welcomed the floaters, although they were happy to use them.

"What do I need to know?" Ann's tone was blunt.

How to win friends and influence people might be a start. He didn't answer right away, sipping the machine coffee, letting it detain his taste buds and beat a confession out of them. The real question was: What did *he* need Ann Crossley to know? He relented and swallowed the coffee down. They were all supposed to be one happy team after all.

"Sir Peter wants me to assist the major from the army base, while keeping him under surveillance."

Her pupils dilated. He tried to break new ground.

"Ann, can I ask you something? What's the deal with Karl — I know his mum is ill, but that's about it."

It was her turn to hide in her coffee. "Just ask Karl when he was last in the province." She stepped around him to the door; their alfresco meeting was over.

An email from Major Eldridge awaited his attention: *Thomas, I'll see you in my office at 10.30 tomorrow. I look forward to working with you. Major C Eldridge.* He stored the email address and deleted the email.

The afternoon dragged without Karl to bounce off, despite Ann Crossley's enigmatic presence. Since Christine's permanent promotion, Ann was the Number Two. Karl had wrung endless juvenile fun out of that one. However, since Ann and Karl had resolved their acrimony, she largely left the two of them to get on with it. Jeez, this whole outfit was turning into one big version of Truth or Dare, without the Truth part.

At four thirty, he reminded Ann about his appointment on the base next morning and the need to do some prep work. He felt a little like a school kid handing in a note from his mum. Down at Stores, he added a GPS tag to the list, just in case Jess decided to go walkabout again.

* * *

Outside, fast approaching five pm, the city seemed to be on wind-down. The suits and the hipsters, the fashion-hungry and the drones, all gravitating towards whichever bar best represented their image.

He stood on a street corner as they trundled past in groups, chatting about their days. Had he ever been like that when he worked behind a civil service desk? Hopefully not. He turned to watch a bunch of drinkers through the faux-Victorian plate glass. A city gent, clutching a pint in one hand, was shouting into a mobile phone trapped between his ear and shoulder. If there was any justice, someone would be stealing his laptop from under the table.

Time to hit Caliban's for a Q&A session with Jess, always assuming she hadn't done another bunk. He pictured Miranda rugby-tackling Jess and bar manager, Sheryl, pinning her down. That was a film for another day.

On the drive over, he tried shuffling the picture cards in his mind. Jess, the major, Karl, Sir Peter Carroll, Ann, Christine and Old Smiler from Engamel; it was too much like hard work. Just when did he — to use one of Miranda's delightful turns of phrase — become everyone's Spy Bitch?

He ran a hand over his face and jolted when some kindly soul behind him beeped their horn. Green light. He glanced in the mirror, considering a quick one-finger salute. He almost missed the light altogether when he saw that the driver behind him was Karl.

It was a haunting smile and it carried him along on the world's shortest convoy. A face like his mam, back when he was a kid. Mournful, that was the word for it; making the best of it and longing for comfort where there was none to be found. He sighed. All this insight after only one session with the counsellor. Another seven, and he'd be weeping into his pillow about the camera he'd wanted as a boy.

Chapter 13

Karl parked up and slowly got out. He looked like an advert for antidepressants — the *before* picture. "Hey, Tommo. I felt like a drink — alright with you?"

"Course!" Better than alright. Miranda had rescinded Karl's life ban, the one she'd imposed when Karl's job had been his one character reference. Plus, Karl could meet Jess and maybe, just maybe, inject a little sense into all this.

The bar was surprisingly busy. He had an immediate theory on that, going by Sheryl's T-shirt and waistcoat combo.

"Hey, Thomas," she beamed. "What would you like?"

He basked in her smile. Karl seemed to be in a world of his own — no Battle of the Banter today.

"A pint of shandy for the lad," he turned to Karl, who merely nodded in thanks. "And a lemonade for me."

Sheryl raised her eyes to the ceiling. "Coming right up . . . boys."

And not, he noticed at the till, on the house.

Karl drew his chair close to the table and propped himself against it. "So how do you rate your first day flying solo?"

Thomas lifted his glass and the chunks of lemon Sheryl had added bobbed about furiously. "In a word: shit. The sooner you get back to work the better — I've no friends to play with."

"Aye, well, won't be long now . . ."

He suddenly felt like the world's greatest arse, realising Karl meant after his mother had died. He fished out a chunk of lemon and sucked at it; it didn't help. "Ann Crossley suggested I should ask you when you last went . . ." he stopped, appalled by his own ignorance; he didn't even know what to call Northern Ireland.

"Home?" Karl gulped at his shandy. When he lifted his head there were tears in his eyes. "Jesus, Tommo, you've forgotten the crisps — see what you're doing to me here!" Karl was laughing, only he wasn't.

Thomas scuttled over to the bar and took his time about it. Out of the corner of his eye he thought he saw Karl pull out a handkerchief. This was not good news; he had enough trouble with his own emotions, never mind other people's. He lingered with Sheryl as long as he dared, while she circled him for sport. Miranda reckoned it was just her way but he'd never noticed her putting in that much effort with other men. Though that was probably what the other men told themselves.

He brought back Karl's holy trinity: ready salted, salt & vinegar, and cheese & onion. Karl was a man who hadn't moved with the times. He repeated Karl's mantra as he opened the bags out. "You can't mess with perfection."

As he sat down, Karl patted the table. Turned out it wasn't a hankie, just a square of white paper. "I've realised I'm not being very fair, leaving you in all this without so much as a helping hand.

"True," he acknowledged. *And you haven't answered my question.*

Karl's took out a pen and held it above the paper, poised. After a few seconds, Thomas cottoned on that Karl was volunteering to be the scribe. He rattled off names for Karl to write down, and then added his thoughts — who trusted who and where the alliances seemed to be. Karl circled names and added arrows.

It was therapeutic, brain-dumping all this on to paper. Now was the ideal time to reveal that he was simultaneously assisting the major and bugging him, while still keeping schtum about the hidden components from the UB40 Scavenger. And of course there was Sir Peter's expressed intention to update Christine with a low-fat version of events.

"To be honest," Thomas stared at the busy page in defeat, "I don't know what the fuck I'm doing with Jess or the components."

Karl scooped an assortment of crisps into his mouth. "Seems to me you're holding a few decent cards, Tommo. Can you not see that?"

"Maybe . . ." he drank some lemonade. "But how do I play them?"

Karl swallowed the last of the crisps and ran his tongue over his lower lip. "If it was me . . ." he pulled out another piece of paper and started to write a numbered list. Karl loved lists. Lists and maps. He was what Sheryl would call 'a visual kinda guy.' The list was very short.

> 1. Tell the major what you've been asked to do and then bug him anyway.
> 2. Tell him that the Land Rover was stolen.
> 3. Ask him what he wants you to do with the photos.
> 4. Do not let anyone else get hold of Jess.

Thomas read through the idiot's guide to problem-solving at least twice, static as a caravan. Karl's face looked like it could break into a smile at any moment, but had chosen not to, so Thomas picked up the paper and folded it into his back pocket.

Karl took another dive into his shandy. "I could, er, really use a proper chat, sometime this week." He looked like he was just about holding it together.

"Yeah, come round the flat. Maybe not tonight, in case I'm babysitting again."

"I'd prefer the club if it's all the same to you — neutral ground."

"Of course. How about tomorrow night?"

"Thanks, Tommo, you're a pal." He downed the last of the crisps. "Now, where are my manners — what are we doing here?"

"Come on," Thomas shifted his chair. "There's someone I'd like you to meet."

* * *

Sheryl rang upstairs and waved them through. Miranda was ready and waiting.

"Smile, boys, you're on TV," she pointed to a screen split four ways.

He didn't know whether to be pleased she'd had it installed or pissed off that she hadn't told him beforehand. He settled for a dignified murmur of approval. "Where's the guest?"

As if cued to his voice, Jess emerged from the side room. "Hello, Thomas," she extended a lettuce-limp hand, which hung in the air like a bad smell. "I feel I owe you some sort of explanation."

That made him feel even more irked. "For what? Leaving the flat without telling me, turning up again without warning or running the risk of being seen and picked up?"

Okay, so it might have been a bit over the top but it filled Karl in nicely, in double-quick time. Karl was still standing in the background — Jess hardly seemed to register his presence at all. Then Karl did a funny thing. He came forward, sidestepped Jess altogether and shook Miranda's hand lightly, touching her shoulder at the same time. It was a curious mix of formal and intimate.

Miranda smiled — not her fake 'how nice to see you — *not*' facial glimmer but a warm, gentle response. "Karl, this is Jess — our . . . guest. I believe you have a mutual friend. Why don't you two have a chat while I thrash Thomas at pool next door?" She grabbed Thomas's belt and hauled him away.

Miranda racked up the pool balls loudly, making it impossible for Thomas to eavesdrop through the open door. He caught a few mutterings but not the substance of them.

"Give it up." Miranda gave the triangle another shake. "I'm sure he'll tell you everything later."

Thomas wasn't sure either of them believed that. She spun a coin. "Call it."

"Tails." He took the cue and leant on the table, pulling back to break.

"Jess said you were the one who came on to her."

The cue ball nearly went airborne, slamming into the pack unevenly. Miraculously, a stripe had been scared down a hole.

She met his gaze. "I didn't believe her of course."

He tried to recover his composure but his reflection was nearly as red as the three ball.

"I just wanted you to know the kind of person you're dealing with."

There was no answer to that; none that would avoid lighting the blue touchpaper. In between losing focus, losing advantage and losing three consecutive games, he tried hard to pick up the occasional word from next door. Midway through the fourth game — convinced that pool-star Sheryl had been giving Miranda lessons — he held the cue in the air like a totem.

"What do you want me to do about Jess, then?"

"I dunno," Miranda seemed pleased and flummoxed at the same time. "Just watch your back."

"That's what I've got you for."

She smiled, took her cue and cleared the table of spots. Somehow, though, she ran out of steam on the black. He squared his shoulders, put on his best Comeback King face and — despite Miranda whistling the opening bars to The Entertainer — set to work. With careful concentration, he put the remaining stripes down methodically. Down to the black now and not even Miranda pushing up her breasts and pouting, glamour model style, would distract him.

"Ahem."

He turned to see Karl and Jess, standing in the doorway like guilty adolescents. "We're all done here." Karl's tone was business-like.

Jess took a step forward. "I've told Karl that I'm going to the funeral. It's what Cecil wants as well."

Thomas looked daggers at Karl, but they bounced right off him. He opened a conciliatory palm to Jess. "Look, we can't protect you if you don't stay out of sight."

Jess opened her mouth and nothing came out. But her eyes said plenty.

"How about a compromise?" Miranda broke the silence. "You lie low until the funeral and that'll give the boys time to figure something out, longer term?" No dissenters, carried unanimously, and Miranda wasn't done talking. "Sheryl's staying here while her flat's being redecorated. There's another spare room upstairs. It's not the Hilton or anything, but it'd keep you out of Thomas's hair." She laughed then, as if to say, 'Because he's so vulnerable.' Jess seemed to share the joke.

"Tell you what," Karl acted like he'd just had a brainwave, although Thomas knew him better than that, "Why don't you pop us your keys and address, and then we can pick up some clothes and personal stuff for you." His face was as earnest as a social worker's. What could be amiss? Jess could hardly object. Karl held out his hand and smiled.

Jess froze for an instant, weighing it up. "Thanks," she twisted her mouth into a smile and handed the keys over to Thomas.

Miranda wangled them some bar food. Jess asked a lot of questions and, for all her innocent abroad act, Thomas could see she was taking everything in. She grew more sullen as the meal went on, outplayed by three people who could evade questions without catching a breath.

Meal over; time to go. He kissed Miranda goodbye — a matter-of-fact kiss, under the spectators' gaze. Then he and Karl left together. Karl didn't speak until they hit the car park.

"Worst double-date in living memory."

Thomas rattled Jess's keys as if he were calling in a cat. "Jess's place is probably being watched — it'd take an expert to get in undetected . . ." he did his best impression of *forlorn*.

"Okay," Karl relented, "give it here. I'll see if I can get someone to deal with it. One suitcase of clothes and personals, a black suit for the funeral and a passport if I can find one."

Thomas frowned.

Karl spread his arms. "Just thinking ahead. Anyhow, can't stop — got to get a postcard in the mail — I had Jess write and sign it.

Only one I had was of Yorkshire, sorry." He pulled out a picture postcard of Scarborough. It was addressed to Amy at a liaison office, as if it had arrived internally. Clever Karl. It might take the heat off for a day or so; and it'd make Jess's reappearance at the funeral seem a little more plausible.

That didn't stop Thomas from picking holes. "How do we know Jess hasn't contacted the victim's family already?"

Karl didn't skip a beat. "Amy was an American citizen, didn't you know? And no doubt our friends across the pond are already watching the post." Karl stepped towards his car. "Get some sleep, Tommy Boy. I'll bring the things to the club tomorrow night — see you at the usual pick-up — seven o'clock."

Chapter 14

The flat felt way too quiet when he shut the door behind him. Funny to think of Miranda at home, in the place that used to be theirs. It all seemed like a long time ago, and now here he was in Walthamstow, end of the line.

He settled in and took the answering machine out of the drawer — one of Miranda's *do not disturb* foibles. Three messages; hang out the flags. First up, his sister, Pat — even her *hello* sounded cagey. Her husband Gordon's job was at risk, and he had to work away for a couple of days. She sounded lonely, even though Mum and Dad were a few streets away. Next, Christine Gerrard — unusual for the boss to ring him at home. Just seeing how he was and what he was up to. He skipped, mid-message and played the last of the trio.

"Alright mate, Ajit here . . ."

"Yorkshire's finest!" Ajit's other half, Geena, had shouted from behind him.

Thomas knew that would have wound Ajit up big-time because he actually came from Lancashire. You could hear the two of them scrabbling for the phone like children. Ajit had the upper hand, and given the size of him those upper hands were massive. "Just wondered, like, how ya doing and when you're next in this part of the world?"

"Oh, give it 'ere!" The phone clattered then Geena's voice cut in, loud and clear. "Right you, when are you getting your arse back home? Ajit's fretting for you! And I'm the size of a bungalow now, *Uncle* Tommy."

Yeah, thought Thomas, and so's Ajit.

"Come and see us soon, eh?"

344

Another clatter — Ajit must have grabbed the phone back. "And bring some jellied eels for Geena. She's into foreign food."

He made a coffee, dug out a biscuit from the tin, one that had not fared well in captivity, and sat down by the phone. His mobile was on, just out of interference range, in case Miranda or anyone else wanted to get in touch. Used to be that his people skills extended as far as Miranda, her family and Ajit. But, since the moors, he'd widened his circle a little. He smiled; must remember that one for the counsellor.

Pat, first. She had an obligatory cry on the phone, but soon pulled herself together. He'd never shaken off the older-brother/lord-high-protector mantle, even though he'd been shit at it. After an update on Mum and Dad, and the kids, Pat had him buttered up so smoothly that he slid right into place.

"No, I promise, I'll come see you soon — when I get some time off. Course I mean it. Tell my little niece and nephew I said hello." No message for her husband, Gordon, though — no point scaring him.

Christine was out, or busy. He thanked her answering machine for the call, said he'd get in early next day to update her, and that he'd be around if she fancied a chat tonight. She wouldn't, and nor would he, but it was one of those things that people said.

It was still the right side of ten thirty, so he gave Ajit a bell, figuring he wasn't on a nightshift. Geena picked up, squealed with delight and did a deliberately piss-poor version of a Chas & Dave song. Miranda's mum and dad loved Chas & Dave, although he'd never tell Geena that.

Ajit must have taken a while to crane his bulk out of a chair. "Hee, Thomas Bladen, as I live and breathe."

"Constable."

"Listen, funny man, I might not be a constable for much longer."

And though he should have been pleased, Thomas shrank a little at the news. Without doubt, Thomas roping him in to do the clean up on the moors would have helped Ajit's standing, and his confidence. After all, it had made the papers. *'Yorkshire Police assist in apprehension of drug-trafficking gang.'* A little more palatable than: *'Yorkshire Police assist in removal of assassin's body and subsequent European conspiracy cover-up.'*

"Well done, mate." Thomas raised his voice to artificially high levels of encouragement. Truth be told, he was happy for him. But, as Miranda had sussed out early on, too much change made him tetchy.

"So, are you coming up or what?"

"Aye, go on then. Not sure when — soon, though, in the next couple of months." It was the closest he got to commitment.

"Nice one. I've got my sergeant's exam soon. It'd be grand to see you, but not worth sacrificing stripes for!"

* * *

He slept fitfully that night, the pale glow of the mobile entering his dreams as a sallow moon over the moors. He was stumbling over unfamiliar territory, a ridgeway he'd never seen before. And right at the top, he saw a caped figure waiting for him. He woke suddenly, the smell of damp air in his nostrils and a last image of the cape's hood lifting to reveal Karl's face gleaming back at him.

First thing he did was jot down the dream, just as the counsellor had asked him. It was probably all bollocks; still, anything for a pal.

Chapter 15

The office clock showed eight, glaring at him as if it couldn't quite believe it either. Ms Gerrard was already in situ, her door ajar.

"Hi, Thomas," she called out without moving. "I brought a *croissant* for you." She pronounced every French syllable exactingly. Education was surely a wonderful thing.

He dropped his bag at his desk then thought better of it and carried it through, closing the door behind him.

"There's a hot choc there as well."

Not *chocolat* — how disappointing. He tried to observe her without looking her over. The latter never went down well, especially since her promotion. The hot chocolate was good, a world away from the vending machine crap on offer. A sip of it went down slow and easy.

"How was Whitehall?" She had a certain economy of speech. Karl did that too sometimes.

"Sir Peter wants you kept at arm's length."

She didn't seem surprised. He'd skipped over 'I want to know what the hell's going on' and landed with 'I'm clear on where my loyalties lie.' It wasn't quite how he'd meant it to come out, but she knew him well enough. Speaking of which, he pulled his eyes back from her legs, signalling at him from under the table.

Over hot chocolate and croissants, he told her about bugging the major and the American from Engamel. Jess didn't figure in the conversation. They parted, all smiles; he nearly leaned forward to give her a hug but she *was* the boss. Plus, he'd heard Ann Crossley arriving in the main office and he didn't want to set team expectations.

* * *

Traffic was snarled up around Liverpool Street, as he battled through and headed north, like a lazier latter-day Amundsen. He called Ann Crossley, hands-free from the car, safely stuck in a jam, and tackled her about Karl and Northern Ireland — the question Karl had yet to answer.

She didn't miss a trick. "He's not as squeaky clean as you'd like to believe."

He took a breath, long and lean, as the driver in front remembered to take the handbrake off. "None of us are, Ann. I'll ring you again once I'm off the army base. Thomas out."

So much for all being comrades now. He reached for some crisps — Jesus, he was morphing into Karl's understudy — and flicked on the radio. There were the usual scandals and politicking, plus some US film star had got drunk at an awards ceremony and ranted on camera. And apparently, shares in the technology sector were particularly buoyant, pending some global alliance venture. Engamel Solutions didn't get a name check, although he did wonder.

* * *

At the army base, Checkpoint Charlie exited the guard cabin and walked slowly around the barrier. If his face were the first line of defence, he was doing a grand job.

Thomas flashed his ID, waited for the card to be returned and generally tried to keep a low profile. From the face on Charlie, even after verifying the ID, the Surveillance Support Unit was as welcome here as they were everywhere else.

"When the MPs arrive, follow them through." The ID card was thrust back, as if the guard had just wiped his arse with it.

And a lovely day to you too. In the distance, a squad or battalion — or whatever they were called — was drilling. There couldn't have been a man among them under six-two. Any of them would have given Ajit a run for his money in an arm-wrestling contest.

* * *

The major was waiting outside as Thomas parked up. He thanked the Red Caps and ushered Thomas inside with his two cases.

First thing Thomas did was sweep the office and back rooms for existing bugs — competition wasn't good for business. After the all clear, he sat down and mentally went through Karl's list of handy hints.

The major was busy outlining what he needed; Thomas didn't pay attention. He was more interested in what wasn't being said.

"So, Thomas, any questions?"

Was he taking the piss? A pro might have warmed up slowly, tried a little subtlety. He couldn't be arsed. "I've been ordered," he thought the major would like that, "to bug your office. Which phone would you prefer?"

The major didn't exactly look surprised, more disappointed. "Why are you telling me?"

Good question. He shrugged. "It's what Karl would do. Right, I suggest you sort out any personal calls while I'm on lunch and then vacate the room while I do my stuff."

The major glanced at two telephones on his desk, and tapped one.

"Everything will be switched off until then, sir."

"Thank you, Thomas."

One item mentally crossed off the list. Next . . . "Oh, you may get a call from Services about the Land Rover we used last week. Someone stole it on Sunday night — from outside my home."

The major blanched; hard to tell under the neon whether it was more guilt or concern. He left the news hanging in the air to see how the major would catch it. In the end, it hit the ground without a whimper. "One more thing, Major — what did you want me to do with the copied photographs?"

"I understood Karl was taking care of that."

He swallowed and turned his face, drawing in the scent of heated polish from the desk lamp. *Liar — Karl would have said so.* He chose his next words carefully. "Karl has been assigned to other work, because of his military connections."

The major snorted a sigh and glanced around the room. "You're sure this office is clear?"

He nodded — silly question; the major looked like he wanted to be convinced.

"Right, this goes no further. Aside from Amy," his voice cracked a little and Thomas thought well of him for it, "there was another technician. I took the decision to get her away from here, and made sure there was no record of her presence, on the day of . . ." he faltered, ". . . the accident."

"Well that's just it. Was it an accident?"

Major Eldridge stared at him like a sentencing judge. He flipped a folder over.

Thomas glanced at the cover. "I don't have clearance for this."

"Just open it, man; you won't get a second view."

It was standard stuff. No mention of exactly what was being tested, a vague reference to mechanical failure and a conclusion suggesting that whatever test had failed was unorthodox.

Thomas backed up a few pages, hoping to find some names to remember. "Mixed rounds."

The major was reading the pages with him, from across the desk. "A random selection, I suspect."

Yeah, Thomas thought, or you've been *told*. He handed the folder back. "There's no mention of a second technician."

"Quite correct. There should always be two — to check the calibrations."

"So what happened?"

"Corner-cutting. The project was behind schedule."

For a man on the periphery, the major seemed to know a lot about it; perhaps it was pillow talk. Thomas picked at a knuckle; he felt no closer to the truth.

"Can we cut to the chase? This is all a whitewash; I get that. So why hold the photos? If the media even got a whiff of this, it'd end up squashed and never see daylight."

The major carefully locked the folder in his desk. "The photos were all I had."

Yeah, besides a fat pension. "Any chance of a cuppa?" Not so much tea and sympathy as tea and strategy.

* * *

He stirred his tea rhythmically, even though he'd skipped on the sugar, tapping the spoon against the china like a séance-bell. Sir Peter did the same thing, using the sound to command attention.

It occurred to him that the major hadn't mentioned Jess's emergency calls — either the one to Karl's mobile, or when she'd rung the major's personal number. Maybe he just needed a nudge.

"Is there something else I need to know?" He waited, blinking to the rhythm of his thoughts.

The major ran a slow hand across his forehead. It had all the hallmarks of a magic moment. "I take it you're referring to Jess. I gave her Karl's number for outside assistance."

And? More blinking.

"She's been in touch since, but I don't know where Karl's hiding her."

He peeled his collar away from his neck. Holy shit; Jess was playing him too. So what was her angle?

"You've been honest, Thomas, so I'll return the compliment. I was hoping you'd be willing to speak to Karl, to get a message to Jess."

He watched as the major's face tightened at the name. Maybe she was putting the squeeze on his marriage — the price you paid for playing away. He clocked the time.

"I'll nip off for lunch and then you can give me a little space here to do the necessary. I don't work well with an audience."

Chapter 16

A staff sergeant provided the taxi service, ferrying him over to the mess hall. He also kept him company over dinner.

"You're not ex-mob then?"

Thomas stalled his fork. "That obvious, is it?"

"It's the way you look around, as if you're working out the angles."

That raised a smile. "Sorry, photographer's habit." He dropped back to his lamb and veg.

"I, er, take a few pictures myself — as a hobby."

Many's the time some part-time snapper had lusted after a lens he'd been carrying, or read the badge and wanted to be friends. He figured they were all after one of two things: tips from the professionals, or a peek over the fence to a future career, if the day job with the MoD, police or whatever, ran out of steam. He got the gist — to an outsider it must look like easy money, playing pretend spies — a long lens here, a microphone there and a few parcels up and down the country.

His mind leapfrogged to Amy — he liked to remind himself of her name so that she remained a person and not just so many pictures. Lying there like broken porcelain in a sea of blood and ash.

". . . So I was wondering what the entrance criteria is?"

He'd learned to tune in at the end of sentences and just wait for the echo.

"Only I'd love to do more with a camera, professionally like."

He swallowed another mouthful. "I can give you a number to call."

"Thanks, I'd appreciate that." The sergeant jotted it down, placing it carefully in a top pocket. Most likely he'd never look at it again.

Thomas knew that he wasn't exactly a walking recruitment poster. Another time he'd have been happy to talk about the relative merits of polarised filters, but today he had other things on his plate — besides the gristle.

* * *

As soon as Thomas returned, Major Eldridge made himself scarce. Everything had been locked away. Thomas's two cases sat on the desk; out of habit he checked the locks and hinges then went to work.

He used a voice-activated phone device, one that also recorded inbound-caller numbers. Later, he'd remind the major to continue using the phone as normal. When that job was done, he took out a different plastic box. This was the bug Christine had removed from her office, not so long ago. He made short work of the second telephone and added a faded plastic tab over one bottom edge to suggest the phone hadn't ever been disturbed. After all, who looked closely at the underside of their work phone? No one. Besides him and Karl, of course.

To pass the time, he took out Karl's four-step guide — only one gem left, relating to Jess. He tried running through the sequence again: Jess rings the major; Jess goes out to see him, but doesn't tell him where she's staying. It didn't play well at all. Something was missing.

By the time the major walked in, Karl's notes were safely away and Thomas was happily browsing the glass bookcase. One of Karl's theories was that your bookcase told the world who you wanted to be, while the books you'd actually read showed how close you were to becoming it. In Miranda's case, she grazed on chick-lit and murders, but her most creased covers held Jane Austen and Thomas Hardy. Funny girl.

The office bookcase held few surprises — military biographies sat cheek by jowl, Churchill was among them; technical books on warfare and the latest edition of *Jane's Tank Recognition* guide; and some historical tomes on the Roman Empire. They all looked in very good condition. In one corner though, peeping out like an anonymous peace protestor, was an ancient copy of *Winnie-the-Pooh*. A sudden image of Piglet piloting the C12 Battlebuster momentarily brightened the day.

The major nodded curtly. Everything was packed away, waiting by the door; no need to state the obvious. But there were things to be said.

Thomas sat down and hunched forward, hands clasps together. He hoped he looked as uncomfortable as he felt. "Major Eldridge, I'm a little confused about exactly what my assignment here is — from you I mean."

It was the major's turn to look uncomfortable and he didn't squander it. "Let me put it this way. In the absence of Karl, you're my best means of locating Jess."

"So in the meantime I turn up with a camera every day or carry a few parcels about?"

"Don't be absurd, man," the major blazed at him. "I'm not interested in how you spend your time. Just find Jess, before anyone else does."

Time, as Sheryl liked to say, to fess up. "Look, I'm confident I can get a message to Jess. I imagine she'll want to attend the memorial service." He was banking on not having to elaborate.

"Can you get word to her today?"

He checked his watch, for no reason other than an early finish might be useful. "I think so."

"Then tell her . . ."

Jesus, please not a love note.

". . . Tell her the best thing she can do is return the papers immediately."

Thomas tightened his jaw and tried not to shout, 'bingo.' "Now, I just need to use your phone then we're set." He didn't wait to be invited.

"Hello, it's Thomas." He looked straight at the major. "Major Eldridge is out of the way. I've networked his phone. I'll do the co-ord when I get back to the office. Really? To whom?" He breathed slow and deep, and put the receiver down carefully as if it were made of gold.

"Why would Engamel Solutions want to view data from your phone tap?"

The major wore a stoic mask. Stalemate. Thomas headed for the door.

"Thomas, tell me this: why are you helping me?"

"I could just as easily ask: why isn't Jess?"

* * *

Back at Liverpool Street, he checked one of the cases back into Stores and trudged up the stairs. Before he swiped in, he peered through the reinforced glass to see who was home.

Ann Crossley was nowhere to be seen — second bonus of the day, after Christine's breakfast. He logged on, checked the major's chosen phone line and played the first of the recordings. Good boy. He'd check the other line he'd bugged from home, outside office hours.

His phone started ringing so he paused the recording. "Thomas Bladen speaking."

"Hi, Thomas, it's Michael Schaefer from Engamel. I wanted to call and thank you for your work today. As a matter of fact, I'd like to invite you to dinner, tomorrow night — anywhere you can recommend?"

He couldn't think of a good reason not to accept and let Mr Smiley sort out the details. It was barely five o'clock, but he needed a shower; he suddenly felt unclean.

* * *

Karl picked him up at Holloway Road tube station, same as the old days — the *before Yorgi* days. He didn't say much as Thomas got in the car, but he'd cued up 'Dead Ringer For Love' so Thomas took it that Karl was in a good mood.

Nothing to it, he told himself, as the car wove through the traffic; just a quiet evening out with Karl. Except that this evening happened to be his first time back at the gun club. Just thinking about it brought the numbness back to his hands. Part of him just wanted this over with, so he could move on.

He returned to the present as Karl pulled up and switched off the engine. They sat there for a while, practising surveillance on the other vehicles.

"Right then, Tommo, shall we?"

Chapter 17

The door to the club seemed heavier, the woman behind the glass more officious. Not that he'd expected a fanfare; he still wasn't even a member. Karl led on, a little diffidently, to one of the pistol ranges. He could hear the dulled thuds and discharges of neighbouring alleys through the walls.

"Any preference?" Karl might have been calling heads or tails to cue off.

"Brownings," he decided. He knew Karl would like that; Karl, with his own pair hidden away somewhere — part of that other life that Thomas had only glimpsed.

* * *

Karl re-entered the room quietly. Thomas stayed fixed on the targets. It could have been minutes, could have been days. The air was heavy somehow, tainted with smoke and spent heat. And oil; that strange mineral-metal combination that seemed to remain on the skin afterwards. He drew back from the wash of senses, mentally rejoining the room as he heard the boxes being opened.

"Here, Tommo, I thought you might like to go first."

He checked the piece over methodically, loaded the magazine and clicked it hard into place. He opted for people targets straight away — no point beating around the bush; it would come to this anyway. He observed his right hand trembling a little before he felt it, up in his shoulder, the jangling dread running up and down his spine. His bladder squeezed — an old fear reflex — but he held it all together and waited. Then he remembered the ear defenders, setting the safety on while he attended to it, every movement measured and controlled. The familiar roar insulated him from the world.

The targets turned and so did his stomach. But there was also a rush of adrenaline, coursing the blood and sharpening the vision. The first shot was the hardest. After that they followed in a steady burst. At the final click, he called "clear" and set the gun down.

Karl hit the button and whirled in the target for inspection. "Nyah." He waved a flat piano hand, so-so fashion. "Better than shite, but don't give up your day job."

Thomas stared at the target. "I'm not even sure what my day job is anymore."

Witnessing Karl in action was like watching an African wildlife documentary, only with guns. Karl stalked the targets. He moulded himself into a predator; he was in no hurry. He took his shots further apart, which lent them greater intensity, each one punctuating the silence between them.

When they finished, he eagerly awaited Karl's first words — the climax to the performance and a reintroduction to normality. Even the target seemed to fly back that little bit quicker for the delivery.

Karl lifted his head. "I'd say the drinks are on you, Tommy Boy — for about the next five years."

Karl suggested trying some Glocks or 38s, but Thomas played safe and opted for another magazine with the Browning. No point pushing his luck. Almost before he knew it, before he was ready in a sense, they were done.

"I have to say, Tommo, that I am impressed."

Thomas did him the courtesy of not interrupting. "Not only are you less shit, after weeks of absence. But your sweating skills are excellent."

On cue, he felt a cold trickle against his back. Nothing more to be said.

* * *

The bar, as Karl liked to call it, was actually a café area within the gun club. Thomas thought of school, of coming back after an illness, and everything feeling different even though nothing had changed. It was space to be reclaimed.

He sat back and felt the dampness in his shirt, beneath his sweater, moulding like plaster to the contours of his skin. When he closed his eyes and heard the gunfire in his head, he saw the targets flickering. It was a welcome change from Yorgi, bursting scarlet amid the heather.

Karl brought over a tray, waddling for effect — a comical waiter. He glanced at Thomas's mobile on the table.

"Listen, Tommo, I've a wee confession." He set the tray down and distributed the goods. "I told Miranda that you and I were meeting tonight and suggested she might want to hold off from ringing you until later. Purely on the off-chance you might find all this a bit difficult."

He felt his cheeks tingling and grabbed a pastry, biting into it savagely, chewing the doughy mass, holding it in his mouth while he poured hot coffee into the mixture.

"Now . . ." Karl continued, "there's been a delay getting the stuff from Jess's home. Even my superpowers don't include invisibility."

Thomas smiled, sipping at his coffee now that he'd burnt his mouth.

"I'll get it to you first thing tomorrow morning — before work. Right-oh, your turn — hit me."

He stuck to the details; that's what he did best.

He told Karl about bugging both of the major's office phones, about dinner plans with Michael Schaefer from Engamel, and the major's cryptic reference to missing papers. "How well do you know the major, from your army days?"

A glow crept across Karl's face. "Major Charles Eldridge — stand-up man, no question about it."

He frowned a little. "I thought his name was Cecil?"

"Well, he must have really taken a shine to you. Cecil's his middle name — some sort of family tradition. Only his nearest and dearest call him Cecil, apparently, and never in front of uniforms."

Curiouser and curiouser. "Wanna come back to mine for a takeaway?"

* * *

"So really," Karl said, holding the takeaway bags, while Thomas fiddled with his door key, "This is our first proper date. You do know that I won't be putting out?"

Thomas swung the door wide and let Karl lead the way.

"Nice place."

People always said that, even if it was a shit-hole. It was right up there with, 'Of course I love you' and 'I promise I'll be careful.'

Karl made straight for the photographs displayed on the wall. "She takes a good photo, your Miranda."

Your Miranda. He liked that.

"I want to show you something."

"Not your etchings." Karl covered himself strategically with his hands.

"Better than that."

With two people, the dark room was cramped. Karl looked without touching, asked questions, seemed to be drinking it all in. He sidled up even closer.

"Actually, I have a collection of war memorial photographs. Dawn and dusk, stark against the skyline. No names visible because that seemed wrong."

"Ever exhibited?"

"Not really. I sold a copy of one once; felt so bad afterwards that I gave the money away to the Royal British Legion."

* * *

Thomas set his albums ready on the living-room table. But *no touching* until the curry was consumed and all the surfaces had been wiped clean.

He'd brought out three of them. The first two were orderly, categorised by theme and labelled with dates and times, as well as a few notes about the camera and settings. Yorkshire featured strongly, as did London's East End and the City after hours. Mostly black-and-whites; frozen faces, frozen time. But the third, smallest album was more random and personal. Like a mix cassette tape that someone had never planned to share with anyone else.

He made two mugs of tea and dug out the last of a packet of shortbreads. Karl had already made sure the albums were out of harm's way.

"How's your mum doing?"

Karl sucked in a cheek. "Did you ever wonder how your life might have turned out, if you'd done one thing differently?"

Thomas sat and absorbed the point.

"Y'see," Karl shifted to one side of the cushion, as if suddenly aware of his own discomfort, "I used to be somebody else. Flew out of Belfast International when I was nineteen and never set foot in my mammy's house again." He drew his hands around the mug and clasped it tightly.

"People on the outside, they don't understand the way things are over there. The way things *were*, so they tell us now. It wasn't just bombs and intimidation; it was straight lines and invisible fences. Religious apartheid — for the same God! What shops you used, what schools you went to, what friends you could keep. Where the wrong secret could get you killed."

The clock ticked away the silence.

"I made a mistake — a terrible, innocent mistake. I took up with the wrong girl. Her brother and I, we used to ride together. Taking cars and that, nothing heavy. But Martin was getting a wee name for himself and building a bit of a gang. It was what you did."

He sounded apologetic as he filled in more details.

"Somehow, Martin had picked up a contact across the fence. A Catholic boy, Francis-Andrew — sure it was all a business arrangement, but we were sworn to secrecy; the kind that threatened a severe penalty if you broke his trust."

Thomas noticed there were no surnames.

"Anyways, from what I figure, Martin and Francis-Andrew formed something of an alliance. Two gangs could have rich pickings if they were good and organised. Me, I was your typical angry young man — I had my reasons mind."

He huffed out a breath, as if the last piece of the puzzle required extra effort.

"It looked like I'd got Martin's sister pregnant. False alarm, not that it made any difference. Martin always claimed he had connections — he wasn't bullshitting. A couple of nights after our little showdown, my ma got a knock on the door, eleven o'clock at night. The kind of knock you don't ignore. I went to answer it even though I was shitting myself.

"There was a man standing there who I'd never seen before. The way I remember him is in a black overcoat, but it may have just been the shadow. Tall man he was, tall and thin. He looked down at me and he said 'Ya have twenty-four hours to leave — just you.' Then he turned and walked up the street.

"I had to hold on to the door handle to keep standing. I really thought he was going to come back and cripple me or something. Ma was in the hallway; I'm pretty sure she heard everything. She just looked at me and went inside; never said a word." Karl took a longer pause now, emptying his mug while Thomas sat frozen.

"Martin and Francis-Andrew are successful businessmen these days, so I hear. Partners, under the table, just like always. And when one of my cousins went to see Martin about my situation, what with my ma dying and all, he gave him a bust lip and a black eye for his trouble."

"I'm sorry, Karl."

He waved a hand at Thomas dismissively. "I used to send money home like fucking Clark Kent and my mammy would fly over, maybe twice a year for a weekend. When it was easier for her to travel south, we'd meet in Dublin. We could never relax though; never knew if Francis-Andrew had friends there."

"What did you do for work?"

"I drifted for a while. There's one or two of my family over here — not many — but they weren't jumping to get involved. So I worked on a few building sites, like every other lad from across the water. Christmas and Mother's Days were awful hard, Thomas. Even now I prefer to shut up shop come December and pretend I'm a Buddhist."

"But surely, under the circumstances . . . ?"

"Unfortunately not. I could just fly over and deal with the consequences," the voice had a harder edge, "but I still have family over there, and afterwards — who'd protect *them*?" He set the mug on the table and propped a hand under his face.

"I'm still paying for a mistake I made a long time ago, and so's my ma. And you wanna know the crazy thing? I really loved her, Jacqueline. It was never just, you know . . . Anyways, she's probably married with a couple of kids now, nice house in Holywood. And here's me, telling you my troubles over an empty mug and a dry throat."

Thomas took the family-sized hint. "More tea?" He clattered the mugs together and stood up. "I wish there was something I could do, Karl."

"There isn't. She can't be moved and I'm running out of time. I'm looking into other options though." The way he said it, it didn't sound promising. Karl cricked his shoulder as if shrugging off the weight of his thoughts. "Listen, Tommo, I'd better be going. Don't bother with the tea — I must have talked your ears off."

"We should do this again sometime — make it a Chinese next time?"

"Aye, right enough. Now, I'm away to business. Jess's flat won't burgle *itself* you know! See you here tomorrow, eight o'clock — and thanks."

* * *

The flat still reverberated with Karl's revelations as Thomas stared at the empty chair. He felt lucky, so lucky, when he thought back to his own collection of crossroads. Those points in time where his life might have derailed. If the kid who'd picked on Ajit at school — the one Thomas had accidentally put in hospital — had recognised him. Or if he'd never had that drunken row with his father and upped sticks to Leeds, never met Miranda there and smacked that sleazy photographer. And if all those dramas hadn't played out — his and Karl's — they'd never have met and he'd surely have been the worse for it.

He made tea for one and fired up his personal laptop, seeking out the anonymising server. He typed in the required URL, retrieved the serial number for the second phone bug from a locked drawer and input the password: SHERL0CK. A list of the major's calls on phone number two cascaded on-screen, augmented with times, durations, destinations and a sound file for each call. There was only one file for an incoming call and he went to it first.

> 'Cecil, I've been ringing your mobile, why won't you answer? We need to talk; I have to see you again.'
> 'You know what I want from you.'
> 'Let's not fight, not when there's so much to discuss.'
> 'I've got nothing more to say to you until I receive those letters.'

Thomas replayed the recording and his ears tingled. *Letters* sounded a bit more interesting — and specific — than *papers*. He parked the other calls and began a web-search for two businessmen in Belfast, with the forenames Martin and Francis-Andrew.

* * *

An hour later, he had a scrappy page of notes for his efforts and he was all done in. Tiredness, though, brought its own inspiration; maybe he'd see just how much support Ann Crossley was willing to give him. He put it to the test, left a message on her work number and climbed into bed. The sheets caressed him with remembrances of Miranda. Every time he shifted the covers, her scent and that indefinable sense of her body engulfed him. He drew it in greedily and reached for the phone.

"Mr Bladen, what a nice surprise." She sounded playful. This could have been the perfect occasion for phone sex, if he'd had the energy.

"I was hoping you'd have called earlier, but I gather Karl turned me into an exclusion zone."

"Only temporarily. As of now, our borders are wide open." She laughed huskily.

"Can you ask your mum and dad if I can pop over this week?" More laughter: the scathing kind.

"Since when did you need an invitation?"

"This is about business."

"Oh. And does this *business* concern me?"

There was an argument on the horizon, moving full steam into view. He suppressed a yawn, in case it was taken out of context.

"I'd like it to. It's about Karl."

"Okay," she softened. "Tell me what I need to know."

* * *

Karl was as good as his word, tap-tapping on the door just before eight. Thomas had been ready since seven. He brought him in and put the coffee on for the third time that morning.

"Good man!" Karl plonked the suitcase and dress bag down beside him on the sofa; he looked like a runaway cross-dresser.

"I don't suppose you found any letters lying around?"

"Letters? No, was I meant to?"

"Doesn't matter." Thomas tried not to show his disappointment. "The major was adamant about getting some letters back," he pointed to his laptop, "when Jess rang him on his private landline yesterday."

"My, my, she does like to live dangerously."

"Doesn't she just. I don't get it, Karl. She wants to see him but she doesn't tell him where she's staying. Makes no sense."

"I guess that's modern relationships for you."

"Maybe." Thomas frowned. He'd never attempted a jigsaw puzzle without studying the picture very carefully beforehand. "Major Eldridge thinks *you've* got Jess and sees me as a way in." He left Karl to think about it and nipped into the kitchen, returning with the coffees.

Karl held his hand up as if he were receiving communion. "Thank you, God, for coffee. Amen."

Thomas rested a hand lightly on Karl's forehead. "Forgive him, Lord, for he knows not much of anything."

"Unless you can talk Jess out of going to the memorial service, in two days' time, I don't see how you can keep the lovebirds apart. More's the pity. But we can do something about her disappearing again."

With some pliers, a screwdriver and very little finesse, Karl fitted the GPS inside the heel of Jess's shoe. They were the only footwear in the case, aside from a pair of trainers — an unlikely choice of footwear for a funeral.

Thomas watched as Karl worked; it felt a little like helping out his dad. "What can you tell me about Engamel?"

Karl set the pliers down for a moment and scratched at his chin. "American and European consortium, looking to develop niche applications for the modern combatant about town."

"You mean weapons."

"Not only weapons. That Battlebuster we waited so patiently for had Engamel components in its defensive capability."

Thomas narrowed his eyes. "Engamel wasn't mentioned in the brochure — I'd have remembered it."

Karl smiled enigmatically and finished with the shoe. "No, they weren't."

"Karl," Thomas said his name quietly, "is Engamel on your list of organisations of interest?"

Karl nodded slowly. "If you really wanna know, they pretty much all are, Tommo. Anyways, I'd best leave you to get to work. Thanks for last night, it really helped to talk about it." He dropped Jess's keys into Thomas's hand. "And listen, I think maybe I'll go back to her flat and see about those letters — she may well have hidden them. I'll only copy them, mind."

Thomas offered the keys up again.

"No need. I've already made myself a fresh set."

Chapter 18

It wasn't exactly skiving. Major Eldridge had wanted him to spend time locating Jess; he'd just interpreted that to mean: *locating Jess where he'd left her and then delivering her clothes*. He telephoned the major and promised to update him later on.

Miranda was waiting at Caliban's. She made a big show of sniffing his neck to smell her own perfume. "Hmm, someone's a lucky lady."

"Yeah, I like to think so."

They went inside. Jess was still in the shower. Miranda reclaimed her seat in the kitchen; Sheryl was buffing her nails furiously. "That girl sure talks. I feel like I've boned the army guy myself."

Sheryl and Miranda giggled like teenagers.

"I can give you chapter and verse. How it started, how he calls her *angel*, how he's going to leave his wife — when the time is right. I could sit an exam."

It really was none of his business but that didn't stop him encouraging Sheryl. And it didn't take a lot of encouragement. *Chapter and verse*, as promised — and no dirty stuff, thankfully. Sheryl had almost wet herself when he'd requested, 'no physical details.' Miranda had patted his head, *poor lamb*.

Jess emerged in her own good time and gave Thomas a disproportionately welcoming hug, which he suffered without comment.

"You've brought my clothes!" She sounded so self-absorbed. Even the way she held up her suit in front of her like some twisted Cinderella scene. Crass didn't seem to cover it.

He told her about the memorial service; doubted she'd really heard him, as she was busy rifling through her suitcase and checking blouses against the suit.

"And you did all this for me," she moved to hug him again but he stiffened.

"It's my job."

She shook her head back like a startled horse and it took her a moment to recover. "Can I go out today?"

"You're not a prisoner." Miranda cut across. "Although it's probably best to have someone with you."

"Thomas can accompany me! Just a *little* walk — and maybe a coffee outside. I'll go and get ready." She gathered up her things and skipped away.

"Well," Sheryl drawled in her native Brooklynese, "Sounds like you've got yourself an admirer."

He shook his head. "Nah, hopefully that seat's already taken."

Sheryl faked a swoon. "Do mine ears deceive me?" She looked directly at Miranda. "Are you two screw-ups officially back on again?"

He watched Miranda through a lens of longing. She milked the moment, then shrugged half-heartedly. He fell back on details.

"I won't be longer than an hour. Do me a favour, while we're out, write down everything Jess has told you. Yeah, even the dirty stuff; I mean it."

Jess looked like she was about to go fishing, using herself as bait. She grabbed his arm and waited for him to lead. He turned to Miranda.

"Won't be long, babe."

Jess reeled him in so close that her breast squeezed against his arm. "I promise to bring him back in near perfect condition."

* * *

They ended up at Whitechapel. He gave her his mini-tour, talking about the galleries and the waves of historical immigrants over the last century and a half. Quite the little guide. And all the while she gazed at him like he was offering the Eucharist. Which reminded him . . .

"I, er, didn't know if you were religious. There's tons of churches round here if you wanted to say a prayer or light a candle?"

"Whatever for?"

Her laughter rattled him. "For Amy." It was the first time that day that either of them had mentioned her by name

"Oh, I see." It was like a switch had flipped in her head. "I, er . . ." Her voice crackled, "I think I'd prefer to just sit and talk, if you don't mind." She took his arm again.

He found a half-decent café, not a million miles from the Royal London Hospital. The café proprietor had somehow thought putting up a picture of the Elephant Man would be good for business.

Jess talked — Sheryl had certainly got that right — but not about Amy. Jess's main topic of conversation was *Jess*. And her specialist subject only covered the last two years. Apparently, joining Engamel and becoming the major's little lady were the most interesting things to have happened to her. Ever.

It was all going swimmingly until he put his size nines in it by asking about her family. She stopped, mid-sentence, and managed to weld a scowl to a smile.

"Let's talk about something else, shall we? Tell me about you." She was all eyes and hands, her touch surprisingly cold. He drew his arm away and her fingernails scraped against the table.

"I saw Major Eldridge yesterday. He seemed to think you had some *papers* in your possession." He chose the word deliberately.

It didn't seem to faze her. If anything she seemed to relax. He sipped at an average hot chocolate and tried to lead the witness. "I take paperwork home too, sometimes. It's easier when it's quiet."

She nodded enthusiastically.

"Did, er, Amy do that as well?" He half-expected another clam-up, but Jess was tripping over herself now to tell him how close they were, and how Amy was such a mouse at Engamel, before Jess showed her the ropes.

"Confidentially," she touched him again and he allowed it, "I think she was a little intimidated by me. The cachet of Oxford, I suppose — very different from Michigan *State* University!"

He watched her spiteful laughter and play-acted silently with her, remembering his mother's advice to never speak ill of the dead. "I'm not sure how it works at memorial services where . . ." he searched for a decent word, ". . . the departed is transferred abroad for burial."

"Do you want to do something after the service?"

"Excuse me?"

"You know, afterwards — we could go on somewhere."

His drink had run out and so had his patience. He grabbed her arm. "Come on, we're going back."

She pulled away from him and a smug smile lit up her face. "I'm not ready yet."

"Fine, stay here, then."

Outside, the blare of traffic shattered the cocoon. He breathed in the city greedily and started walking. He heard the café's metal door

366

crunching back. She was about twenty paces behind him, somewhere between strolling and rushing. He walked on for a bit and then stopped suddenly, tracking her growing reflection in a parked van.

"You were very rude back there," she waited behind him; she sounded genuinely hurt. And just when he was beginning to wonder if she had any genuine feelings at all.

He didn't turn round, less chance of losing it altogether and slapping her. "This isn't a game, Jess. There's a reason someone didn't want you left on the base. Until I know why, I can't resolve this."

She drew level, looking up at him like a puppy in need of a cuddle. "Surely everything can go back to normal after the service?" she stared past him. "Though I suppose they'll need a new technician to work with me."

He didn't speak to her again till they got back to Caliban's. She didn't seem to notice. Sheryl handed him a folded sheet of A4 as he arrived.

"Paperwork," he said to Jess.

She breezed past and headed upstairs, smiling to herself.

Miranda let her get near the top. "Thomas and I are off for a while — business."

Jess galloped back down excitedly. "Can I come?"

"Sorry," she faced her down, "Family only."

* * *

Miranda drove, allowing Thomas to read Sheryl's handiwork. It was mainly what Jess had told him on the daytrip from hell. In fact, a lot of it was verbatim. He tapped the sheet against his forehead: *angel*.

"We've never had nicknames, have we?" He wasn't sure whether to speak about the two of them in the present or the past tense. Present was safer.

Miranda looked up to one corner of the car, found whatever she was searching for in her brain and beckoned him closer. As he heard her words, he fumbled his pages to the floor and she grinned for the rest of the drive.

"Anyway, shouldn't you be at work?" Miranda had a talent for the obvious — that, and nicknames.

"I am, sort of."

She mussed his hair as if to say, I believe you. He checked the mirror — he looked guilty as fuck.

Chapter 19

John and Diane Wright welcomed them with open arms, which made it all easier.

"What's the bother then, Thomas?" John wasn't big on small talk. Not where business was concerned.

"I was wondering . . . if you ever had any dealings in Northern Ireland?"

It was the Internet search that did it. When the two Northern Irish guys both came up positive for interests in casinos — building them, as well as liking a flutter. Tie that in with their import-export activities, and it was a fair gamble that the Wrights might have come across them at some point. He gave John their full names.

John Wright sipped at his tea then dunked a biscuit, sucking at it with relish. "Heard of them, yeah; never done business directly though."

Thomas pressed his hands together as if they were cold. "And, er, what have you heard?"

Diane, Miranda's mum, folded her arms and sighed. John stopped speaking.

"They're serious people, Thomas. Not the sort you'd want to antagonise."

Miranda scooted along the sofa a little. Thomas could feel her warmth pressing against his leg. "They're stopping Karl going home to visit his mum — she's dying. It's like a contract or something and he can't go back without their say-so."

John and Diane looked at each other and drank their tea. Thomas waited for a ray of sunlight, but the forecast was definitely stormy. He cleared his throat. "I think we owe Karl, for what he did for Miranda."

Diane narrowed her eyes. "Hold on a minute, Thomas. *You* owe Karl — it was *your* mess. If you want to get caught up with these geezers," she paused again, tightening her shoulders, "you'd better tread very carefully."

There were only so many ways of taking this forward and he didn't feel like a row. He flexed his thigh, hoped it would prompt Miranda to pitch in with something.

"Thing is, Dad, Karl's alright, isn't he — we all *know* that now." Something about the way she said it caught Thomas's attention. It was as if she was having a separate conversation with her dad that he wasn't supposed to understand. John Wright took an unfeasibly long sip of tea and closed his eyes.

Thomas filled the void. "Remember when we first met, when Miranda and me came down from Leeds? You didn't know me from Adam, but you gave me a chance."

Miranda cleared her throat. "Well, sort of. I did speak to Mum and Dad now and then, from Leeds. I just didn't tell you about it."

He was starting to feel ganged up on. "All I want to do is broker some sort of deal with these people. His mum is dying for Christ's sake. Even an hour — just a poxy hour over there with his mum. Surely they must want *something*?" He surprised himself, hearing the conviction in his voice.

John nodded. "Leave it with us. But why do you wanna get involved?"

Thomas smiled. "Truth? Maybe I've spent enough time with you lot to see how important family is."

"Steady on, Thomas," Diane cut in, "you'll 'ave me weeping." She laughed playfully.

"I'm serious, Diane."

"I know, love," her eyes softened. "I know you are."

Thomas and Miranda went off to make a fresh brew; he made sure she closed the kitchen door.

"So," he lined up the mugs with his back to her. "What sort of things did you used to say to your mum and dad about us?"

He glanced round and Miranda was there waiting. She refilled the kettle.

"I didn't tell them we'd, you know, done the deed."

That was polite, by Miranda's standards. Something about being at her parents' home often dampened her farmyard sensibilities.

"Well, what then?"

"Just stuff — I was a teenager back then. Teenage stuff. That I was safe and I'd met this gorgeous boy from Yorkshire. My very own Heathcliff, all moody and intense, only with much shorter hair!"

The kettle bubbled and frothed and she lifted it off the element just before the switch popped. It always pissed him off.

"For all I knew, they might have killed me when I first met them. I was absolutely bricking it."

"I know," she said, grinning at the memory of that first meeting. "I s'pose I wanted to see whether you really meant all the things you said in Leeds. I know different now." The last sentence sounded like an afterthought.

He took a tray, with mugs and biscuit reinforcements, back to the front room. John and Diane had that stilted look, as if they'd been deep in conversation only a moment ago and didn't quite know how to disguise it. John airlifted a mug.

"So why've those blokes got it in for Karl — some sort of Paddy religious thing is it?"

"Not exactly." He had been hoping to keep Karl's private life out of it, but he saw now that he'd been naïve. He couldn't really expect John and Diane to get involved — and the signs were promising if they were still asking questions — without at least giving them the background.

It was like swimming in Gormire Lake, back home. At first you recoil from the shock, from that hollow feeling in your stomach. But after a while, once you accepted it and started moving around, you got used to it. And that was how he felt, spilling the beans on Karl's past love life.

Diane did the talking. She wanted to know about Karl's background, about when he'd last spoken with Martin and Francis-Andrew. And her radar was finely tuned. "Where's Karl's dad, then?"

Funny you should ask that. "Not sure. He never mentions him. I don't even know his name."

"John?" Diane nudged him.

"Yeah," he re-entered the fray. "I was just wondering if these people know what Karl does for a living? Unlikely I s'pose — given how you secret squirrels like to operate."

Thomas flinched. A little below the belt but no less accurate for it.

Diane paid no attention. "How does that help us?"

John sniffed and bit into a ginger nut. "Well, what if we could shoehorn Karl into another *business*, temporarily? Maybe that would get him safe passage over there, for work."

Thomas could already see the flaw. "But what if they want to know what he's doing over there — apart from seeing his mother I mean?"

John shook his head slowly, like a cat outlining the options to a cornered mouse. "Doesn't work like that. In this line of business, no one *ever* asks. It's just not done. Leave it with us, we'll make some calls — discreet, like — and let you know."

Chapter 20

Thomas washed the suds from his face and let the noise of the shower clear his head. Many of life's more cosmopolitan experiences had eluded him, but tonight he could cross another one off his list. Because tonight he was having dinner with Michael Schaefer — courtesy, no doubt, of his Engamel expense account. Obviously, it wasn't a *date* date, though come to think of it Schaefer had been quick to decline his suggestion of bringing along a partner. *Nah, surely not.*

He turned off the shower and squeezed the water from his hair so it ran down his back. Then he dried off and put on the clothes hanging against the door. If he was nervous before, that little thought just increased it by the power of ten.

When his makeover was complete — having deliberately toned down on the aftershave — he unlocked the door and stepped out confidently. Karl was sat on the sofa, flicking through a Raymond Chandler novel.

"Pretty as a picture, Tommo. If the SSU ever do an in-house magazine, you'll get my vote for the cover."

He struck a pose. "Surely you mean undercover? Come on, then, let's see your toys."

Karl put the hardback down and opened his magic box. Some of the bugs and tracers were standard surveillance kit, stuff Thomas had worked with, day in day out for the last two years. But Karl also had his *other* supplier — the one he never spoke about.

Thomas rifled through the trays like a kid in a sweet shop. Karl sighed and laced his fingers together impatiently. "And you're sure you don't want me to follow you around?"

"No ta," he replied without looking up. "I'm not even sure Schaefer will give up anything useful — it's probably his chance to suss me out."

He suffered Karl's fussing and accepted the compromise; a tracer in his shoe — in case he got lost — and a wire, under his jacket. But finally, after much persuasion, he agreed to one of Karl's *shadow army* remaining on standby. He didn't ask for details; it was better not to know.

* * *

Leicester Square was an unusual choice for a meet-up, at any time — more chance of losing someone than connecting with them. Even in the evening there were still hordes of tourists drifting about. And never far behind them, watching from the shadows: the homeless and the hustlers.

He walked past a burger vendor who was half-heartedly plying his trade. The rich smell of over-cooked onions and under-cooked meat product seemed to sum up tourist London after hours: full of promise but unlikely to deliver.

He was deliberately early and did a couple of circuits, reminding himself what the area felt like and where the nearest tube stations were. It was different, being here without a camera. He had no use for the lights and the chaos, no clear purpose to cling to. Now, wandering around, anonymous and adrift, he was just killing time.

After the second visit to the Swiss Centre clock, he figured he'd head over to the restaurant. It would have been easy to find, even without directions — it looked expensive and exclusive. Miranda would have loved it. He loitered at the door, fiddling with an imaginary cufflink. "Here goes nothing," he announced quietly, for the benefit of the transmitter.

Schaefer was in the bar and made eye contact him as he went inside. So far so good — at least he hadn't been stood up.

"Tommy — come on in!" Schaefer oozed confidence. His handshake was assured and unambiguous, very alpha male. "Glad you could make it — and a little early too. No problem, they're already waiting."

They? He followed Schaefer over to a bar table where two women were sipping champagne.

"Ladies, here's the man I've been telling you about. May I present — Mr Thomas Bladen." Schaefer made it sound like a chat show. To complete the charade, he wrapped an arm around him as if they were old college pals and followed it up with a back slap.

Thomas resisted giving him a slap of a different kind in return and coughed, so that he could check the surgical tape under his shirt was still in place. The two women languidly greeted him; they were dressed barely the right side of decent, and he accepted a champagne glass just to have something else to focus on. Ordinarily he wasn't a fan of the hallowed grape — Christmases at the Wrights and once at an engagement party — his own. But needs must, and all that.

Schaefer was enjoying centre stage, clicking his fingers for another bottle. "We've already ordered," one of the two floozies pointed to a menu on the table.

He opted for the tried and tested; it saved time. He told himself to loosen up, but he was drum tight. Unfamiliar people, unfamiliar location and unknown motives; it all added up to a whole lot of uncomfortable.

Schaefer re-introduced Deborah and Clarity as fellow employees of Engamel Solutions. Thomas wasn't sure if he believed him. Or that Clarity was a real name.

Their table was called and Deborah carried over the champers, clutching it close to her chest. Even the bubbles seemed that little bit more excited. Schaefer had them seated boy-boy and girl-girl at the round table, so the immediate view was Deborah; he had to fight the urge to wipe the condensation off her cleavage. He sipped at his glass and sailed through the starter, skirting the edges of conversation about his work. Schaefer was happier talking about Engamel in any case; the man was a walking promo: blah blah, multi-million dollar; blah blah, world-beating innovation.

They were on to some *like, totally amazing* white wine now, which he didn't have the heart to tell them reminded him of chip shop vinegar. Clarity pressed a hand over his.

"So, Tommy, don't you think London is the greatest city in the world?"

He left his hand where it was and waited for hers to retreat. "I'm not from London. It's alright though, but it's not a patch on Harrogate."

Okay, he might have been exaggerating a little, given that he had relatives in Harrogate. But it gave him a breather as Clarity tried to process the irony without the aid of a safety net. It was a full thirty seconds before she caught on.

"Hey, you're just making fun out of me! Seriously — so which part of London is Harrogate in?"

Bless her heart, she was only 200 miles out. He seized control of the conversation, and went down a familiar route, giving them an armchair tour of Yorkshire, comparing American Football with Rugby and generally doing a flag-waver for the Yorkshire Tourist Board. All material he'd previously practised, bantering with Sheryl at Miranda's bar.

Schaefer's lobster would have made Freud blush. Deborah had followed suit and the two of them ripped into their crustaceans with gusto. Clarity had shifted her chair towards Thomas a little; he noticed, even if the others hadn't. He stuck with small talk and fillet steak. And he watched as Clarity filleted her Dover sole with infinite care, the flip side to Schaefer's Yankee brashness. Somehow, they managed to talk below Schaefer and Deborah's noise level, but nothing much was said.

He felt relieved when everyone opted to skip dessert and fast-forward to coffee, even though the wine was still flowing on the sidelines. He hadn't risked looking at his watch, but his internal clock ran to about two and a half hours. It was a skill he'd honed in childhood, measuring the angry silences of his father.

Okay, so the evening had largely been a waste of time. A good meal though, and somewhere to take Miranda when he won the lottery. He settled his cup down and listened half-heartedly as the Engamel trio laughed at some private joke. Then the conversation cleared like static, and Schaefer leaned towards him.

"If Jessica comes to the memorial service, I want to speak to her." It didn't sound like a request and that got his back up. Rather than confront it head-on, he tried a sideways approach.

"Listen, Michael, if we're going to get those papers back, maybe we need to give her a little breathing space — to grieve and that."

Schaefer's chest expanded a couple of inches. "No, *you* listen, Bladen," Schaefer prodded the table, jangling the crockery. "Five minutes with me and she'll be sending the papers back by courier."

He remained still, although the urge to smile because Schaefer hadn't questioned the *papers* was nearly killing him. Schaefer wasn't finished.

"And don't give me any crap about grieving. Jessica's only interested in herself. Sure, she was close to Amy, but I wouldn't say it was a two-way thing."

Thomas sipped at his drink calmly, hoping for more treasures. Schaefer didn't disappoint.

"I've gone through her file, Tommy — reads like a psychology manual. Only child, orphaned at a young age. Extended family rallied round as best they could, but she ended up in care and sort of missed her turn in life." He sounded almost gleeful.

Thomas turned defence advocate again. "It must be hard to recover from a start like that."

"Tell me about it!" Schaefer took a slug of wine and swung the glass around like a conductor's baton. "Total fantasist. Her application says she studied at Oxford . . ." he paused until Deborah and Clarity had given him their full attention. "Sure, some backstreet outfit near Oxford."

Thomas's brain started somersaulting again. He picked up a bottle and refilled everyone's glass, except his own. "Then how come Engamel took her on?"

This was fast becoming a Q & A session, for the benefit of the tape.

Schaefer slurped some more wine, dripping it on the tablecloth. "Kinda nosey bastard ain't ya?"

He smiled and looked Schaefer right in the eyes.

"Nah, I'm only messing with ya, Tommy, you're okay — you're one of us. At least, I hope you are!" Schaefer flicked a glance to Deborah and Clarity.

Thomas caught it, but couldn't make any sense of it.

"Jessica might be a little screwy but she's got it *all* going on up here," he tapped at his temple. "Genuine eidetic."

Thomas nodded politely. *Not a clue.* As things wound to a close, he took stock. No harm done, a little team-building, a new word to look up and maybe Karl could sift something useful out of the evening's commentary. Time for group hugs and then he could piss off. "Well, thanks for a great meal and everything," he shifted the chair back to stand. Schaefer raised a hand to block him.

"Hey, the night is young. You're not planning on leaving us already? I booked us all rooms nearby."

Oh bollocks. He felt a chill skateboard down his spine. God only knows what laughing boy had in mind.

* * *

The streets of London felt full of foreboding, but Schaefer just breezed along, locking arms with Deborah for mutual support and anything else going, judging by the look of them.

Clarity tagged along beside Thomas. She said nothing. If he were a betting man, he'd say it was odds on she'd been paid to be there. He let Schaefer lead them a merry dance through the darkening streets, staying vigilant for the four of them. After a while he stopped holding his keys at his side, through his knuckles.

"Here we go," Schaefer announced, flinging an arm towards the hotel as if he'd just paid for it out of small change. It would have needed a lorry load of small change.

They stumbled up the marble steps. In a word: palatial. Schaefer showered tips like confetti and collected the room keys.

Thomas hung back by the lifts with Deborah and Clarity, watching as they whispered and nodded in his direction. He blushed, like an idiot; if he got any more out of his depth, he'd be needing scuba gear.

Schaefer sauntered over with a collection of keys and the lift doors opened. The journey took forever and that just made it worse. Someone was pressing against his arse — he didn't dare look to see who; he was too busy sweating.

He remembered being a teenager, and a game of strip poker with male and female friends. Rushing home to put on three T-shirts and extra socks then dashing to the venue, stiff with worry. A bead of sweat meandered down the blind side of his face. He felt every millimetre it travelled, imagined it gradually negotiating the terrain of his face. And all to the faded soundtrack of Celine Dion.

He was last out of the lift, hurriedly wiping his face as the others moved ahead. Schaefer and Deborah fumbled along the corridor together, parting and colliding, like moths against a light bulb. Schaefer opened the door. He was still holding all the cards, and the keys. The room was massive. If Thomas had to guess, it was a penthouse suite.

It took him a moment to realise he was the only one standing at the doorway. No big deal, he told himself — just a nightcap with his new friends. Then he'd collect his key and leave them to it. The *it* bothered him. He stepped inside and closed the door carefully behind him.

Shoes had been scattered across the carpet. He heard laughter and the sound of water. "We're in here!" Deborah's voice teased.

He crossed the room slowly. *Sweet Jesus.*

Schaefer was climbing into a Jacuzzi, au naturel; Deborah was already ahead of the game. She leaned back and the water from her hair ran down her breasts. At first he couldn't see Clarity, then she turned her head from the side of the tub and wiped her nostrils.

Miranda sometimes liked to taunt him — rightly — that he hadn't led a very adventurous life. But even he knew it was coke. He made a flippant comment about sinusitis, for the tape.

Clarity lifted up a tray and Deborah took it. She seemed to hold it there above the frothing water, poised, as if watching for his response. Clarity glanced at him over her shoulder and eased into the tub. And she took her time about it. Then she reached for a champagne glass at the side and patted the water playfully. Schaefer's head disappeared under the water. Deborah finished her line and shifted position to accommodate him.

"No need to be shy, Tommy. We're all grown-ups." Clarity swished a hand through the bubbles. Without warning, Schaefer's head surfaced in front of Deborah, who was all smiles.

He gazed at the three of them and blinked slowly. Back in Sunday school in Yorkshire, there'd been a picture in one of the books. He could see it in his mind's eye now, clear as day. Two roads: two destinations. On one side, a beautiful glowing angel and a road that led to a bright green meadow where Jesus seemed to be having a picnic. On the other side, an indefinable shape, almost human, calling from a path of overgrown trees and shadows. He'd had nightmares about it.

Now, as he watched the three amigos get very amigo-ey indeed, this looked like an adult version of the same thing. Schaefer moved between the two women, his arms around them like serpents. "Well, Tommy, what are you afraid of?"

Afraid wouldn't cover it; try completely intimidated. And curious. And even the teeniest bit repulsed.

As he stood there, like a coeliac at a bread festival, he felt his cheeks burning. In the haze of dinner and naked Americans, he'd forgotten something important. And he hated himself for it. "You do know that Amy's memorial service is tomorrow?"

Of course they knew. He must have looked like a pious schoolteacher.

Schaefer grinned. The slimy bastard actually grinned at him. "Like I always say, Tommy, you gotta live for the moment."

Clarity pouted, Monroe style, and picked up a cigarette from God knows where. "Hey, Tommy, ain't you gonna light my fire?" And the way she looked at him, barely holding it together without laughing, he knew she'd been the bait for the whole evening — the innocent American act.

"Some other time." He wished he'd been wearing a hidden camera as well, not for the flesh, but to capture that smug look on their faces. Although he doubted he'd forget it.

He turned around with all the dignity he could muster and left them to it. As he reached the front door, he called back in a loud and clear voice, "I'll see you at the funeral." But the only reply was the sound of splashing water.

Out along the corridor to the lift. No one else was around. He stabbed the lift button and squeezed his hands, as if that could somehow drain the adrenaline screaming through his veins. He cleared his throat for the microphone. "I don't know where you're hiding, just get me the fuck out of here. As soon as I'm downstairs, I start walking."

The thought of Amy — that twisted carnage of her body — seemed to fade in and out before him as the light flickered through the lift door window; a memory stark and real. He wondered what the Yanks thought of him now — probably pissing themselves about the uptight Brit. Well, bollocks to them.

On the ground floor, the lift door swept open. The stillness and quiet cut through him after the night he'd just had. A receptionist stared from across the desk, bright-eyed and attentive. She smiled and he found the composure to return it and wish her a good night. His mum would have been proud.

* * *

Central London was still buzzing. The combination of neon, lost souls and broken dreams gave the city a poetry all its own. As he walked back to Leicester Square, he distracted himself by selecting lenses and subjects. The way the traffic headlights rolled across the surface of a tree, the jagged slices of light behind an office window blind. It wasn't long before he was in photographer mode, back on home ground.

It wasn't even midnight yet. He could still ring Miranda and meet her at a nightclub. Then again, he didn't really feel like company now. He managed twenty paces into Leicester Square — because he'd started counting them — and then he saw the suit zero in on him.

"Mr Bladen."

It came as a statement. For a moment he flinched; the man looked like police of some description. He flashed his SSU ID. and the suit acknowledged it, calmly leading him away.

"We have a car waiting." The suit walked beside him, not speaking, until they rounded a one-way street where a grey van was parked up. As they approached, the passenger door opened and a familiar face stepped out to greet him.

Teresa. He'd met her two or three times before. He used to think that she was Karl's squeeze, or his boss in the other cloak-and-dagger stuff. He wasn't sure what to believe anymore

"It's been a while, Thomas," she smiled; it carried a whiff of apology.

For the last few months, Karl had drawn an invisible line around his clandestine activities to give Thomas some breathing space. The bitter truth was that he rather missed it. He'd peeked behind the magic mirror and could never properly rejoin the audience.

Teresa waited. He cleared his throat, blinked to show that he was paying attention.

"Anything else I should know, Thomas?"

"Nothing spectacular. Engamel seems to have a very open policy on drugs and team-building."

She didn't push it. Perhaps, like him, she was filing it away somewhere, in case it could be useful in the future. The rest of the debrief, if you could call it that, took place in the van as they drove him home. He said little, not because he had a problem with them; it was just that although he'd worked in surveillance for a couple of years now, the kind of stuff she and Karl were involved in was in a different league.

As the van pulled up, a street away from his flat, Teresa turned to him in the semi-darkness. "I never thanked you for what you did *before* . . ." She left the sentence hanging.

He didn't insult them both by telling her it was nothing, when it had basically fucked his whole life up. And his head. So he just reached for the door handle.

She leant across and tapped his arm. "Until the next time . . ."

* * *

He shut the door behind him and cut her off. Walthamstow was deathly still. He took in a breath and held it, tuning his senses to the street. For weeks after Yorgi's death, he'd looked into the shadows, trying to make out human forms. Totally illogical, as no one comes back from a point blank shot to the head, but when did fear have anything to do with logic? He was past that now, by and large, but he threaded his keys through his fingers again for that secure feeling.

Nothing stirred except the muffled growl of traffic, a block away on Forest Road. He rolled his feet as he walked, dulling the sound of shoes against pavement. A few paces on and he began to breathe again; he was buzzing, ideas spinning like plates. He put his keys away as he rounded the corner and caught sight of the flat. Karl's car was outside, soothing him like a nightlight — the kind his dad had never let him have as a child.

He could see that Karl was reading *Private Eye*. As he drew closer the window wound down. "Special delivery for Mr Bladen," Karl reached into his inside pocket and waved some paperwork.

"You coming in then?" he ambled past and up the steps to his front door.

Karl cut the light and locked up the car. "Tell you what, Tommo, you get the kettle on and we'll swap stories."

* * *

He dished out tea and biscuits, and then went to get changed.

Karl started crooning. "Love letters straight from your heart . . ."

He ignored him, ditched the suit for civvies and made a beeline for the sheets of paper Karl had left on the table. They made interesting reading.

Major Eldridge had poured out his heart in print, while weaselling out of the eternal 'when are you going to tell your wife about us' conundrum. The opening line, *My dearest Angel,* cut no ice with him. Thomas couldn't put his finger on it, but something didn't sit right. He flicked through the pages like a vexed cat. As he looked up, Karl was watching over the top of his mug.

"Come on now, figure it out! I'll give you a clue," Karl put down his mug and cupped his hands like a megaphone, "Something's missing."

He redoubled his efforts, scanning the four pages for anything that wasn't there. No sale. He accepted defeat gracelessly and sat down with his tea.

"No address, Dr Watson," Karl sucked at an imaginary Sherlock Holmes pipe.

He checked again. So what? Still, knowing Karl's fixation on details, where was the copy of the envelope? And then Schaefer's comments about Jess's memory and propensity for bullshitting joined hands to form a chain. He smiled back at Karl and prepared to drop his bombshell.

"Bingo. Jess isn't the major's squeeze, but Amy was. Schaefer said Jess had a fantastic memory and called her eidetic."

It seemed to be the starting pistol Karl had been waiting for. "So she gets the letters somehow, commits them to memory and regurgitates them for everyone's benefit like a proper little show-off. So what does she want from Major Eldridge?"

"Dunno. Maybe she wants justice for Amy? Can't see it from her behaviour so far though . . ." He clicked his fingers. "Of course, if she's as twisted as Schaefer suggested, she might be hoping to *replace* Amy."

Karl took his imaginary pipe out of his mouth. "Let's say you're right, hypothetically. That explains the letters but not the *papers*. Why would Schaefer give a shit about love letters? There's nothing classified in there," he snorted, "unless it's a cunning code."

Thomas bit at a nail as he narrowed his eyes. "Alright," he lowered his thumb, cupping a loose fist. "Let's speculate. What if Jess realises that Amy has mixed random ammo — maybe to speed up the testing, I dunno. Anyway, after it all goes pear-shaped, Jess takes the test sheets or whatever they use, to help cover it up. Major Eldridge showed me some report suggesting it was a factor in the accident."

Karl took a swig of tea, his eyes still on Thomas. "Makes sense. Of course, Jess could also be implicated in the whole mixed ammo thing, so she removes the evidence. And, I know I'm really flying by the seat of my pants here, maybe she's memorised all the data and made a copy."

There was a certain logic to it. "So Engamel wants the data back and the major needs his private letters. And all roads lead to Jess — because, let's face it, she craves the attention and the control."

"She'd be playing with fire though. With all the finance tied up in the development of the Scavenger, Jess would soon become expendable."

"Just like Amy?"

Thomas got a fresh piece of paper and wrote it all down, for his own sanity. The major has an affair with Amy. Amy confides in Jess — or maybe Jess just finds out and gets hold of the letters. Once Amy's gone, she ditches the envelope and the letters become part of her mental wonderland. She also destroys the data sheets from the tests — for whatever reason. And suddenly everyone is looking for her — or looking out for her.

"So who hid the Scavenger parts under our Land Rover? And who took it?"

Karl took a deep breath and sighed. "The major's got to be involved. He knows what we do and he knows me. So he must expect I'll take some sort of action."

Thomas left it there and filled Karl in on the after-dinner entertainment. Karl roared with laughter at Thomas's depiction of the Engamel water-sports team.

"So come on now, weren't you just the teensiest bit tempted?"

"Nah, chlorine plays havoc with my highlights."

Karl took the hint and changed topic. "How do you want to play the memorial service tomorrow?" That was a novelty — Karl sounding unsure of himself. "You know I can't be there, so I thought you might need back-up — people you could trust . . ." Karl seemed to shrink away a little. "I made a couple of calls today." He was blushing. "Miranda will accompany you. As well as Sam and Terry."

Thomas flinched; Karl said their names so comfortably now.

Karl bided his time and didn't speak until Thomas had pulled himself together.

"And what is the master plan they're all working to?"

"It's very simple. If anything kicks off, you'll have a half-decent chance of getting Jess out of there in one piece."

Now he saw red. "Get her away to where? What gives you the right to drag Miranda and her family into this? She was right — this is *your* mess, you and your army pals."

Karl didn't stay much longer. He left Thomas the copied letters for a little night reading and said he'd catch up some time after the service.

Thomas sat there for a long time afterwards, mulling things over. He was glad he hadn't mentioned John Wright being on the case to help get Karl back to Belfast. And was that any better than what Karl had done? He gave up the ghost and lay in bed, pawing through the letters.

It was all there in black and white. Jess was word perfect on the details. Too perfect. He dropped the papers on the floor and turned out the light. He knew he wouldn't sleep for a while, too wound up by Karl's wheeler-dealing.

When the phone went off he pounced on it, snatched the receiver up.

"Hey you, it's me. What are you wearing?" Only Miranda could get a laugh out of that line, every time. She brought him up to speed, on the plan he hadn't been party to. She'd be accompanying Jess on the big day. Sam and Terry would wait at the back — their job was to stop anyone other than Thomas or Miranda taking Jess out of there. God help them, Sam had even asked whether they ought to be tooled up.

"One other thing, Dad rang me — reckons he might have a way forward for Karl's problem with the Irish blokes."

He cupped the phone closer.

"He's putting something together, but he's gonna need Karl's full support."

The sweat was running down his face now. This was all wrong. Miranda's family were too exposed, and it was *his* fault.

"You alright? You're very quiet. If it wasn't for the heavy breathing, I'd have thought you'd fallen asleep on me." More innuendo, even if it was a lovely way to send him off to sleep.

"Sorry, Miranda, I'm gonna turn in — I'm whacked. I'll see you tomorrow. And remember, it's a funeral so nothing *too* sexy." He knew she'd like that.

"Tell you what," she whispered huskily, "I could come round first thing in the morning and try on some outfits, for your personal approval."

It sounded like the best plan he'd heard all day.

Chapter 21

Sex and death; they went together like bacon and eggs. Miranda let herself into the flat around seven o'clock; he'd drawn back the deadbolt at six.

She tiptoed into the bedroom, and eased back the duvet. Somewhere along the route she must have discarded her clothes, because she was as naked as the good Lord had made her. And right now, he felt a touch of old-time religion coming on.

They played the games that lovers play, teasing, testing, letting the ebb and flow of tension and pleasure carry them away with the tide. And when he lay there afterwards and felt the warm comfort of her on top of him, as the pulses of ecstasy faded like an echo, he wondered how they'd ever managed to screw up such a brilliant relationship. And whether, as Sheryl had inquired, there was still hope.

"Right then, Mr Sticky, you get the tea on and I'll wash the sweat off." She could ruin a magic moment in the blink of an eye.

Once Miranda had returned, he showered and pulled on some joggies and a T-shirt. It was barely seven thirty and he felt pleasantly tired, like after a gym workout but with the best exercise regime imaginable.

She nibbled at her toast and gazed around the room, as if she were looking for something. "Karl suggested we pack a bag in case we need to take Jess on somewhere."

"Not to me he didn't." He tried not to sound put out, and failed. Even so, it made sense, but he hoped it wouldn't come to that.

By eight thirty, Miranda was out the door. The meet-up was eleven thirty — she'd left him the address of the place. He figured

Jess had got the details from the good Major, and didn't push the point. One way or another, today was going to be very strange. Might as well take it slowly, in stages.

Once he'd packed an overnight bag, he dug out his darkest suit and put on some Otis Redding to accompany the ironing. He went to town on the tie as well, deriving great satisfaction from smoothing the material. Ironing done, he rang Sam and Terry, to confirm that he knew they were on the team. It was a short call, just long enough to agree a plan to get Jess back to Caliban's in the event of trouble. For one thing, his flat was too small and for another, the bar had at least three exits. Relax, he told himself, how much trouble could a funeral be?

* * *

Ten thirty, he was parking up. Couldn't help noticing the plane trees lining the roads: here was life in abundance. He cut the car radio and sat for a while, eyes closed, listening to the crows high above him and the awkward chatter as people came and went between the cars. And he thought about Amy, a stranger who had left America to seek her fortune, only to wind up dead, for reasons still undetermined.

He felt the hot swelling in his chest, same as when Karl had asked for extra footage on that day in the test lab. His hands were sweating, moist against the steering wheel. He pressed them against his face and breathed in and out through his fingers. What justice would there be for Amy and her family? The only answer was the cackle of crows.

He shouldered the driver's door wide, as if it were a way out of his thoughts. It was still early — all to the good. A chance to check out who else had turned up. As he crunched across the gravel to the waiting area, a car slid past him. He glanced left and saw the side of Sir Peter Carroll's Daimler gliding by. *Great*. Another member of the fan club.

If Miranda were on schedule, she'd be bringing Jess in as close to kick-off as possible. Less chance of a confrontation before the service. So there was no sense waiting outside, best get in and mingle with the other mourners. He hadn't known Amy, but he'd never felt closer to her — they were both pawns to circumstance.

Major Eldridge was right inside the door, wearing a fixed expression that suggested he had nailed a lid on everything. But Thomas wasn't buying it. Judging by the letters, if last night's assumptions were correct, Eldridge was here to see off the woman he loved. Schaefer and the rest of his American trio were there too, making small talk amongst themselves. As he set eyes on Schaefer, the three of them fell silent and turned away. Fine by him.

He exchanged a handshake with the major and struggled for a follow-up line. They stood there, arms at their sides, avoiding eye contact. Now that Thomas knew about Amy and the major — or *thought* he knew — it complicated things.

The major picked up a folded A4 sheet from a pile and handed it to him. There was another picture of Amy on the front, smiling in the hazy sunshine. It looked to Thomas like the kind of impulsive, short exposure that he loved to take of Miranda. Inside the sheet was a bio — where she'd grown up and how much she'd been admired and respected by her colleagues — followed by a brief explanation of the music and hymns chosen for the service. He nodded as he read through the sequence and caught the major watching him. "Good choices," he said — just to see if it got a reaction; it did.

An usher appeared and invited everyone to go through. Major Eldridge led the way and Thomas fell in step behind him. Then he saw Miranda and Jess out of the corner of his eye and held back. Schaefer rushed towards Jess, grabbing for her shoulder, but Thomas blocked him. "Not here," he snarled, "Have some fucking respect."

Miranda flashed him a grin. Schaefer dropped his arm and swept in with his two groupies. There was no sign of Terry or Sam — typical. It was a mistake to have got them involved.

Jess went right to the front and stood beside Major Eldridge, with Miranda in tow. Thomas paused for a moment, unsure how the seating worked. He figured it'd be best if he stuck close to Jess, because a storm was brewing. He opted for the row behind — Schaefer, Clarity and Deborah were opposite him, across the central aisle. Schaefer looked seriously pissed off.

A heavy hand thumped down on Thomas's shoulder. For a moment he thought Terry had finally put in an appearance, but he turned to face Sir Peter. They stared at each other for what seemed like minutes and then Sir Peter smiled softly, as if nothing more needed to be said.

Classical music filtered up from somewhere and the doors at the back opened. Thomas caught a glimpse of the coffin being carried up, front and centre, then he became aware of the minister for the first time. She rose and stepped forward to the lectern, waiting respectfully until the string music faded.

"We are gathered here today to remember Amy Johanson, whose brief life ended in tragedy."

His ears twitched at the American voice, He shifted forward a little. There was a summary of Amy's life, followed by a reading from Psalm 144. Thomas turned to the page and nearly choked at the opening:

> Praise the Lord, my protector!
> He trains me for battle
> and prepares me for war.
> He is my protector and defender,
> my shelter and saviour,
> in whom I trust for safety.
> He subdues the nations under me.

Hardly the stuff of solace and sorrow, more like a rallying cry to the troops. Maybe it was meant to be job-related or the major was making a point. The minister spoke fluidly. She sounded sincere, paused for emphasis and looked out at the congregation every now and again.

Thomas followed, word for word, and at verse seven, the major looked across to Schaefer and held the look.

> Reach down from above,
> pull me out of the deep water, and
> rescue me;
> Save me from the power of
> foreigners,
> who never tell the truth
> and lie even under oath.

He heard Sir Peter moving behind him, shifting towards his ear. "What the hell's going on, Thomas?"

He didn't have an answer so he bent forward as if to shrug Sir Peter off. Schaefer looked livid. Now, more than ever, he hoped Miranda's brothers were close by. The minister asked if anyone wanted to say a few words and Jess's hand shot up like a flare.

A gasp from the American trio echoed around the chapel. Jess squeezed past Miranda and took the stand. She looked about as grief-stricken as an undertaker on Bank Holiday overtime. Okay, so she wasn't exactly smiling, but she wasn't a shrinking violet either. The minister stood politely to one side as Jess unfolded a piece of paper.

Somehow, she managed to talk about Amy while glorifying *herself*. It was sickening to watch, the way she talked about sharing Amy's confidences. The major squirmed like a worm on the hook. Jess went on about how proud they'd both been to work for Engamel and how they'd believed in the vital research work. To a cynic like Thomas it sounded like a loyalty pitch to Schaefer. And he noticed the way she didn't refer to her notes — not once. All in all, it was a marvellous performance; it should have been entitled: Woman Without a Soul.

Clarity was about the only one showing real emotion. She wept slowly into a handkerchief, and for a while Thomas almost forgave how she'd acted the last time they'd met. The moment soon passed, right about the time that Jess stood down. As she did, Jess turned the page over to fold it up and just for a second he saw rows of figures. Unbelievably, this selfish bitch was using Amy's funeral to taunt Schaefer — and anyone else paying attention — with what looked like numerical data. The speech had all been memorised in one almighty *fuck you* exercise.

As Jess sat down, there was more music. This time, a real tear-jerker — Janis Ian's 'When Angels Cry.' Thomas felt emotion rising and choked it back. A solitary tear escaped the barricades, which he managed to ignore. The major's shoulders rose and fell; the poor guy was in real difficulty. Thomas glanced at Jess's face, somewhere between indifference and introspection. He flexed his hand and tried not to think about getting up and slapping her. He wished he were beside Miranda, to feel her hand in his. She always said that weddings and hen parties made her feel emotional — for him it was funerals, every time.

The music drew to a close and the minister concluded the service. The atmosphere was electric. He glanced over, watching Schaefer to see if he would be crass enough to make a move there, in front of an audience. Jess took her own sweet time departing, even waylaying the minister for a few words before she left. She certainly had some balls.

As Jess reached the double doors at the back — first out, naturally, a man stepped forward and grabbed her. Thomas broke into a gallop and Miranda was a second behind him. Michael Schaefer body-checked him six feet from the doors. Six feet from the commotion on the other side.

"Whoa there, tough guy." Schaefer grabbed him forcefully. "I think we'll take it from here." He sounded smug, in control. Right up until the moment Miranda punched him in the kidneys. Then he sank to the floor with a choking, guttural gasp.

Thomas half-opened, half-shouldered the doors. They only moved partway, jammed against a groaning body — stocky, with crew-cut, dark hair. Definitely not Sam or Terry. He drew the doors back and gave them one almighty shove. There was a yelp and swearing, then the doors burst open. Jess was nowhere to be seen, and nor were Sam or Terry.

"My car!" Miranda called, legging it to her Mini Cooper.

He detoured to his own car first and grabbed the emergency bag — this was definitely an emergency.

Miranda wheel-span on the gravel to pick him up and then barrelled for the exit. Fortunately, there was nothing coming in. He rang Sam and it went straight to message — same with Terry. Nothing else for it, but to proceed as planned and hope that they'd managed to spirit Jess away.

As Miranda drove like a demon, he started thinking. Assuming Jess made it to Caliban's, where could he hide her next? If Schaefer had seen the page, like *he* had, then things had cranked up a notch. Maybe, if he could reason with Jess, he could get a copy of the stats or whatever they were to Schaefer, and he'd call the whole thing off? Some hope.

Mentally, he cycled through the few numbers in his address book. In the last few months he'd added one more to make it a round half dozen. Petrov, who Thomas had saved from his murderous brother, Yorgi. He smiled unexpectedly; he'd just had an idea.

* * *

By the time they reached Caliban's he was firing on all cylinders. It was still a chewing-gum-and-string plan, but in the absence of Karl it was the best he could do.

Sheryl was waiting by the door and ushered them in, bags in hand. There were no jokes today, just straight between the eyes *attitude*.

"You better not be dragging Miranda into any trouble, not after last time."

He pushed past her and mounted the stairs in twos and threes. Terry met him at the top. "Thank fuck for that, Thomas, we thought you'd got lost on the way." Terry was nursing his hand; Thomas didn't bother asking.

Jess flounced over and kissed him on the cheek, with Miranda standing right beside him. He shook her off before either he or Miranda decked her.

"Sheryl!" he yelled, only to find her stood behind him. "Can I talk to you in private?" She showed him to her temporary bedroom.

"Have you, er, got a wig and sunglasses — the more fake the better." He didn't mention Miranda's little revelation about her dressing-up box, a few weeks before.

She opened a cupboard full of wigs and extensions. "Help yourself, honey," she said, in the most unhelpful voice imaginable. Once he had what he needed, he shifted effortlessly into 'job mode.' The blood was really pumping now, but it was just a surge against a tidal wall.

"Right, gather round and listen up, we don't have much time. Miranda, grab the biggest coat you can find and put these on as well. Sheryl, once we're out of here, I want you to ring Ann Crossley on this number and tell her to take Jess to this address," he began scribbling on a scrap of paper.

Then he stopped and changed demeanour. "Jess, can I just check something?"

She moved in close, forcing a gap between him and Miranda. He snatched Jess's handbag and turned to one side to open it. Before Jess could lift her hand to stop him, Miranda had it pinned down.

"Don't. I've already put one person down today; I'm quite happy to make it a double."

It gave Thomas enough time to find what he was looking for. He took the sheet out and unfolded it; there were columns of numbers to four decimal places.

"Sheryl, please pass this on to Ann Crossley, to be given to Michael Schaefer." He turned back and flung the handbag to Jess. "When will you get it into your head that this isn't a game?"

Jess gave him a simpering look.

Miranda adjusted her blonde wig. "Where are we going, Thomas?"

"Yorkshire — just you and me." He looked right at Jess, making sure she'd got the message.

The cab arrived quickly. The lure of an extra fiver probably helped. He promised to ring Sheryl later when things had calmed down. It had been a long day already and it was about to get a whole lot longer. Especially when they got to Yorkshire, dressed for a funeral.

Chapter 22

"Do I really have to wear this, now we're on the train?" Miranda hissed.

"Yup," he tried hard not to smile, but it was killing him. With the coat, dark glasses and tumbling blonde wig, she looked like a D-List celebrity, desperate to be noticed.

"People keep looking at us."

He sipped his coffee nonchalantly. "That's the idea."

She huffed back into her seat and rifled through the first of three magazines she'd made him buy her at Kings Cross.

He stared out of the window, mobile in his hand. The second it hummed, he was on it like a cat. He turned to Miranda as he listened, nodding at what Ann Crossley reported. Then he sat back a little easier and tried to play footsie under the table.

"What's made you so bloody cheery all of a sudden?"

He dimmed his voice to a whisper. "Ann's completed the drop-off for me. And she's turning over the paper to the Yank, later today."

Miranda peered over the top of her over-sized shades. "I hope you know what you're doing."

He waited until the train had passed Doncaster before ringing his sister. He had to hold the phone out to cope with Pat's scream of delight. His adding that he'd brought along a surprise only heightened the volume. He swore her to secrecy and arranged a pick-up away from the station, a good hour and a half after their arrival.

It was exciting, being back on home territory with Miranda — like old times. He couldn't help smiling to himself as he packed his Conan Doyle biography back into his bag.

She stirred and leaned forward, resting her hand on his. There was a pause, a moment when time froze and it felt like it had when they were starting over, leaving Leeds for the uncertainty of London. Him, bracing himself to meet her family for the first time and Miranda squished up at his side, like a punked-up prodigal daughter.

What brought him back to the present was the edge of her old engagement ring, driving into his hand. He flinched, and immediately regretted it when she drew her hand away.

"Sorry, forgot. Hope I didn't hurt you," she said, displaying her usual talent for irony. She swivelled the band round, stone uppermost and started to ease the ring off.

"Better take this thing off for a while. Don't want your parents freaking out."

"You know," he gulped, "you could always leave it on."

He stared at her and she gazed back implacably as she wriggled the ring free.

"I think we need to talk that through a little more carefully, don't you?"

The tannoy announced their imminent arrival at York and reminded travellers not to leave any possessions behind. Yeah, he thought, like hope or vulnerability.

* * *

Leeds might have industry and a suitcase full of Miranda memories to its name, but York had culture. The cobbled streets and ancient walls oozed history and charm. He steered her into the crowds — there were always crowds in York, didn't matter what time of the year — and tried not to think about the ring. She took his arm and cranked him close; but it felt like a consolation prize.

"Come on, cut out all that macho bollocks. We will talk about it, you know."

If anything he was annoyed at his own stupidity. What was he thinking? Answer, he wasn't thinking at all. He'd been responding to the moment. And he should have known better.

They found a busy café and took a table outside. There, among the faux Vikings and a hen party on warm-up, Miranda's appearance didn't seem quite so conspicuous. Espresso might not have been the answer to his prayers but it made for a bloody good psalm.

"Gonna show me round York Minster then?"

"Aye, go on, then. But don't go nicking anything — I know what all you thieving cockneys are like."

It was the sort of thing Ajit would say, and he beamed at the thought. Ajit and Geena would meet Miranda again after who knew how many years. Yes, and so would Mum and Dad. Maybe he'd light a prayer candle in the Minster, as back up.

* * *

Pat, his sister, was on time. Even as he approached the car she looked nervy, scuttling out of the car and waiting for him to approach — not her usual animated self. She cried of course. Miranda took off the glasses and put on her best encouraging smile. Pat shook her hand and gave her a polite kiss on the cheek, before doing a double-take.

"Why, it's Miranda, isn't it? How come you're in disguise? I thought he'd found himself a floozy!"

"Not here." Thomas ushered them both into the car. "Take us over to Ajit's place and not a word to Mum and Dad."

He gave Pat a paper-thin explanation for his sudden appearance and skipped Miranda's altogether. Pat played the polite sister and asked after Miranda's family. Miranda seemed to want to help her out and gave her a ten-year update on all the people Pat had never met and was never likely to. And then it was Thomas's turn to talk.

"I, er, needed to get away and Miranda agreed to come with me."

Pat didn't speak for a while. Then, without looking at Thomas beside her, said, "Is this to do with your job? I'm not daft, yer know! Our dad has never breathed a word about what you were up to on the moors, but I read the papers."

Pat dropped them at a street corner. She got out of the car with them and clung to him for a few seconds. He whispered his thanks as he prised her off, and promised to ring her that evening. She didn't look convinced as she drove away.

* * *

He walked Miranda to Ajit and Geena's place, fizzing with anticipation. Outside of Miranda's family, he had few friends. And Ajit had the plus of not being connected to either Miranda's lot, or Karl.

Thomas rang the doorbell and jostled with Miranda until they were both on the step together. An inside door creaked and a broad silhouette filled the door glass. The front door swung in and Geena's puffy face filled the frame. His heart almost skipped a beat.

"Alright, pudgy? Put kettle on, I'm parched."

A smile erupted across Geena's face. "Blimey, Ajit'll bloody wet himself — you should have warned us. Get in then. And who's this lass — surely not the famous Miranda?" She grabbed hold of Miranda as if she were a long-lost relative. "Come on in, love.

Thomas can fetch bags and make the tea while we sit and talk about him."

He followed them inside, pleased and disturbed in equal measure. First thing he did, after closing the door, was draw the curtains in the front room. Miranda took her cue and removed the wig and glasses.

"Going on to a fancy dress party?" Geena laughed, taking Miranda's coat.

"Long story," she replied, making a time-out letter 'T' at him with her fingers.

He searched around the kitchen manfully, determined not to ask for clues. In any case, the chatter and laughter filtering through told him he'd get no assistance. He grabbed three mugs of tea, and choccy biscuits from a drawer, and took them through.

Geena invited Miranda to feel the baby kick and for an instant the laughter stopped. Miranda's face froze and her hand went tentatively to Geena's bulge. Her hand moulded around it gently and Miranda closed her eyes. Then she flinched at the kick and when she opened her eyes, she was a different person. Wistful, maybe. Whatever it was, he didn't know quite how to deal with it. She popped a compact mirror and checked her make-up. He knew she was dabbing her eye and he knew her well enough not to draw attention to it.

The tea was drunk in near silence until Geena finally broke the deadlock.

"Can I ring him, please? Go on, I'll put it on t'loudspeaker."

He relented and they crowded around the phone, which was no mean feat given the size of Geena.

"What're you doing ringing me on duty? I'll be done in an hour."

The speaker also did a neat job of picking up Ajit's colleague's piss-taking. Geena put on her best simpering tone.

"I just needed to hear your voice."

"Nothing's wrong is it?"

Thomas could almost hear the sweat running down Ajit's forehead.

"No, calm down, lover boy. Just pick up a takeaway for *four* on your way home — we've got guests."

Thomas couldn't hold back. "And don't be a mean bugger with the pakoras."

"Blimey, is that Thomas Bladen, photographer to the stars?"

"The very same. See you soon."

Ajit rang off and Thomas went back to his seat.

"Okay." Geena bit into a chocolate biscuit. "Why *are* you up here?"

The notion that his friends could be just as suspicious as he was had never really crossed Thomas's mind. Miranda, too, was looking straight at him now. Whatever he said would reach Ajit, which might implicate the good constable. So he settled for a sliver of the truth. "I can't tell you. And besides, it's better for you if you don't know."

Geena's face lost a whole lot of its welcome. Miranda diverted her, asking about baby names and life *oop north*. He followed Miranda's lead and made another brew to keep the conversation flowing and pass the time.

* * *

Ajit clanged the gate shut, whistling 'London Bridge is Falling Down.' Thomas itched to get to the door before the key was in place. But he sat still, sensing the smile spreading across his face like a sunrise.

The door slammed. Geena muttered to Miranda about the paintwork. The tune, if you could call it that, continued through to the kitchen. Thomas shifted forward in his chair. Footsteps thudded in the hall and the door handle slowly turned. Then Ajit squeezed through the doorframe.

"Ta da!" First thing he did was go over to Miranda and offer his arms. "Come on, then, up you get — let's have a look at yer." He swallowed her in a bear hug and lifted her round to one side. "Oh, you've brought a friend. It's, er, Thomas, isn't it?"

"Dick."

Once Ajit had put Miranda down, he and Thomas did a hearty round of bloke slaps until Geena cleared her throat.

"'Ere, you big lump. Remember me — mother of your unborn . . ."

Ajit nipped outside the door and returned with a bunch of flowers and a box of chocolates.

"Ah bless, he's well trained now." Geena turned to Miranda. "It can be done."

They ate in the kitchen. Thomas and Miranda split a beer between them. Ajit and Geena stuck to orange juice. It must be strange for Miranda, Thomas thought. Okay, so he talked about Ajit now and again, but the last time she saw them — barring their one weekend in London — was years back.

Geena broke off from an assault on her lamb bhuna. "So, are you two like, back together?"

Ajit gave a nudge under the table, like a mini earthquake.

"What? Are we not allowed to mention it or something?"

Thomas was still peeved about the train journey so he said nothing and raised his eyebrows at Miranda. She looked straight at him then to Geena.

"I'm still in the fourteen days cooling-off period; I haven't made my mind up yet."

Geena laughed so hard that she needed a sip of orange juice, which didn't help her any. While Thomas, he just felt very small indeed. And at that moment, he envied the life that Ajit and Geena had — the certainty and stability, even allowing for Ajit's terrified anticipation of parenthood. As for himself, he didn't know what he wanted.

"Hello, Thomas? Are you still with us?" Ajit's voice broke through.

"Yeah," he blinked at a soggy piece of naan bread in his hand. "I reckon we should make tracks soon, Miranda." *And now for the tricky part.* "I'll ring Pat and see if you can stay there tonight; I'll go to Mum and Dad's."

She nodded slowly, as if she'd been expecting this. Ajit raised a hand.

"Don't be a silly beggar — you're both stopping here with us." Ajit and Geena joined hands in a show of solidarity; it hurt Thomas to disappoint them.

"Nah, that's okay. I sort of arranged it earlier." It was a shit lie and even Miranda's little supporting smile didn't make the pill any less bitter.

When he rang her, Pat was happy to oblige, even if her part-time husband Gordon was complaining in the background. But bollocks to him.

"Miranda, time to get your gear back on."

Ajit drove them over to Thomas's parents, taking the scenic route. On his own, Ajit sounded more like a police officer and less like a friend. "I'm not stupid. We don't see you for yonks and then twice in three months. I take it this is work-related again?"

Thomas shrugged. Miranda stayed quiet in the backseat.

"Well, if you need me, you know where I am."

"Yeah, Thomas brightened. "Under Geena's thumb, as usual."

Ajit gave Thomas a playful shove that nearly dented the passenger door from the inside. Pat was already waiting at the drop-off around the corner from their mum and dad's. She looked more agitated than before. Ajit waved from the car as he pulled away and Thomas pondered what might have been if Ajit and Pat had gone through with the teenage thing and made a go of it together. His dad would have really loved that — a copper in the family.

"Gordon's looking after the kids."

That's big of him, considering they're his too.

"Are you gonna tell me what the glasses and the wig is all about? You know mam and dad are gonna ask."

"Not if you let us in with your key, first."

* * *

"Only me!" Pat giggled, quietly ushering Miranda and Thomas in the door.

As soon as she was inside, Miranda took off her accessories and shoved them in her coat pocket. Then she grabbed Thomas's hand.

"Ready?" he whispered and kissed her softly, tasting the spices on her lips.

Pat blushed and eased the door in from the hall. "I, er, found a stranger outside so I thought I'd bring him in."

Their father rose from his chair. "If it's another bloody charity collector they can go wanting. Honestly, Pat!"

Thomas went in first, Miranda's hand still in his. He watched while his father's face changed as he looked from him to Miranda.

"Hello, Dad. You remember Miranda."

His mother poked her head out of the kitchen door and for a moment there was silence. Pat came in and stood beside Miranda. Thomas thought they looked like bodyguards and maybe that wasn't such a bad comparison. You could have heard a pin drop, in sand.

"You both look very smart." Thomas's mother noted, collecting a teacup from the mantelpiece.

"We've been to a funeral today, in London." He stared his dad down: *your move.*

Mam made a break for the kitchen with Pat in tow. Thomas could hardly blame them. Thomas's dad sighed and folded up his newspaper.

"I'll go first, shall I?" Miranda's voice was like a chisel against mahogany. "We had a very pleasant journey, thank you."

Bladen senior scratched at his chin then his eyes crinkled at the edges. "I'll say this for thee, you've got some spirit about you — not like him, stood there like a wet weekend."

Thomas willingly accepted the role of fall guy in order to keep the peace.

"So, are you alright now then, lass? I presume you're speaking to him again."

He winced, thinking back to the aftermath of the moors incident, when Miranda would have nothing to do with him. He didn't need reminding about it now.

Pat called out from the kitchen, asking if Miranda took sugar. Thomas quickly replied on her behalf, just to have the chance to say something that couldn't start an argument. Tea, cake and north-south prejudice — Yorkshire hospitality at its finest. In this house, no one asked what they were doing in Pickering.

He bore the tension as long as he could, then cast a pointed glance at his sister. Pat launched out of her chair and announced that she and Miranda were making tracks. Miranda didn't offer any objection as she got to her feet — lucky cow. She said her goodbyes, complimented his mum on her cake and generally behaved like the perfect guest. He saw her to the front door, making sure her disguise was on properly before she left.

There were maybe a dozen steps back to the front room and every one was laden with expectation and disappointment. It was like returning to the headmaster's study.

"So, how have you both been?" he said.

His parents were squeezed in together on the settee; they looked small and vulnerable. His mother stirred her tea carefully. "Should I make your bed up for tonight?"

He nodded and took up a position alongside them. The TV came on and all hostilities were suspended. He wasn't big on television, but he was happy to embrace the local news and a charming story about a school choir. Eventually, his dad began to pass comment. A few nods and murmurs from Thomas and soon all embassies were on speaking terms again.

When his mum slipped upstairs to sort out the bedclothes, Thomas's dad looked at the closed door.

"So," he turned back to the TV, "everything alright at work?"

"Aye, pretty much. We 'appened to be in the area so we thought we'd pop in." It was neat, connecting the visit to his job, just by association.

"Got summat to show you," his dad stood a little shakily and opened a sideboard drawer. He drew out an envelope, passed it across then lowered himself down to the cushion. Inside the envelope was a set of photographs of garden birds.

"Finches come regular now I've started putting out the right food."

"And what about that whippet you were talking about?"

"Aye, well, mebbe once my leg's back in shape."

Photography had been the one thing they'd had in common while Thomas was growing up. Even after he'd been thrown out and had moved down to Leeds, he could usually count on a friendly reception if he had a camera or prints in his hand. Ironic that photography had brought him into the government job that he knew his father despised.

He turned in at nine o'clock and gave Miranda a call to see if her attempts at happy families had gone any better than his. She said he had a wonderful nephew and niece and it was a shame that he never saw them. And she volunteered that Pat's husband Gordon looked shifty. Ten points for that alone. And just when he thought Miranda was happy to follow his lead, she turned everything on its head.

"If they've tracked us to Yorkshire — and they'd have to be stupid not to — then what happens next?"

He hadn't figured on Miranda needing to know, or on wanting to tell her. "I'll ring you back in a bit."

"Take your time," she said. "I've got a bedtime story to read first."

Downstairs he could hear Ma and Pa talking about him. She was worried and he was reminding her that Thomas was a grown man and could look after himself.

He rang Karl to swap updates and funny stories. Karl got in there first.

"I've heard of a wedding crasher, but never a funeral one. Honest to God, I leave you alone for five minutes and suddenly it's bedlam. How's life up North?"

It seemed that everyone knew where he'd headed. "You tell me."

"Well, I happen to have a little inside information. Jess has been reported as a vulnerable missing person — by the family she doesn't have anything to do with."

He felt his spirits flagging as the call went on. "How long have I got, Karl? The morning, really? No, I'll sit tight and wait it out — might warn Miranda though." But not Pat, not if he wanted a little authenticity.

He gave and got what he needed to, then cut the call. He sat in his old room, gazing up at the cross on the wall. Did his mother still feel the Good Lord was watching over them? Forgive us our trespasses and all that? He was a fine one to talk. He was using his family — all of them — in order to give Jess a head start. He lay on top of the bed, unable to settle. What if Ajit was doing the knock in the morning? Would Ajit be tempted to alert him beforehand? Not if he ever wanted his stripes.

He had to think long and hard about what to say to Miranda before he dared pick up the phone again. She listened calmly, taking it all in her stride. If anything, it made him feel even more wretched.

"And you're not angry or anything?"

"Aw, Thomas, I didn't think I was coming up here on a fancy-dress holiday. I knew you were up to something. And besides, I've just read *Little Red Riding Hood* to the kiddies so I know all about big . . . bad . . . wolves, like you." Fairy stories had never sounded sexier.

"I, er, don't know exactly how it'll go down tomorrow. Sorry and all that."

"Get some sleep. I'll see you in the morning. And listen, about earlier, on the train. I know how you get, after funerals. I promise we'll talk, when we get back to London."

A flash of memory lit up his brain. That was how he'd come to propose, the first time — after her nanna's funeral. Blimey, she knew him so well it was frightening.

He fell asleep easily, perhaps a little too easily. Karl had once told him that when you no longer had doubts, or a conscience, it was time to give it all up. Easy words for the Celtic Avenger. As for Thomas, he wasn't sure if he was numb to the repercussions or just fixated on getting justice for Amy, even if that meant helping out Jess in the process.

Chapter 23

By the time his alarm bleeped at six thirty, he'd been awake for at least half an hour. At seven o'clock, the house began to stir so he showered and made sure his bag was packed; he had a feeling he wouldn't be there for much longer.

The call came through just before eight. Pat was frantic, screaming about the police hammering on her front door and scaring the kids, and all the neighbours watching from the street. After a quick shouting match with his dad, he took the receiver, tried to soothe her and promised he'd come straight over. His father looked daggers at him.

"Is this your doing? I might've known you'd bring trouble up here — again."

His mother peered out from the kitchen but didn't say a word.

"If you've got Pat into difficulty, don't bother coming back here. I mean it."

He grabbed his bag and headed for the door. A burly policeman was already heading up the path; it was Ajit, accompanied by a colleague.

"Thomas Bladen? I have reason to believe you may be harbouring a vulnerable missing person against their will, in contravention of . . ."

Thomas tuned it out and glanced behind him. "She's not here."

Ajit pushed past. Thomas was led away before Ajit went inside, but it was a cert it wouldn't be pretty. By the time they got round to Pat's, a few streets away, a female officer was leading Miranda away to a police car. Thomas was kept in the car behind and the whole circus started to wind down. As they drove away, he saw Pat's haunted face staring out, and he knew that he'd crossed a line.

* * *

He didn't see Ajit again at the police station — probably just as well. Not much to be said, under the circumstances. He wondered if Ajit had known about it the previous night, but that seemed unlikely. And besides, wouldn't he have coughed up the truth about Thomas's companion? Something else best not thought about.

He saw Miranda at the far end of a corridor, being buzzed in for processing. She was holding it together well. With a family like hers, they'd probably been drilled on police procedure from a young age. When the desk was clear, he was moved forward to take his turn. He kept to the script and gave his details in a monotone, wondering how long it would take for the misidentification to get back to Schaefer and Sir Peter Carroll. Well, nothing he could do about it now.

A sergeant took the lead, funnelling him into an interview room where the décor screamed 1980s, but without the feel-good factor.

"Tea or coffee?" The sergeant made it sound like he'd make it his personal business to add the phlegm.

"Coffee, please." No point being an arse about it. They were doing their job and so was he. The drink arrived pronto, along with a constable.

"Reet, can we get down to business? You're not under arrest — you're just helping us with a few inquiries. Clearing up a few anomalies, as you might say."

Like why were the police asked to check on a missing person, only to find that the person they had identified was somebody else? And in what way couldn't this be construed as wasting police time?

He breathed in the aroma of vending machine coffee, with a delicate hint of cream substitute and artificial sweetener. His thinking went like this: Miranda could be counted on to say nothing, which could complicate things further down the line. What he needed was a ready-made get-out-of-jail-free card.

"You're one of them *floaters*, aren't you? Surveillance Support Unit." The way the copper said it, it sounded like a grave insult.

He smiled to acknowledge the point and took a chance. "If I can make a phone call, I can straighten this out." He sat back and tried to look comfortable with his situation, diverting his attention to a rabies poster on the wall while the sergeant made up his mind.

A minute later and he was in the room on his own. He fetched out his mobile and rang Whitehall. The switchboard operator took his name and request, and transferred him straight through.

"Thomas!" Sir Peter's voice was frosty. "Where on earth are you — we've been worried."

Yeah, so worried that you had the police pick me up. He gritted his teeth and danced for the piper. "I'm in Yorkshire, helping police with their inquiries. I understand that Jess has disappeared. I need a favour from you."

Sir Peter Carroll didn't sound too convinced, so Thomas went for broke. "I can either ask nicely or get Karl to make you help me."

It was a low blow, but as Sir Peter was in Karl's debt, it did the trick. "What exactly do you need?"

Half an hour later, a fax arrived at the police station, confirming that Thomas Bladen was in Yorkshire on assignment and that one Miranda Wright was accompanying him. Further, that under Section 6 of the Official Secrets Act 1989, this matter could not be discussed or elaborated upon.

Miranda was waiting at the front desk; she wasn't wearing her blonde wig anymore. He wondered what the first officer on the scene must have thought when she removed the blonde wig to reveal her own blonde hair. They must have thought she was taking the piss. She gazed at him blankly, as if she couldn't quite fathom what she was doing there. They signed the book and headed for the door.

"Did they explain about the fax? I got a photocopy for the family . . ."

She shook her head in disgust. "What are they supposed to do, frame it?" Then she stopped abruptly.

A few paces ahead of them, Ajit was waiting. Miranda flew at him.

"Some fucking friend you are! Then again, maybe you deserve each other — you both put the job before other people." She walked a little way up the road.

Ajit opened his great arms wide. "Look, Thomas, I couldn't . . . I were just doing my job."

"I know." Thomas settled him. "I'd have done exactly the same." Except they both knew that he wouldn't have. "Look, Aj, we're gonna push off — made enough friends for one visit. Will you see that my dad gets this photocopy — should help to smooth the waters."

"What about saying goodbye to Geena?"

"Not this time, mate. Look, I can't stop. We've got a bus to catch for York."

And there it was. Somehow Jess and this poxy job had turned him into a Judas, betraying everyone for the greater good. *Greater good* — he was starting to sound like Karl.

He managed a proper buddies' handshake and promised to ring Ajit later in the week. When he caught up with Miranda she was smiling.

"I deserved a Oscar, back there."

He looked at her, incredulous.

"Ajit'll get over it and I can always ring Geena and explain."

"Come again?"

"Oh, didn't I mention she gave me her phone number while you were our tea boy? She felt we ought to get to know each other, especially after all this time."

His brain was spinning out of gear. "Then what . . ."

She cut across him. "Dad rang. The Irish blokes have agreed to see him about Karl. They're flying in tonight."

Chapter 24

The train journey was long and Thomas's brain was still buzzing. If he could just sort out Karl's problem and get him to his mother before the inevitable . . .

Miranda didn't have a lot to say. Then she spent so long getting the coffees, he began to wonder if she'd changed seats and hadn't bothered to tell him.

"Long queue?" he tried to make it sound funny — the *ha ha* kind.

"Not exactly," her face dropped an inch.

He went through a list in his head, just to check he wasn't in the doghouse again. Nothing stuck so he waited it out.

"I've something to tell you and I'm not sure you're gonna like it . . ."

"Let me guess — Jess snogged you as well?"

But Miranda wasn't smiling. She took a long sip of coffee and sighed, watching him over the cup. He'd done the open comms course, so he knew that guarding the mouth when speaking was more than a little suss.

"Look, whatever it is, I'm fine with it. Honestly."

"You won't be." She put her coffee cup down, but wasn't finished toying with her face. "Remember the money, after the moors . . ."

She flinched at the mention of the subject. Of course he remembered: forty thousand pounds, extracted from Sir Peter Carroll as compensation for Miranda's abduction and his complicity in the clean-up. Danger money, Karl called it. Miranda had been less generous: *blood money.*

"Well . . ." she took a huge gulp of air and let her hands fall away, "the two *Micks* like to play cards, so we're using half of that as stake money."

He didn't know what to say. Half of him wanted to scream at her for what she was proposing; the other half was overwhelmed that she and her family would do all that for Karl. So he leaned across the table carefully, cupped her face and kissed her, long and hard.

She filled him in on the mobile call she'd had during her visit to the buffet car. Martin and Francis-Andrew would be arriving at Caliban's at eight o'clock. The place would be shut for a *private function*. John Wright had gone to elaborate lengths to set the deal up with the help of an old family friend and former business associate.

"I don't think Mum and Dad have ever mentioned Jack Langton to you?"

He sat very still and stared at her, looking for clues. Jack Langton's name had never come up in over ten years. Miranda swallowed softly, blinking as she broke off eye contact.

"Jack's a person who can fix things — he's well-connected." There was pride in her voice and he felt a pang of jealousy. Most importantly, she insisted, Karl needed to be there and at his servile best.

"No problem, I can pick him up and . . ."

Miranda made a face. "Yeah, that's the thing. Mum and Dad think it's best if you're not there. It's just, you know, they want to keep you out of that side of their life. Mum reckons it's better for you too."

He picked at the coffee cup lid and pulled a piece off the rim.

"I said you wouldn't like it."

Ten out of ten. It was stupid. He knew without question that they were protecting him, but even so. Everyone was taking a risk for Karl, and somehow he was excused, like a kid with a note.

"Well at least let me bug the place, in case anything goes wrong."

"Dad and Karl reckon they might check, if they're as hard core as they're made out to be."

He nodded. He felt like a dog put in kennels while the family went off for the summer.

"Honestly, Thomas, it'll be fine. They'll play some cards, Sheryl will serve some drinks in a sexy number and—"

"So Sheryl's going to be there as well."

And then a terrible thought crossed his mind. That perhaps they all felt he simply wasn't up to it. Worse, maybe they had a point. He didn't speak again until Peterborough — spending his time doodling in a notepad and avoiding eye contact.

It never seemed to balance out, not really. Either work was fine and his private life was in ruins or it was the other way round. Or, like now, it had all gone to shit across the board. When did it all get this complicated? He became aware that he was dragging the same line back and forth across the page. When? The day he joined Sir Peter Carroll's merry men and didn't tell Miranda or her family? No, scratch that. It had all started to go sour the day he stumbled behind the façade of the Surveillance Support Unit and got involved in Karl's counter-intelligence games. But the truth was that he loved it, sort of. Stopping the bad guys, like every schoolboy's heroic fantasy. Except the bad guys were real. They deceived, they punished and they killed.

He looked at the page again. He'd drawn a stick-figure girl with a halo above her head. Amy, obviously — Major Eldridge's *Angel*. He was no closer to finding out why she'd died. He tapped the page. When he got home he'd make sure to check the recordings from the bugs in the major's office — both of them; the device that Michael Schaefer knew about and the other one on the second phone. At least he could put his isolation to good use. For some reason, that thought cheered him.

"Penny for 'em?" Miranda called across the table. "You just smiled."

"Just planning my dinner for one for tonight."

"When will you get it into your thick 'ead? Mum and Dad are only thinking of you. Karl's bollocksed without the help of the Micks, and you're well out of it."

"Fine." He tried not to sulk. "I think I'll see Karl before tonight though, just for a quick chat."

Miranda gave him her world-weary look, the one that usually meant surrender. "If you must. He'll be at Mum and Dad's — I s'pose you can come back with me, then Terry can run you home."

Jesus. Why not give Karl a bloody door key and have done with it?

* * *

King's Cross was hassle-free, once you accepted the milling crowds and that indefinable odour of too many people with too little hygiene. He half-expected Sam or Terry to be waiting at the barrier, ready to whisk Miranda away from him. The only thing that greeted him was a sense of familiarity. Yorkshire born, but taken in by London; and as foster mothers went, he had no complaints.

They settled down on the Tube He wondered again why the family chose to live just over the border in Essex if they were so proud of their East End roots. Just something else to chew over while avoiding the real issue. Karl and the Wrights were the only people he had any connection with in London. Not counting Christine Gerrard, who was not only an ex but also the boss, so she was doubly verboten. Tonight's pow-wow felt like a party all your mates were attending that you weren't invited to.

As they waited together for a cab at Dagenham, he sat and read his book, just to piss her off. Petty victories, and all that.

By the looks of things, Karl had made himself pretty comfortable. He didn't stir from his armchair when Thomas entered the room. Miranda wandered off and then, as if by magic, the rest of the Wright clan made themselves scarce until it was just Thomas and Karl.

"Listen, Tommo, I can't thank you enough for this. I mean, if it wasn't for you—"

No, this was too much. "I just spoke to John — he did the rest."

"Well," Karl's face was rosy red now; "that's not how I heard it. And I've no issue with having to scratch somebody else's back in return."

"Come again?" And then the fog started to clear. John helps Karl and Karl owes him, or *someone*.

Chapter 25

At seven o'clock Thomas was sat in his flat, staring at the phone. Neither Karl nor Miranda was likely to ring and say that the Irish fellers had arrived. No, but he wished they would. It wasn't just jealousy, although that figured high in the list; he was also worried about Karl meeting his nemesis after so many years.

Fish-and-chips was keeping warm in the oven and the peas were simmering on the hob. A nature programme he'd recorded was lined up, ready to go. And part of his brain was still doing conjuring tricks. He went to the drawer and pulled out copies of the letters Karl had found hidden in Jess's flat — the letters from Major Eldridge. He took them with him into the kitchen, and carried them back through with the food.

He remembered how, after the big break-up with Miranda, he'd re-read all her letters relentlessly. Even now, he still had them filed away in a box, in chronological order. As well as every Christmas and birthday card she'd ever sent him. Jess seemed that type as well, meticulous, in her way. Except Karl had only found two letters. Surely the good major would have had more to say? He stared at the pages — there must be something useful in them.

After settling to his food, he unpaused David Attenborough and let him go play in the trees with a capuchin monkey. Thomas smiled; his immediate thought was *cappuccino* — the joys of word association. Then, as he went in deep on the vinegar-soaked chips and started coughing, he had a thought. Major Eldridge had signed his letters Cupid: 'C' for both Charles and Cecil, and for Cupid. There was a sense and rhythm to it.

He put his cutlery down for a moment, just as two monkeys got busy with the loving — not so good when you're eating. He dug out another page from the drawer, the sheet where he'd splurged out his conclusions about Amy and Jess. A is for Amy and Angel; there in black and white. He paused the TV and stared out beyond it, as his dinner cooled. If Amy had been the one having the affair, as they'd surmised, a few things made sense — Jess's indifference to Amy's memory, the major's indifference to Jess and his insistence on having the letters back. Plus, no envelope because Jess just didn't have it. Maybe she'd lifted the two letters from Amy's locker and they were the only ones there.

So far, so what? Nothing concrete, short of proving Jess to be a fantasist, especially after what Schaefer said about her and Oxford. The room temperature seemed to lower a couple of notches at his next piece of speculation. Supposing Amy's death hadn't been an accident at all? He whistled a breath. Jesus, what if he and Miranda had been protecting a murderer? Or an attention-seeking saboteur who'd gone too far?

He grabbed the phone. Outside of the high stakes card game, he did have one other contact in London — Petrov, half-brother of Yorgi, the deceased assassin. The only person he could think to entrust Jess to, before he and Miranda hightailed it to Yorkshire, was Petrov, because Petrov owed him big-time.

Petrov picked up first ring. He sounded a little guarded, even after Thomas identified himself.

"It is always good to hear your voice, Tomas. But your friend, I think she is not so good."

He felt his shoulders tense. "I hope Jess isn't causing you any problems."

Petrov drew a breath. "She had an argument on her mobile — shouting very bad things — threatening someone. Then I get a telephone call from an angry man."

He put a hand to his forehead; he could guess the rest. "Do you know who he was?" A part of him was already planning out a route and wondering whether to go prepared.

"He didn't give his name, but when he arrived here . . ."

Arrived there?

"Your friend, Jess, seemed very pleased to see him. I asked her not to go and she said that she is not a prisoner and I am not her keeper. So this, this *Cecil*, he collect her and her things, and I don't expect to see her again."

"I'm sorry, Petrov. I didn't mean to cause you and your family any trouble."

"You are a good man, Tomas, but your work is not good. Do not bring it into my life again." Which sounded rich, coming from a man who had once needed his help so badly.

Thomas ended the conversation, then sent a text to Miranda — *Jess missing again. Get Karl to ring me asap* — and went to his laptop. Clever Karl, fitting a tracker in the heel of Jess's shoe before Amy's memorial service. As long as she had her case nearby — and according to Petrov, everything went with her — he could trace her.

He logged on to an anonymising server and keyed in the appropriate URL. Then he entered the twelve-character reference for the bug and waited while the map loaded. Karl's bug was a high spec device, emitting a GPS pulse about every minute. Better, he could call up any time once the bug was fitted. The first place Jess had stopped after leaving Petrov's house was her own flat — with Major Eldridge doing the driving no doubt.

Thomas closed his eyes and tried to think through the logic. Jess already had her passport and bank cards, and clearly she hadn't stayed at the flat, so what was she there for, for almost ten minutes? Major Eldridge's letters perhaps — why else would he be helping her? Yeah, but in exchange for what — safe passage? How could the major protect Jess from Michael Schaefer and Engamel?

Well, maybe he could ask them himself if he shifted his arse. He printed the map for the last known coordinates and went to his darkroom. Unlocking the door, he reached below the shelf, through the cloth curtain and behind the chemical bottles. The tiny strongbox felt cold to the touch. He carefully lifted it out and produced the key. The small Makarov pistol gleamed under the red light, like a warning.

He was almost out the door when his mobile rang — it was Miranda.

"Is everything okay?" She was whispering. "I can't talk long — I'm in the loo."

"Never mind me," he recovered. "What about your end of things?"

"We're down about ten grand, but it looks like being a long night. I'll make sure Karl rings as soon as he can." There was the sound of a toilet flushing and then the line cut out.

* * *

Thomas talked to himself as he drove, offering up possibilities and explanations then dismissing them without charge. Was Jess in any danger? Maybe, but it was the major who really needed protecting — from her.

411

He zeroed in on Euston, negotiating a succession of temporary traffic lights and diversions to skirt around some roadworks trenches. As the engine shuddered to a stop, he pondered his next move. There were three options on the table. He could just try the last location and hope they hadn't moved since he'd left the flat; he could ring up Ann Crossley at home, and give her the log-in details; or, because he still had the number he'd filched from the mobile that he'd given Jess, he could ring Major Eldridge's personal mobile. In the end, he decided to go for all three.

Ann Crossley — as he had expected — had put her work phone on divert. She was professional, but coy, when he gave her the standard 'I hope I wasn't disturbing your evening?' Nope, Ann didn't seem to do casual, even after hours.

"How can I help you, Thomas?"

He cut to the chase, told her what he wanted to know and recited the details. It didn't surprise him that her laptop was switched on and by her side. Within a minute, she told him what he needed to know. Jess — or at least, her shoes — were in a large hotel, not far from the pub he had tracked them to before leaving home.

* * *

He entered the lobby, smiled at the row of understimulated receptionists and made himself comfy on a sofa, as if waiting for someone. In the bar area, a mixture of tourists and low-budget execs were glued to a footie match on a big screen TV. Lucky sods; he envied them, even though he didn't much like pubs, or football, or drinking.

Short of going up to the desk and demanding the room number, he'd have to ring the major's mobile. He waited another couple of minutes, trying to put together a meaningful sentence in his head. Then he was ready.

"Cecil Eldridge?" the major didn't sound too sure of himself.

"It's Thomas Bladen. I think we need to have a chat — and Jess too."

There was a pregnant pause then the major took in a rush of air. "I owe you an explanation; I've removed Jess from the safe house where you installed her."

Thomas waited, piling on the pressure through the gift of silence.

"Where can I meet you, Thomas?"

"I'm downstairs, in the lobby."

Another pause, while the major presumably tried to figure out his next move.

"I've come alone," Thomas threw him a lifeline. "I just want to talk; with you, first, and then the three of us. After that I'm out of here and you can do what you like."

The line went muffled then became as clear as a bell. "I'll be down in five minutes — stay put."

He watched the clocks inch round, over several time zones at once. Of course, he could have been barking up the wrong tree entirely. Maybe the two of them upstairs *were* a couple after all, and the major was searching for his trousers. Nah, it didn't scan right, whichever way he looked at it. More likely, what they were doing up there was getting their stories straight.

A minute past meltdown, when Thomas was considering taking his pistol on a house call, the lift door pinged open. Major Eldridge looked a little sheepish, but not flustered enough to have been on manoeuvres with Jess. He blushed when Thomas met his eyes, then stiffened as he walked over, like a man facing the firing squad.

"How about a drink?" Thomas greeted him. No sense condemning the bloke out of hand. What evidence did he have, anyway?

"Scotch and soda, thank you."

Thomas took the hint, and adopted the role of butler. They managed to find a table away from the bar and not too close to the doors that opened automatically for no reason at all.

"Shall I go first?" Thomas didn't waste any time; the major tasted his drink and sat there. Time to go fishing. "You were involved with Amy, not Jess. And you've been trying to get back some personal letters that Jess took from her. That's your business. But removing Jess from a secure location puts her at risk *and* the family." He spoke slowly and deliberately, to keep the emotion out of his voice.

"You don't understand."

Thomas rolled his eyes. "Please spare me the two lonely people bollocks — I'm not interested. You chose to drag Karl and me into this. And now you've put Jess out in the open again, just to get some love letters back."

The major smiled, but it was a tired smile, tinged with self-pity. "Look, Thomas, I'm not perfect and whatever you might think, we were in love. I know, a man of my age with Amy — it sounds preposterous."

Thomas nodded; at least he'd confirmed the lucky winner of the major's affections.

"I would have given it all up for her, you know — wife, career. But, with the way things have turned out . . ." he throttled the glass and took a sip, ". . . what sense is there in sacrificing anything now?"

What sense indeed? Thomas gulped at his shandy and said nothing.

"You really don't get it, do you?" Pity had hardened to scorn. "Michael Schaefer would like Jess's head on a plate — I'm trying to broker a compromise."

"Out of the goodness of your heart, I suppose?"

The major shook his head and sneered. "I have my letters now — it's in everyone's interests if the test data can be properly analysed."

Thomas put his glass down. "The data Jess keeps in her head."

The major tilted his head. "Karl said you were sharp."

When was that? "So, what, you arrange a deal for Jess in return for the data and she walks off into the sunset?"

"My dear Thomas, you're miles from the truth. Jess wants to provide the missing data in return for safe passage . . ." he stroked his neck, ". . . to America, working for one of Engamel's consortium partners. Someone like Jess has a bright future over there."

Thomas blinked a couple of times. He felt like he'd bought a cinema ticket and walked in on the wrong screening. "What about the cause of the accident?"

The major seemed to gaze across the lobby, lost in thought. "That's what we need the data for. Schaefer has most of it and Jess has the rest."

Thomas still wasn't getting it. "And you expect Schaefer to share nicely with you once he's got what he wants?"

"It's that or I use the footage you and Karl took — my extra copy, I mean."

Thomas swallowed. "You bastard — you'll implicate the SSU, especially me and Karl."

"Collateral damage, Thomas — unavoidable."

Now he understood why Sir Peter Carroll was prepared to bug the major's phone — no one could trust anybody. He felt like doing a little collateral damage himself and then he remembered Jess upstairs. "And what if the cause of the accident wasn't purely mechanical?" he glanced to the lift.

"Then I'll make sure everyone responsible pays the price."

* * *

The major seemed content to stay there. In any case, Thomas was in no mood for a debate. He stood in the lift, as the doors closed, watching the major head off towards the bar.

The muzak to the sixth floor seemed the perfect accompaniment to his mood — something that appeared to be one thing, but was actually nothing of the kind. He half expected Jess to be at the lifts, but the doors opened to nobody at all, just a disused ashtray beneath a No Smoking sign, as if it was a dare.

He swung the double doors, *High Noon* style, and counted the room numbers along to room 685. There was no light visible beneath the door. He rapped hard and called out his name. Jess mumbled something and he went inside.

The bedside lamp was on, and Jess was in bed. He stayed by the door and stared, lost for words. Did she really think he was still buying her and the major as a double act? Jess began to ease out of the sheets, to reach for her underwear near the bed. She paused, to check he was still watching her.

"Get dressed," he turned to leave. "I'll be by the lift." *Un-fucking-believable.* Literally, in this case.

The minutes ticked by, as he waited. He found he was gripping his gun and entertaining dark flights of fantasy. Consistent to the last, Jess put on an Oscar-winning performance as she arrived, her eyes bloodshot as if she'd been crying. Then again, maybe she had: out of shame.

They rode the lift down with only the muzak between them. It seemed to him that Jess had the kind of issues that even Miranda's magazines would refer to a specialist. Had Jess wanted to *become* Amy? He tossed the idea around in his head. And was that reason enough to kill her?

The major had settled himself with his two new friends, Mr Soda and Mr Scotch. He looked comfortably maudlin. Jess's appearance didn't seem to lighten his mood any. Thomas took a fresh order for drinks and left the two of them alone.

As he waited at the bar to be served, briefly mesmerised by a mid-week European match, he tried to plan his next move. What was his objective here?

Prevent Karl and him from being set up as the fall guys.

Find out why Amy died.

End this bloody assignment ASAP.

So, basically, he needed to get onside with Major Eldridge, while remaining onside with Engamel. As for Jess, the sooner she made it to the US of A, the better for everyone.

A bartender dawdled across to him. She had a face that suggested her name badge, *Bonnie*, had been an ironic afterthought. That, or the weight of it was dragging down the corners of her mouth. Once she'd registered eye contact, she flashed a smile as plastic as the décor and set her training in motion. She filled a tray with three glasses and a packet of crisps; he added a tip out of sympathy — for the customers to follow him. Then it was back to the other two musketeers.

415

The three of them drank quietly. Thomas didn't share the crisps — he felt they didn't deserve them.

"When are you seeing Michael Schaefer?" he looked the major in the face — no sense beating around the bush anymore.

"Tomorrow morning. Until I get his agreement, Jess will stay here, out of harm's way. You're the only other person who knows she's here, Thomas."

That sounded like a loaded statement. He thought about Ann Crossley knowing, and probably Miranda and Karl before the night was out, and mustered his best poker face.

Jess came to life. "Maybe Thomas should stay here with me, just in case?"

Her still-moist eyes reminded him of an anime cartoon. For a moment he thought he could hear the opening bars to *The Twilight Zone*, playing in the distance.

"That's not going to happen." He didn't bother to look in Jess's direction, but he figured she was pouting.

The major walked Jess back up to her room. Thomas was still finding gaps to fill. Why Amy was testing part of the weapon's mechanism on her own, if that wasn't the normal procedure? And where had Jess been when the *accident* occurred? Too many questions and now he was down to the crispy crumbs.

The major looked much more relaxed when he returned to finish his drink.

"Do you think she's a killer, Major?" In terms of subtlety, it was right up there with: 'Shall I take my Viagra now?' But Thomas was past caring. He figured he and the major were both on the same fishing trip.

"I think it unlikely that she's responsible, but she's very evasive."

Thomas squeezed the last dregs of shandy from his glass. "Do you want me to come with you tomorrow, to see Schaefer at Engamel?"

The major paused to consider the offer, probably out of politeness. "No, that won't be necessary. But thank you."

Drinks over, conversation exhausted, time for beddy-byes. He walked to the sliding doors. "Can I give you a lift somewhere?" *Like maybe home to your wife?*

A shake of the head was enough to send him on his way. It could be that the major planned to double back and have one last chat with Jess. Not his problem, Thomas decided; he had other matters to attend to.

* * *

As he stepped back onto Euston Road, a bus trundled past — a portable oasis in a desert of squalor. For all his love of the city, Thomas wasn't a nightbird — not unless he had a camera in his hand. A camera made you look at things differently. Sometimes you saw beauty there, fleeting, captivating. Mostly you saw the ugliness, stark and unveiled. Either way, you saw photographs in the making.

The two young bucks diagonally opposite fell into the latter category. Thomas felt the crosshatch handle of the Makarov pistol tight against his palm. *Not tonight, boys.* And he walked confidently on.

Ten to eleven, time to check his mobile. He remembered now that he'd put it on silent, while playing detective. He rang Ann Crossley first, a combination of professional courtesy and curiosity to see whether she was still on duty. She was, of course; she had the same stilted tone, her gentle Welsh inflections struggling to be heard over the whitewash of an English education. She received his update, asked little and wished him a good night. Fat chance of that, unless . . .

Miranda picked up on the third ring. "Hi, Thomas, I was going to call you. Do you want the good news or the bad news?" "Hit me."

Just what he didn't need, late night riddles. "Hit me."

She laughed at his piss poor attempt to be cool. "It's sorted. The Irish geezers have agreed to let Karl back in for twenty-four hours," her voice tailed off, as if she was rounding for the counterpunch.

"Go on, then . . ."

"We're down about twenty grand." She took a breath. "And it's gonna cost another ten grand as a goodwill gesture, allowing Karl to act as a courier for Jack Langton."

At first, he was lost for words. "Miranda, I'm so sorry." *Her* money, even if she had refused to touch it when he'd extorted it out of Sir Peter Carroll on her behalf.

"It's fine," she sounded superficially breezy. "Besides, what would I want with thirty grand?"

He clenched his teeth to force down the lump in his throat. "So, were these two blokes scary then?"

"Not compared to Jack Langton — did you know I'm his god-daughter?"

"His *what*?" he nearly dropped the phone.

"Only kidding, sort of. Listen, if you haven't already, you better ring Karl tonight. He'd probably appreciate a lift to the airport tomorrow morning. And after that, perhaps you'd like to meet me at my place — or I could wait for you here?"

"Caliban's is good for me. See you as soon as. Bye." He looked at the phone again and hesitated. It must be hard for Karl, finally allowed home just in time to see his mum before . . . He bit at a nail, and fretted over his opening line.

"Karl? It's Thomas. How're you doing, mate?"

"Well, it'll be a while before I want to watch another card game. And I'm thinking of changing my name to Faust!"

"When do you want to be picked up tomorrow?"

"You're a star, Tommo — eight will be fine. It'll give me time to buy you breakfast at the airport."

"What, with your winnings from the table?"

There was a moment's silence. "You don't think I was playing tonight? I'm down as John Wright's man, so I am — I spent the night looking attentive and keeping schtum. Jack Langton wants me to make a delivery on my little trip — I'll tell you all tomorrow."

* * *

Thomas wasn't thrilled to be arriving at Miranda's club, gun in hand. But it'd be safer than leaving it in the car — what a crime report that'd make.

He pulled into the car park and automatically checked out the other cars. Miranda's and Sheryl's sat side by side; the rest of the clan must have left. A pity; he'd wanted to thank them.

He yawned as he jabbed the intercom and waved half-heartedly at the CCTV. The sound of heels clacked down the steps and then the bolt was drawn back.

"Hi, honey, how was your day?" Sheryl widened the door without waiting for an answer, and locked up after him.

"I gather it all went well," he called behind him as he climbed the steps.

"Yeah, pretty much. I'd say Karl scraped a pass; it was all a bit tense at first, but Jack Langton has a way of setting the tone."

Thomas held the door at the top of the steps. "Have you met him before?"

"Met him? I, er, used to run bar for him."

Miranda was sat at the card table, drink in hand, like a survivor surveying the damage. She pushed out the chair beside her with her foot.

"Tea or coffee, Thomas?" Sheryl had already started to veer off.

"Tea, thanks," he joined Miranda at the table. "Tough night?"

Miranda found a smile even though it seemed like it was a long time coming. "So so. And you?"

"Not my best day." He lifted the Makarov out of his pocket and laid it on the table. "Any chance you could stash this somewhere safe for a while? I don't think it would go down well at the airport."

418

"Sure," she didn't bat an eyelid. "Does this make me your moll now?"

He squeezed her arm. Sheryl took her seat and passed the tea across to him.

"Nice weapon — a little small, but very stylish."

"Yeah, I inherited it from my dad."

He watched as Sheryl and Miranda made eye contact. Maybe Miranda had already told her how he'd pulled a gun on Yorgi, on the moors. It would explain the sudden drop in temperature.

Chapter 26

"You didn't have to bring me tea in bed," he peered up at Miranda, bleary-eyed. The clock read something evil past six.

She smiled and rubbed his shoulder as she put the mug down beside him. There was still an edge to her, had been since the previous night. In bed, she'd lain close to him and he, able to read her signals after years of trial and error, just held her close until they fell asleep.

"I don't want you to get involved in Mum and Dad's business."

Bit late for that, he mused, but he kept the thought to himself. He nodded a couple of times and left the airwaves open.

"Only, the card game reminded me of some things; you know, from when I was a kid." She didn't elaborate. "Best you keep out of it."

"Sheryl mentioned last night that she used to work for Jack Langton. Is that how she got the job here?" He leaned over for his tea and yawned, feigning disinterest.

Miranda didn't answer. "Are you coming back tonight?"

"Well," he sat up. "That sounds like an invitation if ever there was one."

She still wasn't playing though. "I don't want your gun here."

Not the declaration of affection he was hoping for. "Fair enough." He read the clock again and wondered how quickly he could get out without it seeming personal.

* * *

It was bin day in Kilburn and it seemed like every cat in the neighbourhood was on patrol for scraps. Thomas sat in his car —

seven fifty — and watched as a scraggy ginger specimen prowled around the black bags. Maybe it was the short tufts of reddish brown hair, but it reminded him of Karl. Karl McNeill, alley cat; it had a certain ring to it.

The man himself emerged from his door at a minute to eight, and then triple-locked it. Knowing Karl, it was probably booby-trapped on the other side as well. He raised a hand in greeting and strolled up with a laptop case at his side and a sports bag over his shoulder.

Thomas got out and opened the boot. "You okay?" Best to see how Karl played it first, before committing himself.

"Aye, Tommo," Karl sighed. "Big day today."

"What's with the laptop bag — is that for the Duty Free?"

Karl got in and pulled the door closed. He didn't speak until Thomas had started up the car. "You really wanna know?" his voice said one thing and his face said the opposite.

"How about telling me now and getting it over with, and then you can pick the music."

"Deal."

Over the ten years or so that Thomas had known Miranda and her family, he'd occasionally speculated about what her family's business involved. Sure, there were the usual tax returns and accountant's fees, but lurking beneath that veneer was a flow of trade and money that came and went like a night tide: you knew it was happening, but you never got to see it. So when Karl mentioned the magic word *coins*, Thomas didn't know at first if he was taking the piss. And Karl, as the bagman, knew very few details, beyond his lap top battery being very expensive, pound for pound.

"And someone just arrives at your hotel and swaps batteries with you?"

"That's the plan. In fact, that's all the plan there is."

It was hard to know how to respond. "And you're okay with that?"

"Truth? It's not the way I'd prefer to work. Remember, I'll be a civilian there. No protection beyond Martin and Francis-Andrew's word." He didn't sound too convinced. "It could be an elaborate set up, for all I know. The hotel has been arranged, along with my flight times, so anything's possible."

"And what about seeing your mum in hospital?"

"It's a grey area. Martin has stipulated that I don't contact anyone else in the family, so God help us if there are any other visitors. I think they'll let me have an hour with her."

Thomas tried to relax his grip on the wheel. "And you trust them?"

"What choice do I have, eh, Tommy Boy?"

"I wish I could help," he jammed his foot down to clear the lights in time.

"You already have — I've saved my cab fare to the airport." And with that, Karl popped the glove compartment and sifted through the CDs, finally holding aloft a Thin Lizzy album, 'The Boys Are Back In Town.' He beamed, as if he'd just seen a photo of an old friend.

Thomas told Karl the bare minimum about his enchanted evening with Jess and Major Eldridge. No point overloading Karl's sense of moral obligation right now. Predictably, Karl offered his full support, albeit at the end of a new mobile number, while he was away.

"I'll try and avoid it, just in case the walls have ears where you're going."

Karl raised an eyebrow and stayed silent.

* * *

Thomas's mood had darkened by the time they arrived at Gatwick airport's short stay car park. Karl picked up on it straight away.

"First time back, eh, Tommo?"

"Uh huh," he busied himself, trying to find a space. And tried not to think about the terrible time when Miranda had been abducted — from that very car — tracked by Sir Peter Carroll's cronies. He managed not to dent the dashboard.

"It'll get easier, Tommo — when you head back here to pick me up."

Thomas smiled; Karl was all heart. "Thanks, I'll put in a good word for you at my next counselling session. And I know just the word." He parked up and carried Karl's sports bag in for him; he steered well clear of the laptop.

The airport was orchestrated chaos; staff who knew what they were doing, passengers who knew where they were going, and the drifters who knew neither. Karl headed to an early check-in. He took the bag from Thomas, went through the admin, answered the security questions politely and deposited said bag, retaining his laptop.

Admin over, Karl wove his way through a throng of happy travellers, in search of coffee and provisions. Thomas followed in his wake. There was a certain delight in not having to watch the clock too rigorously: Karl's flight wasn't for at least two hours. And that was after allowing time to pass through security.

"What if it all goes tits up, Karl?" Might as well say what he was thinking.

"Then I'm on my own and my day job's looking very shaky."

"Shit." Thomas took another slurp of tea and his brain started ticking.

After breakfast, they wandered through the tasteful range of shops and services. There was a strange *goodbye* feel to everything, and Thomas had to remind himself that Karl would be back in twenty-four hours, give or take.

"Will you at least text me where you're staying and where your mum . . . you know." He gazed over the glass partition.

"She's in Belfast City Hospital — palliative care. It's fine to talk about it, really. You're about the only one I *can* talk to on the subject." He shifted the laptop bag to his other hand. "I don't think knowing my hotel is going to do you any good, but I promise to let you know once I'm settled in."

"Come on, let's get you through the sentries so you can stock up on expensive presents." He paused. "How is it supposed to work when you're out there?"

Karl understood immediately. "Someone will ring me at the hotel — that's as much as I've been told."

He walked Karl as far as he could, like a parent taking their youngest child to the school gates. He remembered how pleased with himself he'd been when he'd first figured out a way for Karl to see his mother. Only now, as the back of Karl's head inched along in the sedated conga, to run the gauntlet of a metal detector and an X-ray machine, he didn't feel nearly so clever.

Once 'Alley Cat' O'Neill was half a dozen people along, Thomas went in search of a decent mobile signal. Top of the call list was Ann Crossley, to see if she could get him another appointment with Sir Peter Carroll. There were things to discuss.

Chapter 27

Karl settled in his seat, eyes closed, listening to the drumming of the engines and the chatter around him. The one benefit of such a short flight was a reduced chance of conversation. And he'd stacked the odds further by pretending to be asleep, even during the safety demonstration. Once they were fully airborne, he relented, gazing out on the clouds and marking the distance of years. He remembered now why he'd always hated flying — it had always been there, but he'd never acknowledged it: that first gut-wrenching flight from home.

Ma had seen him off at the airport, mostly for his own protection. "You will ring me when you're settled? You can reverse the charges if you have to."

He blushed against the windowpane as he recalled breaking down, and her flicking his hair from his face and telling him to be brave, to make something out of himself and that maybe Jacqueline would get in touch. But she never had.

Clouds rolled on and the memories rushed in to meet them. He was such a skinny thing in those days — that first day on a building site never seemed to end. He was *Paddy* of course, except to the other Irish. And then, when *the collection* went round — for the cause back home — he donated without hesitation, to avoid attracting attention. And before he knew it, he was invited to the local Irish Centre, a slice of home that threatened to cut through the identity he'd concocted.

Mam got her phone calls regularly, from one of those bent phone-boxes that were common knowledge to certain people. He didn't know who had cried the most, the first time, but after that some unspoken pact applied. He never told her how lonely he was and she never asked.

* * *

When the plane broke cloud cover, Karl felt cheated. He wasn't done with his memories and he wasn't ready to face up to the aftermath. But it was coming, ready or not. Table up, straight-backed chair, firm jaw; coming into land.

As the plane circled in a wide arc, high over Belfast, he looked down upon shades of green that he'd never expected to see again, and rubbed away a solitary tear. Somewhere, down there, he'd told Jacqueline that he loved her.

The flight spiralled in and the engines changed pitch for the final descent. And then suddenly they were taxiing to the terminal, back in County Antrim after nearly two decades away.

* * *

Despite the red seatbelt sign, the woman beside him unfastened hers and glanced around the cabin. He didn't make eye contact, but he watched her closely. Maybe she was on the same package deal: the 'twenty-four hours and fuck off' city break. True or not, she looked ready to sprint to the steps.

He, on the other hand, was in no rush; it would take as long as it takes. And for what lay ahead, it could take forever and he still wouldn't be prepared. After an eternity, the doors opened, front and back, and the cattle disembarked. Soon it was just him, a few stragglers and a woman who needed help with her stick. She'd be about his mammy's age. As he grabbed his laptop and eased into the aisle, he heard a tinny tune playing across the years — 'The Party's Over' by Tony Bennett — his mother's favourite. Christmas, birthdays, even bad news days, Tony Bennett would fill the house. Even the day dad left had become part of the Tony Bennett montage.

The sign read, Welcome to Belfast City Airport. Jesus, he'd been away so long they'd renamed the place. Outside, the air tasted different, felt different as it stroked his face the way a mother soothes a child. He thought there might have been someone there to meet him. Not Jacqueline — he wasn't going soft in the head — but maybe some associate of Martin's or Francis-Andrew's. The absence reminded him how solitary he'd become. Right now, this minute, the only person he could ring and chat about the enormity of his being here, was Thomas — and that call was scheduled for later.

* * *

He grabbed a taxi, just as the rain started; lazy drips smearing the view as they made the prodigal's parade along the Sydenham Bypass. It was as a stranger that he watched, weighing up the risk of a walk-around later on, once he'd checked in.

425

The taxi driver had launched into the blarney from the off, reaching his fourth minute without pausing for breath. "Sure, it's a golden city now — do you come here often?" And then he laughed at the innuendo, probably repeated a hundred times a month.

Karl fended off any probing questions and stuck with the safest line — being back over on business: computers. He looked the part anyway — smart casual. No suit, but not slumming it either.

The driver was still in full flow as they reached the hotel, something about golf at the weekends and again what a golden city Belfast had become. Karl paid him off, faintly embarrassed by the English currency, and went inside. The hotel was mid-range: somewhere between luxury and a doss-house, as befitted the desires of his employers.

As he stood in the foyer, taking stock, he wondered again if the whole smuggled coins routine was bullshit. Think again, he concluded. John Wright might have welcomed him into the fold, but Jack Langton didn't seem the type to do charity work.

The reception desk carried a plaque declaring: 'It's our pleasure to serve you.' Which sounded like a wild boast. On the far wall was a sepia print of a harpist, fingers extended and her eyes closed in rapture. Elsewhere, he clocked a stylised image of St Patrick. All the place lacked was a little sign with an arrow — Shamrock Museum this way.

One of the three wee lasses finished her call, tugged at the hem of her bright green jacket and leaned towards him. "Good afternoon, how may I help you today?"

He played the game, shelled out a few details on paper — false address, false name to match the booking, and false mobile number — and collected his room key. No early-morning call, thank you, no complimentary newspaper and definitely no booking for an evening show. Not in the way that she meant, anyway. She nodded a little uncomfortably and advised him that he'd be charged for each diverted call.

* * *

John Wright had been kind to him, finding a hotel within walking distance of the hospital. Even so, he hunched his shoulders in as he walked, and kept his gaze low. He walked up and down outside for a minute, getting his head together; he wouldn't see Ma until after the exchange, but he wanted to just cross the threshold and burst the bubble.

It was a mixture of the old and the new. A temple to medicine and to hope — for those who believed in such things. The last wisps of euphoria at being back on native soil evaporated as he stepped inside and smelt the sanitised air. Somewhere, in that vast complex of corridors and patients, his ma lay dying. He picked his moment, sidled over to a desk and asked after his ma's whereabouts. The inevitable questions came, but he put his consummate ability to lie into practice and span them a line about being a distant nephew. Once he had what he needed and an assurance that visiting would be fine, he excused himself and high-tailed it out of there. The CCTV was something he'd just have to chance.

The rain outside spattered cold against his face; he kidded himself it was the weather that made him shiver. On the way back to the hotel, he grabbed a local paper, and wondered whether he was already being watched.

As he walked into the lobby, he faked a phone conversation, a ruse to inconspicuously check out the downstairs. No one approaches you when you're on a mobile call; rather, they tend to avoid you. The only visitors were a couple having tea in the lounge. Karl nodded politely, and took his fake call elsewhere. He hadn't thought his contact would be two people but if so, at least he'd had a chance to look at them. The man was bulky, in a suit that had seen better times. The woman, more angular in frame and movement, had been the one paying him more attention. He decided, on the balance of probability, that they were probably guests.

He cut the fake call by the main desk, nixed the phone divert and ordered himself some room service. Back in his room, he switched on the television and examined the phone wires for signs of recent tampering. Part of him knew this was nonsense, but his instincts were so hyped, being back, that it was less stress to follow them up than to ignore them. A cup of catering-standard tea, with sacheted milk and two miniature shortbreads, gave him something to sit down for.

He flicked through the newspaper, not really reading anything, but aware he was scanning for names, while the TV blared on. At five o'clock, someone rapped on the door. He'd ordered room service, but that didn't stop him opening the door carefully, with a fist clenched out of view. False alarm, just fish and chips with mushy peas. He made the guy wait outside while he signed for it then retreated back into his shell.

A presenter on UTV was reviewing the ongoing case of a stolen JCB digger and the ATM machine it had removed from a wall. He finished his meal, wiped the knife clean and put it to one side. Not the best of weapons, more a psychological comfort.

At six o'clock, he made a genuine mobile call. "Is that the Yorkshire Tourist Board?"

"How are you, mate?"

"Oh, fine, fine. Just waiting for the proper business to kick off. Once that's done, I can get on with my own plans."

Thomas waited a few seconds. "Definitely ring me when you need picking up — doesn't matter what time."

In hindsight, that was a funny remark to make, because he'd already told him the details, but like as not Thomas had forgotten, what with the tub of crocodiles he was waist high in. "Anyhow, I'll not keep you — I'll see you tomorrow. If you're a very good boy, I'll bring you back a prezzie."

"A key ring for Miranda might be nice. "

"Alright, I'll see what I can afford."

Thomas laughed then, just as he'd hoped. Jesus, when he thought about the money it had cost — well, cost *Miranda*, actually. He'd make it up to them though, somehow; he'd see to that. Phone call over, Karl went back to his newspaper.

Out of the corner of his eye, he saw the laptop bag stowed under the desk. He'd seen it emptied at Gatwick when they'd dusted the battery for explosives. He wondered what was on the hard drive. He took a deep breath and reined in his imagination. John Wright wouldn't put him at risk — not after everything that went down with Thomas and Miranda.

No, then what about Jack Langton? Langton had humiliated him in front of Francis-Andrew and Martin, painted him as a simpleton lackey and courier. Karl smiled; his conclusions were starting to sound as paranoid as some of Thomas's. True, but when it came to the serpent's nest of the Surveillance Support Unit, Thomas had largely been right.

He took a step closer to the bag, sucking the moisture back from his lips. Three light raps on the door changed his mind. He glanced to the knife and stashed it in his back pocket. "Who is it?" his hand twitched on the doorknob.

"Are you McNeill?" the accent was strong and local.

"Yeah, just give me a minute," he looked around the room. If it was a gunman, what the fuck could he do about it anyway? In no way reassured by the thought, he took off the safety chain, opened the door and stepped back.

The man on the other side of the doorway blinked in the dull hall light. Then he looked left and right along the corridor before taking the first step towards Karl. He didn't look like a killer; matter of fact, he looked even lower-budget material than Karl had been pitched to be. One thing though: he was wearing gloves.

He closed the door behind him. Karl left the TV on, at a level between audible and irritating.

"Where is it, then?"

Twitchy, Karl decided. Maybe this guy was a conscript as well. "It's down there — help yourself."

The stranger knelt down beside the bag and unzipped it. The contents hadn't changed since Karl last saw it, but the guy opened everything very carefully, as if the laptop were fragile. This did not look like a man in the know.

When the deed was done, the guy stood up and wiped his face with the back of his glove; it glistened with sweat. "Did I do everything alright?" his voice wavered.

"Sure, you were fine," Karl assured him, rapidly reassessing the situation and spotting an opportunity. It was only ten to seven. "Do you want to sit down — you look like you're gonna fall down. I could order a couple of drinks up?"

The man licked his lips and took a few more shallow breaths. "Would that be okay? I mean, is that allowed?"

"Sure — whisky?" Karl smiled at him, poor bastard. The man nodded back. "Irish or Scottish?"

The stranger faltered, as if recognising a test. "Whatever you're having."

Karl smiled again and decided to skip the shandy, on this occasion. He played nice on the hotel phone and sat the guy down in a chair. The double whiskies wouldn't be long in coming, but that still left time for conversation.

"This your first job for the business?" Karl felt like he was leaching confidence from the other guy by the second; it was a good feeling.

He didn't reply, but he twitched again.

"Sure, come on. Take your coat and your gloves off, relax a little — you've done your bit." Karl knew the guy would have a delivery to make later, but figured this was probably the hardest part for him.

It was a relief when the drinks arrived — it gave them something to do other than avoid conversation. Now, they could drink *and* avoid conversation. The stranger lifted his glass and snuck a look at his watch.

"We don't have to chat," Karl leaned back casually, catching the TV screen out the corner of his eye. The weather forecast — must be getting on for seven.

The mystery man was still huddled in his chair, only now he was sipping his whisky in rhythmic gulps, like he was in a hurry.

"Hey, don't go rushing on my account!"

He blushed and swallowed. "I, er, have to be somewhere — they'll be expecting me. Besides, you've probably got things to do?"

Karl narrowed his eyes, concentrating hard on not reacting.

By the time Karl closed the door on his visitor, he'd come to a decision. Every instinct was telling him to get out of there; he'd ring John Wright to tell him there'd been a change of plan — but he'd ring him once he was safely touched down at Gatwick. He checked the time — eight minutes past seven. Now was his best chance of getting to the hospital, but what about his bags? Leave them there and maybe they wouldn't be around when he got back. And what if someone was checking the front door, waiting for him?

He peered at the map on the wall and traced the fire escape route out — almost certainly alarmed. He grabbed the duvet and used it to manhandle the laptop into the bag and zip it up. Time to get moving; he'd chance his luck on getting out through the kitchens. If he moved quickly and confidently, by the time anyone stopped him he'd be more likely to get through than be turned back. As he collected his things and opened the door, a gem of an idea occurred to him.

The stairs were always preferable to the lift, more space and free movement in both directions. And easier to turn back if he had to. As he walked down calmly, he concocted the sentences in his head, of how the room service meal had contained a piece of plastic wrapping. And how he wanted to see the chef in private to discuss it, rather than make a scene.

At the bottom of the stairs on the ground floor, he paused and leant round to check the desk. Experience had taught him that it was all about intention and body language. Act as if you're unimportant and people usually treated you accordingly. Not so much invisible as inconsequential.

On the count of four . . . he swung sharp right and kept walking, into the restaurant and up to the double doors at the end.

The maître d' bounded up to him. "Excuse me, sir, I'm afraid that area is out of bounds for customers," followed by a fake and slightly perturbed smile.

Karl put his sports bag down and leaned in towards him. "I'd like a word with the chef about my room service; I thought it'd be better in private rather than out here." He kept his voice steady and low, somewhere between a request and a bollocking.

The maître d' nodded for an instant. "If you'll kindly wait here, sir, I'll go and fetch her."

Karl watched the door swing after him and followed. The three of them all collided on the other side of the door. Karl got in there first and pulled the chef to one side. In the few seconds of meeting her, he surmised that she looked like a decent person — someone who could do with a boost. And besides, she was a brunette.

"Can I have a wee word?" he was all smiles as he let go of her. "I'm a mystery shopper," he revealed, loud enough for the maître d', and anyone ear-wigging, to hear. He squeezed her arm. "I just want to say that my fish and chips was really first rate. Before I make out my little report, would it be asking too much to have a quick tour of the kitchens?"

She flushed and looked to the maître d' who said nothing. "That'd be okay."

Karl turned to him. "And listen, let's not mention this to any of the other staff. Anonymity is paramount in this business."

The maître d' skipped out, grinning like an idiot. Karl stashed his bags in a corner and let the chef show him around. Okay, so he was having her on, but wasn't the joy on her face real? She didn't explain who he was to any of the other staff, and showed him round — good girl. She was maybe in her late twenties, and for no reason at all, he suddenly thought back to the woman in the army test lab: the one who had died.

"I think that'll be fine, thank you," he stopped her abruptly. Maybe it was just the heat and steam, but he could feel the sweat oozing out of him. He drew a twenty from his wallet and handed it to her. And could she let him out the back now, to avoid the reception staff?

The young lad in the car park stamped out his cigarette as Karl emerged. Karl didn't hang around to explain himself; he had an appointment to keep. A cab would have been less aggravation, but also easier to spot. He kept to the backstreets as much as possible and walked at speed.

Chapter 28

Getting into the hospital wasn't difficult. He'd opted for the first point of entry and after that it was a case of finding his way. The searching gave him something to fix his mind upon, something to drive out the only reason for his being there — to say a final goodbye to the only family member he really cared about.

He thought of Thomas, who rarely saw his family, by choice. Strange how the lives of people around us follow parallel trails. As if we instinctively choose friends on the basis of some mysterious fellowship. And that, he told himself softly, was why he shouldn't drink whisky.

He took his time on the final flight of stairs, steeling himself for the inevitable. There was one person at the nurse's station and he was grateful for that. "Excuse me, is it possible to see Mrs McNeill — is, er, anybody with her at the moment?" He tried not to screw his face up at the 'Mrs' part. Despite an unspeakable divorce — and come to that, the rest of the family still might not know about it — she'd never reverted to her family name.

She told him he was in luck, for want of a better term. But, she warned him, Mrs McNeill was very weak and might not be very responsive.

"I'd like a little time with her alone — I've not been able to see her for a while."

She nodded enthusiastically, as if touched by his thoughtfulness. "It's the one from last room, on the left."

Karl walked solemnly through the sickly heat and stale air, forcing a path between the vapour of antiseptic and decay. The closer he came to that fateful door, the more his legs dragged. Until, finally, he was outside, turning the handle.

The light was dimmed and the figure in bed still. It hadn't been that long since he'd seen her face to face — a couple of years at most — and they'd had use of webcams and phone calls in between. Even so, he wasn't prepared for the frail creature before him.

A tiny wail escaped his lips. "Ah, Ma." Before he could say anything further, his eyes had filled up. He put the bags down and approached the bed reverently. The memory of her favourite song rose up like an apparition, and even though his heart began to fracture, he started humming, because he thought she might respond to it.

His mother's eyelid flickered after the first few bars of 'The Party's Over.' Her jaw lowered and her glazed eyes seemed to be trying to focus. He rushed to the side of the bed and held her hand; her skin was parchment.

"Is that you, my brave boy?" she gasped for the words.

The tears came in floods now, echoing back to the phonebox, where she'd told him to build a new life in England, and to make her proud.

He hummed to the end of a verse. "Aye, it's me, Ma."

She squeezed his thumb. "Brave boy," she said, tilting her head towards him slowly, her smile rising gently like a tired moon.

The door catch slowly clicked and a nurse popped her head around the door. "I just need to check on her — I won't be long."

He made as if to get up, but she shook her head and commenced her duties. Her voice was bright and airy, talking directly to his mother in a light, lyrical voice. She looked the epitome of youth. "I don't think I've seen you before?"

He didn't respond.

"Ah, it's lovely for her to have visitors. I gather she doesn't have much family — her son moved abroad, apparently, so her niece was telling me last week."

He turned his face away without answering her and glowered. *Bastards.* Despite years of being away, he could rattle off a list of at least a dozen family members — they couldn't all have moved out of Country Antrim.

When the nurse left, he took a little while to digest his thoughts and surrender to the stillness. There was a peace to be had there in the dulled light — with just the sound of his mother's sighing breaths. He glanced down at her and tenderly laid her palm on top of the sheet. Then he shifted in closer and went back to Tony Bennett, only now he sang the words close to her ear.

A deep smile spread across her face. And although he couldn't hear her, he could see her parched lips moving. He closed his eyes and continued singing to the end, his hand touching hers. And when he opened his eyes again, she was in a deep slumber; for all he knew, it was the final sleep.

"I love you, Ma," he whispered, bending forward to kiss her. It may have been the pressure of him moving, but it felt as if she pushed against his fingers in response. He chose to believe that.

He stayed there in the gloom, saying nothing and seeing little, just feeling her presence. Nothing happened in that time of waiting, except there came a point when he knew it was time to go. He said goodbye for the last time and kissed her again.

"I'm away now, Ma, your brave boy has to go." He stared at her intently, not really sure what he was looking for. Signs, probably, that she wouldn't wake again. Better that than the idea of her thinking, next morning, that she'd only dreamed of him and he'd never made it back. He took a deep sigh; it was over. He'd done what he'd wanted to do and now he'd have to live with the consequences.

He slipped away from her in stages, controlling his movements, so as not to disturb her. He paused at the door, watching the light from the ward reach across the floor to her bed. It always came to this — the parent old and infirm, the child watching helplessly. It was the natural order; only he'd been away for so long that he'd forgotten that.

The bags came out one at the time, his foot propping the door. Then he carefully clicked the door shut behind him and wiped his face again. There was nothing more for him there and everything to lose.

As he passed the other rooms, he saw silhouettes against the blinds, and imagined the relatives preparing for the inevitable — if it was ever really possible to prepare. The same nurse was at the desk. She paused from her paperwork and offered him a consoling smile. He looked away to the door at the far end, and started walking.

As he shouldered the swing door, a shadow approached him: Martin. This was probably it — the long awaited bullet. Well, here on in, he could do his worst.

Martin's hands were in his pocket. He drew them both out together — gloves, but no weapon. "Karl," the word sounded hollow. "I'm sorry about your ma."

He stared him down, didn't reply. Focused instead on not ripping his fucking head off.

Martin sighed. "A lot of water under the bridge, McNeill. Perhaps it's time to lay the past to rest."

Karl squinted at him — was that a glimmer in Martin's eye. He remembered the table knife in his back pocket and wondered how quickly he could plunge it into the bastard. No, he straightened up; he'd be better off getting on that plane and never coming back.

Martin extended his right hand. Karl looked at it, hanging in space like a lifeline. "You should know this, McNeill: Jacqueline never married."

Karl advanced his own hand, but took his time about it. "When you see her, tell her, neither did I."

Their hands met, solid and unyielding, gripping like a death hold. Then the moment passed and Martin withdrew his gauntlet. As he walked away, leaving Karl standing in the middle of the corridor, Karl started walking too, slowly and steadily.

A commotion ahead made him stop in his tracks. Martin looked through the glass of the door, at the uniforms that had filled the frame, then back at Karl.

"McNeill," he snarled, and Karl thought he was reaching for a gun.

But when the door swung in, the uniforms ignored Martin altogether and made a beeline for Karl.

"Karl McNeill? Stay right where you are — Special Branch."

Next thing he knew he was tackled to the wall, sports bag crashing to the floor. Then the laptop bag was manhandled off him, his arms were bent back and he felt the sharp cold of handcuffs against his skin. As they twisted him round, Martin looked on, open-mouthed, then casually made his way out the door.

* * *

For thirty minutes, Karl had sat at the desk, waiting for someone to attend to him. He had been fingerprinted and his hands tested for chemicals, but hardly anyone had said a word. He stared at the wooden floor and replayed the mess in his head, over and over, flexing his hands every now and again as if to dispel the memory of the cuffs.

Martin had looked stunned when it happened; not pleased or satisfied, but shocked. Then again, maybe Francis-Andrew had orchestrated it? Well, whoever it had been, he was really fucked now.

Another face appeared at the window for a matter of seconds and then hastily retreated. He wasn't even sure how it worked anymore — how many hours could they hold him without a solicitor? And what the hell would they charge him with? He closed his eyes and tried to doze, desperate to stop thinking.

The rattle of the doorknob startled him and he sat to attention. There were two of them — both from the sharp-suits-and-short-haircuts brigade. They took seats opposite and slapped a size-zero buff folder on the desk.

"Cup of tea?" the older of the two was Scottish, Glaswegian at a push. He looked to his underling, as if to say, 'Don't get comfortable.'

"Milk and one sugar, please. Any chance of a biscuit?" Humour was always his first line of defence, and right now he needed defending.

The older cop nodded; Junior left the room. "Do you know why you're here?"

He opted for ignorance, in spades. "Nah, I went to hospital to see my mother — she's dying; you can check."

"We already did. But that's not the only reason you're here, is it Karl?"

"How does this work — do I get a phone call?"

"I don't think so, not this time."

He clammed up and tried to play the waiting game. Tea arrived, with a cluster of biscuits on a paper plate. Some of the tea had jumped ship.

"Sorry about that," Junior said, passing it over. "Pre-dunked."

The older guy looked like his face would split if he laughed — with little chance of that happening today.

"Do you like mysteries, Karl?"

He took it as rhetorical and didn't answer.

"Because here's the thing, Karl. I have information that makes no sense at all. There's no record of you entering Northern Ireland — by *legitimate* means — in the last twenty years. Yet here you are today, walking out of a hospital. And you're a floater — Surveillance Support Unit, over in London. But you're also ex-mob, only your file is restricted."

Karl bit at another biscuit. So far, so safe.

"Now, I can live with all of that, but there was residue on your right hand — *chemical* residue. Are you following my drift?"

He tried to subdue the sense of confusion and outrage, half-listening while backtracking in his brain to identify the source of the residue. Taxi? No contact. Hotel and room service? Unlikely. That left the deliveryman in his hotel room . . . or Martin. He nearly cracked a gallows smile; Martin . . . the Judas handshake — bingo, as Thomas would say.

"I take it you've been to my hotel room?"

The Scottish guy smiled, as if to say, 'What do you think?'

A knock at the door interrupted the proceedings. The Scottish guy barked a command as a head poked through.

"The call's come through, sir . . ." the face receded.

The senior officer looked a little crestfallen as he turned to his junior. "He's clean; squeaky clean."

"But what about the residue?" Junior replied and they both looked in Karl's direction.

He coughed self-consciously. What was he going to tell them — keep an eye on prominent local businessmen? He had no proof, beyond gut instinct, process of elimination and a grudge that spanned two decades — a grudge that had now been fed and watered.

"Know what I think, McNeill?" Older cop picked up the file and tapped the edge on the desk, as if straightening the pages. "I think you've been sent here on a job, exploiting your own mother as a cover. And I have to say, I don't like uninvited guests on my patch — do you follow me?"

Karl nodded, out of respect.

"I'm sure you've got some classified need-to-know bollocks to hide behind, but come on, just between the three of us, before they crate you out of here, is there something I ought to know?"

Karl took a sip of tea as they stared at him. "Tell you what, give me your card and I'll get back to you once I'm over the water; seriously."

Scottish bloke's eyes lit up like tallow candles as he passed over a card, face down. Karl smiled back — after all, who doesn't like useful contacts in their line of work?

"What happens now?" Karl figured they were getting near the end.

"Your things will be returned to you and you'll be removed from our soil tonight — someone's flying in to escort you back."

"So," Karl pondered aloud, "as far as anyone else is concerned, I've been arrested and detained. Which means, if anyone finds out otherwise, we'll know where to come." It was clear that the time for talking was over.

* * *

Christine Gerrard was about the last person Karl had expected to see in Belfast.

"Apparently this will ensure you trust me." She handed him a small envelope.

He checked the back, smiled when he saw it was sealed with wax and ripped it open. Inside was a post-it note bearing three letters: KGB. A smile spread across his face: KGB — Kosovo Girl's Brigade. A moniker he'd used once with Thomas when he was trying to gain his trust.

Christine didn't say a lot in the car. Just as well — Karl felt too numb to speak. His ma was ending her days without him. That bastard, Martin, had nearly had him put away, and the way he read it, the only reason he was out now was because Thomas had done God knows what to pull some strings.

The car was heading northwest, out on the A52. He didn't want to say anything, but the Harbour airport was south. Christine seemed relaxed though. His mind wandered back to Stuart Fraser, the older Scottish cop, who'd given him his card. *Bollocks.* He glanced at Christine then reached for his mobile and the card.

"Stuart — it's Karl McNeill. Listen, if you do go to the hospital, please be discreet; none of the family knows I've been here and it's got to stay that way. Sure, uh huh . . . a deal's a deal. Thanks, buddy."

Christine waited until the mobile went down. "We're flying out of Aldergrove, into Brize Norton. I thought it was best, under the circumstances."

It sounded like a loaded statement. Karl tensed up, waiting for a barrage of questions. Not hearing any was worse.

Chapter 29

Thomas paced up and down, outside the Brize Norton arrival doors, toughing it out. At least Karl had been released — Christine had phoned him just before picking Karl up — but that was all he knew. He watched through the glass as the thread of people crossed the barrier

Christine emerged with Karl at her side. Karl appeared shell-shocked and Christine wasn't looking at him at all. The three of them converged and Thomas automatically reached for Karl's bag, as if he'd just been on holiday. He didn't go near the laptop and led the way out to the car.

Christine commandeered the front seat and gave directions, presumably towards a bollocking. No one else spoke. Thomas searched Karl's face via the mirror, as if to read his thoughts. Nothing doing. As the road wore on, a left here and a right there, it became clear that Christine had her own agenda. You didn't get to Bicester along any back roads. As they parked up, he clocked a familiar car on the way in, and decided not to mention it. Christine had obviously planned some sort of summit.

* * *

He let Christine take the lead and fell in line beside Karl. He nudged him, but all lines still appeared to be down. The pub was called The Angel, a bitter reminder of Amy.

Ann Crossley was waiting at a table, four chairs gathered, ready for the feast. He could imagine her guarding them fiercely and whipping out her government ID as last ditch crowd control. She got to her feet, generously offering to get in a round, crisps and all. The rest of them took a chair. It felt like the prelude to a séance. Then he remembered Karl's mum and didn't feel quite so amused.

Christine folded her arms and waited. Karl looked like he was waiting for an explanation as well. Thomas waited for Ann Crossley to return, and tried to think of something credible to say that would satisfy everyone.

"Right," Christine received her glass, "who'd like to tell me what's going on?"

Thomas opened his mouth to bite the bullet, but Ann Crossley clunked her G & T against the table. "Well," she paused, looking in Thomas's direction as if seeking inspiration. "Karl has been visiting his mother on compassionate leave. However, Thomas became aware of a potential threat to him, which could have been connected to the support being given to Major Eldridge . . ."

He nodded emphatically. *Could have been connected — only by a surrealist.*

". . . Thomas took appropriate action and alerted the major. Unfortunately, by then, matters had become somewhat complicated." She stopped talking, as if unwilling to go that final step and tie everything up in a ribbon.

Christine looked to Karl. "Anything to say?"

"No, ma'am," he stared ahead, as if he had something better to do.

"And how about you?" Christine asked Thomas, third time lucky.

He flicked a glance to Ann Crossley in the vain hope that she had some more gems up her sleeve. Turned out she did.

"Did anyone see a sign for the Ladies?"

"I'll show you," Christine pushed against the table dramatically and headed off, Ann trailing in her wake.

Karl let out a deep sigh as they watched their colleagues disappearing. "Well," he turned to Thomas, "I don't reckon much to yours." He moulded a smile, which Thomas reflected like desperate semaphore.

"How was it out there then?"

Karl shifted in his seat. "Like seven shades of terrible. Honest to God, Tommo, you're never really prepared for death. Except maybe your own." He took another weighted breath. "I'll not be back there in the foreseeable future."

Thomas stared at the table. "I should have checked Jack Langton out properly myself first — then I'd have known that he's had business dealings in Belfast for years."

Karl's face tightened. "Imagine if you hadn't intervened. There was me, arrested by Special Branch, with Semtex residue on my hand. Quite a tip-off."

"Yeah," Thomas blushed again, "Thing is, Special Branch were already watching you. They knew you were coming before you landed. As soon as I'd filled in the blanks about Jack Langton, I went to Major Eldridge and he pulled some favours in."

Karl raised his glass. "Well, that explains the look of shock on Martin's face. He probably thought I was setting *him* up. I'm very grateful to you, Tommo. I reckon Martin had someone waiting for me at Gatwick." He nodded and they both took a gulp of amber liquid. "Hey, heads up, Mr Bladen, here come our dates again. Remember, don't be too forward."

Thomas was still laughing as the women sat down. The frostiness between Christine and Ann Crossley had lifted; he reckoned they'd had a private team talk. He pondered the wider ramifications as Karl grazed on the crisps. Then he came to a decision: these people were supposed to be allies. "Anyone got a piece of paper?"

Karl obliged. Thomas took out his trusty pen and drew three separate circles. Everything could be reduced to a diagram — he'd read that somewhere. He labelled the three rings: Army Base, Engamel and Secrets, and prepared for a deep dive.

A mobile trilled into life. "Mine," Karl confessed, reaching into his jacket. He turned to one side, but didn't leave the table. "Yeah? Ah, Fraser, good man — how d'ya get on?" There was a pause; Karl sat deathly still. I see, thank you for telling me. Okay, I'll speak to you tomorrow about the residue. No, it's fine. The family will make all the arrangements — I was never there today."

Thomas felt the blood draining from his face. Karl cut the phone and carefully placed it back inside his jacket. "As you've probably surmised, my mother died a short while ago."

Christine reached over and touched Karl's hand; he tolerated it. "I think I'd like to go now, Tommo, if you wouldn't mind?"

"Sure." He looked to Christine, who muttered something about getting a lift back with Ann.

* * *

"You don't have to baby-sit me; I'll be fine . . ."

"I know," Thomas pulled into the supermarket car park. "But I'd prefer it this way — think of it as Yorkshire hospitality."

"Suit yourself. In that case, grab something you like drinking, while you're in there. I think we need to get royally hammered tonight."

That was the thing about Karl; because everything seemed like a joke to him, you never really knew when he was being serious. So

Thomas grabbed a bottle of Southern Comfort, along with some food, just to be on the safe side.

* * *

Back at the flat, Karl kicked off his shoes and wiggled his toes. "What do we know, then, Tommo?"

He refilled their glasses — a small measure, following several previous large ones. Karl shifted forward and hunched over the same three-circled page, gazing at details they'd added between them.

"So, the major's willing to make a deal with Michael Schaefer? You do know what he is?"

Thomas grinned, enjoying the sensation of heat stampeding across his face. Oh yeah, he knew what Schaefer was all right.

"Project Director, my man. Research projects . . ."

Thomas pressed his eyebrows in, concentrating to think. "The Scavenger — UB40, or whatever you want to call it — that's probably one of *his* then." He took another sip of Southern Comfort and rolled the sweet goodness around in his mouth, pressing his lips together as it slid down. "Do you think Jess really has all that data stashed in her head?"

Karl waved his glass to and fro, like a conductor's baton. "It's not unheard of. From what you said, she's a bit of a mimic, so why not figures as well? She's also a conniving minx if she's destroyed the original records."

Two hours down the line and all the drink was gone, along with most of Thomas's deductive reasoning. He lay back in the armchair, lolling his head to one side to hear Karl better.

". . . I'll not let it go; I'm telling you that. But I'm not stupid, oh no; I'll not go see Jack Langton all guns blazing." He grinned for a moment and then his face hardened. "I'll sort him out, good and proper, that's a promise. And then I'll sort out Martin and Francis-Andrew — I've nothing to lose now."

Chapter 30

The last thing Thomas remembered was Karl swearing vengeance like some Mafia Don. Only, where Karl was concerned, he knew it wasn't just a drink-fuelled rant. It worried him so much that it almost distracted from the killer hangover.

As he sprinkled the painkillers out on his hand and winced as the water gurgled into a glass, he realised that he'd slept right through till morning. No nightmares, no early morning wake-ups. Although it had been a *drunk* sleep, which was a contradiction in itself.

He stumbled out of the bathroom, praying for the paracetamol to kick in. Karl was still dead to the world on the sofa. It was seven thirty and there was only one thing to do: real coffee, hot and strong. On the way through, he grabbed the piece of paper that had made so much sense the previous night. Most of it was just scrawl, but one question — written down early — stood out: Why had Amy tested the mixed ammunition alone? He nodded to the page — good point — and eased his head back up again.

Karl surfaced just as the coffee mug landed on the table. He rolled over, tried to uncrumple his face and stretched an arm beyond the duvet. "You know, I can't even send flowers; not unless one of the family informs me about the funeral in time." It was as if Karl had kept the conversation from the previous night on pause.

"Do they have your address?"

"Not exactly," he craned the coffee in, took a gulp and then returned for the two tablets waiting on the table. "They have a PO box number."

Thomas stared at him: You're kidding? But Karl clearly wasn't.

"What's on the agenda today then, Mr Bladen?"

Thomas teetered on a bow wave of incredulity.

"What do you expect me to do — sit at home? I've been in mourning for twenty years, Tommo. And there'll be time enough for that again in the future. Now, where are my trousers?"

That sounded like an opportune moment to leave him to it and hit the shower.

* * *

Karl gazed around as Thomas pulled into a parking space. "I used to share a flat not far from here."

Thomas recognised the familiar memory-lane theme tune and said nothing.

"On the other side of Euston Road, mind; quite bohemian it was. The neighbour had this big, beige Persian cat — it never went outside; used to sleep in her bedroom." He smiled; a hook line for Thomas to clamber on board.

"Would you like to be alone with your memories?"

Karl opened the door. "No thanks. What I want to do today is break some eggs — are you with me? Listen, if we hurry, we might even snaggle some breakfast in the hotel — we could try charging it to Jess's room."

Thomas's stomach twitched in sympathy; the coffee was definitely wearing off. "Let me do the talking, okay?"

The glass doors slid back silently; the reception staff didn't react. Thomas left Karl at the sofa and ambled over to the desk.

"Hi there," he got the greeting in first. "Can you call Room 635? Thanks."

"What name please?" The last of the caffeine percolated through his brain. "Jess . . . Sanders." Fingers crossed she hadn't gone in under an assumed name. He looked over his shoulder; Karl had buried himself in a complimentary newspaper.

"I'm sorry, sir. Miss Sanders checked out early this morning."

Thomas blinked slowly, taking it in. He kept it together, nodded his thanks and walked back to Karl. "She's gone," he flopped down beside him. "Any suggestions?"

"Yeah, first we see if the restaurant will serve us and then we'll check Jess's room out."

Two teas and muffins later, they were riding the lift, Karl pretending to tap along to Beethoven on a synthesiser.

"What are we looking for?" Thomas watched the light flickering through the floors.

"Dunno, Tommo. But a fiver says we find a pair of shoes." He started whistling, proving that there was something even worse than synthesised Beethoven. The flute strangling continued as they exited the lift, but the tune changed — something folky. Karl led on past Room 635 — closed — and along the corridor. As they spied a gaggle of cleaners at the far end, Karl stepped up the pace.

"Excuse me, please, I need to get into Room 635."

At least, that's what Thomas assumed he was saying, in a language he surmised was Eastern European. His brain made the link with Yorgi and the corridor seemed to become narrower. He breathed rhythmically through his nose, standing his ground against the past, and hoped Karl would stop gabbling.

One cleaner, who was strikingly beautiful, began to follow Karl as he walked back to the room. Thomas decided that two men going with a woman on her own was a bit suspect, so he stayed put and tried to smile. The other two women began a private conversation, undeterred by his gooseberry act. *Come on Karl, shift your arse.*

"Tommo!" Karl called melodically behind him. The cleaners broke off conversation and started laughing.

As he turned, he saw Karl waving a pair of shoes, as if he were playing hunt the bride. Thomas passed the cleaner and saw the very top of a rolled banknote, crushed in her hand.

"Right then, that's us outta here. And you owe me a fiver."

* * *

"Next?" Thomas unlocked the car.

"Tell you what, why don't I meet you at the office — I'll get the tube. I need to ring my new friend in Special Branch."

Thomas watched him go and took out the piece of paper they'd scribbled on. The question about Amy had been pretty damn important the night before, but now he couldn't quite figure out why. Time to make a call of his own.

Miranda only picked up on the fourth ring: never a good sign. His brain had already started doing somersaults. Was she with someone, was Jack Langton nearby — the usual mixture of paranoia and confusion.

"I enjoyed your text last night. Touchingly romantic, but piss-poor spelling — were you drunk by any chance?"

Shit. So drunk that he didn't even remember sending it. "Er, yeah, sorry about that. Karl stayed over and . . . you know. Didn't I ring you earlier?"

"Uh-huh. How is he taking it?"

He took a big breath. "Well, he seems okay, but I know him better than that. And he's determined to settle some scores." He stopped there.

"Anyway," she sounded particularly chipper. "I'm glad you rang, especially after last night's text proposal. Because there's something I need to say to you."

What?

"Your *thing* is still here, in my safe; I want it out of here today."

He pulled into traffic; it was like floating, nudging along with the other bubbles, drifting up Euston Road and beyond. That part of him that always seemed to be thinking, and assessing, went to work on the major and all the other players. A spiral of conflicting ideas turned slowly in his head, all centred on Amy. Somehow, if he could understand why she died, he could impose some sort of order. Euston Road gave way to Pentonville Road, but it didn't come with any answers.

It was like photography; change the lens or the filter and the same composition looked completely different. It evoked a different response from the viewer. Well, he was the one viewing this now — so what was he looking at? Where could Jess have gone? She must have been somewhere on the base, else why would the major have needed to get her out? Could she and the major have been seeing each other after all? He tried it on for size; it didn't fit. Nah, nothing in the major's behaviour so far supported that. His best hope was confronting Jess in front of the major.

* * *

When Karl put in an appearance in the office, Thomas was still puzzling. Ann Crossley looked over at the door, acknowledged him and then went back to her work — whatever actually was right now. On balance, Thomas preferred it when the two of them were at loggerheads; this new entente cordiale was doing his head in.

Karl made a beeline for him and patted him on the shoulder. "I need another favour — not right now, but in the next week or so."

"Fire away."

"Funny you should say that. I need visual surveillance on Jack Langton. All photos with cross-hairs superimposed. At home, family, business — the full package. Think you can handle that? I'll pay you . . ."

Thomas gazed into his eyes. "I can handle it. You can fill me in at the club, later this week."

Karl sat down and started dialling. "Major Eldridge, it's Karl McNeill here. I take it Jess is with you? Yeah, I know. I'm fine, thank you." He kept everything matter-of-fact. "I agree — where? Just like old times then; we'll see you both at noon."

Thomas watched from the vending machine, straining to pick up the gist as he navigated through the selection options. When he'd collected a third 'delicious' beverage — for Ann Crossley — he manhandled them back, detouring by her first. Karl rose up from his desk.

"Better drink that quick, we're heading out."

* * *

"Is this for real?" Thomas took a step back and tilted his head. Karl looked right at home, standing between the twin guns at the top of the steps that led into the Imperial War Museum.

"It's worse than you think, Tommo. This is the site of Bethlem Hospital — the original Bedlam. The major and I used to meet here, in the old days."

It didn't sound like an invitation to further discussion. "And what's today's objective?"

"Find out what the hell is going on, that's what." Karl clutched a carrier bag in one fist, raising it aloft as if it held week-old fish. "The shoes were left behind because someone didn't want us to know where she'd been this morning. A simple sweep would have picked up the bug in her heel."

"Well, it's twelve o'clock so where are they?"

Karl turned to the great doors, from where the major emerged, Jess close at hand. Her face lit up at the sight of Thomas; a sentiment he didn't share. Karl waited for the happy couple and led the party of four away, to the Peace Gardens next door.

"I never had you pegged as a man of peace, Karl." the major looked decidedly uncomfortable among the white pillars and stones.

Karl seemed lost for an answer, so Thomas obliged him. "From the very beginning, *you* came to *us*, both of you. And since then you've told us everything except the truth." He looked directly at the major.

The major seemed unfazed. "Are we all square, Karl?"

"Yeah," he held out the carrier bag. "Electronics deactivated and removed."

Jess made a grab for the shoes and scowled at the major.

"Now, Thomas here has some questions for Jess. It'd be easier for everyone if we could just get on with it."

Jess gazed at Thomas earnestly and then took a step towards him.

"Where were you when Amy died?"

She stopped in her tracks. Everyone froze on the spot, but Thomas caught the signal that the major threw her way, even if he didn't understand it.

"I was outside." Jess spoke quietly. "We had a visitor."

The major turned to her slowly; clearly, this was all news to him.

"Mr Schaefer came to see me; it was my lunch break."

But not Amy's? "Go on. What else?"

"He's always been very interested in us; we were trying to finish all the tests ahead of schedule. Mr Schaefer promised us a bonus if we completed the full spectrum of scenarios early."

"And how would you do that?" the major's veins had come out on parade.

"We worked it out between us," she sounded proud of her own intelligence. "Coming in early and finishing late, splitting our lunches."

Major Eldridge stared, rigid with malice. If he'd been carrying a gun, Thomas reckoned he'd have shot her. "How much?" He hissed.

"Five thousand pounds each." Jess seemed bemused. "Amy said we could go away on a cruise together."

Thomas stared. She couldn't help putting herself in the middle of the picture. Amy was dead, but Jess was still painting herself as the orphan. He gravitated towards one of the pillars, aware that Karl wasn't far behind him; it was starting to feel like a business negotiation. "All this for five grand?" The knot was coiling in his abdomen.

"You don't get it, do you, Tommo? Schaefer was willing to take shortcuts, to risk lives for five grand apiece. But that's not the half of it; we've more digging to do."

Jess and the major were right where they'd left them, not talking to each other. Thomas wondered how the major was taking the knowledge that his mistress had been sacrificed on the altar of expediency. "What's Schaefer giving you for the data you stole?" Simple, blunt, unambiguous.

"No." Jess screwed her face up into a ball. "I never stole anything. Mr Schaefer asked me to memorise the data; it was one of my extra jobs, right from the beginning. Sometimes he'd visit and quiz me to check — it was our little game."

Thomas looked at Karl, who shrugged off control of the conversation. He tried again. "So what's in it for you now?"

"Mr Schaefer's promised to take me away." She smirked. "Don't worry, not romantically, silly! He's offering me a new job in America — a fresh start. Mr Schaefer says that there are opportunities with other consortium partners."

Yeah, Thomas thought, and Mr Schaefer's a scumbag who . . . He stopped, mid-thought, and stared at the stark, white pillars of marble. Bingo. Jess was a rare talent; Schaefer could move her around like a human memory stick. The clever bastard. And of course, once she was in the US, she'd be out of the picture. "When are you next seeing Schaefer, Major?"

Major Eldridge answered. "Tonight, to confirm the arrangements. Once Jess is safely through passport control, I'll hand over both copies of the DVD. Karl — I'll need yours back."

Thomas took a breath; surely the major realised that Jess's departure would cast suspicion on him? Or maybe a cover-up was better than everything coming out in the open. Yeah, that would make sense: a mutual cover-up.

Chapter 31

Getting Jack Langton's details from the Wrights wouldn't have been difficult — one phone call, basically. But better they were kept in the dark. Miranda too, come to that. This was a private job for Karl and it would have to stay that way. It was hard to remain hidden these days. What with the Internet and private investigators. Thomas had once fancied himself as a private dick — part Sherlock Holmes and part Masked Avenger. Back when his career at the SSU looked to be coming to a premature end, he'd seriously considered it. *Note to self: be careful what you wish for.*

The office in Dalston was a portal into a murky world. From the outside, it could have been a minicab outfit; tinted windows with gig posters plastered over them like camouflage. It looked the kind of place you check your shoes on the way out — and your pockets.

He went inside and took a seat, waiting for the woman across the desk to stop glaring at him.

"'Ave you got an appointment?" she dared him to reply, opening her desk diary to confirm the obvious.

"No. I was just passing." Like anyone ever sees a private investigator on the off chance.

"Wait here," she flicked her hair extensions over her shoulders and went to a door at the back.

Peter Tosh was crackling through the radio, pulsing the speakers: 'Coming in Hot.' Thomas felt himself nodding to the rhythm, thinking about Ajit and simpler times. Then he went all self-conscious, wondered how he'd look to the receptionist, like some twatty, inverted racist, *white* guy, thinking he was all 'street.' It didn't spoil the music any.

Hair Girl still had her head poked through the open doorway, playing mutter-tennis with whoever ran Lyon Investigations. She glanced back, checking him out, finished her conversation and then swaggered back to her desk. "Boss says you can go in."

Nice. He walked stiffly past her, rapped on the open door and went in, closing it behind him. "Thurston Lyon?"

The West Indian guy laughed, as if he'd just thought of a howler. "That's what it says on my door. You here to do business?"

Thomas took out a printed page and passed it across.

Thurston looked at it carefully, turning it over, but finding the other side blank. "He owe you money?"

"Something like that. I need his home address and phone number, same for business, car registration and which pubs he drinks at in Hackney and Clapton."

"And then what?" Thurston straightened, the scent of money in the air.

"That's my employer's business." Like Karl had told him, the less he said, the more convincing he'd appear.

Thurston sucked at his teeth. "Is he some kind of gangsta?"

Thomas held his poker face. "The worst kind."

Thurston Lyon laughed again. "In dat case, I need to apply an extra charge — for health and safety."

"When and how much?" Thomas cut to the chase.

Thurston's eyes danced left and right. "Give me two days."

"I need it by this time tomorrow — I'll call you."

"The price just went up," he raised three fingers.

Thomas took £100 from his jacket and flattened it on the table. "I'll speak to you tomorrow. If this works out, my employer could put more work your way." He paused, like Karl had told him to, and then promised that Martin — using his full name — could be a very generous client.

Thurston's eyes flickered, but, as far as Thomas could determine, it wasn't a name the private detective recognised.

Thomas left it at that and walked out, leaving the door yawning behind him. As he reached the street, he glanced back to see Hair Girl scurrying into the office. They looked like they could do with the business.

On the way back to the car, he made a call. "It's done."

"Nice one, Tommo. By the way, Christine's trying to reach you. Our glorious leader requests the pleasure of your company at Whitehall. I'll see you in the park afterwards."

* * *

451

Thomas supposed he should have got used to the cat's cradle of allegiances by now, but it still rankled. He worked for Christine, and Christine worked for Sir Peter Carroll. But Karl — who worked with him, for Christine — also pulled Sir Peter's strings. Then there was Michael Schaefer, working for Engamel and spying on Major Eldridge, with Sir Peter's consent. And finally there *he* was: everybody's best friend. Well, maybe not Schaefer's — Thomas hadn't heard from him since Amy's memorial service.

Once again, they kept him waiting in the lobby at Main Building. He thought about taking out his diagram to try and decipher it and decided against it, in case the CCTV took an interest.

And what if he *had* proposed to Miranda by text? Still possible she was kidding, but he might have sent it and then deleted it somehow. If he'd proposed, would that really be so bad? Ajit and Geena were happily settled in their semi, awaiting their firstborn.

Then he remembered his last proper conversation with Miranda; the one where she told him to remove his gun from the premises. No, Ajit was definitely a happy endings sort of bloke. He used to feel the same way about himself, but lately he saw only shadows.

He managed to solve three clues from the *Times* crossword in the ten minutes it took someone to collect him, and he reckoned one of those was probably wrong. The silent treatment in the lift didn't faze him anymore; it was just another facet of the *not-so-great* game. On the way up, he tried to concoct a progress report for Sir Peter; no doubt one was expected.

"Thomas, take a seat." The Old Man continued with his paperwork.

From Thomas's vantage point, it looked like a report of some kind. *Don't bite; don't give him the reaction he wants.* He gazed around the office, settling on the portrait of Churchill — arch defender of Great Britain. And, if you believed the Net, an early proponent of a United States of Europe, and patron saint of federal nutcases.

"Michael Schaefer has concerns about your loyalty." Sir Peter's head was still down.

It speaks. He ran a thumbnail between his teeth, as if sharpening a talon. "Schaefer wants to take Jess out of the country, before the inquiry is complete."

Sir Peter glanced up; he didn't look at all surprised. "Karl McNeill is a loose cannon, Thomas. You'd be wise to keep your distance, especially when he creates problems for himself — and for the department. This is still my organisation and you'd both do well to remember that. This is not a sport for solo players."

That riled him, as it was supposed to. "Why did you send for me?"

"I think you ought to know certain things; things other people aren't telling you."

"Like Schaefer risking lives to rush through the Scavenger tests?"

Sir Peter snorted. "That's old news, Thomas, and such a worm's eye view. I'm disappointed. I thought you were smarter than that by now."

Thomas tilted his hands open, inviting all the goodies into his lap.

"There's much more at stake than a revolutionary weapon." Sir Peter shook his head slowly, side to side. "You're being used, Thomas. It wasn't a coincidence that you and McNeill were on the base — *he* arranged it with me." And there was that look again, the one that implied, I'm always ten steps ahead of you.

Thomas stared him down. His father used to have a similar look whenever they played chess; right up until the day Thomas checkmated him. Then they never played again. He narrowed his eyes. "Say you're right — so what? Isn't it better that the reasons behind Amy's death are out in the open?"

"Do you really think a fully-funded military research programme will grind to a halt because of a project director's inability to control one of his staff? Open your eyes, Thomas!"

One by one, the pieces slid together. It didn't really matter who carried the can — Amy, the major or Schaefer. The wheels of industry would continue turning, regardless. The great and the good would have their new toy.

What he couldn't figure out, from this sitting at least, was which side of the line Sir Peter stood. Time to find out. "You could stop Jess leaving the country — revoke her passport or something?"

"Could I now?" Sir Peter puffed himself up and squeezed his fingers together, daring Thomas to figure it out.

Oh Jesus. His jaw widened. "Unless you're one of the people who wants Jess out of here."

Sir Peter smiled, like a vulture witnessing a car crash. "Congratulations, Thomas; you're finally starting to see things as they are. I'd no more want to impede Jess than I'd have wanted to stop Karl McNeill at Aldergrove."

Thomas swallowed, and Sir Peter's eyes took on a hypnotic gaze.

"Schaefer is a liability. McNeill realises that; it's time you did as well."

He couldn't tell if that was supposed to be a statement or a warning.

Sir Peter folded the file cover down. It looked suspiciously like the one that Major Eldridge had shown him on the base. "We're all parts of one organism, Mr Bladen — symbiotically interlinked for the good of the whole. And what's true for people and organisations can also be true for nations. You do see that now, don't you?" This was starting to sound like a recruitment speech.

"Was there anything else, sir?"

"That will be all. Take care, Thomas. For all our differences in the past, I wouldn't like to see you come to any harm."

He made his way outside, switching his mobile on in the lift. He picked up a message at the door, from Michael Schaefer. And he didn't believe in the Coincidence Fairy today.

* * *

Karl was ready and waiting in St James's Park, sat on their usual bench and toying with a domestic camera. "You look like a man with something to say." He pulled a muffin from a bag at his side.

Thomas received the bounty and slowly rotated it. "Have you ever lied to me?"

"Never," Karl was abrupt. "I may evade the question and hold things back, but there'd be no point deliberately lying to you. What's on your mind?"

He parked the use of *deliberately* and picked at the muffin, pulling off the chocolate chunks first, like a child. "Our leader reckons you arranged the photography gig at the arms fair." He stalled, waiting to be proved wrong.

"It's true."

Thomas cursed under his breath. "And the reason is . . ." He left a gap a mile wide.

"Quite simply, I was hoping to have a nosey — see if there was anyone there that I recognised from files."

He'd whittled away most of the chunks. "And I'm s'posed to believe you?"

Karl grabbed a muffin for himself. "You can believe what you like, Tommo. It happens to be the truth."

Truth. He'd started to wonder if anything was true anymore. "Coincidence, then, that your former Major was on the base as well?"

"No, no. I knew that in advance. I expected to make contact with him in the afternoon; as we discovered, he knew we were on site. And then of course, there was Amy." Silence followed. "Look, I promise you this, I would only keep something from you if I thought it was in the long-term interest."

"So you won't mind telling me while I dragged my arse over to Dalston, using a second-rate private eye to get information I could have found out myself?"

"Hey, hey, there's nothing second-rate about Thurston Lyon. He's good at what he does, and if anything goes wrong, he's one step removed. It's a sensible false trail, should we need it. You did remember to give him Martin's full name? You might want to mention it again when you collect the info tomorrow."

"Yeah, well," Thomas shrugged his shoulders, "if he's up to it."

"Not a worry there; Thurston's like a Mountie — he always gets his man."

"So you've worked with him before?" He figured he'd push it.

"Well," Karl took a muffin-sized bite, leaving a thin crescent; "After a fashion. I've not met him personally — I always use a go-between, someone I can trust."

"What? Someone like me?"

"Jesus, make your fucking mind up, Tommo. You want to get involved — but not *too* involved. *And* you want a private life, away from all the cloak-and-daggering. So I keep you at the edges, for your good as well as mine. Now, are we done playing Q & A? I need a sandwich — I'm all sugared out."

Chapter 32

The neon sign for Caliban's shone out, defying the rain that spattered against the roof and overflowed the guttering. Thomas straightened his coat and wondered what sort of reception awaited him.

The bar was packed, but Sheryl's neck craned up as he eased the door inward. She nodded; he went straight over.

"Miranda around?"

"Go straight up, honey." She had a talent for saying one thing and letting her face tell a completely different story.

As he turned from the bar, a camera flash went off. He flinched, started chambering a fist.

"Relax, they're just tourists — Germans, I think, or Polish."

It looked like a full crowd. And it didn't take Brain of Britain to realise it was Sheryl they were taking pictures of. And she was milking it like a Little Dutch Girl.

The door upstairs was closed; he tried the handle — locked. It felt stupid announcing himself, but he did anyway. Miranda was slow in answering, as if she had something better to do.

She cranked the door open about a foot. "Romeo, Romeo, wherefore art thou, Romeo?" That was far as she managed without laughing.

And yet, when he saw her standing there, laughter cascading through the air like poetry, he almost wished he *had* proposed again, properly. But he knew that those little moments of magic were only that: moments.

"You feel like a nibble?"

He blushed. God, he was useless at playing it cool. The first time he met her, when she was seventeen, he'd broken out in a sweat.

And he'd never really recovered since. "Sorry, I've got a meeting with Karl and Jess." Then, to pre-empt whatever caustic remark she was cooking up, he added, "She's being sent abroad."

"What, like an endangered species? Come on, coffee's hot — if you've got the time." She sounded just a little hesitant and he loved her for that.

"Yeah, always time for coffee," he followed her through.

First thing she did was open the safe and return the Makarov pistol to him. It nestled in his palm, cool against his clammy skin. They spoke a little about Karl as they drank their coffee. Miranda wanted to be certain that Karl understood she and her family had known nothing about Jack Langton's overseas business.

"Please give him our condolences and tell him I was asking after him. It wouldn't hurt you to bring him here for an evening."

He smiled; how times had changed — a few months back, Karl had been banned from the premises and now she was sending out invitations.

"And you can relax, about last night. It's okay, babe, I knew you were pissed — you called me Randa. You only ever do that when you're drunk."

He nodded, and reminded himself to remember that.

"And just so you don't go torturing yourself, it was a nice text . . ."

He kissed her, the polite kind — a supreme act of self-control.

"Anyway, I think you're already married — to your job."

The weight of the Makarov, inside his jacket, tended to support that.

* * *

He had hoped to meet Karl beforehand, but he was already running late. Couldn't very well leave Caliban's without spending a little quality time with Miranda. So by the time he arrived at the restaurant — that *same* restaurant near Leicester Square — and scoped them from across the street, the party looked to be in full swing. He caught the Engamel trio through the bay window; saw that Deborah and Clarity had dressed a little more demurely this time. A little, but not much. Schaefer looked to be in for a busy night; there didn't seem to be an American word for *subtle*.

Karl was there too, holding court, palling up with Michael Schaefer. It was all like some garishly detailed Hogarth drawing. Jess was at one end of the table; she looked lost, out of her depth. Until she spotted him, that was. She waved enthusiastically as he approached, which left him little option but to go inside.

A single seat awaited him, next to Jess. No sign of the major. As Thomas sat down, Karl broke off from his captivating monologue. "Major Eldridge won't be joining us, he has some domestic crisis."

"Got that right!" Schaefer laughed into his beer.

By the look on Schaefer's face and the one he gave Deborah, it reeked of a stitch-up. Thomas didn't bother commenting. Schaefer was a little cool with him at first, skimming over the misunderstanding at the memorial service and 'that feisty blonde.' Miranda would have gotten a kick out of that.

He kept his cool and let Schaefer's mouth run its course. From the looks of things, Karl had dug himself in, good and proper. It wasn't worth spoiling the mood unless there was something to gain.

Jess seemed happy to split from the main party, free to talk about her favourite subject: herself. Specifically, her new life in America. "Of course, you'll be able to visit me once I've settled into my new job. Isn't that right, Mr Schaefer?"

Schaefer lifted his head, and with some prompting from Deborah, muttered: "Sure thing, honey — whatever you say." Then whispered something to his gang that produced a peal of laughter.

Jess carried on, oblivious. "I was sorry that things never worked out with Cecil, but sometimes it's for the best. Don't you agree?"

Thomas chased his starter around the plate and just nodded. He wasn't practised at listening to two conversations simultaneously — if you could call Jess's 'let's talk about me' monologue a conversation — but Schaefer and les femmes were doing their damnedest to suck Karl into their comfort zone. He just hoped Karl could see that as well. They locked eyes, for a second, and Karl winked at him over his glass.

The main course signalled a change in the proceedings, with Schaefer taking centre stage and praising Jess's gift. "You're a special little lady and we're lucky to have you."

Clarity and Deborah formed an applause section, with Karl joining in off the back of them. And though Schaefer and Karl were still doing some kind of 'men of the world' routine, with Deborah flirting with both of them, Clarity seemed to have slipped through the gaps. She smiled softly and Thomas studied her face, trying to reason out what she was doing with these people.

Jess had moved on to outlining her holiday plans, once she was States-side. Schaefer had fed her a complete travelogue, everything from New England in the fall to Christmas in Oregon and all points in between. In essence, he'd sold a tourist's fairy tale to a fantasist, which had a certain justice to it.

Thomas took to whispering with Jess: conspiring, to be more accurate. She loved it, of course, pulling him in close so that her hot breath landed on his face. And that perfume, if he wasn't mistaken, was the same floating scent that had haunted the accident scene like a wraith — probably something else she'd taken from Amy.

"I really thought Cecil would be here tonight — I know he wanted to be," he tried his luck at the wishing well.

Jess leaned in again. "Mr Schaefer thought it was best if he stayed away, in case it upset him. What with Amy and I being so close, and this being my last day and everything." There was a slight twang to her voice, faux American, as if she were already morphing into her new identity.

He let it pass. "So you're flying tomorrow?" It never hurt to check the facts.

"Of course, silly," she squeezed his arm, feeling his bicep. "And you're coming to see me off at the airport."

"I am?" No one had mentioned seeing her off the premises.

She seemed flummoxed for a moment, as if the house of cards was wobbling. She drew her hands back. "Anyway," she smarted, "it's all arranged, so you have to be there."

Right that minute, he could have taken out the Makarov and shot Schaefer with a clear conscience. Jess might be deluded — and there was little doubt of that on tonight's performance — but Schaefer was vermin.

Jess made another play for his arm. "You will be there?" she pouted.

"Wouldn't miss it for the world," he patted her hand, aware that Clarity was taking an interest in them now. "About your memory trick . . ."

Jess cut in straightaway. "It's not a trick," she bustled, affronted. "It's a *gift*."

"Sorry, my mistake." He poured more wine for her. "I think it's fascinating. I mean, how long can you retain things for? I bet you have trouble keeping it all in."

She beamed. "It's all quite logical, really. Anyone can learn it to an extent, but I'm a *natural*." Again, that last word was mangled into a mid-Atlantic drawl — genuine shudder fodder. "I store a picture in my head and revisit it periodically. The key is to frame the image in detail and keep it fresh. I write it out from scratch a few days later and compare it with the original — I've never achieved less than one hundred per cent."

"Are you sure you wouldn't struggle to recall some things, a little bit?" he tapped the words out on her hand.

"I would not!" she grinned, sloshing wine on the tablecloth as she flattened out a napkin. "I'll prove it to you."

He laughed, just happening to have a pen to hand, and leaned across to block other people's view. Her eyes looked up, to the left, at some faraway place. Then she started to write with remarkable speed, small neat columns of data, adding the row and column headings afterwards. It didn't take long.

"There," she said breathlessly.

Then, as he stared at her, open mouthed, she moved in and kissed him. As her tongue explored his mouth, he sat as rigid as a virgin on her wedding night, one hand clawing at the napkin to drag it under the table.

Schaefer banged on the table. "Hey, Tommy, there's people here, okay?"

Jess disengaged. He didn't have to fake the embarrassment; it was there in spades as he suffered the scathing laughter from the other end of the table. Clarity wasn't laughing though; she stared intensely, as if she were taking everything in — the seen and the unseen.

"You do like me, don't you, Tommy?" Jess pressed against him and he shifted round to make sure the gun stayed on his blind side.

"I'd like you even more if you could remember all those figures; it would really help me in *my* job."

"Well, alright," she whispered huskily, "if you promise to wave me goodbye at Heathrow." She nodded as if she'd just agreed something with herself. "I'm going to contact Amy's family once I get my new apartment. I think they'll be glad to know that Amy had a good friend over here."

He held his hands still, fighting the urge to slap her.

"And maybe, when they've got to know me, they'll invite me to stay with them for a while."

Oh Jesus. She really was up there in her ivory tower, unable to make sense of the world below.

"I need the gents," he declared, like a plea bargain, and stood up.

"I'll join yer, Tommo." Karl looked over. "If you'll excuse me, ladies."

They giggled on cue. Schaefer remained with his harem.

"When do we get to leave?" Thomas headed straight for the stalls.

Karl broke wind, muttered something about 'better out than in', and unzipped at the urinal. "It won't be much longer. Dessert, coffee — forty-five minutes, max," he spoke over his shoulder.

"I feel like a bloody escort service." Thomas finished up and yanked the chain.

"You looked like an escort!" Karl joined him at the sinks. "Now, let's get back in there and be on our way."

* * *

460

Jess had insisted he walk her up to her room and everyone else had colluded. It felt like Karl was pimping him out.

She took his arm as they left the restaurant, allowing him to steer her to her hotel. She was past tipsy, but not bladdered. The delicate state where Miranda would normally be unguarded and adventurous — not something he wanted to think about while in Jess's company.

"Would you like to pop in for a nightcap?" If she was aiming for seduction, she'd overshot the target by about a mile.

"I'd better not. I still have things to do before tomorrow."

She threw her arms around him again and made a clumsy lip lunge. This time he was ready and turned his cheek. "Good night then."

Downstairs, the Engamel team were waiting along with Karl. Schaefer checked his watch as Thomas arrived. "Well, Tommy, you're either a fast worker or you struck out." More laughter.

Karl kicked off a round of goodbyes and then the two of them made their escape. When Thomas turned to make a final farewell, he noticed Clarity's guarded wave. At this rate he'd be needing a minibus for the fan club.

"How'd you get on?" Thomas clung to the door handle of the taxi as it performed centrifugal-force experiments on Shaftesbury Avenue.

Karl leaned forward and checked that the secrecy button was on. "Schaefer's got Major Eldridge in his sights as the fall guy. And without all the missing data, it doesn't look good for him."

"I don't get it though — the major's not part of Engamel or the research, is he?"

"Whatever the official line is, take it from me, he's involved."

Thomas shook his head to try and clear it. "Hold on, then, so is Eldridge friend or foe?"

"Nah." Karl replied. "It doesn't work like that, unfortunately. But I happen to know that the major wants the data, to prove that the Scavenger wasn't ready for the advanced tests."

"Ergo: Schaefer is in some way responsible for Amy's death." That should have been a conversation killer, but Thomas's inquiring mind was still inquiring. "What stopped the major attending tonight?" He watched Karl closely.

"Nothing. Schaefer had incriminating evidence sent to Major Eldridge's home — to his wife in fact. Only it was intercepted and I warned the major."

* * *

461

The taxi dropped Karl off at King's Cross, nowhere near his flat in Kilburn. Thomas understood the combination of privacy and paranoia to the point where he didn't even feel the need to comment.

"Are we still tubing it to Heathrow tomorrow?" Thomas asked as Karl was out the door."

"Wouldn't miss it for the world — give me a call on the mobile when you surface." And then suddenly Karl was away, scurrying down the stairs like a commuter on speed.

"Where to next, guvnor?"

He cringed inwardly and muttered, "Walthamstow Central tube station." Sod it — Schaefer was paying. Late-night London was ablaze with neon and awash with the sort of people you'd avoid by daylight. They all whirled by in brief snatches of tragedy and comedy. Scenes that lured a photographer out of a warm bed. Note to self — charge up his phone for the morning . . . phone; that reminded him. He still had Karl's mobile from the base *and* he hadn't checked the major's two landlines for a day. A little unpaid overtime when he got home, then.

The walk from Walthamstow Central always set his senses on overdrive, but stupid to get another cab from there for a few minutes' walk. He bunged the cabbie a fiver tip, promising himself to get half of it out of Karl in the morning, and pulled his jacket in. The Makarov was eager for action and an amusing scenario played out in his head; some fuckwit mugger would step out of nowhere and make a very bad decision indeed. It amused him because he wasn't into all that macho toss at all; he'd done a little boxing at school — out of some crazy idea that he'd take his dad on — but Walthamstow didn't need a vigilante. At least, not this one.

Past the burger bar, sidestepping the alcopops gang and on beyond the old cinema. Now the street lighting became more sparse and the side roads scattered off the main road like lures for the unworldly traveller. He gripped the Makarov, stroking his thumb along the hatching on the handle until he found the embossed star. Now he was the sheriff again, and the sheriff always wins, right?

Left, down Greenleaf Road, crossing over to face any oncoming traffic, his mind acutely aware of everything around him. Out to the middle of the road, where the gardens looked overgrown, walking at a steady pace and checking side to side. He could have jogged home in half the time but that sent out all the wrong signals.

Along the street and up the five steps. Then pause and check behind, before opening the door. It still didn't feel like *his* door, not when he knew that Karl had replaced it a few months back when some scumbag smashed it in. The last time Karl had spoken of it, the guy responsible was still employed in some government department, still looking over his shoulder for Karl. Justice of a sort.

* * *

It wasn't the beer that had made his head spin — Thomas had managed to keep his consumption to a minimum. No, it was Karl's comments about Major Eldridge — all coagulating together into a misshapen mess.

Yet there was still one mystery: who had taken the Land Rover? Logically, the major, but he would have soon discovered that the Scavenger parts had been removed. So why remove the vehicle and why hadn't he mentioned it? Something else to add to his notes.

He plugged in a charger to Karl's mobile, using a universal socket thing, and sat down in the kitchen to await the kettle. The room needed redecorating, same old paint job since he'd split with Miranda; same old four walls. Why did he stay in that flat? He didn't know his neighbours, didn't socialise there, and couldn't even guess at the local shopkeeper's name. Well, maybe the owner of the takeaway, at a push. Half a life, Miranda had called it — the worse half, because she reckoned he mostly lived through his work.

And what was his work these days? He grabbed the kettle and made the tea, blowing the cup to breathe in the steam. Maybe Miranda was right, not that he'd tell her. Tonight, punch-drunk by half-truths, lies and counter intelligence, he felt crowded out of his own existence. He took his tea to the front room, but his conclusions followed him. Keen for a diversion, he plonked the mug on a coaster and sent an off-the-cuff text to Ajit: *Are you losing all the weight that Geena's gaining?* Added the obligatory smiley face and fired it off. Probably a good idea to check Karl's magic mobile as well, just to make sure the market bought adapter wasn't in danger of overheating.

As he crossed the room, he felt a sense of disquiet. No reason for it, but something nagged at the back of his brain — a piece of logic that eluded him. He turned Karl's throwaway phone on. There was a recent text from Major Eldridge: *Thanks Karl. I knew you wouldn't let me down. My offer still stands.* And one voice message. Probably more of the same and, given the text, he was anxious to find out what the offer was. What could the major give to Karl? And then it hit him, the one thing Karl didn't have — a door back into the army. *Shit.* He dialled in and sat down uncomfortably for the message.

"It's Jess," the voice was insistent. "I've been thinking about you, Tommy. I need to speak to you on your own, before I go away tomorrow — it's really important. I feel awful not telling you before, but I was afraid it would change things." She left her hotel room number, in case he'd forgotten.

463

He finished his tea first — it wasn't as if Jess was going anywhere tonight. And he rang Miranda first, a quick five-minute chat, just to see how she was and whether she was missing him. Adolescent stuff. An itch that needed to be scratched, every once in a while.

"It's not even eleven yet — did your dinner party fizzle out?"

"Yeah, we ran out of blondes." Especially the feisty kind.

"Terry called me today — wanted to know how long you planned to keep your stuff at you-know-where . . ."

He laughed, then she did as well. A good point though. Why hadn't Karl taken the Scavenger parts away? "Dunno, I'll speak to you-know-who tomorrow."

"You're such an arse."

"I know. G'night, babe." It was like a hug in a call — the sexy kind.

And now for the human chameleon. He was put through by the hotel switchboard. Jess picked up and he heard the TV fade to the background. They swapped pleasantries, agreed that the restaurant meal was great and then he steered the conversation back to the point.

"Well," Jess needed a run-up. "Don't be mad at me; I should have told you something before. Only Mr Schaefer was rude about me when you and Mr McNeill were in the bathroom. He called me a photocopier."

Thomas suppressed a chuckle and offered his sympathies.

"Thank you, Tommy, I knew you'd understand. Anyway, where was I?" She found her way back to the spotlight. "Clarity and I worked together before, just for a little while, on a project to develop a vehicle."

"I see," he said, not seeing at all. "Out of interest, what was it?"

There was a long pause, followed by a loud sigh, as if she'd drawn the receiver closer. "I know I can trust you — it was codenamed C12. I reported to Clarity, and after three months I was suddenly transferred over to the UB40, working alongside Amy."

"Thanks for telling me, Jess. Look, I'd better go — I'll see you tomorrow — why don't we get there early then we can have a coffee together, just the two of us?"

"Tommy, that night, at your flat — I wish you had taken advantage."

He put the phone down carefully and lifted his hand away, as if it were toxic. She'd make someone, somewhere, a wonderful stalker.

As his laptop booted up, he took out the log-in details for the server and sat, ready. The usual procedure — an anonymising server first and then calling up sound surveillance for the major's two office phones. He started with the one the major knew about. It was run-of-the-mill stuff, mainly day-to-day comms and a couple of family calls.

Mrs Eldridge gave the impression of being a real blue blood, the sort that Christine Gerrard's mother would have welcomed with open arms.

Line two was a little light on recordings — which made sense now that Jess was out in the open. The final file held a nasty surprise. It was a landline call from Karl, thanking the major for his assistance in Belfast. So far, so what? Then things took a sharp detour. Thomas listened, rooted to the screen as the vocal peaks and troughs played out for him like dancing daggers. Major Eldridge was offering Karl a deal: the deal of the century in fact. If he got the data out of Jess, to hold Schaefer accountable for Amy's death, then the major would *guarantee* a way back into the army.

Thomas's first instinct was to ring Karl, there and then, and have it out with him. Then again, Karl hadn't responded other than agreeing to give the matter consideration. He bit on a fingernail and replayed the call. Was it really his business what Karl did? Point and counterpoint rolled around in his head. He logged off and shut the laptop down, leaving the arguments to fight it out in his dreams.

Chapter 33

Thomas floated up from the depths of sleep, gradually becoming aware of the wind outside. Safe in his bed, he pictured the rubbish being blown up the street. As if God Himself was clearing up the place, once and for all, and making a bloody racket about it. He heaved his eyes open; it had to be early, the sun hadn't put in an appearance. He rolled to one side and the alarm clock glared back in the semi-darkness, silently screaming: five twenty-five.

He smiled. Somewhere out there was the prospect of a sunrise, waiting to be photographed. If he got a shift on, he could be at Epping Forest for the dawn, to watch that pale brilliance streaking through the tree line. Or he could relax back into the mattress, close his eyes and spend the next hour or so in warm comfort. No contest. He sprang out of bed and tiptoed around the flat, as if in fear of waking himself. In times gone by, he used to leave Miranda little notes on the pillow — dragging her along had always delayed things and often started an argument. Now, there was no one to tell, but there was still a rush of excitement. He was a kid again, lugging his rucksack to the front door in Pickering, where Ajit's dad would be waiting outside.

Final bag check: flask, camera, emergency chocolate bar — no point wasting time on a shower — and out the door. He could see right up the street, sense the onset of the day. His mother would have called it a holy moment; he could live with that assessment. A quick bite of past-its-best snack bar and then a gratuitous door slam for the benefit of his neighbours. Lower the rucksack carefully into the passenger-side foot well, and chocks away.

* * *

The A406, heading east, held few surprises and almost no companions. Just a postal van trying to break the land-speed record and a bunch of lads probably heading home after a trip to the pleasure dome. You could love all humanity at a time like this, when it was sleeping. Only when the teeming masses came to life, clogging the roads and his head, did humanity degenerate into liars, cheats and arseholes.

At the first sign for Epping he gave a cheer. Didn't matter that he was alone in the car; it was just one of the rules. Like apologising for farting when you didn't mean it, or wondering how your ex spent her weekends, when you didn't really care. Traditions you follow, stuff that makes you who you are.

Now came the second wave of elation: where to park, where to walk and how to frame the shot? Occasionally he'd seen other snappers out there, plus the odd wayward soul, seemingly from nowhere. No possessions or car, as if they'd materialised at the roadside. Always male, and he never stopped for them.

He guided the car in, with that delicious muffled sound of tyres on dirt. The wind rocked the car gently in welcome. He took another bite of the sad snack bar, grabbed the camera and started walking. Many photographers — according to the chat rooms — already knew what they were looking for, so it was a case of matching the picture in their heads. Thomas tended to fit into the other category, treating spontaneity as a gift from circumstance.

If you waited long enough, cleared out your mind of all the dross about your job, your bank balance and — God help us — your relationship, the picture would come. Never failed, like a child wishing for a present that the parents had already bought and hidden away.

Up the ridge, a pallid sky awaited, shimmering blue grey at the edges, with a last star or two and a vanishing moon. One massive beech tree, stark before him, reached out to the cosmos, dominating the frame — it had to be. The wind blew on, rattling the branches, daring technology to capture a moment of stillness in a ballet of movement. Withering leaves flickered to some jazz rhythm he hadn't connected with. He paused a little longer, then: one beat, four beats, steady now, seven beats . . . nine beats — *snap, snap, snap, snap*. No checking until he got home though — a golden rule, seldom broken. Commissioned photos were different of course, and he'd had one or two of those over the years. But the unanticipated, gifted pictures were magical. And Pandora's Box could only be opened once he was back at home. Otherwise, he might spot an error and try to correct it, might try to manufacture *natural*. That never worked. Even if you achieved a better composition, it ended up stilted and hollow to the trained eye.

He strolled back to the car, closed the door and poured his tea. When he'd been a young boy, his dad had done this with him. That was one memory of home he treasured. Although, as the years had wound forward through the trials of adolescence up to when he was kicked out of the house, he'd almost convinced himself that he'd imagined it. Not today though. Because this morning, right now, he remembered how he *felt*.

The drive back to the flat was tinged with sadness. Time for work, time for school: it was all the same, all lining up for someone else's parade. He smiled as he spotted the first super-commuters and lorry drivers, patting his camera at the lights and telling himself that he wasn't like the rest of them. And almost believed it.

* * *

Second exit from the flat, time became important again. He finished the flask of tea in lieu of breakfast, and promised himself he'd do a proper shop later in the week. The forced march, up to Hoe Street, got the blood pumping. If he could collect some data from Jess, and get the info from Thurston Lyon, it would have been a successful day.

He swiped himself through the barrier, tried to forget that this could track his movements, and scanned the free newspaper as he walked. He carried both mobiles — his and Karl's throwaway. And before he'd left the flat, he'd copied the accident footage to a disc, just in case. They'd probably put that on his headstone: Here lies Thomas Bladen — just in case.

First call, McNeill residence. "Good morning campers, rise and shine."

"Ah, Tommo, I'm glad you caught me early. Afraid I can't make the John Denver fest."

"The *what*?"

"Leaving on a jet plane; catch up when you can."

Thomas leant against the wall to avoid the slipstream of people swarming past, and waited for an explanation. "Because?"

There was a deep sigh from Karl. "Stuart Fraser rang me late last night. It seems that my cousin Marion contacted the authorities, asking after me. Apparently, Martin sent flowers to her house — on my behalf, as I'm supposed to be in custody."

Thomas pushed his suspicious nature down.

"So Marion has been asking all sorts of awkward questions, such as when was I in Belfast and what have I been arrested for. Poor Stuart has had to take cover behind a 'no comment' statement and now solicitors might be involved. The upshot is that I need to lay low this morning and straighten everything out. I've left a message to put

Christine in the picture. You'll be able to cope on your own, won't you?"

"Sure," he said, except he didn't think so. "I'll call you as soon as Jess is on her way."

"Thanks, Tommo, have a nice time."

It felt like a good sign that Karl could still muster sarcasm. "Yeah, you too." So, he'd be Billy-no-mates among the Engamel crowd. Not counting Jess — and he wasn't. He jumped the first available train and did some mental juggling.

It went like this. Karl knew that both of the major's lines were bugged, and *he* had rung the major, not the other way round. Maybe Karl wanted Thomas to know about the deal? So did it compromise their working partnership? Possibly. Or perhaps it just showed how desperate the major was to hang Michael Schaefer, which didn't make him a bad judge of character.

The train juddered back and forth, back and forth, moving thoughts around his head like ball bearings in a child's puzzle. Every time he thought he'd achieved equilibrium, something set off another thought ricocheting against its neighbour. As the train surfaced at Gloucester Road, he dredged up a text from Jess. He scrolled through the warm welcome, to the meeting point in Terminal 4. And got out at South Kensington to get a ticket extension to Heathrow.

More passengers with cases were joining the train now — the ones who couldn't, or wouldn't, afford the Heathrow Express. No, this was more his style, especially if your idea of fun was crowd control. The connecting carriage door burst in and a shorthaired dude with a stripy waistcoat and a battered guitar began a round of introductions. Soon, the entertaining Aussie started belting out his own little bit of happiness. From Thomas's end, the bloke didn't sound bad, if you could hear him above the tutting chorus. Aussie Bloke was lost to the music and into his act, serenading a few and trying his luck with anyone willing to give him the time of day, and some change. Thomas dropped him 40p, just for being a trier.

* * *

At Terminal 4, he wove his way through the United Nations, sidestepping the barricades of suitcases, surfboards and boxes mummified in brown tape. If he'd had the day to himself, he could have happily hung around, immersing himself in the sounds and colours and excitement of travelling. But the only excitement today was the prospect of getting useful data out of Jess.

There was no surprising her at the rendezvous; as soon as he arrived she was all over him like a rash.

"Tommy!" she quivered, flinging her arms around him.

469

For reasons he couldn't fathom immediately, she was wearing a headscarf and dark glasses, like a child's idea of an incognito film star.

"Where shall we go eat?"

That newly acquired mid-Atlantic tone was already starting to grate. He played safe and turned the attention back to her; it didn't take much doing. She'd slept well, and her bags were already checked in. Engamel were arranging for everything from her flat to be shipped over by sea. What she really wanted for breakfast was pancakes and syrup. She led the way confidently, having memorised the map.

And speaking of memories. "How did you get on with that test I set you?"

"Oh, let's not talk about that right now, Tommy, not before our last meal together." She breezed along, pausing at anything with a reflective surface, to check herself out.

After the second or third time, he realised who it reminded him of — Miranda, in disguise, when they'd set off for Yorkshire. He gave up trying to fathom what was going on in Jess's mind, and just hoped it included wanting to help him. Two armed police officers glanced sideways at her but let it go. He already had his hand on his ID card, ready to intervene with an explanation. Roll on the final gate call.

They soon arrived at the cafe and settled down to their last supper, in breakfast form. He'd half expected to see an Engamel handler there, so things were looking up. As he sat, watching the same families walk up and down for third time, he had an idea. "I'll be back in a sec." Before Jess could object, he added, "It's a surprise."

She beamed and lowered her glasses. Then he waved with just his fingertips and disappeared into a gift shop. *Gift* was a little strong; a gift to commercialism, certainly, but that was about it. He found a teddy that was midway between cute and extravagant, swallowed hard as he passed over his credit card, and snuck the carrier bag into his jacket. Then he used a passing family as camouflage and returned to their table from a different direction, clocking her as she stared out, Labrador-like, desperate for signs of him.

"Wotcha!" he pressed a hand against her shoulder blades and felt her mould her back into his palm. "I just wanted to get you a little going away present." He placed the bag in front of her and sat down to watch the show.

She scrabbled to take her glasses off and peered feverishly into the bag. Fair enough, it was a good teddy, but it didn't deserve the floods of tears she christened it with.

"It's beautiful, Tommy — I love it!" she was staring at him now, drinking him in.

Did it feel a little manipulative? Yeah, but he was beyond that point by now. Checking the upload from Karl's mobile earlier, and seeing Amy again — what was left of her — had removed any final shreds of conscience.

After a minute or two, with no offer of data pages forthcoming, he realised he'd struck out. He tried not to show it in his voice. "When are the others arriving?"

Her face reddened and she brushed her hand tenderly over the teddy bear. "Mr Schaefer is expecting me down by the check-in."

"Well, let's not keep him waiting."

Jess carefully untied her headscarf and put it in the bag with the glasses, followed by the bear. Then she pressed the top of the carrier closed and looked up at him, as if dismayed at her own regression.

He stood and she followed, walking close beside him, prisoner and escort. She didn't look at mirrors now; she just faced forward.

* * *

Schaefer looked seriously pissed off, gazing in all directions like a hyperactive sentinel. As soon as he laid eyes on them, he lifted his mobile to call off the search. Clarity and Deborah quickly emerged from different directions, through the crowds.

"You're late." Schaefer had a talent for the obvious.

"My fault," Thomas took the flak. "I asked Jess to meet me for breakfast and we got talking."

Schaefer's face turned barley white. The two harpies looked worried too, particularly Clarity. It was hard not to enjoy the moment. The party of five moved off along the concourse, two prisoners now, and Schaefer leading the way. If Schaefer was wondering about Karl's absence, he was keeping pretty quiet about it; all he seemed interested in was getting Jess through security and away. Away from Thomas, most probably.

Deborah and Clarity were sharing whispers. Thomas stayed alongside Jess, slowing when she slowed, keeping her company. One suggestion was all it took to divert them to a coffee shop. After all, as Thomas innocently pointed out, Jess had *plenty* of time yet.

They crowded around a table the size of a footstool. Jess ran true to form, like a wind-up doll, chatting about her new apartment and the new neighbourhood. Reciting enough facts and figures to impress an inquisition. Impressed they may have been, but they were not entertained.

"Hey, Tommy," Deborah burst in at one of Jess's pauses for breath, "you ever think of transferring overseas?"

Jess's eyes shone like headlights. Thomas blinked at Deborah, as if sending her a message in Morse code: *bitch.* Schaefer's shoulders lifted to accommodate a sickly smile.

"The way I hear it, Tommy's more of a stay-at-home kinda guy. Outdoors can get pretty rough, don't you find?"

Thomas's brain bounded the stepping-stones. His first thought, following after Sir Peter Carroll and his big mouth, was the standoff out on the moors, months before. Mentally, he squared up to Schaefer and nodded for the benefit of the audience. "Yeah, last time I was outdoors I shot a man." He figured Schaefer knew all the details anyway.

"What d'ya do that for?" Deborah was laughing — at him, and probably at the looks of horror on Jess and Clarity's faces.

He looked her full in the face, deadpan. "Because he deserved it."

Then suddenly she wasn't laughing any more. And nor was Schaefer — this must have been new information for him.

"I thought you guys weren't licensed to carry a piece."

Thomas opened his jacket and flicked it with his hands. "We're not, usually. That was a special occasion — protecting Sir Peter." He finished his coffee and rested back in his chair; time to flip the tables, try and fill in a few blanks of his own. "So, what will happen to the testing if Jess is moving on?"

Schaefer's face took on a swagger, the sort of look that made Thomas want to slam a door into him.

"I'm sorry, Tommy," he inclined his forehead forward, like a bull about to charge. "That's privileged information."

Jess was watching Thomas intently. She seemed to eat when he ate, drink when he drank. He figured he'd better play it cool or she might side with him, take up against the Yanks and refuse to go — not a good career move for either of them.

Fortunately, the clock was still ticking and Jess showed no sign of doing a runner. A real pisser about the data though.

"Hey," Jess suddenly brightened, "I can write to you at home."

Deborah and Clarity warmed up a little. Jess waited until she had their full attention. "I still have your address from when I stayed over."

Schaefer grinned like an idiot; no practice required. "That's what I love about you Brits — all that stiff-upper-lip bullshit on the outside, but behind closed doors you're no different to the rest of us."

Thomas's eyes bored into Jess, waiting for her to qualify her statement. She didn't. She milked it, happy to ride his reputation if nothing else. After that, the clock couldn't move fast enough.

It was a slow walk to the security gate — with Jess hanging loosely on his arm, like a dead pheasant. He didn't bother shrugging her off; if she needed to act out this last fantasy then so be it — he was past caring what the Americans thought.

One by one, Jess shook hands with the Engamel farewell party. Thomas though, she singled out for special treatment. As the last hand retreated, she called him forward to walk her to the door. Then she turned in front of him, so that she walked into her, and pounced. Her arms slithered inside his jacket and around his waist. She reeled him in and kissed his cheek, moving her lips to his ear. "Thank you for picking me up, that first night."

He felt something flat being slid into his inside pocket, something very much like an envelope. Then she withdrew her hands and cupped his chin, drawing a final kiss from him before she broke away, sobbing, and went through the door. He straightened his jacket and turned to face the Engamel cheering section.

"Goddamn, Tommy," Schaefer clapped his hands together. "You're a real dark horse! Okay people, how about a little drink, to celebrate a successful conclusion to a difficult situation."

No one had mentioned Amy, and Thomas wasn't about to. Especially when there was every possibility that Jess had slipped him something useful. He bore their false bonhomie and took a gamble, reckoning Schaefer was such a cocky bastard that his contempt for Major Eldridge lay just beneath the surface.

"Do you still want me to maintain sound surveillance on the major?"

"Sure, why not?" All he lacked was a Stetson to tilt and some stubble to strike a match against, the prick. Schaefer played to his gang, as if they were discussing whether to torment the fat kid after lunch. "Now come on, Tommy, are you sure you won't have a proper drink?"

Thomas raised his orange juice and emptied the glass. "Not for me thanks, I'm driving this afternoon — work." He didn't elaborate, and no one around him seemed to care enough to pursue it. He did the decent thing, waiting for them to finish up, and they took their time about it. Schaefer and Deborah excused themselves for the loo, leaving Clarity behind like the kid sister cramping their style.

"Know what I think?" she tried to tempt him.

"Nope," he said flatly. It didn't seem to deter her any.

"I think there's never been anything between you and Jess. Wanna know why?" She didn't wait for him to reply. "She still talks to me, sometimes — she mentions you the same way she used to mention the major, sorta exaggerated, for effect. Because she's never had any feeling for either of you. It's all bullshit."

"What's your point?" Okay, so he was a little bit interested now.

"I've got you figured out, Thomas Bladen. You're actually one of the good guys."

He tried his best half-second smile. "Don't be too sure of that."

She touched his arm. "Nobody wanted Amy to get hurt."

His mouth curled up at the edges. "She didn't get hurt — she *died.*"

Clarity checked to see if the other two were returning. "Look, all I'm saying is: don't make this into some personal crusade. The assignment will finish soon; it's not worth making enemies."

He took a long time to think about that, on the tube back into London. It was getting to the point where he didn't know who was threatening whom. And, call him paranoid, but he wasn't about to open the envelope anywhere that had even a gnat's chance of being within sight of a camera. He checked the time on his mobile. Jess would be in the departure lounge by now, probably trying to hit on some poor sod sat on his own. Still enough time to get to Thurston Lyon's place, but later than he'd have liked — should have driven into town first.

At Walthamstow Central he sprinted for the stairs and out the exit, dialling Karl as he slowed to get his breath back. "I'll be in my car in ten minutes then on his road."

"Ten-four, good buddy!" Karl did a poor American accent.

"How did you get on with *your* new buddy?" It always paid to talk in riddles, so Karl could say as much or as little as he wanted to.

"Fraser? Yeah, it was interesting. He's going to attend the funeral on my behalf. Well, on his as well, hoping to run into Martin again."

They were skirting around the obvious. "How about we meet up tonight, after I do my info collection in Dalston?"

Karl must have considered it for all of three seconds. "Yeah, okay. Tell you what, I'll meet you in Hackney and we can drive in together."

* * *

Thomas reached his car, checked the time again and opened the envelope while the engine was running. By the looks of things, Jess had come through for him. Yeah, she was as still mad as a fish but, judging by the numerical content, here was the evidence that the major was so desperate for. He sat in the car, tapping the envelope against the dashboard, wondering. Would this be enough to get Karl back in combats?

Chapter 34

Dalston, like so many parts of London, always seemed to be busy. It might be what politicians would politely call *economically and socially deprived*, but there was a buzz about the place. It was another closed community, as far as Thomas was concerned, but even looking from the car at the lights, there were a million photo opportunities going on. The surly faced woman, heaving bags of shopping across the street with her grandson/nephew indifferent to her struggles, as if his earpieces drowned out his conscience as well. Two girls, because that's what they were, wheeling baby buggies.

He wound the window down a little to take in the sounds of the street; the heavy beat musical backdrop, the spicy food wafting along the street. It made Walthamstow seem second-rate. There was community there too, but he never got to see it. Most of the time E17 was just somewhere to park his car. And speaking of which, it was time to negotiate the back roads near the housing estate and head in on foot.

Some kids were playing football on the green outside the flats. As he passed, one or two stopped to stare at him, firing questions with their eyes. He let them get on with it. Life turned the volume back up on the high street, leaving little space for private thoughts. He pushed the door, and this time there was no music. There was something *amiss*. Nothing out of place, just an atmosphere, as if he'd brought in a bad smell. Hair Girl was watching the door intently. He raised a hand; it made little difference. She must have buzzed or something, nodding to him to go straight in without him opening his mouth. He threw her a smile but it bounced off her face and shattered.

The office door creaked inward. He found himself checking the corners of the room, searching for a tangible reason for his own jumpiness. As soon as he set eyes on Thurston, he stopped searching. The man had scuffmarks across his face and purple bruising on his jaw. One arm hung higher than the other, as if crying out for a sling.

Thurston Lyon didn't speak. He leaned forward with some difficulty, and wrenched back a desk drawer, waiting. Thomas flicked the remaining £200 on the desk. Thurston's eyes never left him.

"The price gone up, brother. I need another two hundred pounds."

Fuck. He didn't have it. He stood there, wondering what to do next, trying to remember what he had in his wallet. "I've got another £100 and that's it." It was easy to show an honest face when you were telling the truth.

Thurston mulled it over and lifted the envelope up. Thomas took out his wallet so Thurston could see he wasn't bullshitting.

"I hope it was worth it."

Thomas was startled. So much venom in so few words. He put the envelope in his jacket and buttoned it up. Then he remembered Karl's words of wisdom and reiterated Martin's full name and the prospect of further investigations.

"I don't think so, mister. You are bad luck."

Nothing much he could say to that. But he thanked him again and went on his way. Hair Girl sucked her teeth at him on the way out; he figured it wasn't a local version of 'have a nice day.' On the way back to the car he dived into a newsagent and grabbed some crisps. Lately he was living on snack food. Note to self: do some shopping.

More footballers of the future stopped to gawp at him. He did wonder what the fuck had happened to Thurston. But hey, what was he going to do about it now anyway?

He got in the car, locked it and sat for a moment. The mobile was on and no one was ringing; may as well check Thurston's handiwork. He bent forward to extract the envelope. At first, they were just dark shapes, like crows flapping their wings. Then the shapes rushed in, crowding out the light. He registered one white guy and one black, and the iron bars they were carrying. Instinctively he crouched down, one arm above his head as the crowbars converged on the windscreen. *Holy Fucking Christ.* The car shook at the first impact, and the next; then he was shaking so much he couldn't register any more. The glass creaked like thin ice, fracture webs jigsaw-ing the light from beneath his arm. It may have been six impacts, maybe more.

Then, when he fully expected the whole thing to collapse in on him, they stopped. They didn't run off though. They looked down on him cowering there, admiring their own handiwork, and bust his headlights for good measure before they jogged away.

His mouth was moist; he tasted blood, metallic and warm. In blind panic and unable to cry out, he'd bit into his own lip. It was quiet outside. No nosey neighbours, no good Samaritans — fuck all. He couldn't stop shaking, fingers trembling as he crushed his mobile in both hands and pressed two thumbs together. One lad, who looked like he'd been playing football earlier, ran past and jeered.

"Karl, I need your help." Thomas didn't remember saying anything else, but he must have, or else how would Karl have found him minutes later?

He didn't get out of the wreckage until Karl arrived in a screech of wheels and brakes.

"Come on; let's have you out of here." There was a hard edge to his voice. He helped Thomas into his own car, put the seatbelt on him and then made another call. "I have a priority collection and repair . . ." He glanced at Thomas. "Hold on, Control, I'll tell you when I'm at the end of the road." They took off, slowing down briefly at the first junction so Karl could call in the details.

Karl drove to a pub a few miles away and parked up outside. "We could skip the club tonight?"

Thomas hadn't spoken up until now, just nodded here and there. "I thought they were going to kill me."

"I know; I'm sorry."

Thomas tilted his head; that didn't sound right somehow. Why would Karl be apologising? He kept it together, pulling Thurston's envelope out.

"You open it," Karl broke eye contact.

He slid his fingernail beneath the seal, watching as the bloodstain from his nail smeared across the crisp white paper. It was a single page, neatly folded into three. He bent it open for both of them to see, and his jaw dropped.

STAY OUT OF MY BUSINESS.

Karl took in a mass of air and blew it out again, like a subdued roar. He took the page and screwed it up into a ball, crushing it tight. Then he stuffed it into the door pocket. "I'll have him."

Thomas felt like there was another voice inside him now; a weaker, younger voice that nonetheless was going to be heard. "You used me."

Karl put a hand to his face, as if shielding himself from the accusation, or from the truth. "I didn't know this was going to happen; I swear to you, Tommo. I'll fucking have him though, and that's a promise."

Thomas turned his head slowly and stared at Karl through a haze. Then he pushed his head back against the seat and closed his eyes. It felt as if a single tear was rolling down his left cheek, on his blind side. He wanted to brush it away, but he stayed deathly still, trying to take it all in.

* * *

Karl turned to the passenger seat. "We don't have to do this, you know."

"Yeah, we do." They'd been sat in the car park for at least five minutes, Thomas's eyes boring into the heavy-duty door of the gun club. Out the corner of his eye, he saw Karl's brow furrowing. "Come on," he pulled on the passenger door, letting in a rush of autumnal air. It had been raining again, the damp scent of leaves and change adulterated by the grimy stench of the city.

Thomas was out the door, leaning on the car, pressing against it as if it were a talisman. It wasn't the thought of the guns that reassured him; it was the environment. Somewhere he could be in absolute control — how often did that happen in life? Answer: never.

As Karl paid their way in and they waited for their IDs to be returned, Thomas thought back to Dalston. Did they rough up Thurston to set *him* up? Or had Thurston tried to cut a deal with Jack Langton and paid the price for his insolence? Maybe it didn't matter; either way — neither of them had come out smiling.

Karl didn't bother to offer him a choice of handguns, opting for a pair of Baby Brownings. Thomas smiled when he saw what was in the box. He could palm the gun in one hand. Karl let him go first, obviously some psychological bullshit or an act of penance on his part.

As usual, there was no talking; that suited him fine. He still felt like a jackass for getting emotional over a little thing like terror. Hard to know what was worse really — the shame of cowering there while they destroyed his car or the humiliation of Karl seeing him like that. He tensed his legs, settled into his pelvis and relaxed his grip a little on the handle. It weighed about the same as the Makarov pistol in his hand, but it felt different. No more thinking. He entered the kill zone and instinct flooded out thought and reason, honing everything down.

Four shots rang out, each a hammer blow that reverberated inside his ribcage. Bang. Bang, bang, heartbeat steadying, sweating over, bang. All done. The gasping click of the empty chamber like a death rattle of some other self, the one he left behind in that private underworld — the one that was afraid. And as he surfaced from the moment, he gazed upon a dark certainty: Jack Langton would have to pay.

Karl's marksmanship was below his usual exemplary standard. Thomas watched from the back of the room, noticing how Karl never seemed to get comfortable. Still, as he knew from personal experience, guilt played havoc with your concentration.

"I meant to ask," Karl finally set the pistols back in their box. "How did you get on with Schaefer at the airport?" It was the closest they'd come to a normal conversation since the emergency pick up.

"He's still a prick. And he wants to maintain the voice tap on Major Eldridge."

"Even with Jess away? Interesting. I mean, she's hardly likely to ring him long-distance."

No, Thomas thought, not *him*. "What's your thinking, then?"

Karl clicked the lid shut. "Maybe he's just being cautious. Unless he's got something else to worry about?"

Thomas reached into his jacket and remembered Karl's none-too-private chat with the major about army recruiting. He didn't say anything, just whipped out Jess's envelope and flopped it on the lid.

Karl stared for a few seconds then reached out a tentative hand. A huge smile spread across his face as he straightened out the pages. "Jesus, Tommo, you're a miracle worker."

He grinned and withstood the pat on the back.

Karl pocketed the envelope. "I'll make us a copy before I hand this over."

There was no follow up about any deal. Thomas let it pass and waited for Karl in the corridor. No doubt about it, the place was beginning to grow on him. Karl returned, minus the weapons, whistling 'Mr Postman,' and led them through to the café area that Karl liked to call 'the bar.'

"What's he going to do with it?"

Karl looked up from his coffee. "The major? Assuming the data's accurate, he could go to the inquiry and accuse Schaefer of negligence."

Thomas shook his head, he couldn't see that happening.

"Or," Karl mused, "if he's the kind of man I think he is, he'll want something a little more personal and conclusive."

In a word: revenge.

"Look, Tommo, I'd like your help with Jack Langton." Karl waited, checking his reaction before he continued. "As far as everyone is concerned, I'm under lock and key. I can't very well turn up in Jack's local watering hole. And besides, it's not quite what I had in mind."

Thomas gazed at his right hand, stroking the tiny graze where he'd slipped as he got out of the car. As Karl had dragged him out. "Whatever it is, I'm in."

Karl's eyes narrowed and a twisted smile played upon his lips. "Jack Langton already thinks Martin is prying into his life. As far as he's concerned, *you* were some nobody snooping around on Martin's behalf and he's sent you both a clear message to stay away. Now I'm going to tip Jack over the edge."

"What's the objective, besides the obvious?"

"Well, I'm hoping Jack will go looking for Martin, big time. After that they can fight it out between them." Karl checked the clock. "Time I was dropping you home — you got anything to eat?"

"Sort of — but what about my car?"

"Ah, yeah, I'll arrange a replacement for the time being. Come on then, drink up, I'm getting hungry."

* * *

They opted for a curry; Karl paid. As they sat waiting for two bhunas, pilau rice and a couple of garlic naans — squinting to follow a football match that neither of them gave a shit about — Thomas wondered how Ajit was doing. Maybe he'd call and clear the air.

Karl gave him a nudge, "D'ya think you and Miranda will ever settle down?"

Cue nervous laughter. "Only if I quit my job."

"Not very likely, then."

Somehow this didn't seem like the time or place to reveal his innermost thoughts and feelings. "And what about you, Karl — think you'll ever leave the SSU and seek gainful employment?"

Karl nodded towards the counter and leapt up to collect. "Well, I knew this one was coming. My answer's the same as when you asked me in the mess hall."

"But the major—" he stood to join him.

"Look, Thomas, it may surprise you to learn that I've told you more than I'd tell him. It suits my purpose to have him think I'm itching to get back into camouflage. Now, come on, let's get this back to yours, we can have that ice cream in your freezer for pudding."

"Huh?"

"I checked last time, when you were taking a leak."

"You looked in my freezer?"

"Sure, I'm one nosey bastard — how do you think I got the job?"

* * *

Ten minutes later they were sprawled out on the sofa, devouring bhunas. The TV was showing another wildlife programme, all massive skies and photogenic carnage.

480

"Divide and conquer, my friend," Karl dropped in another comment from out of nowhere. "I'll meet you at work tomorrow and take you to your temporary car."

Thomas felt like saying it was the least Karl could do, but he was enjoying the company too much to want to ruin it.

"Then you can do a clandestine on Jack Langton, while I'm away at the army base. And best you leave the Makarov at home."

Chapter 35

Karl had given him a head start, digging out Jack Langton's details. You just had to know the right people to ask.

The Ford Focus smelt of new car. It was immaculate — untouched by ungloved hands, probably. He had a good play with the controls, reminding himself of the time he'd gone with Miranda to buy her new Mini. The salesman had ignored her and spoken only to him. Miranda had dealt with it by insisting on speaking to a woman instead. And, as usual, she got her way.

It had been days now since he'd heard from her. She'd have taken it for granted that he was immersed in work. He watched Karl disappear out the supermarket car park — with the mystery deliveryman in tow — and reached for his mobile. As texts went, it wasn't exactly Shakespeare. The sentiment was there though: *Hi M, how's life in the fast lane? Tx*

* * *

He took a run through Jack Langton's neighbourhood, making sure of the fastest routes to two major roads if he needed them. Forest Gate was remarkably lacking in forest. Lots of big houses though — mostly converted into bedsits, judging by the clusters of overflowing wheelie bins. He clocked the house in question, parked up and waited.

A large man in chinos and a polo shirt squeezed out of the front door. Thomas watched as the guy lumbered down the street towards a high-end BMW — the personalised number plate had been a bit of a giveaway.

Thomas counted the beats as the BMW passed, and started up his trusty new Ford. It wasn't exactly chase of the century, and Thomas gave him enough rope to hang himself. The Ford had an inbuilt low profile; he could have been a sales rep or a teacher, anonymously making his way across town.

Jack Langton drove with one hand, a tree trunk of an arm elbowing out of the window. And naturally, he thought his favourite radio station was too good not to share. The BMW pulled into a bus lane and stopped outside a convenience shop.

Thomas swung in at the next left turn and scrambled out of the car to take up position. Jack Langton was on the phone the moment he got back, newspaper tucked under one arm like he hadn't a care in the world.

Two snaps later, Thomas ran to complete the world's fastest three-point turn, ready for the BMW to pass. As he rejoined the main road, the BMW was just clearing the lights. It was a simple equation: if he caught up with Jack Langton, he'd stick with him; if not, he'd return to Chez Langton for some background surveillance on the family.

He scraped across the lights and made up the distance, three cars behind. It was a perfect position to be in. Close enough to watch the BMW's turns without the need for knee-jerk reactions, and far enough back to be invisible. He played follow-my-leader for nearly half an hour, including a stop-off at a café for a sandwich, heading somewhere in no great rush.

The BMW looked out of place by the flats — a rose among rundowns. Thomas watched Langton stepping lightly into the building and up the centre stairs, catching a glimpse of his silhouette through the glass as he tracked him through a long lens. Up and left, coming out at the second floor, moving along the balcony. Thomas captured a couple of side profiles and counted down the numbers of the doors, wagering with himself that it would all end up with a woman. Jack Langton slowed — number seventeen, unlucky for someone.

Jack rapped at the letterbox — no key — and waited calmly, packed lunch in hand. The door opened and Jack turned towards it, blocking the view with his fat head. *Shift over, you bastard.* Jack bent down and a slim arm curled around his shoulder for what looked like a polite kiss on the cheek. *Just move, will you?*

Thomas froze, button poised, ready for a second's clearance. Bingo, he caught a glimpse of a face and squeezed the button. He heard two bleeps and then he lowered the camera. As Jack wriggled past the woman Thomas's eyes confirmed what the camera had already revealed: it was Sheryl, Miranda's bar manager.

He didn't hang around, made a pact with himself to get as far away as possible. Maybe sweep past Chez Langton on the way home. He felt like a kid who had woken up too early on Christmas morning, only to find out that Father Christmas was actually just his dad. Sheryl and Jack Langton — it made his skin crawl just thinking about the maths. It explained a couple of things, though. Now he understood why Jack had given Sheryl a bar job, and probably why she was working for Miranda. *And* why the Wrights were so accommodating to her.

The road signs couldn't gallop towards him fast enough. He stopped at a set of lights and slapped the dashboard, examiner style. That must have been what Sheryl meant, back when Miranda had been abducted. For the first and only time, Sheryl had threatened him with a couple of phone calls that would sort him out — no prizes now for guessing who she'd have called.

He shot back to Walthamstow for printing and editing. The image of Sheryl was pinpoint sharp; even Karl would recognise her. He checked his watch — too late for lunch, and time to check in.

* * *

Karl was in a good mood. "So, Mr Bladen, any news from the front?"

If you only knew. "Yeah, I caught Jack Langton as he left home and I've managed to get some distant headshots. His car stands out a mile — personalised plates."

Karl picked up on it straightaway. "Great. If we can find out where he goes, it'll give us a choice of possible strike points."

That sounded ominous. He felt himself cringing silently. He closed his eyes, like a kid bracing himself for bad news or a bollocking.

"Is there a problem, Tommo? You weren't seen, were you?" There was concern in the voice, but it was hard to tell who for.

Jesus, that was something he hadn't even considered — what if Sheryl had seen him?

"I don't think so. Nah, it's fine, I reckon. It's best I do some more surveillance."

"Good man, Tommo, I knew I could rely on you."

He said his goodbyes and stared at the photo dangling from the printer. There was nothing else for it — he'd have to see Sheryl. Next call . . .

"Miranda Wright, and what can I do for *you*, Mr Bladen?"

There wasn't time to run through a menu, more's the pity. "Just a quickie," he knew she'd like that. "Just thought I'd say hello. By the way, I was, er, driving near East Ham on a job and I could have sworn I saw Sheryl. She must have a double."

"Doubt it. Anyway, she lives up that way. Sweet though, you asking after her. I'll tell her you called."

"Nah, don't do that." He started sweating. "You know how she is with me; it'll only encourage her."

"Okay. Don't worry, your secret's safe with me — I'll protect you."

"Good." A little too emphatic — time to change the subject. "So, when are we getting together again?"

"Well . . . I was gonna invite you round to Mum and Dad's, but I wasn't sure if you still felt weird about the business with Karl?"

He smiled; that was the least of his worries. "It wasn't their doing. Go on then, pick a night and I'm all yours — as long as I'm not working." He paused, in case she wanted to have a pop. But no, Miranda rarely questioned his job anymore. She still didn't like it but she knew it was a lost cause.

"How about tomorrow night?"

"Deal."

"Fish and chips, and a few hands of cards."

"Brilliant. I'll bring some beers."

"Anyway, gotta go. I can't stand here talking to you — Sheryl's off today so it's just a barmaid and me. Don't work too hard, Thomas."

Thank you, God. Next stop: East Ham.

* * *

Jack's BMW was nowhere to be seen. Thomas checked all the surrounding streets before parking up, not far from his original spot. This was all a gamble, but maybe his luck was in today.

He took the stairs, running through opening lines in his head. Nothing too cocky, but no sense beating around the bush. Mind you, she could just tell him to fuck off. That thought didn't help his confidence any as he edged along the balcony.

At the door, he heard the faint sounds of jazz. Funny, he'd never had Sheryl pegged as a Miles Davis fan; he'd always seen her as more of a rock chick. He rapped the letterbox twice and stood back a little, shifting from foot to foot.

The door pulled back. Sheryl opened her mouth, but said nothing.

"Can I come in?"

She looked smaller, less certain of herself, as she nodded and led the way. He carefully closed the door behind him.

"This is a surprise. How come you know where I live?"

485

That was going to take some explaining. He sat down on the sofa. "Any chance of a cup of tea?"

"Sure," she looked perplexed.

He rode it out and gave nothing away. As she hadn't mentioned Miranda yet, he figured she was still running through the options.

"What can I do for you, Thomas?" She passed him a mug. She wasn't smiling so he followed her lead.

He bobbed his head side to side, searching for an easy opening; then he gave up the search. "It's about Jack Langton."

She shrank back, grabbing her chair like a safety line. "Go on."

He sighed and sniffed in rapid succession, as if desperate for stale air. "I know you two are involved — he was seen coming up here, earlier."

She gulped at her tea, the cup hovering mid-air. "And that's *what* of your fucking business?" Her eyes glowed, pools of molten hatred. "Are you here on some kind of work assignment? Don't lie to me because I'll ask Miranda — don't think I won't." But her voice had lost its usual edge. He figured she was bluffing.

"She doesn't know I'm here; *no one* knows I'm here. I just want to talk."

"I heard about Karl," she lowered her eyes. "I'm sorry he got into trouble in Belfast."

Now he was pissed off. "Got into trouble? Jack Langton set him up! Special Branch arrested him."

One look at her face told him she wasn't going to let that be dropped at her door. "Oh, what, and you're here to even the score?"

He sought solace in his tea; this was turning into a bad idea gone worse.

"Come on, Thomas," she goaded him. "Why are you here? You looking for information? Blackmail? I'll make it really easy for you — Miranda doesn't know that Jack visits me. Happy now?"

He blushed, like an idiot. "Blackmail? No." He was floundering now.

"I think you'd better go." She looked vulnerable; this was a side of Sheryl he hadn't seen since Miranda's disappearance.

"Wait up, just give me five minutes." He waved his hand like he was trying to hold back a stampede. "Then, I promise I'm out of here and no one gets to know, not from me." And this, he told himself, was why he was so shit at cards. "These are the photos." He pressed them flat on the table and smoothed the creases. "No copies and no files." He tried reasoning. "Look, Jack Langton isn't safe to be around."

"You think I don't know that?" She picked up the page to look at it.

"Then why are you . . ." he grabbed at the first phrase to hand, ". . . having a relationship with him?"

"A *what*? You think he's my boyfriend?" She leaned back as if to spit out her reply. "You asshole."

He blinked a couple of times, as if he could see the Angel of Conscience standing before him. "You're right." There was one thing he hadn't tried yet: the truth. "I was trying to even the score with Jack. A couple of days ago, I was sniffing around, trying to find something about Jack that would be useful, to help Karl. Next thing I know, two geezers are panel beating my car while I'm still inside it."

"Look, Thomas, I don't get involved in Jack's business."

He ignored that. "So this morning I decide to follow him, and now here I am."

"What are you planning to do — confront him? Because take it from me, he's not a guy to cross."

"Has he hurt you? Is he one of those pricks that likes to knock his girlfriends around?" His shoulders tensed.

Sheryl started laughing. "Miranda always says you have a vigilante complex. But you've got it wrong this time, big time. Jack's not my boyfriend — he's my father."

Hostilities quickly ceased. "What does his wife think about it all?"

"The short version is that she doesn't know. Oh sure, she knows I exist, but she thinks I'm some kind of step-niece or something. We've only met once."

She brought the cups through and he followed her. Jack's tinfoil was neatly folded on the kitchen table. "If you have to ask, then I won't be telling you." She picked the foil up and stuck it in a pedal bin, flicking a remnant of white powder from her fingertips. "So, what are you going to do?"

"He owes me for my car and he owes Karl for a whole lot more."

She shook her head. "Jack doesn't back down. Ever. And he doesn't care who he uses or hurts." She pointed a finger towards the pedal bin, dagger straight. "You think I want him to bring that crap into my home?" She turned to face him. "Why are you really here, Thomas?"

"Okay: confession time. I was hoping to convince you to tell me about Jack Langton's movements. In return for . . ."

Sheryl folded her arms protectively. "Your silence? You're gonna use me just like he does. I thought you were better than that."

He swallowed and paused, as if listening to himself. "I am. It's your choice. Either way, Jack will get what he's due." They faced each other like Samurai.

"And you'll never tell Miranda about any of this?"

487

He nodded. "Besides," he reminded her, "you know my secret too now, and when Jack gets a visit . . ."

She squeezed herself. "I want Jack out of my life for as long as possible."

He smiled. Sir Peter Carroll had told him, during his interview, that every surveillance assignment was a problem to be solved. This was no different. "How often does he bring the packages over?"

"Every week or so. He doesn't need to — I think he does it to show me he can." She lowered her head. "I've no idea where the stuff comes from and it never stays here. He keeps scales and bags in the drawer."

Thomas put on his best poker face. "I think I can find out where he gets it." He stepped forward and hugged her; it seemed the right thing to do. For a moment, he felt he had lost the fear of her, stepped around her Siren persona, the one who led innocent men to their doom. Well, maybe not entirely innocent.

But as he moved away, she lit that touchpaper smile and he reddened again like an idiot. He was pleased though; equilibrium was restored.

"How will I get in touch with you?"

"Let me have a mobile number and I'll text mine to you," he said.

She snorted back laughter. "You really are one cautious son of a bitch."

He was already edging towards the door.

* * *

It was a mile or so before he pulled in and rang Karl back. They were trying out a new system: if the call wasn't picked up by the third ring, hang up. The way things were going, he was holding much better cards than he'd started the day with.

Karl picked up with one ring to go. "What's the score then, Tommo?"

"Are you okay to talk?"

"When have you ever known an Ulsterman who wasn't okay to talk?"

His first thought was: when he's in custody. But he let it pass. "I've found a way to track Jack's movements." He didn't elaborate and Karl knew the drill by now.

"That's grand. Unfortunately, I have bad news. They're shutting down the testing on the base and moving it in-house to an Engamel facility. The major was very coy about it; I can't figure him out. I was so sure he still wanted Schaefer's blood — now I don't know so much."

"P'raps they've offered him a deal too. Let's face it, if everything came out in the open his career would be bollocksed, along with his marriage."

"Aye, maybe. I thought he was bigger than that, though. Anyway, enough of me going on — where are you now?"

"London. You?"

"Like the song says — working my way back to you. The major and I finished our wee chat and now Christine would like a word — in person. And guess what, you're invited."

Pound to a penny, Ann Crossley would be on the guest list too.

"I'll head over." He pulled out Karl's giveaway mobile and texted Sheryl, confirming his name and a few keywords from their discussion.

* * *

He swiped in and mounted the stairs, two at a time, past the other security doors that he didn't have access to. How simple life would be, he thought as he rounded the last flight, if all the intelligence agencies — and the floaters — could pool their resources properly. Then he laughed at himself; it was the kind of bullshit Sir Peter Carroll might come out with on a television interview.

Another swipe, a twist of the handle and there he was, safe and sound. Christine's door was closed, lights on, and Ann Crossley was nowhere to be seen. There was little point in creeping to his desk, but he did it anyway. He figured he'd wait for Karl and they'd go in together, like Butch and Sundance.

Christine's office door opened. "Will you come in please, Thomas?" Only it didn't sound much like a question.

He locked his laptop then thought better of it and brought it with him, closed, under one arm.

Christine offered him a seat, the one next to Ann Crossley.

"Aren't we waiting for Karl?" He heard the warble in his own voice and felt even more of an arse.

Ann smiled encouragingly. "He won't be long — I'm sure he won't mind."

He bit at a nail, trying to organise his thoughts, dividing his knowledge into two piles: the *do not discuss* and the *only discuss if you have to*. Christine moved a file around on top of her desk; it didn't seem to be going anywhere. He felt a twitch coming on, every time that file circled round.

"Can we make a start, then?" He looked up earnestly. "The suspense is killing me." Okay, it was stupid but so was this.

"You're aware that your assignment is to be concluded?" Another statement, this time from Ann.

"Yeah, I gather Major Eldridge has closed it all down."

Christine and Ann exchanged *the look*. The one that made him feel like a child in a roomful of adults.

"That's inaccurate." Christine fiddled with the file again. "The order came from Sir Peter Carroll. He wants our resource withdrawn."

That would make an interesting dilemma for Karl. Thomas smiled to himself, tongue pushed tightly against his lower front teeth.

"However," Christine cleared her throat, "I'd like you to continue to support the major — and Engamel — at my discretion."

It could have been his imagination, but the room temperature just dropped a couple of degrees. He had no problem bypassing Sir Peter, but he was curious. "Might I know the purpose of . . . ?"

Christine stared him down. "Let's not play games, Thomas. There's unfinished work there."

Now, that could mean the major's quest for justice for Amy, or it could mean the completion of the testing. He was still pondering what to say when he heard the distant slam of the security door. He relaxed a little; the cavalry was here.

There was no whistling as Karl approached — just rapid heavy footfalls. He came straight in. "Sorry I'm late — where are we?"

Christine obliged.

Karl waited his turn. "The major confirmed that things have moved on as we anticipated. Any testing of the Scavenger will be relocated to Engamel's Regional Headquarters, as they're under pressure to ensure that the consortium deal stays on schedule."

Thomas uncrossed his legs and leaned forward. "The what?" Now it was a three-way shared look, and he still wasn't invited. "Is there any point in me being here?" He picked up his laptop, ready for the off.

"Sit still, Thomas." This was Christine's other voice. The one that used to say: *you could have made an effort* or *you need to get out of those clothes*. He didn't know whether he felt aroused or defensive.

"You do know that Jess worked for Clarity, before she was assigned to testing the Scavenger? And what they worked on together was the C12 armoured vehicle?"

"This is true, Tommo." Karl rode the wave. "Bet you didn't know which bit of it though?" He didn't wait for a reply. "They worked on the main gun."

Christine looked disappointed. "The consortium will be announcing the live deployment of the Scavenger in designated international conflict arenas. Meantime, development will progress to an upscaled version for the C12."

Thomas faced Karl. "You knew from the beginning, didn't you?"

"No." Christine leapt to his defence. "But I did, once Ann had briefed me."

He blinked once, like a camera capturing evidence. "You've used me." He waved a finger at the two women. Then he pointed at Karl. "And you. Just to get close to your old buddy, the major."

"It was necessary." Ann Crossley seemed about as contrite as a war criminal on extended vacation in South America.

"Nothing's changed, has it? Same old bullshit — you send me in like some sort of decoy and watch what crawls out from the shadows. Meantime everyone gets on with the real job and I'm left in the dark."

"It worked though, Tommo — that's what matters."

Thomas sniffed. Karl had a point, even though it choked him to admit it. "So what's the next move?"

Ann moistened her lips. "My Engamel contact may need protecting, if she decides to break cover."

"You're talking about Clarity." It was hardly a Sherlock Holmes challenge, but he still felt a sense of satisfaction.

She tilted her pen towards him, like a glass.

"I presume," Karl's voice was sombre, "That you'd prefer it if I supply any defensive capability independently?"

Christine made a face. "I'd prefer it if firearms weren't necessary."

Meantime, Thomas had done some thinking. "So, this *deal* goes ahead even though the Scavenger is unsafe?"

All three of them shared the same weak smile. Christine picked up the file, leant across and put it out of reach. "That's the nub of the problem, Thomas. We," she indicated the three of them, "and the people we represent cannot be seen to be obstructing the Scavenger. Neither can we be seen to be endorsing — or assisting — its deployment."

Ann knew her cue. "And no agency is willing to act as a whistle-blower."

"And that's why I'm here?"

Ann tried hard to sell it to him. "All you need do is be there to support Clarity, if she needs it."

"How's she going to get in touch?"

"Karl gave me a mobile number to give to her."

He raised his eyebrows in Karl's direction. Now he understood why Karl hadn't claimed his phone back.

"Look, Tommo, whatever you think of me, or any of us, if we get this right we'll save lives and put a dent in Michael Schaefer's future at Engamel. Political expediency is a secondary consideration."

Judging by the look on Christine's face, Karl was in a minority of one. Well, two now. He nodded resolutely. "Okay, I've heard enough; I'll await her call."

Chapter 36

Thomas didn't feel like sticking around after the meeting. In any case, the three of them seemed to have lots left to talk about, judging by the way no one else followed him out.

He reconnected the laptop and booted up. Meantime, he grabbed a chemical coffee from the machine and escorted it back to his desk. The screensaver floated in front of him like a one-fingered salute. The Surveillance Support Unit crest bobbed about the screen, complete with the motto *Omnes Sensus*: All the Senses. Yeah, he thought, sipping slowly, all of them except common sense.

Emails first, a toe-dip back into reality. Then maybe a sniff around the SSU phone bug on the major's comms. Thinking about it only irritated him off, reminded him of the major's secret offer to take Karl back into uniform. Was that how it was going to be for all three of them still at Christine's desk? Her off to the Foreign Office and Ann Crossley doing a similar deal with Naval Intelligence?

He didn't have any answers. Jesus, he didn't have a full set of questions. He was still the only one playing against the house. He passworded his way through and watched the messages stack in his in-tray. There were a mess of emails eager for his attention. One, sent from Karl just before the meeting, read: *If I don't get to see you before we go in, stick around afterwards. I need to talk to you.* Yeah, right. *Next.* The Liaison Office, short and sweet — advising that he'd missed a health appointment with the counsellor.

A quick glance at the office door — blinds still drawn and no sign of movement. Straight through to an answering machine, bloody things. "Hello, yes, it's Thomas. I really must apologise for missing this week's session. Too much going on at work." *That managed to*

493

sound both lame and ambiguous. "I'm fine and everything — I'll definitely be there next time." He just got it all in before the beep. After that he breathed a little easier and gulped down some more caffeine.

There was some domestic email traffic from Christine, keeping the team informed. Usual nonsense — performance assessment dates, a reminder to use only the latest templates and the server to find them on. Plus an unbelievable email about a teambuilding event, workload permitting. The title alone was enough to make him choke: The Unified Team.

He scanned up the list of emails, working his way to the present. One ominous entry sat atop the list, like a blister. Not to be ignored, but to be treated with caution, sent in from Whitehall. *Please contact me as soon as you receive this. Sir Peter Carroll, Director-General — Surveillance Support Unit.* Just in case Thomas had forgotten the natural order of things.

The call went straight through — no switchboard — and was picked up on the third ring. Sir Peter was that cultured mixture of civilised behaviour and ruthless manipulation.

"Thomas, I appreciate you calling back. I wonder, are you free to join me? Shall we say thirty minutes' time? Excellent, I'll see you then."

Karl would have to wait. This was less an appointment than a command performance. Even if Karl's people did on occasion pull the strings where Sir Peter was concerned, it hadn't improved Thomas's position. On the one hand, the Old Man used to have a soft spot for him; and on the other, Thomas was a means of getting things done. It seemed to be the theme of the day. He left a note on Karl's desk — *summoned to Whitehall, speak to you later* — and headed out the door.

* * *

He could have jumped in a taxi and reclaimed it on expenses, but entering the Tube network always held a fascination for him. It was like shedding a skin, becoming anonymous. Give or take the traceability of an Oyster Card. Hard not to think of Sir Peter tracking him like a badger on the move. Except, of course, they were a protected species and he wasn't.

Surfacing at Embankment, he donned another skin — teacher's pet. He'd barely made it through the security doors when a guard approached him.

"Sir Peter's ready for you now." She sounded calm and unequivocal, walking him to the scanner and then escorting him up there herself.

"It's very kind of you to show me the way," he caught her smile and returned it, gift-wrapped.

"I've, er, put in an application to join the SSU." She didn't qualify the statement.

"It's never a dull moment," he smirked, for reasons she'd never fathom.

Three, four, knock on the door. The guard turned smartly and walked away, glancing back at the bend in the corridor.

He went inside. Sir Peter was standing by a window; he seemed to be gazing through the blinds, beyond the blast-proof glass at the real world below. "Shall I tell you something, Thomas? I still bring in a camera, on occasion. Some mornings, I watch the Thames, flowing like an artery through the city."

Thomas closed the door and waited there. "You sent for me, sir."

"Some things never change. That great river — whatever we call it. Whether it's flowing in London or England or the United Kingdom, it doesn't change the river."

Thomas figured the philosophy lecture was just for openers and sat down. "You forgot to add *Europe* to your Thames list."

"Indeed I did." Sir Peter crossed the room and took his chair behind the mahogany desk. "You mistakenly think you understand the rules because you persist in seeing things in black and white — Mr McNeill the hero and I the villain."

He cupped his chin in one hand and propped his elbow on the chair arm. "A woman is dead because someone was more interested in cutting a few corners to a sales target than in the risks. That's the cold truth — black, white or grey."

"I agree with you."

Thomas lifted his head and sat a little straighter.

"But I also recognise that the Scavenger will one day be a valuable asset, once the problems are ironed out. What's needed is more time."

He heard the rest of the speech in disbelief. The high points — if he could call them that — hit him like a set of knuckles: align himself with Michael Schaefer, distance himself from Major Eldridge, and accept a temporary assignment at Engamel.

Reading between the lines, the major must have kept secret the data that Thomas had retrieved from Jess. Which suggested he had a plan of his own.

Sir Peter Carroll leaned in, hands resting on the desk. It had all the hallmarks of a sermon "We want the same things, Thomas. You simply need to see this in a wider context."

He found himself nodding, mainly at his own decision to have it all out with Karl, once and for all. He smiled and Sir Peter smiled back, mistaking his motivation.

"I'm glad we had the chance to talk. That'll be all then; keep me informed."

* * *

The *Guard du Jour* was waiting at the lift. "So, any tips for me, Mr Bladen?"

He stared at the lift buttons for inspiration. "First, make sure that you enjoy your own company and don't need a social life. And learn to read people carefully, lass."

He received a broad grin for his trouble. "Maybe you could talk me through a few things, over a drink sometime?"

His lips squeezed together. "That was the first people test — I'm spoken for."

* * *

It probably should have surprised him to find Karl loitering outside in the street, but he was all surprised-out for the day.

"You took yer time, Tommo. Come on, let's take a wee walk."

They made it as far as the nearest pub that met Karl's exacting standards. Karl opted for a cross between a sandwich and a full meal. Thomas, grateful for the chance of real food instead of snacks, plumped for some stew.

The food arrived and Karl led a full assault on his plate while he talked. "What's on your mind then? You've got a real face on you."

"Are you going back to the army?" However gruffly he'd tried to say it, he still sounded like a petulant teenager rowing with his girlfriend.

"Nope." Karl gulped down a mouthful of food. "I already told you. It suited my purpose to let the major think I was keen on the idea."

"So you lied to him then?"

Karl bit into his wrap, exercising his right to remain silent.

"Sir Peter wants me to work at Engamel for a while."

Karl shook his head. "That's not good news. Either he's getting desperate or Schaefer has something up his sleeve. Anything else you wanna talk about?"

Once he'd started, it just kept on coming. The major holding back on Jess's data; Sir Peter seemingly at odds with the major; Schaefer being made of asbestos. And then there was the business with Jack Langton. He stepped lightly around the quicksand, letting

Karl know the bare bones. It felt strangely exhilarating, being on the controlling end of the equation.

"So, I'll be able to find out when Jack Langton is next on the move, but it'll be short notice." He took a dramatic pause and shovelled in another mouthful of stew. "I've also discovered his delivery point."

Karl waved a knife in the air, singsong fashion. "Well played. We could hit him there."

The light from Karl's knife seemed to flicker across his face. Maybe that was the thing making Thomas squirm.

"Yeah, about that — not enough time."

"Pity. Anyway, with what you've put together, we could at least disrupt Jack's business."

Thomas was warming to this by the second. "What have you got in mind?"

"Well . . ." Karl jabbed towards his plate. "If we knew exactly when Jack was doing his rounds, we could put the police on to him."

Thomas felt a chill clawing up his spine. First priority: keep Sheryl out of it. But maybe Karl was on to something. "It would take some coordinating."

"I'm sure a man of your abilities and *connections* could work out a way to involve the Met."

Thomas got the message loud and clear: Ajit. Karl must have learned about his job in the police during the business on the moors. Best book a call to Yorkshire, later. Odd, though, that Karl should want to bring in the police. "Say Jack Langton *is* picked up by the police, how does that help you turn him against Martin and Francis-Andrew?"

"Wait and see. What car did you say our Mr Langton drives?"

"Beemer — a sporty one."

"Well there you are then. Odds on he's got a family car tucked away somewhere as well. We need to know what it is, and we can hardly ask Thurston Lyon to do a recce."

"I'll do a run-by tonight, on the way home."

"Nice one. Listen, I know I've been a bit off lately, what with . . ." Karl's mobile rang — saved by the bell. "Hello? Ah, Stuart, thanks for ringing me back." He didn't speak again for a minute, nodding slowly as if coming to some terrible conclusion. "You did the right thing. Yeah, send it straight over. Bye." He didn't take his eyes off the phone, didn't move again until the bleep announced the text. Then he hit the button and gazed at the pixels, ashen faced.

"Are you okay?" Thomas put down his cutlery.

"Take a look." Karl passed the phone over. "Stuart went to ma's funeral, to see whether Frances-Andrew or Martin turned up. Someone else did — my father."

Thomas stared at the screen. "When did you last . . . ?"

"A long time ago." He sounded younger, trapped in some memory he'd rather not visit again.

Thomas sighed and returned the phone. Life was a cruel bastard. Karl hadn't seen his dad in years, by the sound of it; Sheryl wanted to disown hers; and as for him, he hardly ever spoke to his family, let alone saw them. And the last time it'd ended up as a police matter. Something else he'd have to tread around carefully when he spoke to Ajit later.

* * *

"Is that Ajit of the Yard?"

"By 'eck, is that the famous Mr Bladen, the one who went foreign?" Then, in a change of tone, "no, it's for me."

Thomas smiled. The bickering from Pickering was one of the great constants in his life.

"Sorry, just the little woman . . . *ow, give over!* So, we're still talking then?"

"Course we are." It sounded like the first hurdle was a low one.

"Only, wi' Geena and Miranda on the blower, I was starting to feel left out."

Blimey. "Yeah, it's er, actually a work-related thing I'm ringing about." He heard a piece of furniture creak into submission as Ajit made himself comfortable.

"Should I get me notebook and pen?"

"Might not be a bad idea."

"Ee, I were only taking the piss. 'ang on." Then there was hissing and scrabbling about. "Sorry, that were Geena — I'm not allowed to swear int' house now. It's practice for when baby comes. Right, I'm ready."

"Okay, I've got this tip-off — drug related. But I don't know *when* yet. And I have intelligence that can help you nab a nasty bastard, if we get the timing right."

Ajit took notes and asked pertinent questions, which Thomas did his best to deflect. He wondered whether Ajit was enjoying this as much as he was. The old duo, back on the same side.

"It's unusual," Ajit made a noise somewhere between a sigh and a grumble, "I'll grant you that. But it's not a problem. We have procedures for this sort of thing. Of course, you could speak to the London coppers yourself."

"No," he snapped. "I can't be involved — because of my job. Anonymously would be best, but if not, then I know I can trust you."

"Righto, mum's the word. And you'll let me know when?"

"Yeah, on the same day, probably." *Which is why the boys in blue need to be ready.* Thanks, Ajit, this is really important to me."

"Should I ask: is this purely work or personal?"

Thomas paused. "So, how's Geena?"

Ajit coughed politely. "Well enough, let me put her on."

She didn't stay on the phone very long. Long enough to tell him that Miranda was a good sort — as if he didn't know that already — and that it'd be lovely to see the two of them again. If he could manage it without the fancy dress next time.

"Anyhow, I'll leave you two boys to chat. Take care of yourself, Uncle Thomas."

Ajit didn't have a lot else to say. He was fired up though, Thomas could tell. Which was all to the good.

Chapter 37

The answering machine was winking when Thomas got out of the shower. He always checked, on the off chance. He pulled a towel off his head and hit the magic button.

"Are you picking me up at the club tonight or meeting me at Mum and Dad's? Let me know what your busy schedule will allow. See you later, babe."

He turned a yawn into a grin and wandered into the kitchen whistling a Four Tops' tune. This was already showing every sign of being a great day and it wasn't even seven o'clock.

Washed, dressed and crammed with toast, he fired up his laptop to check the major's phone lines. There was one call from the previous night, a late one — to Michael Schaefer. He was either very sure of himself or hoping for early retirement, threatening to blow the whistle about Amy's death and go public like that. Schaefer didn't back down, reminding the major that he knew about his affair with Amy. Then the major made a counter bid for top dog.

'I have the remaining firing mechanism, from the second Scavenger."

Thomas clicked the pause and recoiled from the screen. No the major didn't, but *they* did. So why hadn't Karl brought it up again? Something else to discuss with the Celtic Wonder.

He let the recording run its course, made some scribbles on that very creased piece of paper he'd been carrying around for days, and powered down the computer. Something had to give, and soon.

Even with the radio jabbering on, against the backdrop of London traffic, Thomas couldn't help thinking about Karl — specifically, about his dad. About all those years Karl had lived in exile, hardly able to see one parent and shunned by the other. Life hadn't dealt Karl a very fair hand. Which naturally made Thomas think of Sheryl.

Ajit was supposed to be on early shift today. If he was true to his word — and you could bank on that with Ajit — then the call would go through to London today. And then it'd be a waiting game. Sheryl had said there was no set pattern to Jack Langton's appearances, sometimes twice in a week, or weeks without showing up. Funny that he'd never seen Jack Langton at Caliban's though.

* * *

Maybe Lea Bridge Road wasn't the smartest move of the day, but he couldn't face the gridlock of Seven Sisters. And besides, the back roads were always more interesting, once you got there. He switched radio stations and caught the tail end of some political piece; it made his blood run cold.

"Of course, the modern theatre of war has changed beyond recognition and technological capabilities have had to change in tandem. These days, the challenges are flexibility and speed of response. New materials, new technologies even — that is the way forward."

Somehow Thomas managed to stick with it to the bitter end: 'And I'd like to thank Major Charles Eldridge, DSO.' The words that came to mind were *shit* and *fan*. And the question that came to mind: what was Thomas going to do about it?

He rang ahead to Karl, on hands-free.

"I heard it was coming last night, Tommo. I didn't ring you — thought you had enough going on. It puts our contact in a very difficult position. Get in as soon as you can. And if the major rings you, *don't* answer it."

* * *

Three worried faces greeted him as he entered the office. Ann Crossley was on her way out, mustering a smile as she passed. "You'd better reprioritise your workstack."

Karl and Christine were in mid disagreement, which was a novelty.

"All I'm saying here is let *me* talk with the major. I'll get him to see sense."

"For the last time, Karl, we are past that. The radio interview was a warning — to Schaefer and everyone else. You either follow my orders or you find yourself a new section — understand?"

"Ma'am," Karl barked fiercely.

501

"Right," Christine looked at them both. "I don't care what went on in Belfast, I'm not interested. If there are any loose ends, you better tie them up quickly because as soon as Clarity calls, you start running. Thomas," she pointed at him, "your phone stays on 24/7 from now on. Karl will be available to assist you whenever you need it."

As if that was ever in doubt. She froze for a moment, like an old computer, trying to process more information than it could handle.

"Permission to speak?" Karl managed to stay just the right side of sounding like a twat.

She flashed a weary look that Thomas knew intimately. "Well?"

"Look, we're on the same side, Christine. You have your orders, but I'm already pegged as a stroppy bastard. If I were to speak with Major Eldridge it would be without your approval, if it ever came out."

Christine glanced Thomas's way and he nodded slightly, willing her to make the right decision. She narrowed her eyes.

"I'm going into my office and I don't want to be disturbed. Keep the personal calls to a minimum." She blinked in Karl's direction and started walking. "Thank you."

Thomas gave Karl a little space to do the necessary. Maybe Christine wasn't so inflexible after all. He put his mobiles on the desk and unwound a serpents' nest of chargers — work official, personal and work unofficial. At this rate, he'd need a bigger desk.

A mobile erupted into life. He snatched at it and checked the screen: number unknown. Not good news. It could be the major or it could be Sheryl — only one way to find out. On the third ring, Christine lifted her office window blind aside, staring out at him. He took a breath: shit-or-bust time — again.

"Hello?"

The line crackled. "Hey, Thomas." Sheryl sounded lost, unable find her way back from somewhere.

"I'm here," he emphasised, like a parent to a child waking from a bad dream.

"Jack rang — he's coming over later." She gulped. "You promised . . ."

"I'm on it, leave it to me." He let Sheryl ring off, looked over at Christine and shook his head slowly, until she closed the blind. Then he grabbed his own mobile and speed-dialled Yorkshire. "Aj, it's Thomas. That little problem I told you about last night?"

"Aye, well . . ." Ajit retreated. "I've not spoken to anyone yet." He was apologetic, with a hint of belligerence. "I were called in early — big police operation — I can't talk now."

He got in quickly. "But what about the Borough Intelligence Unit?"

Ajit didn't respond. All Thomas heard was background chatter and the jet-stream swish of traffic. He let it rest there. His fingers tapped the desk, frantically beating out a call to his brain. Jack Langton would be on the move any time now.

"Karl." He swivelled round to meet him. "We need to talk — outside."

* * *

He stood back against the brickwork, hyped up by the cacophony of London chaos and his own desperation.

"I'm waiting, Thomas." Karl leant back, coiled like a cat.

"That call was my contact — Jack Langton is picking up drugs today."

"Fantastic. Let me know the moment the police have picked him up. I've still got something to sort out on my side before I'm ready to make a move.

Thomas searched the grey London sky for inspiration. Nice try, anyway. "I need a massive favour, Karl." He paused, to gauge the reaction. "My mate in Yorkshire couldn't pass the info on in time."

"Ah well, it'll have to be another time. Shame though . . ."

"No." Thomas pressed a hand against Karl's arm, as if afraid he was going to walk away. "You don't understand — it *has* to be today."

"Steady on there, Tommo. What do you expect me to do about it? I've already told you I can't be involved — as far as Jack's concerned, I'm still rotting in a cell."

"I know you have contacts all over the place," he watched Karl's face change, reading him back. "I need someone to relay a message through formal channels — someone who will be listened to at the local Borough Intelligence Unit. All I'm asking for is someone to call."

Karl held his gaze. Then he straightened up to his full height and his chest seemed to sag. "They'll want something in return."

Thomas had figured as much, but Sheryl was as close to Miranda as he was and that was good enough reason to proceed. "Can we do it now?"

"That's a big ask . . ."

He stood his ground, imagining Jack Langton leaving his house and Sheryl waiting at hers, trapped.

"Let's take a walk." Karl didn't wait for an answer, heading off towards Middlesex Street.

"I wouldn't ask if there was any other way . . ." he let the sentence finish itself.

"Rules first. You're on your own with this. All I need to know for our little operation is when — or if — he's under lock and key. Next, you don't *ever* ask me again. And lastly, you'll have to convince them to take action — tell them it's a code five priority."

Blimey, a magic password. He nodded solemnly. "I really appreciate this, Karl. I know it's . . ."

Karl physically stopped him. "Save it for the phone box." He dug out a handful of change.

When they got there, he turned his back while Karl dialled.

"Right, I'll see you later." The door shrieked open.

He grabbed the phone and pressed it close to his ear.

"Internal Communications." The voice was male and nonchalant, daring him to play this game through.

"I have a code five emergency."

The voice on the other end didn't respond.

"Sorry. I'm new to this. I have a code five priority, requiring police assistance."

"Please state your name, caller."

He huffed down the phone, the sound roaring in his ears like a spring tide. "There isn't much time. I can give you all the details, but I can't give you my name."

"I think you may have the wrong number."

"Wait." He pre-empted the click. "This is a direct threat to one of *your* operatives." *Bollocks, should have said 'our.'* "At least let me pass on the information, for the Borough Intelligence Unit." The phone was silent. For all he knew he could be on loudspeaker. Almost certainly being recorded.

He chose to believe they were still interested, threw in another load of coins and went through the salient points — Jack Langton and his drug dealing, his car, the pick-up point and the need to catch him in the act today. Then he had an inspiration and added that Langton might be armed — that was payback for the windscreen.

"It will be looked into. What's your number?"

"Hold on a moment." He pulled out a slip of paper from his jacket and read out Karl's throwaway mobile. The voice didn't say anything more; maybe he was expecting some other code word. The line went dead.

Thomas put the receiver back and pressed the sweat between his palms. Then he picked it up again and dialled a random series of numbers before replacing it, just in case the next person got curious. As he turned to leave, the dampness across his back pressed cold against his skin. And his world had shifted a little closer to Karl's.

* * *

Coffee was the only sure-fire cure for the adrenaline tremor in his hands. Thank God for railway stations. He'd just sat down with his Americano and a healthy chunk of carrot cake when the magic mobile went off.

"Hello?" He could barely squeeze the word out.

"The BIU has been advised; the matter will be looked into."

"Thank you — will someone . . .?"

"You'll be informed if there is any development."

He took a large gulp of coffee and let the heat permeate his mouth, circling in waves through his abdomen as he swallowed. It took a moment to realise that the call had finished. His imagination was still in overdrive. What if he joined Karl in that secret army of his?

The lure of hidden knowledge had always been there, even back at school when he discovered that two of his teachers were meeting after hours. He'd memorised several of their car number plates, so when two were parked up in a side street, it didn't take much to check out all the nearby pub and restaurant windows. He smiled now, thinking about it — that delicious feeling of power at school the next day. Telling no one, not even Ajit. Maybe that was the appeal of the Surveillance Support Unit: knowing other people's secrets without them knowing.

Time to juggle mobiles again. "Hi, Miranda."

"About bloody time; I was beginning to think you'd forgotten me."

"Not a chance! So, what's your pleasure tonight — picked up at Caliban's or star crossed lovers at Mum and Dad's?"

"Blimey, you are in a good mood — did you get a gold star for spying today?" She sounded like a primary school teacher talking to a five-year-old. He let it pass.

"Something like that. Any pref then?"

"Tell you what, I'll make my own way over. I'm a big girl now."

He laughed down the phone, aware that people around him were probably peering over their lattes by now — sod 'em. "You certainly are, if memory serves me right." Her laughter cascaded into his, filling him with a heat no coffee could ever match.

* * *

He was whistling as he re-entered the building, a mobile in each pocket and one inside his jacket, like some hi-tech gunslinger. Still imagining Karl's handshake of congratulation when everything went down as planned.

Ann Crossley was by the vending machine; no one else was around.

"Where's Karl?" He noted Karl's approach to the clear desk policy — laptop away but plastic cups and chocolate wrappers still there.

She looked at him and squinted. "I thought he was with you, working?"

He played the odds in his head and settled for a safe bet. "Yeah, I thought he might have finished ahead of me."

"Why don't you ring him?" Her eyes shimmered.

"It can wait." He aimed for *casual* and left her to it, plugging his mobiles back in at the desk and arranging them for easy reach. If Christine was still in her lair, she gave no sign. That was fine. Being under Crossley's eager gaze was enough.

Ten thirty came and went, with no calls and no Karl. He busied himself, checking the major's call log with headphones on. There was nothing remarkable, other than a distinct lack of calls with those nice people at Engamel. Mrs Eldridge had seemed jittery though; perhaps she knew more than was good for her.

The report template stared back at him from the screen. He made a couple of stabs at it, then pulled out a writing pad to organise his thoughts. Christine would need to see *something* for his days since the base accident. On the plus side, there were some unsocial hours to claim for, plus the lockdown and a night on the base: hurrah for paperwork.

Eleven fifteen. Jack Langton could be on his way to a police reception. Unless he'd changed his plans or they cocked it up somehow. He caught himself drumming on the desk again.

"Is there something on your mind?" Ann Crossley swivelled towards him.

He smacked his lips and swung round to face her. "How do you . . ." he searched for the right words, ". . . keep your working priorities separate?"

She tilted her head and smiled. It was the sort of smile that used to wind him up. "It took me years of practice, Thomas; years of practice. Is there something *specific* I can help you with, in Karl's absence?"

It happened again, that blurring of accents. Whenever Ann Crossley got a little too interested in something, those Cardiff high notes became audible, like a poker tell.

"No, I'll figure it out — thanks anyway." He jerked the chair away, pondering the twist of fate that had partnered him with Karl. Another day and another detail, and he'd have been swapping secrets with Ann Crossley across the desk, as the civilian help for . . . Naval Intelligence, wasn't it?

In the end, he cobbled together the reports as best he could and decided he'd talk it through with Christine. No point giving her more information than she needed, and no point in wasting too much energy on it beforehand. He smiled, that could have been Karl talking.

He was halfway through making a to-do list for that evening's jaunt to the Wrights when the balloon finally went up. Wary of being watched, he reached across for the mobile calmly, tasting the inside of his mouth.

"Your information has been acted upon, with a satisfactory conclusion. We will call you again."

"Thank you." He gazed around the room, grinning as if he'd just won first prize in a phone-in.

Ann Crossley looked over and just nodded at him. He felt like yelling to release the pounding in his chest, but he didn't. He took some slow, deep breaths — just as the counsellor had taught him — and moved on to his next call.

Sheryl sounded years younger. "Hello?"

"It's Thomas — it's done."

She burst into tears and he squeezed his jaw tight as he listened. He knew what it felt when the tide had finally shifted in your favour. That first morning after the moors, when he'd woken up in Pickering, knowing Miranda was safe and Yorgi was lying on a slab somewhere, he'd wept out of sheer relief.

"Listen, I've got to go. I'll see you at Caliban's sometime."

"Yeah," she sucked in a breath. "What will happen . . .?"

"I don't know. I can try and find out, if you want?"

"No, better you don't. I couldn't face being disappointed right now." She snorted a laugh. "Anyway, thanks again, Thomas. You don't know what this means to me."

"Don't mention it." He blushed and thanked one of his mother's saints as Sheryl put the phone down. A call to Karl's mobile went straight through to voicemail. He did his best to hide his excitement, relaying the message word for word.

Chapter 38

It was fast becoming a day of surprises. Ann Crossley had invited him to lunch — a first. They settled for a pub that Karl would have approved of — the décor anyway, if not the clientele. The features looked original, but the drinkers were mostly a bunch of bankers.

Crossley did the honours, fetching back a couple of soft drinks and the promise of hot food. She smiled a lot, which didn't suit her. It was on the cards they'd be playing question time so he made a pre-emptive strike.

"What got you into this line of work, then?"

She sipped her juice and paused, mid-air. "I did languages and politics at university. It was a logical step." She shrugged, as if to say it was something that just happened.

He didn't buy it. From the little he'd seen, just about *no one* ended up in the SSU by chance. She looked at him, waiting. He'd already trotted this routine out to Karl, no qualms about it because it was the truth.

"I worked in Central London, at a civil service desk. But I'd always done photography. And one day Sir Peter Carroll and me were in a lift after work. . ."

She laughed, the way people usually did. As if to say: 'Is that what *really* happened?' But it was. He hadn't even considered it as a permanent option until after the second weekend job. And even then there wasn't much to tell. Turn up, use a better camera, sit on his arse all day not talking to the people around him, take some long lens footage, and then hand in his camera and go home. Of course, he knew he was good. He knew he could impress them without trying too hard.

The food arrived. He broke off from his thrilling monologue and made short work of the gammon. They flipped a coin, best of three — she paid and he'd owe her for next time. This was turning out to be a brilliant day. All it needed now was Karl to burst in with a box of chocolates. Speaking of which . . .

"You, er, seem to be getting on better with Karl these days."

"Ah, the elusive Mr McNeill. I was wondering how long it would be before he joined the conversation." The laughter sounded genuine. "We haven't always hit it off — let's call it professional rivalry. But I've always respected him, in the main."

He was itching to probe deeper and find out whether there was more to it. But hey, what was she going to do — sign a confession?

"The thing is, Thomas," she did it again, bending the second syllable of his name. "Someone like you is in a strong position to get his career going — from this point on. I mean, you don't want to be doing this for the rest of your life, do you?"

It could almost have been one of Christine's old scripts — or her mother's.

"It'll do for now. I'm afraid I don't have any great ambitions — they didn't teach us that at my school." Not if you weren't paying attention, anyway.

"I used to have all that working-class pride in my veins too. Then I got a scholarship and saw my potential. It's never too late, you know."

He put down a chip, firm and golden against the rim of the plate. "This is starting to sound like a recruitment speech."

She was all smiles again. "Would that be such a bad thing?" she said, finishing her drink.

* * *

At three thirty, Karl put in an appearance at work. "Any more news?"

"Nah. All quiet on the Western Front. Where have you been?"

Karl sauntered over, waving to Ann Crossley who returned the favour and pretended not to watch him. He made sure he stood with his back to her and bent forward over Thomas's desk. "I was getting this sorted." He produced a ring box.

Thomas clicked back the lid. Inside was a bullet, polished and gleaming, and engraved with a harp." He tilted it so the ceiling light ran along the surface. It looked like a work of art. "For Jack?" he hissed. "You are kidding?" Judging by Karl's face, clearly not.

"Too subtle, do you think? I was going to go for a shamrock, but I thought this said it better."

Thomas strained his eyes to try and fathom out the point. "Why?"

"Because, Tommy Boy, someone would only do this if they didn't care what Jack thought about it. It's a 'fuck you' message — loud and clear."

"Fine. I get it. He'll link it with the Belfast firm. But how are you going to get it to him, especially now he's inside?"

"That's where you come in. Fancy a little unpaid overtime tonight?"

He made a face. "I'm supposed to be meeting Miranda."

Karl nodded, tongue between his teeth, as if he were tasting the air. "Not a problem; I won't be needing you until late. I'll call you on the magic phone."

As soon as Karl went off in search of chocolate, Thomas cranked out an email to him. Stupid really, sending an email to the desk behind him, but it was liberating to have control over a conversation with Karl, at least at the start.

Crossley took me to the pub for lunch. I think she wants me to join her gang. Care to top that?

Karl shuffled back to his desk and an email pinged in. Thomas heard his laughter, and the sound of him scuttling away again. And then the grinding of the vending machine. More footsteps, and a chocolate delight landed on his desk.

An email followed soon after. *Dessert beats the main course — I win!* Three lines below he'd added, like an afterthought: *Of course, you're a free agent. In this office, you're the only one of us who is.*

* * *

He left the office early, to get a bag together at home. Mindful that Clarity's call was overdue, he packed the Makarov pistol, as well as a black balaclava and face paint.

At the flat, he checked both bugs on the major's phone lines once more. Funny that Major Eldridge hadn't contacted him lately, despite acquiring the missing data from Jess. So why had the major gone to ground since then? Something else to obsess about in traffic.

* * *

The cut-through, avoiding Forest Road, was as treacherous as a politician. Snarled up, bumper-to-bumper, he went over the day's events aloud. More pluses than minuses, for sure, but fewer answers than questions.

One thing bothered him unreasonably; something he'd always let pass before — who exactly did Karl work for in the *evening* job? He'd figured it was connected to Karl's army days, so maybe Army

510

Intelligence? And was that the same as MI5? And what was all that stuff about Code Five? He drummed the steering wheel as the lights changed. That settled it; he'd grab a few minutes on John Wright's computer and do a little sleuthing.

Might he not be better off though, remaining in the dark while Karl, Ann and Christine performed in their three-ring circus? He chewed that over as some stupid bastard in a plumber's van tried to play 'pick a lane.' Did he really want to know about Karl? Of course he bloody did. Knowledge was power. And power was control.

* * *

Diane Wright was outside the front door when he pulled up — must have been waiting.

"Sorry I'm late — traffic was a 'mare."

She laughed at his attempt at a cockney accent. The lingo still sounded wrong coming from his lips.

"There's one extra at the table tonight," she looked hard at him, as if he were supposed to know something.

He grabbed his lucky bag and followed her inside. The front room door yawned open so he poked his head in. Everyone turned towards him. The full family were there, Miranda, sitting seductively at one end of the settee, gave him a little wave. So did the person next to her: Sheryl.

Diane squeezed his shoulder as she passed through to the kitchen. The warmth in her fingers thawed him a little, but not much. He set his bag down and checked it was zipped up. *Right then, best foot forward.* "Everything all right?" he asked the room in general, trying to play it cool.

"We're celebrating," Miranda nodded to two champagne magnums, one already opened. "Help yourself to a glass."

The weight of their attention made every step across the room drag. "Just a small one. I'm working later on." Best to get the bad news out of the way early on. He braved a look at Miranda — she wasn't pouting. That was a first. All eyes followed him as he measured out a small glass.

"How d'ya do it, Thomas?" Sam broke the silence.

"Sam!" John barked. "What did we agree?"

"Sorry, Dad, it just slipped out."

He turned to face them, sipping at the champagne to cool his face down. Sheryl and Miranda parted company on the settee, leaving him the middle space.

"Sit your arse down," John tipped back his lager.

He sat, a thorn between two roses, and sipped his drink. Everyone seemed to be looking at nowhere in particular, like at a wake.

"Oh, for fuck's sake, someone say something." Miranda ended the deadlock with her usual light touch.

Sheryl leaned forward and pressed Thomas's arm. "I told them about Jack Langton being my dad."

John Wright lowered his glass. "I did wonder sometimes, but it's not the sort of thing you ask — not of Jack anyway."

"I'm gonna look in on the kitchen." Thomas got up, trying to ignore the fevered whispers behind him.

"Alright, love?" Diane was counting out the plates. She smiled; she didn't seem to need an answer. "This must be your worst nightmare — stuck in the limelight."

He leant against the breakfast bar, empty glass in his hand.

"Never you mind, Thomas. You did a good thing. Give 'em a few minutes and they'll find someone else to pick on."

As if by magic, an expensive lace-up boot was tapping on the floor tiles. "Not sure I like the idea of my bloke preferring my mum's company to mine."

"Well maybe you should try treating him better." Diane grinned.

"Bloody cheek. Treat 'em mean, keep 'em keen — that's what you taught me."

Even over dinner — shepherd's pie, coincidentally, one of Thomas's favourites — Sam and Terry were still eyeing his every move.

"Thing is, Thomas," Terry spoke through a mouthful of churning potato, "this makes you an even darker horse than we thought. Which is saying something."

"Let the man eat in peace." John had the final say, but he looked as proud as a season ticket holder when the Hammers won the FA Cup.

Thomas stole a glance at Sheryl, wondering just how much of her soul she'd unburdened before he arrived.

Sheryl peered back, uncharacteristically quiet, with the same expression she had worn at her flat. The tension was breaking him out in a sweat. "Sorry," she mouthed, "I had to tell them."

By the time they'd finished dessert, the atmosphere had lifted. Diane fetched out two packs of cards from the special cupboard, opened one and confounded the menfolk with Find the Lady. Both Miranda and Sheryl were immune to the trick.

Poker was the big event. The solemn appearance of the box of casino chips seemed to cast an invisible shadow over the frivolity. The Wright children watched the box as it proceeded to the table, now covered with green baize. The whole thing was almost a religious experience.

There were no family allegiances when it came to poker, and very little talking unless someone was trying to soften you up or psych you out. Thomas had long since decided that Karl would be a natural poker player. Maybe he'd wangle him an invite for Christmas.

Thomas played cautiously, studying his opponents as chips piled up in the middle of the table. Miranda ran her tongue along her lip for his benefit. He took that as a sign she was bluffing and upped the bet. It was a short-lived strategy.

As he folded, out of chips and out of luck, a call he'd been waiting for finally came through. No one commented. He took it outside the room.

"Tommo, are you available?"

"Give me ten minutes — you picking me up?"

"Yeah, better to have just the one vehicle. I'll be outside."

He made his excuses, grabbed the bag in the hall and went off to change in Miranda's room. Dressed head to toe in black, he kept the balaclava and face paint in his pocket and called a goodbye to his hosts. Miranda muttered something about waiting up for him, and that was that.

Karl was already parked up, similarly attired. "Good to see ya. Hope I didn't spoil your evening any?"

He smiled. He didn't know exactly what he was getting into, but the mere fact he was doing it with Karl made him feel safe. Like a teenager who trusts his mates implicitly. "So what's the plan?"

"Simple really. The Langton household have another vehicle. I want to do to them what they did to your car. Then I put this . . ." he tapped the ring with his gloved finger, ". . . through his letterbox as a message."

"His wife will be terrified — seems a bit unfair."

Karl looked across as the streetlights blurred by. "Tell that to my mother."

There was no talking on the rest of the journey, and little to discuss. Thomas would act as the lookout while Karl neutered the car alarm and punched the windows.

"Thomas, are you armed?"

"Jesus, no. What do you take me for?" He stopped then because he remembered the Makarov waiting for him back in Miranda's room.

"Only asking."

"Why, are you?" Mrs Langton was hardly public enemy number one. Not her fault she'd married a thug.

"Not armed as such but I'm equipped to defend myself."

"From what?" Now he was starting to worry.

"Just a precaution, Tommy Boy. Jack Langton isn't an idiot. He'll probably think he's been set up — hopefully by Martin and Francis-Andrew. By the time he gets home, he'll be sure of it. Anyway, could be he'll have someone staying over at the house to protect his wife."

* * *

Karl parked on a corner, offering a good vantage point in three directions — one of them facing the road where Jack's house stood. "Right, here's yours," he passed Thomas a walkie-talkie. "Very simple. You see anyone, and it's one tone. Anyone you think is suspect and it's two tones. Anyone suspect heading *my* way and you drive towards me and beep the horn. Smooth, mind — no amateur dramatics. I get in the car and away we go — got it?"

Thomas watched the darkness, glad that he'd opted to leave out the balaclava and face paint — tricky to explain if someone passed by. It was close on midnight now, nothing to see but curtained lights blinking off.

He couldn't put his finger on it, but there was something satisfying about this. He'd missed. His senses strained against the glass, rigid with tension and also loving it.

Then his walkie-talkie two-toned. That wasn't part of Karl's pre-flight safety sequence. He started up the car and pulled out, crossing the side street. He cut the lights and let it move slowly forward. Half way down the road, a figure walked out, waving an arm to slow him down. As he drew level, Karl got into the back of the car, behind him.

"Slow as you can and don't over-rev. I'll tell you when to stop." He lowered the rear window, letting in the cool night air. "Steady now, pull alongside the people carrier, on the right."

At first the vehicle looked undamaged, until Thomas noticed four flat tyres.

"Get ready, I've posted the bullet. So it's two strikes and then we're out of here." Karl leaned out of the window and swung back with what looked like a hatchet, smashing through the windscreen then swinging the other way for the driver's window.

Thomas didn't hang about, pulling away smartly to the sound of a ferocious dog barking somewhere behind them. He couldn't speak, could only focus on resurrecting the headlights and creating some distance. Karl wound the window up and sat back with a contented sigh.

"Nice work, amigo. The car was too new for me to chance the alarm so I settled initially for puncturing all the tyres. Then I thought

514

'no, fuck it,' his boys did it to you. That was one loud alarm though, eh?"

Thomas shook his head. He hadn't heard anything apart from broken glass and the pounding in his chest. "An axe though?"

"Listen, at least I didn't put a bullet *through* the windscreen."

He couldn't argue with that.

"Have you time for one drink, Tommo?"

"Yeah, I'd like that."

"Grand. I hope you're not just saying so because of the axe on the back seat."

* * *

It was, as Karl had promised on the way in, the kind of joint where people dressed head to toe in black didn't raise any concerns. Basically, they were just glad of the business — any business. Two blokes at the far end were playing as good a game of darts as two people can play when they're really pissed, with as many darts landing in the wall as on the board. The barman watched them with a blank, bored expression plastered across his face.

Karl got in the provisions and directed Thomas as far as away from human contact as possible. "Here's to you, Kathleen Victoria McNeill." He raised a half-pint solemnly.

Thomas nodded, glancing at the pub lights turned golden through his glass. Karl was still lost in the moment, so he did the decent thing and left him to it.

"You know, back there on the job, Tommo, I think we shared a bit of a magic moment."

"Yeah," he filtered through the pile of crisps for three of a similar size. "I'll give you that. It was just like old times. Probably did me some good."

Karl nodded appreciatively then emptied his glass in a single pour. "I want you to know, Thomas, that I have always held you in the highest regard."

"What's your next move, then, apart from a shovel full of crisps?"

Karl laughed quietly but that distant look hadn't left his face. "Ideally, I'd get the chance to deliver some payback to Martin and Francis-Andrew — about twenty years' worth. I'm banking on tonight's trail of breadcrumbs leading Jack Langton straight to Belfast. Stuart Fraser could be a useful contact for stirring things up across the water, pointing the boys back towards Jack Langton. Just add hot water and stir. Me? I'm a regular *Yojimbo*."

515

Thomas knew he was expected to ask and chose not to. "Well, just don't go doing anything stupid — otherwise I'll end up being partnered with Ann Crossley permanently."

"Hey listen, she's come up in my estimation in the last few months."

"Now I am getting worried!"

"Relax, Tommo, I don't plan on going anywhere for the time being. Right, come on, let's get you home to the fair Miranda."

* * *

First thing Thomas did in the car was turn his mobile back on and check his voicemail. He was disappointed. "Tell me something, why doesn't Clarity just get in her car and keep driving?"

Karl turned the radio down even further. "Same reason Sir Peter Carroll wasn't deposed as head of the Surveillance Support Unit when you exposed him. It's not the way things are done, not when there's something bigger at stake. Sir Peter is of more use to us in Whitehall, and right now Clarity can get more done on the inside at Engamel."

Thomas looked at the mobile screen again.

"It'll be soon." Karl promised him. "Just you make sure you're on the ball."

He mock saluted; there was no smile in return.

"When the call comes in, ring me before you get on the road."

"But I thought you wanted to stay out of it."

Karl waved a hand, so-so fashion. "What I want and what has to be done can be very different things. Remember, Tommo, I'm on standby too. And listen, make sure you are fully equipped — do we understand each other?"

"Crystal." Thomas felt his trigger finger move involuntarily. "I'll see you." He got out of the car and walked up the drive.

The lights were still on in the Wrights' house. Time check: nearly one am. Now was one of those times when he wished he still had a key. Nothing else to do, but knock and hope someone was up.

Miranda eased back the door with the chain on. "Are you the tall, dark, handsome stranger I ordered online?"

He smiled wearily and she took the hint, closing the door to reopen it without the chain.

"We all waited up. Sam and Terry are throwing a bit of a moody — probably women trouble."

Funny, he'd never known them to have any trouble with women. He followed Miranda in and muttered something about how nice a cup of tea would be. He was still blushing from what she'd muttered in return as he entered the front room.

Diane, John, the boys and Sheryl all sat to attention. "Everything all right, Thomas — with Karl and that?" John got in there first.

He nodded and grabbed a seat. Almost immediately, Terry and Sam stood as one and headed for the kitchen. "Something I said?"

"Take no notice Thomas, those two have been acting up all evening." Diane swept a hand in the air, in their wake.

"Maybe it's their time of the month — they've synchronised." Sheryl grinned.

Miranda returned with a mug in each hand. "Kettle's boiled if anyone else wants one — the Brothers *Grim*," she nodded to Thomas, who'd first coined the phrase, "are still out there, bickering about something."

The conversation died down again. Diane and John gave up the cause and said their goodnights. Only then did Sheryl start talking again. "Will Jack go to prison?"

Thomas figured that she'd filled Miranda in about the drugs, otherwise she wouldn't be asking him openly.

"I don't know." He felt bad saying it, wished he could reassure her it would all go away. But he didn't bullshit his friends. "It all depends on whether he had the stuff on him when he was nicked." He stopped and drank his tea.

"Well, I'll leave you two lovebirds alone. I'll see you in the morning."

"Here we are, then." Miranda leaned against him, both hands clasped around the mug.

He tilted his head and squeezed his shoulders back, feeling the relief as the tension shifted. "Are you still cool with Sheryl, now you know she's a Langton?"

"Let's just go to bed." She spoke through a yawn. And the way she said it, there wasn't a come-on for miles around.

His bag was waiting in her room, unopened. There was no preamble; all those pretences had been scoured off by the years. She escaped from her jeans and stepped into the en-suite, leaving him to it. He waited until he could hear her peeing before he checked the bag again, making sure the Makarov was there and loaded.

He tried the bathroom door and went inside. And even though no good would come of it tonight, he couldn't resist drawing her hips towards his and wrapping himself around her. She tasted fresh, like the perfect after-dinner mint. But sleep was the only thing on the menu.

Last thing before lights out, he plugged the mobile in and turned the glow to the wall. Then he hit the light switch and lay there, Miranda's leg against his, strong and sensuous. He closed his eyes and relived the craziness of the day. He felt wrung out by the end of it

517

and turned towards Miranda in the dark, smiling at the sound of her sleeping. With any luck, they'd get a lie-in. The way the day had gone, he was definitely feeling lucky.

* * *

It took a few seconds to realise that the ringtone was his. Miranda squirmed under the duvet, muttered and elbowed him sharply. He was wide-awake now, scrabbling over the side of the bed for the phone. Miranda hit the light, behind him.

"Hello?" It could be any one of three, four if he included Karl in the list.

"It's Clarity. I'm at Engamel. You need to come *now* — I can't talk." She cut the call.

He slumped out of bed to his knees and hit speed-dial. Karl picked up second ring, sounding impossibly alert.

"Thanks, Tommo, I'll do what I have to then get on the road. I'll see you there. Stay sharp."

As he dragged his clothes on, he was intoxicated with excitement. If he was anything, he was a creature of purpose and here was a purpose he could relish. He unzipped the bag and dug out a torch and the Makarov. As he turned to holster it in a side pocket, Miranda was sitting up in bed, watching him.

She didn't say anything at first — she didn't need to. Her face was a collage of disappointment and concern. He would have been more concerned too, if he'd had the time.

"Is it always going to be like this?"

He figured she knew better than to expect an answer. "Go back to sleep; I'll ring you later." He didn't bother qualifying that because it would only raise questions he didn't have answers to. As he reached the front door, he heard another mobile going off. Probably Sam or Terry's — women trouble after all, then.

Chapter 39

The door closed, like the great divide — on one side, Miranda and her family; and on the other a place of shadows and intrigue: Karl's world. He connected the mobile to the hands-free unit and started up the car, heading for the M25 London Orbital Motorway, to pick up the M40 for Chipping Norton and the Engamel Facility.

It was four thirty in the morning and he was wired from a lack of decent sleep, thoughts whirling in his head to the sound of the engine. And the further he travelled, the less anything made any sense. Why had Clarity rung him now? And what was he supposed to do — turn up at the gate like a minicab and whisk her away? Nah, Michael Schaefer wasn't the amenable type. There was no plan and another ten miles of driving made no impact on that.

The mobile kicked off again. He clicked the button and prepared to shout — the earpiece being safe and sound, back in the box. It must be Karl unless Clarity was ringing with an update.

"Yeah, it's Thomas. Go ahead, I'm driving."

"Thomas?" The voice repeated, as if weighing him up. "This is Internal Communications — we spoke before. I did say we'd talk to you again."

Even though he didn't count himself as a believer anymore, religious education at school had taught him three things: 1) Fight the good fight with all thy might; 2) Jesus loved him just the way he was; and 3) There were no coincidences, just the unseen hand of God. Or, in this case, the unseen hand of someone else.

"What do you want?"

"Perhaps we can be of mutual assistance again. Are you still there, Thomas?"

He winced — rookie mistake, giving his name away. "Yes, I'm here. Look, I'm a bit busy right now." No response. Then he remembered what time it was. "How did you know I'd be up and about this early in the morning?"

At first there was silence. "You're driving one of our vehicles."

Logic checked in. The car must have a tracer on it, and that meant they probably knew his destination. "Do you know who I am?" he heard his own voice pitch upwards.

"No, Thomas; I don't. But I still think we can help each other."

For the next fifteen minutes that calm, objective voice instructed him on what to say at Engamel's security gate, and how to find his way around the building, and what to watch out for.

He couldn't be sure what *he'd* given away — certainly not Karl's involvement. But whoever they were, they understood the situation more clearly than he did, and they had their own objective: protect the operative.

Once he was on the M40 he rang Karl, starting with the standard failsafe. "You free to talk?" The background noise sounded like a small lorry.

"No. McNeill out."

End of discussion. Now, that was a weird one. Formal. Like maybe Karl had company and didn't want him identified? That would rule out Christine, Ann Crossley and the major, unless there was someone else present. He rubbed an eye with the ball of his thumb; he needed a coffee.

* * *

Thirty-one . . . thirty-two, he caught himself counting the lampposts, imposing numerical order on the unknown. "Chipping Norton," he read the sign aloud, as if to confirm it, and gripped the steering wheel tighter. The mobile was no comfort — Karl out of reach and Miranda further away than ever.

He watched for the exit, and after that the nondescript minor road snaking through the countryside like a threat. The sky was pale and clear. It held the promise of a good day, if he could figure out what one of those was anymore.

Warning signs informed him he was on private land with strictly no unauthorised access. The speed bumps were so far apart that he took them for pressure sensors. *Coming, ready or not.* Beyond the road, fenced in on both sides, he saw discreet steel and glass buildings, scattered across the landscape.

A new sign appeared, warning of *extreme* tyre damage to the unauthorised. Then a shining oasis of brilliance erupted up ahead — a reception desk and sentry box combined. He pulled alongside, gave his name and arced his Surveillance Support Unit ID card across the glass. This was never going to be a surprise raid.

There was no preamble, just a check of his name against a list and a caution to follow the signs. Then a button was pushed and a wide row of spikes in front of the car dropped below the surface of the road. The instant he passed through, a yellow arrow appeared on a display board, pointing straight ahead. A few yards on, another came on in sequence — this was electronic 'follow my leader.' He kept to a steady speed and trailed the arrows for another fifty yards, arriving in an empty parking area where a flashing rosette shone out from the tarmac in a parking bay.

He parked dead centre, engine off. It was an edgy kind of quiet, like before a storm. Nothing stirred. Common sense suggested he'd be under CCTV surveillance so he kept his hands visible, far from the handgun. As soon as he was out of the car, a light appeared above a door. He locked up and took a slow, steady walk towards it, checking out the terrain in case he had to make a sudden about turn.

As expected, the door opened automatically, closing behind him as the lock set. Past the point of no return now.

"Keep walking, Tommy." Michael Schaefer's voice ricocheted through the speakers. "Sorry to drag you out of bed at this hour," he sounded almost pleasant.

Thomas thought about that as he advanced along the corridor. Why wouldn't he be? Clarity might have been the one to call him, but not so long ago Schaefer had offered him a job. So why did Schaefer want him there?

The doors he passed had colour codes and card-swipe mechanisms, and the sort of handles that suggested biometric security.

"Next door on the right — come on in, we're all waiting."

Uh oh. That didn't sound good. He touched the door and it levered in effortlessly. The first thing he saw was Schaefer, glass in hand.

"Hey everyone, Tommy made it to the party!"

He looked behind Schaefer, remembering the advice on the phone call to stay sharp; one fire exit on the far side, difficult to get to unless he went through Schaefer — always an option though. He was so focused on his own thoughts that it took a moment to realise there were other people in the room. Sitting down to one side, as if awaiting judgement: Clarity and Major Eldridge. The major wasn't in good shape at all.

"I think his arm's broken." Clarity spoke quietly.

"Can you believe this asshole, Tommy?" Schaefer pointed at the major with his glass. "Who the fuck does he think he is — pointing a fucking gun at me." He freed his hand from behind his back and let the baseball bat hang down. "And what about you, Tommy?"

He swallowed hard, playing for time or an angle, whichever proved to be more useful. "I got a call to come here, Mr Schaefer. I assumed you needed to see me."

Schaefer's gleeful laughter poisoned the room. "It's about time I got some respect around here. That's right, Tommy, *I* sent for you. That job I offered you has just become a promotion. But first you need to prove your worth."

He looked over at Clarity and the major, then back at Schaefer very slowly. "I'm listening."

"A little radical action is needed to keep the Scavenger project on track. You see Tommy, there's a bright future for the right man. All he has to do is eliminate the competition."

Clarity glanced back at him. He looked away to the far windows. *Where's Deborah?* "Mr Schaefer, I'd really like to work with you . . ." *Work on you, you fucker.* ". . . But I'm not sure I understand your meaning."

Schaefer's eyes narrowed and his mouth widened. "You said you'd used a gun before, didn't you?"

Thomas put a hand to his mouth; he wasn't pretending. This guy was out of his tree. "How much money are we talking about?"

"Name your price, Tommy — whaddya say, 50K a head plus bonuses? There's only the four of us here, no cameras in this room and this is private land. Do I have to spell it out for you?"

He flinched a little as he felt the moment slip away.

Schaefer shook his head with disgust. "Nah, I thought not. I'm disappointed, Tommy. I really hoped you'd come through for me. Hey, the cavalry has arrived." He looked down to his left. "Let me patch them through."

A wall screen fizzled into life, showing a Land Rover stopping on its own rosette of lights. Thomas's jaw gaped as Karl and Sir Peter scurried towards the building.

"Come on in, guys — the party's just getting started." Schaefer spoke aloud, eyes still on the monitor screen, obviously miked up.

Thomas watched through gritted teeth as the screen switched to a different camera. There was Karl's Land Rover — the one Thomas had last seen parked outside his flat — sat on the tarmac, out some distance on another side of the building. The front of the vehicle was clearly visible and so was the canister underneath.

He checked the room again. Schaefer was staring intently at a screen. Major Eldridge's eyes were closed. Clarity sat close to him, one arm draped over his shoulder.

He stood adrift in the standoff and folded his hands together. "Shouldn't we get him an ambulance?"

Schaefer sniffed the air indifferently. "Tell you what, Tommy, as soon as we've taken care of business, you can do whatever you like." He reached across to a release button and the door swung inward.

Sir Peter stepped inside, Karl lagging behind him like a servant. The major roused a little, took sight of the latest arrivals and sank back against Clarity.

"You had the Land Rover all along?" Thomas threw it in Karl's direction in the hope that some of it stuck.

"I'm sorry, Tommo. I needed to be sure about Major Eldridge, once it was obvious who'd put Jess and the remaining Scavenger off the base. I thought I could smoke him out, along with anyone else involved."

"So what the bloody hell's it doing here then?"

"It was my decision, Thomas." Sir Peter announced to the room, as if addressing an inquiry. "It's here as collateral."

Schaefer gestured to Sir Peter then at the major. "Now you see why I wanted you to join the team, Tommy? You don't think like these guys — Sir Peter has told me *all* about you."

He glared at his boss, who stood there calmly, withstanding his contempt.

"Okay, enough Limey chit-chat, let's get to the main event. What sort of damage limitation are we looking at here?" Schaefer spoke directly to Sir Peter.

Thomas gazed back at the screen. Why would Karl be stupid enough to bring the Scavenger firing mechanism over to Engamel? Simple: he wouldn't. And maybe that was why he didn't look Thomas in the eye.

Sir Peter was still talking with Schaefer, as if no one else was around, like the transatlantic special relationship gone wrong.

"Holy shit," Karl blurted out, and everyone followed his line of vision.

Schaefer must have pushed another magic button because the monitor was split-screen now. On the right-hand side was the miraculous Land Rover; and on the left, some sort of military hardware. Thomas choked on a breath as the armoured vehicle sharpened into view — it was the C12, no question.

The C12 swung hard left and as soon as the turret started turning, it was painting by numbers. He knew exactly where Deborah was now and what was coming. It was still mesmerising, watching as the big gun fired.

The direct hit was a foregone conclusion. Even so, everyone in the room jolted as the Land Rover exploded into flames. Schaefer let out some kind of Texan cowboy whoop, and both Thomas and Karl made a move towards him, at least until the baseball bat put in a reappearance.

Sir Peter looked lost, as if Schaefer had deviated from some prearranged plan. "Michael, let's be reasonable. What are you looking for?"

Thomas wanted to block his ears, but his hands had tightened by his side.

"It's like this — *Peter*, old pal. The next phase of the Scavenger development cannot be hampered by past events."

Jesus, this guy has no soul. His eyes widened to take it in.

"What we need is to finish the clean-up operation. That crazy bitch Jess is stateside now and as for the last remaining Scavenger test model . . ." He pointed his bat at the screen, where the smouldering wreckage told its own story. "Which leaves three little details. One — the second encrypted disc of images from the range accident. What you might call Amy's finale."

Thomas felt his mouth dry and his muscles start throbbing. The only thing holding him back was whether Schaefer was packing a piece as well as the bat.

"Two — the test data, which I gather Jess gave to Tommy as a leaving gift. Let me guess, Major Eldridge? Am I right?"

No one spoke. No one had to.

"And lastly," Schaefer was really playing to the gallery now, "There's all of you. We're the only ones who know exactly what happened. And let's face it, an inquiry ain't getting in the way of business." He reached for his glass again.

Thomas was already doing the maths: how much run up he'd need to get over the counter and start pounding the shit out of him. He looked around for a surprise weapon — nothing doing — then remembered the torch. Yeah, and then what? Apart from Karl, no one else seemed to have a problem with all of this.

Sir Peter muttered something to the major, who nodded slowly and opened his coat. Clarity reached in and pulled out the plastic case.

Thomas watched the scene play out in slow motion. The DVD went first to Sir Peter, who calmly walked it across. As he passed, Thomas felt a twinge, an urge to pull the Makarov and take them both down. But he was banking on Karl being smarter than Sir Peter and having some kind of backup plan. Although that hope was waning by the minute.

Karl had edged to the right a little, his face was a mask of calm. Thomas had seen that face before, just after Mrs Langton's car won a weekend pass to the glaziers.

Schaefer tilted the plastic case as if he could read its contents by eye, and smiled his smug bastard smile. "Nice work, boys. And now, the test data." He put the bat down on the counter, as if indicating that the rules of the game had changed.

Sir Peter opened his tailored coat, and retrieved an envelope. The major sank a little, as if someone had just put his mother on eBay. "It's for the best, Charles."

"Wise move guys. Now, we have one final problem. The Scavenger is a multi-million-dollar deal. Maybe billions, once we get to full deployment."

"It's not ready!" the major shrieked. "It's unsafe. I won't let you . . ."

"You won't do shit." Schaefer pulled out a gun and gave it some air.

"Now, Michael," Sir Peter folded his hands together. "There's no need for that — let's talk terms. I propose limited deployment — with an addendum to the user manual that ammunition must not be loaded randomly — just until we sort this glitch out. We cannot afford any more collateral damage."

As Thomas turned towards Sir Peter Carroll he felt his hands go cold.

Karl had found his voice at last. "Poor Amy died because *he* wanted to meet some godforsaken delivery deadline and now you're gonna allow him to go ahead?" He shook his head violently. "No way, not a chance."

Thomas stole the moment and pulled the torch out, flinging it towards Schaefer. It wasn't exactly an assault, more of a distraction. It did the job though. Schaefer blocked it with his hand and by the time he'd looked up again, Thomas had him in his sights, the Makarov pistol resolute and unwavering.

"Put it away, son, before you write a cheque you can't afford to settle." Schaefer faced him down, drawing his own weapon.

"Nah, *you* put it away." Karl had seen the Makarov and raised Thomas a Browning, catching the Yank in a three-way standoff.

Schaefer tried to play it down. "Say, Peter, I'm disappointed," he laughed aloud, like he was waiting for everyone else to join in. "I thought you could control your boys."

The old man's face turned a shade of apoplectic. "You will both stand down immediately!" he roared. "I order you."

Thomas glanced towards Karl, who took a moment then nodded slowly. "Do as he says, Tommo. Sir Peter is our superior."

Thomas recoiled like he'd been stabbed. When it came down to it, even Karl was willing to knuckle under to preserve the double-edged relationship his *people* had with Sir Peter. He stuffed the weapon in his pocket and turned to Karl silently — no sense in wasting any words.

Everyone else seemed to be focused on Schaefer. Meantime, Thomas caught the flicker of the monitor screen before it fractured into eight squares, each one a different camera view. Something flitted across three of them, like a shadow. Then the shape stopped moving and hunched down.

I spot details that other people miss. That was the line he'd sold Sir Peter Carroll at his SSU job interview. He wasn't kidding. He watched the stand-off play out around him and an instinct awoke. Something triggered, like a lyric sung before the full song is recognised. The Internal Comms caller had told him to protect the operative.

He looked back at his oppo. *Fuck.* "Karl, get down — gun!" He launched himself across the space between them, taking Karl to the ground. Seconds later, a bullet punctured the window and hit the wall.

Karl rolled Thomas off him and hunted around to retrieve his Browning. Thomas was ahead of him, levelling back at Schaefer, untroubled by conscience.

Schaefer's hands were wide in protest, and neither one held a gun.

"You better call her in," Karl kept low, signalling to Thomas to do likewise, "or I'll put a bullet in her."

"Er, Deborah, you heard what the man said," Schaefer sounded as convincing as a car salesman on a Friday evening.

"Sorry, Michael," Deborah's voice had shed its playfulness. "There's been a change of plan. It looks like the clean-up is gonna be more thorough than we anticipated."

Another bullet zinged through the glass, into the ceiling, popping one of the strip lights.

"She's got us pinned down," Karl spoke directly to Thomas then turned towards Schaefer. "How many exits out of here? And for God's sake cut the microphone."

Schaefer reached above the desk. "Done. There are three ways out of this block — assuming all the doors still work — but she knows that."

"Mr McNeill, it's time you took care of this." Sir Peter sounded sombre.

"Sir," Karl acknowledged, as if they'd reached some kind of accord. "Right, Michael, give your gun to Clarity."

Schaefer skidded the pistol across the floor and Karl intercepted it.

"Tommo, swap this Browning for your peashooter — you're more used to it."

He did as asked, checking the clip and pressing his skin around the handle. The adrenaline began to surge. He knew what was coming, and this time he was ready.

"Right, here's how we do this. Thomas and I go out the fire exit; I don't suppose we can help the alarms. Mr Schaefer, we're relying on you to hold Deborah's attention. And if you warn her, Schaefer, you'll live to regret it — that's a promise." He looked directly at the major, who nodded darkly.

Thomas crawled forward until he and Karl were shoulder to shoulder, facing the fire door. He felt blood pounding through his arteries.

"Ready, Thomas?"

He nodded, unable to speak, eyes glistening.

"When we get outside, make for the first embankment then we'll split two ways. Schaefer," he twisted his head back, "the agreements made here still apply — if we get Deborah out of the picture."

Chapter 40

Four . . . three . . . two . . . one . . . GO! Thomas watched as Karl barrelled through the fire escape, claxons blaring after him. He wasn't long in following Karl, straining every muscle to keep pace, forcing himself to look beyond the mirage of Yorgi's face lurking at the back of his mind.

He slammed flat against the damp grass, panting into the moisture and dirt. Then he heard Karl's call and twisted round to catch the finger movements, directing them in a pincer movement.

"I'll draw her fire and then you run like the wind."

Time didn't slow down. It intensified, compounding focus, like a long lens. A gun went off behind him and he lurched towards the trees, colours blurring around him. He smashed against tree bark, one palm outspread to receive it like a blessing, crouching low, hand stinging, tracking all directions for movement.

There was no trace of Karl behind him; he was alone. He held his breath and listened. Then, caught between desperation and urgency, he got ready to move.

"Over here, Tommo!" Karl's voice carried in the air, punctuated by a gunshot.

Karl had drawn her out as planned. Through the trees, Thomas saw his car — the one Karl had procured for him. Another shot rang out — hopefully return fire — and that made up his mind for him. He belted towards the vehicle, hitting the unlock button mid-sprint. His hands were shaking as he hurled himself inside but he got the engine to start first time, curving backwards to open out the tarmac ahead of him. He set the safety on the Browning in his lap and roared off, taking the kerb so fast that his head smacked against the roof; it didn't delay him any.

Soon he was flying over the embankment and crunching down the other side, ploughing through the gears to get up speed. There was no plan, no strategy, other than to get to Karl.

He knew the sound of a Browning, homing in as Karl fired a volley at the femme fatale. As he got closer to the target zone, he could see Karl's position — and Deborah's — through the windscreen. Then there was a dull explosion and the car twisted round. He pulled the wheel, but it was no use — the tyre had burst and physics was running the show now. The wheel snapped back and the driver's door arched over him. He thought he saw Karl's face, framed momentarily through the glass, then the sky whirled by, over and over, as he tumbled inside the car. He tried counting the rotations, as if that would somehow help. He lost count after three and closed his eyes against the nausea, trying to hold his arms in and keep still as possible.

As the car slow-somersaulted for the final time and rocked to a standstill, he heard shouting. Then a sickening lone shot rang out, like a mercy killing, and Karl was nowhere to be seen.

He pressed against the headrest, blinking as the blood seeped down his face. Something was getting closer. A dull static filled his brain, like a broken machine. He wanted to sleep, wanted to let it all slip away from him. But the sharpest pain, in his thigh, wouldn't let him be. It felt like a chunk of metal, wedged tight against his skin, puncturing it. He reached down and felt the back of the Browning. It took two breaths to prise it out from under his leg; he'd been lucky.

He wiped the blood away with his left hand and forced himself to focus. The shape became steadily clearer, and Deborah's laughter left him in no doubt. She was dressed head to foot in combat gear, hobbling towards him like his crippled nemesis. He moved his hand over his gun and released the safety catch, waiting and watching, as she closed in on him for the kill.

He remembered the times before, when he'd held a gun. As a boy, confronting his own father, and then with Yorgi, over the moors — shooting *him* out of rage. He knew that Karl needed his help now — might even be dead — but he pushed those thoughts aside. Right now it was just the hunter and the hunted: simple as that.

Deborah was a hand's grasp from the passenger door. He stayed very still, propping the gun against his leg and angling it upwards. The laughter hadn't stopped — she was really on a roll. And now it was time for the punchline.

Their eyes met and in that instant he felt something. Maybe respect, maybe a fleeting twinge of conscience. It made no difference. He tensed up and squeezed the trigger, exactly how you're

529

not supposed to. It didn't impede the bullet that hit her at close range, punching her backwards with a muffled scream.

He caught his breath, realising in that instant that he was more vulnerable than ever. He wasn't sure where the bullet had struck her — and she could be wearing a vest. Terror shook him, his hands scrabbling frantically at the handle to push with all his might until the battered door gave free.

As he slid to the ground he saw her feet beneath the other side of the car, laid out like a corpse. He kneeled to stand, the ground swirling around him. Then he heard her moan and knew that it would not be over until she was no threat at all. He stumbled around the front of the car, reversing roles now, stalking her.

She lay, contorted, clutching her abdomen, blood smeared across her torso and hands. A look passed between them; the look a gazelle gives the lion when it realises there is no more room for manoeuvre. She coughed, and it sounded a little like tears, although he didn't imagine that she had any. His gun arm was out, scenting her through the barrel, his gaze unblinking. She fumbled towards her own gun on the grass and her fingers trembled, but she didn't have the strength.

He rushed forward and stamped down on her weapon, leaning over her, the Browning quivering slightly in the breeze.

"Do it!" She gurgled, her hand still extended for the weapon he was standing on.

He kicked her hand away and let her scream again. "Yeah, but I'm a civilian."

"Tommo!" Karl's voice was weary, raw.

Thomas picked up the .38 automatic and ran over, blinking back tears. "I knew you'd be wearing a vest."

"Yeah, but I hit my bloody head — it's killing me. Is Deborah . . ?"

"She'll live, probably." He pulled out the mobile and flicked through his call register. "It's Thomas. The operative is safe. We need an ambulance urgently."

Karl dragged himself to sitting. "What? Have you joined the team now?"

"Nah. Just a favour for a friend." He helped Karl to his feet.

They waited together beside Deborah, Karl using his field skills to make her as comfortable as possible. Neither of them spoke to her; she was hardly going to dictate a letter of apology. The ambulance wasn't long in coming. A cynic might suggest that the clean-up crew had been waiting around the corner, waiting until Karl and Thomas had done the dirty work. And if that were true, it would be just like every other day in the Surveillance Support Unit.

He followed Karl's example and let the medics have a couple of minutes on him, before returning to Schaefer and the others.

"You okay, Tommo?" Karl held out his hand for the major's gun.

"Yeah," he returned it willingly. "Better than okay, actually."

"If it's all the same to you, I'll tell the major that I took his gun — it saves a lot of complication."

"Fine by me. I'm not looking for a mention in despatches."

"Well, Mr Bladen, you deserve a medal as far as I'm concerned. Will you settle for a shandy and a bag of crisps?"

"Deal."

* * *

Thomas saw it through different eyes now, the way the wheels turned in the aftermath. Sir Peter, the major and Michael Schaefer all playing together nicely, while he and Karl were consigned to the shadows. He preferred it that way — the less he knew about the handshakes under the table, the easier he would sleep at night.

Miranda had been to his flat three days running — a personal record, since their split up all that time ago. She didn't ask any big questions and it saved him having to lie to her. He phoned Karl every day, just talking around things instead of confronting them. According to the Celtic Wonder, Deborah had admitted that Karl was one of the jobs she'd been paid to take care of. He also said that she'd undergone surgery and was expected to make a full recovery. Thomas felt nothing about it. And Karl's confession that he'd visited her in hospital only prompted a vague sense of disbelief. But he knew that was how things were in Karl's world — no absolutes, and a backdrop of permanently shifting grey.

Word also reached him — via John Wright — that the case against Jack Langton was pretty watertight. There was a good chance he'd go to prison. The rumour was that other things had caught up with Jack at the same time — he'd be looking at a hefty sentence, even with a decent lawyer.

* * *

"You seem very pleased with yourself." Miranda's talent for the obvious didn't diminish the feeling any.

"I managed to have a chat today with my new overseas friend."

Miranda murmured and went back to sifting through a pile of DVDs. "Rom com, thriller or black-and-white?"

He laughed. The chances of finding a romantic comedy in that lot, unless she'd hidden it beforehand, were exactly nil. "Anything, you choose." He sat back and watched her foraging through the DVD cases. Life was good.

"Speaking of phone calls," Miranda's voice wavered, "I talked to Geena last night. She wanted to know how we'd feel about being godparents, sort of."

He shrugged against the upholstery. "Blimey, that's a bit premature." But he stopped himself from ruining the moment. Nice that Geena — or more likely Ajit — had put them at the top of the list. Although he figured it was a very short one anyway.

"I know, babe, but it's nice to be asked. Anyway, we could always . . ." Miranda didn't get to finish her sentence because the doorbell rang. "I've got it," she trilled and headed for the door.

Meantime, he sneaked a peek at the DVDs she'd approved. He was still shuffling a trio of them when Miranda returned with a visitor: Karl.

"Any chance of a cuppa — I've brought my own biscuits and everything."

Thomas smiled. But, as he still hadn't subscribed to Coincidence Weekly, he signalled for Karl to follow him through to the kitchen. "How's things then?" he kicked the door shut behind them. Miranda would understand.

"Yeah, pretty good, Tommo. I come bearing news — and you'll likely not appreciate it." Karl opened the biscuits and helped himself to a plate from the cupboard.

Thomas sorted the mugs and spoons, relying on Karl and the redemptive powers of confession.

"Sir Peter Carroll met with Christine Gerrard this week. Seems he's flexing his muscles a little. He wants us back on the job Monday."

"That was the plan anyway, wasn't it?" he pushed a mug across to Karl and picked up the other two."

"Nah, he wants us back on the *same* job. I'm to report to Major Eldridge now and you, my friend, are to report to Michael Schaefer."

"You've got to be kidding."

"Do I look like it? Oh, and while I'm here, could I have that mobile phone back?"

They went through to the front room. Miranda muted the TV and gave up on the remote. She grabbed a mug from Thomas and a couple of biscuits from Karl.

"You two look like you won the lottery and then found you'd burned your ticket."

Karl took up residence in an armchair. "Does she know . . . ?"

"Oi. I am in the room, thank you very much."

Karl looked suitably shamefaced. "No offence, Miranda — force of habit."

"Tell her, Karl. I want Miranda to hear what we did last week."
He didn't know how this was going to play out. Fuck it, Karl could
decide what she ought to know.

Karl put his tea down and looked straight at her. "Thomas saved
my life last week. He put himself between a threat and me, and he
shot her."

Miranda's face grew rigid. And even though Thomas could only
bear to look at her sideways on, he recognised the dullness in her
eyes, and he was sorry for having started it. Miranda turned to him
and he sensed she was on the verge of tears. He knew that because
one look at her and he felt the same way.

"The thing is, Miranda," Karl's voice had changed, picking up
on the mood shift, "we need to finish something that started with
Amy, at the Army Base. And I'm here to ask Thomas to trust me to
do right by her, and by him."

Wow. Thomas hadn't seen that one coming — a speech to the
jury from Karl.

"Look, I won't stay any longer. I can see that you both might
need a minute — if I can just have the mobile then I'll be away."

Miranda casually brushed her hand across her face, crushing the
tears as she stood up. "Nah, you stay put, Karl. It's about time we got
past this. I know how much that business on the base affected
Thomas — you too, I s'pose. So you finish your tea and sort out what
you need to sort out. I'm just walking down to the chippie — I'll get
three cod and chips, shall I?"

Chapter 41

Same reception desk at the Engamel Facility, same arrows at the roadside. But it all led to a different block, far from the car park where the Land Rover had lost out playing who's hardest with the C12 armoured vehicle. From where he parked, this time, he couldn't even see the furrows up the embankment. Or maybe they'd re-laid a shitload of turf since his last visit.

The side door was unlocked. As he walked through, glancing in at windows along the corridor, there was office space, technical classrooms and a comfort lounge, all filled with the great and the good and the name-tagged. It didn't take long to find Michael Schaefer, not when he had his name above the door.

"I'm really pleased you made it, Thomas."

He nodded. Maybe this was American for contrite.

"They won't let me see Deborah. Sir Peter and his cronies have closed ranks — for all I know she's been spirited away."

Yeah, like Jess. "Is that why I'm here?"

"What?" Schaefer paused as if thinking about what he'd just said. "Shit, no — did I come across like that? Sir Peter thought I needed support staff for the next couple of days, until the big announcement. And we couldn't think of anyone more appropriate than you."

He shuddered, and was only stopped from replying by the sight of Clarity some way behind Schaefer. Judging by the hand gesture, she wasn't happy with the aftermath either.

With the welcome speech over, Schaefer handed him a schedule sheet. First thing Thomas noted was the product launch, two days away, and the location: Larksford Army Base. Back where it all began. If it wasn't for Karl, who had schooled him over cod and chips, he could have cheerfully lamped the Yank. But Karl was already on the case, apparently.

"So really you're my personal assistant — just for a couple of days. I'll need you to take some promotional photographs, and to go back through any archives we can use — once you've removed Deborah from them. I want a really classy portfolio for the guests."

"Guests?"

"That's what I love about you, Tommy. You never see the bigger picture. You're so . . ." he searched for the right word, ". . . ambitionless! Must be some Limey working-class thing. We'll be presenting to the investors and our corporate partners, representatives from the military — the people who will take this project forward and make it a success." He did everything but wave a little flag. "Clarity will show you where everything is. I've gotta go to a meeting."

Thomas stood aside so Schaefer could strut off, and waited at the doorway, wishing he had the Makarov to hand.

"You may as well say it," Clarity peeled herself away from the keyboard and stood before him, like the accused. "You'll feel better afterwards."

He couldn't see that happening until the assignment was over. "Best I don't, under the circumstances — I'm just the hired help."

* * *

Erasing Deborah from video footage and a series of photographs proved to be strangely therapeutic. Often, she was just a figure at the edge of things, but once or twice she'd been the one making promotional presentations. He worked around that by splitting off and running her vocals through some software, and then cutting the footage to turn her into an unseen voiceover. As far as Engamel was concerned, she never existed.

Clarity left him to it and laughing boy didn't return until late afternoon. So he worked at his own pace, painstakingly editing out the past to meet the needs of the present. And, with Clarity keeping her distance, he took the opportunity to make copies of everything for himself. Have memory stick will travel . . .

He was on his way out the door when he encountered Michael Schaefer in the corridor. A hand blocked his chest. "Hey Tommy, lucky I caught you." It felt about as coincidental as Christmas in December. "I forgot something — Major Eldridge has requested that you and Karl McNeill don't contact each other until this is over. I've been assured of your cooperation."

He nodded and pushed past. 'Assured of cooperation' sounded like another way of saying, 'We're monitoring your calls.' Same old bollocks, only with a two-hour drive back to London to look forward to.

Outside, the fading sunlight gleamed off his old car, delivered to his flat the night before. The replaced windscreen and bodywork were actually an improvement on the original. He got in and shut the door on the world, checking his mobile before he set off for home. There was one text: *Fancy a meal out tonight? Meet me at Caliban's. Mx.* He pinged back a *Y* and did the rest of his thinking on the road.

The security staff on the gate waved him through, with the kind of detached professionalism that suggested they couldn't give a shit about him. He returned the sentiment.

* * *

Sheryl clocked him as soon as he walked through the pub door. He was relieved to see that predatory look on her face — things hadn't changed between them. "Hey there," she called over, luring him to the bar. "The fair Miranda awaits your pleasure upstairs."

He took the steps one at a time. That nagging instinct that something was amiss was playing in his head like a familiar tune. "It's only me," he called up. No reason, other than to convince himself that he was in control.

"This came today, for you," she passed him a courier package. "Wanna tell me what's going on?"

He shrugged, took the package and opened it in front of her. She stared without comment as a mobile phone saw the light of day — the same mobile Karl had taken away last time they'd all met for cod and chips. When he switched the phone on, there was one new text. Miranda sidled up as he hit the magic button. *Don't rock the boat. Just go along with it. See you in 2 days. J4A.* He nodded and turned the phone off.

"Ready to eat?" Miranda picked her coat off the chair.

"You certainly are." He gave her a winning smile and pocketed the phone.

* * *

"Terry and Sam still feel bad about deceiving you, by hiding the Land Rover and everything, for Karl."

It was the 'and everything' that interested him. So where was the remaining Scavenger firing mechanism now? He kept his thoughts to himself; the Wright family had been dragged far enough into this. "What's the latest with Jack Langton?"

Miranda made him wait. She sipped her wine and ran her eyes over him. "Dad spoke with Mrs Langton — did you know she's

Jack's second wife? Course you did," she answered for him, in the way that he hated. "You must know all about him."

He counted to twelve. No sense having a row with Miranda because of some scumbag. "No, I didn't. I just wondered what's happening and how Sheryl is about everything." Out of habit he checked the surrounding tables to see if anyone was paying them any attention.

She went back to her meal. "What's J4A?"

He followed her lead, and didn't look up. "I'm guessing: Justice for Amy." Then he raised his eyes and caught her smiling. It might have been the wine, but the blood swarmed to his face.

"Don't get me wrong, Thomas, it's great that you always try to do the right thing. But what happens when you get out of your depth?"

He grinned stupidly. "That's when I call in Karl."

"Hmm," she tapped a nail against her glass. "I've noticed that the more you hang around with Karl, the more aggro it seems to make for me and you." She dropped her cutlery and raised her hands a little. "I know he's a good bloke. He just always seems to have an agenda."

"True," he conceded with a grin, "but he means well."

She didn't share the joke and they finished the meal under a cloud. He paid the bill, insisting that the waiter brought the card machine to the table.

Miranda dug out a tip. "Fancy coming back to mine for a nightcap?" She was matter-of-fact about it, so he didn't feel bad turning her down.

"Not tonight, babe, I've a long drive tomorrow."

She snapped her handbag. "You wanna be careful, or you'll end up alone — like Karl."

Chapter 42

Schaefer had insisted on seeing all the proofs. Thomas drifted to one side as he pored over the options to decide which images would make it into the final presentation portfolio. "I gotta hand it to you, Tommy. Your work's good. These shots of me and Clarity are pretty smooth — it's like Deborah never existed." There was a smirk on his face, as if he wanted to say more. Then Schaefer flicked through a series of images and stopped short. "This your idea of a joke?"

Thomas held the corners of his mouth down. He knew what Schaefer was looking at. A high-resolution solo he'd cleaned up from the CCTV. A composition he liked to call 'smouldering Land Rover.'

"Asshole," Schaefer muttered aloud. Then he did what Thomas had expected — rechecking the whole series carefully, to ensure there were no more hidden surprises.

By four o'clock, the deed was done. The glossy portfolios were printed on site and boxed, ready for the big event. Clarity hadn't been around all day, so Thomas got to see Schaefer close up, watching him as he put the final touches to his speech.

"What happens tomorrow — for me, I mean."

Schaefer stopped typing, unable to hide his irritation. "You?" Then his face lit up like an incendiary. "You can pick me up here at eight am and drive me to Larksford."

Eight in the morning. That meant a bastardly early start for a two-hour drive, plus another hour over to the base, with Mr Smug for company.

"Oh, and Tommy, put on a suit. You can at least look the part of a loyal employee. And I want you where I can see you."

It felt like the last day of school, albeit one that began with the alarm clock shrieking in the dark. A small price to pay though — after today, there'd no more skivvying for Engamel. He did the shit-shower-shave routine before his brain really moved into gear, then struggled into the suit he'd pressed the night before. A pity he didn't have a Surveillance Support Unit tie for the finale. He chose a grey one to match the morality.

He kept to the speed limits — speeding was for mugs and emergencies — and promised himself a coffee at the halfway point. He wasn't relishing the prospect of revisiting Larksford. Maybe Schaefer had chosen it to make a point, as if declaring to one and all that he didn't care about anything except the project.

Next roadside services, eighteen miles. *Thank Christ for that.* He tapped at the crucifix he'd put on for the day. Mum would be pleased. He flicked on the radio to keep alert and wound the window down a little. Roll on, caffeine and sugar. As the sun eased through the clouds he began to smile at the absurdity of the situation. How did he get from being a snap-happy teenager in Yorkshire to temping for a weapons manufacturer? He smiled all the more at the answer, and adjusted his crotch as the familiar roll call of memories flooded his brain: Miranda — pure and simple. All roads led back to her.

* * *

He followed the slip road traffic into the services car park. Three minibuses of students, who looked like they were on an outing for soap and water, had spilled out on to the tarmac. He watched them as he parked up, playing a familiar game of spying out which ones were involved together and who the loners were. A couple of young women spotted him and launched into a clinch, prising themselves apart to glare at him, daring him to disapprove. Time for refreshments.

He sat in the cafeteria, to avoid getting crumbs on his suit. On the table beside him, Karl's giveaway mobile was giving nothing away. He was ahead of schedule by fifteen minutes — time enough for caffeine and reflection. And all without resorting to Karl's 80/20 rule, 'Always drive at 80 mph for 20% of the time.' The dick. *Well, best be getting on; don't want to be late on my last day.*

* * *

It was too much to hope for that Michael Schaefer would be waving at the security gate, ready to go. No, Thomas had to play follow the lights one last time and then await his master's orders. He thought about Schaefer's words as he stood at the main reception.

Did he really lack ambition? Nah, he decided. He just had different objectives. Like seeing Schaefer held accountable — that was worth putting on a suit for.

Michael Schaefer arrived through a double door, wheeling an aluminium trolley. Four boxes filled the two shelves. "Tommy, will you get these loaded?" He pushed the trolley out. There was a set of keys on one of the top boxes. "We're taking a different vehicle," he pointed in the general direction of the car park.

One scan of the cars on offer was enough. It had to be the Jaguar. Schaefer was just that kind of man. At least the driving detail wouldn't be so bad. He trolleyed out the boxes and stowed them away. Judging by the amount of catalogues they were expecting a good attendance.

He expected Schaefer to be watching him, and when he took the trolley back he wasn't disappointed. Schaefer caught up with him at reception. "Not even curious, huh, Tommy?"

He smiled softly; no reply was a silent victory. Once they were in the car — which did indeed drive like a dream — Schaefer was Mr Convivial. It was as if the Jaguar's air-con carried some sort of truth serum — the man could not stop talking. Mostly it was anecdotes about the important people he'd dealt with in the past and the after-show parties that he'd enjoyed.

Thomas nodded where he was supposed to, or feigned shock, or interest. Truth be told, he didn't give a shit one way or the other. He let Schaefer ramble on while entertaining fantasies of crushing his head in the car door. It helped to pass the time.

* * *

Schaefer finally shut up when they reached the Larksford perimeter. After the security check, a Land Rover escorted them to an enclosed compound. There was no sign of Karl's car.

"What time are we leaving?" *Might as well see how the land lies.*

"Yeah, about that, Tommy, you may have to make alternative arrangements — I have a flight to catch first thing tomorrow morning. I'm due a little R & R."

Nice. He got out of the car. Schaefer sat there and it took Thomas a moment to realise he was waiting for the door to be opened for him.

Have it your way. Maybe Karl could tip off passport control.

"Take the boxes through and then you can start setting up the chairs. The guests won't start arriving here till noon. I'll be back in an hour."

The floorplan revealed that seventy people were expected; the rows of seats set on a graduating dais so that none of the attendees risked missing the excitement. It was a spacious room, strangely corporate for an army base.

From outside, Thomas could hear the background noise of day-to-day soldiering, but inside it was unnaturally quiet. One of the fluorescent strips hummed rhythmically, buzz-clicking every minute or so.

With the seating in place, he positioned the lectern and donned the wireless mike for a sound test, skirting the rim of the room and running through the numbers. Then he moved on to the portfolio boxes, carefully positioning a sealed folder on each chair in the upright position, as per the plan. Michael Schaefer's copy he opened, to insert his printed notes as a back-up in case the comms failed — tragic as that would be. He was still digging through the last half box of spare folders, when the double doors swung in behind him.

"I'm sorry," he lifted his head out of the box, but couldn't be bothered to look round. "The presentation isn't due to start until noon. Refreshments are available in the hospitality suite — you passed it on the way here."

"Away with you, Tommo! They'll check for peasants — I'd never get past the waiters." Karl rested one hand flat against the door. "Listen, I can't stop — I'm not really allowed out. Just wanted to show my face."

"How d'you know I'd be alone?"

"It's called surveillance, Thomas," he winked. "I'll catchya later."

Around eleven o'clock, Sheryl called Thomas on his mobile. "Hey, I can't talk long. Miranda's just nipped out. I gather you were asking about Jack Langton and it kinda killed the mood."

"Yeah," he sighed heavily, signalling he wasn't up for any righteous piss-taking today.

"I won't be making a habit of this — just wanted you to know that he's been refused bail in case he skips the country. His lawyer keeps me informed."

"Does the lawyer know . . . ?"

"He just does whatever Jack tells him to, like everyone else." There was a short pause. "Well, not everyone! Anyway, gotta go — I'll put in a good word for you with Miranda. Bye."

He walked the chairs for the third time, straightening the line, and rechecked all the comms connections. There was nothing left to do but await Michael Schaefer, only he wasn't the waiting type. Schaefer answered his mobile, apologising to companions in the background.

"The room's ready. And I haven't eaten since seven o'clock this morning."

"That's terrific," Schaefer's voice rattled from two doors away. "Wait for me." He rang off.

Thomas was admitted into the corporate suite on condition that he didn't speak to anyone. Schaefer allowed him a toilet break, and a soft drink and some sandwiches — to be taken back to the presentation room.

Half an hour to go, and sadness consumed him. The emptiness in the room was Amy, a voice that no one else could hear. Sod it, he'd take one of the folders with him, from the spares. As he crossed the room, he spotted a brown envelope by the door. He walked over quietly and inched the door open — there was no one there. The cacophony from the hospitality suite seemed to rise and fall like the thrum of a wasp's nest.

He picked up the envelope and slit the seal with his finger. There were three pages inside, each one a four-photo display. The backs were adhesive. It didn't take much to add them to the last pages of Schaefer's personal presentation pack. Maybe that, and shoving a glossy folder in his jacket, was all he could do, but at least it was something.

* * *

The stream of worthies flowed in like a tide of effluent. He nodded to Michael Schaefer and stood by the door, like a good servant. If he really concentrated, Thomas could still hear the strip light's tinny protest. All Schaefer seemed aware of was the horde, susceptible to his charm offensive — with the emphasis on *offensive*.

"Ladies and gentlemen, my name is Michael Schaefer, Engamel project director for the urban utility armament — *The Scavenger*."

Cue carefully chosen music and polite applause. Thomas let it all wash over him. Schaefer sounded every bit the consummate professional, somewhere between Samuel Colt and PT Barnum. It must have been an easy audience, judging by the way they applauded whenever Schaefer took a choreographed pause. He asked them to hold any questions until the very end, so as not to spoil the chilled champagne in the break. Cue more applause.

Thomas watched from the safety of the wall, wishing he'd rigged up a private camera. This was business with a diamond edge. Sure, armies needed weapons, but the way these people talked about product deployment, concept realisation and marketing strategy, they could have been discussing a games console. And let's face it, to this lot — who had as much chance of seeing active service as Sir Peter

Carroll had of being called up again — it *was* all a game. And the game was called profit.

Break time. Schaefer led the guests past Thomas, on their way to the executive trough. No one said a word to him; he was invisible. He knew the schedule — everyone back in thirty minutes. Which didn't prepare him for the large, ominous shadow he saw, approaching through the glass. Sir Peter nodded curtly to him, the way Thomas imagined a lord might acknowledge a servant at Christmas time. "Go outside and help Mr McNeill." *Friendly as ever.*

Karl was wheeling a large grey box, very carefully. "Thanks, Tommo. The major offered, but he's only the one good arm — hairline fracture in two places."

Another PR triumph for Michael Schaefer and Engamel. Once they were inside the room, Sir Peter took his leave to go join the champagne set. Thomas stared at the heavy-duty grey box. Karl didn't venture any clues.

"Nice suit." Karl gazed out at the empty seats.

"You too." Thomas nudged him. "Nervous?"

"Nah. I got a good feeling about this."

"Jack Langton didn't make bail, by the way."

Karl hummed thoughtfully. ". . . Everything's going my way."

* * *

Sir Peter was first through the door, followed by a worried looking Michael Schaefer.

"Of course you're welcome here, Sir Peter — I just wasn't expecting you," he insisted, hastily dropping the subject in front of the staff.

Thomas stood at the opposite side of the room to Karl. He counted everyone back in — plus two. Major Eldridge had his arm in a sling. It suited his uniform, somehow — like a reminder of what the job was really about.

Schaefer said a few encouraging words about Sir Peter Carroll and thanked Major Eldridge for his support, even making a joke about the major's injury. Thomas would have given a month's wages at that moment, just to have a decent lens on the major's face.

The good major smiled and told the audience some fabricated bullshit about a riding accident. Schaefer applied his rapier wit again and recommended the major stick to tanks. Everyone lapped it up, except anyone that mattered.

With each pie chart and demographic display, Schaefer turned a page. Thomas edged round the side of the room, moving closer towards him for the magic moment.

"And now, ladies and gentlemen, if we look at the costs — projected over a five year model, we will see . . ."

Schaefer stopped talking. It took the audience a few seconds to catch on, but he was soon the main attraction. Thomas glanced, sideways on; he knew what Schaefer was thinking. Sure he did. Was everyone now looking at pictures of a dead girl? Were they also being confronted by crisp images of her flesh charred and scattered, her bone fragments embedded in the wall like human shrapnel?

Schaefer cleared his throat and it sounded like a squelch over the mike. He gripped the lectern with one hand and flicked through his notes. "Let's skip that page for now. Moving on . . ." He flipped to the next page: another set of photos. The sweat was gathering on his fret lines, beads of panic. By the third page, his breathing was the only sound in the room.

He closed the folder. "You know what?" he waited a moment, judging their reaction, never once looking in Thomas's direction. "Let's take some questions."

Sir Peter Carroll raised a hand. "Is there a 3D model available today, to show us what the Scavenger looks like in the flesh?" He seemed to cling to the last word.

As Schaefer opened his mouth to speak, Thomas looked over at Karl and caught his nod. Then he looked back at Sir Peter, who smiled right at him. And he finally understood. Even Sir Peter had a line that couldn't be crossed, and that line was the armed forces themselves. So the dagger had passed to Thomas to make the first incision.

He coughed aloud and walked towards Michael Schaefer, closing in on him like a hawk. When he reached the lectern, he turned and addressed the audience.

"We can do better than that — we can show you a working mechanism."

There was a ripple of excitement from the seats. Schaefer's gasp seemed to catch in his throat — with any luck it would choke him. Karl unclipped the sides of the box and lifted them away to reveal the Scavenger firing mechanism, built into a weapon.

Schaefer wasn't about to give in without a fight. "Yes, ladies and gentlemen, this is a prototype, of course. But it's an accurate approximation." He crossed the floor, half-prowling, half-galloping. "We're all very proud of this." He touched the barrel, tentatively at first, then spread his hand wide as if claiming it."

"And when will the Scavenger be available to order?" one audience member couldn't contain her enthusiasm.

"You can order it now," Schaefer was gaining ground by the second. "As we Americans say, it's basically *in the bag*. We're just making some minor adjustments, based on test user feedback."

That was a low blow, and Thomas felt it in the pit of his stomach. One look at Karl's face told the same story. No, he couldn't let Schaefer get away with that.

"Mr Schaefer," Thomas put on his best deferential voice, "you're welcome to perform some test firing."

"I . . . er . . . don't think that's necessary today."

But the audience had other ideas. Thomas had played to the gallery and now the gallery wanted to play as well. A woman rose up from the audience and tucked her folder under her arm. "Actually, I'd like to see what we're getting for our investment."

Michael Schaefer swallowed. "Erm. Ladies and gentlemen, we . . . er . . . didn't envisage firing a live weapon in a roomful of people."

Thomas had to fight the urge to smile. He dug his nails in and thought of Amy; that hardened his mood perfectly. Now a different emotion spiralled inside him. He straightened up and faced Schaefer. Karl was watching; Karl was always watching. But he could live with that.

Karl turned towards Sir Peter Carroll. Thomas missed the beginning of the exchange, but not the conclusion. Karl walked over to the Scavenger and bent down to retrieve a large box. He crossed the room, drawing their attention like a magnet. He went straight to Thomas and stood with his back to the audience, presenting the box to him.

Thomas undid the two latches, snapping them free with sudden movements to generate the most noise. The lid groaned open. Inside was an ammunition magazine, set into a foam surround. On top of the magazine was a taped note that read: WARNING: MIXED CALIBRE CONTENT — RANDOMLY SELECTED. He felt his heart smashing against his ribs, vibrating up to his Adam's apple. Karl's face was stoic. It was all up to Thomas now.

He lifted the magazine up and held it high, as though it were an icon. There was instant applause. Those poor bastards must have thought it was all part of the show. The note was on the shadow side, only visible to Schaefer and Thomas. He turned towards the lectern and saw the strain on Schaefer's neck as he carried the magazine towards him. There was no way Schaefer could have missed the warning about the ammunition.

Thomas kept on walking, parading the magazine back across the room so Karl could snap it into place. Sir Peter left his seat and strode towards them. It could have been Thomas's imagination, but it looked like a march — straight and synchronised.

"That will be all, gentlemen," Sir Peter saluted them and, without a glance between them, Thomas and Karl both returned the compliment.

Thomas led the way through the oncoming surge of people, numb and deliriously happy. This had to be one of the best days of his life. He got it now — why Karl and the others needed someone like him on the team, someone without any competing allegiance, who wasn't beholden to a chain of command outside the SSU. He could do the things they weren't able to — as a civilian, as a person of conscience. No one had bought that from him, because it wasn't for sale.

As he and Karl reached the door, Thomas turned to see Schaefer and the Scavenger surrounded. Sir Peter's voice rang out, clear above the throng. "Shall we take this outside — do you want to do the honours, Michael, or shall I?"

That was it; Schaefer was fucked. Even he wasn't crazy enough to risk a bloodbath in front of the Scavenger's backers. It was tempting to stick around for the punchline, but Thomas was an SSU man today and orders were orders.

He turned to Karl and shook his hand, hard and tight, cementing their bond. As if to say, 'It's us and them, amigo.' But the only words out of his mouth were, "Any chance of a lift? I need to pick my car up from Engamel HQ. I don't think I'll be needed there again."

Chapter 43

"I think this might be her," Miranda got up from her chair and craned her neck towards the trail of souls meandering through Arrivals.

The hard-core travellers had bustled through a good ten minutes ago — these were the waifs and strays. Thomas didn't comment. He stood up and straightened his jacket, standing close enough to Miranda to sense the heat between them. It was time.

"Come on," he set off briskly, dulling his own excitement; this secret squirrel stuff was addictive.

The woman looked lost. Scratch that, she looked weighed down and in need of a friendly face. He waved, continued walking and introduced himself and Miranda as the welcoming committee.

"Did you have a good flight?"

She nodded. What was she supposed to say? She looked like she wanted to cry. He picked up her bag and led off towards the car park, leaving Miranda to work her magic. By the time they got to the car, he could hear laughter behind him — the kind that dissolved barriers and healed wounds.

Traffic was a pig of course, but that was fine. It gave them all space to make the adjustment. By the time they reached the mean streets of Kilburn, he'd decided how to play out the last hand. He pulled up and asked Miranda to do the honours.

As their passenger got out, she leaned forward to Thomas and kissed him on the cheek. "For your trouble," she placed a bottle of whiskey in the car.

"It was no trouble at all, Jacqui," he smiled, wiping away her tears from his face as if they were his own.

Miranda walked her up the path and knocked on the door, but she didn't hang around. Thomas got out and stood beside her, felt her arm circling around him and mirrored it.

Karl opened the door, saw Jacqueline and gazed at her. Then he turned and raised a grateful hand to the couple. Thomas nodded and got back into his car — job done.

THE END

The author would like to thank the following people:

Anne Derges, Cathy Lake, Christine Butterworth, Clive Aplin, David Brown, Elizabeth Sparrow, Helen Rathore, Jasper Joffe, Jeremy Faulkner-Court, Kath Morgan, Kelly Aplin, Martin Wood, Sarah Campbell, Sue Louineau, Susie Nott-Bower, Villayat Sunkmanitu and Warren Stevenson.

BOOK 3:

CAUSE & EFFECT

For Warren, the voice of reason.

Prologue

Harnell Street. A Tuesday morning. Playgroup is closed for the day, Janey is out of ciggies and that bloody kid won't stop screaming.

"Just shut up will you?" she snaps, as little Jacob bawls on defiantly. She feels her hand trembling; she waits for him to look away. It's stupid but she can never bring herself to hit him when he's staring at her.

Jacob's in luck — Janey's remembered the twenty pound note in the emergency tin — the one that Jack Langton used to top up when he came round to collect his post. She scrabbles at the back of the cupboard, pops the lid and leaves it clattering on the Formica. The Queen seems to smile at her from the twenty and she can't help smiling back. Sorted.

"It's all right, Jacob; we'll go out and get some sweeties, yeah?"

He cuts the racket at the sound of the magic word. Now he's smiling too. She's rough with him as she gets him ready because it's all she knows. And he doesn't make a fuss because it's all he knows as well.

It starts raining when she's halfway up the road. Jacob's all right, lucky bastard — the plastic cover fastens down, safe and sound. Janey hunches forward, rolling the buggy along like a penance. The street is deserted. This is the East London that regeneration never quite reached.

She relaxes her grip as the shop comes into view. "Nearly there, darling." She dangles a hand in front of the blurred plastic and little Jacob squeals excitedly. Without stopping, she wriggles her phone out of her jeans. "Greg, where's my money this week?" She doesn't wait for an answer. "Don't be bullshitting me — your kid's gotta eat." It's a short call — promise extracted, there's nothing more to say. "That was *Daddy*, Jacob," she says with spite, "being an arsehole again. He'll be over later, if you're a good boy."

She reaches the shop, parks the buggy up so Jacob can watch the cars, and nips inside. The girl serving on the till is no quicker than the old cow in front of her. So back out Janey comes and sure enough the little sod is kicking off again. He wants to see the cars properly and his buggy cover is all steamed up. His choice then; he can get wet watching the traffic. She unfastens the cover and legs it back inside before anyone can take her place.

Janey doesn't hear the screaming at first. It's a woman rushing into the shop that alerts her. The buggy hasn't moved, thank God, but Jacob . . . She rushes to pick him up and stops, paralysed. For a moment she's certain there's blood pouring down his face, and then she realises it's paint. Someone has sprayed her baby's eyes. And now the two of them, mother and son, are screaming together.

Chapter 1

At seven-thirty the alarm went off. It was the rule. It didn't matter how wasted Ken Treavey had been the night before, there had to be some standards. He got up, shuffled to the bathroom and wrung out his kidneys in preparation for the next onslaught. He generally avoided the mirror these days, but sometimes he'd catch a glimpse of the man he used to be — that straight-backed, eager servant of the crown. Then his memory would paint in the beret and army fatigues — those were the really painful days.

By eight-ten he was ready. A crisp shirt and fresh creases in his trousers. Cereal, toast and tea — all to the backdrop of Radio 4 and issues of the day he used to care about.

He locked up his digs — *flat* was too grand a word — and moved briskly down the steps before any other doors opened. Sometimes he'd pick up some shopping for one of the old-timers. Not now though — this early time was sacrosanct. His shoes clipped rhythmically against the stone steps, stepping out in a marching gait.

Sometimes when he drew his first breath out on the street, inhaling the decay and neglect, he wondered how he'd ended up like this, far from his native Glasgow, slumming it in London. An ex-wife and a daughter he could scarcely pick out of a line-up, living in the North East and sending down a new photo every Christmas.

He picked up the pace, soothing himself with the tap-tap-tap against the pavement. The man in the corner shop gave him a nod and watched without comment as he picked up a tabloid, a four-pack of lager and some provisions. A brief exchange of words — usually about football — hand over the cash, and he was on his way. 'As you were.'

His shift as a nightclub doorman didn't start until eight in the evening, so the wide expanse of the day stretched before him. The world played out in a tape loop; cars and commuters clogged the streets. A gaggle of schoolgirls, all hormones and horoscopes, drifted past on their way to a local comprehensive. He smiled and they looked through him — he wore a different form of camouflage now.

There was a spring to his step as he re-entered the block. On a good day the tabloid could fill up nearly an hour. He took the steps two at a time, ears pricked for sounds of life. Upstairs a radio was blaring out what passed for music and that bawling baby along the landing was testing her lungs again. The familiar soundscape of what he called home.

He halted at the top step, aware that something was different. It took a moment to register that the black rubber mat outside his door was slightly skewed, just enough to bring him up short. He approached warily — no wires on show and only a faint bulge in the centre of the mat. He held his breath and eased the mat away, inch-by-inch, until he saw a small padded envelope. He turned it slowly, examining it at arm's length, reading his name and flat number on the front.

Safely indoors, he rested the envelope on the kitchen table and put his shopping away. Never more than a couple of steps away from it, he circled it like prey as he boiled the kettle and poured the tea. Now he was ready.

The envelope contained a folded piece of paper — the good quality kind, with no marks on it. The page showed a phone number, a time to call and details of the phone box he had to use. The last line read: 'Work opportunity.'

He stood the folded page on the table like a tent and sat facing it, sipping his tea. Someone knew all about him — where he lived, what his routine was and that he needed money. They hadn't wanted to be heard by the neighbours otherwise they'd have used the letterbox.

* * *

At one thirty in the afternoon, overfed on a menu of tabloid opinion and daytime television, he left the bedsit, giving himself half an hour to make a ten-minute journey. He plucked out two hairs and set them top and bottom of the locked front door, half-convinced that some bastard planned to rob him while he was out. Then again they could have done that earlier. Or maybe it was some elaborate plan to mug him at the phone box. He took along the knuckle-duster that accompanied him to the nightclub, just in case.

The world seemed different now, foreign and foreboding — cars he didn't recognise and blank faces. He dropped into the corner shop for some chewing gum, and paid with a tenner to get a handful of change. After walking past the phone box three times, he creaked the door back and took a good look inside. Nothing out of place, just the usual smell of stale cigarettes and sweat. He could hear his own breathing echoing in the old-style kiosk. *Only curious*, he told himself, *following the trail to see where it leads*. He stood and waited, chasing the sweep hand of his watch as it counted down the last couple of minutes.

The phone number picked up on the first ring. "Who's calling?"

"Ken Treavey." No point in subterfuge; they knew his name anyway, and more.

Silence. He closed his eyes, straining to hear. He felt like lighting up a cigarette, even though he'd given up six months ago. Was anyone still there?

"Very good. Take down these details."

Now he could breathe again.

Two hours' time, across town — no explanations. He took it to be a test of his ability to follow instructions. He could live with that — at least until he knew about the job and what it was worth. It wasn't as if he had anywhere else to be, apart from his regular TV date with *Trisha*.

* * *

The pub had two exits, one on the main street and another out to a side turning where traffic-calming bollards choked the road down to single file. Not a problem, as he'd come by Tube, but he noted it anyway. He didn't like crowded bars, although the thrill of the unknown excited him just a little and the prospect of some ready money tipped the balance.

He'd arrived early and waited across the street. Five minutes before time a Daimler pulled up. The suited gent in the back clocked him instantly and they stared at one another through the traffic. The suit exchanged a few words with his driver, who let him out — like a proper chauffeur — before gliding off. The suit went inside the pub.

He waited until the last minute and nipped through the traffic. The man was at the bar; he held out a hand as Ken approached.

"A lager for you, Ken?"

He smiled. The mind games had already started. They had all the gen on him while he knew nothing about them, but at least they were buying. The suit took a single malt, the expensive kind, and gestured to a table. He grabbed his lager from the bar and sat down with his back to the room, surveying the saloon by its reflection in the window.

"Your service record was impressive."

He had grown used to *was* now. Faded glory and years gone by. Even so, he wondered what they knew about his history and how they'd got hold of it.

"I'll come straight to the point. I'm looking for someone like you — I need a man killed and I'm willing to pay you £10,000." There wasn't a pause.

The voice had been monotone, a trick way of speaking without anyone else hearing. Ken sipped his lager, taking it all in. As he lifted his eyes, the suit met him face on. He liked that — no bullshit.

"And why come to me?"

The suit nodded, as if appreciating that he'd cut to the chase as well.

"Your past recommends you."

He narrowed his eyes and read the sentence two ways. Someone he'd served with, maybe? Or did they mean his actual army record? "You havnae answered my question. Why me?"

He could see the suit was put out, even though he tried to mask it. Seeing through masks was a skill that could save a life — catch the difference between innocent bystander and insurgent.

The suit cast a casual glance behind him and moved in close. Ken read the tension on his face — the barely parted lips and the rigid jaw.

"It needs accurate timing and it cannot look too . . . clinical. You've done this sort of work before, I understand? If the rate is acceptable you'll be contacted with further details."

Ken lowered his pint. "I need to know more."

The suit checked his watch and eased down the last of his malt. "The man you're going to kill is a murderer." He put his glass down and it rang out a hollow note. "Now, do we have an agreement, in principle?"

He knew there was no sense prevaricating; he'd have to make a decision. He gripped the hand floating before him and sealed the deal. The suit nodded and the colour came back to his face.

Ken watched him leave and returned to his lager, his hand trembling slightly as he lifted the comforting liquid to his lips. He'd killed people for less in the past, in a roundabout sort of way. Ten grand. He'd be able to send Steph some of the child support he owed her. Maybe they could start over . . . *Aye, that'll be right!*

He checked whether anyone was taking an interest and thought about another pint. Maybe this was all some kind of wind-up. And even if the suit was on the level there was no saying he'd actually go through with it. His hand throbbed a little, as if to remind him of the pact he'd already made. It was up to them now.

Chapter 2

Thomas Bladen glanced at the dashboard clock: seven a.m. The street was empty, apart from an old moggy patrolling its patch. He watched it sidestep some rubbish to disappear through a gap in the fence. Beside him, slumped in the passenger seat, Karl McNeill was dozing off the sweet tea and supermarket doughnuts they'd brought to the stakeout at six. Another happy Wednesday.

He shifted in his seat to get comfortable, and tried not to think about the warm bed at Miranda's that he'd left behind. With any luck, their quarry — on the Benefits Investigation Team's surveillance list — would show his face by seven-thirty, confirming he lived with the single parent claimant. Then they'd collate the evidence and move on to the next welfare desperado. This would have been a new low in assignments, except it was their second turn at the Benefits shitty stick in twelve months. Maybe that was why other government departments called them *floaters*.

Karl stirred in his sleep, lip quivering. He reminded Thomas of a dog by the fire, dreaming earnestly.

"Come out, come out, wherever you are," Thomas whispered, finger poised by the camera. The edge of a curtain barely flickered, but he was on to it before it was fully open. A series of bleeps immortalised the happy couple on digital. He counted under his breath; ready to give Karl a nudge if nothing had happened by the time he reached fifty.

Finally the front door opened and a bloke emerged, fresh as a daisy in a business suit and the sort of hair Thomas hated — gel, for Chrissake. As if to say, 'Yeah, I work in an office but I'm so unique.'

Prick. He trailed the subject through a lens, capturing every self-assured step to a garish yellow Peugeot.

Karl woke up as the pus mobile roared away. "Morning, Tommo, what did I miss?" He cricked his neck and adjusted his crotch. "Any joy?"

"Yep. Show's over, maestro. Were you working late again last night?"

"Right enough — until the wee, small hours."

He nodded. Karl's other job was keeping him busy then. The one he knew never to ask about unless invited.

"Relax, Tommo. Just eavesdropping and observation — no individuals were harmed in the making of *that* film."

He cupped his hands over his ears and feigned horror. Yet having already ridden on Karl's counter-intelligence merry-go-round, he was interested. Who wouldn't want to know someone else's secrets? After all, what else was surveillance? Only . . . Karl's world was not without consequences, and he had the scar on his arm to prove it.

He escaped his thoughts and handed over the camera. Karl flicked through the shots, grading them in a series of grunts.

"Nicely done. Okay, who's next on our list of fraudsters?"

"*Potential* fraudsters . . ."

Karl grinned and returned the camera. "Ah, Tommo. You're like a dog with a Socialist bone. That'll be your Yorkshire roots. Of course, back home in Belfast we didn't do politics." He winked.

Thomas stowed the camera in its case and started up the car, backing it out of the parking bay with infinite care. "Grab the list and tell me where we're going."

His phone trilled into life. Karl stared at it for a second then thought better about answering it. Thomas cut the ignition and carefully applied the handbrake. John Wright, father of the fair Miranda, didn't waste words.

"Sorry to ring you so early, Thomas. I need to see you. Come to the house after work and bring Karl if he's free. It's connected with Jack Langton."

That was a shocker. Last he'd heard, Jack Langton was in prison — and Thomas had helped to put him there. He confirmed a time and cut the call. Now came the tricky part.

"Listen, Karl, how do you fancy a takeaway after work tonight — in Dagenham? You can drive."

* * *

Thomas's hand was on the handle before Karl stopped the car. He got out and glanced at the upstairs window, looking for signs of movement. Karl followed him to the front door and they stood together, not making eye contact.

Diane Wright, matriarch of the family, greeted them with a smile. He noticed it stopped halfway up her face — always a giveaway.

"Well, don't just stand there. Terry and Sam'll be here soon with food. It's a curry night."

He ignored whatever John called out from the living room and made a beeline for the kitchen. Miranda was propped against the breakfast bar like window dressing.

"Alright babe?" She picked up on his mood straight away and shifted a little, arching her back so that her chest rose.

It was all he could do to stop himself from undressing her. He took refuge in his curiosity.

"Has John said anything? All he told me on the phone was that it's to do with Jack Langton and I should fetch Karl along."

She shrugged and kissed him, exploring his mouth and grinning against his face as he absorbed the sensation. "You always were a soft bastard. Well . . ." she slid her thigh against his, "some of the time."

"Ahem." Diane cleared her throat. "When you've finished getting reacquainted, we're in the living room. Sam's just pulled up."

"I know how he feels!" he whispered to Miranda, eliciting a peal of laughter.

By the looks of things Karl had made himself at home. Deep in conversation with John, he paused to meet Thomas's gaze, offering nothing. Sam's key turned in the door, breaking the tension, and soon the delicious aroma of food and spices permeated the air.

"I took a bend a bit too fast and I think one of the curries has leaked."

Diane organised the chaos, directing Sam and Terry to the main table where plates and cutlery were waiting. John and Karl hadn't moved; they sat together like tribal elders.

When everything was dished out the family gathered around the table. Karl took a seat between John and Diane, which put Thomas's back up. As he and Miranda sat down opposite, he wondered if they were choosing sides.

John tore at a naan bread, dipped the shred in curry and took a bite, waving the remainder in the air. "So, I've got this favour to ask." He sniffed. "Thing is, Jack Langton wants some help and I can't really refuse."

Thomas coughed as he bit into a cardamom seed. "Aren't you forgetting it was only a few months back Jack tried to fit Karl up in Belfast?"

He looked at Karl, who raised a hand. "Hear the man out, Tommo."

John coated more bread in curry sauce. "Jack's got a sort of niece down Bethnal Green way and her boy was attacked. He's only a nipper and Jack thinks the kid was targeted because of the family connection."

He hated stating the obvious. "Jack's doing eighteen months for intent to supply . . ."

Everyone around the table fell silent while he connected the dots. Jack needed someone on the outside to look into it. Thomas had suddenly lost his appetite; the thought of doing anything for Jack's benefit turned his stomach.

Miranda moved closer. "What would they need to do, Dad?"

He almost smiled; she knew how to play a difficult hand. Never mind all that East End girl bollocks she traded on at her bar, Caliban's; she was as sharp as a blade. It was bloody obvious where all this was going.

Diane smiled again, as if to really sell it. "The police are already involved, but there isn't any obvious link to Jack and he wants to keep it that way. He asked John to find someone *on the level*, to talk to one or two people and report back to him."

He pushed his plate away. "You want us to sort some mess of Jack Langton's?" He shot a glance at Karl by way of an apology.

Karl shrugged. "Sometimes these things have to be done."

Thomas blinked a couple of times, puzzled. John laid out the bare bones of it while Thomas went back to his food, studying Karl all the while. How did Karl square all this? Jack Langton was a scumbag who believed Karl was languishing in a Belfast prison where Langton had set him up for smuggling, handling explosives and having God knows what on his hard drive.

"So, what do you think?" John's voice brought Thomas back to the table.

"Just this once," Miranda insisted. "And you'd be helping Mum and Dad out."

There'd been no need to up the ante. "How's this gonna work? Is someone giving us a list of names to check out?"

"Yeah . . . about that." John Wright actually blushed. "Thing is, Jack will want to see who he's dealing with. Face to face like. He's got a prison visit due soon and I thought we could go up there together. I need confirmation tonight so I can get the visiting order sorted out."

It was a done deal. John left the table and returned with beers from the kitchen, which he passed around to the men. Thomas stuck to juice. John popped a can and left it untouched on the table.

Thomas found John's gaze unsettling. He remembered the time he and the Wrights' runaway teenage daughter had turned up on their doorstep all the way from Leeds. A speech was coming.

"I know you're not happy about this. But when you got into that bother with the Serbian geezer . . ."

"Yorgi was Albanian," Karl cut in.

"Whatever he was," John bristled, his eyes still on Thomas, "he was a problem. I gave you a gun, remember?"

He was hardly likely to forget — he still had nightmares about it.

"That gun was Jack Langton's. I told him Miranda was in danger and he gave it to me — no charge, no questions asked. I owe him for that and now he's calling in the debt."

Thomas glanced around the table. "Let's get it over with then."

Sam and Terry cleared the table for a traditional family game of cards, but Thomas sat it out. He could sense that his luck wasn't in. Karl decided to call it a night so he walked him to the door.

"You gonna be alright, Tommo?" Karl patted his shoulder.

"Never mind me, what about you?"

"I'll be fine. John cleared up a couple of things when you were taking a piss. I'm on hand to keep the wheels turning and to watch your back."

Thomas checked behind himself and mimed removing a dagger from between his shoulders.

"Sure, you're a funny bastard, Mr Bladen. I'll see you by Mile End Tube in the morning. Don't let Miranda keep you up too late." He waited for Thomas to flip him the finger before he turned away.

564

Chapter 3

Thomas loved to watch Miranda in the dim light of the early hours. She always seemed to sleep so easily. Maybe she had a clear conscience — lucky girl. Once upon a time, he mused, he had had his life carefully orchestrated, with Miranda and her family in one corner and the Surveillance Support Unit diagonally opposite. Now it was all overlapping circles and tonight, with Jack Langton in the mix, he couldn't even see the lines clearly.

She shifted under the covers and slowly opened her eyes. "I can feel you staring at me. I'm surprised you've got any energy left for surveillance."

He blushed, remembering that he hadn't wanted sex until she'd persuaded him. Chalk that one up to Jack Langton's malign shadow.

"Do I need to draw you a map?" She teased back the covers.

No second invitation required. As he leaned across he spotted the old engagement ring on her bedside table and closed his eyes for a moment to skewer the memory. Then his hand touched her flesh and he decided to let his brain take a break while his instincts ran the show.

* * *

It all seemed like a distant memory at eight fifteen, while he froze his tits off as the rain spat down on the commuters. *Come on, Karl, where the bloody hell are you?* He left Mile End for Burdett Road, scanning every passing car, and dived into the nearest newsagents to grab a tabloid. He stood under the awning and flicked through the pages. It seemed like the entire paper had been given over to Sidney Morsley, on trial for abducting and murdering a seven-year-old girl. He managed about half a page on 'Monster Morsley' before he binned the paper and started walking up the street.

A text came in from Ajit, his childhood friend from Yorkshire: Geena getting bigger by the day. Still bricking it. Ring soon. Aj. He put his phone away; more lives spinning around him.

He heard the car horn first. Karl's Ford Escort drew alongside and the window descended. "Sorry, Tommo; I got waylaid. Get in, it's tipping down."

"Thanks, I hadn't noticed."

Karl closed the window, sealing them back in their bubble. He yawned like a walrus. "Apologies, amigo. I got back late again and overslept."

Thomas reached for the schedule, still in the glove compartment from the previous day. "We're cutting it fine if we want to set up outside the laundry."

"Nah, we'll make it. This car's never let me down yet."

He held on tight. To be fair to the man, Karl knew his way around the backstreets, even if he didn't know his way around a gearbox. There was no talking while Karl was in mission mode, so he watched the world flash by and tried to figure out what was bugging him so much.

Finally, with a flourish of gear changes, the car whinnied to a stop. Karl folded his arms triumphantly. "Piece of piss. Now, who are we stalking first?"

He read from the list. "Ms Paulette Villers, suspected of earning undeclared income . . ." He flicked the page and held up a photo for Karl's scrutiny.

"She's a wrong'un — look at that hair."

It was ten more minutes, half a packet of mints and Karl trying — and failing — to do drum solos to Led Zeppelin before there was any action.

"Heads up, Tommo — here she comes now."

Paulette Villers bustled along the street, her coat pulled in tight. His lens did not lie, picking out a bruise across one side of her face, raw as a piece of meat. He felt his shoulders tighten as the woman passed and disappeared through a side entrance. He got the shots, including the scratch marks on her neck above the collar.

Karl lowered his own camera. "I know what you're thinking, but it's not your place to go sticking your oar in."

"No, not *my* place . . ."

"Come on, Tommo, we're not social workers. If she shows up here the rest of this week, we've got her bang to rights and then we're done with her."

"One phone call, Karl — that's all I'm asking. You have contacts — a copper who happens to be around. Someone to ask if she's all right. Then it's her choice."

Karl sighed. "Just this once. You'll owe me, mind."

"Deal." He smiled. Owing Karl would mean only one thing: more surveillance work — off the books. He'd missed it since he and Miranda had been spending more time together. Karl's morally ambiguous world of counter-intelligence proved the point that knowledge was power, especially when it was hidden.

* * *

It was a late lunch — a sandwich and a coffee in the car, as they staked out the sandwich bar where they'd bought them. Karl was economical with his words and Thomas realised there was one subject they hadn't broached. Jack Langton; the elephant in the back seat.

At one thirty they wrote off the lunchtime cash-in-hander as a no-show; and it seemed like the ideal time to ask about private work. Karl reminded him of the rules. He saw them in his mind, clear as black and white.

1. Karl would only tell him what he needed him to know, which wasn't a great deal.

2. Payment would be in cash like the previous times.

3. Karl would decide what to share with their SSU boss, Christine Gerrard.

"So we might still be doing official work, just not on the books?" He nibbled at a crust, waiting for Karl to elaborate on who was covered by 'official.'

"Nice try." Karl crammed his sandwich wrapping into a cardboard cup.

"One more thing . . ." He collected up as much litter as the bag would hold. "I don't want Miranda to know I'm freelancing again."

"Fair dos." Karl turned the ignition. "I've got a request of my own. Anything you find out about Jack Langton — run it by me first, okay?"

Chapter 4

The days fell in line like the names on their assignment sheets as they made their way through the different locations. Guilt or innocence? He kept his thoughts to himself, unlike Karl, and let his camera make the judgement.

Even though Karl had insisted he was happy to cover on his own during the prison visit, it didn't sit easily with Thomas. The whole set-up had crossed a line for him. He kept his distance from the Wrights — Miranda included — in the run-up to the appointed day.

Karl provided two evenings of low-level surveillance work, to pass the time he said — a basic 'point and shoot' affair. Thomas was glad of it. He could have done background checks if he'd wanted — a call to the restaurant and then run a couple of number plates past Miranda's police contact. But he had enough to think about.

He swapped texts with John Wright the night before their trip to Wormwood Scrubs prison, arranging to meet him outside. None of this was John's fault; objectively, he could see that. No, the more he thought about it — and he had thought about it, a lot — Jack Langton was pulling the strings and everyone was dancing. Even Karl.

He travelled in early to check out the local area. As well as a prison Wormwood Scrubs was also the name of 200 acres of nearby common land. He'd read up about it online, amused to discover it had once been London's duelling ground. Maybe it was a sign of things to come. The other thing he'd noted was that the prison was originally built by convicts, which tallied with his opinion that people were often the creators of their own misfortune.

The Scrubs Park didn't compare with the Yorkshire moors, but the undulating warble of a skylark high above him was a welcome reminder. He faced the distant line of trees that pushed back against the skyline, holding the city at bay, closed his eyes and took a breath, steeping himself in the sounds of nature. It was all going to be fine. He was just doing a favour for a friend, visiting some bloke in prison. End of story.

He opened his eyes and changed direction and the prison building marred the view. A German Shepherd dog came bounding towards him and stopped about ten feet away, ears alert, staring intently. He stared back, wishing he'd brought a camera along — maybe the Canon with the USM lens. Then again, he couldn't see that going down too well at the prison gates.

The dog wagged its tail slowly and he tried to remember whether that was a good thing. Ajit would probably know. All those years in the North Yorkshire Police must have taught him something. Maybe he'd ask when he next got round to phoning him.

A high-pitched whistle caught the dog's attention and it abandoned him to his thoughts. He wondered if Jack Langton had any inkling of how it was he'd ended up behind bars. All it had taken was a little evidence gathering and one phone call. Like Karl had said, 'In life as in comedy — timing is everything.'

* * *

John Wright was already waiting on the street outside the main gates. He looked like he was there under duress. "Morning, Thomas. I hope you've got your paperwork with you." A nervous smile undercut the humour.

Thomas patted his pocket then shook hands, and listened as John prattled on about the weather and the trains. Other people started arriving so they followed them around the barrier, through the arch, and into the imposing Victorian stronghold. He stepped in behind John and showed the staff his passport and a phone bill as proof of identity. It was only when someone noticed his Surveillance Support Unit ID around his neck that they decided to 'randomly' search him.

You could tell a lot about the people queuing to visit a prison: the anxious mothers, the cagey partners, and especially the children. They were the easiest to read and fell into two groups: the ones with fear in their eyes, who didn't really know what was going on, and that other category. Judging by their faces those poor bastards had seen it all before and took it in their stride; this was normal for them.

Successive doors were unlocked and then locked behind them, drawing them deeper into the belly of the prison. John hadn't made eye contact since his search, and when Thomas tapped him on the shoulder he looked haunted. Well, well — another item to file in the

Bladen archives. He knew about John's ambiguous relationship with the Tax Office, but his behaviour today suggested there was a side to John he knew nothing about. On balance, he preferred it that way.

The corridor led into a locked room with glass walls, like a long holding cell. A prison officer stared blankly, scanning the line for anything untoward. Thomas gazed back and their eyes met briefly, trading indifference.

They were ushered forward just as the kids started getting restless, through the barred doorway towards Jack Langton. The visiting area was cavernous and neglected, tainted by the tang of bleach and boot polish. As he followed John, who clearly knew the drill, his eyes were drawn to flaking paintwork and clumps of dead flies that blotted out patches of the neon strip lights.

They waited opposite an empty chair for a couple of minutes, without explanation — no one else seemed bothered so he didn't ask. Then at some unspoken signal a door was unlocked and the prisoners flowed in under the watchful eyes of the prison staff.

Jack Langton would have been easy to identify even if he hadn't seen him before. He looked as though he took full advantage of the prison gym and swaggered a little as he made his way to the table, cocky bastard. All around them chairs were scraping back for happy families and lovers' reunions. Jack looked like he was about to open a business meeting.

Thomas offered to shake hands, but Jack tilted back and folded his arms.

"Best not — I can do without a strip search today." He laughed and Thomas couldn't figure out whether he was kidding or not. "Appreciate you both coming . . ."

"I've heard a lot about you, Thomas."

A chill raced down his spine. *I fucking hope not.* He put on his best poker face and sat there, listening to Jack and John getting pally, concentrating. He paid close attention because every few sentences a clue floated by amid the shorthand of familiarity — people they'd known from years back.

"Thing is, John, she's a good kid and she knows not to touch it. But sometimes people get curious. Maybe Thomas here could sort it for me?"

Thomas took a breath and leaned in. "Sort what?"

"Ah, some stuff at Janey's." Jack rubbed at his nose with a thumb. "It might need taking to my house for Ray — he'll know what to do with it."

Thomas felt around his collar. The room had suddenly become a couple of degrees warmer. "You understand I'm clean, Mr Langton? I can't be involved in anything . . ." he left the sentence there.

Jack raised a soothing palm. "Course not. And call me Jack. Just some things of mine she's holding for safekeeping. Paperwork and stuff."

"Is that alright with you, Thomas?" John's voice wavered a little.

"Yeah, as long as we're all clear." The bullshit alarm in his head was clanging.

"Right then." Jack Langton thudded his arms on the table. "Let's talk about Jacob. There are some people I want you to talk to."

And John was playing secretary, counting on his fingers, bobbing his head as each name was mentioned. . . John Wright — the man Miranda had terrified him with, back in Leeds when they were first getting acquainted.

"He's not some sort of hard case, is he?" Thomas had asked, when he'd convinced her to return to London with him.

"Nah, not like that. He's the real deal though."

Well, he seemed pretty fake now.

"Like I say, John. Write the details down when you get out. My brief, Elizabeth Locke, will be happy to help if he needs more information. You know Janey's address — you always send Jacob something for his birthday."

As they stood up to leave, Jack thanked them for coming. Like they had a choice. "One more thing, John." Jack made it sound like a throwaway comment, but Thomas knew better than that. "Tell Sheryl to get in touch."

Thomas turned away to shield his face. Sheryl — Miranda's bar manager and Jack's daughter that no one was supposed to know about. She'd given him the attack of conscience that led to Jack's conviction.

Away from the prison gates, John Wright was a humbled man. As soon as they were back on the street he brushed the dust off his coat sleeves.

"Those bloody places give me the willies."

Thomas laughed and shook his head. "Fancy a coffee, John — or a pint?"

"Yeah, a coffee sounds good."

It didn't take long to find a proper café. Not that he had a problem with the corporate chains. As long as the coffee was good, he didn't give a tinker's where it came from. This place was a *real* Italian café. The blackboard menu looked authentically retro, although the prices had kept up with the times. He approached the chrome counter and let John find a table.

Balancing two strong coffees and a couple of cheese rolls on a tray that wasn't up to the job was no easy task. He wasn't trying to impress John exactly — his own dad was a perfectly serviceable parent, only John was like the best bits without the crap. Right from that first day, when he'd brought Miranda back to them, John had treated him as one of the family. No 'keep your hands off my daughter' threats. Just a polite word about what he expected of him and nothing more was said.

He finished reminiscing and settled the tray. "How do you think it went?"

John sniffed his coffee and then grimaced. "Hard to say. I don't like poking around in Jack's business — the less I know, the better. It wouldn't be the worst thing in the world if you drew a blank on what happened to Jacob."

Thomas squeezed his roll for a bite. "Isn't it better that we get a result and then you're all square with him?"

"Yeah, until the next time," John took a gulp of coffee and poured in more sugar. "Sorry for dragging you into all this."

"It's okay, John; it's done now. And Karl's there to back me up."

John nodded, stirring his mug mechanically.

"And besides, it's not as if . . ." He felt his phone buzzing and picked up, turning away towards the window.

Christine Gerrard, his boss, was on the warpath. "My office in one hour." She sounded less than thrilled.

"I've got to go, John." He downed the rest of his coffee and grabbed the roll.

"Let me give you Janey's address and we can talk later about Jack's solicitor."

* * *

He left John in the café and hotfooted it to East Acton station, wondering why Christine sounded so pissed off. Once he made it on to a Central Line train, he looked at John's piece of paper. One side had Janey's address scrawled across it and the other, written in advance judging by John's neater handwriting, was a short list of names: Janey, Greg, Andrea Harrison, Natalie Langton and Charlie Stokes — who'd earned two question marks. Although now he thought about it, Jack Langton hadn't mentioned anyone called Charlie.

He made the journey over to Liverpool Street ahead of schedule, not that he expected any prizes. On his way into the building, he brushed shoulders with two colleagues from the first floor. He'd seen the MI5 bods around. They waited until he'd passed and muttered, 'floaters' when they thought he was out of earshot. Nice.

Karl was still out on the road, flying solo with the Benefits Investigation Team. The only person in the main office was Ann Crossley, now the official number two — a detail that kept Karl constantly amused. She managed an indifferent wave from behind her laptop.

Christine's office door at the far end of the room was open. He went over and played nicely by knocking first. She invited him in and gestured for him to close the door.

"Care to tell me what you were doing at Wormwood Scrubs this morning?"

He kept his paranoia in check and tried to reason it out. Mobile phone footprint? Nope — switched off until they were back outside. He hadn't used a car either. He completed his thinking aloud. "Those new ID cards we got a month ago."

She said nothing, but he read her like a book, always had done — between the covers once upon a time.

"Thomas, I give you a certain latitude with your private life."

Judging by her face it was his turn to say something.

"We all have our secrets." He didn't say 'Bob Peterson'; he didn't have to.

She huffed. "Look, if it's something that might reflect on the team — or the Unit — then I need to know about it."

"It doesn't."

She peered over her reading glasses. "Is it connected with Miranda, or Karl?"

He yielded what he hoped was an inscrutable smile.

"Thomas," she said wearily. "I can only protect you if I know what's going on."

An interesting turn of phrase. Protect him from what?

She took off her glasses and folded them carefully on the desk. "I've said what I need to and let's leave it at that. Fancy a coffee outside?"

"Sure." Only right then he wasn't sure at all.

They strolled out under the watchful gaze of Ann Crossley. Sometimes he marvelled at how civilised they were together. Christine was an ex, even if it was ancient history. The last interest he'd shown had been purely professional, when he'd found out about her and the very married Bob Peterson. It still made him smile to think how Bob had been transferred from London, with Christine promoted in his place. A good day's work. Last he heard 'Uncle' Bob was back in Southampton with his unsuspecting wife.

Liverpool Street station was bustling; a swarm of people pouring from the escalators at street level. It would have been a great picture. Christine made a beeline for a carbon copy coffee house —

matching decor at every turn and staff who all looked like they deserved something better.

"My treat." She reached across him in the queue to pick out pastries and a hint of French perfume grazed his memory.

"Cappuccino, please," he said to the pierced lovely behind the counter, who beamed at him when Christine turned her head.

He carried the tray over to a table, which she brushed with an extra napkin. "So how are you? We haven't caught up in ages." She glanced down at her iPhone, resting on the table with her keys.

"We never *catch up*? Why are we here?"

She adjusted the tray to line up with the table edge. "I've been asked . . . that is . . . Sir Peter Carroll has requested I make you available as a courier. Ordinarily I'd assign anyone from the team . . ."

Logic kicked in. "Only, you want something from him — or your *people* do?" He wondered why Christine's friends in the Foreign Office might be taking an interest in the Director General of the SSU.

She blushed and he warmed to that. The lady still had her scruples.

"You're free to say no, of course, after . . . everything."

He sipped his coffee and the foam tickled his lips. Everything. The reality had been a lot messier. Six months ago he'd been just another name on the surveillance team. Now he knew that Christine, Ann and Karl had additional allegiances and all were engaged in an intelligence tug-of-war that surfaced from time to time. And as for the great leader himself . . .

He licked the sprinkles from the rim of the cup. "Tell him I'll do it," he promised, because he didn't have a good enough reason not to. And this way she'd hopefully back off from his prison visits.

"Thank you, Thomas; I appreciate it. Can you head straight over to Whitehall? He needs you there today."

"What about the Benefits Investigation Team and Karl?"

"This takes priority. It's an urgent collection and delivery. And let's keep this between ourselves — just like your personal appointment today."

Chapter 5

There was a time when he'd enjoyed attending Sir Peter Carroll at Whitehall. Those occasional summonses, from the Director General himself, used to make him feel valued.

Things were different now. Ever since Karl and circumstance had opened his eyes, he viewed the interaction more as an audience, albeit complicated by Sir Peter now answering to Karl's people, whoever they were. It didn't pay to think too much about it.

He jumped the Tube at Liverpool Street and threaded through the underground network to surface at Westminster. This time, as he approached Main Building, he felt something different: a sense of foreboding. Could he really trust the DG anymore? He smiled to himself — answers on a postcard.

The guard at the front door eyed him up as he entered the foyer — nothing new there. A sign showed the building's alert status as black, which matched his mood. The security desk received his ID card with thinly veiled contempt — this was another place where *floaters* weren't welcomed with open arms. He'd never quite figured that one out. Was it because the SSU only came into being at the time of The Falklands War, twenty years or so ago, lacking the pedigree of the other departments? Or maybe it was the belief that the SSU was a dumping ground for anyone who couldn't hack it anywhere else in the service.

A quick phone call and a scan of his hand, and then it was the familiar stand-and-wait routine while an escort came to fetch him. Meantime, he counted the seconds. To think he used to be impressed with all this. The seat of power — what a joke! In the last few months Karl had educated him about a power struggle across Europe that had nothing to do with governments. A *Shadow State* whose tendrils reached into the military, multinationals and so-called democracies. Even though he didn't subscribe to a 'United States of Europe' conspiracy, unlike the nutcase websites Karl had directed him to for fun, there was definitely something to it. Everything always came down to money and power.

His escort arrived and she chaperoned him to the lift for the top floor. Sir Peter Carroll, always the man at the top.

"I've not seen you before, Mr Bladen?"

Her voice startled him and he smiled. She was from the northeast — a Geordie by the sounds of it.

"I'm not a regular here. This is more of a command performance."

She let loose a three-second smile and visibly relaxed.

"Congratulations, by the way." He nodded to her engagement ring.

"Well-spotted. Aye, only a couple of months to go now," she confided. "Best day of a girl's life, apparently."

"Your other half must be bricking it."

"I reckon he is!"

Out of the lift it was back to business. He led the way, noting that the CIA liaison office had moved three rooms along since his last appearance. He stood aside to let her knock on Sir Peter's door, already ajar.

Sir Peter looked up from his desk, large as life and twice as ugly. "Ah, Thomas! Do come in; I've been expecting you."

He smiled to himself. Same old shit. He took the empty seat.

"I've rung for coffee."

Thomas didn't have much to say; the history between them filled the silence. "You sent for me?" It came out a bit chippier than he'd intended.

Sir Peter flustered a little. "Yes, Thomas. I need someone I can rely on to obey instructions implicitly." Subtext: know your place.

He nodded, a reflex action, and let his attention drift to the familiar painting of Churchill on the wall behind the desk. If that piece of art could talk.

" . . . So, as I say, it is a small matter and I need it done today."

A brown envelope slid across the desk. "Collect the package from room 402 on your way out."

A knock on the door interrupted them. Thomas instinctively grabbed the envelope and folded it in his pocket. Engagement girl brought in a tray with two coffees then closed the door behind her without a word.

"You'll also be needing this." Sir Peter snapped a key down on the desk. "Follow the instructions."

He could see that it had been newly cut; the edges gleamed under the office strip lights. He dragged it across the hardened skin on his thumb and gulped his coffee down.

Sir Peter set his cup down. "Well, I won't keep you. Ring me when the job is complete."

Once he was out in the corridor, he slit open the envelope and read the contents. On paper this looked like the easiest job in Christendom; he'd fallen for that one before. As he waited for the lift he played mental somersaults, pondering why the Old Man had insisted on him for such a routine job.

The fourth floor was a hotchpotch of government offices. He found room 402 without difficulty and rapped on the door. A muffled voice called him in by name. More head games, more subterfuge and more bollocks. Room 402 was little bigger than a cupboard.

"Sign here, please."

He gave his autograph and studied the man opposite, noting how the sweat dappled the redness of his bald head. The stranger adjusted his glasses and peered back.

"You have your instructions?"

He nodded curtly.

Evidently satisfied with the paperwork and sphinx impression, the man went through a door behind him and promptly returned with a bulky parcel. Thomas was still putting his gloves on.

He was surprised by the size and weight of it, feeling the hard plastic case through the packaging. The authentic looking stickers and travel stamps were a nice touch. The guy behind the desk didn't get the joke.

Having got what he came for, he headed straight out the building. If he was carrying currency again, they'd put in more effort than the ripped bag on the Leeds retrieval six months before. Maybe that was progress.

He took a short walk to Victoria Station and wandered through the complex to find a weighing machine, where he carefully weighed the package. Next, he tracked down a hardware shop in nearby Ecclestone Street and bought a tape measure. He detailed the dimensions in his notebook and then visited the gents in the station. In a cubicle he took photos of the package from all angles.

He also took a couple of close-ups of the key before sealing it in a small padded envelope, adding the PO box number and address from the label to his notebook. According to his instructions, the key had to be posted off after that day's collection. All that was left was a short trip over to Charing Cross Station to deposit the goods at Left Luggage. By the time he called Sir Peter back, it was only three thirty.

"I'll come down to meet you and then why don't you consider your work finished for the day?"

Thomas wasn't fooled by the sudden attack of generosity, but he wasn't going to argue either. Especially when he had inquiries to make on Jack Langton's behalf.

Sir Peter was waiting as he neared the building. It seemed strange to find the Old Man outside in daylight on London's busy streets. He seemed diminished without his desk or his Daimler.

Thomas slipped him the receipt in an awkward handshake. He was mindful that Karl's people still had the Old Man under surveillance. Sir Peter muttered a few words of thanks and then scurried back inside.

Karl picked up on the second ring. "Jaysus, Tommo, I was beginning to think they'd kept you in prison."

"Sorry, there were one or two complications. Not much point coming out to you now. I'm going to head over to . . ." He stalled, distracted by the little padded envelope. " . . . Janey's and see what I can find out. Do you wanna meet at Caliban's?"

"Miranda's place?"

"Unless you know another one. Hopefully I'll have an update for you."

"Good, and you can tell me what Jack Langton said."

"Chapter and verse."

"I'd expect nothing less. Listen, why don't you see if Jack Langton has any post at Janey's flat? It might give us more insight into his world. Catch you later."

578

Chapter 6

Janey's maisonette on the housing estate wasn't hard to find. The front garden was littered with the ghosts of toys past and fresh bouquets of flowers left by the door. He shuddered as he pushed the gate. Last he'd heard the little boy was still in hospital.

He rang the doorbell and strained to catch what was on the radio. The sound cut and a silhouette gradually appeared against the frosted glass. He gave out his name as she closed on the handle and opened the door. He figured Janey must be in her early twenties, but the last few days had not been kind to her. She glanced at him and blinked a couple of times, as if to recollect why he was there. Then she bent down to scoop up the flowers and went inside, leaving the door open for him.

"The solicitor said you'd be visiting."

That pissed him off, given that he hadn't spoken to the solicitor yet — something else to discuss with John Wright. He trailed her into the kitchen, where she put the kettle on and went to fill a vase. As she turned back, she must have read the look on his face because she shook her head.

"No, it's okay — Jacob's still in hospital. It's just people's way of showing respect. A week or two ago they couldn't give a shit about me and now it's 'alright Janey' and 'hope your son's okay.' If I had a quid for every miserable bastard round here who's complained about my kid or me, I'd be off to Majorca for a fortnight." She laughed at her own joke.

The tea was average. He declined a biscuit as there were only two left in the packet.

"So, you know why I'm here. Jack wants to find out who did this to Jacob."

"You're not one of his usual boys." She smirked. "He's always *Mr Langton* to them."

He blushed; he hadn't even thought about it. "Like I said, I'm here to help." He took out a notepad and told her he wanted to chat for a bit and make some notes as they went along. It was ten minutes before he got anything useful.

"Jack's little Jacob's godfather. Funny, innit? The godfather! I don't see Jack that often now — before he went inside, I mean. Maybe once a month. He picks up the odd bit of post and keeps a change of clothes here."

Thomas's pen quivered. She cupped her mug with both hands and rocked slowly.

"Look, Natalie's a nice woman and all that, but I gather it ain't all hearts and flowers at home so I don't ask. Here, how's all this gonna lead to the bastard who hurt my boy?"

"I'm not sure." He picked up his underwhelming tea. "You said Jack keeps clothes here?"

"In a little suitcase, on top of the wardrobe in the spare room. I don't go near it — Jack wouldn't like it."

At his insistence she showed him the room, although she wouldn't take the case down. He decided to call it a day and was heading out the front door when the toilet flushed.

"Jack said you lived alone."

"Yeah, well, I do." She squirmed. "Only Greg *is* Jacob's dad and he's been supporting me — well, both of us — through all this. You won't tell Jack, will you?" Her eyes reached out to him. "Only since Greg left Jack said he's not really . . . you know . . . supposed to stay over."

"I'm just here to look into the attack on Jacob. How is he by the way?"

She sniffed and pulled the front door closed behind her. "He's in Moorfields Eye Hospital. Jack arranged for private care there. They're still not sure if there'll be any lasting damage."

It was too much for her and she fell forward in a flood of tears. He caught and held her as she sobbed in spasms.

"I know I haven't been the best mum in the world to him, but I swear it's gonna be different when I get him home."

"I'm sure you do your best," he soothed her. "It can't be easy being a single parent on the breadline."

She eased herself away, wiping her nose on her hand. "Specially when his dad is such a waste of space."

He paused at the end of the garden, one hand on the gate, aware that she seemed very keen to have him off the property. "I nearly forgot; does Jack have any post to be collected?"

It was a knife-edge moment where it looked like she could jump either way. After a few seconds she slipped around the door and returned with a bunch of envelopes held together by a rubber band.

She held them out to him and he passed back a fiver as he took them. "Buy something for Jacob." She took the cash and slid back inside. Even from the gate he could hear the shouting match that followed.

Chapter 7

He expected Caliban's to be empty before five thirty but the bar was heaving. It took a moment to realise that the talk was a mixture of English and German. Sheryl homed in on him straight away and cocked a slow, suggestive finger, reeling him in to the bar. The punters loved the show, laughing and offering encouragement — mainly by gestures. He was glad he'd stuck to French at school.

"Take no notice, honey." She fetched him an orange juice. "Sam and Terry have done a deal to get a few coachloads of tourists here."

He tried not to look at her Stars & Stripes t-shirt. "Is business that bad?"

"Hey, I just work here — you'd have to ask Miranda. But no good business ever turns down good business."

He braced himself to mimic her *Noo Yawk* accent. "And you can take dat one to da bank."

"Damn right you can!" She flicked a finger skyward. "She's all yours."

Two young guys were at the pool table upstairs. They looked him over then continued with their game while they muttered in German. He walked through and knocked on the reinforced office door.

"Who is it?"

"It's me." He took a sip of juice and pressed his tongue to the roof of his mouth to prolong the sharpness.

"Are you gonna huff and puff if I don't let you in?"

"Only if you want me to."

The door unlocked, revealing a vision in designer jeans and a white blouse; her blonde hair was tied back and crowned with reading glasses.

"It's a good look — sort of sultry secretary."

"Wanna step inside and look over my figures?"

He crossed the threshold and found a convenient spot for his glass, leaving his hands free. She met him halfway.

"You do know," she licked her top lip and made it glisten, "that this is now a soundproofed room?"

Was this a genuine come-on or another tease? When he'd almost given up on the idea she reached for his neck and pulled him close.

"No speaking," she said, undoing his buttons with practised ease.

* * *

Once he'd readjusted his clothing, he finished his juice and stared at the edge of the desk that had just been so accommodating.

"You know, that little boy lost face can sometimes be irresistible."

"I'll try to remember that."

"Sorry, it doesn't work that way. Anyhow, I won't ask how your day has been, because I'm guessing it just got a lot better!" She checked her blouse one final time and made a show of fixing her bra.

He kissed her until he needed to breathe. Then he unlocked the door and left the office. The German pool players had gone. He suddenly realised that if the room were truly soundproof he wouldn't have heard her inviting him in. Those lads would have something to talk about on the coach back to Germany.

Karl arrived around five. Sheryl sent him straight up with a tray of drinks and crisps. Miranda joined them at the table.

"Someone's had a busy day." Karl nodded in Thomas's direction.

He avoided Miranda's gaze. "How was your day at the office?"

"Grand." Karl's hand hovered over the crisps. "I was expecting you though."

"Christine needed me for something and then I got off early." He flinched as Miranda's foot rose up his calf under the table. "I went to see Janey to get some background."

"And?" Karl's notebook was ready and waiting.

"The kid's in hospital. Janey's got this on-off thing with her ex, Greg. Can't see him harming his own kid unless it's to get cosier with Janey, which would be pretty sick."

"I'll check him out anyway," Karl concluded. "Is that it?"

"Not quite. Janey reckons all isn't well in the Langton household. Jack keeps a case at her place — he told me it's for paperwork but she said it's a change of clothes."

He grabbed a swig of orange juice while Karl was thinking.

"Was there any post at the flat?"

He handed it over and his mobile went off.

"Alright, Thomas?" John Wright sounded bad news edgy. "I've 'ad a message from Ray Daniels. He's Jack's . . ." he seemed to be fishing for the right word, " . . . deputy — taking care of things till Jack gets out."

Thomas waited for the punchline.

"He wants you to fetch that suitcase from Janey's and take it round to Jack's missus tonight."

Thomas greeted the royal decree with silence.

"Are you still there? He says it's just a one-off thing, and he'll owe you."

"I'm gonna need a cupboard for all these IOUs." He checked his watch and gestured for Karl to stand up. "You better give me Jack's home address. Incidentally, I gather you spoke with Jack's solicitor, Elizabeth Locke?"

Karl twitched and then shook his head.

He took the hint. "Do you wanna give me the details for the other people Jack mentioned? Save me ringing his brief tomorrow."

One look at Karl's face told him Ms Locke wasn't a stranger.

* * *

Thomas didn't like surprises; they usually became problems. Karl stayed in the car, in case word got back to Jack Langton that a bloke with a Belfast accent was poking around. Last Jack knew, Karl had been arrested in Belfast; best he carried on thinking that.

Janey answered the front door hesitantly. He made the decision for her, stepping back from the porch so she could go and get the case. She was gone a couple of minutes, returning with the type of old suitcase Thomas remembered from childhood.

It was brown and scuffed with patches at the corners. The sight of it transported him back to holiday B&Bs in Whitby. His mum and dad arguing outside and his sister, Pat, pinching his leg to get his attention from whatever book he had his nose in.

Janey passed the case across with some effort and he carried it to the car, his leather gloves creaking against the weight. Karl already knew the address from his previous run-in with Jack Langton. The way Thomas saw it, Karl never forgot anything; or forgave it, probably.

"Whaddya reckon to the case, Tommy Boy?"

"Too heavy for clothes and I can't see that it'd be locked, or why would Mrs Langton want it home?"

"We could always park up somewhere and check."

"If it's all the same to you I'd rather not."

"It's your call, Tommo." Karl said it casually, but his body language suggested 'wrong answer.'

Chapter 8

Karl pulled up a couple of streets away from Jack Langton's house.

"Don't be any longer than you have to."

Thomas got out, grabbed the suitcase from the boot and started walking. The street whispered working class respectability, with trimmed hedges and satellite dishes.

The gloves were making his hands sweat and his arm throbbed with the weight so he started switching every hundred steps. It gave him something else to think about. The house was called *Xanadu*. In a toss-up between Coleridge and Olivia Newton-John, he figured on the latter. Jack's Range Rover sat outside, the windows clear and sparkling — unlike the last time he saw them after Karl had set about them with a hammer.

He put the case down by the hardwood front door and hit the doorbell. Mrs Langton was at the handle before the chime had faded. He motioned to the case, by way of introduction.

"Can you bring it through?"

She didn't look feeble, more the able-bodied and full of trouble kind. If the Lycra she had on was for an exercise class, she hadn't managed to work up a sweat yet. He remembered there being two young children in the family though they weren't in evidence.

"The kitchen will be fine. Thank you, er . . . ?"

"Thomas." He was pretty certain she knew already.

"Can I get you a drink?"

It was a relief to get the gloves off. "Nah, it's fine. I won't stop."

"Someone waiting for you?" She traced a finger along the kitchen top, as if she were doing am-dram.

"Something like that." He noticed she hadn't shown the slightest interest in the suitcase. A large drink was already waiting on the counter, with a bottle of tonic to keep it company.

She gave out a sad little sigh and reached across for her drink, stretching her credibility and everything else in the process. He moved out of reach and breathed in Chanel; not what he normally associated with Pilates.

"Anyway, I'll leave you to your evening. Can you let Jack know I've delivered the goods?" He noticed the way her eyes flickered at hubby's name — something else to file for future reference.

He was halfway up the road when he remembered his gloves. Idiot. Stupid of him to have taken them off there. He sprinted back and composed himself before he rang the doorbell. Mrs Langton was faster than ever.

"Blimey, you timed that well . . ." Her face cycled through surprise, fear and indignation in a matter of seconds. "What do *you* want?"

"Sorry — I forgot my gloves."

"Wait here." She dashed inside and then practically thrust them at him.

He thanked her and kept walking until he heard the door slam. He figured she might be watching him through the curtain, so he put on a show and rang Karl as he walked up the street.

A BMW slowed as it drove past — one occupant. The car stopped in the middle of the street and a woman in Lycra and a fur coat lifted a heavy case into the boot before getting into the car.

He clocked the number plate and read it aloud for Karl. "Could be nothing; could be something."

Karl ferried him to Caliban's and they played detective on the way.

"Why attack a child?" Karl asked for a third time.

"Maybe it's really Jack's child?" He was running out of ideas.

"With his niece? Isn't that illegal — even over here!"

"Okay then, it's a warning for Jack. Next time it's one of his own kids."

"For what?"

"Dunno." Thomas rubbed at his temple. "What about Greg?"

"Maybe he's got another kiddie out there and this is some kind of vendetta? Hell hath no fury, and all that."

"What, blinding a kid? I can't see it." He stopped when he realised what he'd said. "Did you make that call like I asked?"

"Paulette Villers? Uh-huh. Someone will look into it in due course."

* * *

Miranda was behind the bar, chatting with a woman who thought a busy pub was a great place to bring a nipper for the evening. Miranda saw him and wandered over.

"All sorted?"

"Yeah." He looked over at the mother and child as an excuse. "I nearly forgot; Ajit wants us to go up to Yorkshire before Geena has the baby."

"I know — she spoke to me a couple of days ago."

"You up for it?" He read her face: wild horses couldn't drag her to Pickering again.

* * *

After the sudden frost at Caliban's, he wasn't surprised to end up alone at his flat. Miranda used to like Yorkshire. Then again, it hadn't been kind to her lately. Especially the last time, when the police had turned up on his sister's doorstep and carted Miranda off for questioning. Him too, although he'd long since forgiven Ajit for doing his constabulary duty — another shining example of his work and personal lives colliding.

He prepared his special dish — *kitchen surprise* — anything quick and edible. He carried resurrected lasagne and steamed veg through to the living room with a glass of water. If he was going to live like a monk tonight, he had the meal to match. A flick through the TV channels sent him scurrying, mid-lasagne, to the DVD cupboard. He didn't make it through the ads before the phone rang.

The Wrights' number. Must be Miranda saying goodnight from her folks' place.

"Well, hello there!" He opted for unusually cheery.

"Thomas, that you?" The male caller sounded confused. "It's John. Natalie Langton rang me — Jack's wife."

He glanced at the bay window curtains to check they were drawn. "Not here; on my mobile."

John rang back. "You took that suitcase straight over." It was more a statement than a question, so he didn't bother to reply. "Only the contents are light by half a kilo."

"You *what*?" Thomas felt his hackles rise. Clearly, they weren't talking about a few extra shirts.

"I didn't know, Thomas — honestly."

He remembered Janey insisting she'd never been near the case. "So now what?"

"Well, they want the missing half kilo back."

"That's gonna be bloody difficult then, as I don't know where it went and I *really* don't want to know what it was in the first place."

He took a large gulp of water. "I'll have to look into it tomorrow after work. Now, can I have a word with Miranda?"

He heard voices and then Diane grabbed the phone. "She, er, decided to stay over at Sheryl's. Said she wanted to be left alone."

"By me, you mean?"

"You know Miranda, Thomas."

After he got off the phone, he rang Karl, mobile to mobile.

"Hey, Tommo! I'm glad you called."

"You won't be." He filled Karl in about the underweight suitcase.

"Hmm, tricky. Tell you something else strange. Mrs Langton is away for the night in a hotel in Suffolk. And you'll never guess who's keeping her company — Ray Daniels."

"How do you know all this?"

"Vehicle check though the ANPR system — the car is registered to Ray Daniels. I'm in the hotel car park with a long lens, metaphorically speaking."

Thomas quickly solved the clue: someone else had reported back to him. "So what do you want to do with this new information?"

"You're the front man for all this — I'm the back-up, remember? And the wee boy sat out there in his car is a trainee; I'm showing him the ropes from afar."

"So the information only comes to you — that is, us?"

"Right enough. Okay, gotta go — you can tell me tomorrow what the master plan is. Laters."

"Hold on, I want to ask you about Elizabeth Locke . . ."

The line went dead. He let the DVD play out then returned *The Trouble With Harry* to its appointed slot in the cupboard — comedies, top left. Though entertaining, it hadn't stopped him from thinking.

He listed all the names on a piece of A4: Janey, Jack Langton, Natalie Langton, Ray Daniels, Greg, little Jacob, Andrea Harrison, Elizabeth Locke, and the unknown Charlie Stokes. He drew a circle around Jacob and one around Jack, linking them with a dotted line. There had to be a connection. He closed his eyes and asked aloud, "What don't I know?" Then he laughed at himself. What *did* he know?

It was still dark when he opened his eyes next morning. As he eased out the tension in his spine, he felt something jab his shoulder blade. He shifted *The Moonstone* by Wilkie Collins and set it carefully at the edge of the bed. Miranda was on his mind. Was it so big a deal to head up to Yorkshire for Geena and Ajit's sprog? On his way out the door a text came through from Ajit: Don't leave it too late! That settled it — he'd talk to Miranda and finalise some travel plans.

Chapter 9

Every assignment was another manila envelope of expenses and timesheets, filed alongside his annual appraisal in one of Christine Gerrard's box files. He wasn't knocking the job itself, only the sense that he was killing time. Ajit and Geena, about to venture into nappy rash territory brought his own circumstances into focus.

The Tube station steadily sucked in the commuters it had spewed out the day before. They fell into a rhythm, trudging in step so that everyone made it to the platform without incident. He squeezed on to the next train, reading the front page of a newspaper from the seat opposite. The headline didn't pull any punches: *Monster sentenced today*. Child murderer, Sidney Morsley, had his final day at Crown Court.

He stared at the faded photo, taken years before, of a man on a fishing trip. Hard to believe what some people were capable of. He caught his reflection in the tunnel darkness. *He* could talk — he'd shot two people: Yorgi, a psychopath for hire who had threatened Miranda; and Deborah, another nut-job — from technology developers, Engamel — who had tried to kill Karl. They'd both deserved it — no question.

His mobile trilled into life as soon as he reached daylight at Mile End.

"Ahoy, shipmate; any chance of you grabbing a couple of bacon butties on your way round to the car?"

The café smelled of stewed tea and spilt fat — he could have stayed there forever. It looked like a one-man-band, the guy nodding to him dolefully as he went up to the counter.

He gave his order and grazed a tabloid on the counter, flicking past the day's top story to see what else was going on in the world. He'd developed a habit of checking the business pages for anything interesting in electronics and new technology. Karl reckoned that several tech companies had a keen interest in the *Shadow Europe* — the one that didn't need overpriced buildings in Strasbourg and Brussels. He'd arrived at the sports pages when he saw the chef's spattered outfit looming towards him.

"There you go, chief." Two sandwiches wrapped in tin foil were presented to him.

Karl's grunge-mobile was ready and waiting outside the newsagents, hazard lights flashing wildly.

"Come on, get in; I want to show you something." There was a hint of glee in Karl's voice.

Thomas put the sarnies by his feet and let Karl have his moment of intrigue. The car sped off as soon as he closed the door.

"Okay, you were on at me to nod the plod towards Ms Villers and her bruises?"

He nodded. "And?"

"I'm coming to that. Knowing you as I do, if you saw the guy and you thought you could take him, you'd probably want to give him a smack — am I right?"

He considered the proposition for about three seconds and nodded a little more enthusiastically.

"But what if," Karl took his chances with a late turn that made the brakes shriek, "things were not quite as they seem?"

The car stopped at their previous spot, overlooking the laundry. Within five minutes, punctuated by Karl saying nothing and pointing occasionally to keep Thomas focused on the road ahead, a familiar figure crossed their line of vision. This time Ms Villers was hand-in-hand with someone special — a woman. Thomas started behind the lens and Karl leapt on it.

"So what do you think, Tommo? Could you take on a lesbian in a fight?"

He took a flurry of pictures and then lowered his camera to see the joy on Karl's face. "Is this a problem for you?"

"Hold your heterosexual horses." Karl failed to wipe the grin off his own face. "You're the one who paled at the notion of two ladies together. Me? That's some of my favourite DVDs."

"Prick."

"Not in those films. My point, Mr Bladen, is that we don't always get the full story and it's wise not to go blundering in."

"It's still domestic abuse."

"Right enough, and I've put a word in with the boys and girls in blue."

"How did you know she had a *partner*?" He baulked at the 'L' word.

"Another training exercise, last night. I like to keep my apprentice busy."

He noticed Karl's crumpled shirt beneath his jumper, and the grubby cuffs that looked at least a day old, but said nothing.

"So when do you need me for the next private job?"

"Will a morning suit you, later this week? Say I pick you up around four? I'll fill you in nearer the time."

As in: four a.m. and keep your week clear. Shit.

"I've been thinking about Janey's kid." Thomas let his camera range past the laundry in search of Victorian architecture. "It'd help if we knew what the police know." He heard clapping.

"Bravo! Uncle Karl is already following up that line of inquiry."

"When we see Janey tonight about the suitcase, maybe we could take a look at Jacob's buggy?"

"Interesting. What's your angle?"

"Not sure. It's the only evidence — your lot have labs, don't they?"

"That's what I like about you, Tommo, You've never pressed me about my colleagues outside the SSU."

"Like you're always telling me, Karl — need to know. Right now, I don't."

"Let's celebrate your self-control with a bacon butty — I'm famished."

He felt the light bulb go on in his head. "When can I have Jack Langton's post back, so I can take it over to Natalie?"

"Soon. There's a slight snag — nothing major. Now, where's my brekkies?"

Chapter 10

Ken Treavey heard the package scrape through his letterbox. By the time he got to his door and opened it to the night he was alone. He waited there a minute or so, listening to the hum of the city and feeling the chill against his bare feet. This was it then.

He felt his way back to the bedroom and put the bedside lamp on, squinting against the burst of light. He tore at the envelope and looked for treasure. Instead, he found pieces of a puzzle — a left luggage receipt and a key that presumably went with it; a map; a cash card; a note with a PIN number, a name, a time, and the words: 'Remember to make it look amateur.' He saved the best till last, tipping the rifle rounds on to the duvet. They clattered like brass and copper jewels under the lamplight.

First thing in the morning he'd visit the PO box across town, as arranged. Checking the map against the street guide confirmed his suspicions: the courthouse. He picked up the cash card and cradled a bullet in the other hand, parodying the scales of justice — everything had its price.

* * *

It felt strange breaking routine, travelling different roads to reach the PO box. He made it seem casual, waiting fifteen minutes after the place opened. The padded envelope was smaller than he'd expected and his curiosity almost overcame him. It was only the thought of the money that swayed him. He checked the balance afterwards, hardly daring to move as the card disappeared into the machine. He didn't breathe again until the balance showed on-screen — £10,000. Twenty quid would do for now.

He kidded himself he could make a run for it and disappear. Not a chance. He retrieved the magic card and picked up his money, grinning. When was the last time he'd had cash to squander? The padded envelope was burning a hole in his pocket so he treated himself to a coffee. Inside, he found a lonely corner and checked his post: one key and no explanations.

* * *

After collecting the parcel from Left Luggage, he made straight for the observation point. He'd always called them that until he was set up and ready. London's noisy chaos blurred around him, as if he were a ghost. When he'd been in uniform he never liked to eat or drink beforehand, but now he compromised and pulled out some chewing gum. A hit of mint at the back of his mouth sharpened his wits. Time to get to work.

No one paid him any attention as he approached the block of flats. He blended in, moving unhurriedly like he belonged there. The hard part would be getting out afterwards. He climbed the stairs in twos, the case held tight against his body. As he mounted the final flight of stairs on the top floor he drew out the Ingersoll key, ready.

The well-oiled lock gave without effort and he carefully closed the door behind him. There was a sound now, like the rush of wind, only he couldn't be sure if it was real or inside his head. He breathed slowly and made the final echoing ascent.

Instinct took over, dropping him to his knees as soon as he reached the rooftop. Sounds magnified — a plane's distant roar threatened to smother him. Traffic played like an urban symphony. He crawled to the roof edge and peered over with a pocket scope. Just as they promised, he had a clear view of the walled yard, where a security van was currently unloading its cargo. Not his target though — he was waiting for the final directive.

He slit the wrapping around the parcel carefully and slid the two sections of paper apart. They went into his bag — to be burned later. The name hadn't come as any surprise. Who else was high profile enough to warrant a ten thousand pound price tag? Knowing the identity made it easier — an abomination against God and Man. He smiled. If only his father could see him now, following in the family tradition and doing the Lord's work after all.

He opened the case; it was a .300 Winchester bolt-action rifle, adapted by the looks of it but similar enough to the NATO model he was used to. They'd done their research. A picture of Sidney Morsley was taped to the inside of the case, staring blankly at his executioner. He fitted the weapon together and loaded the ammunition: four bullets.

Time moved in waves, alternating fast and slow, toying with his watch. Eventually he heard the bleeps of another vehicle reversing into the yard. He hunched in and kept the rifle sight fixed on the back door of the court, waiting for Sidney Morsley's final act. The door unlocked and then . . . Christ, he wasn't expecting a woman in front of the target. He wavered for an instant and then committed, squeezing the trigger to drop her. She screamed and fell to the ground, a perfect distraction for everyone else. A fluid movement of the hand then the second round chambered and plunged into Sidney Morsley's torso, swiftly followed by the third. Messy. Morsley was down now, doubled in agony — a sitting duck in a pool of blood. The final bullet struck somewhere in the vicinity of the heart, if he'd had one.

He broke up the weapon and felt the warm touch of the barrel through his gloves. He felt more alive than he had in years. He scrabbled on the ground and retrieved three spent casings but the fourth was nowhere to be seen — too late now. He crawled back to the door, pushing the case in front of him.

When he reached the top floor the sirens kicked in and so did the panic. The first flat along the landing was boarded up and grilled with a shiny new lock. He tried his key and almost collapsed in relief as it turned, releasing the door. There was little light inside, only a dusty haze. It felt safe there although he knew it wasn't. He found a back room and forced the case in behind a hot water tank, taking a moment to calm himself. He left soon after, keeping his head down, moving once again through a world where he didn't belong. He felt his guts twist, but it wasn't conscience — he needed a drink.

Chapter 11

Thomas gave Janey's bell two short rings. When the door opened she smiled a little and led him in. He heard Karl's footsteps behind him as he went indoors and imagined her smile evaporating.

"So, how's Jacob?" He thought he'd start with the easy questions.

"Ah, getting there. They reckon he can probably come home in a couple of days. I really miss him."

Her voice was rising in pitch the closer they got to the living room. He nudged the door to find Greg sprawled across the settee like he owned the place, a can of lager by his feet. He clipped Greg's foot and he took the hint, sitting up and lifting his can out of the way. Pausing in the middle of the room to make a point, Thomas leaned towards him. Karl seemed to instinctively block the exit.

"I need to ask you about the suitcase Janey had on top of her wardrobe." He felt like an idiot, spelling it out, but Greg must have been a moron to think no one would notice something was missing.

Greg's face contorted, as if he were weighing up his options. So Thomas upped the ante.

"Jack Langton's wife spotted the case was light and Jack won't be pleased if she has to tell him. It's better for everyone if you hand it over."

Greg folded. "I was nosing round the flat when Janey was out and there it was. I just did it, spur of the moment."

"So where is the bag now?"

"I sold it."

"You did what?" Janey piped up, shrill as a cry of pain.

Greg turned towards her. "You know I got debts. It seemed like a golden opportunity — a lucky break, yeah?"

"And what if Jack thinks I did it?" She gripped the sofa.

"I was gonna take care of it. Once I had a buyer for the rest, I was gonna make it look like a burglary while you and me was at the hospital. Ain't no one gonna report a missing stash, are they?"

Thomas was halfway impressed; Greg had a few brain cells after all. "Who did you sell it to?"

"I can't tell you; I gave my word. Don't look at me like that, Janey — I did it for us. We can get away and start over."

"Are you mental, Greg? Jack'll come after us. He knows my family." Her voice could have scratched glass.

Thomas waited, trying to stare it out of him. "It's this simple, Greg. You tell me now and we'll try and sort this, or Natalie tells Jack and he sorts things out his own way. What's it to be?"

Janey started crying. Thomas squeezed his hands together: *we'll try and sort this*. Jesus, he could feel Karl's disappointment emanating from the door.

"Charlie Stokes — I sold it to Mr Stokes."

Thomas heard a bell go off in his head. Karl cleared his throat and mimicked pushing a buggy.

"Yeah." Thomas's brain clicked into gear. "Janey, we want to take Jacob's buggy away for a closer look — we'll have it back to you before he needs it."

She did as asked, muttering that the police had already checked it.

He stood right over Greg. "How much did you get for it?"

"Five grand, minus what I owed."

Thomas shot a glance to Karl, who shook his head and flashed up enough hands for Thomas to feel sick. Greg was indeed a moron; they'd never be able to buy it back for five thousand.

He let out a sigh that could wake the dead. "Right, we are out of here."

"What about the missing bag?" Janey's voice wavered.

He didn't have the heart to tell her they were both fucked now, thanks to Greg, so he sold her a lie until he could think of something better. "We'll work on it."

Karl stayed tight-lipped until they were back on the road.

"Go on, say it."

"Do I need to? You're getting us involved in a shit storm that's nothing to do with us, Tommy Boy. Unless you have a five figure sum stashed away — always assuming this Charlie Stokes hasn't already moved the stuff on — we've got nothing."

He wondered where the drop-off would be for the buggy. Going on past experience, Karl's clandestines favoured supermarket car parks. He played the counting game, watching the seconds tick by until Karl broke the silence.

"You can't save Greg from his own stupidity, and to be frank with you I don't hold with drugs. I've told you before, they're one of the ways the European cartel funds its operations." Karl looked pensive. "There's something else we haven't considered — the drugs might not be Jack's at all."

"You know something, don't you?" It was a moment before he realised his knuckles were whitening as he crushed them together.

Karl had spotted it too. "Tell you what, how about we grab ourselves a drink and go do our thinking somewhere else? I know the perfect place."

Chapter 12

The pub's lights streamed across the pavement, highlighting the scarlet paintwork. Thomas recognised it from the time Karl had taken him there before. He rubbed at his scar self-consciously as Karl pushed the swing doors.

The place hadn't changed and nor was it ever likely to, unless some developer ripped its soul out. The saloon bar walls wore regimental shields like medals. He would have stayed awhile for a history lesson but Karl pointed him towards the bar and took out a mobile. Meantime, no one paid him any attention and that included the barman.

He waited, browsing the labels on the optics and fighting the urge to wave a fiver in the air like a one-fingered salute. Eventually the barman made the supreme sacrifice, finishing his conversation and ambling over.

"Two shandies and two bags of crisps please."

Karl ended his call as Thomas reached the table. "Sure, just give me a bell when you're outside."

Thomas slid a glass towards him. "What did I miss?"

"They'll pick up the buggy and we should get the analysis pronto, as a favour."

He chalked it up as another debt. Item one on his mental checklist was Charlie Stokes. Typically, Karl was a step ahead of him.

"The word is that Mr Stokes is one nasty piece of work." Karl took a mouthful of shandy. "What? You were at the bar so long I had time for two calls."

Yeah, Thomas thought, and look which one you made first. He whipped out a ballpoint and paper; he always thought better visually.

"Could Charlie be behind the attack on little Jacob?"

"Maybe." Karl pawed at the crisps. "Why though, unless he was after scaring Greg into lifting the drugs to settle his debt?"

"Doubtful — Greg only found them recently."

"Aye, so he says."

"Then why stop at one bag and why now? Jack's been inside for a while."

Karl shrugged. "Beats me. You ponder on that; I'm off for a piss."

Thomas lifted his head and casually scanned the room. No one else was drinking alone. He envied them their camaraderie. The swing door caught his attention — a silhouette against the glass, immobile and poised. The old fear slithered to the surface. Yorgi may have died on the moors but was there unfinished business with the people he'd worked for?

A stranger entered the saloon and looked straight at him. He returned the favour, sizing him up. The bloke seemed indifferent, skirting the room to end up at the bar. Karl returned, phone in hand and stopped, halfway across the carpet. The stranger stalled too and Thomas tried to fathom what was happening. Karl seemed to change tempo, smiling at the stranger as he approached him.

Their voices stayed low and Thomas watched, fascinated, as some part of Karl's private world gate-crashed the evening. The stranger ordered a drink, which Karl insisted on paying for, and the two of them came over. Karl reached across to grab a nearby empty chair.

"Thomas." Karl laid a hand on the stranger's shoulder. "Ken's a friend of mine — from the old days."

Ken didn't seem to be in on the joke. He took a seat and dived into his beer. Karl tried again.

"It's been a while. I didn't know you were living in London now."

Ken didn't reply until he'd downed most of his pint and had to surface for air. "Been moving around, Karl — you know how it is. Spent a lot of time in the north, only things don't always work out." His eyes fixed on Thomas. "And how do you come to know Karl then?"

He went for cryptic. "We work in the same office."

"Never had you figured for a desk job, Karl," Ken took on a mocking tone. "The way I heard it, you left the forces under a bit of a cloud. Still, needs must I suppose and at least you've remembered the old days." He gazed around the bar.

If that was meant to be bait, Karl wasn't biting.

"Anyone fancy another drink — Tommo?"

"Here," Ken pulled out a crisp twenty. "This round's on me — have what you like. Where are you from, Thomas? I cannae place the accent; it's not all London."

Not many people noticed — or cared. Miranda reckoned it was only the odd inflection on a few words by now. He felt his chest swell a little. "Yorkshire, only I've been naturalised."

"Aye, well, don't lose touch with your roots. That right, Karl?" Ken gave him a playful slap on the arm.

As Thomas left the table, a mere errand boy for drinks, he heard Karl asking if Ken needed any money.

"Do I, fuck!" was Ken's defiant reply

Returning to the table with Ken's lager and crisps, he played the silence game to see what the tide brought in. Answer: very little. Karl was tight-lipped, while Ken had a haunted look about him, which Thomas hoped a few more beers would exorcise.

Eventually Thomas gave up and went to the bar for a set of darts. He played against himself, last man standing. The walks back from the dartboard showed him that conversation had resumed in his absence, though not much of it. Karl looked rattled and Ken was getting progressively more out of control. Finally, he stood up, leaned over Karl and hissed, "Don't forget, you owe me." Then he staggered off to the gents, colliding with the back of someone's chair and offering an incomprehensible apology in his wake.

"Everything all right?" Thomas teased his thumb against a dart.

"Champion." Karl's face didn't agree. "Listen, Tommo, do you fancy working tonight?"

"Sure." He watched Karl's face start to relax. "What time?"

Karl checked his watch and deliberated. "About two a.m. You might wanna get a nap in, given it's barely ten. Either that or some strong coffee."

"Do you and your mate need some space?"

"Ken?" Karl laughed. "If I know him, he'll be out the back door and away by now." Karl's mobile trilled. He glanced at the number before he answered. "I'll come out now." He brightened and nodded to Thomas. "Perfect timing. Could you give me a couple of minutes?"

With Karl outside he made a beeline for the gents. Turning left from the exit instead of right, he found himself in a yard — crates stacked against the walls and heavy wooden gates at the far end. Ken must have been keen to disappear.

Karl was already in the driving seat when he got round to the car. He spotted him pocketing a key as he got in.

"Tommo, your friend from the old days — Ajit, was it? Do you trust him?

"Yeah, of course," he said without thinking. He wondered where this was leading.

Karl started playing with the key again. "I mean *really* trust him, like you trust Miranda?"

He felt his face burning. "No. I don't trust anyone else like that — not even you."

"Good man." Karl nodded slowly and started the car, dropping the key down by the handbrake. Thomas got a good look at it and the hairs on his neck stood up.

Chapter 13

Thomas flinched. Karl was slow to respond to his mobile alarm until a sharp nudge did the trick.

"Right, time to switch. You'll be in the driving seat for a change." He got out and let Thomas lever himself across.

Rain was already spattering the windscreen; the windows had misted up. It didn't help that the inside of the car smelled like a kebab graveyard.

"Where are we heading?"

Karl read a text and sucked a tooth. "I'll navigate as we go." He fetched a battered street guide from under the seat.

They were near the Thames; Thomas was sure about that, though not much else. He followed Karl's monotone directions, arriving near a block of flats.

"Okay, give me five minutes and then start the car. If anyone spooks you — especially if it's the police — drive off and I'll make my own way back. I'll leave my phone here, locked. Worst case scenario, try flashing your badge."

Thomas smiled, recalling the one and only time an SSU ID had headed off a parking ticket. These days it'd be more likely to double the fine.

Karl exited the car quietly and headed into the shadows. Now came the waiting. Thomas tripped his mobile to silent and read another text from Ajit: Don't they have phones in London anymore?

A pair of headlights swallowed the street by degrees. He slipped down in his seat, slowly and casually, waiting until the stream of light had passed. Sure enough it was a police car, the rear reflective chevrons shrinking into the distance. He was beginning to join the dots and he didn't like the emerging picture. He trawled through his phone and brought up the image of the Ingersoll key from the gents at Victoria Station.

Time ticked down so he turned the ignition, startled by how loud the engine sounded in the darkness. He flicked the wipers sporadically, clearing the view for trespassers.

Karl cut it fine. He walked quickly, carrying a long case. Thomas craned the passenger door open as he approached and Karl hefted the case behind him with some difficulty.

"Drive." Karl stared ahead. "Take a left up here and then the second right." He was back to map-reading again.

Thomas's brain was already slotting pieces together. The key, the size of the case and the last minute job offer all pointed in one direction. He needed to be sure though.

"Why don't we go back to my flat?"

"Good idea, I'm bushed." Karl was only half-listening.

Once he'd crossed back over the Thames there was no further need for directions so he tried to fill the void. "How long did you and Ken serve together?"

"Two years, give or take. Look, can we change the subject?"

* * *

Walthamstow was its pretty self, even in the early hours. Vagrants slumped together at Bell Corner, waiting for something to happen. Lloyd Park stood silent, the trees swaying gently in the wind and rain. He thought it could make an interesting composition, lit from one side and with a fog filter. But he wasn't that type of photographer.

"Listen, Thomas, I appreciate your help. I know we've gone a little off-piste."

He didn't answer. All he could think about was getting the cargo inside.

Karl laid the case down on the coffee table and finally took his gloves off. "A cup of sweet tea before bedtime would be nice."

Thomas played mother, leaving the kitchen door ajar. When he returned with two mugs of the brown stuff, Karl was dozing on the sofa. He gave him a shove.

"Huh? Thanks pal. I must have dropped off. Shall we give the lock a try?"

Thomas sat beside him for the big reveal.

Karl flicked the catches and lifted the lid. For a moment they both stared silently at the weapon. Thomas sank back into the sofa.

"Did you know . . ?"

"You think I'd willingly bring this into your home? Say the word and I'll take it away tonight."

"It's late." His eyes stayed anchored on the rifle. "It's leaving here tomorrow anyway."

Karl announced he was off to the loo, leaving Thomas with a dilemma. He wanted to photograph the case and the gun, and get a look at Karl's key again. Sure, he could ask him, but why show his hand so soon? He listened to the revolving wheels of circular thoughts and paranoia. Something else the counsellor had picked up on — his inability to trust people.

Decision time. He went to a drawer and took out a pill from a plastic container. "Sorry, Karl," he whispered, stirring it into Karl's tea.

By the time he brought out a spare duvet and blankets for the sofa sleepover, Karl was already groggy. Thomas stared at the keys and change piled up on the table; he figured he'd give Karl an hour to be on the safe side.

At four-thirty he couldn't stand it any longer. All roads led to the same nightmare conclusion. Sir Peter Carroll had set him up — the fucker — and Karl was the recovery man. He got up, listening hard for Karl's heavy snoring.

The streetlight cast a silvery glow in the front room. Nothing looked real, which about summed up the situation. He checked the empty mug first then took the Ingersoll key into the kitchen to photograph it. He went back for the case, amused at the sight of himself in surgical gloves. If Karl woke up right now this could look very suss indeed.

Once the photo session was done, he stumbled back to bed and set both alarms. From what he remembered of those sleeping tablets Karl wouldn't hear an earthquake.

Morning caught up with Thomas around seven. He didn't attempt to move Karl until there was hot, strong caffeine at the ready.

"Come on — it's half seven. Time you shifted your arse."

Karl rolled back the top of the duvet and wiped his eyes. "Is that coffee I smell? Fantastic. I've been thinking. I want to test fire the rifle."

As Thomas stared into his mug of roasted goodness an idea leapt out. If Karl was after ballistics then he didn't know where the rifle came from. Time to enlighten him.

Karl didn't speak until the end. "Why didn't you tell me, Tommo — that night after Caliban's?"

"It was only a job until today. I had no proof of anything. And besides, we've both had stranger requests."

Karl's face was a study in disappointment. "Either we take the rifle to the shooting club, or . . ." He paused to let him fill in the blank.

"We go somewhere more private — the scrap yard?" Miranda's brothers' scrap yard in Wapping.

"Perfect, and it means I can still meet Ken at midday."

"You're kidding me? Despite everything I've told you you're giving it back to him?"

"It's a little late for a lecture on ethics." Karl reached for his coffee. "And by the way, your rubber plant over there — or whatever the hell it is — might be a little *sleepy* for a while."

Thomas coughed quietly.

"For future reference, when you've secretly stirred something in, leaving the liquid swirling is a bit of a clue. Shall we cut the crap now — I'm on your side, remember?"

He really wanted to believe that. "So what's going on? Jesus, Karl . . . a gun — the Old Man had me deliver a gun . . ." He couldn't say the 'm' word.

"Let's start with what we know." Karl smiled to sweeten the pill, but it still left a bitter taste.

He printed off the two photographs of keys while Karl got his brain into gear and his trousers on. The photos were identical, same serial number and scratch marks.

"It's a special Ingersoll key – for municipal locks. Ken gave it to me in the pub when you were playing darts. Next question?"

"Why not confront Sir Peter today?" Even as he said it he knew the answer. Karl would want to know everything so he could exert the maximum leverage with it.

"I'll make you a promise, Thomas. When we get to the bottom of it you decide what we do about it. I'm serious. Now, are you going to ring Terry or shall I?"

Thomas picked up his phone. "What about ammunition?"

"Leave it to me. This rifle is like an old friend."

Chapter 14

Thomas tapped the steering wheel and stared at the locked scrap yard gates. Already past eight thirty and no other bastard had shown up. Karl, he could forgive — at least he had bullets to collect. He stifled a yawn. Jesus, what a world he inhabited.

Another text came in from Ajit: Are you avoiding me? And speaking of guilt and avoidance, he hadn't contacted Miranda for a while either. Funny how spending time with Karl tended to push everyone else out of the frame.

He was on the point of ringing Terry when a cobalt-blue Peugeot roared up. Terry gave him a thumbs-up, got out and unlocked the gates. He looked hung-over. Thomas drove in after him. Karl had been quite specific about the depth of target he wanted, so they made a scavenger hunt around the yard.

By the time Karl put in an appearance, fifteen minutes later, they'd assembled an assortment of boards, posts and a couple of old car doors, ready for the build phase.

Karl took charge, instructing them how to reinforce the planks with wooden pallets so that the target stayed upright. Once it was all set up, he paced away what seemed like a ridiculous distance and turned, shifting his head from side to side like an owl. Finally, he made a line in the dirt and returned to his car.

"So what is it?" Thomas waited until Karl had set the case on the ground.

"The weapon?" Karl flexed his gloved hands. "A Winchester .300." He fitted the weapon together, screwed the silencer on and then strode away to his mark.

Thomas cleared off to grab a brew with Terry.

"Thanks again, Tel."

He shrugged. "You'd do the same for one of us."

True enough. Like the time he warned them off Harwich Port when he was working with Customs & Excise.

Karl took three shots and then came over to join them, holding the spent casings aloft in a bag. "If I'd been more organised I would have brought along ballistic gelatine to go with the biscuits."

Thomas delivered his most unimpressed face. Karl in the know was just about bearable, but Karl showing off was a step too far — not that Terry showed any interest. Tea break over, the three of them returned to the target. The three bullets had punched holes right through the wood and both doors, into the final block, where Karl carefully prised them out.

"You can imagine the mess they'd make. Right-oh, Tommo, We've got what we came for. I'll be in touch."

* * *

Thomas fortified himself with a bacon roll and a chocolate muffin, and trudged through the benefit claimants' list alone. By the time he reached the stalking ground he'd already missed the first few.

He ran his tongue over his lip and tasted fat residue and salt. Was it coincidence that Ken had found Karl in the pub? Karl hadn't seemed thrilled to see his old oppo. And why choose Ken at all? He started picking away at the chocolate chips, weary of his own thoughts. At this rate he'd be asleep before the afternoon shift.

Radio 3 offered up Grieg's *Peer Gynt Suite*, which conjured up memories of Christine Gerrard and her spacious car seats. That wasn't helping either. He rubbed his eyes and checked his watch again: eleven fifty-two. Karl would be on his way now.

A builder's van drove past and Thomas started the car. Nick Barrowby should be on board, suspected of working cash-in-hand. And, by suspected, the docket recorded that *information had been received*. A tip-off, maybe by a disgruntled recipient of sub-standard tarmac.

The van logo matched the sheet. All he had to do was follow at a discreet distance and catch him in the act. The van stopped opposite a building site of a garden and four men got out. The youngest, sporting baggy jeans and a fake branded sweatshirt, matched the photo on the sheet.

Thomas knew to wait it out. Arriving wasn't evidence of illegal working, any more than being with Miranda constituted a stable relationship. He bedded in and let the camera do its work.

Barrowby pushing a wheelbarrow. Then fetching out tools. At this stage he could still be helping out a mate and walk away. Thomas almost willed him to be *that* man. But the observer in him knew that the job was the job. He simply collected the data and some other schmuck made the decisions.

After the first batch of photos, Thomas's mobile rang. Pisser. He placed the camera down in the passenger foot well with infinite care and then picked up the call.

"Thomas? It's Ajit — where have you been? I've left messages . . ."

"Aye, sorry Aj. I've been working extra hours." He winced; that sounded lame.

"So, are you coming up or what?"

There was desperation in the voice. He could picture Ajit's family crowding around him, suffocating him with kindness and tradition. They were good people, but God help Ajit as the son bringing a potential heir into the world. Particularly if Ajit's dad had anything to do with it. Bloody hell, Ajit taking up with an *anagareja mahila* — English girl — was enough of an adjustment for them.

"I'll be there, Aj. Can Geena hold the baby in until the weekend?"

"You do remember that Friday is the due date?"

He didn't, and he felt bad about it. "I'll check with Miranda." He gave Ajit a cast iron guarantee, which bumped Miranda up the list.

"Is that a tall, dark stranger?"

"Hi, Miranda," he flustered. "Have you got a minute?"

"A minute? For you, I can spare five — when can you get here?" Cue background laughter, which told him that Sheryl was within earshot of at least half the call.

"Ajit wants us up at the weekend." There was no laughter now. "You are still coming?"

"I said I would, didn't I?"

"Great, gotta go. I'll call you with train times. Ta-ra babe." When it came to ending their calls he often felt like a dick. They didn't do *love*, but 'laters' hardly seemed to cover it.

He lifted the camera again and leaned through the gap in the seats. The van was still parked, but no one was around. Nick Barrowby could have gone home. He could call it quits. Maybe a five-minute rest of the eyes would help decide . . .

"Oi!"

He stared up as an old codger hammered out a rhythm on the driver's window. He took the hint and lowered it.

"You've been here nearly half an hour, asleep outside my house. This is a residential area you know."

He blinked slowly. "Sorry mate — must have dozed off for a bit."

"Right, well, can't be too careful. I've made a note of your car. We don't want the neighbourhood getting a reputation."

He reached for his SSU ID and kept a strategic thumb over his name.

The resident's demeanour changed. "Oh, I see. You're on a stakeout, are you?" He looked up and down the street. "Is it the woman along there with the kids?" He flicked his head to the left. "Different fathers, and neither of them takes an interest from what I hear."

Like Karl said: never let a good opportunity go by. "Listen . . ." He leaned towards the open window. "Any chance I could pop in for a few minutes?"

It was disturbingly easy to gain access to an upstairs room. In five minutes of photography Nick Barrowby was well and truly shafted. He ticked him off the list, using Karl's patented 'G for Guilty' shorthand. Once the job was complete, he thanked his host, sidestepped a cuppa because he'd seen the sterilised milk downstairs, took a leak and then went on his way. Last thing he did was remind the bloke to keep schtum and stay vigilant, and not to let any strangers into his house again. A time check showed it was nearly one p.m. With any luck, Karl would rendezvous with him at the next location.

* * *

Karl's car was just pulling in as Thomas arrived, so he joined him. Mr Paul Tomlinson wasn't hard to track; he could have been followed at a light stroll. They watched as a man, old before his years, lurched unsteadily on two sticks. Karl's head bounced side to side, scrutinising every step.

"He's consistent; I'll give you that. There's a definite rhythm to his movements."

Thomas twisted in his seat. "Doesn't this bother you? When you think of all the assignments we've had . . ."

Karl considered the point for about four seconds. "Nah. They send us and we turn up to do the job. End of story."

Mr Tomlinson shuffled along the street and shouldered his way through a pub door.

"You know what I'd do?" Karl carefully replaced his lens cap.

Thomas smiled; he knew all too well because they'd both read Conan Doyle. "A Study in Scarlet — smoke bomb through the window."

"Right. Then see how quickly he moves."

"So, what, he can't be really disabled because he likes a drink?"

Karl stiffened. "Fancy a pint? I'm buying." And before Thomas could answer he was halfway out the car.

They locked their cameras in the boot, for all the good that might do, and cut across the council's idea of a play area. Municipal irony came in concrete. He followed Karl in silence, grabbing the pub's swing door as Karl let it go behind him. Mr Tomlinson stood out like a sore thumb, standing behind a chair with his two sticks leant against it.

"Any news?" Thomas set the drinks down on the table.

"What, with Ken? Funny thing; he wasn't pleased to see the case, pretty spooked by it actually. Think on that — I've gotta nip outside."

Their quarry sat down and didn't move. Thomas was glad; it seemed unreasonable to hassle a bloke in Tomlinson's condition. Still, like Karl said: the job was the job. Evidence based reporting — once you began to make subjective decisions, it was a slippery slope leading to bias and poor judgement. Amen.

The saloon door rattled and Karl bustled in, whamming a newspaper down beside Thomas's elbow — it made grim reading. Either a reporter had got clever, or she had contacts. The shooter's location had been identified as a block of flats. Thomas wondered if child killers merited a lofty word like assassination. The leader page made it clear that access to the roof was only possible with a security key.

"Something troubling you, Thomas?"

"I made that possible."

Karl seemed nonplussed. "Well, you're hardly complicit. Anyway, some would say you deserve a medal."

It didn't make him feel any better. "What did Ken do in the army?"

"Not here." Karl finished his drink and headed out the door.

Thomas was a second or two behind him; Mr Tomlinson had been outranked. Outside, grey clouds masked the horizon.

"Come on then — Ken?"

"I'm sure you've worked it out — he was a sniper. My, my," Karl walked back towards the cars, "what have we got ourselves in the middle of?"

"Karl!" He grabbed his arm and spun him round. "I'm going away for a few days — I've got too much in my head. Ajit and Geena are about to have their first baby and . . ."

Karl nodded sympathetically. "Of course. Do what you have to — just don't do anything rash. I'll square your trip with Christine and call you if there are any developments. Go home."

Chapter 15

Miranda had thawed a little since the last time they spoke, but not by much. He understood. Yorkshire hadn't covered itself in glory on the last couple of visits, but he still got nostalgic for the old days in Leeds when she lived in a bedsit on Hyde Terrace. He kept, captured in celluloid, fond memories of love's young dream and the move down south to start a new life together. And what a life it had become.

He tore himself away from the photographs on his wall and picked up a sports bag; he was already wearing the rucksack. Karl had offered to drop him off at Euston Station, but he'd chosen the Tube. Walthamstow had a touch of *dirty old town* about it, but he liked that. There was honesty on those unswept streets — that and litter.

The tide of commuters had long since rolled through Walthamstow Central. Passing through the barrier he could hear the whirr of the escalators — like his own thoughts, circling without resolution. He descended into the labyrinth, half-wondering if Miranda would actually show up.

He surfaced at Euston and immediately texted Ajit: Nearly on train — speak later. Then he joined the throng in the station hall and started looking for a special blonde.

"I bought you a book."

He opened the bag and read the cover: *The Spy Who Loved Me*. He wasn't sure if she was taking the piss, so he kissed her anyway and then dragged her off in search of snacks. By the time they were on the concourse, he was £15 poorer; a small price to pay. He felt like a teenager again, heading home to Yorkshire. Miranda waited until they found their seats before she put a major spoke in the works.

"I'm going to stay in a hotel. You can join me if you like."

He gave up trying to read her face. "My sister's expecting you."

"Yeah, I know, but I thought this way I won't get under anyone's feet."

He did a sweep of the carriage from his seat. She looked up, raised her eyes and then went back to her magazine. Once what she called his *gentle paranoia* had subsided he settled into the journey. The soothing rhythm and flow of an ever-changing view allowed his mind to wander unfettered.

"When you're finished, I'm trying to read." She smiled impishly as he became aware that his foot was rubbing against hers.

Time for a crossword. He delved into the carrier and pulled out a book of cryptics. He liked the sense of order and structure, and their strange algebra. It seemed to him that much of his life was about cracking codes, solving problems, or bringing order to chaos. He itched to ring Karl, but now was not the time for a declaration of war with Miranda — especially as she'd already mentioned she was here under protest.

"All right, let's get a room tonight and then see how we go."

She lowered her magazine like a drawbridge. "How long are you staying?"

Good question. "Dunno." He'd assumed Geena's sprog would keep to the timetable, given Ajit's punctuality. Against his instincts he wanted to tell Miranda about the case and the rifle, and everything he was running away from. He knew it wouldn't do any good though.

"You were miles away." She glanced down at the crossword he'd started filling in with little targets. "If you're offering, I'll have a large coffee, milk and sugar."

"You're the boss." He returned her smile. Trains — was there anything they couldn't do? The buffet car gave him some thinking space; there was bad news to deliver back at the table. He'd need to time it carefully

"Did I mention Dad's picking us up at York?" He passed Miranda her coffee.

"You *are* kidding?"

He slid into his seat. "Well, I could hardly expect Ajit to come and fetch us when Geena might go into labour at any moment?"

"So you'll tell him about the hotel then, before you get home?"

"Yeah." He gazed out the window. "I'll tell him."

The sight of York Minster catapulted Thomas back through the years. Mum liked to make a pilgrimage there at Christmas and Easter – probably still did. She would dress in her church clothes, with Dad pressganged into a shirt and tie. Meantime he and his sister Pat would have to be on best behaviour. The routine never varied, including the arguments on the way there and the festive tug-of-war between the tearoom and the pub afterwards. In his mind's eye he watched his younger self, traipsing round the shops with his sister, mimicking the adults and taking sides. He recalled the gaggles of carol singers and the roasted chestnut pedlars, and weaving through the crowds with Pat, breathing in the sugared air together. York had always been a place of sanctuary.

"Are you fit?" Miranda clutched her bag, packed and ready to go.

He nodded, dumped everything back in the carrier and turned to the luggage rack. Outside, there was a bustle of people even in the early afternoon. That was the magic of York – never empty and never dull. Dad was nowhere to be seen and he regretted not planning an overnight stop in York – a halfway house between the old life and his present one.

"Do you think he's forgotten, or d'you reckon he's still in the pub?" Miranda pulled her coat in close.

Visitors and students streamed past, jostling together as taxis homed in on the prey. Once upon a time he and Ajit had talked about getting a flat in York. In the finish, he'd overshot York by several hundred miles while Ajit had never really left Pickering. Funny how life worked out.

Miranda threw a quiet strop and went off in search of coffee, leaving him to guard the bags. He nudged them together with his foot, and texted Ajit: In York awaiting Dad. No sooner had he sent it than an earlier text came through: Where are you? Aj. Good old modern technology.

Miranda returned with one cup of coffee, so they shared. He couldn't tell if this was punishment or intimacy, but at least it was coffee. He spotted the hazard lights as the car approached.

"Well don't just stand there, get in." Dad leapt out, kissed Miranda awkwardly on the cheek and gave him a manly grip of the arm.

Miranda had opted for the back seat, alone. Thomas turned round, periodically, to make sure she felt part of the conversation, but he may as well not have bothered.

"So, how's things, Dad? Taken any good pictures lately?"

His father took the bait, distracting him with talk of the Rievaulx Abbey ruins, St Mary's 'Dracula' church at Whitby and the moors, a mental guided tour.

"Now, I 'ope you're hungry because your mam's done a bit o' baking."

Miranda coughed and he felt her knee pushing against his back.

"Actually, Dad, er . . . we've made plans for tonight."

Chapter 16

The old family home in Pickering felt overcrowded. Pat, with Gordon — her feckless shit of a husband, the two bairns, and Mam, all crammed into the front room. Dad's seat was waiting for him and Mam leapt up to welcome them before scuttling into the kitchen to put the kettle on. Pat, naturally, made a huge fuss of her *daft brother* and Miranda waited beside him for her turn in the spotlight.

Dad changed into slippers and then nipped into the kitchen, presumably to deliver the bad news in private. Soon after, tea was served with a slice of cake and a sprinkling of attitude.

"It's lovely." Miranda played nicely, although she didn't use her name and would certainly never call her 'Mum.' Thomas had been on first name terms with John and Diane Wright from the moment he clapped eyes on them.

"So, where are you staying?" His mother made out like she didn't care, and fooled no one.

"We're at the Best Western," Miranda parried. "We managed to get a special deal."

Thomas glanced at Pat, who was trying hard not to laugh. This was like watching a lioness face down a crocodile at the watering hole. "How's work, Gordon?" He opted for a soft target.

"So-so." Gordon looked at his watch none too casually. "Well, I'd best be off with the kids – come on, say goodbye to Nana and Grandpa."

The children swamped their grandparents and then approached Uncle Thomas for their customary pocket money; after which Miranda handed out chocolate. Then, without a word between Pat and her husband, Gordon took off with the kids. The front door slammed, carrying the children's voices with it, and Pat seemed to relax, motioning for Miranda to sit beside her. Thomas winked at Pat; unless he was mistaken battle lines were being drawn.

"Right, lad, let me go and fetch them photographs." Dad left the field early, clearly in no mood for bloodshed.

Thomas filled in, asking about the extended family – uncles, aunts and cousins he'd had nothing to do with in the past decade. When that rich conversational vine had withered, he shifted the focus to Ajit and Geena. All he could get out of Mum was, "It'll likely be a big bairn, judging by the size of him." It was said with affection and it helped ease the tension.

While father and son pawed over photographs, Miranda delved into her case to deliver a Harrods bag to Thomas's mother.

"Just a little something."

"How thoughtful." She melted.

By five thirty they were away to the Best Western. Miranda confirmed her double room at reception.

"So you knew I'd stay with you?"

"No . . ." She paused. "I booked it for me, and to add you if required."

Required? He didn't like the sound of that. She did the necessary at the desk, insisting it went on her credit card, while he tried not to look — and feel — like an afterthought. Once they were upstairs, he rang Ajit at home.

"At last! I thought you'd got lost after York and ended up in Ripton. What are you both doing tonight then?"

Ajit insisted on picking them up at the hotel, so Thomas booked an early meal for two beforehand. Dinner was fractious; the staccato conversation managed to say nothing at all. He felt himself withdrawing; he'd expected Yorkshire to be a challenge, with everything else going on, but not like this. He figured she'd tell him eventually — she always did.

Ajit was punctual to the minute; he had the look of a condemned man about him.

"You've cleaned the car!" Thomas squeezed into the passenger seat behind him.

"He's a cheeky bugger." Ajit beamed at Miranda beside him. "So how was it wi' the Bladens?"

No reply. On the drive over, Ajit chronicled Geena's two false alarms, her mania for tuna and inflatable ankles.

"Bloody 'ell, Thomas, I'm going to be a dad soon." Ajit sounded like he still couldn't believe it.

Thomas went in first. Geena looked immense. "Are you sure it's just the one kid?"

"'Ullo love," Geena adjusted the cushion behind her. "Put kettle on, will you?" She slapped a nearby chair. "Well, come in, Miranda."

He left them to it and joined Ajit in the kitchen. They jostled together among the cups, seventeen-year-olds again.

"How's your job, Thomas? Don't worry, I am covered by the Official Secrets Act."

* * *

Time among friends twisted the minutes and folded the present in with the past. Ajit had been the first to know when he and Miranda had decided to go to London and had lent him the money for the tickets. Now, as he relaxed in their company, he felt maturity creeping up on him. Soon Ajit and Geena's lives would change forever and revolve around sleeplessness and feeding times. He listened to them talking about baby names and stole a glance at Miranda. Were they next? Wasn't that what couples did?

"And then . . ." Geena tapped Miranda's knee, shaking the chair as she rocked with laughter, "Ajit's mum suggested I have a 'traditional' home birth with all the women of the family in attendance! I said, 'Bugger that — I want a hospital with a dishy doctor on standby.'"

"We're having it in the Malton," Ajit explained.

"Oh aye," Geena erupted into laughter again, "*we.*"

"You're gonna be there in the delivery room?" Thomas looked at Ajit incredulously — Ajit, who got rattled at the sight of a needle.

"He better be!" Geena answered for him.

Miranda had left the room without leaving her seat. He knew that look in her eyes — a storm was approaching. "Right." He put down his mug. "Time we left you good people to your bed. Do you want help getting Geena out of her chair?"

He rang for a cab and waited at the door with Ajit wedged beside him.

"Listen, sorry about Miranda; I don't know what her problem is today."

"How d'ya mean?"

"Never mind, it's been a long day. We're seeing my folks tomorrow, but ring me if anything's happening."

The taxi journey was a crypt on wheels. He kept his mouth shut until they were back in their hotel room.

"Couldn't you have made an effort? I know you didn't want to come, but it's not their fault."

"No." She stomped around the room, searching for a hairbrush. "It's yours. I told you I'd rather not be here, but you insisted I come along to play happy families."

"What *is* your problem? Have I done something to piss you off?"

"Just leave it. I'm tired; I'm going to bed."

He didn't need surveillance skills to work out it wasn't an invitation.

Chapter 17

He was out next morning, camera in hand, and returned with pictures of two chaffinches and the back end of a squirrel. Miranda was in the shower. When he pressed his ear against the door so he could hear her trying to sing, he thought he heard her crying. She emerged from the steam wrapped in towels, her face a little blotchy. Somehow she could still make pissed off and unhappy look good.

After breakfast they went walkabout in Pickering, a busy Saturday in a typical market town with endless opportunities for not talking to one another. They got to the café early. The place could have doubled as a lace museum. There were only four chairs at the reserved table. Apparently Pat, Gordon and the kids were out for the day. Knowing Gordon it could well have been a trip to the garden centre.

Hostilities had abated by the time his parents arrived. Miranda broke new ground by calling them Helen and James. He watched the three of them struggling and went on the offensive.

"What's the latest with Pat and Gordon?"

His father faltered. "Well, she doesn't say a lot. I think they're managing . . ."

"And what about you two?" Mum returned fire.

He was all out of ideas after the previous night. When make-up sex was off the table, he knew they were in bad shape.

Helen advanced further into enemy territory. "You've had years to sort yourselves out. If you'd stayed in Leeds — or come back to Pickering — things might be very different now."

"Excuse me, I need the loo." Miranda stood up and glared at him.

He made the most of her absence by defining a few boundaries. They were all enjoying a nice cup of tea when his mobile came to the rescue.

"Alright, Thomas?" Ajit's voice echoed in the earpiece — a classic corridor conversation. "Geena's been taken into hospital, on account of her blood pressure — a precautionary measure."

"So it's not the big push, then?"

"No, but I think she'd be glad of that now. Complete bed rest until the baby comes. She came in first thing this morning and she's already bored out of her skull. Do you feel like popping in to cheer her up?"

"In hospital you say?" He mouthed 'Ajit' for the benefit of everyone at the table. "And where are you again?"

"The Malton, like I told you yesterday."

"The Malton?" He repeated it for effect. "That's miles away."

It had the desired result. The journey over was punctuated by Thomas's efforts to include Miranda in the conversation and a fat lot of good it did him. They were dropped outside and he walked off to the front desk, threading his way to Ajit, with Miranda trailing behind him.

Ajit looked elated to see a new face. "It could be up to a week they reckon — she's nowhere near ready," he muttered outside the room.

"I bloody well am," Geena called out. "Are you coming in or what?"

The room smelled of some aromatherapy spray — the scent he had noticed at their house. A stuffed piglet, Geena's from childhood, was propped up on a pillow.

"Does Percy know he's getting a sibling?" Thomas flicked its ragged ear.

A medic put her head around the door and asked them to leave while she did a quick examination. Miranda was first out and the three of them decamped to the corridor. Ajit tried small talk about her business and Thomas listened in. Miranda was so self-contained. She didn't need looking after and that scared the hell out of him.

The medic emerged and passed on a message for Miranda to go in alone. She went pale at the news, glancing behind her up the corridor. Ajit caught Thomas's eye and nodded towards the drinks machine.

"Girls' talk!" Ajit nudged him without turning back. "Is she alright?"

"Dunno." Thomas was relieved to have Ajit on his wavelength. "She's been in a funny mood since we left London." He dug into his pocket for a handful of change.

"P'raps she's broody." Ajit stroked his chin. "I've 'eard that some women get that way when one of them has a bairn. Maybe you want to think about that, Mr Intelligence."

He concentrated on carrying the coffees back while his mind turned somersaults. They'd never discussed having kids — apart from joking about what terrible parents they'd make. And now his job always seemed to get in the way.

Ajit knocked on the door before they went in. Geena was in tears. Thomas meekly handed Miranda her coffee; she'd have given Medusa a run for her money. Ajit moved around the bed to Geena's side and Thomas looked on.

He felt the walls closing in, as if a haze had filled the room and only he could see it. He heard each shallow breath, felt his heart pounding and knew he had to get out of there. Without saying a word he closed the door behind him. A few paces on he dropped his cup into a bin, inhaling the sickly aroma of machine coffee and creamer as it hit the plastic liner and burst. *Jesus.* He felt the sweat in his hands as he switched on his mobile.

"Hey Karl, it's Thomas — any news?"

"You could say that. I got a look at the police report — ballistics confirms what we already knew. I'll tell you more when I see you." Karl's phone paranoia kicked in.

He took a Judas breath. "I'll come back today."

"Well, that'd be useful but I can hold the fort here until you're ready."

"No, it's settled. I'll ring you from the train." As he slumped with relief against the wall, he felt his rucksack digging into his back. Inside were his camera, his passport and his keys — all the things that mattered.

He dragged himself back along the corridor and tried to lose himself in justifications. Jack Langton was depending on him and so was Karl. Besides, Miranda might be grateful for an excuse to leave. He cleared his throat and went inside, a few steps from the door.

"I've just spoken to Karl. Sorry, I'm needed in London."

"No." She spoke quietly and didn't say anything else.

He couldn't tell whether she was objecting or if she didn't believe him, so he waited. She was quiet for a time, taking it all in. And just when he thought she was okay with everything she flipped. A complete meltdown; screaming, flailing at him, resurrecting every injustice he'd ever inflicted on her — and there were many. Telling him how he put his fucking job before her every time, and now he'd treated his only friends the same way.

"The truth is you need your job — you're lost without it. You run back to London. I'm staying on at the hotel."

Ajit stared at the floor. Geena grabbed his hand, pulling him close, crying and crying without saying a word, until finally Miranda told Thomas to get out.

He shut the door and kept on walking, telling himself it wasn't cowardice but self-preservation. Either way, the rush of air past the automatic doors was the purest oxygen he'd ever known. When he reached York he rang his sister. He wanted to get in his side of the story first, and he passed on Miranda's mobile number so Pat could keep an eye on her.

"Oh, Tommy." Pat's voice sank. "Whatever's wrong with you?"

"I don't know, Sis." He told her the signal was breaking up and cut the call.

At York, he collected a couple of Southern Comfort miniatures to anaesthetise him for the rest of the journey. Not being a big drinker had its advantages. He woke as the train arrived in London, a sweet taste on his lips and a bitter one on his conscience. The therapist, who he'd stopped seeing, had once asked him if he saw a way back to the person he used to be. Before he'd been dragged into the Surveillance Support Unit quicksand like all the others. "No," he whispered on the train, "there's no way back now."

Chapter 18

Karl met him at Euston Station. "Jaysus, Tommo — you look like shit. Is everything okay?"

Thomas threw him a sardonic smile and followed him to the car. Karl rattled off a relentless briefing while he drove.

". . . I acquired a photo of a cartridge the police recovered from the scene, found in a drainage channel. Ken must have missed it — sloppy. It matches the ones from our test firing. You realise what this means?"

"Yeah, I'm definitely an accessory to murder." When Thomas closed his eyes he saw the bullet holes that had penetrated wood and metal in the scrap yard. He opened the window to escape the faded scent of spilt orange juice from the back seat.

"Stop the car – I'm going to be sick." He was true to his word.

Karl sluiced off the kerbstone with drinking water while Thomas sat there, head in his hands.

"You wanna talk about it?"

He shook his head slowly. "I wouldn't know where to start." He held out his hands and rubbed some water across his face before taking a swig.

"That's all right, Tommo — you keep it. Listen, if you don't feel like going home, do you fancy a drink?"

It wasn't like he had anywhere else to go. "Sure. Where does the police report leave you with Ken?"

"Treading carefully. He's clearly implicated although I'm still waiting for his version. But I think what you're really asking is whether I'd turn him in?" Karl looked him right between the eyes. "Not a chance. I hope I haven't offended your moral compass."

He didn't bother responding.

* * *

It didn't take a detective to predict the choice of watering hole. He wondered if Karl was secretly hoping to run into Ken again. He doubted it — life was rarely that tidy. As they entered the regimental bar the manager called Karl over. Thomas fell in step.

"Mr McNeill!" He stiffened a little, as if passing sentence. "This was left for you — hand delivered. Please don't make a habit of it."

Karl reached for the envelope and ordered two shandies. Over at the table, he checked it for signs of tampering and then slit the top with his car key. He extracted a single page from the ragged edge and folded it flat on the table so they could both read it: SORRY TO DRAG YOU INTO THIS. NO ONE ELSE I COULD TRUST — KEN.

Half an hour and one game of darts later, Thomas felt brave enough to put his mobile back on. Ajit's text read: How could you? There was no word from Miranda, which was about what he figured he deserved. He was still reliving the scene in the hospital when Karl returned from the gents.

"No good news, I take it?"

He snapped back into work mode. "We need to get the buggy back to Janey. You can explain the science again to me on the way."

"Not much to tell. The paint colour is obsolete according to some database, and the chemical analysis of the flakes on the buggy confirms the paint was manufactured before 2000."

"So how does that sit with Jack Langton's theory that it was a premeditated attack?"

"It's an anomaly, I grant you. And we still don't know it *was* about Jack. Greg owed money to Charlie Stokes — he as good as said so. Something to discuss next time you see Jack in prison?"

Heading across London, he turned down *Deep Purple* and reached for his phone again. No voice messages but one new text: I need to see you tonight — Diane. That was unexpected — a summons from Miranda's mum.

"Listen, could you drop me off at my place first and deal with the buggy on your own? I just received an invitation I can't turn down."

* * *

When he went inside for his car keys he spotted the answering machine flashing. He hit the button and stood in the shadows, waiting. Pat didn't pull any punches this time — Miranda deserved better, he was totally selfish, and the topper: she was ashamed of him. Join the queue.

It stood to reason that Diane Wright had heard from Miranda. They were close. Not like her to get involved though. She usually stayed well clear of their chaos. He was either in line for the mother of all bollockings or something else was going on. He got in the car and put his foot down.

Chapter 19

His palms tingled as the sweat met the dank air outside, each step from the car talking him further from safety. Diane was quick to answer the door, solemn faced and drawn.

"Come in, Thomas."

He followed her to an empty living room. Diane noticed he was looking around.

"John's in his office. We agreed this was better coming from me. Sit down. Coffee all right?" Her voice trailed behind her.

He leapt up after her; he thought he might as well get it over with.

"Look, Diane, I'm really sorry about leaving Miranda in Yorkshire. There was stuff I needed to do for Jack Langton and it couldn't wait."

She faced him down, saying nothing, and pulled out a couple of chairs. The kitchen it would be then. She seemed lost in thought, or maybe she was waiting for the right moment. Either way, it was killing him.

"I know I fucked up." He felt his voice go brittle.

She yielded a long sigh, put down her coffee, and cupped one hand over the other as though she were shielding something fragile.

"Miranda's been under a lot of strain lately." She raised a finger when he lifted his head to speak. "It's been hard keeping you in the dark, but Miranda talked with Geena and then she rang me."

A wave of dread hit him. "Is Miranda ill?" His breath caught in his throat.

"No . . ." She stalled. "Not *ill*." The way she said it hinted at bad news. It wasn't long in coming. "You remember when she went to Bermuda?"

How could he forget? They'd parted company — again — and she'd been seeing some up-and-coming footballer, apparently. What was it with her and footballers? And then, almost out of the blue, that was all over and she announced — in a phone call, mind — that she was off to Bermuda on a modelling job.

"Yeah." He felt his shoulders locking. "I remember."

"Well . . ." Diane swallowed hard and pressed her hand flat over the coffee mug. "Around that time she found out she was pregnant."

His brain went into slip gear. "Why didn't she say something? I didn't know . . ." He started conjuring with the implications.

"No, she wanted to think about it and make her own decisions. As it turned out," her knuckle whitened, "events ran their own course and she had a miscarriage. Early stages, that can happen."

His mouth dried. "I'm so sorry." The pieces fell horribly into place. How volatile she'd been about Ajit and Geena, and then, God help him, he'd insisted she go with him to Pickering. He pressed a hand to his mouth. They'd made her a godparent and he'd left her there with them, about to go into the delivery room. And she'd never said a word. "Christ, I've been such an idiot."

"You hurt her badly, but you weren't to know." She drew a breath with difficulty. "The thing is, there were *complications* and now she may not be able . . ." Diane looked like a broken woman.

He smudged a finger against one eye. "What do I do?"

Diane seemed not to have heard him. "Maybe some good has come out of this." She stared at her hands. "Miranda doesn't want any more secrets; only she couldn't face telling you. So now you know."

"Okay." He faltered. "I'll talk to her tonight. I dunno; we'll see a counsellor or something. I'll find some way to make it up to her."

She stared at him and reached out a hand. "You don't get it — it wasn't your baby."

Everything moved into slow motion, like the time he'd been shot. He was aware of standing up and walking, but it wasn't really him. Diane said something about staying, only the words rushed past him. It took all his concentration to put one foot in front of the other, get into the car and drive away. He had nowhere to go.

"Karl, are you busy?"

"Twice in one day — people will start to talk." He cut the comedy routine when he got the measure of the situation. "I'll meet you at Holloway Road Tube station. You've got your passport?"

* * *

What he felt was a heavy grief, about everything, now that the covers had come off. Miranda must have been seeing the footballer before they'd broken up, during her sex embargo. There was anger too — at the world — especially people like Sir Peter Carroll and Jack Langton. Tonight he'd settle for targets and guns.

Karl chose Browning 9mm pistols. It had been a while since Thomas had faced down static targets but the body remembered. Muscles tensed and then settled in that curious way Karl had told him about. The ear defenders entombed him with his thoughts and he lined them up like targets to take them out one at a time. It was all he could cope with. By the time he reeled in his handiwork, the burden had lifted a little.

Karl waited until Thomas had emptied two full magazines and then signalled that their session was over. It wasn't quite therapy, but it came close. He set the pistol down and wondered: was this who he was now — the kind of man who needed a gun to feel in control of his own life?

"Do you, er, want to try some other equipment?" Karl carefully closed the lid on the Brownings.

He shrugged; he didn't know what he wanted, other than to not go home. Karl returned with a pair of SIG Sauers.

"I'll tell you this, Tommo, you've got an edge about you tonight. Whatever's bugging you, it's doing wonders for your hand-eye coordination."

"You have a fair idea what it's about."

"Let me just annihilate your score and then we'll get us a beverage."

It still amused him that a private shooting club offered drinks and snacks. He watched as Karl sauntered back to their table with the goodies, silently acknowledging persons unknown.

Thomas picked at his pastry. "Incidentally, what happened to Jack Langton's post that I lifted from Janey's?"

Karl's face pinched in. "Oh, right. It was mostly nonsense, apart from one interesting item. It's in code, so we've been busy having a crack at it."

"Oh?" He gave him his full attention, intrigued to hear there was something Karl and his cronies couldn't do. "Tell me more."

Karl's eyes seemed to glint. "It's a piece of brilliance — both simple and complicated – like a Vigenère code. It requires a key word; but we haven't figured it out yet. We've tried variations on names — wife, Jack himself, their kids, even Jacob. Basically, anything we could associate with him. No dice."

"What about 'scumbag'?"

Karl laughed, raising his coffee in a toast. "That was one of my first choices."

Thomas swallowed. "Try 'Sheryl.'"

Karl took out his mobile and made the call in front of him — that was a first. He spelt out Sheryl's name and waited a minute or so, with the phone at his ear. Finally, Karl nodded and ended the call. "I'm impressed. Honest to God, Tommo, you ought to be in intelligence." Karl was all smiles but he wasn't laughing.

Disparate details were aligning in Thomas's brain and a disturbing picture was emerging. "Let's play a game." He dug out a pen and paper. "I'm going to write three statements down. You don't have to add anything, just tell me if I'm right. Deal?"

Karl nodded; he didn't look happy about it. Thomas gave every sentence careful consideration, adding to Karl's discomfort. He could see Karl reading the words from across the table.

> 1. Jack Langton is at the end of a Shadow State supply line.
>
> 2. The merchandise at Janey's flat belongs to the Shadow State.
>
> 3. Both Jack and Charlie Stokes were already persons of interest to your people.

Karl took the list and re-read it. "I wouldn't contradict any of your conclusions." The façade slipped a little. "Look Thomas, you have to understand . . ."

He cut Karl off. "How could I do that without the information?"

* * *

Back at his flat, Thomas searched Vigenère ciphers on the Internet and gave himself a headache. He flicked on the TV to fill the void and fixed a microwave meal from the freezer. Hunched over the table and shovelling shepherd's pie into his mouth, he replayed the events of a shitty day. Did anyone tell him the truth anymore?

'Let him who is without sin cast the first stone . . .' his mother used to say. He thought about the times he'd driven past Christine Gerrard's flat once they'd split up, coincidentally around the same time Miranda returned from Bermuda. Or that evening, working late with Christine, when a friendly drink nearly became something more.

Just after eleven pm he switched his mobile back on. There was a text waiting, all in caps: GEENA HAD A BOY. 8-3. SEND FLOWERS. AJIT & GEENA X.

He got in the car without a destination in mind. London seemed emptier because Miranda wasn't out there somewhere. About the only thing he knew was that he'd be keeping well clear of Christine's

Hampstead flat. If Bob Peterson were there tonight, he'd be getting a free pass.

He couldn't deny himself a drive past Caliban's and, as he gave a sad salute to the neon sign, an idea struck him. Maybe Karl was doing his own surveillance on Janey and Greg tonight. The thought took hold, gnawing away, leading to only one conclusion. As he drove into Janey's housing estate he spotted someone weaving along the pavement, obviously pissed. Greg's idea of supporting Janey and their boy was by getting bladdered. No sign of her; she'd probably be at home waiting by the phone.

He pulled in and backtracked, twenty yards or so behind him. He figured the least he could do was make sure Greg made it home in one piece. The trouble was, other people had a different plan. At first it was just two shapes, up ahead, moving out of the shadows. Greg stopped, his carrier bag clinking as he stood there. It was only going to go one way and Thomas had to make a split second decision. He started running towards them.

Greg went down and by the time Thomas got there they were kicking seven bells out of him from opposite sides and yelling that he should have kept his trap shut. Greg was hardly moving — not a good sign.

Thomas ran into the first one at full pelt, knocking him flying. The second lad — they looked about early twenties — put up two fists and wanted to make a night of it. Whatever else they were, they weren't fighters. He sidestepped a half-hearted punch and returned the favour with interest. He felt his knuckles connect with a satisfying crack.

The lad may not have been a boxer but he knew how to take a punch; he recovered, charging back for a second wave. Thomas dodged a first punch that never came, unlike the second that winded him. He doubled over and pulled back, furious with himself for being fooled so easily.

The first one was up on his feet now and spoiling for revenge. Greg was no use whatsoever; Thomas saw him out the corner of his eye checking his bag for damages.

"You're gonna be sorry . . ." They advanced towards him.

He straightened and faced them down, crushing his fists in. *Not as sorry as you.* The would-be boxer was around five feet nine, giving Thomas a two inch height advantage and a better reach. The guy flinched back when he launched himself towards him, but the other one, bigger and broader, made a wide circle round.

Thomas turned and retreated to keep them both in his field of vision, forming an unholy triangle. That's when he heard the unmistakeable *shikk* of a flick knife tasting the air. The shitty day had just got worse.

The boxer held out a hand to stay stab-boy, but things had gone too far. Thomas felt the inside of his mouth turn to sand. Chances were that they'd only cut him, as a warning. But warning or not he would make it his personal business to really fuck them up. He watched knife boy's eyes, waiting for him to make the first move, having already decided on a throat punch or a kick in the bollocks.

A bottle smashed somewhere behind him and, to his immense relief, Karl McNeill came forward.

"Put it down, son or you might hurt someone."

Knife boy didn't look convinced although he edged back a little, still sizing up his chances. "This is nothing to do with you."

"I'm making it my business." Karl waved the broken bottle back and forth.

Thomas turned back to the boxer, surprised — and a teensy bit impressed — that he hadn't run off. One look in those eyes told him that they were both packing some sort of weapon.

"He said put it down."

They all turned to see Ann Crossley, facing them, arms extended with a pistol at the end. Knife boy dropped his weapon as if it was molten and started walking away. His accomplice followed suit. Karl was quick to pick up the knife but he didn't try to stop them.

"I'll leave you boys to have a chat — I'll be in the car." Ann holstered her weapon and zipped up her jacket, cucumber cool.

Thomas stared at Karl, aware that his mouth was open.

"What just happened here?"

"Come on, Tommo, we better get him home. We'll talk about this another time."

Chapter 20

He stared at the alarm in disbelief — six fifteen — and made the best of it by dragging his weary arse out of bed to order flowers online for the new Mummy and Daddy. He skipped breakfast and was out the door before seven, beating the rush into the capital. Too restless to take photographs, he walked around St Paul's Cathedral and gave a fiver to a beggar to make himself feel better.

Karl arrived for the pick-up at eight fifteen, in high spirits judging by his whistling. Paulette Villers was first on the day's Benefits' hit list and Karl opted for their previous vantage point. Thomas was determined not to mention the previous night.

He blew across the camera buttons for dust, paused, and then removed the lens cap. "What's put you in such a good mood?"

"Irony and information. Guess who manufactures the SSU's ID cards now?"

He shrugged; he couldn't give a shit. Doubtless, Karl would regale him with a tale of corporate conspiracy if he waited long enough.

"Give up?" Karl lasted ten seconds. "Engamel, that's who!"

Thomas sneered at the news.

"Yeah." Karl huffed a breath and folded his arms. "I thought that'd give you something to think about."

Engamel — manufacturers of the Urban Ballistics UB40, also known as The Scavenger. The weapon a woman had died for needlessly, a few months back — when, for once, Sir Peter Carroll had done the honourable thing and stood up to the Euro-Cartel.

Thomas bit at a thumbnail, cradling his camera with his other hand. "Anything more from your army mate, Ken?" He waited for an update, which never came.

When Paulette Villers arrived with her partner, she was limping. Karl picked up his camera.

"See." Karl pressed into the eyepiece. "That's what I don't get about domestics. The other lass gives her a beating and then helps her into work — her *illegal* work. The mind boggles."

They captured the footage, mapping every step and glance. Thomas focused on Paulette's companion. Once the target had entered the building, the other woman waited a few seconds, flapping her arms against her coat to stay warm. His camera picked out her anxiety and the uneven stance.

Thomas lowered his lens. "Listen, do you fancy doing a sandwich and coffee run? I didn't have breakfast and I'm famished."

Karl held out his hand for cash. "I'll give it back to you later, scouts' honour."

He watched him leave and returned to his vigil. Something didn't sit right; that familiar tension was creeping over him, subtle as seduction — instinct. Paulette's other half was still there, checking both directions from the corner. Paulette Villers rushed back out of the laundry, grabbed the woman's arm and they cautiously made their way up the side street.

He was out of the car before he really registered what he was doing. There was no plan; only a sense that something was wrong and he might be able to help. But even that was an afterthought.

"Paulette, wait . . ." He was only a few paces behind them now.

Both women turned and then pulled closer together, shuffling up the street like wounded animals.

"Look, I wanna help." He stopped moving.

"Leave us alone. He'll see you and then we'll all be in trouble."

He? That threw him. "I'll be here on Monday, early — if you want to talk." He didn't wait for an answer. A silver Saab cut into the side street. He sized up the driver effortlessly; well-built with cropped, greying hair — a geezer who'd use an old-fashioned gym and wouldn't be seen dead in a leisure centre. A mastiff of a man; the sort of bloke you didn't fuck with.

Thomas turned his head away slowly, so that he could get a look at the number plate sideways on — one for Karl to check out later. He told himself it was probably nothing, until the Saab stopped in the road. He crossed over to get a better look and saw the two women, now parallel with the car, slowly get inside.

Karl was waiting by Thomas's locked car, without breakfast. "There was a queue at the café, so I didn't bother." He didn't speak again until they were moving. "I'm waiting, Tommo. This had better be good."

Thomas passed over the number plate and assembled his thoughts aloud. "I know it's a stretch, but I've been right about stuff in the past, haven't I? You set the ball rolling with your comment about 'domestics' and when Paulette left the laundry and they both started walking . . ."

Karl closed his eyes, as if asking for intercession. "Where is this going?"

"If you can check out the Saab's owner."

Karl smiled, cat-like. "You used to do that kind of thing privately."

"Yeah, well, I think you proved conclusively last night that we're a team. And besides, your contacts will be quicker."

Karl made the call at their next observation session. By the time a Nigerian family — based on the clothing and the notes — exited number 43 and locked the front door behind them, proving fairly conclusively that Mr Liang was subletting, he had his reply.

"Well, well," Karl lowered his mobile. "Looks like you were on to something. You had a close encounter with Mr Charlie Stokes."

That was two hits on the radar; it was definitely time to speak with Jack Langton again.

* * *

Ninety per cent of surveillance was sitting around waiting for something to happen, but it wasn't the worst part of the job. Every assignment demanded some interaction with their hosts and that could only mean one thing: meetings.

The review was scheduled for three thirty — a crap time by anyone's estimation. Karl checked through the paperwork en route. They agreed a 'no questions' pact to get out by four-thirty, so they could visit the SSU office at Liverpool Street.

Karl must have been working a night shift again; he'd taken dressing down to new depths and could have passed for a benefit claimant himself, like the one they'd just followed to a doctor's surgery. Despite that, Karl was relentlessly upbeat.

"Don't you get a thrill from it? With each assignment we become someone else."

Thomas shrugged. "Same shit, different department."

Undeterred, Karl hummed a *Disney* tune on their way through the turnstile. Second floor, sharp left, and along the corridor to the glass-walled meeting room. Welcome to the goldfish bowl.

Not the last in, but close. Someone muttered, "Floaters," as they took their seats. Karl retaliated by coughing, "Wankers." At three thirty on the dot Dawn Yeates rose from her chair and hushed everyone. As she turned towards the whiteboard, the beads in her hair clattered together.

"Let's make a start. Karl?" She looked over her shoulder and smiled. "Perhaps you'd like to kick off?"

Thomas glanced at Karl, who was smiling back. Was this some kind of magic moment? He gave a succinct progress update, highlighting their successes and the gaps. This was Benefits Investigation Karl, who spoke the language of the locals — *claimants*, *suspected* and *benefits, recipients*. Thomas sat back to enjoy the show.

Dawn Yeates lapped it up, showering him with praise and suggesting tactics. Karl took notes. After that, feedback Friday went round the table like a Mexican wave. Some of them sounded like big game hunters reflecting on their kills, while one pair — clearly ex-coppers, lamented that they no longer had the power of arrest.

The latecomers put in an appearance close to the end — another SSU team, based over in West London. Thomas had never really spoken with them; he only knew them by their surnames — Malone and Iqbal. They sounded like injury lawyers. Malone always seemed buttoned-up, her skirts safely below the knee, while Iqbal's smart suit belied his position. Thomas suspected that he'd been assigned on the grounds of ethnicity and language skills. Or maybe the pair of them weren't in favour with the SSU.

He waited outside for Karl to finish his schmoozing. The good folk of the BIT passed him without a word. Even their West London SSU cousins only managed a murmur of courtesy. Karl emerged with a folded piece of paper in his hand.

"Right. Time to visit our real family!"

Chapter 21

By the time they reached the Liverpool Street building it was well after five. Naturally, Christine and Ann were still working.

Karl nudged Thomas. "It's like a double-date."

Christine ventured out from her office. "Thomas, could you spare a minute?"

She reached behind her desk and lifted an A5 envelope from a pile of papers. He received it without comment and slid out the contents.

"Standard visual surveillance," she explained. "Where he goes and who he speaks with."

He stared at the photograph, waiting for her to state the obvious. Bob Peterson — the married Bob Peterson, her ex, now banished back to Southampton.

"What am I looking for?"

"I'm not sure."

He didn't bother asking if this was on the books, given that Bob Peterson had been the boss for a brief period.

"I'd like to end your assignment with the Benefits Investigation Team."

The deal with Sir Peter was that he and Karl always worked together. "And Karl?"

"It's up to you. As long as you report back to me — and me alone — you can run it however you like."

He could almost feel Karl drumming his fingers at his desk. "When?"

"With immediate effect, unless you have any objections?"

Three or four. He decided to stall her. "I'd prefer to stay put for the next couple of weeks . . ."

"Oh?"

Now for the tricky part — eyes down and keep the voice low. "Miranda and I are having problems . . ." That at least was true.

She tapped her fingertips — corporate empathy. "Try not to let it interfere with work. I take it this means you'll be visiting the prison again?"

He smiled a little; now for the last minute save. "I don't mind working weekends if you think the target warrants it."

It was her turn under the microscope. She didn't stay there long.

"Weekends will be fine." She nodded. "We'll talk again – Karl's waiting for you."

Karl was busy at his laptop as Thomas emerged, and immediately started packing up. "Fancy a wee drink?"

* * *

The Swan was good and local; shandy and crisps, and the luxury of seats facing the doors. He'd noticed that Karl preferred his back to the wall when there were crowds. They sat for a while and watched the show — the city boys and girls, out to impress; the office workers trying to shrug off the day's drudgery; and even — God love 'em — a couple of MI5 blokes from their building, almost blending in. He nudged Karl and they raised their glasses to the second cousins from the first floor.

Karl chose his moment carefully. "Have you spoken to Miranda since you left Yorkshire?"

He shot him a leaden glance.

"Understood." Karl lifted his hands away from the force field. "Only I've got the weekend off, if you're at a loose end . . ."

"Actually, I've got a job lined up."

"Not another wedding shoot?"

He pretended to enjoy the joke. "Something like that."

* * *

Friday night was the worst; rattling around in the flat with his mobile burning a hole in his pocket. Twice he thought about ringing Miranda; he'd revisited their last car-crash conversation in his head until his cheeks burned. Pat had given up leaving messages and Ajit and Geena were now knee-deep in nappies. And anyway, he was probably still in the doghouse.

The doorbell rang; a flick of the curtain confirmed the welcome visitor.

"Alright, boss? Chicken Jalfrezi, pilau rice and a Peshwari naan."

He carried the booty into the kitchen, laying everything out on a plastic tablecloth. Already in the hallway were a camera and a road atlas ready for the early morning jaunt to Southampton.

Christine had struggled to fill a page. Bob Peterson's home address, the SSU office there, his children's school, and the charity Mrs Peterson had last worked for. The handwritten notes also detailed locations of the nearest supermarkets and the number plates of both the Petersons' cars. All in all, it looked very much like a private inquiry.

Chapter 22

It was no great hardship being on the road at six thirty a.m. He enjoyed his own company — something the moors had taught him. Just as well because Miranda and he were on opposite sides of a crevasse. The Reichenbach Falls had nothing on this *final problem*. He gazed at the pale horizon and wondered how to draw a line under the past when it still cast a shadow over the present.

By eight thirty the weekend traffic around Southampton was chock-a-block. Erring on the side of caution, he had parked up in good time at the end of the street. Bob Peterson was only five minutes out from Christine's schedule; she'd certainly done her research. Bob did the whole family bit — waving and smiling to the wife and kids before he pulled the 4x4 off the drive and went a-hunting.

Thomas stayed well back, trailing Peterson to the supermarket. The 4x4 slotted into a space but Thomas still kept his distance, waiting until Bob had been inside the supermarket for a good five minutes before he nipped over to the petrol station for some snacks and a piss. On his way back across the tarmac, he stopped to tie his shoelaces and slipped a shop-bought transmitter out of his pocket, attaching it under the rear wheel arch. The handheld locator read Uncle Bob's stationary position loud and clear; he was all set.

Thirty minutes later the target emerged with enough food to last a nuclear winter. Thomas let the camera tell its own story, as Bob Peterson carefully stacked plastic containers in the 4x4. What had Christine ever seen in a dick like that?

He trailed him home, letting him off the leash more now that he had the tracker in place. As Thomas arrived, Bob was carrying the last of the containers inside. He stared at the house, unclear what he was looking for, when Bob was suddenly back on the road. Only this time, he wasn't hanging about.

First stop was a nondescript SSU building. Not hard to spot though, when you knew the signs — like the grilled car park and the reflective film on the office windows. Peterson was only there ten minutes; his next port of call was a multi-storey car park.

Thomas gambled on covering the front exit and decided he'd give him twenty minutes before checking out the shopping centre on foot. The radio offered up a discussion panel show with the topic: do we have a culture of snooping? Concerned citizens phoned in to trade certainties and insecurities, pooling their outrage at future plans to fit microchips in wheelie bins. The second course covered supermarket loyalty cards and what data they might hold. It passed a pleasant quarter of an hour without putting a scratch on the Regulation of Investigatory Powers Act 2000.

A quick jaunt on foot through the multi-storey yielded nothing. He checked his own parking bay, did a quick tally up of how much time he had left, and went walkabout again. Mixing with the shoppers was the closest he'd got to normality since he ran from Yorkshire. He watched them with a cold eye, moving among the couples and families in search of his quarry.

He kept the handheld screen at his side, glancing at it every twenty paces, not that he could do anything now if Bob started driving. It all seemed like a bastard waste of time, unless he wanted a great deal on a new phone or to chat with one of the honeys trying to extort money for charity.

And then, like a gift from God, there was Bob — sitting in a café with a woman. He could only see the profile, but she didn't look like wifey, and in any case Bob had left the missus at home.

He walked on, checked there was no one following him and regrouped his thoughts. Christine wanted photographic evidence but would she really want *this*? Sod it: the job was the job. He slipped an Olympus mu-10 out of his coat and did a practice run, further along the precinct; walking past a shop with his camera nonchalantly by his arm, tilted to the shop front. It wasn't his finest work on playback, but it was better than nothing. He set off slowly to avoid jogging the phone around.

It was a punt, a fly-by, and he didn't dare turn his head until he was clear of the row of shops. The footage was far from perfect — at best he figured on pulling off a couple of decent images. A shame about the fat bastard who'd cut across his line of vision, but that's *Joe Public* for you. Bob would be at least a few minutes behind him — probably with his mystery woman — which gave him time to get into position.

Peterson's car was on the fourth floor, tucked away in a corner. And naturally the nearest lift was out of order. With the blood still pounding in his head, Thomas checked the tracker was securely in place and looked around for a vantage point. He wanted to get a clear shot of the woman too, not that he expected Christine to like it. He took pleasure from that without knowing why.

Ten more minutes and he'd be risking a parking fine. *Come on, Bob. Shift your arse.* The surveillance mantra must have worked its magic because Bob Peterson arrived a couple of minutes later. The woman held back by the stairs, still in the shadows — smart. Maybe she was too smart. He did the best he could without a flash and, seeing as Bob was setting off solo, he legged it back to his own car to try and beat the parking rap.

Back at the car he turned his mobile on, expecting Christine to have texted for an update. There was a message, but not from her: *Can we talk? Mx.* The familiar dilemma: work or Miranda. He moved the car, fleeing the city centre to find a quieter backstreet without permit parking. The phone stared back at him, awaiting his decision. A text would have sufficed, but she deserved better than that.

She picked up on the third ring. "Hello, Thomas."

After the killer opening line — "How are you?" — he stalled.

"Are you free for lunch?" She sounded edgy or tired — he couldn't tell which.

He took a deep breath. "I can't; I'm working."

"Oh, I see."

"But I'm free later," he winced at his own enthusiasm.

"Ring me later then and I'll see what I'm doing. Take care, Thomas."

Her voice was hollow. He was about to ring back and renegotiate the terms of the truce when the handheld caught his eye. Bob Peterson was on the move, out of the city.

A quick flip through a street guide and he'd worked out a reasonable intercept point, assuming Peterson kept to the same course. Any thoughts of Miranda were put back in their box; there was a job to do.

The tracker signal died without warning. He ran through the probabilities. Peterson could have discovered it or the bloody thing might have fallen off somewhere. It had happened to him once before on a job. Whatever the cause, he was buggered. Might as well head for home and try again on Sunday. Not much for a morning's work — not good at all.

A couple of miles up the motorway he spotted the blue lights behind him, cutting a swathe through the traffic. He slowed again, out of habit. The chequered car drew alongside him and signalled for him to pull over. He played it cool and glided to the hard shoulder, pushing the tracker screen under his passenger seat when he came to a halt.

The über-cool patrol car nestled in behind him. He was no petrol head but this was a car to die for. Miranda's brothers would have been wetting themselves. He kept to the drill and waited for the knock on the window, clocking the two coppers behind him as they talked among themselves for a minute or so.

He felt for his Surveillance Support Unit ID in his jacket and then checked his phone was turned off. The passenger door of the police car squeaked open and a burly figure loomed towards him.

"Do you know why I've stopped you, sir?"

Stopped him? By the way they bombed up the motorway they were hunting for him. He shook his head and smiled, playing innocent. The conversation reminded him of a fly-on-the-wall documentary — the sort of thing Karl loved. It was the standard checklist: driving licence — clean (and nigh on immaculate), road tax, insurance and MOT all up to date. Burly cop seemed perplexed.

"There's a marker on our system against this vehicle . . ."

Now he flashed his SSU card. Less a loyalty card and more of a 'see, we're on the same side' card. It made sod-all difference. Burly cop gave it a cursory glance.

"What sort of marker?" He stared at the copper's buttons, wondering how you tell real ones from fake.

"Can I have your keys, sir? It won't take long."

The cop went back to sit with his chum. Maybe he could ring Ajit for some advice? Then again, he was hardly flavour of the month there.

Judging by the rear view mirror, the traffic cops were having a conversation with no winners. He imagined they were listening to a third party feeding them instructions by radio. Finally, the driver took her turn, jangling his keys in her hand as she walked over.

"Can you follow us down to the nearest services?"

It was a question with only one answer.

As they entered the services, nose to tail, he noticed the faces of other drivers — the freaked out, the intrigued and a bloke in a van who gave him two thumbs-up. He parked beside supercar and heard the numbers counting in his head, slow and steady. The police car became his sole focus.

He wound down his window and looked across, smiling. A parallel pane descended.

"If you could wait here." The window rose back.

He put on the radio, dropped the numbers routine and thought about the marker on his car. Perhaps Karl could look into that. The sight of a 4x4 approaching with a number plate he recognised dispelled any further questions. Bob Peterson was the guest of honour. It was tough to know what was worse, being caught out — and by Peterson of all people — or the realisation that his target had played him brilliantly. He could hardly lamp Peterson in public with two coppers present.

Bob Peterson nodded to the police officers, stopped his vehicle so that it blocked Thomas's car and took his time getting out. Then he reached behind the driver's seat to retrieve a package. He left his driver's door wide open and motioned to Thomas to join him.

Peterson waited for Thomas to draw level with him. "Two things — one, this is the package Christine is expecting; and two, leave Christine alone."

Thomas took the package and circled back to his car without a word. Peterson had sounded stone cold serious, which suggested he might have a reason for behaving like a possessive arsehole.

"I mean it, Thomas," Peterson called behind him. "I'm always three steps ahead of you."

Like he couldn't have been satisfied with two — dick. Back in his car, Thomas watched Peterson pull out his phone, make a quick call and then walk briskly back to his 4x4. He made a two-fingered matey salute to the cops and then drove off.

Thomas turned to the cops, who looked as bemused as he felt. He got out again and stood by the police car.

"Am I entitled to know what the marker is on my car?"

The driver deferred to her colleague.

"Must be a glitch — the database probably needs updating. All I can tell you is that your vehicle is flagged 'of interest' if seen in the Southampton area. Sorry about that."

"I'm here on an assignment." He showed them his ID card again. "So being stopped makes it difficult to do my job."

"I'll pass it up the line," the driver promised half-heartedly.

He called it quits and decided to grab a coffee in Motorway Services Shangri La. They were gone when he came out, but they'd left a contact card under his wiper blade. He couldn't work out whether it was a warning or if he'd made a friend.

Chapter 23

The London bound traffic was as sluggish as his thinking. Nothing made any sense. He had no idea who Bob Peterson was with, or why Christine cared. Then there was Peterson warning him off from Christine. And lastly, what was so important about the package in the boot? He toyed with the idea of ringing Christine, so he could deliver the package, and then thought better of it. Whatever it was could wait.

Miranda hadn't rung him back so his first call was to the answering machine at home. Geena had got there first.

"You're forgiven for being a dickhead. Now, go make your peace with Miranda — if she'll let you. You really hurt her, you know."

Yeah, he knew. He dialled Miranda's mobile; judging by the background noise she was at Caliban's.

"Hiya, it's me. I just got back from . . . work."

"Do you fancy a bite?"

There wasn't a hint of innuendo and he missed it.

"I'll come over now if that's okay?" He waited to hear whether the thin ice would bear his weight.

"Yeah, okay."

It was a short drive over from his phone stop. He thought about picking up chocolates, but nothing quite said 'sorry for abandoning you in your worst nightmare.' He decided to pay for lunch instead.

Caliban's felt like enemy territory as he threaded his way through the jungle of people to the bar. Sheryl, Miranda's manager and confidante, was the greeting party.

"You made it then." She'd clearly cancelled her fan club membership. "Look after her, Thomas — she's been through a lot."

"I know," he muttered, already on the defensive.

"No," she shook her head, "you don't. But I do. I was there in Bermuda when it happened. She stayed with me afterwards."

He went upstairs and knocked on the office door.

"It's open." Her voice wavered.

He saw the picnic she'd set up on the desk and wished he'd brought chocolates or flowers. The plastic gingham tablecloth was a nice touch.

"I thought you might prefer somewhere private." She gave a tiny smile and swept her hand towards the empty seat.

But there was a third, unwelcome guest: the past. They met as opposing armies, advancing and retreating sporadically. Until, finally, all the effort to *not* say something drowned out the conversation.

"So where are we?" He broached another silence.

"You know where we are."

He gazed in all directions, like a hapless tourist, eliciting a smile. It lasted until his mobile started buzzing. She shot him a killer look of disappointment and shrugged. He checked the number, purposefully setting his mobile on the edge of the desk. Typical — it was Christine.

"No, really," she insisted. "Take the call. I mean it."

"Hello?" He looked away.

"Thomas? It's Christine. I need to see you."

"Can it wait?"

"Would you drop by the office, say in about an hour?"

His eyes drifted across to Miranda, weighing up the odds.

"Okay, I'll see you then."

All things considered, Miranda was pretty good about everything. She didn't fly off the handle; she even backtracked a little, which caught him off guard.

"I'm not trying to change you. Well . . ." She smiled for a millisecond, "I've given up on that. Oh Christ, Tommy, have we made a mess of everything?"

It was his turn to smile now. "We're still talking — and lunching."

She offered more wine, but he waved away the bottle.

"Better not; I've got some work to take care of."

"For Jack Langton?"

"No, I've got some work stuff to deliver for Christine — from this morning."

"Without Karl?" Now she was fishing with depth charges.

"Yeah, just me this time."

"You watch your back. While you're busy trying to save the world, who's looking out for Thomas?"

"Well, you — I hope!"

Her face reassured him he'd come up with the right answer. She reached across and forced the rim of the cork into the wine bottle.

"Hadn't you better get going? Duty calls and all that."

"I've a few minutes yet." And he gazed at her earnestly.

By the time he got into his car the landscape had shifted. They hadn't shagged; they hadn't even kissed — not properly, but there had definitely been electricity in the room. That, and hope.

* * *

The Liverpool Street underground car park was practically deserted. All the high performance cars were nestled in an area designated for the Security Service — his MI5 neighbours on the first floor. Nearby was one space, hardly ever claimed, for MI6 that read: *Secret Intelligence Service.* Karl had taken a picture once. Christine's Merc looked lonely so he parked next to it.

His trusty rucksack held the spoils of the day — camera, mobile phone footage and Bob Peterson's package. He could hear it rattling a little as he walked and felt the box inside nudging against his back.

He took the stairs two at a time, letting his steps act like a metronome to his thoughts. On the second floor, the office was eerily quiet. Karl's desk looked bereft without him, despite the mess he'd left behind. Out of habit, Thomas scooped up the vending machine cups and chocolate wrappers, dumping them in the bin. A notepad page lay next to the keyboard with GVA and a set of numbers next to it.

He took his time getting to Christine's office, weighed down by the sinking feeling that he'd just been paid overtime to do some domestic gumshoeing.

"Thanks for coming, Thomas." She didn't look up from her laptop.

"I was stopped by the police — something about a database marker?"

She swallowed. "I don't think Bob has ever forgiven you for . . . the altercation."

A smile stretched his face when he recalled landing a couple of punches on Bob Peterson — both beauties — back when the inner workings of the SSU were still a mystery. Well, *more* of a mystery. So Bob still held a grudge — good.

"Anyway . . ." He brought his rucksack forward and noted the sparkle in her eyes. "Bob turned up and gave me this for you."

Now she stirred, one eye on his hand as it reached into the rucksack.

"Would you like my report now?"

He moved around the desk so they could both see the screen, and connected up his camera.

"Wife and kids." He provided the narrative and watched her reactions.

"I can see what you're doing," she insisted.

It didn't deter him. "Big shop at the supermarket — going in and coming out."

"What about inside?"

He hadn't thought about that. "Too much risk of exposure," he lied. "It would help if I knew what I'm looking for."

"You're a surveillance officer," she snapped. "I don't pay you to ask questions."

Touchy. He changed tack and told her about the vehicle tracker on Peterson's car and how the signal had died.

"I think he was expecting me. Maybe the police tipped him off before they stopped me." He waited for another dressing down but it didn't come.

Christine turned her attention back to the screen.

"I went looking for him in the shopping centre, near where he parked." He noticed she was barely breathing now. "I found him in a café . . . with a woman."

"Oh?" She coughed a little.

"Yeah, I had to improvise. The quality's not great. Do you want to see it?"

"Can you upload it to my laptop?"

"Sure." He reached into his rucksack for the cable.

They watched the camera connect to the computer and he looked away as she authorised the security override. The film was amateurish, barely in focus for the café window and hampered by some passers-by with remarkably large heads. The woman's face was obscured but not the profile. He looked at Christine again and figured it out.

"Do you want to tell me what's going on?"

Her silence told him plenty. She'd needed someone to film her there with Peterson — maybe it was emotional blackmail, or something to send to his wife. The dots connected a circuit and a light bulb came on. She was still involved with Bob Peterson, or wanted to be.

"Oh, Chrissie." He heard the ragged edge to his voice.

"I don't need you to fight my battles or to save me from myself."

No, he thought, only to do your dirty work.

"So Bob has no idea?" He sighed; of course he bloody didn't. "And you've done what . . . told him that I'm the jealous ex, following you around?"

"It wouldn't be the first time."

Disappointment decayed to pity. "I'm *concerned* for you, is what I am."

"Save your breath, I'm a big girl now and I can look after myself."

He pulled the camera lead free. "I'll get prints to you. Is that it now?"

"No. I want the surveillance job in Southampton completed."

He wondered if she were simply playing Bob Peterson for information. That somehow this was legitimate surveillance on an authorised target. But something in her eyes, some trace of the obstinacy he remembered from their own ill-fated relationship, assured him this was also personal.

"Okay then, you're the boss."

Her lips drew tight, as if to remind him that was never in any doubt. The package stayed on the desk, unopened. "Thank you, Thomas." She opened her office door and stood aside so he could leave.

Chapter 24

Back home, having shrugged the chip from his shoulder, he researched GVA on his laptop. Karl didn't usually leave notes on his desk, however badly scrawled. The search took less than three minutes, allowing time for the kettle to boil. GVA was the airport code for Geneva. As was the norm with Karl, a new piece of information only created more questions. Still, lucky sod — it was a better gig than *spot the boyfriend* in Southampton.

While he was busy pondering a choice of takeaways the phone rang.

"It's John. Natalie Langton wants to discuss the missing half kilo with you."

"When?" His finger strayed across the menu to Jalfrezi.

"Tonight. Watch your back, Thomas. Jack Langton may be the one pulling the strings, but take it from me — his wife is an expert at pushing people's buttons."

* * *

He dressed up for the appointment and put himself on best behaviour. Logically, he had nothing to fear; all he'd done was deliver the case. Even so, his guts were churning on the drive over.

Ray's car — the one Natalie had got into with the case — was nowhere to be seen. He was glad of that, until he rang the doorbell and she appeared in a low-cut number.

"Come in — Thomas, wasn't it?"

He faked a smile; she knew damn well. She made it through to the kitchen before he'd had a chance to close the front door.

"What can I get you?" Her voice echoed along the passageway, a little on the shrill side now he thought about it.

"Nothing for me, thanks — I'm driving." He felt like adding, 'and you're married,' but he let it pass.

She returned from the kitchen, hips swaying, and pointed him through to the lounge. A massive white leather three-piece filled the room, which was quite an achievement. A flick of a switch and *Sade* poured from the speakers, sweet as honey.

"So, Thomas." She moved the glass away from her face. "How much do you know about Jack's business?" Her lips parted to receive his answer.

"Me? Nothing. I'm just helping him out — a favour for a mutual friend." He didn't elaborate about John Wright; he was more interested in what she wanted him to know. People always wanted you to know *something*, especially if they were selling a lie.

"A smart man like you — aren't you just a little bit curious?"

"Killed the cat." He smiled again, forcing it up into his eyes. She looked like she was waiting for more, so he moved the Bladen charm up a notch as she sipped her drink.

"I can see Jack likes the finer things in life." He paused, waiting for that coy smile to dance across her face.

"Look." She leaned towards the edge of the sofa. "The missing half kilo is making problems for everyone."

He nodded. "I can imagine. What do you want me to do?" Simple and direct; he reckoned she'd appreciate that.

She swung her legs up and stretched out. "It'd be best for everyone if we had a full case again. I'll pay out for it if I have to but I'd rather not, and I don't care how you get it — do you understand?"

"I think so." His stomach flipped again. Oh bollocks, this was all heading in the wrong direction. Best to play the part all the way to the curtain. "What's in it for me?"

She didn't miss a beat. "My gratitude. You'll find I can be very grateful."

He blinked a couple of times as she faced him with a warm smile and cold eyes. Maybe Jack Langton was safer in prison.

She smoothed her top needlessly; from where he sat there were no imperfections. "Just get the half kilo back before word gets around and I'll make it worth your while. I wouldn't want anyone thinking they can take advantage," she rearranged her window display again, "just because Jack's inside."

He was out the door in less than twenty minutes. *Sade* was still waxing soulful and somewhere, he surmised, Ray Daniels was eyeing up Jack's throne — among other things.

Karl telephoned at close to midnight.

"Any chance of a Sunday meet up?"

"Could be tricky." He wiped an eye with the heel of one hand. "I've, er, got a job on tomorrow." He took the plunge. "Surveillance on Bob Peterson in Southampton. You remember Bob?"

"Does Christine think he's still active for *them*?"

Karl never named his enemy. Thomas had heard him call it a cartel, a Shadow State and even Shadow Europe, but there was never a clear definition. Smoke and mirrors every time.

Another pause so Thomas went for broke. "Are you in?"

"Of course I'm bloody well in. We're partners, aren't we?" There was a warmth to his voice now.

"Okay then, partner, where have you been in the last twenty-four hours?"

"Geneva, as you probably worked out. I realise it can't compare with the glamour of Southampton, but someone had to make that sacrifice. Anyhow, call me when you're leaving tomorrow and pick me up."

* * *

Thomas had the dream again — the one where he caught Christine Gerrard and Bob Peterson together at a hotel. The one where he lamped Peterson and kept on pummelling him until he was a crimson pulp. Only this time Karl was there too, taking photographs.

Chapter 25

He woke exhausted; nightmares always wore him out. There was nothing easy about this Sunday morning.

Karl passed him a bag when he got into the car.

"I picked up something on my travels — I sampled it for quality purposes."

He peered inside: handmade chocolates. "Thanks; I didn't know you cared."

"I don't — they're for Miranda. I thought you could use all the help you can get."

He didn't dignify that with a response. Instead, he gave Karl the low down on the Peterson job and shared his speculations.

"Okay, Tommo, I can understand her wanting to force Peterson's hand — what the heart wants, and all that. But he's connected to the cartel, albeit at the bottom of the food chain, so there has to be more to it."

"Then you're saying Christine is somehow working him?"

"I'm not saying that — you are."

It would have been smarter to use Karl's car, but he wanted to see whether the police stop in Southampton was a one-off. He had half a mind to ring the number on the card left under his wipers, to see what happened.

Sunday in the Peterson household was hardly a web of intrigue. The whole family went for a swim, while Thomas dissuaded Karl from a little housebreaking. Later, the Petersons trundled off to a burger bar — the posh kind — while Daddy read the paper and Mummy kept the children entertained with drawing pads. Through a long lens it all seemed like domesticity, but Karl wasn't buying it.

"Christine must know *something*, or at least suspect."

Thomas thought about the padded envelope she hadn't opened in front of him.

"Could we find out what Bob and his teams are working on?"

Karl frowned. "I prefer not to spy on other SSU teams. It's like professional incest."

He nodded, noting that *prefer not to* wasn't the same as saying *no*.

* * *

After the burger bar the Peterson family went straight home. Thomas figured there was only so much fun a family could take. He suggested they give it another thirty minutes, no more, and sure enough Bob Peterson was out in twenty-five. They tracked him back to the Southampton SSU office, where he disappeared into the rabbit hole and kept them waiting.

Thomas nudged Karl, who was practising surveillance on a pigeon.

"What do you think Christine suspects . . ?" He was dropping a pebble for ripples.

Karl lowered his telescope made from a copy of Private Eye. "I think she suspects he's up to something." That was all he said.

Thomas reached for Radio 2 — something soothing that didn't require any concentration. As he settled in to enjoy *The Drifters*, the metal gate beside the front entrance started rolling up.

"Pool car." He started his engine.

Peterson emerged from the underground car park in a silver Ford Focus.

"We should call it in to the boss." Karl was already reaching for his mobile.

Thomas nodded — what harm could it do? By the sound of things Christine was keen to continue the information gathering. He gestured to Karl to up the volume and asked the crucial question: "What's our primary objective?"

Christine was unequivocal.

"I want to know exactly what he does and who he talks to — understood?"

"Ma'am." Karl ended the call. "Methinks Peterson is out of favour."

He clocked the sign for Southampton Docks. "I'm pulling over."

Karl was unperturbed. "It's your call."

They watched Peterson disappearing into the distance. Three steps ahead . . . Peterson knew to take a different car and he knew

Thomas's number plate. He'd be going to the docks — Thomas was sure of it.

"How about the wife? While we're tracking Uncle Bob, she could be anywhere."

"Nah." Karl rooted around in the glove compartment for food. "I've already checked her out and she's clean. Besides, where would she stash the kids?"

This called for some lateral thinking, which he did in silence. He grabbed his mobile, ignored Karl and rang Christine with the pool car's number plate. Peterson's pool car was easily located when they got down there, thanks to Christine, but the great man himself was nowhere to be seen. No problem, Thomas already had a plan.

"We get him paged."

Karl was all ears. "I like it — some kind of emergency. We need him somewhere we can see him along with anyone who's with him."

"Yeah, well, as long as we're not worrying the guy about his wife and kids."

"Ah, Tommo, you're all heart. Leave it to me." Karl climbed out of his sweatshirt, wrapped it around his fist, and then got out of the car. "This'll do nicely." He picked something up and went across to Peterson's car. Without another word he cracked it down hard on the windscreen, chipping it in the centre. Then he knelt down to see to two of the tyres before getting back in the car.

"What?" Karl lifted his hands in exasperation, the sweatshirt smeared in brick dust hanging off his arm. "That ought to do it. Now we just get Christine to page him."

"Are you taking the piss? We could have paged him ourselves."

"Yeah," Karl smirked, "but now . . ."

Thomas caught Karl's logic train. "Now he can't drive it away, so either someone comes to collect him or someone has to give him a lift."

"Spot on. So let's split up and find out who his date is."

Thomas found a sheltered spot in the Mayflower terminal and rang Christine. A few minutes later, Bob Peterson's name hit the tannoy.

"Surely he'll know it's a set-up?" Thomas muttered into his mobile.

"Possibly, but he won't ignore the call." Karl's voice crackled and whinnied outside in the car park.

"And you can't be seen?"

"I have done this before Tommo, once or twice."

"Yeah, but this is against one of our own."

Five minutes on, and with no sign of Bob Peterson, Thomas was getting restless. Maybe Peterson had figured it out and gone

654

straight to his car; he could be surveying the damage and updating the police national computer database.

He was about to make another call to Karl when Bob Peterson arrived at the helpdesk. He looked relaxed, even when the man behind the desk relayed the bad news. A woman appeared beside him, standing close, as if they were a couple. Maybe they were. Busy, busy Bob.

And speaking of bobs, the blonde had her hair styled in a bob cut. As she turned to look behind her he realised he knew her. The hair was different now and she wasn't in uniform, like the time he'd met her in Leeds. He felt as if someone had wrapped a thick blanket around his shoulders, closing him down. He circled the pillar to find a spot behind a plant tub, taking pictures on his phone. He didn't hang about, fleeing to the nearest gents so he could check the pictures and contact Karl.

The toilet resembled some kind of septic tank disaster. He closed the cover and rested a foot on top, as if to literally keep a lid on things. The picture wasn't great, but it *was* her. The same woman he'd met in Leeds when he collected a Document Security Bag for Sir Peter Carroll, months back. He stared at the image and then sent it on to Karl. Shortly afterwards, he rang him, speaking in a shout-whisper.

"What's the score, Tommo?"

It felt like two-nil — to the opposition.

"Did you get the image I sent you?"

"No, it sometimes takes a . . . hold on, it's here now."

The line went quiet; all Thomas could hear was a pulse in his head and swirling static in the earpiece.

"Right, got it. Listen, we have a problem."

"You're telling me, Karl. I've seen her before . . ."

The outer door of the gents swung in and Thomas immediately cut the call. He stayed perfectly still. He heard deliberate breathing, as if someone were trying to compose himself. Then the bleeps of a mobile phone pressed into action.

"Hi Julia, it's Bob. No, everything's fine, darling. It's just work . . . I know I said I'd be back before three . . . let's not do this now . . . yes, I know. Look." The word ricocheted off the wall. "We'll talk later. I'll be back as soon as I can. Okay?"

He heard a rhythmic tapping like fingernails against the side of a sink.

"Okay, love you; bye."

It sounded like Bob Peterson did a good line in irony. The thing Thomas noticed after that was nothing. No footsteps, no one washing their hands or taking a piss; not even — thank God — someone going into the neighbouring cubicle.

There was just shallow breathing. What if Peterson suddenly appeared, looking over the top? Photograph him? Make a break for the door? Lamp him one? He thought about flushing and walking out — Peterson was hardly likely to keep him captive in a lav. Except . . . being seen there was tantamount to an admission of guilt.

He breathed slowly through his nose, nice and easy, and started counting down in his head. One-eighty, one-seventy-nine . . . At one-forty-eight the main door squeaked open and footsteps retreated. He texted Karl — He's coming out now — turned the phone off, and finished his countdown. He figured Uncle Bob would want to see to his car straightaway. As he eased through the crowds he thought back to the mystery blonde who had been with Peterson. Did he know her name?

Outside, the distinctive aroma of Southampton Water blended perfectly with diesel and drizzle. The cruise ships and ferries might promise glamour and prestige — at a push — but that didn't change the backdrop.

His phone rang as soon as he put it back on.

"Where the hell have you been, Tommo?"

"Hiding in the toilets."

"Peterson's made a couple of calls — I couldn't see the numbers at this distance. It looks like he's leaving his car here to be collected — the two of them are moving away. Hang on, I think he's having a tiff with blondie."

Thomas swallowed. "I'm out now; where do you need me to be?"

Karl seemed quieter than usual. Thomas followed his lead and stayed in position until a people carrier arrived and whisked the unhappy couple away.

"Did that go well?" He honestly didn't know.

Karl was non-committal. "We got what we came for — we know who Bob Peterson's contact is. Christine ought to be pleased."

They found a café on-site, now Bob Peterson had gone. Karl was well into his second coffee before he shared anything useful.

"You remember my trip to Geneva? She was there too."

It seemed like a good time to mention he'd seen her in Leeds. He picked up a spoon for his coffee and it lingered, mid-air, as a thought congealed in his brain.

"So the mystery blonde is one of your people?"

Karl stared at him blankly — his *keep out* sign.

"How should we play this?"

Karl chewed his muffin thoughtfully. "You report back to Christine and then it's her call. I'll convey the same information to other quarters."

Thomas plunged the spoon. "Do I tell her about Leeds?"

"'Sup to you, partner."

It was the most uneven partnership he'd ever heard of.

"Bob will be really pissed off about his car — and he might have seen mine — so the police could be lying in wait. Perhaps we should head back to London by train. I can pick it up in the next day or so . . ."

Secretly he was hoping Karl had access to false number plates.

"Don't worry, I've got it covered. I'm just waiting for a call back. How about another drink? Tea for me, ta."

Which explained why they were still hanging around the port. When he returned from the counter, Karl was on the phone. There was a time when he would have stood back and waited, but Karl did have legs. The call ended quickly.

"Make yourself comfy — they could be another half an hour."

"They?"

Karl put on his inscrutable grin.

* * *

Thomas watched as the final flap of tarpaulin was secured over his car sitting on the recovery vehicle. "I have to say, you've excelled yourself."

Karl took a bow. "They'll drop us off in a lay-by, well past the city limits, and you can take us on from there."

"You really do think of everything!"

"If only . . ."

Chapter 26

Christine took the news stoically and said not to bother coming into the office, which told him she was probably there. It seemed an opportune moment to mention his next prison visit and to her credit she didn't ask for details, which saved another layer of subterfuge.

And so ended another weekend. Or it would have done, had he not dragged himself back to Walthamstow and seen a blue Mini Cooper parked along the street. It was the best news he'd had for days.

As he opened the door he caught a whiff of Kung Po chicken — luring him along the hallway to the front room.

"Well, this is a surprise."

Miranda was perched on the arm of the settee.

"Are we celebrating?"

"More like turning over a new leaf."

He searched her face for a smile, found one and breathed a little easier. It lasted until she added, "and I thought we'd clear the air."

It only took one bite for Thomas to realise that this was no ordinary Kung Po.

"You picked this up at your local Chinese in Bow." He closed his mouth for a moment to savour the tender cashews mingled with the meat. "Luckily for you I was coming home."

She finished her mouthful. "No, luckily for you I first checked with Karl that you weren't already booked for the evening."

He let it pass; it was hard to be churlish when the food was so good.

"Ice cream and fritters afterwards?" He thought he'd push his luck.

"Of course, once we've had a little talk."

It didn't spoil the food any, but he wasn't in a rush to finish. Miranda didn't actually say a great deal; she left that to him. He had little to say that wouldn't start a row. As far as he knew this was going to be a quiet night in, watching *The Matrix* again. He gave her twenty seconds of thoughtful silence and she took the hint.

"If we're going to move forward we need to be completely honest with one another."

When he really thought about it, there was only one solution.

"You know what? Let's not. Be open, I mean. We each have our secrets and I reckon it should stay that way."

"Thomas, I'm not asking about your bloody job—"

"I know. And I'm not asking about the past. Done is done and raking over what's gone is not gonna help either of us."

It all came out in a rush and Miranda suddenly reached over and kissed him while he still had the taste of chicken in his mouth. It wasn't passion exactly, more a sense of connection. And there was still the prospect of two kinds of dessert.

* * *

Over breakfast he showed her Jack Langton's list of suspects.

"Do you know her?" He prodded at Andrea Harrison with a butter knife, blotching the paper.

"Doesn't ring any bells."

It was a long shot but he was disappointed. Advance intelligence was a tactical advantage — another of Karl's pearls of wisdom. He'd have to settle for a Q&A session in the next day or so.

"I wouldn't have thought Jack was the gallery type." She got up to clear the plates. "I'm going to take a shower. There's room for two in there . . ."

He glanced up at the clock. Surely fifteen minutes wouldn't do any harm. Karl could always read a newspaper.

* * *

Thomas picked up the text on his way out the door. Karl's message was succinct: Detour to the office — by request. He pictured the scene awaiting him; Christine, or Sir Peter, or even — but hopefully not — Bob Peterson himself.

The drive in was the usual blend of frustration, stop-starts and death-wish cyclists. Remembering the road works at Tottenham Hale, he'd bitten the bullet and cut through Stratford instead to pick up the A11. Unfortunately, half of London decided to join him.

As Newham begrudgingly gave way to Tower Hamlets he got a deeper sense of Old London Town. The garment wholesalers and discount warehouses rubbing shoulders with those mobile phone shops that managed to stay in business even though you could buy everything cheaper online — like they had. Mile End, Stepney Green, Whitechapel and Aldgate East . . . He marked off the Tube stations and drank in the words. Every one brought him back to Miranda; she was London to him. Mile End — turn left to get to Caliban's; Whitechapel — opposite the London Hospital where Miranda's Nan had spent her final days.

Dragged along in the slipstream of traffic, he started thinking about rainy childhood Sundays in Yorkshire. Playing *Monopoly* as a family and laughing at Dad winning second prize in a beauty contest. And the terrible caravan holiday in Cleethorpes, where it poured down day after day and Dad hit the bottle.

The van in front hit its brakes. He tensed up; he'd been drifting, driving on autopilot. A radio news bulletin warned of traffic jams in the city. *No shit, Sherlock.* He heard the sirens up ahead. Once the van had moved he could see lurid emergency lights — two police vehicles and an ambulance. A motorcyclist was down, poor bastard. There was a man standing perfectly still, staring into space — probably the driver. A police officer was already taking measurements.

He wondered who was doing the photography. That would be a *real* job, instead of spying on benefit cheats. The rear view mirror smiled back at him. Karl's words had taken up residence in his head.

He watched the drama unfolding, like every other ghoul as they edged past. This was how life was — a series of accidents, lucky and unlucky. Meeting Miranda — top of the plus list. And Bermuda . . . Bollocks, why did he have to start thinking again? The lights shone a lucky shade of green and he swung round towards Liverpool Street without answering the question.

The underground car park swallowed him, drawing him into the nether land of the Surveillance Support Unit. His brain locked into work mode. The office door smelled of polish, or maybe it was the carpet. Unnaturally clean, like an adman's fantasy. He wondered how they went about vetting the cleaners. Maybe Karl's people were missing a trick — cleaners were surely the ultimate in invisibility. Perhaps that'd be their next assignment.

He had the space to himself so he caught up on his emails, including the one from Karl that duplicated his text. There were no surprises: refresher training dates, performance review dates for his e-calendar and a request for volunteers to provide feedback on new equipment: another day in the service of the Crown. He heard the lift outside shunt to a halt. Only one set of footsteps exited; the rhythm confident and unhurried. He didn't bother turning round.

"Hi, Thomas — you got my message. Come through."

Christine collected him en route, unlocking her door and plonking two bags on a spare chair. She didn't fire up her laptop, waving him round to the seat opposite as she emptied her mobile from her coat.

"I spoke with Karl last night, about the situation. Thank you for your email by the way. I think we'll put the Southampton surveillance on hold for the time being."

If there was a subtext it eluded him. He'd bide his time; people always showed their hand if you waited long enough.

"Karl says you're assisting him on something. The prison?" She arched an eyebrow. "Just make sure I'm in the loop, okay?"

That was rich; to keep her in the loop he'd have to know what was going on. In the absence of any better ideas, he tried a stab in the dark.

"Is Bob Peterson a risk?" She could take that however she pleased.

"At this stage, he's a medium priority, but I'd planned for this contingency."

There it was — the management speak, so beloved of the movers and shakers. Maybe she picked it up from all the mentoring Peterson had given her, back when she and Thomas were trying to prove her mother wrong about the class struggle.

"Something else on your mind, Thomas?"

"I was wondering how it all works now — between the three of you." He stalled, suddenly aware that she might think he meant Mr and Mrs Peterson, instead of Karl and Ann Crossley.

The lift door clunked open in the distance and he heard welcome voices — Karl and Ann flying the flag once more for team spirit. They came right into Christine's office, and then things got strange.

"Please wait outside," was not something he had ever expected to hear from Christine. From her mother, maybe, back in the day; but not from her.

The door closed discreetly behind him. Well, two could play at secrets. John Wright picked up on the fourth ring.

"Morning, John; any more word from Jack Langton's solicitor?" He waited for John to start talking and then cut across him to catch him off guard.

"Have you got any info on Andrea Harrison?"

"We used to know her, years ago," was hardly intelligence coup of the year. But the way John said those few words let Thomas know that something had gone awry, way back when.

The meeting of the allies was over in fifteen minutes. Karl emerged first.

"All set, Tommo?"

661

"Well, unless Christine wants me back in there . . ."

"Nah, she doesn't. I'll fill you in when we're on the road."

Two chocolate bars from the vending machine and they were on their way. Karl had a quiet sense of purpose about him — no jokes and no cracks in the façade.

The lift opened, ushering in the damp of the underground car park.

"You do realise I signed the Official Secrets Act?"

"It's not about trust; you know that by now. It protects you, Tommo."

Yeah, but from who, or what?

He unlocked his car; Karl could ride shotgun today. They waited on the ramp as the metal grid raised, the links shrieking as they disappeared into the housing.

"Needs oiling," Karl said. "Maybe that'll be our next job."

"You'd know before I did."

"Touché, Mr Bladen. Okay, where are we?" Karl pulled a clipboard from the passenger door. He answered himself. "Just off Old Ford Road."

Chapter 27

"Next up is Dorothy Kinley; elderly and living with her niece, Monica."

It sounded like a far cry from the usual 'shysters and innocents' they'd been dealing with for the past few weeks. Karl read the case notes aloud and he clapped his hands in glee.

"A proper challenge, Tommo — at last!"

The 'case' as Karl kept referring to it, in Sherlock Holmes fashion, hinged on whether the niece was a full-time carer. On the face of it, a bugger to prove or disprove, but — once again — a tip-off had activated the Department of Works & Pensions radar.

"It says here Dorothy was completely housebound for a long time, and now she pops out occasionally, mostly to pick up her pension."

"So, does she actually need the carer?" This one was making Thomas really uncomfortable.

Pension day. They set up and waited for the procession to the elephants' graveyard. Mrs Kinley left her maisonette on schedule, as if she'd read the file. Her ambling gait was hard to detect under her oversized coat; she reminded Thomas of one of the Sand People from *Star Wars*. She kept her head down — or else it was osteoporosis — clutching a handbag to her chest and concentrating on every step.

He waited until he was past her line of sight and then took to his camera, capturing the rest of her journey.

"This one's a sod for details. What else can we do, other than time her?"

Karl considered that for a moment. "Tell you what, how about you go and get me a couple of stamps? Would you mind? God knows we've got the time and I've got bills to pay this week."

Thomas smiled at Karl's legendary distrust of the direct debit system. The banking system, he'd said, was at the dark heart of the European Shadow State. Then again, he also said that prawn cocktail crisps were an aberration.

Outside, Thomas slowed his pace so that Dorothy didn't think he was stalking her; the effort was exhausting. There was a queue in the post office, almost to the door. Some of them were chatting, putting the world to rights. As he took his place a couple of spots behind the target he listened to a litany of complaints, largely about the speed of the post office queue.

Dorothy collected her pension and moved past him, without so much as a smile — the miserable so and so. He managed to get to the second counter, avoiding the woman with her lethal shopping trolley immediately in front of him. He grabbed Karl's stamps and nodded to the ladies in the queue, who clucked like a flock of hens. Good to know he still had appeal.

This was all starting to feel like a monumental waste of time. Old Ma Kinley was up ahead on her return journey, approaching her nearest point to the car, filling the frame if Karl was taking a secret photo. He took his eyes off her for a couple of seconds, to negotiate some dog shit, and when he looked back she was down on one knee. He legged it and caught up with her, pronto.

"Are you okay?"

She nodded, mumbling away, her handbag clutched in a death grip. No wonder she fell; she had no way to steady herself. Despite her protests, he insisted on helping her up and seeing her home. He didn't bother to explain how he knew the address. He could hear her breathing heavily, her arm shaking in his hand.

When they reached her gate, she wriggled free and thrust out a hand to bar him at the threshold. There was gratitude for you. He waited until she'd slammed the door behind her.

He was feeling pretty pleased on the way back to the car, until he saw Karl walking towards him.

"Ready?" Karl was rubbing his hands together.

"For what?"

"Mild-mannered Dorothy just dropped to the ground."

"I know, I helped her home; I think she was in shock."

Karl smiled. "In shock? She will be. When I ask for my £30 back. Like I was saying, she *dropped* to the ground and picked up thirty quid in marked tenners wrapped up in a rubber band."

His eyes widened. Karl had just set her up. Not quite the 'collect evidence impartially' the Benefits Investigation Team recommended.

"How did you come to have marked banknotes on you?"

Karl shrugged. "Force of habit."

There was no time to talk tactics, so he let Karl take control of the situation. Karl lifted the latch on the gate delicately and the two of them stood at the door. He rang the bell and nothing happened. Karl ducked below the frosted glass and whispered instructions.

Thomas rapped the letterbox and peered through. "Hello! I was with you when you had the fall. I just want to make sure you're okay." Crouching low, he could make out two stockinged feet at the top of the stairs. They weren't in any sort of hurry.

"Shall I get you a doctor?"

"No!" The voice sounded more like a yelp.

The feet disappeared and he let the flap go. At least she'd heard him and responded — now what? Karl started counting down from ten. At zero, Thomas lifted the letterbox again and caught sight of someone squatting on the stairs and looking back at him. The niece, he presumed, and blessed with the same level of social skills.

He waited; she'd soon realise he wasn't going anywhere and she could hardly expect the old lady to come downstairs.

The niece took her time about it but gradually approached the frosted panel.

"We're fine," she said through the glass. "Aunt Dot's in bed, resting. You've got to go now. It's upsetting her." She hovered by the door.

Karl scribbled on a piece of paper and passed it up.

Thomas mouthed the word *twat* at Karl but delivered his message anyway. "Look, your aunt picked up some money that was my friend's. He wants his thirty quid."

This was starting to feel like harassment. He looked down at Karl, who mouthed the final script.

"The notes are marked. I want them back or I'm calling the police."

He cringed. This was a new low — worse than following a disabled man into the pub. Maybe they'd been on this assignment too long.

The letterbox flap popped open and three ten-pound notes were ejected. Then he heard footsteps galloping upstairs.

Karl collected his money, examining each note carefully. "One's different — not to worry." He took out a small notebook and wrote in the new bank number. "Anyway." He folded the money into his wallet. "It's all job and finish, and I'd say we're done here."

Conversation resumed back at the car.

"Shall I start?" Karl walked around to the passenger door. He got in and waited for Thomas to join him, then grabbed imaginary lapels, as if he were a barrister. "One — the speed with which Dorothy Kinley rushed to get the cash. Remember, you didn't see her from my vantage point. It wasn't a fall; she knelt down and shoved the readies in her bag just before you showed up. Two — Dorothy went to bed quicker than a one-night stand. Three — and this is the killer — the niece had the money on her when she came to the door. Maybe she filched it out of the old dear's coat, I dunno. But there's something wrong there, however you look at it."

"So you're saying that if Aunt Dorothy can move that fast — with the aid of gravity — she doesn't need a full-time carer?"

"Now who's judgemental? All I'm saying is it merits further investigation — by the grown-ups. I'll let BIT know later, maybe *after* work." Karl winked.

"Dawn Yeates? Surely you're not fraternising with our temporary boss?"

"Merely socialising."

It occurred to him then that Dawn Yeates might be another of Karl's contacts. Perhaps that was why they'd been picked for the assignment. Karl was giving nothing away, so he checked his mirrors and set a course for the nearest café.

"So . . . where are you taking her tonight?"

"Well, it's a toss-up between the Roundhouse Theatre, or a pub."

"And Dorothy Kinley?"

"I doubt she'd join us — she finds it hard to get around, unless money's involved."

"Dick."

"I'll tell Dawn about our concerns, only I'll skip the finer details."

"What d'you think will happen?"

"More surveillance, probably. Or they'll call in the niece for an interview. Even if she is stealing money from her aunt, it's hardly dawn raid material."

"I see what you did there . . ."

"So when do you plan on speaking to Ray Daniels, Tommo?"

"I'm seeing Andrea Harrison tonight, but Ray Daniels is on my list. Why the interest?" He stared across the table. "Do you know something?"

By the look on Karl's face, whatever it was it was toxic.

Chapter 28

The sign said it all: *Andrea Harrison*. Not even the word 'gallery.' The lettering screamed modernity and Thomas knew instantly that he wouldn't like whatever she was selling. He pushed the glass door and stepped into her world.

Andrea Harrison was leaning on a counter, set along one of the longer walls. Mobile in hand, her finger pointed down at a catalogue.

"I suggested seventeen thousand, but he won't budge."

She looked over, as if sizing him up. A flick of the head told him he'd failed the assessment. He should have brought along a camera — maybe an Olympus OM1 with a sizeable lens that looked the part.

He turned his back on her and browsed through the industrial sculptures and something made out of rounded glass that looked like a child's nightmare. Moving from exhibit to exhibit, he picked up snippets of conversation and filed it all away. At the far end of the main gallery room there was an open doorway. Discordant synthesiser music plagued his memory — something from the eighties probably — music from Thatcher's dream. He grimaced, peering through. Footsteps quickly followed behind him.

"Sorry about that; I'm Andrea Harrison — welcome to my gallery. Are you looking for anything in particular?"

He smiled, mostly at the reply he wanted to share with her. But no, he was here on business.

"I'm Thomas — Jack Langton sent me?" He posed it as a question, but he knew it had all been arranged through John Wright.

She took a moment and then led him back to the glass counter.

"What can I do for you, Thomas?"

He gave her the Bladen smile, along with a sanitised version of his meeting with Jack Langton. As icebreakers went, it cut through the glacier. She offered coffee and when he agreed she took out two pouches from a drawer. The machine was as stylish and over-engineered as everything else in the gallery, including her.

"What do you think of it?" She gazed around her domain, soaking up his attention.

He noticed the faded streak of crimson in her hair, glittering in the spotlights.

"It's . . . different." He saw no sense in bullshitting her.

She seemed amused. He figured it gave her a sense of superiority. So this was art? He couldn't imagine any of the stuff here getting past the door at Leeds Art Gallery. Londoners — they'd put up with any old shit.

"Is there somewhere we can talk privately?"

"Here's fine. Besides," she glanced over to the doorway, "I have artists working on-site — they prefer to stay in the shadows." She patted a leather stool beside her.

The coffee was good, much to his surprise; although the ginger biscuit with it was so small it was frivolous. Maybe it was some sort of statement, like everything else around him — style over content.

"I suppose you already know about me and Jack?"

He blushed in ignorance, which she, in hers, misinterpreted.

She blew across her coffee. "It's common knowledge; we used to be an item, back in the day."

He waited for her to continue, noting how she flicked her hair, as if to brush away the memory; fat chance of that.

"We're good friends now — and partners too. Jack came to my rescue when I started the gallery — he found me some backers . . ." She changed topic abruptly. "John said you were coming because of some poor child." She sipped her coffee, eyeing him all the while. "But I don't see what any of that has to do with me."

He shrugged. "Jack asked me to speak with you — and others." She nodded; satisfied she wasn't the only fish in the net.

"So what do you want to know?" She raised her empty coffee cup for seconds, which was a perfect excuse to ask for the loo.

He stepped through a doorway at the back and kept on walking. Two welders in a side room paused from their work and nodded to him. He found the gents, took a leak and then phoned Karl.

"Have you cracked the world of modern art yet?"

"Industrial and urban street art, actually — *specialised* bollocks. Honestly, Karl, you wanna see some of the prices. I'll be at least another half an hour; all I've learned so far is that Jack Langton bankrolled her in the beginning."

"Drug proceeds, most probably. A bit of a punt with the gallery but a great way to launder dirty money, especially if you own the building."

"Good point. One last thing, Andrea Harrison and Jack used to be an item."

"How quaint you Yorkshire folk are. Ring me when you're free. Over and out."

The welders were away on a tea break now; probably Earl Grey. A pity — he wanted to ask what it was supposed to be, although he imagined that was part of the sell.

Andrea had the next coffees lined up and offered him a quick tour.

"The Crocodile is one of RT's more experimental works." She quoted from a script she knew too well. Every artist was reduced to initials; he supposed the important ones had earned their three letters. It mostly washed over him, like a timeshare presentation he and Miranda had once been to in the West End. He made a mental list, in case she asked him anything: sculpture, metalwork, permanence and impermanence, decay, contrast, urban . . . He stopped walking, mesmerised by two artworks, placed side by side. The piece on the right was electric blue, sprayed flame streaks against a painted wall, flowing down into the shape of a supine form.

"Ah, yes — *Naked Flame*. A lot of men like that one; some ladies too."

He nodded agreeably, but his eyes were on the frame next to it. *Naked Heat*: a flame dissolving into entwined lovers — in blood red spray paint.

"Are these by RT as well?" He turned and studied her reaction.

She smiled, tour over, and returned him to his coffee. Now that he'd shown genuine interest, her demeanour changed, even if the biscuits didn't. This time he grabbed a handful.

"I noticed that some of the pieces don't have a price tag."

"Yes, it's one of RT's foibles. The purchaser suggests a price and RT considers it. Sometimes he accepts it, sometimes he offers an alternative and sometimes he rejects them outright. It's how he likes to do business."

"And a little mystique is good for the brand?"

She laughed. Put on, of course. He decided to play along.

"Those pictures — do you call them *pictures*? — they've really got something. Is he a local artist?

"RT? No, not any more. He lives in Spain and only visits once or twice a year with new pieces. How long have you worked for Jack? I've never heard of you before."

"I don't actually work for him; this is more of a favour for a friend."

"Yes . . ." She snapped a miniature biscuit in half. "Jack receives a lot of favours."

"What can you tell me about your dealings with Jack? I mean, would anyone you know . . ." He let the sentence hang there. He didn't know how to end it without accusing or insulting her.

"A man like Jack makes enemies . . ."

He could hear the pride in her voice.

" . . . Yes, I think that's why he enjoys this sort of art; it's confrontational — not to everyone's tastes. He appreciates the context and its potential."

"So Jack is a working partner, as opposed to a silent one?" Now he was digging in the dark. But dig long and deep enough and eventually you'll strike something solid.

"Jack's a very private man. Even so, he has a lot of money tied up here, for which I'm very grateful. It's a cutthroat business and there are only so many seats at the top table. Look at the Saatchis."

If that was supposed to impress him, it fell wide of the mark — by about fifty yards. All very interesting but it was getting him nowhere.

"Has anyone been in touch with you, here, about Jack — since he went away? Or maybe something out of the ordinary happened recently?"

"The attempted break-in? I informed Jack's solicitor and Ray Daniels. Nothing was taken; I think it was drunks pissing about."

He couldn't help thinking the swearing was for his benefit, to show she was like him. She couldn't have been more wrong.

"Yes," she continued, "you'd be surprised at the reaction a gallery like this can generate." She stopped and looked right at him.

"Does anyone live upstairs?"

"I do. I can show you if you like?"

"Maybe some other time." He checked his watch.

"I'll hold you to that, Thomas."

"And nothing in the post — for Jack, I mean?"

She blushed and he knew straight away this was another of his drugs drops. Interesting — Sheryl, Janey and now Andrea — how Jack kept the ladies at his beck and call.

A postwoman came into the gallery with some envelopes and a small parcel. As he was nearest to the door, he did the chivalrous thing and stood up to collect the mail. The postie smiled and handed over the goods. Andrea leapt from her seat.

"I'll take those," she insisted, with the forced politeness that told him something else was going on. She placed them on the glass top, unopened.

Occasionally, he liked to think that lady fortune was smiling on him. It didn't happen often — meeting Miranda and her family was top of the list. Another had been getting no worse than a flesh wound from one of Karl's trigger-happy adversaries. When a pair of potential punters breezed into the gallery, fortune gave him a cheery grin.

Andrea left her coffee and her table manners at the desk, winding a circuitous route round to the couple. It looked like a routine to showcase the goods and suggest she wasn't in a hurry to sell anything. He listened, fascinated, as the three of them talked *texture* and *depth*, throwing *authenticity* and *statement* into the mix. Jesus; if his dad could see him now. 'Nowt but a lot of middle-class ponces,' is what he'd say.

As the three culture vultures waltzed around the urban scrawl, he casually leaned forward and fanned out the envelopes. It was hardly a shock to see a letter addressed to Jack Langton at the gallery, but the postmark was a showstopper — Spain, where RT the aerosol artist was based. He tidied the pack and headed off clockwise around the gallery, one eye on the sales party. He picked up that they were restaurateurs on the hunt for some urban degradation. He smiled to himself; they could always move south of the Thames. He was nearing *Naked Heat*, a car key palmed in one hand to get a paint sample, when Andrea zeroed in on him.

"Can we continue our chat some other time?"

He put his key hand in his pocket.

"Sure, name the time."

"I'm free tonight. Shall we say nine? Would you mind seeing yourself out?"

"Nine o'clock it is then." He took another glance at the *Nakeds* and detoured around them, patting the Crocodile's head on his way out.

Chapter 29

Karl said he'd collect him at Hackney Downs station. It gave him time to collect his thoughts. Why would a jumped-up graffiti artist in Spain send Jack Langton a message by attacking some kid Jack hardly ever saw? DNA — he made a mental note. Could they get a sample of Jacob's DNA and one of Jack's? Nah, he was letting his imagination get ahead of him.

He clapped his hands, prayer-fashion, to stop his mind wandering. RT lived in Spain and came over once or twice a year. When was he over? Andrea must know the geezer's full name; maybe Karl could get a passport number from it. He couldn't help noticing how much he was relying on Karl's expertise. John Wright knew what he was doing when he brought Karl on board.

The next logical move was to get a red paint sample. He could nip back to the gallery and wait until there was an opportunity to take a scrape — probably no one would notice on a wooden canvas — or Karl's people could just buy the thing. Or there was a third option that made him laugh just thinking about it.

Karl wasn't at the station. Instead, he directed Thomas by mobile to the nearby Pembury Tavern. The shandies awaited.

"Well, well, if it isn't the art critic of the week!" Karl opened a celebratory bag of crisps as Thomas took his seat. "How d'ya get on?"

"I'm not really sure."

"Why don't you tell your Uncle Karl all about it?"

Karl offered him a pen and paper so he could map out the mosaic of the problem. He'd liked Roman mosaics as a child — the way that tiny, insignificant tiles all contributed to a bigger, more imaginative picture.

"This artist, RT; he uses spray colours. Bright red, sometimes."

Karl seemed less than impressed. "This is the fella you said lived in Spain."

"Yeah, most of the time. We need a sample of the paint he uses. Also, I was hoping you could find out when RT was last in the UK."

"Smart thinking, Tommo, except RT isn't much to go on. Also, how do you expect to get a paint sample undetected?"

"I'm going back to Andrea Harrison's at nine tonight. We'll be upstairs, so it's an ideal opportunity for you to do some breaking and entering."

"Alarm systems?"

"Probably. I thought you could improvise. I know it's sketchy but if I can keep Ms Harrison busy — talking," he added hastily.

"Maybe. CCTV? Tell me that at least."

"Not that I saw. Can't imagine anyone wants to be filmed buying that tat."

"*Concept* tat." Karl went into screensaver mode, gazing at his shandy for longer than Thomas was comfortable with. "Okay," he announced, "let's give it a go. One stipulation: if I make any noise, I want you to come down alone."

"Deal." Thomas sat back in his chair, less reassured than he'd expected to be.

The rest of the day's snooping passed much like every other day in the world of Benefits investigations. Villains, suspects, the misunderstood and the vindicated, all paraded past them to a tedious beat.

* * *

He checked his watch — twenty-fifty — and carried on talking with Karl on his mobile as he walked up the road. And to think Miranda said men couldn't multitask.

"I still don't see why you can't tell me what you're planning, Karl."

"Trust me; it's better that way — keeps things spontaneous and plausible. You have your wee drinky upstairs and remember, keep it zipped up."

"Funny boy." He cut the call.

He felt sweat down his back as he rang the gallery bell and blinked at the headlights of a taxi rumbling by. Peering through the door he could see a light at the far end of the gallery room. She seemed to be taking her time; maybe it was a long walk down two flights of stairs. To his intense relief she was dressed casually. Jeans and a cashmere jumper didn't scream 'on the pull' — not in his world anyway. She turned to the wall, out of view, before unlocking the door.

Bollocks — that was probably an alarm. Pessimism turned to joy when she locked up after him and didn't reset it. Industrial art, he decided, looked very creepy in shadow.

She didn't say much on the way up, only that the kettle was on and she hoped he was hungry because she had nibbles. He pictured Karl smirking. Of course she did.

Her apartment was a collector's paradise. There wasn't a stick of furniture that wouldn't have graced a high-class glossy. What surprised him was the range of styles and how old and tasteful everything was.

She caught him gazing at the sideboard in her lounge.

"It's *rococo*, 17th century. You were expecting tubular steel and exposed brickwork? That's just my day job."

Even so, he noticed one or two miniatures with RT's signature on them.

"Make yourself comfortable."

She led him to a pair of large sofas, one each side of a pale blue coffee table, like two banks of a river. She sat opposite. The food was arranged in small dishes. Moroccan, by the looks of it, or something Middle Eastern. He recalled trying a Moroccan restaurant with Miranda once in Leeds. Gave him the trots, although that could have been the beer.

"I used to travel a lot," she explained. "Dealing in furniture and room decor. I do a great lamb tagine — do try the borek." She lifted a plate of pastries; the aroma alone made it hard to concentrate.

"How did you meet Jack then?" He figured he'd start at the beginning.

"You first," she teased, threatening to draw the plate out of reach.

"Like I said," and sighed with relief as his fingers wrapped around a borek, "we have mutual friends. I'm not part of Jack's circle and that's what he wanted, someone objective." He opened his hand; now it was her turn to share.

"Oh, I met Jack years ago." There was a glow to her face as she recollected. "I saw him at a club a few times and there was something about him. You never quite knew where you were with Jack — he never tried too hard. Made a change from the other regulars. But you're not here to rake over the past."

Now that she looked straight at him, Karl had a point. She was an attractive woman, educated by the sounds of it, although clearly happy to mix with the peasants. And she was waiting.

"Alright, I'll level with you." He reached for some couscous, hoping he looked au fait with the cuisine. "I first met Jack in prison — he, er, asked me to go and see him."

She smiled a little and nodded, as if she knew what Jack's requests felt like.

"Anyway, you were on Jack's list. You *know* about his business, Andrea?"

"I know not to ask. Jack's very loyal to those who show him loyalty. That's good enough for me."

He regrouped. "Does he get involved much in the arts scene?"

"Yes, to some extent." She lifted a bottle of wine from a cooler but he shook his head and settled for juice. "Some people meet Jack and form the impression that he's a philistine — don't quote me on that. They're wrong and I think he trades on it. He takes a genuine interest in the gallery and the artists we promote — he even comes to a show once in a while." She raised an index finger and took a gulp of wine. "Take RT. Jack's been out to Spain to visit his artists' commune more than once."

"I liked his stuff. It had . . ." He searched for a word, and was mortified by the dead-end he'd arrived at, ". . . authenticity."

"You mean you liked the nudes. I modelled for him once, actually." She paused dramatically and held her breath.

"I could see that working." He looked away for an instant, wishing he could think of something else to say. Time for more food. "I mean, I could see RT's artwork working on the street."

"Exactly!" She slowly turned her glass. "Contemporary and yet naturalistic."

It was easier to stay on safe ground, so when the lamb tagine appeared he turned the conversation to photography. Now he could talk about the Merrion Street Gallery in Leeds, the pictures that inspired him and the ones he still liked to take.

"I sell photography occasionally. If you have anything special I'd be happy to take a look. Any friend of Jack's . . ."

Except he wasn't a friend. He couldn't tell whether she was humouring him or trying to buy him off. When the wine bottle rattled again he stuck with mixers and let her gradually fill herself up. A few more eats, Middle Eastern music in the background, and he could almost relax. It was all turning into a pleasant evening, right until he heard glass smashing somewhere below stairs.

Now he understood Karl's reluctance to share the plan.

"Stay here." He glanced around the room and grabbed a small metal sculpture in his hand, holding it like a cudgel.

"Not that!" She gasped.

He put it back down and picked up a poker from the fireplace, just in case it wasn't Karl downstairs.

"Are you going to ring the police?"

He thought he knew the answer already; her face confirmed his suspicions. She didn't want the Bobbies prying into her affairs, or Jack's. Table for one, then.

He crept down the stairs in twos, the blood pounding in his heart. As he peered through the doorway, poker at the ready, Karl, all in black, in a ski mask, was scraping paint off *Naked Heat*.

"I hope this is the one you meant; I couldn't see any other red ones like this."

"Jesus."

The glass door at the front looked like it had imploded. Other pieces of artwork had been damaged by Karl's entrance. He was an equal opportunity desecrator.

"Right, all done. Just one more thing, Tommo," Karl stepped clear, motioning him to one side. "Sorry about this and stay down for a bit."

Next thing he knew, a fist had swung out of nowhere, connected, and sent him flying backwards until the floor kicked him in the spine. Still conscious but dazed, he heard Karl retreating into the night, an apology wafting behind him.

Chapter 30

Taking Karl at his word he lay still, eyes closed, listening to the sound of his own breathing. He tried counting up to five thousand, only he kept losing the thread. At some point he heard a voice, echoing through the semi-darkness, growing louder. When he opened his eyes Andrea was standing in the doorway, arms limp at her sides as she surveyed the scene.

"I'm okay." He lifted his head on the off chance she was interested.

She stepped over the debris and helped him to stand.

"We'd better get you to A&E."

"Shouldn't we wait for the police?"

"No need. I phoned Ray and he's on his way. Did you see them? Did they take anything?"

Her Florence Nightingale act needed more work. He danced around the details — two people, probably, and no one spoke. Maybe they just wanted to cause damage, or else he had scared them off.

"I'll make some coffee." She seemed to be talking mainly to herself.

They remained downstairs, sipping caffeine in the wasteland. He got it together enough to rescue *Naked Heat* from the mess, found a broom and started sweeping up. It wasn't like forensics was going to make an appearance and it helped tidy away anything incriminating.

Naked Heat looked a little rougher around the edges now.

"I don't suppose it'll be worth as much."

"Don't you believe it!" She lifted the artwork and hung it back on the wall. The frame was cracked and some of its gloriously red paint was scuffed and chipped. "This will make wonderful publicity, especially with RT coming over for a new show in three weeks."

"RT?" He pressed fingertips lightly to one side of his face. "You never told me what his actual name is."

"Rodrigo Tollinger — RT to those who appreciate his work." She wobbled a little, a sure sign that the coffee hadn't straightened her up. She nodded, as if agreeing with herself. "Tell you a little secret, Thomas. It's not his *real* name. Changed it by deed poll years ago, a good career move." She opened the cupboard where the little biscuits lived and brought out a brandy miniature, shaking a little as she siphoned its contents into her cup.

In the spirit of generosity he put it down to stress.

"Somehow Rodney Tompkins doesn't quite cut it."

He never liked to be around drunken people. Drink made people do funny things. Many of the worst arguments with Miranda had been a three-way affair between the two of them and a bottle of something.

He did the chivalrous thing and saw to another couple of coffees; Andrea poured the dregs of her first into the second. Then he made himself useful again with a dustpan and brush. Full marks to Karl for taking pride in his work.

By the time a Range Rover pulled up outside, depositing Ray Daniels and a nameless thug on a lead, all that was needed was a 24-hour glazier and the briefest of explanations. He kept things simple, taking the lead as Andrea seemed in no fit state to answer Ray's questions. No, he hadn't seen the bloke clearly before he laid him out, and now that he thought about it there were two of them, possibly three. The geezer who hit him seemed to be looking for something; said nothing, and then it was lights out. End of story.

He allowed Ray to drop him off at Accident & Emergency, along with Andrea who insisted on exorcising her guilt by waiting with him at the hospital for two hours. By the time he'd been patched up and received some painkillers he'd also bagged an invite to RT's opening night. It'd please Miranda, hopefully.

After the once-over from A&E, he loaded Andrea into a minicab and phoned Karl.

"How's the face?"

"Sore — you shitbag. I need picking up."

"I'll be there in minutes."

He laughed. "You don't know where I am!"

"Ha! You don't know where *I* am. I'm in the hospital car park – I followed the Range Rover from the gallery and I've been bored stupid waiting for your call."

The journey to his Walthamstow flat provided ample time for a debrief. He went first, passing on Rod Tompkins' name, plus the

678

Rodrigo Tollinger alias. Karl promised to follow it up with a passport check.

"There's something dodgy there — I just can't put my finger on it yet."

"What, Tommo? You think he attacked Jacob with paint from his own studio?" Karl's voice of reason sounded like the case for the defence.

Lea Bridge Road flickered by, strung together with orange streetlights. He watched them for a while before replying.

"He's coming back over in three weeks. I'll confirm the date and maybe you can get me the flight details?"

Karl gave a mock salute. "Aye, aye, skipper. I'll add them to my to-do list. You did some great work tonight, Thomas. And all it took was a smack in the face."

He gave Karl a crooked smile and touched his throbbing jaw.

Chapter 31

Saturday morning, ten am. Thomas woke to the sound of the letterbox choking on the weekend post. He dragged himself out of bed, shimmied into some jeans and stumbled to the kitchen. Kettle on, he went to see what the day had brought him: two bills, an uninvited investment opportunity and a postcard from Yorkshire — Rievaulx Abbey, its magnificent shell of a building basking in sunlight. Judging by the rounded handwriting Geena had been the scribe.

Visiting hours for Godparents are nine am until seven pm. Bring presents. Come and see Ajit pretending to be a proper dad and gagging at changing nappies. We miss you both. Geena & Aj x

Since when did she start calling him Aj? She'd signed his name too. Chances were that Ajit didn't know she'd sent it. Ajit and him had got themselves a right pair of clever uns.

The answering machine was flashing like a distress call. He compromised with an instant coffee and hit the button.

"Hey, stranger; you coming over at the weekend?" Miranda sounded upbeat. "Ring me before I get a better offer."

After arranging a late lunch with her, he turned his attention to Karl.

"Well, sleepyhead — I was expecting a call from you first thing." Karl gave him a short rundown of events since they'd last spoken: RT's red paint was now at the lab; RT's movements, past and present, expected by Tuesday lunchtime; and a background check on the gallery and its finances should arrive sometime Wednesday.

Thomas tapped the postcard against the edge of a table. Only one call left to make. Andrea Harrison was more emotional than the previous night. He felt bad for that, until he remembered Jacob and what the priorities were.

"I've rung RT in Spain and he was devastated. Then he decided that he needed to be strong and inspire confidence in his collectors. He's going to bring his new exhibition forward a week."

He took a sip of caffeine heaven and listened to her wittering on about the new arrangements. *The opportunity of more publicity was just a coincidence, naturally.*

Chapter 32

Karl leapt at the chance to take him back to the indoor shooting range. He didn't ask why and Thomas never ventured an explanation. They couldn't talk at work and lying on the phone was too easy — he was living proof of that. No, ironically, Karl was less defensive when firearms were around.

"Something on your mind, Tommo?"

He took the pistol from its box and set it down. "Apart from a SIG Sauer?"

Karl smiled and edged towards the door, beyond his peripheral vision. More used to Karl's Brownings, it took a little while to adjust. He loosed five rounds into the target, taking his time. The first two were so wide of the mark it was a wonder the paper target hadn't logged a complaint. The next three were all in the upper torso and the rest of the magazine scattered nearby.

He waited until Karl was on his mark and about to put ear defenders on.

"Why aren't we confronting Sir Peter about hiring a killer?"

Karl's hands paused by his head. "We need to know why. Once we know what's behind it — or who — then it's the right time to bring everything out in the open."

Thomas rubbed at his scar. There was nothing more to be said, but Karl insisted on saying it.

"I won't pretend that what we do is heroic. We make a difference though."

Lately Thomas had begun to question that.

* * *

The first thing Thomas noticed about the gallery, as he approached the curve of the street, was how normal it looked. Obviously, the glass door had been replaced — flawlessly, a carbon copy. Well, silicon. It was only when he pushed the door and he felt its weight that he recognised toughened glass. At least it was modern.

Andrea was all over him like a polite rash, kissing both cheeks.

"Thomas, it's so good to see you; let me get you a coffee."

Amazing what taking a punch could do for trust building. The politicians could learn a lesson there. As Andrea wafted a vapour trail of expensive perfume around him, a couple in the far corner were gazing at *Naked Flame* and *Naked Heat* in rapture.

"The publicity has done wonders for the exhibition." She was all aflutter. "We kept it out of the newspapers — except the local — and word has spread throughout the art world."

He nodded, eyes still on the punters.

"Suffice it to say there is *great* interest in RT's new show."

"Listen, mind if I use your loo? It was a long walk over," he added for effect.

"Sure, sure," she dismissed him, craning her neck to eavesdrop on the art lovers.

He wandered towards the *Nakeds* to catch some of the conversation.

". . . And of course," the leather-elbowed one insisted, reeling his other half in closer, "it would be an investment."

Yeah, that about summed it up. Thomas sidled past, made his excuses and went through to the gents to take a leak. Washing his hands, he caught sight of himself in the mirror and surveyed his face. The bruise had lingered and he needed a shave. He reached into his pocket for his keys and felt something plastic. It was the UV pen he'd used that morning to mark up his new camera, the case, the additional lens, and the manual.

As he walked back to the main gallery, pondering the amount of money a scumbag like Jack Langton might be earning while sitting on his arse in prison, he noticed that the room to the left was open. Only this time there were no 'emerging artists' working — if you could call it that. He couldn't resist a peek at what passed for creativity in their world bubble. He'd be quick, he promised himself, just a nose around and then out.

The room was strangely sterile, especially with the light off. He flicked on his Maglite key ring and waltzed over to the metal monstrosity, noticing the fierce red slashes up one end. That shade of red was really starting to bug him. It was stupid and childish but he felt like making mischief. He pulled out his UV pen, crouched low where it would be difficult to find, and wrote in tiny letters: FRAUD.

Andrea was in full flow when he returned, the three of them stooped over the Crocodile. Definitely some sort of crock. They all spoke the same language, passing superlatives around like a tray of canapés: challenging, progressive, subversive, and the dealmaker – *quixotic*. That was the word that finally had them reaching for their credit card and him for a sick bag

Andrea spotted him when they moved to the counter to conclude their business. He kept his distance, busying himself while delivery details were confirmed and plastic money changed hands — how apt. Then Andrea walked them to the door and reminded them about RT's opening night, assuring them that RT loved to meet collectors of his work. She sighed as she closed the door, like the cat that got the credit card payment.

"Listen, I don't think I can make it when RT flies in on Sunday. I'll be at the show though and I'd love the chance to meet him without the crowds. By the way, how come there's no poster up for the show?"

She threw him a pitying smile. "That's not how these things are done. And besides, RT doesn't like to give too much away; it spoils the great reveal." She made the word sound theatrical. "Would you like to see the pieces we've had in storage?"

"I'd like nothing better."

Chapter 33

"What do you think?" Miranda paraded around the kitchen.

This would be her third outfit and Thomas knew the wrong noise or facial expression at this point could spell disaster.

"Perfect." By which he meant he'd liked to unzip it in private.

"And you're going like *that*?"

He smiled; she'd pretty much dressed him.

"And what are we looking for tonight?"

He squeezed her waist — clever girl. "Just keep your radar on."

* * *.

It took them ages to find a parking space. They could have taken a cab and claimed it on expenses from Jack Langton, but he liked the security of his own car. He could leave when he wanted and, judging by the thrum of the music as they approached the gallery, that could be any time soon.

Miranda nudged him as he hunched his shoulders a little. "Well, at least the music sounds promising."

He couldn't tell whether she was taking the piss. A peer through the glass door confirmed his worst suspicions — he wondered if a copy of the Guardian under one arm might have helped him blend in.

The heavy door swung in and they eased through the throng. A pseudo-punk in a carefully torn and repaired jumpsuit zeroed in, introduced herself as Citizen Virtue, and ushered them over to the drinks.

Miranda muscled in before Virtue could finish her 'what can I get you' speech, grabbing a glass of white wine. "An orange juice for the boy." The women laughed and Thomas let them enjoy the joke.

He took a couple of sips as he gazed around. It was impressive — laser light across the ceiling, someone's idea of a musical joke on the hi-spec speakers and the heady scent of money in the air. No wonder Jack Langton was a patron of the arts.

He gave Miranda's elbow a gentle tug and they moseyed around the exhibits. He pointed out the *Naked* series to her and paused at the latest addition — *Naked Ambition*, a nude wearing a crown. And where was the great artist?

They left the main gallery room and wandered out back, through the fluorescent bead curtain that now adorned the doorway.

Andrea was easy to pick out. To her credit, she hadn't gone down the 'apocalypse at C&A' route that many of her contemporaries favoured. And the metal bow tie and diamante waistcoat were nice touches.

He worked his way over gradually, wondering what Miranda thought of it all. She was savvier than him; more cultured, less uptight about all the razzamatazz. Maybe that was why she had her own business, while he was a peasant holding a camera.

Ah, the camera. He missed the anonymity of being behind a lens, where every face became a willing victim, unwittingly revealing something else about themselves.

He contrived things so that she'd spot him first. It wasn't difficult.

"Ah, Thomas."

He turned his head on cue, motioning to Miranda, like they'd arranged in the car. He'd barely got the cheek kisses over when Andrea blossomed again.

"You must be Miranda. You take after Diane but you've got John's eyes."

That was a surprise — on first name terms with her parents. Andrea wasn't finished with her charm offensive.

"What a stunning dress. You'd better keep an eye on her tonight, Thomas!"

And there it was again, that little laugh that told him she was already merry. RT arrived at her side like a bad smell. They swapped stiff introductions and Miranda put in a few comments about his work that seemed to please him, while he fiddled with the tassel on his ethnic hat.

"Andrea suggested we talk tomorrow evening about Jack's . . . concerns. Perhaps we could make it dinner for four?"

He could see that RT was much more interested in Miranda than the conversation. Miranda seemed to pick up on it as well.

"What drives your passion for urban art?" She sparkled under the gallery lights.

RT was soon in full flow about urban decay, cultural identity and other toss. Andrea drew Thomas to one side.

"What do you think?" She waved a discreet hand around.

"Seems like a good crowd." He floundered, unable to read the question.

"The unveiling is in fifteen minutes. RT likes to do something dramatic."

Thomas drifted back to them, guiding Andrea and depositing her there.

He put his arm over Miranda's shoulder and eased her forward. "We'd better have a good look around before the main event."

"I was just getting somewhere," she hissed.

"Yeah, that's what it looked like."

She shook her head. "No, stupid; he was telling me about his trips over from Spain. Jack's very generous, apparently — pays for everything."

"How come he told you that?"

"I think he wanted to impress me."

He had to admit, it really was a stunner of a dress.

By now the place was so crammed with people that a full circuit was impossible. Instead, they went with the flow, moving inexorably towards the side room where RT had placed four burly security guards — two male and two female — one at each corner. Looking at the wires, he figured it was going to be one theatrical push of a button and then the cloth would fly to the ceiling.

The crowd eased apart to let RT approach the veiled exhibit. Thomas was suddenly bursting for a pee and trying to remember the location of the gents, now that the decor had changed. He decided to stay for the big reveal and then answer the call of nature. Miranda stood close by, grabbing his arm.

"This had better be good," she whispered.

The music stopped, electro-jazz giving way to a murmuring that reverberated around the room. RT unzipped his top and fingered a pendant with a bright red centre. The four guards stood to attention and crossed their arms, hip-hop style. Without any preamble RT hit the button and the silvery fabric ascended to the ceiling. The crowd went wild before they'd even seen what was on show. Everyone seemed to join in with the hysteria — all except one person. Thomas stared at the piece, open-mouthed. It was a sculpture of metal and brick with bright red slashes.

He smiled a mile wide. The same piece he'd seen several days ago, when he'd signed his name on it in invisible marker. A piece RT couldn't have created because he was in Spain, and couldn't possibly have brought over because Thomas had already tagged it. Yep, modern art really was bollocks.

They stuck it out until just after eleven, when the first wave of guests started leaving.

"Thank you so much for coming, Thomas." Andrea teetered by the door, drawing a shawl around her shoulders.

"I really enjoyed it, especially the unveiling." The build-up of glee was killing him.

"See you tomorrow evening then. RT is so looking forward to it."

"Wouldn't miss it for the world." He escorted Miranda off the premises. A breeze stirred, but inside he was glowing. Secrets, he loved them — as long as they belonged to someone else.

She pulled him a little closer. "What's gotten into you tonight? When we arrived you looked like this was the last place on earth you wanted to be and now you're like the bloke who found a tenner in the gents."

"Better than that."

He waited until they were in the car before he spilled the beans.

"Seriously?"

"One hundred per cent: fake. Not only did I see it before, I can prove it." Now he told her about the security marker.

She grinned. "Can you vandalise a piece of rubble? I love it — that's priceless! What does it tell us though? How does it help with Jacob?"

"Well, it's a reason to distrust RT and Andrea Harrison. Plus . . ." He held up a finger. "We don't know whether Jack Langton is in on this scam or not. We'll find out tomorrow."

He turned to Miranda, expecting her to look impressed. She wasn't.

"What? You think I should keep schtum about it for now?"

"I dunno, babe. Just remember you're about as good at cards as Dad."

She nodded, yielding him that. She patted his thigh. "So, you see, you don't always need Karl around."

"Not for some things." He pressed his hand on hers.

Chapter 34

"You look shattered." Karl slurped tea from a polystyrene cup. "That girlfriend of yours shouldn't take you out gallivanting on a school night."

Karl had already heard the fruits of their discussion with Andrea at RT's big night. One stewed tea later, he was ready to say his piece.

"We know conclusively that RT wasn't in the country when Jacob was attacked, based on his passport." He broke off for a bite of a fried egg sandwich, leaning forward in time to save his jeans from the drips, if not the floor of the car.

"And the red paint wasn't a match, so he's not our man."

"Not directly, anyway. But this art scam changes the landscape." Karl churned his breakfast with every syllable.

"I don't see how."

"It's another reason to wonder what else is going on in Jack Langton's universe."

"He's really got under your skin, hasn't he, Karl? I mean, I know he didn't do you any favours when you went over the water . . ."

Karl took a savage bite of his egg sandwich and didn't reply.

Thomas turned his attention to the world beyond the windscreen. "We'll see what RT says tonight. I can't wait to hear his explanation."

"Quite the little team we're building up, huh?"

* * *

His heart wasn't in the day job — not today, anyway. Collect the evidence, log the details and document any observations; all for someone else's evaluation. He knew the drill so well he didn't have to think about it. In fact, the predominant thought was that this was his SSU career low point. Sometime in the not too distant future he'd take that up with Christine.

Lunch was an extra-large bag of chips, shared.

Karl scooped up the deep fried ambrosia of the gods. "All I'm saying is that Jack Langton's not an idiot — far from it. Look at the evidence." He waggled a vinegar soaked chip in the air. "Drugs, clearly; art and property; and let's not forget the gun he supplied to Miranda's Dad."

"For me." Thomas added.

He wondered how much Andrea really knew about Jack's past. Karl listened without interrupting; partly, Thomas surmised, because he was still focused on the chips. Had RT been forced into the arrangement? Did that put him back in the frame for Jacob? Some sort of retaliation and in a way only Jack would understand?

"You're neglecting another possibility, Tommo. Uncle Jack might not know anything about the art scam. Now," he cupped his chin with a greasy hand, "imagine how pissed off he'd be should his investment be exposed as a fraud. You might want to test that theory tonight over dinner." There was a hard edge to Karl's voice.

"You don't like these people any more than I do, which is saying something."

The remnants of the chip bag were offered over.

"It's different for me though, Tommy Boy. The English class struggle is your fight, not mine. Jack Langton . . ." His eyes narrowed a little at the name. "He's the enemy. Same goes for Charlie Stokes."

This was new; calm and controlled Karl making it personal.

"I've told you before, Tommo. Drug trafficking is just one of the ways the Shadow State funds its activities." Karl's lips curled into a sneer. "It's all big business — and big businesses cross national borders. They'll invest in anything that favours and furthers their interests. If I had my way I'd take them out of business permanently. Unfortunately, my orders are to gather enough information to *turn* individuals in the distribution network and track it back to source."

"And you're fine with that?"

Karl didn't answer.

* * *

The Dolan brothers were a joint investigation with a difference: identical twins. A logistical nightmare; they dressed alike with the same hairstyle and mannerisms. Karl's suggestion that they forcibly tattoo one of them didn't find any takers at the briefing.

So far they'd spent an hour watching a pizza delivery back door.

"Roland Dolan, Tommo. Jesus, that's practically child cruelty, right there."

Thomas tapped the clipboard. "Is this really a good use of our time? Couldn't you find out their mobile numbers, ring one and see who picks up?"

"It's not a crime to carry your brother's mobile phone around, or to answer it. Not unless it's a deliberate attempt to—" Karl stopped speaking.

A car pulled alongside the mopeds; one occupant — Charlie Stokes. The unnamed Dolan approached, leaned his face in the passenger window and withdrew with some sort of package.

"Extra anchovies?" Karl had picked up a discreet pair of binoculars.

The car didn't wait, and nor did Dolan. He added the package to his rear pannier, revved up and shot off in the opposite direction.

Thomas started the car. The moped had a head start and they had additional ground to cover. But it beat sitting there, reeking of chips. They had two things in their favour: the mystery Dolan didn't know he was being followed, so he wouldn't be speeding, and Karl — the human road atlas.

"Cut around and turn left onto the main road. If he's turned left we'll catch up, and if he's turned right we'll see him go past us."

"And if he turns off before we see him, we're buggered."

"Don't worry, I've got a Plan B." Karl reached into his bag of tricks and pulled out a handheld radio. It was tuned to a police channel. "In case we lose him and want to call it in."

Thomas hoped it wouldn't come to that. Police involvement was the last thing they needed. He reached the high street and eased out into traffic.

"Okay, so he's got a package, but he could drop that off any time."

"Nah, That'll be drop number one and I want to see where it lands. Quick, up there – indicating right."

Karl was spot on. Same last four characters of the number plate. They trailed the moped for another half mile, under Karl's direction. As the pizza delivery boy pulled up, Karl made Thomas slow down.

"Give me a sec." Karl unclipped his seat belt and wriggled through to the back seat just in time to take a big, obvious photograph.

Dolan turned towards him, helmet still on, and gave him the middle finger.

"Round the block, not too quickly; I want the little scrote to be on his way. Right now, I'm more interested in identifying the address he's delivering to."

* * *

Thomas had done enough surveillance over the past two years to know that there were good days and bad days. This one fell into the latter category. The dice didn't roll in their favour. The next two claimants on the list weren't where they were supposed to be — either that or they were masters of disguise — and a quick call to Dawn Yeates came to nothing because she was in a meeting.

By five o'clock there were more ticks under 'to be continued' than 'evidence completed.' Karl was mightily pissed off about it.

"Think I might go back to the delivery address tonight. Pity you're not available."

Thomas felt a pang of . . . jealousy? Yeah, something like that. Karl was on to something and meantime he was back over at Andrea Harrison's for dinner and deception. At least he had Miranda for company.

He managed a quick shower at home and put on the 'going out' clothes that he'd ironed that morning before leaving for work. Miranda picked him up at eighteen forty-five sharp, and let him drive her Mini.

On the way over they talked about RT's rogue sculpture.

"Other artists have done it as well," Miranda insisted. "I was chatting with Sheryl today and she looked it up on the net." She caught his look of disapproval. "You know you can trust Sheryl. Like I was saying, Andy Warhol used to sign blank canvases and so did Kosabi."

"Yeah, but were the punters — and the investors — in on the act?"

"Dunno. All I'm saying is that maybe this is all part of the modern art experience."

He sighed, unconvinced.

Miranda had planned in advance, ringing ahead to know which wine to bring. She'd also arranged for flowers to arrive earlier in the day, which Thomas would be paying her back for. He told her that Jack Langton would be picking up the tab, courtesy of the initial £500 John Wright was holding for him. She looked surprised, proof that even their family had its secrets.

As they walked up the street together, he started playing house in his head. These properties were way out of their league. Even so, his flat in Walthamstow and her flat in Bow, combined, would surely pay for something decent. The sight of an Aston Martin, one of his dream cars, brought him down to earth with a thud. He was an interloper — a peasant in paradise — and about to be the bearer of very bad tidings.

"All set?" She took his arm for the last twenty yards.

The upstairs curtains were drawn and glowing golden. He imagined Andrea up there, plumping cushions and tending to her coq au vin.

Miranda rang the bell and peered through the glass. "All tidied up; you'd never know there'd been a show. It's a better job than the cleaners we use at Caliban's — maybe I should get their number."

He knew she was making small talk for his benefit. She could always read his mood. This was smoke and mirrors territory. Andrea seemed like a decent person, but that didn't mean he wouldn't use any leverage to get information out of her. He rationalised that it was all for little Jacob, although that was only half the story. They were *bent* — no two ways about it — and he would get to the truth.

RT came downstairs to let them in. Miranda handed him the wine and his eyes lit up when he saw the label. RT carefully locked up after them, which made Thomas smile, and then led the way upstairs. He gabbled on about the show and a couple of media interviews that he had lined up, speculating about what the critics might say and how it all created a trail to the money.

RT clutched the Rioja Reserva to his heart; clever of Miranda to fetch along some quality Spanish plonk. Upstairs, things were a little more formal than his last visit. Andrea had dressed up as well. She seemed genuinely happy to see them both. Then again, she had no reason not to be — yet.

He still hadn't figured out how to play his ace. This would be far from easy.

"How did you meet Jack?" RT fired the first salvo.

He skipped the prison visit by royal command, and started talking about Miranda's parents, following it up with a familiar version of how he and Miranda hooked up together. It was painting by numbers — two runaways in Leeds and love's young dream. He didn't mention the bloke whose nose he'd broken on Miranda's behalf, or the Bladen family feud that bubbled along like a river of discontent.

At the point when he felt he was on the ropes Miranda cut across them.

"How do you find living in Spain?"

She talked about going there a couple of times with the family when she was younger, though not in Cuenca; and once, it had to be said — and she bloody well said it — when she and Thomas had needed some cooling-off time.

Naturally, the artist in residence loved all that and began waxing lyrical about the light and the warm evenings and the *ladies* there. Thanks to RT's self-promotional tour, dinner was a little late. No matter, Miranda and the wine had oiled the wheels.

"Thomas takes urban photographs," Miranda announced, swinging a wine glass wildly over her food.

He followed her lead and told them about his early morning shots of London and the failed attempts to get on one of the dailies.

"I did say I'd be happy to take a look at your portfolio," Andrea insisted. "It's the least I can do."

He ignored the momentary scowl from Miranda and decided there were some roads he didn't need to go down. Besides, Andrea might feel differently before the night was out. He had a vague sense of how he wanted to do it. Cosy up to RT and Andrea a little more, ask for another look at his new *creation* and then go straight for the jugular.

Dinner was followed by more wine — which he declined because he was driving, and which Miranda declined because she had an early start for stocktaking. That didn't put the brakes on either RT or Andrea. By the time the chocolate torte was a pleasant memory he was beginning to wonder if they'd manage the stairs okay.

"I'd love a private view of your work." Miranda tapped RT's arm and he flickered into life like a Christmas tree. "We couldn't stop talking about it after we left your show."

Andrea was happy to bestow the favour. She led the way with RT bringing up the rear behind Miranda, charm dripping from every syllable. Down the stairs they clattered, Thomas gripping a tiny torch from his pocket. They started at the Crocodile in the main gallery room. It was all very jovial until he noticed Andrea steering the conversation round to the decor at Caliban's — ever the saleswoman. A good deal of time was spent beside *Naked Heat* and *Naked Ambition*, so that Andrea could regurgitate the tale of Thomas's bravery and the damage to the works. Her delivery was sales pitch perfect.

"And that's what makes these pieces of urban art truly original. They've literally been impacted by their environment."

RT found it hilarious. Thomas bit his tongue. *Laugh on, while you still can.* He felt his pulse quicken as they passed through the beads and approached the side room.

"I hope you don't have a secret camera on you." RT was drooling all over Miranda.

"Girl Guides' honour." She saluted with three fingers.

RT mumbled a glib remark about seeing Miranda in uniform and Thomas seriously thought about giving him a slap.

"Here we are then." Andrea swayed a little, having long since made her peace with Bacchus and the sacred grape.

She unlocked the door. Thomas couldn't so much as look at Miranda. RT ushered them in, still in shadow until Andrea flicked the switch and the strip lighting clicked into life. The sculpture was covered again, only this time RT was without his magic button so he had to settle for a switch on the wall. The tiny motor whirred, drawing the silvery cloth to the ceiling, where it juddered to a stop and flapped gently, suspended on a fine metal cable.

RT unclipped the rope to let everyone draw close. "I haven't thought of a proper name for it yet." He took Miranda's hand. "Maybe you could come up with something?"

Thomas unclenched a fist and moistened his lips. Christmas had come early this year. "Actually, I think I can help you there. How about *fraud*?"

RT gave a chuckle but didn't get the joke. Miranda passed Thomas the portable UV light from her bag and then cut the lights so he could deliver his coup de grace.

"So there's no way this came over with you from Spain."

Miranda threw the lights back on. The colour had drained from RT's face. Andrea was looking a little peaky too.

"I warned you . . ." RT began, before thinking better of it.

Andrea was slower off the mark, but soon several steps ahead of him.

"What do you want? Name your price."

Miranda came to the rescue. "Why don't we go back upstairs and discuss it?"

Black coffee was now the order of the day, with the two giant sofas territories around a negotiating table. RT hunched up, hands tightly together, unwilling to say the first word. Andrea made a couple of false starts — it was no big deal; other people did it. And besides, no one benefited from the truth coming out whereas *everyone* stood to gain if the genie stayed in the bottle.

Thomas swirled his coffee, in no doubt now that Jack Langton knew nothing about it. Miranda jumped into the fray.

"If there's a problem, maybe Thomas can help."

Ouch. That wasn't in the script. RT and Andrea held a staring contest until finally Andrea cleared her throat.

"Jack was instrumental to RT's success."

The word reeked of something more suspect.

"I was hiding away in Spain, pretty much. I'd got into some difficulties down in Kent, so I decided to start afresh. Anyway, I met Jack out in Spain and we got chatting. I told him more than I should have, but he said he might be able to smooth things over for me. And when he found out I was an artist and he saw my work, well, he couldn't do enough for me.

"All he wanted in return was for me to keep an eye on things for him in Spain. Most of the work is actually mine; sometimes, though, I only provide the ideas and the outline; maybe some sketches too. I had a couple of new pieces exhibited in Japan like that, because of the distance. Jack's been fine with it in the past . . ."

Another pause; things were going down a notch.

". . . But this time there were problems in Spain. What you might call distribution issues. I knew Jack would want me to prioritise sorting them out, so the artwork had to wait."

"It's what he pays you for," Andrea chipped in.

"What about Natalie Langton?"

RT looked over to Andrea for moral support. He didn't get any.

"Natalie doesn't get involved with Jack's business," he continued. "Ray's the man, only he and I don't really see eye to eye. So this sculpture . . ."

"Fraud."

"Yeah, fraud." RT's laugh was hollow and heavy. "It was supposed to herald a new phase of my work. There's been a lot of interest since Jack went to prison — notoriety by association, I suppose."

Miranda placed her coffee cup next to his. "We're just trying to find out who might have a grudge against Jack Langton, because of the attack on the boy."

RT nodded like he understood, or cared. Thomas suspected neither was the case. He finished his coffee and eased forward. Time to go. He nudged Miranda and they stood up to leave. Andrea tried a last ditch attempt.

"How about this: you say nothing to Jack about the sculpture's provenance and I'm sure we can find a couple of pieces of RT's work. One each?"

"There's a couple of smaller works," RT conceded. "*Naked Trust* and *Naked Need*."

Andrea went to fetch their coats. "Why not sleep on it?" Her Turkish slippers made no sound on the rugs. "And if you wanted to realise their value, we could arrange a private sale. No one outside this room would ever know about it."

Thomas helped Miranda on with her coat.

"And these two pieces are your *own* work?"

RT didn't say anything. Maybe he couldn't remember.

* * *

Thomas passed the walk back to the car wrapped up in thought. Modern art was everything he'd expected — artificial and bogus. No, give him a decent landscape or a Pre-Raphaelite: that was real art.

"Do you want me to drop you back, if you're stocktaking first thing?"

"You really are naïve. That was for their benefit. I couldn't very well get plastered, now could I? Your place will do very nicely; maybe I should leave a bag there or have a couple of drawers to myself. What do you reckon?"

"Have you ever considered a career in intelligence, Ms Wright?"

"Well, the intelligent thing would be to take up Andrea Harrison's offer." Before he could object, she added, "the pieces could stay in the gallery — on loan. They'll feel you're properly on-side then, so you might learn more about Jack. What do you think?"

"I think maybe we should swap jobs and I'll run the bar."

"I'm sure Sheryl would enjoy working under you."

He blanched. "Let's not go there. For what it's worth, I doubt either one of them is connected with Jacob, but Karl is taking more of a personal interest in Jack than I expected."

"Is that a problem?"

"For me? No."

"Me neither." She brushed her hand down his arm. "We all want this sorted as soon as poss, so do whatever it takes."

Chapter 35

Ken stared out of the passenger window. The driver of the 4x4 wouldn't look him in the eye and had hardly spoken to him since he picked him up after midnight. The rifle was in the back somewhere and now a scratched up pistol nestled in Ken's gloved hand. The other held a set of keys.

"You're clear about where to go?"

Ken nodded and closed his fingers, engulfing the small weapon. It looked old, second world war or fifties, and there wasn't an identifying mark on it. The 4x4 pulled in and the driver put on the interior light. Ken could see the sweat on his face now.

"I'll be here for fifteen minutes. After that you're on your own."

The light blinked off.

* * *

He pocketed the gun and let himself out, closing the car door behind him with a *chunk*. Having studied the map several times he knew the route by heart, winding his way through the alleys of the housing estate. There was no name this time, just an address, keys and a time limit. It didn't sit well with him, but another £10,000 in the account would help to ease the pain.

The back gate was the only one with *PERV* painted across the front. Someone had tried to paint it over but what was left shone a garish green in the ambient light. He inserted the key and teased it round by degrees until the lock clicked. The gate swung in, silent as night; someone had seen to that. The ground floor maisonette was pitch black with heavy curtains that kept the world at bay.

He set to work on the back door with the two remaining keys and slipped inside, taking a moment to orientate himself. The bedroom was second on the right and a thin strip of light beckoned at the end of a short corridor. In a couple of breaths he was at the door, listening, waiting for the perfect moment to strike. He smiled; he'd always had an instinct for the kill.

The handle gave way under his touch, releasing more light around the door; his other hand slipped the pistol free, ready.

There was a man sitting at his computer; his back was towards him and the screen betrayed his depravity: kids.

"Jesus!" Ken gasped.

The man turned around and made a grab for something behind him. Ken was dazzled by a flash of silver as a hunting knife swung out towards him. He bumped back against the door, closing it. In a split second he made a decision and pocketed the gun.

The blade slashed wildly but he could tell it was for defence. When it came down to it most people had a natural aversion to blood — even someone else's. Ken wasn't most people though. He sought his moment, waiting until the blade was the furthest distance away and rushed in, one hand up to block as he punched him in the throat with the other.

The man dropped to the floor choking, fighting for breath with the blade still in his hand, and tried to scrabble backwards until the computer blocked him. Ken grabbed the hand with the knife and squeezed the fingers tight against the handle. He felt the body shuddering uselessly as it struggled against the inevitable. He forced the arm in at the elbow and levered it under until the blade glimmered beneath the victim's ribcage.

Ken didn't speak and he didn't hesitate, using his whole upper body to thrust the man's hand against his abdomen, tearing through his flesh in the process. He maintained the pressure and stared into his eyes, watching the agony and recognition on his face. Then he twisted the blade and tried to remove it. The victim's body sagged but he didn't die easily, lurching forward with the last of his strength to end up in a bloodied final embrace.

Ken felt the dying breath against his face and shoved him away in disgust, smashing him against the computer stand. He stood up and gazed at the blood; so much blood. Time to leave. He drew a cuff over his hand and turned the door handle, fighting the urge to vomit. As he reached the back door he grabbed a long coat that hung there and pulled it tight around himself, wearing the skin of his enemy.

It would have been quicker to just leave, but he locked the back door carefully and opened the gate. There were four people waiting across the way, three women and a man. Ken touched the pistol through the coat; the people never moved. One of the women called out.

"Is he dead?"

He nodded, turning to lock the gate behind him.

"We'll give you ten minutes before we ring the police."

There was nothing more to be said. The 4x4 was waiting, although he was sure he was late. As he opened the door and climbed inside, his coat opened. The driver stared at him in horror.

"What did you expect? It's done. Take me home."

Chapter 36

Whoever said take refuge in dreams had never spent time in Thomas's nightmares. Childhood — again. Caught out in the front room with the gun he'd found wrapped up at the back of the greenhouse. Only this time he knew it was loaded.

Dad lurched forward and Thomas retreated, waving the pistol from side to side to warn him off but it only made Dad more determined. He could smell the booze on his father's breath and the stench choked him. His arm twitched, the pistol rattling in his hand.

"Stay back! Stay back." The tears were streaming down his face now.

His father never spoke, but a guttural moan accompanied each step, that of a creature in torment.

"No!" Thomas screamed as the hands reached towards him, closing his eyes as he pulled the trigger. The whole house trembled and one of the York Minster plates on the wall smashed to the floor. Then the walls broke apart and blinding light burst in . . .

* * *

He juddered awake. Miranda grumbled and turned over. Something was buzzing. He licked dry lips and scrabbled under the covers to retrieve his mobile — set to vibrate so he didn't wake up in a panic. Nil points.

"Tommo, it's me. Get up."

"Huh?" He peered at the phone, squinting at the glare. "Karl, it's not even six yet."

"Put News 24 on and call me back."

The dream was still percolating through his brain as he dragged on some clothes and stumbled to the TV in the front room. It didn't take long to get the message. The ticker tape across the screen read: 'Convicted paedophile murdered at home.' Meanwhile, the presenter was adding details. The victim, who'd served time in prison, had been found at home after reports of a disturbance. There was no sign of forced entry to the council property. The police refused to comment on their investigation — what material might have been found at the ground floor flat, or the precise cause of death.

Thomas's blood ran cold. He'd seen enough; he muted the sound, pulled the door to, and rang Karl back.

"How did he die?"

"They're not releasing details. Don't make plans after work. I might need your help."

"Course."

"I've got a very bad feeling about this, Thomas."

* * *

Morning. Proper morning. Sat next to Karl, having yawning competitions and watching the laundry for signs of Paulette Villers. The target repeated the script from their previous stakeout, only this time there were no new bruises. Or else, he reasoned, she'd done a better job of hiding them.

"What is her partner's name?" Thomas fired off the shots.

Karl flicked through the paperwork. "Lemme see here . . . Rachel Perry — all legit. Are you gonna try another rendezvous with Paulette after she stood you up last time?"

Thomas thought back to the twenty minutes he'd spent in the café, on show and conspicuous.

"Might be worth a go. It could help us get some intel on Charlie Stokes, before I go and ask him for Jack's drugs back."

"You're really gonna do that?"

"Yeah, after I get the okay from Jack. Besides, I want to try and get Greg off the hook. Got any better suggestions?"

"If the SSU ever lays you off, you might wanna try Social Work."

In the finish they tried a different tactic altogether for Paulette Villers, driving past, out in the open. Maybe she'd react, run off . . . do *something*. Unfortunately there was no box on the evidence sheet for 'stared blankly at me as I passed her.'

"She's either a very cool customer, or she's scared witless."

"Thank you, Professor McNeill."

"Hey now, you're close. I have studied psychology."

"Really?"

702

Karl looked affronted. "What, you think everyone across the Irish Sea just reads Roddy Doyle and drinks pints of the black stuff? That's when we're not listening to Van Morrison, of course."

"No, I think you drink shandy."

"Okay, Mr Philistine, where to next?"

* * *

The day played out like a series of misadventures. Roland Dolan — presumably — was nowhere to be seen, which made Thomas wonder if Paulette Villers had warned him they were onto the plot. There was no logic to it other than the link with Charlie Stokes.

Elsewhere, they failed to get anything conclusive on two supposedly single mothers, a sickness claimant that Karl insisted had 'a very lively limp,' and a man who may well have done small building jobs on the side, but who had spent his time in the lens today watching TV with his hand down his trousers.

"Manual labourer." Karl elbowed Thomas in the ribs. "Listen, fancy knocking off early to get a little shut-eye before we go out tonight?"

"Fine by me. Will you tell Christine, or shall I?"

"If you drop me back to the office, I'll pop up and see her — you go on your way."

Thomas wasn't going to pass up an invitation like that, although it bugged him that Karl was the de facto superior in their partnership. Then again, when had it ever been any different?

The drive through East London before five p.m. was a treat. He'd forgotten what it felt like to crawl through Stratford in pre peak-time traffic without losing your rag. He wondered if you could be a London driver and a Buddhist. Somewhere, at the back of his mind, he recalled Karl saying that he'd once gone out with a Buddhist. Now there was a match made in Nirvana — a pair of joss sticks and a pair of Brownings.

He made it through Leyton, steadily gaining ground until Hoe Street funnelled him to Forest Road and then home. He slept easily, surfacing just before the seven pm alarm. A shower, a cheese sandwich, a strong coffee and he was ready to face . . . Well, that was the big question — to face *what?*

He picked up Karl at Marylebone as planned. He didn't bother asking him why there, or how come Karl had put a holdall in the boot.

"All eventualities." Karl faked a smile, closing the passenger door behind him.

703

Thomas knew the score. Based on last time, if Ken were implicated he'd end up at the military pub. Maybe not tonight, but some evening over the next few days, so Karl — *they* — would be there to meet him. In a twisted way it was a welcome distraction from the Jack Langton situation.

Parking was a nightmare but eventually they found somewhere and sat for a while, watching the illuminated door.

"I, er, don't know how this is going to pan out — you do realise that?"

He nodded. That's what life with Karl was like. "Only one way to find out."

By the second hour, he wondered if Karl had called it wrong. The Evening Standard boasted front-page photographs of a police forensics van and the ubiquitous crime scene tape roping off the back door. More details had emerged. The police had removed a computer and bags containing 'relevant items.'

He went back through it as the conversation withered and died. He'd craned his neck at the door so often he was starting to worry about repetitive strain injury. Thank God for the cryptic crossword.

"Nearly ten-thirty. Let's call it a night. Same time, same place tomorrow?" There was a tinge of desperation in Karl's voice.

He nodded, collecting the four empty glasses to deliver them back at the bar. The pub wouldn't be getting rich on them tonight.

"I'm heading off for a piss, Tommo. I'll see you out the front."

From the swing door he took a last look at the walls. So much history; what must it feel like to carry the burden of all that heritage? Karl reckoned some of the regiments went back to the 1700s and beyond; another thing Karl had studied in his spare time.

The air was cold outside; an autumnal breeze that carried a hint of the winter to come. He didn't want to wait outside the door — too many memories of childhood and Dad. So he edged round the corner and leant against a wall where he could see the car.

There was barely time to register the running footsteps and then *wham;* someone had him pinned against the brickwork with his arms by his side. Ken Treavey looked like he'd been to hell and back, and then stayed on the bus.

"Where's McNeill?"

He stared into manic eyes and kept it brief.

"He's just coming out the pub."

Right answer. Ken Treavey released him, patting the air between them.

"I just . . . I just need to see him. He's got to help me. He *owes* me."

And the way he said it told Thomas all he needed to know. Pissed and pugnacious — never a good combination.

"Come back to the car — you two can talk there."

Ken Treavey deliberated for a moment and then followed him. He climbed in the back and Thomas passed him the newspaper. The headline seemed more lurid under the streetlight.

Karl came up to the car, saw Ken and got in. "Drive, Tommo."

They took a scenic tour of London while Ken Treavey spilled his guts. It was either the weight of his conscience, or the whisky bottle Karl had produced from his coat pocket. Whatever it was, Ken let it all pour out of him. That first, fateful meeting in Central London with the man in the Daimler, the way they seemed to know his background and his life — it all added up to an eel trap. One way in and no way out.

Ken did most of the talking, but Karl managed to coax a few extra details like the first note under his mat and the later ones through his letterbox. Ken ranted, and cried, and swore he never meant to get involved in the business of killing again. He told them how he nearly took a swing at the stranger in the 4x4, who collected the rifle only to exchange it for another weapon.

In the absence of instructions Thomas made for the North Circular Road, heading clockwise. Midnight approached and Ken was still in confession.

"I can't go on, Karl. I can't do it again. This last one was a bloodbath. I need to get clear."

He slumped back into the shadow, groaning, while Thomas drove on.

"I'll need to think on this, Ken." Karl spoke so quietly that Thomas wasn't sure Ken had heard him. "What you're asking, well, it would need planning. You can't just disappear — given what you've done, you'd be a liability for them."

Thomas gestured to the sign for Finchley, but Karl shook his head.

"Nah. If this is going to work then everything has to carry on as normal — for now. I'll tell you where to turn off so we can drop him home. This is just an evening out with a couple of pals. He's in no fit state to do anything tonight anyway."

Hardly surprising, Thomas thought, since you've been anaesthetising him. It wasn't long before they heard heavy snoring behind them.

"I'll talk with him properly when he's sober — find out how it all works."

Thomas nodded and took a turn-off for Tottenham. Karl reached into the glove compartment for a street guide, reading it by torchlight. He navigated the car through the back roads to Stoke Newington, calling out left and right turns at places where Thomas couldn't even read the street names. Maybe it was deliberate.

The car finally juddered to a halt near a housing estate, not far from a kebab shop. Karl turned to the back seat. "He's still sparko. I'll have to get him back into his flat. I could use a hand."

The two of them roused Ken and dragged him out of the car. He seemed to revive once he was outside, insisting that he buy everyone a kebab. To Thomas's surprise, Karl took him up on the offer and the three of them gravitated like moths towards the neon. Ken waved a twenty in the air. The poor sod at the till, who Ken repeatedly called *Abdul,* took their orders and went off to prepare the delicacy. Thomas managed to call out 'no chillies' just in time.

Ken pocketed the change, took several bites of his fiery kebab in rapid succession and then launched into a unique rendition of *Flower of Scotland.* Thomas quickly realised that they were visible and memorable — in case anyone came round asking questions. If Sir Peter Carroll was involved, Daimler and all, anything was possible.

As they steered Ken home, he entered the repetitive phase of drunkenness, telling Karl over and over that he knew his old oppo would see him right. Karl didn't reply, which suggested he didn't share Ken's optimism.

Ken's shoes scuffed on the steps and, as he rolled up his sleeves Thomas caught a glimpse of a tattoo and wondered if Karl had one that matched — comrades in arms and all that. Making the most noise, Ken shushed his companions and then laughed at nothing. Thomas reckoned it would all end in tears.

Finally, with some assistance, Ken got his front door key in the lock. As the door gave way and he staggered inside, Karl held a finger up for Thomas to wait there and went in after him. *Flower of Scotland* echoed again, followed by the sound of a kitchen skirmish. Thomas listened, aware of the night air against the back of his neck.

"Enough!"

That was Karl's voice, clear as a bell, and then exit one agitated Irishman clutching a white plastic bag. "Let's get out of here, Tommo." He squeezed the top of the bag tighter. "Don't ask unless you really want me to tell you."

He could see bloodied clothes inside, pressing against the plastic. No further questions.

"I'll drive you home if you direct me."

"Are you sure? It's out of your way." Karl still had the bag in a stranglehold.

"Yeah, it's fine." He started up the car and waited to be given his orders.

It wasn't so much a plan that Karl put together on their journey over to Kilburn, more a collection of jigsaw pieces, incomplete, but telling. Two of them led directly to Sir Peter Carroll: Ken's meeting and Thomas delivering a weapon, whose purpose was no longer in

706

any doubt. Then there was the choice of Ken as some kind of — executioner? For all his bluster and *Rule Britannia*, Sir Peter had his connections, so why get someone like Ken to do his dirty work? Except that Ken had previously served in the armed forces with Karl.

"What do you think, Thomas? Sir Peter Carroll is surely smarter than that."

He couldn't fault Karl's logic, although he did have one question.

"Despite what you know, you're still willing to help him?" His gaze went to the plastic bag.

Karl sighed, long and hard. "For the time being. I don't expect you to understand."

"What, being a civilian?" Thomas managed a wry smile. "I understand loyalty, but there's such a thing as morality."

Karl's shoulders seemed to broaden. "Let me ask you this: was it moral when you tried to kill Yorgi out on the moors?"

He crushed his hands to the steering wheel. "No question. He had it coming."

"Some would say the same about a child murderer and a convicted paedophile."

That was about all the conversation Thomas felt like having for a while. When the car stopped, Karl unbuckled his seatbelt and carefully manoeuvred out of the passenger seat with the bag. "I'll just grab my other bag out of the boot. Listen, we need to see Ken again soon. Maybe tomorrow morning before work?"

"Can't — I'm back at the prison."

"What tangled webs we weave, eh Tommo? Right you are; we'll rendezvous later and compare notes. Goodnight, and thanks again."

He drove home with the window open, the breeze cold against his face. It kept his senses sharp and stopped him from drifting. Something was bothering him; something Ken had said. There was only one person he knew, connected with Sir Peter Carroll, who drove a 4x4.

Chapter 37

Before heading for the prison Thomas visited the heathland again. It didn't help much. Jack's oppressive effect seemed to meet him at the gates and he found himself rehearsing what to say. Although he knew the drill better now, he didn't think he'd ever feel comfortable doing this — especially solo. This time he showed his SSU ID at the reception desk before joining the queue. Christine would likely find out anyway.

John Wright had made it clear that Jack knew all about the missing drugs now and was not a happy man. In the absence of John's company he eavesdropped and observed the other visitors, mentally filling in the blanks.

"You behave nicely when you see your dad, and remember what I told you — keep your mouth shut and I'll take you to the zoo later."

He glanced at the woman's outfit; a little too alluring for a prison, unless she was trying to show hubby, and the prison staff, what he was missing. Odds on, there'd be a bloke waiting for her at Regent's Park.

An older woman edged forward, eyes down, a loose fist clutched to her chest. He shifted position until he could make out the beads around her neck and figured she was holding on to a crucifix. Good luck there, luv, if she was hoping God would intervene.

He worked his way through the people around him, putting two and two together. Assumptions dressed up as deductions — it helped to pass the time. John reckoned Jack Langton was becoming paranoid. First the attack on his niece's boy, then losing half a kilo of coke, and now Andrea Harrison's gallery had been done over. Idiot's logic — look for a common denominator and then string everything together. Like Karl had said: correlation is not causality. Still, it suited him to have Jack Langton on the back foot. Hopefully it would make him more manageable.

The visitors' hall had the same sanitised despondency and dismal decor, only it felt a little brighter. It took him a moment to work out they'd replaced the duff neon strip light in one corner; it didn't lighten the mood any.

Although he had asked to see Jack Langton on his tod he knew he wouldn't be the one calling the shots. He pawed at his pocket where he'd stashed his ID and pictured Christine watching him blip on a screen map.

Maybe it was an optical illusion but Jack seemed to have a bigger table and slightly better chairs: king of the mountain. He felt Jack's eyes on him from the second he entered the arena, weighing him up.

"Thanks for seeing me like this." Thomas extended a hand, shook and then took his seat.

"Well," Jack folded his arms and smirked to himself, "it's not like I had somewhere else to be. So, what's on your mind?"

Thomas gave a cursory glance around. It wasn't every day you asked someone for several grand to buy back their stolen illegal drugs.

"Shoot." Jack leaned back and laced his fingers behind his head.

He gave it to him straight, both barrels. If Jack was perturbed about his merchandise going missing he didn't show it.

"I've talked with Natalie, erm, Mrs Langton. She's gonna set up a meeting with Ray."

"Was it Janey?"

Now it was Thomas's turn to play poker.

"Nah, course not." Jack did his thinking aloud. "Janey wouldn't do that to me — she's loyal."

Thomas said nothing; not every problem was his to solve.

"Greg, eh?" Jack sucked at his teeth. "Well, that's for another time. Who'd he sell it to?"

"Charlie Stokes."

Jack's jaw tightened.

Thomas swallowed. "Natalie said Ray thinks there's a reasonable chance of buying it back."

"Right." Jack changed demeanour, bringing his arms forward to rest on the table. "Offer him fifteen K then. It's worth more because of the purity, but Charlie won't want any bad blood between us again."

The word 'again' pinged on Thomas's radar. Talk turned to Mrs Langton, which threw him off balance.

"She's a good girl, is Natalie. And Ray will look after you. You can trust him."

Maybe, Thomas thought, but *you* can't.

"So what's your next move — with the boy?"

He could tell Jack was enjoying this. Maybe the telly wasn't up to much. He trod carefully.

"Well, I've ruled out any connection to Andrea Harrison. I also met your artist mate from Spain, RT. He's clean too."

Jack cracked a broad smile. "Bit of a poser, eh? Dependable though. I couldn't see him biting the hand that feeds him — I'd break his jaw. But that's good to know."

"Of course, you have to check these things out." There was a lull in the conversation, so he made good use of it. "Jack . . ." He strung the word out to suggest subservience. "What do you know about Charlie Stokes? Anything we can use?"

"Lemme see now." Jack rubbed his hands together slowly. "Ex-army; some fancy regiment — don't ask me what. Marines or something. His patch borders mine and we have an understanding; we keep out of one another's way. His delivery service is mostly a side line." Jack's voice, low anyway, now sounded like an ad for throat lozenges.

"Do you know the Dolans?"

Jack stretched back and sniffed. "Kevin Dolan used to do some work for me, until Ray showed up. Last I heard Kevin had gone up north — apparently he got into some bother with a skirt. He was like that. Why d'you ask?"

He shrugged. "No reason. One of the twins does deliveries for the pizza place."

Jack's pupils enlarged; this was new information to him. "Yeah, I'll bet he does!" He cracked a smile. "That'll be Roland. Charlie took the place over a year or so ago. It sounds like you've taken an interest in Mr Stokes?"

"I'm just following all lines of inquiry like you asked me to." He could feel his pulse jumping in his throat.

Jack smiled again; a gold tooth gleamed under the strip lights. "Good." He folded his massive arms. "You've got your head screwed on. What's your dad do for a living?"

He didn't have time to make up a lie. "He was a miner; drives a minicab now."

"A grafter. Like father like son, eh? My ol' man worked down the docks. Long hours and shit conditions. He used to see all sorts coming in under the table and he wised up in the end. Taught me a lot, my dad."

Debrief over, the talk became more casual. Jack did a nifty line in the lives of those around him. "Geezer two tables back, over my left shoulder?" Jack didn't even bother to look round. "What do you see?"

Thomas glanced over. "Bloke talking to his mum?"

"She's there cos his wife refuses to come . . ." Jack winked and then dished the dirt on half a dozen fellow inmates.

Thomas breathed a little easier when one of the prison staff called out, "Five more minutes!" He asked Jack what he planned to do when he got out, seeing as they were mates now, and all.

Jack was clearly a man full of ideas. ". . . And I thought I'd take Natalie and the kids away somewhere — Marseille maybe, or Gambia. The bloke I share a cell with was talking about it this week. Course, she'll probably wanna bring her mother along. Then again, she can look after the kids, like now."

Jack found his own musings hilarious, so Thomas let him get on with it. Like his French teacher at school used to say: 'It's your own time you're wasting.'

They shook hands at leaving time and to Thomas it seemed they were both prisoners now.

"Listen, how'd you like to earn a few extra quid?"

"You're paying me plenty." Thomas shrank back into his chair; it was starting to feel like a hostile takeover.

Jack nodded. Thomas wasn't sure whether he'd passed a loyalty test or dodged a bullet.

"Keep an eye on Natalie for me, will you? I'd like to be kept informed." Jack held his gaze in a chokehold.

* * *

The grey skies of Acton were a welcome relief from Jack's spidery lair. He walked quickly to put some distance between him and the Scrubs. Karl was quick to pick up the call.

"How goes it, Tommo?"

"Let's just say if you are ever banged up in prison, I won't be visiting you very often. Incidentally, Natalie's mum came up in conversation. How was your morning?"

"Productive and disturbing, in equal measure. I met with our friend and he explained a few more things. Not on the phone — I'll tell you when I see you." The call tailed off, although he could still hear Karl breathing. "I'll pick you up at Dalston Junction, soon as."

* * *

The Dalston pick-up was short-lived. He wondered whether Natalie's mother should join the list and Karl had an interesting take on it.

711

"Get someone else to do it; it's just background. Learn to delegate."

He was about to ask for suggestions when the penny dropped. They were in Dalston, home to a bona fide private investigator by the name of Thurston Leon. Perfect, if the bloke could get over the beating he got on the last job Thomas had given him.

"Mr Leon has never let me down yet." Karl was reaching into his jacket.

No, Thomas thought, and thanks to mugs like me he's never even met you.

"You'll be needing this." Karl pulled out an unsealed envelope filled with notes. "£200, to be going on with."

"So you knew about Natalie Langton's mother?"

"Much as I would like to claim omniscience, Tommo, I was thinking more about Charlie Stokes, but let's work our way up the food chain. You go and charm Leon; I'm going shopping."

The receptionist was new, or filling in. Her blonde hair looked like an explosion in a *Clairol* factory. The earrings and lipstick was 100% celebrity magazine. If she were waiting to be discovered, she'd made it as difficult as possible by hiding in Dalston. She looked like she had somewhere better to be and, simultaneously, had no chance of getting there.

"Can I help you?" Her clipped attempt at culture had the opposite effect.

"I'd like to see Mr Leon."

"I'll check if he's free."

He drifted off to the waiting area, glancing between the lettering on the window, and set himself down in a cane chair. The magazines on the table were an eclectic mix — old editions of *Caribbean Times*, *The New Yorke*r and some computing mag with the cover missing. Someone had made a trip to the charity shop.

He heard half a conversation. Celebrity Girl's accent seemed to have slipped a couple of notches.

"Woz he like? I dunno; he's a bloke. See for yourself."

The office door opened a crack. Thomas looked up and the door widened.

"Well, brudder; I never expected to see your face again. The only reason I'm not throwing you out on the street is because of the bonus you sent me after our last . . . adventure."

Thomas smiled, realising that Karl must have sent the cash. The last time Thurston Leon had kept tabs on Jack Langton he had suffered a beating; while Thomas had fared little better, with his car getting crowbarred while he was still in it.

"So what ye want?"

"I have some business — if you're interested?"

Leon let go of his door and it creaked open.

"You better come inside."

It wasn't exactly the espionage job of the century, and even then Thomas played it down. Just a simple case of keeping an eye on Natalie Langton's mum for a few days, albeit with a few conditions. He picked up Leon's business card.

"I want everything by email. I'll be in touch with my email address."

That is, once he'd created one. It was all done and dusted in ten minutes, and he left there £200 lighter. Karl wasn't around when he got back to the car, so he checked his mobile. There was a text from his sister and an update on the Yorkshire bairn — happy families everywhere he looked.

Karl finally put in an appearance with two carrier bags.

"Sorry, too good a chance to miss. I thought I'd treat myself to something special tonight. Fancy joining me for dinner?"

"Your place is tiny."

"I know; that's why I thought we could use your kitchen."

He glanced at the bags. "That looks like a lot of food."

"Yeah, about that. I thought it might do Ken good to get away from his usual patch. And without alcohol on tap he might open up a bit. What do you reckon?"

It all sounded like a done deal. "Okay, you better let him know."

Karl shifted from foot to foot. So that had already been taken care of then.

"Any more surprises?"

"Er, well, I took the liberty of inviting Miranda as well."

"Fuck me, Karl; why not make it a party and have done with it?" He smiled a little, to let Karl know he was kidding, but Karl's face was hard as marble.

"Thing is, Thomas, I might need her help."

Chapter 38

They were en route to the Dolans' place when Karl took a call on his mobile.

"Right; I see. No, we can come in now — absolutely, no problem at all. We're on our way." He switched off his mobile and kept it in front of him. "Dawn Yeates wants us to go straight to the office."

"Which reminds me, how did your *meeting* go? Did she turn up?"

"Cheeky bastard; of course she did. It was all above board. Listen; more importantly there's been some movement on the Monica Kinley front. It seems they've called her in for an interview. Dawn wants us to make statements."

"How's that, exactly?"

"I dunno. No doubt she'll explain everything when we get there."

Dawn met them at reception and took them through to a back office on the ground floor. Thomas could see something had changed — maybe Karl's dating technique had put her back up.

The office was big enough for one large table and four seats; no windows and no sign that a cleaner had been anywhere near for a while. The bin, squeezed into one corner of the room, was already choked with plastic cups; all in all, a classic interrogation room. It didn't help that Dawn directed the two of them to the seats furthest from the door. She sat opposite, her mobile resting on the table in front of her.

"When did Monica Kinley come in?" Karl's voice had an edge to it.

"She's here now. The preliminary discussion raised sufficient concerns that I've asked a social worker to do an emergency visit with the police."

Thomas was starting to feel a little side lined. "So what has she said?" The word 'entrapment' loomed large in his head.

"She said that you knocked on her door . . ." Dawn folded her arms and waited.

". . . After I helped her aunt home — she had a fall."

"Yes, Monica said that too."

Thomas had a sense of something unspoken in the air.

"Look, Dawn." Karl slapped his fingertips down on the table. "It's unorthodox, I grant you. But we could hardly leave the old lady lying in the street. Thomas wanted to make sure Dorothy was okay. We did offer to call a doctor, but Monica wouldn't have it."

He watched the two of them play a watered down version of the 'angry silence' game — first person to speak is the loser. They were amateurs, compared to his parents.

Dawn's mobile trilled into life. She was out the door, mid-greeting.

Thomas turned to Karl. "What is going on?"

Karl fiddled with an imaginary Stan Laurel tie. "Beats me."

Fifteen minutes later, Thomas had explored the tiny room in detail and concluded that there were no cameras or listening devices. He'd even checked the bin to be on the safe side. The room was exactly what it seemed — an eyesore. He sat beside Karl, facing forward: exam conditions. Though God only knew what they were being tested for.

Dawn Yeates returned in a flourish, almost smashing the door against the back of an empty chair. "I'm sorry to have kept you." She loitered by the door, as if guarding an escape route. "There's been a development. I need you to wait a bit longer. I'll organise some hot drinks and a biscuit."

When she returned again she wasn't alone. One of the boys in blue was behind her, notebook in hand.

"Karl, could you come outside please. I need to separate the two of you to give statements." Dawn stared down at him. "The police forced entry to the property and Dorothy Kinley was found dead. "Looks like she's been dead for some time."

"Weeks. Months, probably." The copper couldn't hide his glee. "And to think you boys are supposed to be the observant ones."

Two separate statements, a review of their evidence sheets and a difficult conference call with Christine Gerrard sucked the life out of the day.

"Come on, Karl," Thomas muttered, as they eased their way past a line of grinning bastards, "we can hardly blame ourselves."

"How could we not have spotted there was something amiss with the sprightly Mrs Kinley?"

The conversation continued in the car, on the way over to Liverpool Street.

"Wrapped in plastic sheeting, apparently. Grim, but hygienic." Karl waded through the details.

Clearly, he'd gotten more out of his copper than Thomas had. The lass he'd given a statement to had only said, at regular intervals, "and you really had no idea?"

He drove to the underground car park, still conjuring with the implications. "So why dress up as her aunt to collect the pension in person when she could have had it paid straight into an account?"

"I suppose, when it comes down to it, she's not a criminal mastermind. She must have thought it was a good way to show Aunt Dorothy was still alive."

"This won't look good in the papers."

"Rest assured, the SSU won't get a mention. Christine will see to that."

"Well, that might be difficult in a murder investigation."

"Who said anything about murder? A fiver says it's natural causes."

"Bollocks. Unless you've seen a police report . . . Have you?"

Karl drew a thumb and index finger across his lips.

The chances of Karl revealing a hidden alliance were infinitesimal to nil, but it was worth the accusation to see the look on his face.

"I'll be off now to get Christine to authorise a car for the night. I'll see you at your place in about an hour."

"What about the food in the car?"

"Take it with you; I'll bring the fish — and Ken."

* * *

Maybe Thomas should have expected Miranda on his doorstep. She'd waited outside this time, parked in his usual spot.

"Table for four?"

"Apparently so. Karl's doing the cooking, if he turns up in time."

"I'm sure we can give him a helping hand. What are friends for?"

That was a very good question.

* * *

Sober, Ken was a very different proposition. He arrived in a shirt and tie, spick and span like some of the blokes Thomas had seen

716

at the military pub. Those trousers looked like they could cut paper. He'd even brought along chocolates, bless 'im.

Karl settled him in the front room and then made himself scarce, leaving it to Miranda to drum up conversation. Thomas loved watching Miranda in action; she had the gift of the gab, just like her mum and dad. Ken asked if the Mini was hers and soon they were talking about cars. Ken liked a bit of Grand Prix and Miranda had picked up enough gen from her Dad and the boys to maintain the flow.

He sat with them for a while and then judged it was safe to check on the kitchen. Karl stood at the eye of the storm with all his ingredients chopped in separate piles. Thomas recognised the plantain from Walthamstow Market.

"It won't be authentic Salt Fish and Ackee, but you'll love it." Karl dropped a wooden spoon on the counter.

Thomas put it on a stand and wiped up the mark. "Do you want to tell me what's going on and why you've dragged Miranda into this?" He pulled the kitchen door closed. "Does she know about Ken?"

"Of course not. What do you take me for?"

"Right now? I'm not even sure. Where did you learn to cook like this, anyway?"

"To be sure, sir," Karl parodied his own Northern Irish accent. "Did you think we only cooked potatoes?"

"Listen . . ." The word caught in Thomas's throat. ". . . Don't put her at risk, okay?"

The kitchen suddenly felt claustrophobic. He left Karl to it.

Dinner was served with great occasion. Karl did everything but ring a bell. Thomas forgave him that because the food smelled fantastic. Maybe Karl had done a spell in the Catering Corps.

"Okay, Ken." Karl cut through the chatter. "Permission to speak freely?"

"Granted." Ken played along.

To Thomas's eye, while Karl's army oppo didn't exactly look at ease, it was the most relaxed he'd seen him without singing.

"You get your money by cash card, correct?" Karl picked out a fishbone.

"That's right — a £300 a day limit."

"Hmm. Not much time to stockpile cash before you need to be away. You know why they gave you a card?"

"So I can't empty the account in one go?"

"Well, there's that. But also . . ." Karl looked to Thomas, inviting him in.

"They can see where and when you make each withdrawal."

Ken carried on eating. "That's clever, but how does that help me?"

Karl seemed to stall for an answer, so Thomas took the heat off him. "What if you weren't where the card was — like a blind?"

"What is it with you two? Are you some kind of double act? And while we're about it, exactly what part of the civil service are you in?"

Thomas took a swig of juice. "Doesn't matter. What's important is finding a solution to your problem."

Miranda coughed quietly. "If the cash card was cloned you could have two people using them at different locations."

Karl came to life again. "Why stop at two? How about six, all around the country?" He was already running with the idea. "It would need coordination though. I imagine it'd be a small window before that sort of usage was flagged up somewhere."

"What?" Ken rubbed his forehead. "You mean have several cards and then I can get all my money out?"

"No. It doesn't work like that; your limit would be the same but it'd give you a head start in your disappearing act."

"Aye, I see. Well, I thought I'd go to—"

"No!" Karl snapped. "Better you don't tell anyone, including me."

"So what if another *job* comes up in the meantime, before you get this plan of yours sorted?"

"What can I say, Ken? I'll put this together as quickly as possible. Until then . . ."

Ken loosened his tie. "Have you got any drink here?"

"Cameras," Thomas piped up. "Some cash points have little cameras in them. Easy to tell which card was actually used by Ken."

"Well some of them, yes." Karl patted the table, as if to say *play it down*. "If anybody was really that keen to track someone."

Thomas stared, wide-eyed. Of course Sir Peter would be keen; he'd spy on his own mother for Queen and Country, and then turn her in.

Karl took a breath. "Okay, who's for ice cream? Miranda, would you care to accompany me to the shop? You two, you're on washing-up detail."

As soon as the front door slammed, Thomas cleared the plates away. Ken remained at the table, as if he needed permission to move. Thomas sussed that this was a bloke who didn't make friends easily.

"You can switch the telly on if you like. I'll put things into soak. Fancy a brew?" He reckoned he knew the kind Ken really wanted, but that wasn't going to happen tonight.

"You into photography as well?" Ken followed him out, gazing at a moody black and white of fishing boats at Whitby.

"Yeah, got my own little dark room here."

"Is that how you and Karl became pals? Nothing personal, Thomas, only something about you doesn't make sense. Don't get me wrong, I am grateful and everything, and I'll not forget it."

He could feel the unspoken word: *civilian*.

"I don't know what Karl's told you, and I was pretty hammered that night outside the pub, so God knows what I was ranting about. Even so, you don't seem fazed by any of this." Ken scowled. "I can't figure you out."

"Does it matter?" The guy was beginning to make him nervous. Karl's dinner guest had killed two people, after all.

"Mebbe not. And what about Miranda? How does she fit into all this?"

"Karl's the one with all the answers. Ask him when he gets back."

"I bloody will," he said, and they both smiled. Finally, they had something in common.

Thomas would have been hard pushed to say which of them was more relieved at the sound of Miranda's key in the door. They'd struggled gamely to find something in common. It turned out Ken had no interest in photography or rugby. Guns, probably, but Thomas gave that a wide berth.

"It's chocolate chip — it was either that or some low fat nonsense." Karl joined the gentlemen's club while Miranda carried on to the kitchen.

During ice cream and coffee Thomas brought out a notepad. Karl seemed more confident and Miranda more subdued, suggesting they'd had words in the car. Thomas was reduced to secretary.

Karl said he'd take charge of cloning the cash card, and insisted that Ken keep a low profile until they contacted him again. In the meantime Miranda would speak to her family about rustling up some unconnected people around the country. She promised to get a list back to Karl pronto.

"Here." Karl passed Ken a slip of paper. "If you ever feel in real danger call me and I'll come get you. Emergencies only."

* * *

Everything was done and dusted by ten-thirty. After Karl took Ken away with him Thomas and Miranda lay sprawled together on the settee, listening to Paul Young's *No Parlez*.

"Did Karl say anything to you in the car?"

She smiled. "I never knew you were the jealous type."

Of course you did, he thought. "Seriously."

719

She adjusted a cushion. "He wanted to know if Mum and Dad could get a cash card cloned and he asked for a favour, if it came to it — a bed for Ken, for one night."

"He's got a bloody nerve . . ."

"You know Mum and Dad are happy to help him. He's helping you with Jack Langton. That's what friends do. Or didn't they teach you that in Pickering?" Her face grew serious. "Out with it, Thomas. I can always tell."

He let go of her. "Would you have felt differently about me, well, about us, if I'd killed Yorgi on the moors?"

"Oh, let's not go back over old ground."

"No, this is important. You wanted to know what's bothering me."

"You were trying to protect me — and anyway you didn't kill him."

"But what if I had? What sort of man would that make me?"

"Is this because Karl and Ken were in the army together?"

So he told you that at least. "No, listen." He swung her legs off him and sat up to face her. "Supposing I had killed Yorgi — like I wanted to?"

"What do you want me to say? I'm glad he's dead. He deserved to die." She pulled her knees up under her chin and then brushed at her fringe. "Let the past go. No more talk about guns and monsters tonight. Karl can deal with all that stuff."

He followed her to the bedroom, wishing she were right.

Chapter 39

Karl picked him up from Bethnal Green Tube, an hour later than usual, a sandwich in foil waiting on the passenger seat. Thomas didn't bother to question the change of rendezvous. Karl always had his reasons.

"Fried egg, not ten minutes old. We're celebrating. I've had mine already."

The crumpled tin foil on the floor was proof of that. He busied himself with the celebratory sarnie and let Karl turn evangelist.

"So . . ." Karl yawned out the word. "We're on track for Ken's disappearing act."

"When?" Thomas licked lukewarm egg yolk from his fingers. "Because once Ken's safely out the way there should be nothing stopping us talking to Sir Peter Carroll."

He finished his sarnie and folded the foil neatly into a square, placing it in the door pocket.

"That wouldn't be my preferred course of action, Thomas."

"Easy for you to say — you weren't the dumb bastard who transported the murder weapon." He stopped speaking and waited for his brain to catch up. "Ken said someone collected the rifle. How did he kill the second bloke?"

Karl turned a defensive shade of red. "All I did was give him the rifle when we recovered it."

Thomas smiled at the bluff. "That wasn't what I asked you. Answer the question."

Karl fidgeted a little in his seat. The engine was still running but they hadn't gone anywhere. He glanced skyward, huffed and turned off the ignition.

"I wanted to do this later."

"Let's not fuck about, Karl. Miranda's family have gone beyond the call for your army mate. From where I'm sitting you owe me big time."

Karl folded his arms and stared at his knees.

"Glove compartment. I was gonna show you later once we had a coffee break."

Thomas clicked the button slowly and deliberately. The flap lowered like a mouth that wanted to say something. He smiled; a brown envelope — how could it be anything else? The first image was a long lens of a front door, part way along a balcony — Ken's, presumably. The next showed someone standing at the door with his back to the camera. The third, of someone handing over a small package to the stranger, had part of Ken's face in shot. Thomas paused to look at it, sensing Karl looking at him.

"They told Ken when to be ready, so he beeped me before he opened the door."

Thomas noticed the shadows under Karl's eyes.

"When did you last get a decent night's sleep?"

"Honestly? The day before Ken showed up in my life again. You'd better go on."

Happy snap number four was Ken receiving a package in return. Thomas figured it was the replacement weapon. He was about to flick to the next photograph when Karl grabbed his wrist.

"You need to know that I had absolutely no idea about this."

Thomas wrenched his hand free and revealed the last picture. It was Bob Peterson. Now he remembered Ken muttering about a visitor in a 4x4. The power of speech momentarily deserted him. Only momentarily.

"What the fuck is going on?"

Karl started the car. "I don't know. Truly. Now do you see why I want Ken out of the picture?"

Thomas breathed into his hands, slow and steady. "I think we have to assume the worst. Peterson's not an idiot — and he's well connected." He knew Karl would be insulted by that. "I'll need to talk to him."

Karl reared back in his seat. "Hang on a minute; let's not be hasty."

Thomas put the photos back in the envelope. "I take it you have copies?"

"Yep."

"Good, then I'll keep these. Maybe I can use them as leverage with Bob."

"Or collateral."

"Come again?"

"I hate to break the bad news to you, Tommo, but he may well have a set with you in them."

"Jesus, Karl. I need coffee."

Chapter 40

Thomas was developing a fascination with the news, searching the bulletins and Karl's tabloids with grim determination.

He wondered why Karl permitted the nightmare to continue, but that presumed Karl controlled anything anymore.

He took Miranda's advice and they went back to Andrea Harrison to agree to her proposal — two artworks in private ownership, on loan to the gallery, with a discreet sale should they ever require it. He had no intention of collecting on the deal, but Miranda had done an Internet search and the maths so they were able to talk numbers to her. It all added to the illusion that they were on the make.

RT's relief that night had led to an evening of Anis-fuelled revelations. Miranda made the ultimate sacrifice with her liver, saving Thomas's head as the designated driver. Once Andrea had practically passed out, RT couldn't stop talking. Not quite a distribution timetable, but a couple of names and entry ports, and some ingenious methods of concealment and transportation. Now Thomas understood why RT was so valuable to Jack Langton. The Spanish climate was great for cannabis plantations.

* * *

Karl disappeared for a day. He'd warned Thomas the previous night that he'd be phoning in sick and suggested they meet after work. Work that was now down to Johnny No-Mates. At least, it would have been had Christine not instructed Thomas to swing by the office and pick up Ann. It was starting to feel like musical chairs.

The East London traffic was unforgiving, every hesitation punished by some cunning bastard trying to edge him out of the lane. Ah, those chirpy cockneys. Like Barry Manilow he 'made it through the rain' and parked up underground.

He got into the lift and hit the button for the second floor, watching as the door closed with precision and counting the six seconds in his head. No sooner had the lift started than it began to slow. First floor: MI5.

The lift door slid open and an Asian woman in a smart suit got in.

"It's Thomas, isn't it?" She delivered the line so casually that it was clear she knew who he was.

Just as he recognised she was British-born, educated, and knew where to shop. Then again, maybe MI5 gave out a clothing allowance. His eyes drifted down to her belt and he read the ID card hanging there: Rupindra Tagore. He nearly said, 'Like the poet,' but no one likes a smart-arse. Besides, his brain was already preparing for a forward roll. In two years he'd never seen someone travel up from the first floor. Maybe she was lost on her first day.

They smiled with their eyes, saying nothing, playing the diplomacy game. He was first out of the lift and then it was follow the leader. Past the vending machine and sharp right. He swiped her in; since it was obvious she wasn't there by accident. She headed towards Christine's office and Ann raised her head from her desk like a meerkat.

"Hi, Rupee! How are you?"

He held back to watch their brief exchange before Rupee took a seat at Christine's desk.

"Right then." Ann watched him, watching her. "I'm all yours." She locked her desk with a theatrical flourish and picked up her bag. "I do hope Karl feels better soon."

* * *

At first, being out in the car with Ann Crossley was like sitting an extended driving test. He went through the assignment sheets, brought her up to speed on progress and actions outstanding, and then suggested a takeaway coffee before they took another crack at the Dolans.

She seemed amenable, but he could never quite make her out. Karl was Mister Cloak and Dagger, no question about it. Ms Crossley, on the other hand, didn't even leave a shadow. Here was a woman who created spread sheets voluntarily. From the way she conducted herself, she evidently thought she was destined for better things. Maybe she was already laying the groundwork for a move to

MI5. He gave her the benefit of the doubt. She had saved his arse when Greg took a kicking — an event that Karl had never really explained. *Quelle surprise.* It was the not knowing about Ann that really bothered him: gay, straight, politics, lifestyle? Nothing.

Subject Dolan came into view on his pizza moped. Ann waited for Thomas to finish taking a batch of pictures.

"Don't you ever want more than this?"

He pondered that. Did she mean working in the SSU or working with Karl?

"I'm not sure what else I'm good for." He chose the words deliberately — good *for*, not good at.

"Someone with your abilities, Thomas?" The first syllable of his name betrayed her Welsh roots. "I'm sure an opportunity could be found."

He shrugged off the compliment. Sir Peter Carroll had said much the same thing, several months ago. And look how that was working out for him.

"Karl won't be here forever. Europe may be calling for him."

Interesting, given Karl's recent trip to Geneva.

"I meant to ask," he ricocheted the conversation. "How did you get on with the Southampton job?"

She blushed — a fleeting flare of conscience. "I'd rather not talk about that . . ."

"We're on the same team, aren't we? Besides, we both know Bob Peterson has already met with a contact from . . . what would you like me to call them?"

She smiled. "You really are relentless. That's why I know you could do more."

"RAF Intelligence? It's not quite my style."

"No, I agree, not yet. But with the right mentoring . . ."

"Dolan's on the move." *Saved by the bell.*

Thomas followed the same course as before, assuming that Dolan had a regular delivery route. Sure enough, the moped took an identical turn and Thomas slotted in behind a bread van. He figured it would be the same address as last time, so he veered right and put his foot down in search of a parking spot. He didn't say anything and neither did Ann, as they waited ten doors away on the opposite side of the road. The moped's rasping engine grew louder until it pulled up by the same olive-coloured front door.

He dropped the window enough to allow the lens to breathe, racking up shots while Ann checked through his paperwork. He gave her a running commentary.

"Dolan is off the moped, pannier unlocked, pizza box extracted, knocking on the door now . . . same bloke as last time — skinny, shirt and tie, head like a pencil rubber."

Crossley didn't laugh; she coughed a little instead. Stick to the job at hand.

"Delivery being made, money changing hands."

He cut the soundtrack once he realised what was actually going on. The man at the olive door took delivery of *something* but it wasn't pizza. And it looked like he'd put something back inside the box before returning it. This was what Karl called a game changer. And frankly, he should have seen it before. Whatever young Dolan was delivering, he was also collecting merchandise for Charlie Stokes.

"Did you get everything on film, Thomas?"

He smiled at the word 'film.'

"Yeah, everything I need." *Not that you'll see all of it.*

He was itching to ring Karl, but not under supervision. Off they went to the next job for more of the same. It wasn't Ann's fault. She wasn't terrible company; she just wasn't *good* company.

They had lunch on the move, although she did spring for sandwiches from a deli. It was odd being around her outside the usual four walls. She didn't do informality.

"I'm not really your cup of tea." She broke into their silent sandwich time in the car.

He blinked a couple of times, hoping she'd pick up on his personal Morse code for, 'do we really need to do this now?'

"We all work in the same department, but you stick to Karl like he's some sort of *player*."

He pursed his lips. 180 degrees off target. Karl wasn't that at all, which was exactly why he trusted him . . . most of the time.

She cleared her throat. "All I'm saying is, Karl doesn't have all the answers."

He couldn't resist taking the piss while he was finishing his sandwich. "When did I become such a valuable asset?"

"Ah, you were always that, Thomas. Only Christine missed her chance and Karl got to you first." She proffered an open bar of chocolate and he snapped off a couple of pieces.

* * *

At four p.m., when Thomas had started wondering if the car clock was on a go-slow, Karl rang his mobile. The first thing he said was, "Can you put Ann on?" so he passed the phone over.

Thomas waited, mute, while Ann nodded and uh-huhed. Finally, she passed his phone back, still on.

"Are you running on schedule, Tommo? If so, I'll know where to find you. I have a copy of the timetable about my person."

"Of course you do."

He wasn't surprised when Karl turned up not long afterwards. Ann accepted a lift to Mile End underground, to make her own way back to Liverpool Street, leaving the air easier to breathe.

"Okay . . ." Karl took a deep breath. "Here's the fruit of my labours."

Inside a padded envelope was a collection of white plastic cards, indistinguishable from one another, each with a magnetic strip along the length.

"And these will work?" He did a quick count: nine cards altogether.

"They should do. Realistically, even two plus the original would be plenty to give Ken enough of a smokescreen for a head start."

"How do you plan to distribute them?"

Karl's silence gave him his answer.

"I don't have that many friends."

"You don't need to, Tommo. How do you fancy an all-expenses paid trip to Birmingham? Even better, I'll make it a freebie trip to Yorkshire, as long as you spend an hour in Brum on the way."

"Because?"

"It's pretty central — ideal for distributing a few cards."

"And what about the others?"

"I was coming to that."

Karl had been busy. There were seven mobile numbers on the list. The last number stuck out like a sore thumb — it was John Wright's.

"You've got to be kidding."

"Like you said, Thomas, you don't have a lot of friends. And neither do I — not like this. People we can trust: no questions asked.

Thomas went through the list again. "Anything else I should know?"

"Now you mention it, there is one other challenge."

Karl reached into his bag. Clearly he was doing this by degrees. Knowing Karl, he was saving the best – or worst — until last.

"How will people know which cashpoints are safe to use — without cameras?"

Karl cleared his throat. "That is indeed the challenge. The information is best guess, I'm afraid. See page two."

Thomas flicked over the page where cashpoints were listed in groups of five. No longer the self-assured espionage agent, Karl was adrift, planning on the hoof.

"So I gather John and Diane got the cards cloned for you."

"I couldn't very well use my own people, under the circumstances."

"No, but you bloody well used mine."

* * *

Thomas got back to the flat and decided he'd give himself half an hour for a shower, a change of clothes and then out again. The flashing light on his answering machine had other ideas.

"Thomas, it's Christine. I'm at the office. Call me whenever you get this."

He checked the time, took her at her word and went for a shower first. Afterwards, he set the stopwatch on his mobile and dialled in, his hair still wet and a towel around his shoulders. She cut to the chase.

"I wanted to apologise for Southampton. There's more going on than I'm able to discuss."

"It's fine; you don't owe me any explanations."

"I know." Her voice regained its edge; she was the boss again. "Even so, I wouldn't want you to misjudge the situation."

Here it comes.

"The surveillance on Bob Peterson was sanctioned by Sir Peter Carroll."

Like that was any kind of recommendation.

"So why are we talking now?"

"I wanted to say something. If you do what *we* do, there's always a price. Back when I met Bob——"

He cut in, mindful of the time. "When we were still together, you mean?"

"Bob was the price I paid."

She'd sidestepped his point, but he wasn't finished with it.

"I think you'll find I paid a price too."

"We were hardly a perfect match and if we'd still been together when Miranda reappeared in your life, we both know what would have happened."

The timer was running low and so was his patience.

"I'm sorry, Christine — I need to be somewhere."

"Okay. All I'm saying is think carefully and stay your side of the line."

It sounded halfway between a warning and concern. He put the receiver down. That was ten minutes of his life he was never going to get back again. He hung the towel on the rail, making sure the line was level, and then got on the road.

* * *

Miranda's car was already outside the Wrights' place in Dagenham. He rang the bell and the door gave a little, on the latch. He went inside.

"Anyone home?"

729

Miranda, Diane and John were in the front room.

"I'll put a brew on, shall I?" He wandered through to the kitchen and listened for tell-tale footsteps behind him, which weren't long in coming.

"Alright, babe?" Miranda's voice reached him before she did.

He didn't answer until she was facing him, and he didn't need to say a word.

"Karl didn't put any pressure on me or Dad."

"Is that s'posed to make me feel better?"

Miranda moved around him, setting out the cups and fetching milk from the fridge. They waited together in silence, glances passing for sentences, and then took a tray through.

Diane went first. "It's a favour for a friend — a friend who has looked after you and Miranda. Is it the fake cards that are bothering you?"

"Hardly. It's the whole bloody principle of you and John having to call in favours of your own for Karl. You don't know what this is all about."

"We don't need to know." John stirred into life.

"What's the matter, don't you trust us?" Miranda shot him a poisonous glance. "Or is it your precious job again?" She crossed her legs.

She got up to answer the door, leaving him hanging; she'd played this game before as well. The Indian takeaway helped to defuse the tension. John went to help sort out the food, which left Thomas with Diane.

"It's not a problem, Thomas."

Maybe not for you.

He didn't stick around after the curry.

Chapter 41

Days later, the balloon went up. Thomas caught an item on the early morning news about a drink-driver who had left a pub and ploughed into a family walking home. One of the two children — already on the critical list — had succumbed to her injuries overnight, a few days ahead of the sentencing. Thomas was certain — this was the one. He rechecked his bag before he went to work.

The call came through around nine a.m., just as Thomas and Karl were doing another observation on Paulette Villers. Karl turned up the volume on his mobile so Thomas could hear. Ken sounded wired.

"They put a note through my letterbox, first thing. I'm to be ready for the next few days. It's not as organised as the last two jobs. Are you still there, Karl?"

"Where are you now? Are you safe?"

He could see the change in Karl. One moment they were joking about Paulette Villers doing her laundry at work for free and now Karl was icily calm.

"Stick to the plan, Ken. Where are you?"

"I'm on my way to the shops. Same routine, like you said."

"Okay, Ken. From now on, keep everything you need close to hand. We'll drop by as arranged, straight after work. Try to stay calm — and sober — until then. One more thing: don't ring me unless it's urgent. Goodbye."

Karl touched his fingers to his lips.

"The truth is, Thomas, I'm out of my depth. I can spirit Ken away, right enough, but I can't give him a new life. I reckon they'll turn off the tap to his bank account after four days, tops. Honest to

731

God, I intended to put something together for him financially — with more time. Do you think John and Diane would be able to lend me some money? You know I'll pay them back."

"You must think a lot of him."

"He'd do the same for me, no question."

And yet, Thomas thought, you've never mentioned him in two years.

"So what do you reckon?" Karl looked up. "About the money?"

"How much will you need?"

"I dunno. Two thousand, maybe? More would be better, obviously."

"And then what?" He felt the heat rising up the back of his neck. "How you gonna pay them back, and what if you can't?"

"I've just said, haven't I?"

"I get the army camaraderie, but why are you so keen to fix his mistakes?"

Karl snorted and shook his head. "No, Tommo, you don't get it at all. Camaraderie, my arse. You see it on-screen and it's all heroics and medals. But out there, in the shit and the shadows, when you don't know what's coming round the corner, you put your life in the hands of your regiment. That means something, even once you're out on Civvy Street. Christ, if it wasn't for Ken I wouldn't even be here having this conversation, okay? Now, will you help me get the fucking money together?"

"Yes." He patted Karl's shoulder with a smile. "When you put it like that, how could I refuse? Drop me off at Caliban's."

Miranda's car wasn't parked in its usual spot next to Sheryl's. The front was locked so he went to the side and pressed the intercom.

"Hey stranger, what are you selling?" Sheryl sounded like she wanted to play but he wasn't in the mood.

"Can you let me in?"

"Sure, come right up." She was a fast learner; she cut the banter and met him at the top of the stairs. "Is everything okay? Miranda's not around. Anything I can do?"

Yeah, if you've got a two grand float in the till.

"Lemme get you a coffee. You look like you could do with one."

He followed her on the promise of caffeine.

"I was sorry to hear you've been dragged into Jack's world."

He raised a mug to her. "Seems only fair as I helped put him in prison."

"Something else I'm sorry you had to get involved with, not that I don't appreciate it. Miranda shouldn't be long — wanna shoot some pool while we wait?"

She teetered forward a little, daring him to accept the challenge.

"Go on then."

"Great. I can use one hand if you like?"

Somehow Sheryl always found a way to make anything sound salacious. Maybe Miranda had given her lessons. He racked up the balls and slammed the cue ball into the pack. No planning, no finesse; he wanted to lose himself in the game and stop thinking. Two stripes down and he entertained fantasies of victory; it didn't last long. Sheryl knew her way around a pool table like Karl knew his way around an armoury. All it took was one mistake in the jaws of a corner pocket and then Sheryl went to work.

"You know . . ." She leaned on the table and looked over her shoulder at him, her pose reminiscent of a French film Miranda once took him to. "I could always teach you."

"I prefer to learn by experience."

She laughed and promptly sliced the cue ball, ricocheting it into a middle pocket. He didn't waste the opportunity; the odds were that this would be his luckiest break of the day. Maybe she'd slipped something in his coffee because he was leading by two games ahead when he heard Miranda's voice downstairs.

"We're up here!" Sheryl sang out. "Thomas is showing me how to play pool — York*shire* style."

Miranda's footsteps padded up the stairs. "You'll be needing a flat cap then. She turned to him. "To what do we owe the considerable pleasure, Mr Bladen?"

"Beats me." Sheryl conceded the game by grabbing the black and plunging it down a pocket. "I couldn't loosen his tongue. Anyone fancy fresh coffee?"

Good girl; she knew when she wasn't wanted.

"No, ta."

"Back soon. Be nice to one another."

Miranda scooped up the cue ball and rolled it across the baize.

"Shouldn't you be out working, or have you and Karl had a lovers' tiff?"

He stopped the ball and span in on the spot, watching it going nowhere.

"Karl needs some money for Ken."

She took it well, as if finding two grand at short notice was nothing for her.

"All my money's tied up in this place. You could always ask Jack's wife for help." She flashed a smile, as if to say, 'Kidding.' "Or we could ask Mum and Dad . . ."

"I was thinking more of Andrea Harrison — and our paintings."

He stepped away from the pool table and waited for the storm. She took all of two seconds to make her mind up.

"Yeah, alright then. It's not like we ever intended to collect on the deal."

He felt his shoulders sag a little. "Miranda, I could kiss you. You are amazing."

"That's what they tell me."

"Hey!" Sheryl pitched up with two mugs. "Did someone mention kissing?"

"No time for coffee; me and Thomas are about to be artful." She patted Thomas on the arse. "Come on, no time like the present — let's go see Andrea."

* * *

Thomas drove, to save Miranda the London congestion charge. After all the shit his job had put Miranda through, it was the least the Surveillance Support Unit could do.

"How much time do we have?"

"Us? All day. Karl can cover for me. Ken? Probably two days, three max."

Traffic brought them to a standstill so they played one of their favourite games: reminiscence. Their walk down memory lane started in Leeds, where they first met all those years ago. Miranda went first.

"You ever wonder what would have happened if we'd stayed in Leeds?"

"I'd have a criminal record, probably."

"How d'you figure that then?"

"The bloke I hit. I broke his nose. I heard about it from Mum and Dad after I wrote to them."

She nodded. The bloke who'd had plans for her to be his topless model when she was barely seventeen. She laughed. "And you never thought to tell me, even after all these years?"

"Would it have made any difference?"

"Too right; I'd have bought you a better Christmas present as a thank you."

"You're definitely okay with this, Miranda? Still time to change your mind."

She shook her head. "No thanks. And what about you, Thomas? Be honest now, aren't you just the teensiest bit tempted by the cash? Those artworks ought to be worth four grand a piece."

Only now, locking the car, did he give it any thought.

"Nah; truth is, it's enough to know that Jack Langton *doesn't* know. He's a scumbag and I don't want anything to do with him or his money. But if it helps Ken and Karl then I'm prepared to hold a candle to the devil this time."

Chapter 42

Andrea and RT stood together, schmoozing a punter while Virtue — from the opening night — took photographs. Thomas held Miranda back by the door and moved her to one side to get a better look at the camera: a Minolta Dynax 5 — not bad at all.

RT had another of his 'arty' hats on. Thomas wondered whether he enjoyed dressing up like a dick, or if it was an essential part of being 'an artist.' By the looks of things Andrea and RT were at the end of the sales presentation. It was all smiles and, "please take a catalogue," before the mark checked his gold watch and departed. Virtue waited around and Thomas spotted Andrea palming some cash to her.

Andrea didn't acknowledge them until both players had left the stage. "How lovely to see you." Her face suggested she meant it. "Coffee?"

RT only had eyes for Miranda and Andrea didn't seem fazed when Thomas explained why they were there. If anything, RT seemed chuffed that they appreciated the value of his work.

He stuck to the details without justification: quick sale, cash buyer and ASAP. He didn't ask if she'd be taking her usual commission; that was a foregone conclusion.

"I'll call you tomorrow," Miranda pitched in.

"You'll come for drinks, of course." Andrea's suggestion gave RT the sweats.

"We'd love to," Miranda simpered, "but Thomas has some business to take care of for Jack. I'll pop over tomorrow to collect the money."

That seemed to take the sheen off Andrea's pearly white smile.

* * *

He dropped her off after a celebratory lunch, pausing to check in with Karl. It no longer seemed to matter that she hadn't got out of the car yet.

"Jaysus, I was beginning to think you had gone into witness protection."

"Nah, just lunch. I think the money for Ken is sorted now."

"How the hell did you . . ?"

"I didn't — it was down to Miranda."

"Hey, Karl!" She waved at the phone.

Thomas coughed and grabbed at her hand. "I'll explain when I see you. I'm at Caliban's. Where will I find you?"

Karl's rendezvous point was a coffee house. Thomas settled for a latte; he was almost caffeined out. He filled Karl in about the great art sell-off.

"I'm speechless. I don't know what to say."

"Firstly, clearly that's not the case. And secondly, there's nothing to say."

"And Miranda did that for me? Remind me to send her some flowers."

"In your dreams. Now, what's the plan for collecting Ken tonight?"

The more Thomas listened, the less he wanted to hear. They'd pick Ken up from his workplace at the end of his shift, approximately one thirty a.m., and then deliver him to John and Diane's place. That stuck in Thomas's throat like a stale crust.

"Come on, Tommo, who else could I trust with this? Your place would be known to Sir Peter — from the time your door got smashed in."

He went silent. Sir Peter was somewhere at the heart of this yet Karl hardly mentioned him. Something to be sorted out when he got back from York.

* * *

London after hours was a city transformed. The gin houses of Hogarth's time might have gone — crack houses now, more likely — but foxes weren't the only predators lurking in the shadows. He had to think twice before leaving his Makarov pistol at home.

He was at the front door with his bag in hand before the last stroke of midnight, allowing himself ninety minutes to rendezvous with Miranda at Caliban's before catching up with Karl for the big push. The only noise was a distant car's sound system pissing off the neighbourhood. What would it be like, he wondered, to close the door

736

on your life and simply disappear? He felt his lip curl into a half-smile; a new life with a few grand, courtesy of RT's daubs.

The mobile sat in the car's hands-free cradle; it didn't have anything to say. He followed the road down to the park, edging the line of trees. Walthamstow High Street was almost deserted, apart from a couple of drunks in search of their lives. He made a beeline for Leyton and crossed the scar of the M11 link road. He remembered photographing the protestors as the bulldozers moved in on the shells of empty houses, and then trying to flog the pictures. In the end, a single picture made it into a left-wing magazine, although they forced him down on the price — power to the people.

Leyton became Stratford without a fanfare and then more late night traffic, in dribs and drabs, drivers shitting themselves at the sight of a police car parked up at the roadside. He instinctively tapped his coat pocket for his SSU ID. Force of habit. This time of night anything was possible.

First port of call was Caliban's, where the lights shone out against the darkness. He rang from the car and Miranda said she'd be right down. Her travel bag looked heavy, but a few grand could do that, as he'd learned once doing a courier job for Sir Peter Carroll. It took a moment to realise someone was following behind her: John Wright.

Miranda got in the front.

She patted the bag on her lap. "Eight grand."

He stared at her with an unspoken question about the ten grand total she'd originally texted him, and she stared right back. He gave up and turned round to John.

"Evening, Thomas."

There was nothing to say on the drive over; everyone knew the score. Karl would meet them in his own car and then join them in theirs to wait for Ken to come out. Karl flashed his lights as they approached and got out to move a pair of road cones. He climbed into the back seat and shook John's hand. The car clock read one-ten. Thomas watched Karl in his mirror, checking the clock against his watch — a big bastard of a watch. Maybe it was army issue.

"Even if he's late, we'll wait it out. Remember, as far as anyone there is concerned, it's just another ordinary working day."

Thomas smiled a little in the semi-darkness. Nothing was ordinary around Karl; he was the epicentre of the extraordinary. At one thirty-six and five seconds, not that Thomas was counting, Ken emerged carrying a holdall. He looked around, evidently clocked a car he was expecting, and signalled.

Karl got out and went over. Through the window it was clear that there was some kind of disagreement. Eventually Karl handed over a small box, which Ken thrust into his holdall.

Thomas warmed the engine up. As soon as Karl and Ken squeezed into the back seat Miranda passed over the envelope.

"Eight grand. Spend it wisely."

Ken looked to Karl, who nodded his approval, before taking it.

"I'm in your debt, you two."

Karl took command. "Okay, here's how this works. Ken, John and I will go in my car. You two are off to Birmingham tomorrow. Ring in sick first thing, Tommo. Say a family situation has come up."

Thomas watched as the back seat passengers filed out and transferred into Karl's car.

"What's the matter?" Miranda poked his arm. "Won't they let you into their gang? Back to yours, then."

He was fading by the time they reached Walthamstow. It had been a long day and his head was filled with questions. As Miranda opened the front door he clocked the envelope on the floor — two return tickets to York. Karl had kept his word.

Last thing before bed he checked that the cash cards were still in their hiding place among the DVDs, and that the list of contacts and mobile numbers had lain undisturbed beneath the cutlery tray. He was out like a light, lulled to sleep by a perfume that hadn't changed in ten years.

Chapter 43

He left a vague message at Christine's work number before seven am, promising to ring her later. After that he checked in with Karl to get the green light for Operation Bank Fraud. He didn't ask about Ken. That was beyond his remit now and on reflection, maybe Karl had done him a favour.

Cards retrieved, list secured, bags already packed, they were out the door by eight, travelling the Tube with the rest of the cattle. Miranda had a steely calm about her that was both unnerving and alluring. There was no talking in the Underground crush, and even above ground at Euston she didn't have a lot to say. He watched as a new mobile phone — probably from Karl — emerged from her pocket while she checked the departures board.

He left her to her calls; no doubt arranging the pick-ups at Birmingham. It was a little early for coffees, but he got them anyway, along with muffins. If she were standing in for Karl she might as well go the whole hog.

* * *

They grabbed a table on the train and were soon joined by a suit with designer glasses and a laptop full of spread sheets, and then a woman whose choice of book — judging by the cover — suggested she wasn't keen on thinking. Mr Laptop sodded off at Milton Keynes so Thomas spread himself out a little.

Seated opposite Miranda, sipping their coffees in silence, he thought they looked like a couple at war, or strangers. And yet, he mused with a smile, they couldn't have been more in sync — not clothed, anyway.

Once Chick lit Queen had taken the hint and moved somewhere else, he asked the question that had been eating away at him all morning.

"What happened to the other two grand?"

"You can't expect people to pay for their own travel when they're helping *us*."

He knew that she meant *him*, but let it pass.

"But if there's any left . . ." She second-guessed him. "I'll treat you."

If? Blimey, were they all travelling first class?

They reached Birmingham New Street and jumped ship. He'd forgotten how much he hated the station; the platforms looked as if a committee of muggers had designed them. They squeezed up the narrow stairs and surfaced onto the main concourse, sidestepping travellers clustered under a screen in search of their late-running train.

Miranda took her mobile out and walked on a few paces. She glanced over her shoulder and signalled for him to follow her.

"No offence, but leave some distance. These are people from Mum and Dad's world."

She went back to her phone and he trailed her out of the station. It wasn't difficult to stay on the periphery; it was what he did on every other working day, which was why he couldn't help noticing details.

The first contact was a black guy in his early fifties. Somehow that surprised him; he wasn't proud of it but there it was. Judging by her body language, Miranda already knew him. Thomas enjoyed her sleight of hand as she deposited the card in the bloke's coat pocket. The two of them walked up the street to a café, where Miranda gave him a hug before they parted company.

Thomas had followed on the opposite side of the street, so there was nowhere to go when the bloke walked past.

"Alright, mate?" The bloke winked at him.

Thomas clocked the London accent and crossed over to rejoin her.

"You could always show me today's itinerary."

"Where's the fun in that? Besides, it's better like this: 'need to know' and all that." She was quoting from the Karl McNeill rulebook.

He let her make all the running, and she led him a merry dance through the Bullring to a café on Edgbaston Street, where he managed to grab a coffee with her, albeit at separate tables. From there they looped round to the Odeon, dropped another card off and wandered back towards New Street Station. Five strangers came and went and he realised she didn't want them to see one another either.

Miranda started fiddling with her mobile phone again.

"Problem?"

"Nothing I can't handle . . ." Her face suggested otherwise.

"Anything I can do?"

She cast around a final time for the no-show.

"With one condition. You don't check up on this afterwards — ever."

"Deal."

"Someone's supposed to be flying into Birmingham International, but their flight's been delayed."

"So we'll head over there?"

She started walking back into the station.

* * *

He did the decent thing at Domestic Arrivals and made himself scarce — but not invisible, and avoided the screens, even though it was killing him. Instead, he rang Karl to pass the time.

"Only me checking in. How's work?"

"Same old bollocks. I plan to stalk the mystery Dolan again later. Roland or Donald: that is the question."

"Sorry, forgot to tell you — it's Roland."

"Oh?"

"Prison talk."

"Well, thank the Lord for incarceration. How are you finding playing second fiddle to the capable Ms Wright?"

"Yeah." Thomas evaded the question. "Listen, this will work, won't it?"

"Don't see why not." Karl's voice trailed off, a sure sign he was focused on something else. "Right, must dash. The scales of justice won't tip themselves."

He considered buying Miranda an 'I love Birmingham International' key ring, clocked the price and thought better of it. There was an art to surveillance and it was a hard thing to switch off when there was so much of interest going on around him: bored children, anxious parents and the solo travellers who were always harder to interpret and more intriguing as a consequence.

Miranda and another woman crossed his line of vision. They looked comfortable together. The woman was suited and booted, her vivid auburn hair a striking contrast to Miranda's blonde. They stopped abruptly at Miranda's prompt and turned in his direction. He assumed it was an invitation.

"This is . . ." Miranda paused and blinked, ". . . my cousin, Philippa."

Both women found this hilarious. He sighed, waiting for *Philippa* to say something.

"Well." Miranda stirred, "I won't keep you. Thanks again and have a safe trip."

"You must come up some time and do bring . . ?"

"Thomas." His lips barely moved.

She tilted her head slightly, still looking at him.

"Not bad at all, Miranda."

He watched her leave and moved closer to Miranda, while his brain whirred on. Maybe a solicitor; Scottish, probably. She didn't sound like Karl, anyway.

"Reet then . . ." Miranda was taking the piss out of Yorkshire. "'Ow d'you fancy a trip oop north?"

They caught a train back to New Street Station and then on to York. There was only one bank card left in the set and Miranda handed it to him. He'd picked York because it would be teeming with people. Leeds would have done, but York was also easier for travelling on to see Ajit, Geena and the sproglet.

* * *

The Connaught Hotel was a decent, middle-of-the-road establishment; not dissimilar to places he'd stayed at on assignments outside London — clean, welcoming and not too up itself. The bloke on reception didn't blink an eye at their casual appearance — this was Tourist Town after all. He offered them a map of the city and some discount vouchers, which Miranda seized upon. The only thing that almost took the smile off his face was Thomas asking if he could pay in cash. A more up-market establishment might have insisted on a deposit by card, but the Connaught clearly had more trust, or fewer scruples. Thomas paid in advance and bunged the bloke a fiver for his trouble.

They went in under Miranda's name — her first name, anyway — which made him feel like a trophy boyfriend. After the day's excitement it was a fun game to play, and it helped take his mind off the final hand to be played that evening. Upstairs, the flowery wallpaper extended right along the corridor in a flourish of chintz. He couldn't work out if it was intentionally retro or whether the place was long overdue for a makeover.

Miranda opened the room door, dropped her bags and flopped down on the bed.

"Pretty good timing." She checked her wristwatch.

A Christmas present from him, three years back — nice touch.

"When do you want to eat?" He walked around her carefully, placing his bag down on the floor at his side of the bed. "Only I don't want to wait until after . . ."

"Give me a few minutes to freshen up and then we can go."

She raised her arms so he could pull her up. It felt like an invitation and he had to fight both gravity and desire.

* * *

Dinner was a pub special. He figured it would draw less attention to nip out from there to a nearby cashpoint than interrupting a meal in the hotel. The place was heaving and they blended in nicely, just one more couple on a leisure break. Miranda had added to the effect by bringing the hotel leaflets with her.

"Fancy doing the tourist trail tomorrow before we go to Pickering? What time did you tell Geena and Ajit to expect us?"

He sipped his half-pint of shandy quietly.

"You did ring Ajit?'

"Not exactly."

"Great. So what happens if no one's home tomorrow?"

He faked a smile. "We'll catch a bus to Scarborough instead."

"And they say romance is dead."

He checked his watch — seven-twenty: around half an hour to go. The food arrived quickly and that was a bonus. You couldn't really go wrong with fish and chips, and more to the point neither could a chef.

Miranda seemed to relax a little with food on the table.

"Where do you think Ken will go?"

He listened for the satisfying crunch of knife against batter and inhaled a waft of steamy vinegar. Bliss.

"Well, he's Scottish; maybe he'll find some quiet glen and lie low for a bit, and then disappear abroad with a new identity."

Miranda lifted her glass of Malbec.

"Where would you go, if you were in his predicament?"

He gazed at his chips for a second or two. "Canada. Halifax or Winnipeg."

"Bloody 'ell, I like how you've already thought about it. Talk about be prepared — you must have made a brilliant scout."

"Never joined; Mam couldn't afford the uniform."

At ten to eight he was getting restless. There were two cashpoints likely to be camera-free, according to Karl. The man had more contacts than a discount optician.

He lifted his chair back and play-acted for an imaginary audience.

"Just popping out for a sec."

"Okay."

Outside, a group of students in rugby shirts jostled along the street and launched into a rendition of *Ninety-nine Bottles of Beer*, starting at forty-one; presumably where they'd left off.

He waited until they had moved on, and chose the cash machine on the right. It was two minutes to eight. Now came the moment of truth. He took the card out of his pocket, blank as Ken's future, and made a show of looking for something in his jacket. At eight pm he inserted the card, tapped the number in carefully and waited. The main display appeared on cue; he selected £30 cash and held his breath, counting in his head as the machine went through its routine. Finally, it returned his card and spat out the money. There now, that wasn't so bad. He planned to cut the card up later and spread the parts in three different locations.

His food was waiting for him with a plate on top, and he turned to the last of his chips.

"All sorted."

"Then let's go back to the hotel, rent a movie and celebrate."

Chapter 44

Thomas woke in the early hours and tiptoed across to the window. York was still sleeping off the previous night and he watched as a police car wove through the maze of streets. His mind drifted through the previous day's events and he wondered about Ken. How long would it take Sir Peter and his cronies to realise that something suspicious was going on with the bank account? It stood to reason that it was already being monitored. According to Karl, banks across Europe acted with impunity and did things that would make your hair curl.

He stayed behind the curtain and checked his mobiles — work and personal. Both were stony silent so he went back to bed. As he lay there, softly serenaded by Miranda wheezing in her sleep, he tried something his counsellor had once recommended.

'When you're overwhelmed by too much thinking, imagine each thought as a brightly coloured ball. Instead of trying to keep them all in the air at the same time, mentally throw them up and catch just one. Focus on that and let the others go.'

He smiled at himself, remembering the look of incredulity he'd given her when she'd offered him fantasy juggling. He closed his eyes now and up they went. The thought that landed in his lap was Jacob. He got up again, dressed and grabbed a handful of change.

Downstairs he took a seat at the public Internet computer, wiped the child-sized fingerprints from the keyboard and readied a small pile of coins. The pages crawled but eventually he was able to access his most recent email address. Thurston Leon, the private investigator he'd paid to snoop on Natalie Langton's mum, had emailed a reply. Apart from some ultra-right wing tendencies, she was spotless. At least it was someone he could cross off the list.

When he returned to the bedroom Miranda was busy checking her mobile.

"Your phone rang while you were out. Don't worry, I didn't touch it."

"Which one?"

"Search me!" She slipped her t-shirt off her shoulder.

Tempting, but some other time. Karl had sent a text: Tried ringing but you must be busy — the eagle has flown the nest. Thanks again — K.

He took first turn in the shower and Miranda was still messing with her phone when he exited from the steam.

"Updates on the cards," she explained. "One failed, but I can't tell you where or I'd have to kill you."

It would have been funny if it hadn't conjured up the image of a white plastic bag filled with bloodied clothes. He changed the subject.

"You're sure you're okay about seeing Ajit and Geena again?" He left the 'b' word out of the equation and watched her fateful sigh.

"Yeah, I should be."

* * *

His mobile phone gate-crashed breakfast. This time it was the work mobile who wanted to be his friend.

"Thomas Bladen." He spoke softly, easing back his chair to make an exit.

"Ah, Thomas, it's Sir Peter. Are you free to talk?"

"Yes, sir; just give me a second."

He gagged the phone, gestured to the door and mouthed 'duty calls' to Miranda. She looked unimpressed. The clock near the front desk read eight fifteen — the Old Man must be on overtime; this was never going to be a social call.

"How soon can you be at my office?"

He glanced back to the glass doors, where he could just about see Miranda.

"I have some things to tie up — would eleven-thirty be okay?"

"Very good — and come alone."

He turned off the phone and made the condemned man's walk back to the restaurant.

"Everything all right?" Miranda seemed extra bright and breezy.

He sat down and took a gulp of orange juice before he answered.

"Do you believe in déjà vu?"

* * *

Miranda was better about it than he had a right to expect. He figured she was probably relieved too. They were packed and out of the hotel in fifteen minutes without a cross word spoken. Or almost any other kind.

York station was awash with end of season holidaymakers and students with more luggage than sense. He ducked past an idiot carrying a surfboard, found a corner away from the noise and rang Karl.

"Missing me already?"

"We have a problem . . ."

Karl was the voice of reason. "It was only a matter of time, although they're pretty quick off the mark. Then again, it may not be connected with yesterday."

"Yeah, he probably wants to promote me."

"Actually, it might be something *I* did."

Thomas started sweating. "Text me on M's phone."

"Will do."

A series of messages arrived as the train sailed through Doncaster. It seemed Karl had been creative by using the genuine bank card in Southampton, as close to Bob Peterson's home as possible. It felt good to know Karl was fighting his corner.

Thomas decanted the essentials into his rucksack, including Karl's photos that he'd taken along for safekeeping. If Karl was right, he had a feeling he'd be needing them soon.

Miranda's generosity continued when they reached London. She took his bag and left him the rucksack. "You can come over tonight and collect it — ring me."

He waved her off, reflecting that life always seemed complicated in London — on a bigger canvas. He wouldn't have it any other way.

* * *

This time there was no waiting at the front desk of Main Building. ID, hand scan and welcome to the citadel. His escort was the Geordie lass from before.

"Mr Bladen — I never expected to see you back so soon."

She remembered; how sweet.

"Me neither."

Sir Peter's door was closed. He rapped staccato and went in. The Old Man smiled, but he'd done that in the past so it cut no ice with him. Thomas waited; he was good at that — better than most.

747

" I expect you're wondering why I asked to see you so urgently?"

He decided to box clever. "I assumed you need something else couriered. I've got an overnight bag." He lifted the rucksack for effect and noted the lack of coffee on offer. More waiting.

"Thomas, I'd like your assistance with a problem. I want you to support Bob Peterson and meet with him today in Southampton. I'm pleased at your initiative."

That read one of two ways. Thomas pressed his tongue against his lower teeth so hard it made his jaw ache.

"I'll book a pool car from Liverpool Street then and take my instructions from Bob when I get there."

"No need." Sir Peter clapped his hands together once, as if he'd just thought of something. "My driver, Phillip, will take you. He's expecting you. The sooner you're down in Southampton the sooner you can get started."

Chapter 45

Thomas got to the Daimler before the chauffeur had time to get out.

"I'll sit in the front if it's all the same to you?"

Phillip started the engine.

"Would you like the radio on, Mr . . . ?"

"Thomas." He cringed. "Just Thomas."

Phillip was a classical music man. Rachmaninov formed the backdrop to their departure from London, the sombre tones and sweeping piano lending the south of the city more grandeur than it deserved.

There were questions on Thomas's mind, mostly about loyalties; but to ask them would reveal his own. He settled for, "have you worked for Sir Peter long?"

Phillip smiled, the way people do when they're remembering something. "You could say that — I served with him in the Royal Navy. You?"

"Two years or so in the SSU. You could say he recruited me."

Phillip lowered his window. "You can relax. I'm just the driver."

Spending time with Karl had taught Thomas that nobody was *just* anything. Conversation didn't resume properly until the signs for Southampton.

"We met before, Thomas." Phillip followed the sat-nav, spiralling in towards Bob Peterson's building. "About six months ago."

The penny dropped. It was that fateful day Thomas went to see Sir Peter to deliver his ultimatum. Reflecting on it now he couldn't help wondering how much had changed.

"I'll give you my number. Call me when you're ready to be picked up, or if you decide to stop overnight."

Phillip passed over a laminated card, bearing the crest of the Surveillance Support Unit. Thomas tapped a corner against his palm.

"Perhaps you know my friend, Karl McNeill?"

"Perhaps I do." That was it; nothing more. "We're here now."

Thomas took a moment outside the building, running through his options. Playing it straight would be easiest — show Peterson the photos and find out what *he* knew. If they could just get over hating one another's guts.

He buzzed up and some underling promised to come down and collect him. Thomas turned from the camera — force of habit — and wondered if there was another, less obvious one hidden in the brickwork. This was the SSU after all.

* * *

The office was bigger than Liverpool Street's, with twenty-six desks — he counted them. Bob Peterson was cordial, that was the word, meeting him in the open plan office. A light handshake, a dismal offer of machine coffee and then Thomas was whisked away along the corridor, coffee in hand.

Peterson's domain had an air of headmaster's office about it. A map of the British Isles covered part of one wall, the thick green line encompassing a chunk of the southeast. Thomas figured the team was a regional hub and everything inside the line was Bob's. He always was the territorial kind. Another map covered Southampton in detail. Peterson caught him looking at it and gestured to a round table where a notepad was already waiting.

Thomas took a seat and thudded his rucksack on the chair next to him, ready to produce the photographs of Ken's flat. Peterson sat opposite and the two of them clutched their coffees, ready to draw.

"I'll start, shall I?" Peterson flipped open his notepad. "I don't like you and the feeling's mutual. But whatever our differences — personal and professional — Sir Peter Carroll has *requested* that we coordinate our efforts."

"I still don't know what the job is."

"Don't you?" Peterson took a large gulp of coffee, which Thomas hoped was still piping hot, and wrote down a name on the page: Ken Treavey. "Our task is to locate him. Anything you want to say about that?"

Several things actually. He thought about protesting his ignorance, or querying why this was an SSU job. But all that was bullshit. Besides, he had a better plan — find out if Peterson had any photos, goad him into ending the meeting, and get the hell out of

750

there. He took the photos from his rucksack and laid them on the table, face up.

If Peterson was surprised he did an excellent job of not showing it. Much as expected, he got up and retrieved some photos of his own from a desk drawer. "Now we're on a level playing field." He passed them across.

There were three photos; probably the best of the bunch, Thomas surmised. Him, close to Main Building carrying the package and two in Victoria Station. He could see Peterson studying Karl's handiwork.

Thomas drained his coffee. "This is a set-up. We were the couriers and now it's our problem to locate . . . what was his name?"

Peterson laughed. "You must take me for a fool, Thomas. But like I've already told you, I'm three steps ahead of you."

"And your wife too?"

"Watch yourself, Thomas. Christine's not here to protect you now."

He took a breath and tried to let the red mist clear. "The day I need protecting from you . . ." He couldn't think of a punchline, other than punching him. Tempting, but unproductive. "Let's cut to the chase." He placed Peterson's photos carefully into his rucksack. "I have no idea where Ken Treavey is, and maybe it's better for both of us that way."

Peterson folded his arms. "I'm listening."

"Why you and me, Bob?" He took delight in using the name. Now he'd asked the question aloud, the ideas came thick and fast. "Sir Peter knows you'll follow orders to the letter, and he knows I don't trust him an inch. This is a fool's errand."

"Then what's the point?" Peterson eased back a little and picked up a pen.

"Maybe there is no point, other than that Sir Peter's seen to be doing something while we're at one another's throats."

"Can you make some inquiries?" Peterson's voice sounded plaintive.

Thomas pitied him; it must be a bitter pill to swallow that *he* was the solution to Peterson's problems. He nodded and stood up to leave.

"Give my best to Karl. I gather he knew Treavey once upon a time." Peterson couldn't resist a parting shot.

"I'll be in touch. Give my best to Christine — if you see her before I do."

Peterson flinched in his chair. For one sweet moment Thomas thought Peterson was coming up to meet his fist. Sadly, it wasn't to be. He was on the phone to Phillip before he got to the end of the corridor.

Chapter 46

After Phillip dropped him off at Liverpool Street the first thing Thomas did was access his mobile messages. Miranda had checked in twice to make sure he was okay and her dad had managed 'call me' sometime on the drive back. He rang him first.

"Where have you been?"

"Southampton."

"Are you still down there? I need you in London — Natalie's been in touch."

It was beginning to get chilly. He let John do the talking.

"Natalie wants you to meet with Charlie Stokes to discuss the goods. And she said Ray Daniels will act as a sort of go-between."

"When?" He looked over at a taxi.

"Tonight?" John didn't sound convinced.

"Let me speak to Karl first and I'll ring you back."

He took a chance and walked round to the car park, using his ID card to release the side gate. Karl's car was there, taking up space, and the bonnet was still cooling off. Christine's car sat nearby, as cold as his opinion of her now he'd seen Bob Peterson.

It wasn't a huge surprise to find Karl, Ann and Christine deep in conversation as he approached the office door, but it still smarted. Now he knew how the young, skinny Ajit had felt at junior rugby practice — always the last to be picked.

The meeting broke up abruptly as he entered the room, or maybe it just seemed that way. Christine was last to acknowledge him, which made him wonder if Peterson had been on the phone. He decided to call her bluff.

"Can I have a word?"

"Of course." She led the way to her office.

He gestured for Karl to wait for him.

"How is everything?" She sounded concerned.

"You tell me. Sir Peter rang me this morning. He sent me to see Bob Peterson about finding a missing person."

"Really?" Her brow dipped. "I thought you were on compassionate leave?"

"Yeah, so did I." He blinked a couple of times, making space for her to say something. When he realised silence was the only answer on offer he knew it was time to leave. "You know what? It's been a really long day and I could do without the subterfuge this time. Don't you trust me yet?"

Her lips parted and she looked away. "It's not that. I want to keep you safe."

"I can look after myself." He wrenched the door open.

"Not against these people. Karl agrees with me."

* * *

Karl took him to The Swan and somehow managed to find them a table.

"I'll get these, Tommo. Shandy and crisps?"

"Ah, you remembered!"

Even though Karl played it cool when Thomas mentioned meeting up with Charlie Stokes, he could see he was guarded.

"Come on; out with it."

Karl hunched in over a pile of crisps. "Our man Charlie is a cut above Jack Langton. Keep your wits about you. Anything you notice might be useful."

"Then you think I should go tonight?"

Karl hadn't moved. "It could . . . erm . . . be really useful if you met him — and the sooner the better."

Thomas sat back and laced his fingers together, waiting. It occurred to him that John Wright was waiting too, but that was *his* problem. "Well?"

"Charlie acquiring some of Jack's drugs will cause ripples. The franchises are not supposed to compete and that instability is a golden opportunity for us. Our problem has always been getting close to Charlie to gain any intelligence. He's shrewd."

"So are we. I've still got the bug you gave me, at home. I can ring John on the way."

Karl didn't need a lot of convincing.

* * *

Thomas changed his clothes while Karl got the coffee on.

"Are you sure you're up for this?"

He opened his hand to show Karl the device. Subject closed.

"I'll be on standby. I can come in heavy if need be." Karl sounded spooked.

"It'll be fine. Ray will be with me . . ." He smirked. *Good old Ray — Mark Antony to Jack Langton's Caesar.*

"Don't underestimate Charlie Stokes." Karl moistened his lips, despite the coffee, "His profile isn't pretty. He's psychopath material."

"Thanks for that. I'd better get going before I change my mind." For all his concern, Karl didn't try to stop him.

* * *

He arrived at *Xanadu* shortly after eight pm. Ray came to the door, in a rush, and corralled him into his BMW.

"Mr Stokes doesn't like to be kept waiting. You keep your mouth shut unless he speaks to you, and it's *always* Mr Stokes — got it?"

"Understood."

Ray Daniels was agitated, no question about it. And he didn't look the small talk type. But everyone had their soft spots.

"Nice car."

"Yeah, benefit of the job." Ray upped the speed. "Jack Langton says presentation is everything. Incidentally, you did a good thing, looking after Andrea during the break-in." He reached into his suit jacket and pulled out pristine banknotes. "Three 'undred quid there — ought to buy you a new coat."

Thomas grabbed the money, pretending to marvel at it.

"Thanks . . . Ray."

Ray perked up a bit.

"We'll be there soon. Just follow my lead and do like I told you. Remember, fifteen K and that's it."

The car left civilisation behind, bumping over a dead-end to bounce across wasteland. Up ahead, Thomas noted at least three buildings — remnants of some sort of factory. It hadn't escaped his attention that Ray seemed to know his way around without the help of sat-nav, but he did like the man asked and kept his mouth shut.

The car pulled under cover, losing the comfort of moonlight. A train rumbled past in the distance, wheels screeching against the rails. Ray got out and stretched. Thomas joined him and they stood there while Ray had a smoke.

Thomas wondered if he was armed — whether that was the way these people behaved. He figured Ray was about five feet ten; shorter than him anyway, but broader. Another gym fanatic. What was it with the East End boys and their pecs?

"Let's get on with it." Ray flicked his cigarette and Thomas watched the orange glow as it arced into the shadows. "You coming, or what?"

The main building was a ruined shell and it led out to two more substantial structures. Thomas kept his hands together, like a prisoner, and counted his steps. It helped to have something to focus on. Right turn, flash of moon, left turn, into the building and then a change of footing, broken glass and cobwebs. And that smell? Grease, or engine oil; something industrial.

"Is that you, Ray?"

The voice reached them before the doorway. Charlie Stokes appeared to be alone. It looked like a supervisor's office, frozen in time from the 1970s; a semi-nude stared down from the wall to remind everyone it had once been April. Thomas tried not to stare back.

"Wait here." Ray elbowed him in the ribs, making him flinch, and walked over to chat in private.

After a couple of minutes, Ray called out. "Come through, Thomas."

Ray was seated at a large metal table. Charlie was pouring three slivers of scotch.

"Sit yourself down."

Charlie waited and then loomed over him. "I know what you're thinking. Why am I in a dump like this?" He laughed and Ray laughed with him. "They used to make all sorts here. Lathes and drills, then it was parts for conveyor belts — proper machinery. Now, what's left is potential — posh homes, a casino . . . the works. I've had this place for years."

Thomas pulled his chair in close and felt in his pocket. He waited until Charlie took his place at the table and then slipped out the bug and pushed it until he felt the magnet attach. A piece of piss, until he gripped the scotch and saw that his hand was shaking a little. Ray saw it too and seemed amused. Charlie had emptied his glass and was heading back to the bottle. Thomas covered his glass and shook his head.

"No thank you, Mr Stokes."

Thomas caught the look they shared and stared blankly past. His heart pounded in his chest. These two blokes weren't strangers.

Charlie rejoined them. "Right. Let's get down to business."

Thomas sipped what was left to steady his nerves and delivered the message from Natalie, except he had to say it was from Jack: fifteen K for the return of the drugs and to cover any inconvenience.

Charlie smiled. "Let me show you something."

Ray shifted his chair back, but Charlie shook his head slowly.

"Just Thomas. We won't be long."

He forced himself out of the chair, shooting a glance at Ray, who didn't meet his gaze.

"It's this way."

Charlie led him through two more dilapidated rooms, into what must have been the production area. Wooden benches, caked in grease, stood idle. A neon strip light blinked desperately like a cry for attention. Charlie kept on walking.

"Through here."

Thomas heard a rattle of keys then the shriek of metal as bolts scraped back. Charlie went straight in so he followed him. In front of them were half a dozen plastic kegs, sealed tight, on pallets.

"You know what this is?"

Thomas shook his head, although his instincts told him this was more cartel merchandise held in storage. He stared at his feet, noticing how the cement on one section of the floor seemed newer than the rest. About six feet by three feet — big enough for a coffin.

"I think you do know. Look at it."

As Thomas lifted his head he felt the sweat gathering at the top of his neck.

"I don't need Jack Langton's poxy half kilo, but why would I sell it back for below the market value? Do you think I'm stupid?"

Thomas felt Charlie's grey eyes reaching into his psyche in search of an answer.

"No," he yelped. "But Jack will owe you and maybe that'll be useful someday."

Charlie stared him down; the light went out of his eyes.

"I'm only kidding!" He slapped Thomas on the shoulder. "How did you get mixed up with Jack anyway?"

They left the compound and Thomas stood back while Charlie locked his treasures away.

"I'm a friend of John and Diane Wright's."

Charlie leered at him. "Ah, are you Miranda Wright's bloke? You and Ray have got something in common then." Charlie's laughter bounced off the walls. "Come on, I feel like another drink."

He wasn't the only one.

Ray had made himself scarce so Charlie poured two drinks and carried them through to the office.

"You're a photographer, right?"

He nodded dumbly, shocked that Charlie had done his homework.

"Yeah, that's what I heard. Anyway, cheers." The glasses collided and Charlie's — twice the volume — emptied in seconds.

"You tell Natalie I'll accept the fifteen K this time and — like you said — Jack owes me. Word for word?"

"Yes, Mr Stokes."

"I'll be keeping my eye on you, Thomas. Mind how you go — you can find your own way out." Charlie turned his back and the bulky frame stole most of the light.

Thomas walked slowly and deliberately, half expecting Charlie to have a change of heart and come charging after him. He found Ray outside, smoking.

"What did he say?" Ray's lips pulled on the cigarette.

"He agreed to the price."

"Did he say anything else?"

"Jack owes him."

"Jack won't like that one little bit." Ray's grin turned orange.

In the car Thomas noticed his legs shaking. Ray noticed it too.

"He's a scary fucker, is Charlie Stokes. Natalie thought I ought to come along to look after you, and as a mark of respect, on behalf of Jack."

Yeah, Thomas thought, but you knew your way around.

Natalie Langton was delighted with the news. Jack owing Charlie didn't seem to bother her at all. Thomas left them to it, grateful to leave their troubled world behind him.

* * *

He stood in the shower a long time when he got home, trying to rinse away the fear. Later, he rang Miranda just to hear her voice. He didn't talk for long because Charlie's comment about Ray and Miranda was running through his veins like a poison. After a quick update to John Wright, Karl was the final call of the night. He came right to the point.

"I get it now — why you leave me on the periphery."

Chapter 47

Keeping Bob Peterson at arm's length proved easy. Peterson called him, first thing, and explained that he intended to stay in Southampton and have Thomas be his eyes and ears in London. To buy himself some time Thomas promised to visit Ken's flat after work.

He hadn't slept well and the train ride into work was gruelling. It was never a good sign when he needed chocolate to keep body and soul together before he'd even made it back above ground. Everywhere he looked people wore earpieces to cocoon them from their commute, the wires trailing discreetly inside a coat, making it harder to identify if it was a genuine iPod — or worth stealing. The train rocked side to side, crashing his brain against the same thought: Miranda and Ray.

Today was a repeat list of benefits claimants — a mop-up of those they'd missed altogether, and a continuation of surveillance on some of the others.

"Trouble sleeping?" Karl edged into the conversation with more care than he applied to the traffic.

"I thought Jack was intimidating, but Charlie — he's in another league."

"He's smarter too. No criminal record — implicated, but nothing that sticks."

"I dunno how you do it, Karl. It's day and night for you. When did you last take a holiday?"

"Apart from my European break in Geneva, you mean?"

The welcoming sight of the café ended the conversation. Still time for breakfast before Paulette Villers was due at the laundry.

The door had an old-fashioned bell above it. Thomas headed to the counter and grabbed the newspaper. Two fried egg sandwiches and teas ordered, he took the seat with his back to the window so Karl could keep watch on the world.

"Even the news is spoiled," Thomas lamented. "Thanks to you I'm forever reading between the lines now."

Karl fiddled with the salt cellar. "All I did was open your eyes to what was already going on — and you asked me to, remember?"

"I know." He cheered up a little when the tea arrived and started flicking through the paper. There was no mention of a killer on the run, or a European conspiracy, but he knew they were facts of life.

The sandwiches weren't long in coming and the magical hit of bread and butter, egg, and sweet sauce were balm to an otherwise shitty day. Thomas was going back over the Bob Peterson situation, in between bites, when Karl's face brightened.

"Don't look now, Tommo — I think our luck is changing."

He waited for Karl to elaborate — which he didn't. The door pinged and Paulette Villers stood over them.

"I'm ready to talk — tomorrow, at two pm. You know our address. Only . . . can you leave me alone today? I've got things to do — private things." She didn't hang around.

"What do you reckon?" Thomas squeezed his bread against the plate, smearing yellow and brown together.

"Yeah, I'm up for that."

"No, I mean the part about leaving her alone today. What is she doing?"

Karl was already reaching for his mobile. "Hello, Ann? How would you like to make an Irishman very happy?" He got up and took the call outside.

The carousel of claimants — Karl's phrase of the day — gradually thinned out as the hours slipped away. It was Thomas's turn as the lookout, so Karl practised surveillance on the insides of his eyelids.

"Karl?" Thomas stretched his name out like a yawn.

"I'm not asleep."

"I wanna ask you something. A straight question without further discussion?"

"Uh-huh." Karl hadn't moved.

"Miranda and Ray Daniels . . ."

"Oh, that." Karl shifted a little in his seat. "Let sleeping dogs lie, Thomas. The past is the past."

"Any other clichés in your bag?"

"I thought we weren't discussing this?"

"We're not. But Charlie Stokes also knew I was a photographer, so I'm wondering where he got that from?"

"I told you he was smart. And as for Ray Daniels, you and Miranda had enough going on and it wasn't my place to say anything."

"That's never stopped you before." He arced his camera along the horizon. "I'll be glad when this business with Jack Langton is over."

Karl didn't reply. The subject appeared in the frame, so Thomas dropped the subject and got to work.

* * *

Dinner at *Caliban's* hadn't been part of the plan but Karl had a point — it was local and they deserved some sort of reward for a hard day's surveillance. The bar was a tourist magnet again, only this time the coach outside had French number plates.

Thomas followed Karl across the car park. "This'll be perfect for you. They speak French in Geneva."

Karl made a pretence of holding his ribs. "Look, I should have told you about Miranda. I know you've done a lot for me lately — for Ken. So I'm gonna repay your trust a little because I know how much you love secrets. I won't repeat myself. Ready? I went to a NATO building in Geneva."

"Holy shit!"

"The very same. Now, by my reckoning I owe the two of you dinner."

Inside, Miranda sauntered over and directed them to one of the three reserved tables. At Miranda's minimal sign language Sheryl brought the menus. "Nice to see a friendly face for a change, guys." She dealt them out like cards. "Any progress on Janey's kid?"

Thomas tapped Karl's boot under the table. "You know her?"

"I know *of* her. By the way, when are you seeing Jack again?"

"Soon. I'm gonna go on my own again."

They settled for 'poulet et croustilles,' as the menu put it, mainly because Miranda admitted she had over-ordered. And, like Karl said, you couldn't really get chicken and chips wrong as long as it was actually cooked.

Karl hung around longer than Thomas expected. Miranda and Sheryl alternated their company with helping out at the bar. Thomas liked it that way — no space to talk over anything work-related. The weight across his shoulders lifted as the evening went on. Even when Karl went outside to make a call it didn't disturb him.

"I suppose we should see Ajit and Geena at some point . . ." He tested the water with Miranda.

"Maybe once Jack's out of your hair?"

He made a face.

"No progress with Jacob then."

He shook his head and sought solace in his shandy.

"Eliminate the impossible . . ." She leaned in and kissed him.

Sherlock Holmes had never felt so sexy.

Karl returned with a flourish. "Remind me to buy Ann Crossley some flowers." He glanced at Miranda and carried on regardless. "Our boy Dolan . . ."

"Roland," Thomas corrected him.

" . . . Went to the same olive-coloured door address, collected something and delivered it to . . ." He drummed on the table and then stopped for the punch line.

"Paulette Villers!" Thomas stole his glory.

"Very good, Tommo. Maybe she's gonna hand over some evidence tomorrow."

Miranda squeezed in close to whisper in Thomas's ear. "Shall we go back to yours?"

Chapter 48

The morning's work was just a prelude to the main event of the day. They broke for lunch at twelve-thirty to talk tactics. Thomas was all for bugging Paulette's home, but Karl thought they'd be pushing their luck.

"Domestic surveillance is always more risky. People behave erratically at home — things get moved and knocked about."

That meant relying on naked charm. Thomas laughed at the thought — another title for RT. He wondered how Karl would make use of the information he and Miranda had gleaned about Jack's Spanish operation. Karl had talked in a general way about 'turning' Jack to use him against the Shadow State, but had left out the details.

"How long do you think we'll be there, Karl?"

"In and out in half an hour, tops."

* * *

Thomas parked around the corner with five minutes to go. There was a metallic tang in his mouth and moistness under his arms, and he loved it. They were finally making headway against the monsters. Maybe, by some miracle, Paulette had something that would link Charlie to the attack on Jacob. Yeah, and maybe Bob Peterson would emigrate to New Zealand.

"Remember, Tommo, let me do the talking. And do whatever you can to make her feel at ease."

Thomas immediately took his SSU ID off and thrust it in his pocket.

Paulette was at the door as soon as they knocked — obviously waiting. It looked like a small place for a couple, although someone was big on interior design. Smooth lines and muted lilac tones contrasted with burgundy — not what he'd expected of a potential benefit fraudster.

"Rachel's upstairs. She'll be down soon — she's a bit uncomfortable about all this."

Karl nodded. "We appreciate you inviting us here. It's just a chat, nothing official."

Thomas cleared his throat, but Karl ignored him.

"Okay . . ." Paulette took a deep breath, which didn't stop her trembling. "I'm not working in the laundry — honest."

Karl opened his hands wide, just like the textbooks said to do — non-threatening and inclusive. "We have seen you going there regularly."

"I have to be out of the house at certain times. It's somewhere to go. Sometimes I help out a little bit, that's all. Charlie makes me leave." She looked to the far wall. "A couple of times I came back early and . . ." There was a *thump* upstairs. "It's only Rachel." But she flinched. "You said you'd help us . . . I'll make some tea — kettle's not long boiled."

Karl waited until she was out of the door. "I need to put some pressure on her — don't contradict me," he growled.

Thomas felt himself withdrawing into the role of observer. This was another, ugly side to Karl. Paulette was vulnerable, and Rachel so scared she wouldn't even come downstairs.

The kitchen door opened and Paulette brought through a silver tray, holding it close by the handles, as the mugs of tea slopped on to its shiny surface. Thomas had a flashback to the café after his first prison visit with Jack.

He muttered to Karl, "Ask her about Jacob."

Paulette put the tray at one edge of a coffee table and doled out the mugs. Tea oozed out from the base of each one across the dark wood. It struck Thomas as strange that she'd gone to the trouble of a tea tray but hadn't cared about the table.

"Who's Jacob? Drink up."

Thomas stared at his milky tea — southerners rarely made a decent brew. Karl drained the cup without pausing for breath, a man on a mission and a dog with a bone.

"Tell us about the times you came home too soon."

Thomas looked at his watch; they'd need to get back to work soon. The Benefits Investigation Team had its agenda too. He took a gulp of sweet, sickly tea, detecting the unmistakeable tang of sterilised milk. He had to squeeze his eyes shut to take it down, like when he was a child at his Gran's house; Sunday teas as torture.

Within seconds Karl began to sway in his seat. His face was dappled with sweat. "I don't feel so good."

Thomas stared at his half empty mug. "What have you done?"

"You've got to finish all of it."

Karl lurched out of his chair and stumbled over the edge of the coffee table, careering into a lamp. Thomas reacted instinctively, letting go of the mug as he rushed to Karl's aid. He heard the smash of ceramic against wood but it didn't slow him down any. Karl was groaning now, struggling to get to the door.

A door opened upstairs and someone rushed down, only it wasn't Rachel. It was one of the toe-rags who'd given Greg a kicking. Thomas dragged the front door open but there were already two men waiting for them.

"It's not my fault — he made me do it!" Paulette screamed behind him.

Thomas felt the fist jar against his back and fell headlong into Karl and out on to the street. He felt woozy but conscious enough to know they were screwed. He closed his eyes and let it happen.

* * *

Play dead. He felt like he was flying, arms dangling in the air. Then he hit the ground and rolled into a cave. Someone sealed the cave up. Maybe it was Joseph of Arimathea. The ground lurched beneath him, only it wasn't ground. His hands touched a smooth wooden surface. *Think, Thomas — think.* He forced his eyes open and recognised the dark belly of a van. His brain stalled as he tried to work out how he'd got there. The body beside him was Karl's; insensible, rasping.

Thomas dug a nail into his own palm. The pain felt dull, far away, but it was something to cling on to. He chased the pain and found it, added a key scrape across his knuckles to bring it home.

What did he know? There had been three blokes and that bitch had set them up. He heard muffled voices behind his head. And a radio. He couldn't make out the words so he eased forward and pressed an ear against the metal panel. All he got for his trouble was a pounding vibration through his skull, so he retreated. There wouldn't be much time. He could only think of two things to do.

He put his hand in his pocket and the raw skin scraped against the seam. Once he'd separated the ID card from the holder he put the card between his teeth and carefully took his boot off. He wanted to sleep now, but he couldn't, not yet, not until he'd finished. The card went in his sock and he put the boot back on, feeling the rounded plastic edges pressing against his sole. He slid along the floor and his boot tapped something hard. Manoeuvring 180 degrees he felt his way around the spare wheel and dipped into his pocket again for the holder. Down it went, out of sight. He scratched his initials and

Karl's into the wooden floor and dragged the spare wheel over a little to cover it. Under the circumstances, it was the best he could do.

Chapter 49

Thomas woke to the sound of banging against the van.

"Wakey, wakey!"

The door retracted and daylight flooded the interior. He struggled to his knees and blinked against the glare, trying to cover his face. Someone — no, it was two people — wrenched his arms forward and dragged him out, smacking his shins against the ground. He cried out and they laughed.

"The other one's still under — we'll have to carry him."

Even with his eyes closed, Thomas recognised Ray's voice. They walked him, arms out to the sides like a crucifixion, into the hangar-like shell. Ray came around to face him, leering at him in the semi-darkness.

"Surprised to see me?"

The punch, though half expected, doubled him over.

"Get the hood. Oh, for fuck's sake."

He saw someone scrabbling about on the ground and the hood was pulled down roughly over his head. The stench of diesel choked him; the stupid bastard must have dropped it on the ground. Time to sleep again.

* * *

He jerked awake and reached forward, but his arms were restrained. He moved his fingers and felt the radiator. A quarter-turn on his wrists and the cable ties dug into his skin. Holding his breath he sensed his own terror, like a presence beside him.

He pushed back with the heels of his boots to try and ease the pressure on his shoulders. It helped a little, but not much. All he could do was wait and try to keep calm.

The sound of footsteps crushing glass stirred him. Someone was standing close by, their breathing steady and rapid — someone was getting off on this. When the hood was wrenched off he saw Ray and Charlie standing over him. He didn't bother saying anything.

"Time for your medicine." Charlie tilted his head back and tried to open his mouth.

He resisted, so Ray got handy with his fists again. When he cried out Charlie squeezed his jaw until he relaxed and opened his mouth. The liquid slithered across his tongue, leaving a chalky aftertaste. When he'd swallowed he suddenly smelled orange peel, so strongly he started coughing.

They replaced the hood.

"We'll have a little chat later."

Through the cloth he felt Charlie's face close to his.

"Come on, Ray, the other one should be ready now — he's far more interesting."

* * *

Thomas breathed in and out in tides, and the world floated around him in darkness. Somewhere beyond, *they* were watching him. Someone was always watching; had been his whole life: the voices from the dark and the one voice that could pierce his defences with a single word.

He was in the water now, swimming against the tide, and the creature — he never looked back but he knew it was there — was gaining on him. Faster and faster he swam, reaching for breath, trying to escape the shadow in the darkness that would overwhelm him. He screamed in rage as it engulfed him, swallowing him whole, fighting, clawing for breath as he slid into its guts.

* * *

Light bleached his world. Two faces came to meet him, but they weren't saviours.

"Let's try again."

A huge hand slapped him hard across the face and he fell away until the wrist restraints bit in, jarring his shoulders. No point calling out — he'd tried that before. One of them spoke and he heard someone else replying with his voice. They wanted to know all about Jack, and Natalie, and it was funny to tell them about Natalie and Ray. But the big one, Charlie, was angry then. And now Ray was angry too.

Charlie's was the dominant voice. "I told you not to get involved with Natalie. Just like I told you not to pick on the kid."

"That ain't my fault — those stupid lads were only supposed to spray the buggy. Anyway it did the trick. Jack's so paranoid now that he's given me more control so I can run things."

Thomas closed his eyes while they argued with one another. How long had he been here? Hours? Days? His brain tried to figure it out, only every thought slithered free. The world had gone quiet again so he risked opening one eye. The faces had gone and there was a bucket not far away, reeking of piss. On the floor nearby were four broken cable ties. He shut his eyes again and slipped away.

"Medicine!"

This time he didn't resist the road to oblivion. The voices retreated and he began to float again, until he heard a scream, fearful enough to scare the living and the dead. As if in primal response, something stirred deep inside him; coiling, besieging his organs to break free. Another scream and he screamed back, out into the darkness.

He opened his eyes and he was still in darkness. And there was still screaming — his and Karl's. He called his friend's name but it made no difference. Someone ran into the room and knocked over a container. It rattled around on the floor.

"Shut your fucking noise." Ray, again.

He heard the fateful click that could only be a gun. And then his own voice begging for life.

Bang. The wall exploded by his ear, showering him with dust and brick fragments.

"Next time it will be you and then Miranda will be all alone." Ray's laughter scorched him, peeling away his defences until there was nothing left but despair

The monster breached the waves and vomited him up on a shoreline thick with oil. He twisted and turned, rolling in the slick as he tried to get free, but every breath drew in more viscous poison. Death would be slow unless he took that courageous step. He leaned into it and fell, face first, into the inky blackness. The smell permeated his skin, rippling through him until it spewed out again.

He choked up the vomit through stinging tears and felt its heat against his chest. He tried to lean sideways to avoid the stench from the hood. Sleep overtook him again.

He dreamt that someone was hitting an old-fashioned dustbin lid with a hammer, and then there was yelling. Someone was telling him his own secrets about the bugging device and about Karl. And then there was nothing.

The world tilted forward, before he realised he was moving backwards against the radiator. A hand pressed down against his shoulder, then two clicks, and he could move his wrists again.

"You're safe now. Save Karl."

Something hard pushed against his foot. He was alone again. He waited a long time, or it seemed that way, until he lifted the hood. His legs throbbed in protest as he rolled forward to his knees, coming to face with the pistol.

Instinct took over. He staggered to his feet and felt the silencer to make sure it was on properly. As he stumbled towards the doorway where he'd heard Karl screaming, something moved behind him to the left. He turned and fired, listening for the satisfying *thwap*. Whatever it was back there dropped like a stone.

His hands began to tingle the closer he got to the doorway. It didn't matter how many of them were in there, they were all as good as dead. He saw two silhouettes at the far end of the room, stark against the windows. Point and fire; dead and buried.

More voices came from beyond the building, hidden by torch beams. He stood against them, holding back the storm, and the last words he remembered were, "Put down the weapon and get on the ground — do it now."

The torches converged on him and he complied. Now he was flying again, flying free.

Chapter 50

Thomas woke from a dreamless sleep. Light filtered through the blue curtains; he figured it was morning wherever he was. His hand felt sore and then he noticed the Tube in his vein. There was no sea and no monsters. As he raised himself to sit up, the mother of all headaches decided to throw a street party in his skull.

When he gazed around the room everything looked unfamiliar, until he saw the armchair in the corner. Despite the throbbing in his head he couldn't help smiling.

"Miranda?" he rasped.

She shrugged off a blanket and rushed to his side, looking like she needed the bed more than he did.

"Can I have some water — and a painkiller?"

"Let me tell them you're awake."

When Miranda left he stretched out in bed — no broken bones anyway, although that hand, with scratches across it and a needle going in, was stinging like a bastard. Miranda returned — with Christine. She handed him a painkiller while Miranda poured some water.

"Well," Thomas tried to see the funny side, "this is awkward." The current and the ex, along with a fractured memory. Not good at all.

"I'll give you two a moment and then someone will come and unhook him." Christine turned back at the door. "Remember what we agreed, Miranda."

He was grateful when the pain subsided a little. Miranda said he'd been there a day, but he couldn't make out when that day might have started from.

"And where are we, exactly?"

"Safe house in Hertfordshire."

A stranger knocked and entered the room. He gave Thomas a cursory once-over, nodded to Miranda and then removed the cannula to the accompaniment of some choice epithets from Thomas.

"Drink as much fluid as you can."

The orderly left while Thomas was still wiping away the blood with a tissue.

"I grabbed some things from the flat . . . once I'd heard . . ." Miranda fetched some clothes out of a wardrobe.

"What did they actually tell you?"

"You're better off talking to Christine."

Walking took more effort than he'd expected. Miranda supported him on the short journey to the main room and left him at the door. He gripped the handle and went inside. Christine had her back to him. Karl leaned over to look past her.

"Ah, Tommo — the man himself!"

She turned aside, revealing Karl wearing a dressing gown. Christine waved a finger at Karl. "Two minutes, and then we need to get everything straight."

Karl mock-saluted behind her back as she left the room.

"Alone together at last. How much do you know about what happened?"

Thomas saw now that Karl was nursing an arm close to his chest. He squeezed his eyes shut to concentrate. "I shot three people . . . fuck! I killed Charlie and Ray." He opened his eyes and looked straight at Karl as the truth hit him. "I'm glad."

Karl had his mind on other matters. "How did you get yourself free? More importantly, how did you get a gun?"

Thomas recounted the few details he had any faith in. Then Karl delivered the killer punch line.

"Evidently Charlie and Ray were already dead. Unless you shot them, propped them up, and then shot them again for good measure."

"I don't understand; they were right by the windows — I couldn't miss them." He stopped then as he remembered the familiar, Scottish voice — *you're safe now.* "Ken Treavey." His eyes widened. "Which explains the gun."

The door handle rattled and Christine returned, this time with Ann Crossley and Bob Peterson. Christine moved over to the dining table. "Shall we?"

They sat down together, a party of five. Christine filled in the blanks — and there were a lot of them. How, when Thomas hadn't come home and neither he nor Karl had answered their mobiles, Miranda had called the SSU and everywhere else she could think of until she obtained Christine's mobile number.

The SSU ID cards had given them a location, and then Bob Peterson had provided what Christine called *an assault team* to rescue them. Bob smiled then, and Thomas couldn't tell if he was being smug or conciliatory. Bob's team, whoever they actually were, had discovered two very dead people and another one wounded. A thorough search also revealed, as Bob explained, "a significant quantity of chemicals, which I've removed to secure storage."

Karl looked distinctly unhappy. "I'd like to have a wee chat with you about that."

Ann seized the moment and spoke directly to Karl. "A raid was executed at the house with the olive-coloured door — a home chemist had set up business there, for Charlie Stokes. They gave you both Scopolamine," she explained, not that Thomas understood anything from it. "Plus some other compounds. It interferes with memory and renders you open to suggestion."

Christine glanced at her watch. "Let's move on. Knowing we'd be pressed for time, Bob, Ann and I have already agreed an *official* version of events."

Thomas listened without comment to the mixture of half-truths and lies. It was a paper-thin fairy-tale: he and Karl had been looking for someone on behalf of Bob Peterson and stumbled upon a criminal connection, with unforeseen consequences.

The triumvirate of Bob, Christine and Ann had decided that Sir Peter would know nothing about the drug seizure or any connection to the Shadow State. Charlie Stokes wasn't even mentioned by name.

And from the looks of things Bob and Christine had managed some sort of reconciliation — even if only in their working relationship. Thomas sneered to himself; Bob's wife must be thrilled.

Christine didn't mention Ken Treavey either; maybe Bob had left out the finer details. Maybe he needed more painkillers.

"Well . . ." Bob stopped talking and Thomas realised he'd zoned out again. "That seems to be about everything. Any questions?" Bob smiled in Christine's direction and rested his hands on the table, near hers.

It seemed rude to disappoint him. Thomas coughed to get everyone's attention.

"What about the dead people?"

Bob didn't miss a beat. "What dead people? We only found you and Karl there."

Thomas felt the beginnings of a smile. Bob had the drugs and Christine's support and the glory. Yep, three steps ahead, just like he promised. But he was still a tosser.

"I think we'll end it there." Bob left the table. "Christine and I will see Sir Peter. He may want to speak with the rest of you afterwards."

* * *

Thomas sat down at the kitchen table. Miranda was seated opposite, with Karl and Ann either side of them. Four mugs of tea were on the table, untouched, while two rooms away the grown-ups were presumably redrawing the map.

"Is someone gonna say something?" Karl finished stirring his tea and put the spoon down next to it.

Miranda smiled across the table and Thomas suddenly thought about Ray Daniels. "I'm totally lost here. I don't know what we can and can't talk about." He glanced first at Miranda and then at Ann.

Miranda fidgeted. "Listen, if you three need to discuss work I can make myself scarce . . ."

"Karl?" Thomas stared daggers at him.

"The little boy is home now," Ann announced, out of the blue. "I kept an eye on things while you were away, Karl. I forget to mention that we intercepted the van — that was how Bob knew it wasn't just your IDs there — a smart move, leaving a message in the back."

Thomas had heard enough. "I'm going to get some air in the garden. You coming, Miranda?"

Outside, the autumn trees were all browns and copper. The grass was still wet and he trailed a foot across it to feel the dampness against the top of his trainer. The painkillers were doing their job nicely but he couldn't settle. There were things to be said and no easy way to say them.

"Ray Daniels is dead."

Miranda's face twitched for an instant. "Did he suffer? I hope so."

That was unexpected. He didn't push the point; she'd tell him in her own good time — or not. When he explained about Ken's return she suggested they ask for their money back. At least she'd kept her sense of humour.

"So what do you want to do when all this is over?" He threw an arm around her.

"Does that mean you're done with Jack Langton?"

"I dunno." The question unnerved him because he didn't have an answer. "I'm getting cold. I don't suppose there's another way in?"

"There is, as a matter of fact; I'll show you."

They reached a side door.

"You certainly know your way around."

"I remembered from last time."

Her face said it all. He caught the inference straight away. This was where she'd been held in exchange for the papers Yorgi's brother had stolen from him. More inescapable history.

"I'm sorry."

"You weren't to know. Shall we see if Karl wants to cook again?"

As they entered the corridor, Sir Peter was leaving the dining room.

"Ah, Thomas! And Miss Wright."

The combination of bluster and bullshit riled him, but he felt Miranda's steadying hand on his shoulder.

"I wonder if I could speak to you alone for a moment, Thomas?"

He shrugged Miranda's hand free. Who was he to disappoint a willing audience?

* * *

The table seemed larger, but maybe that was because there were only three people in the room; Christine and Bob had made themselves scarce. Karl was already seated at the head of the table, funny but true.

"The floor is yours, Mr Bladen." Karl opened his good hand.

Thomas threw him a glance that said, "really?" Karl nodded. He felt a tremor in his hand and flexed his fingers. "We could have died, clearing up your mess."

"That was regrettable. I knew nothing about it."

"You knew about Ken Treavey though." He paused, waiting — in vain — for Karl to jump in. He levered himself up. "I can't do this your way, Karl." He leaned against the table for support and then eased himself back to freestanding. "Ken was none of my business until you got me involved. Now two people are dead — that I know of — and the trail of evidence leads back to you."

Karl found his voice at last. "We have photos of Thomas leaving Main Building with a large parcel, along with its dimensions. We have a photo of the Ingersoll key, a match for the ballistics as well as Bob Peterson twice replacing the weapon."

To Thomas it sounded like a Royal Flush laid out on the table. But Sir Peter's face suggested he had a killer hand of his own.

"Excellent work, gentlemen. I knew I could rely on you."

Thomas sat down again; it didn't make any sense, unless . . .

"You wanted us to find out?" That made even less sense.

Sir Peter raised himself to his full stature. "Are you aware of Eva Fairfield?"

"The Home Office minister." Karl made it a statement.

Sir Peter stared across the room, as if seeking inspiration. Thomas figured absolution was a more likely objective.

"Eva had a request and she made it very clear I was in no position to refuse. Sidney Morsley murdered a little girl and she wanted justice. Real justice. There was a distant family connection. *Blood for blood.*"

Karl was ahead of him. "But you had your misgivings so you laid a trail for us."

Thomas shook his head. "It wasn't conscience, Karl. He couldn't bear to be under her control — he had too much to lose." He glared at Sir Peter. "At least it was personal for her, but you — you don't have a conscience. And why choose Ken?"

"Because of you, Thomas. I knew I could rely on your mistrust, and your loyalty to Karl. I involved Bob Peterson, as a contingency, because — unlike you — he'd do exactly as I told him and not ask questions."

Thomas's hand was throbbing again, aching to become a fist. Karl took one look and spoke again.

"And what about the second murder?"

"Eva contacted me again — a series of *incidents* would take the media's attention off Morsley, to say nothing of the saving to the British taxpayer. Public opinion seems to be on her side."

"Un-fucking-believable." Thomas had heard enough. "You really are a monster. I'm going home, Karl. You do . . . whatever . . ." He pushed away the air between them.

"Hold on, Tommo — let's think this through." Karl showed no sign of moving.

Sir Peter adjusted one of his cufflinks. "Name *your* terms, Mr Bladen."

Thomas reached the middle of the room and faced the negotiation table. The bastard was smiling. He wondered if Karl would intervene if he made a move on him. Even Thomas knew he was more valuable where they could see him. "You give Ken Treavey his life back. And this . . . Eva Fairfield? She has to go — within a month. You take care of this, Karl. Or, so help me, I'll find another, more public way to resolve this."

He left them to it.

Chapter 51

It hadn't occurred to Thomas that Miranda would hardly have been given directions to the safe house. Ann drove, and he listened.

"Bob asked me to give you this, recovered from the site. He said he hasn't watched it."

Thomas held the DVD between his fingertips, as if it might contaminate him. Someone had written his initials on it in permanent marker.

"Karl has his own and Bob gave him the others, as a show of good faith."

"Others?" he felt a knot in his stomach.

Ann glanced over earnestly. "Charlie Stokes kept meticulous records. Apart from you and Karl there were at least a dozen more victims."

"And the chemist?"

"Arrested and detained."

Thomas fell silent, thinking about a suitable punishment for Roland Dolan and Paulette Villers. They'd each played their part.

Miranda told Ann where to pull over.

"We'll call you in a few days, unless you're fit for duty before then."

"Understood. The sooner I get back to normality the better." Even he smiled at that; this *was* normality.

* * *

There were five messages at the flat, but there was something he had to do first. Miranda assured him she understood when he disappeared into his darkroom with a laptop and some headphones.

There were fragments of memory floating around in his head and it wasn't enough. He needed to make sense of everything and the only way to do that was to face his demons.

The footage was grainy with sound — a typical CCTV rig. Ray and Charlie were difficult to decipher unless they got close to the radiator; there must have been a mic on the light fitting. That also explained the constant low hum in the background.

He felt a twinge in his guts when the two figures approached on-screen and force-fed him the poison — the 'medicine.' The body remembered. As the sweat prickled his forehead he got up from the laptop to catch his breath. He fast-forwarded until he saw the prisoner straining to get free, screaming about the darkness, the contours of his face briefly visible as he strained forward against the hood.

Ray asked the questions. Sometimes Charlie observed. He seemed to like doing that. He'd prompt Ray in a whisper then stand to one side to watch the whole thing at close quarters, studying the prisoner.

Thomas made notes of the questions and any keywords in his responses. Those he could understand, anyway. He worked through the interrogations methodically, searching for confirmation of a half-remembered dream.

Charlie and Ray, facing off. "I warned you not to get involved with Natalie. Just like I warned you not to pick on the kid."

Ray had stood his ground, a pit bull to Charlie's mastiff. "Jacob was a happy accident. Now Jack's wound tighter than a spring and I'm in his bed."

Charlie had stormed off, but Ray stayed, squatting down next to Thomas. "Absolute power — that's the drug, Thomas. I can do *anything*. I could cut you now and you wouldn't even remember — or choke you." He grabbed him in a stranglehold and all Thomas could hear was himself choking. Then a gasp of breath as Ray released him. "I own you." He leaned back and head-butted him, the *crack* smashing Thomas against the radiator.

Ray turned around for the camera and stared back from the grave. Thomas clicked the mouse to pause the footage, matching the gaze of a dead man. It wasn't justice, but it would have to do.

He watched the rest of the recording with a clinical eye, writing down details as if it were another SSU job. His detachment only faltered again when Charlie had come to see him alone. Once the hood was raised, on-screen, Thomas had a fleeting flashback.

"Ray doesn't understand, but I do." Charlie waved the bug in front of Thomas's face. "I would have picked you up anyway after your interest in Paulette and young Roland. You're more than a Benefits snooper, though. Karl, I already knew about, but you . . . the Cartel will be very interested in what you've got to say."

Thomas noted, to his shame, that he answered all Charlie's questions about Karl and their counter-intelligence work. He didn't reveal much, thank God, because he still didn't know a great deal — full marks to Karl on that front. He slipped the headphones off again and rubbed his eyes.

Miranda rapped on the door lightly. "Thomas? I didn't want to disturb you but Karl just rang — I didn't answer it. I'm popping out for some food. I'll be back in half an hour."

He let her know he was okay and checked the time. He'd been in there nearly two hours. When he heard the front door click behind her he ventured out into daylight and rang Karl back.

"How are you holding up, Thomas?"

"I'm fine." He actually meant it. "How's the arm?"

"Sprained, I think. It seems I put up more resistance than was good for me." Karl sighed like a carthorse. "I should never have got you in so deep."

"I'm fine," he repeated, a little sharper than before. "Occupational hazard." He read the silence and knew there was more to be said.

"It's been decided that Ray Daniels is officially only missing. It's useful to have a phantom out there — it'll keep Jack Langton on his toes as well."

Once again, expediency over the truth. Thomas gripped the phone.

"Ray was responsible . . . for Jacob."

"Ah well, justice has been served on that account. He was a dead man walking — Charlie too. Once they'd interrogated us I couldn't have risked compromising other operatives. If it hadn't been Ken, or you, I would have killed them myself."

"Is that supposed to make me feel better?"

Karl didn't answer. It didn't matter; Thomas understood. You could never really negotiate with monsters. Maybe Eva Fairfield saw that as well. Silver bullet, wooden stake, Browning pistol, or counter-intelligence — choose your weapon.

"I'll get my DVD to you. I've made notes as well but it's best to be thorough."

"Your notes will suffice, Thomas; I trust you." He said it like he meant it. "Destroy the DVD — you might find it therapeutic! Be seeing ya."

Thomas smiled. "Soon, I hope."

Time for one more call. He kept it brief and Natalie Langton never knew what hit her.

"It's Thomas. Charlie Stokes is dead and Ray's gone. I'm seeing Jack in a few days to give him the news, so you have time to pack if you want to leave."

He didn't have to spell it out for her. She begged and pleaded, said that Ray had used her and that Jack didn't need to know. Both were probably true.

"Please — I can pay you, Thomas; I've got money here."

"I'm not for sale."

No, but she was. Maybe Karl could use her as a spy on the inside, to keep tabs on Jack when he got out of prison. She took the deal; it was the best offer on the table. He'd text Karl about it later.

By the time Miranda returned with a curry he had plates on the table and *An Inspector Calls* cued up in the player — an old-fashioned morality tale. His hand smarted from snapping his DVD into shards. Karl was right — it felt good.

Chapter 52

Although John had offered to accompany him to Wormwood Scrubs Thomas decided to go alone. Better to say his piece in relative privacy. He watched the swarm of commuters moving through the network, untroubled by the myriad of cameras — overt and covert — or the electronic footprint they were leaving. Maybe the populace was better off living in ignorance; give him the unadorned truth any day.

He picked up a tabloid as he left East Acton Tube and browsed the first few pages while a bus thundered by. Home Office minister Eva Fairfield had decided to step down from her role and seek out new opportunities. He smiled skyward: how noble of her. The article reported that the Home Secretary was saddened by her departure and felt she had made a unique contribution. That was one way of putting it.

His Surveillance Support Unit ID card won him the hands-on treatment again from the prison officers' welcoming committee. He didn't make a fuss; it wasn't like he planned on coming back. He followed procedure and then did the slow shuffle to the visitors' hall to await an audience.

Jack Langton had the same swagger as the late Mr Stokes. Thomas smiled and offered his hand.

"Any news?" Jack blinked a couple of times, as though seeing something different.

Thomas stared, keeping his voice monotone. "Charlie Stokes is dead — there'll be no more trouble . . ."

Jack grinned from ear to ear.

" . . . I haven't finished. Ray Daniels has disappeared."

The tip of Jack's tongue poked out of his mouth, tasting the future. "If Ray's not around, there's a vacancy — if you're interested?"

Thomas's face hardened. "No. I know what he's capable of."

"Well, look." Jack leaned back, fingers laced behind his head like he owned the place. "I owe you, and I'm a man who keeps his word. Name your price."

"Really?"

"Within reason, yeah!" Jack was grinning again.

"Stay away from the Wrights in future, and Sheryl. Not even a postcard. Your word, remember?" Thomas got up to leave. "Because I know everything about you now, Jack — *everything*."

THE END

My thanks to the following people:
Anne Derges, Christine Butterworth, Clive Aplin, David Brown,
Elizabeth Sparrow, Jasper Joffe, Martin Wood, Paul Sullivan, Sarah
Campbell and Warren Stevenson.

My thanks to the following organisations:

Inside Time
The UK Cards Association

Characters and Notes

The UK Surveillance Support Unit loans out specialist and support teams to other government departments, including law enforcement and intelligence agencies. Those other departments refer to SSU staff as 'floaters' — it's not a term of endearment.

The Shadow State is a European infrastructure outside of the legal and political process. It functions as an alliance of corporations, politicians, the military and business leaders, operating as a clandestine United States of Europe. It is also known as 'the cartel' and trades in various commodities, including drugs, technology, information and weapons.

Main Characters

Thomas Bladen is a Yorkshire-born photographer, who brought runaway Miranda back to her family on London when they met in their teens. He has been with the SSU for nearly three years. He has five numbers stored in his phone and that's probably two more than he needs.

While always at peace on his native and elemental Yorkshire moors, Thomas's home is now London, where the East End and the north-east of the capital are inextricably linked with Miranda.

London is a city of contrasts — 2000 years of history and culture layered like rock strata and shaped by subterranean forces. As a photographer he sees the hidden beauty in the ancient streets of a modern, thriving city; as a surveillance officer he sees everything other people don't want him to.

Karl McNeill left Northern Ireland in his teens and joined the SSU after leaving the British army in circumstances he has never revealed. He is part of the intelligence war against the Shadow State. His closest SSU ally is Thomas, but he is not above using him, if the ends justify the means.

Miranda Wright is Thomas's lover and his Achilles heel. She owns Caliban's, a bar in London's East End. She also has secrets to hide, even from Thomas.

John Wright and **Diane Wright** are parents to Miranda and her two brothers. They met in a casino and have an ambiguous relationship with the tax office. Their motto is *family comes first* and they treat Thomas as one of their own.

Ken Treavey served in the British army with Karl, who owes him a debt that Ken wants to collect.

Sir Peter Carroll is the Director General of the SSU. He is also under the control of Karl's people, following his exposure as a member the Shadow State.

Jack Langton is a small-time drug dealer and crook with aspirations, buying his way into respectability by investing in the modern art scene. Currently in prison, he has no idea that Thomas and Karl helped put him there.

Charlie Stokes is Jack's business rival with big ambitions and a penchant for cruelty. With Jack in prison, Charlie thinks it's an opportunity to expand his empire.

Ray Daniels is Jack Langton's associate and takes care of things while Jack's in prison, those *things* include Jack's wife.

Glossary of British Slang Terms

British slang: US equivalent

'appened: happened
'ead: head
'eck: heck (expression of surprise or emphasis)
'em: them
'un: one
aggro: stress
arse: ass
arseholes: assholes
arsed: bothered
asap: as soon as possible
Bagpuss: popular 1970s children's TV character
beddy-byes: bed (childish)
benefits: similar to welfare (but more generous, can include payments for unemployment, housing costs, disability etc) paid by the British government to eligible claimants.
bhuna: a type of Indian curry
Billy-no-mates: someone who is friendless or alone
bladdered: very drunk
bollocksed: ruined / helpless
Brize Norton: an airbase in England
colandered: peppered with holes
comms: communications
co-ord: co-ordination
cuppa: cup of tea
d'ya: did you
des res: desirable residence — a nice place to live
don't 'ang about: don't delay
dunno: don't know
friendlies: non-competitive soccer matches
fuck a duck: an extreme exclamation
guvnor: the boss
heffalump: a fictional elephant in Winnie-the-Pooh stories
hold up: wait a second
int': in the
joggies: sweat pants
loo: toilet
mam: mom
Meccano: steel and plastic construction set for children
Mechs: mechanised infantry
Mick: slang for someone who is Irish (derogatory)
miked up: wearing a microphone

MoD: Ministry of Defence (equivalent to Defense Department)
muzak: artificial 'elevator' music
naan: type of Indian flatbread
narked: irritated
oop: up
oppos: work buddies
ow: how
ow's: how is
p'raps: perhaps
pakoras: deep-fried meat or vegetables in batter (Indian)
paracetamol: painkiller
Peshwari naan: delicious stuffed Indian flatbread
play footsie: secretly rub someone else's foot with your own
plonked: placed something without care
ploughing: plowing
poxy: lousy
prat: jerk (derogatory)
pref: preference
prezzie: gift
Proddy: Protestant (religious)
recce: reconnaissance
reet: right (accented)
ridgeway: track or path
s'posed: supposed
schtum: silent (Yiddish)
Semtex: a type of explosive
shag: have sex with (verb) / someone you've had sex with (noun)
shandy: ale or lager mixed with a soft drink (often lemonade)
shite: crap
skivvying: doing menial work
slotted: shot and killed
snaggle: acquire/get
snogged: smooched/kissed
so's: so is
sod 'em: screw them
sodded off: departed/left
soz: sorry
squaddie: an army private
summat: something
suss: weigh up someone's character or motives
sussed out: figured out
t'loudspeaker: speaker phone
ta: thank you
tannoy: speaker
telly: TV

trier: someone who tries hard
trolley: gurney
trolleyed: wheeled
two penn'orth: two pennies worth (small personal opinion)
tutting: expression of disapproval
twatty: like a jerk (derogatory)
UB40: old name for UK unemployment benefits claim form
whatshisface: what's his face (when you can't remember)
wi': with
wotcha: hello/hi
yer: you
Yojimbo: a classic Japanese movie about a masterless samurai
yonks: ages (from *donkey's years*)

Thank you for reading this book. If you enjoyed it please leave feedback on Amazon, and if there is anything we missed or you have a question about then please get in touch. The author and publishing team appreciate your feedback and time reading this book.

Our email is jasper@joffebooks.com

www.joffebooks.com